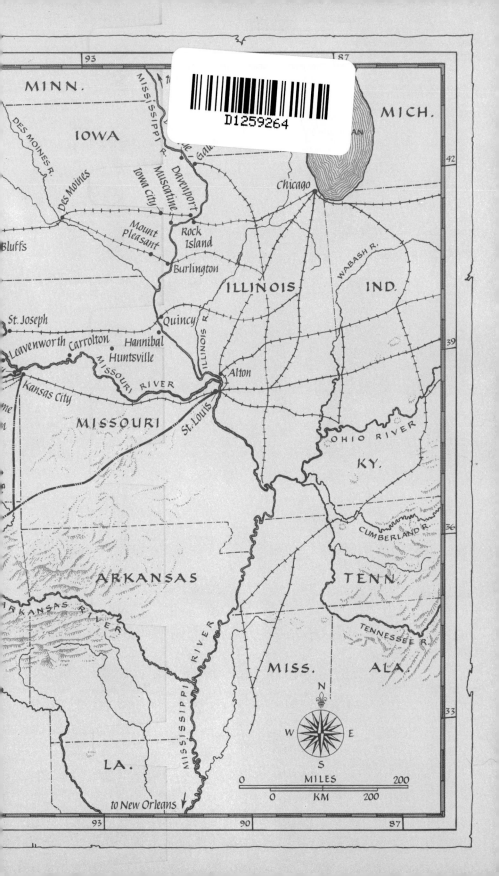

HEARTLAND

Robert Douglas Mead

HEARTLAND

DOUBLEDAY & COMPANY, INC.
GARDEN CITY, NEW YORK
1986

Library of Congress Cataloging in Publication Data

Mead, Robert Douglas.
 Heartland.
 I. Title.
PS3563.E168H4 1986   813'.54   81-43557
ISBN 0-385-14774-0

I dedicate this book to those of my name, known and unknown to me, who have preceded me in the infinite journey: through whose loins have been transmitted to me that life which for a time defines the part I step in the endless dance.

I am a stranger with thee and a sojourner, as all my fathers were.

Contents

Author's Note

There must be as many ways for a book to begin in its author's mind as there are books and authors. This one began for me in childhood, in a few tales told and retold within my family, concerning some of my forebears. When in the course of life I attempted to shape these familiar tales into a book, I could not feel the novelist's usual freedom to recast events for my convenience: I was constrained, I started from certain facts and events, they were for me fixed, given—so things had happened, in this order. On the other hand, I found that I would fulfill my writer's obligation by trying to discover, imagine, and communicate *why* the known actors of my familiar events, in the contexts of their lives, history, associates, should have behaved as they did— what their real (as distinct from professed) motives were—what, finally, moved them to act and react. That is among the reasons for writing any book, maybe the only reason: to *find out* what happened— to *find out* why and how, in all the senses.

The book that follows, therefore, is fact and fiction in equal measure, faithful to all known historical events, both public and private, yet freely inferring the inner substance of motives known only (if at all) to their possessors. It is a novel that treats always with respect the evidentiary standards that make history worthy of our trust; and, at the same time, it is history cast in the form of a novel—a somewhat old-fashioned, 19th-century kind of novel, perhaps, as befits its subject, but a novel all the same. That is among the reasons why the family at the center of my narrative bears the name Pride, not my own. The two families are parallel, perhaps equivalent, one inspired by the other. They are not identical.

I have taken the Indian names that figure in my narrative as I found them in treaties and other documents, without attempting to impose a consistent style. They represent many different, mostly unrelated, languages, transcribed by official translators whose knowledge of the original must generally have been imperfect. What these transcriptions have in common is that they indicate, often by hyphenating every syllable, the meaningful elements of the original; and all vowels are sounded, and sounded in roughly their French, not their English or American, values (because the intrepid French fur traders and their half-breed offspring were most often the intermediaries between the languages). Thus, for instance, the name I have written as Pat-so-gate I hear as *pah-tso-gah-teh,* with equal stress on the four syllables.

I owe more than conventional thanks to many individuals: historians, living and dead, whose researches have assisted my own, some of whom have further helped by responding to questions arising from their work; scholars of the many specialized disciplines into which my inquiry has lead me; librarians and archivists in Philadelphia, Washington, and numerous repositories in Illinois, Iowa, Kansas, Oklahoma, Colorado, California, and Montana who have guided me to relevant materials in the collections entrusted to them. Above all, I wish to record here my gratitude to my wife Thulia for loving help and encouragement, in ways beyond counting, in this and every work I have attempted in the course of our life together.

Robert Douglas Mead

Paoli

HEARTLAND

I

Peakers Depart

He opened one eye, cautiously, and looked out. The sky beyond his window, looking west, was smoothly gray, lightening, no longer velvet-black. Through the blankets he pressed the coarse cover of the patchwork quilt against his cheek and waited, lying on his side as if still in sleep, but today the feeling did not come—oh, of a kind of soft fog that filled and wrapped his mind and all his joints loose and strengthless as if already exhausted from the work of the day. This morning he was perfectly awake, a tingling coursed the surfaces of his flesh, like, what was that word, galvanic. He slid a little deeper in the bed, tugged the covers up tight, and stretched and felt his feet curving over the end of the mattress in the cool of the sheets, and the soft air from the wide-open window caressed his cheek and forehead. He tried to remember the moment of going to sleep but could not. He had lain on his back, hands joined under his head, the candle out on the bedside stand, and looking up into the darkness of the room, imagining the day ahead when they would start, yes, actually start after all the months of planning and waiting. He held his breath, listening, but the house was still silent. He would wait a little more and listen for the clock on the parlor mantel and count its chimes when they came. Five o'clock, that's how the light looked, it might be five o'clock by now.

—I'm going to Pikes Peak. Today I'm going to Pikes Peak.

The words seemed to shape his lips of themselves and the sound of them, not whispered, vibrated in the bones of his head, and in a rush he flung the covers back, swung his legs out, and his heels landed with a thump on the rag rug. He stepped across to the window and leaned on the sill, taking in the morning air in gulps and studying the sky. Starting to get some light in it and color, first palest hint of the beginning of blue—clear, it was going to be a clear day, blue sky and cloudless, a glorious day to be going somewhere, halfway to the end of the earth or beyond, so folks thought, though the distance he'd calculated from his maps was not much over a thousand miles from Davenport and good traveling all the way by the Santa Fe Road and the southern route; sixty days more or less at the ox-team pace, say early July, and they'd be in the mountains digging the gold.

He leaned far out to look, bracing his hands on the window frame, and could just see, out in front of the house at the edge of the road by the picket gate, where he'd left the loaded wagon last night, brake set: dew stood in droplets on the heavy canvas stretched between the wagon bows, and ran in slow rivulets down the sides. And say, wasn't it a sight with its two coats of sky-blue paint on the body and the bright red on the spokes and felloes of the wheels and the new top shining like a summer cloud! Fifty dollars he'd given old George Staffelbach for it in March, down by Horse Island on the River Road, good cheap if he did have to spend a month of evenings since with his father out in the barn, fixing it up till it was good as new and stronger, too, and then a good part of last week in the shop, shaping a spare axle of aged oak from their own wood-lot up the hill.

Sun, descending the river bluff, rounded the house, lighting one end of the wagon top, and a breath of steam lifted and crawled lazily along the surface of the wet canvas. From the top of a tree up the hill behind the house a redbird flung its whistling song at the sunrise and a hundred bird voices answered in a pulsing, chirping chorus that a flock of crows took up, roosting in trees along the top of the bluff, in a discordant babble of raucous cries. As if on signal the kitchen door creaked open, slowly, and shut, and Ozias McDonald came around the side of the house below Isaac's window and shambled down the slope toward the barn, a squat figure, shirtless with his red union suit half-buttoned and the unlaced tops of his brogans flapping at the cuffs of his high-water jeans. Too lazy or half-asleep for the side trip to the outhouse, Ozias braced himself against the side of the barn, belly sagging over his waistband, to relieve himself, and steam rose from the iridescent stream. Kept a gallon jug hidden in his room—to send him off of nights, as he once admitted when his breath reeked high in the morning as a barrel of last year's cider—but at least he got up mornings to do his chores and never yet ran off in harvesttime as some others had.

Ozias hawked a gob at the barn wall, held a match to the blackened clay of his pipe bowl and, sending up a blue puff of smoke, set his bowed, arthritic legs moving again and disappeared around the back of the barn to pitch down hay for the cows, first chore of the day. Isaac drew his head in, pulled the nightshirt up and off, and dropped it on the floor. Filling the basin on the washstand, he leaned to splash

his face and hair and work a lather from the thick cake of his mother's
yellow soap.

Dried and half-dressed, hair combed and brushed, he paused to take
the steel mirror from the dresser and consider whether he should
shave. The hair covering his cheeks was curly and silky-fine, transparent in the rising morning light and almost invisible; fuzz. On the
other hand, those were definite beard-like bristles on his cheekbones,
lip, and the point of his chin—but of the same golden hue as the rest
that made them hard to see. Angling the mirror, he tried a smile but
did not like it; then set his jaws till the muscles bulged and drew lips
and brows together in the serious, penetrating look of a man going
forth to meet the world, and liked it better. Why, there wasn't a thing
he couldn't do, and wouldn't do, too, now his time had come. He
propped the mirror on the dresser-top and stropped the razor.

The kitchen door opened again and after a moment shut, and his
mother emerged, a slim figure in a poke bonnet, moving with quick
steps in a straight line for the barn, followed at a trot by the new girl
with the pails—Treenie, she called her, as a name that could perhaps
be taken for more American than her own, Katharina, and had not
attempted to learn or pronounce the rest of it, which sounded something like "whole-shoe" and was Dutch, meaning German, no further
comment needed. Ozias met them halfway up, pitchfork shouldered
like a musket, and silently lifted his wool hat by its shapeless crown.

—Mister McDonald! Mrs Pride saluted him in her carefully modu-
lated, gentle voice that nevertheless carried, uphill, through window
and wall, implicit in the two words the accent of Vermont that
twenty years in the West had not effaced, of the place that was still for
her what she meant when she said home.

—You'll be pitching the corn down to the hogs now, she observed, I
expect—a plain statement not quite question or command, partaking
of both, confirmed by the fork on his shoulder. Ozias nodded and
replaced his hat, labored on up the hill. We'll leave the milk pails for
you by the barn door, she called after him.

Pulling the skin tight, Isaac cautiously scraped at his soapy cheek.
Ozias had entered the crib built into the slope above the fattening pen
and a cascade of golden ears rained down on the earth among the
waiting animals. It was a chore, feeding them, first thing, from which
Isaac this special day had been excused. It was one of the things he
was not going to have to do now, no, not ever again.

Mary followed the girl slowly up the slope—the morning's eggs to
hunt, the chickens to feed, breakfast to get ready, the stove already
heating with the first wood burned down to coals. If only they could
get and keep good, reliable, American help, but it was always the
same: tell them the tasks one by one, lead them along and set them to
it, and come back afterward to see how they had done—and half the

time Mr McDonald asleep on the milking stool, head cushioned against the cow's flank and still not dressed like a Christian for his day's work, and little Treenie dreaming out the window while the bread scorched!

This morning of all mornings Mr Pride would be long in his bedroom at his private prayers. In their early years in the West she had been gravely fearful for the condition of her soul—Husband off preaching three and four days a week and trying to make a farm in between, raising up children in a comfortless land and the neighbor women to nurse through, the kitchen garden to tend with the girl, and when the cows freshened forty pounds of butter a week to churn and barrel up in the icehouse for the merchants at Davenport—it did not seem that any moment was left her from new-year to year-end for any but material thoughts: things of this world.

A momentary flash of light glanced at her eye under the wide brim of the bonnet, she lifted her head and the morning sun slapped her face, and looking up she saw: Isaac unmindful and precarious on the windowsill of the bedroom over the kitchen, a mirror in his hand, examining his face by the morning light, vain as a girl—or not a girl neither but a man, a man's vanity, a boy on the way to manhood. At least for once he was up and stirring without having to be called. And now he was twenty-one and free to go according to law, impatient to depart, wasting his substance on a vain journey to the gold regions, the prodigal son; and wasted the whole spring fitting up his wagon, and looked well enough standing out in front on the road, but paid too dear in the first place to that Dutchman, Mr Staffelbach—and spending the last of his money on supplies to carry, and Mr Pride abetting with a camp stove from LeClaire's foundry and the two best yoke of oxen at no charge—. But if her son made his journeys to the ends of the heathen earth, they still had their work to do, the same work every day—*they* could not pack up and go.

—Treenie! Mary called as the girl lingered, looking up, like her, at the boy with his mirror in the sunlit window. We've eggs to gather, and chickens to feed, and the men—. No time—

The girl, startled, went skipping up the slope empty-handed, and Mary plodded after.

Isaac let himself through the front door and out the gate, climbed in the wagon to look once more before it all began. They had loaded toward the back, leaving space enough in the front of the wagon-box for him and Andy to sleep, if they had to. In front of the tailgate to be handy to get out were all the cooking things, clothes in a square tin trunk and blankets in boxes, and the big wall tent rolled up on top. Then a barrel of flour, paper-lined, and a hundred pounds each of bacon and dried beef, lightly salted, in tin-lined boxes; and two kegs of sorghum syrup and one of sugar, a barrel of potatoes, dried apples, green coffee, salt, matches, soap, six half-gallon cans of axle grease; and some delicacies his and Andy's family had insisted on putting in —a couple of hams, two crocks of head cheese, a gallon of strained honey from his mother's hives, a small box of grape jam in jars, another of home-canned beans and peas, a firkin of his mother's butter, well salted; and a big dried-fruit cake Mrs McHarg had made last week and promised would keep. And: six kegs for water, filled, two kegs of powder, fifty pounds of lead in bars and two heavy drawstring leather sacks of ready-molded bullets and two small, tin-lined boxes to hold the caps; and sacks of oats and shelled corn, a hundred pounds each, for the cattle, for when they got into country where the grazing was scarce; a couple of axes and shovels, a bow-saw, a hand-adze; and somewhere under all, the new spare axle. Something over half a ton it came to, a light enough load for this broad-tired Western wagon with two yoke of his father's well-fed oxen to pull it, even on the muddy roads of an Iowa spring. Isaac had wanted to cut back on the beef and potatoes, calculating to get fresh meat with his gun, and didn't like vegetables anyhow; but his father insisted they outfit with enough of everything to last the whole way and something over, and anything too much would help see them home or sell at good profit. He was shipping them by boat to Leavenworth City; and three more barrels of his own good flour, to make up what they'd have consumed by then.

Late the last week they'd been ready at last to pack up and go, but Mr Wood, who was to be the train's captain at least across the Missouri and maybe beyond, had deemed Friday an unlucky day for beginning a journey. Then it was Saturday and Isaac's father had ruled that if they loaded they were not to violate the Sabbath by traveling, and they had waited out the two more days and packed on Monday; and now it was Tuesday, third day of May of the year 1859, a lucky day in a lucky year, or so Isaac pronounced it and meant to make it so.

There was woodsmoke in the air and, as he re-entered the house, other smells: the penetrating, faintly sour smell of sliced ham frying in the skillet, under that the pillowing sweetness of biscuits in the oven, hot iron and steam and smoke. As he came in, his mother was placing a stick of stovewood in the firebox. She clanged the door shut with the wire-handled plate-lifter, and stood up, smoothing a wisp of hair along the side of her head.

—A good morning to you, Isaac, she observed, the corners of her mouth lifting in a small smile. You're up with the chickens, it seems.

—I was checking over my outfit, Isaac said.

—And wear it out with looking, if you could, his mother rejoined.

Well! She turned back to the stove, slid the skillet toward the back, and stirred at the pot of mush with a wooden spoon.

Treenie mounted the steps to the back porch, stamping her feet. She set the empty pail down and came in, small face flushed under the tightly drawn checked kerchief, breathing quickly and muttering something about *"erzürnende Hühne."* She untied the kerchief, tucked it in the band of her apron, and gave her hair a shake.

—Treenie, Mrs Pride said, voice clear, slow, and emphatic, we'll give Isaac his breakfast first this morning, needn't make him wait for prayers since he's here—the men coming soon enough, I expect, and his long journey to begin today.

The girl stood motionless a moment, her flat face assuming a look of obedient blankness, brow drawn together as she sorted the command from its explanation.

—Yess, Missuss Pride, she answered carefully, with a drawn-out hissing of sibilants.

The girl took a bowl from the hutch, ladled it full of mush, and set it on the table by the honey crock and a pitcher of fresh milk still warm from the cow.

—Six kegs full of water! Isaac said through a mouthful of mush. That Father says we're to carry clear across Kansas, for the cattle, in case ever we have to camp between streams. Dried up and leaked away, I don't doubt, before ever we come to the dry part of the road! But that's well enough—

He waggled his empty spoon at his mother, who was serving fried eggs and dripping slices of ham onto a plate. Treenie stooped at the oven door, hands wrapped in a towel, and brought forth a pan dotted with steaming, golden-brown biscuits.

—No, those kegs won't be wasted, no, sir! Isaac continued as his mother set the plate before him and stood back, arms folded on her breast. Cause we'll use those kegs to carry the gold home in, that's what we'll use them for, think of that, why, it might make a thousand pounds, and all in gold. And then the things we'll do! Buy in the mortgage on the farm from Ebenezer Cook and buy the mill back from Fred and tear down the house and build it new and twice as grand—or no, we'll *keep* it to live in while we build and then after, for tenants or renting out. We'll build in the trees at the top of the bluff where we can look out and see the boats coming and going on the river and the engines and cars crossing the bridge from Rock Island, about twice the size of Squire Newcomb's house in town, and four stories high with a glassed-in tower on the top, so big it'll cover a whole acre of ground and one big room for just nothing but taking baths in. And a new harmonium for Lizzie. And—Treenie!—a chain of pure gold just to tie up your hair—

With a rustling of the striped gingham of her apron, newly sewn on her machine and stiff, not yet washed, his mother crossed the kitchen and stood behind his chair. She placed her hands gently on his shoulders and leaned forward as if to embrace him but held back.

—Ah, Isaac, Isaac! she said, voice lingering on the syllables, almost crooning, how you do run on—but only to get your courage up, and ours too, I expect. But you know I wouldn't envy the Newcombs or anyone what's theirs—why, I've all the house right now I can live in or care for, and if ever we require another room or two we can build on ourselves, with a couple of men, as we have always done—and when I want a bath, I'll have it warm and cozy with the tub beside the stove in my room. And gold! This land is all the gold I want, and will go on yielding back its gold as long as we have strength and wisdom to plant and crop—and for you too, once you've made your journey and seen what the world is and come home again. But—and smiling now she drew back and returned to the stove—to hear you go on I'd think, if I didn't know, you'd caught the gold fever sure, same as some others hereabouts, and as they write it in the papers.

Leaning back in the chair, silenced and thoughtful, Isaac poured himself a fresh cup of coffee. Treenie held out the biscuit pan but he shook his head. A wisp of steam rose from the cup. The windows were clouding over with warmth from the stove and its cooking and the steaming water in the reservoir at its side. Perhaps in a month, with the heat settled in and more men around to be fed and the labor accelerating toward harvest, the stove with much commotion would be carried out to what they called the summer kitchen, a sort of shed, broad-roofed but open on all sides, around which his father had trained up grape vines. Another thing he would not do: high out on the Plains by then, driving the wagon along the Santa Fe Road, and most across Kansas.

Gold fever: it was the latest of many—there had been, in the years following the War of Independence, an Ohio fever transmitted by the promise of land bounties to former soldiers; an Iowa fever that Isaac's father Abraham had taken; a Kansas fever burning hot now five long years, since new millions of acres of Indian land had been opened; and now another spell of the gold fever, raging a year, since someone found pure specks of the metal in the sands along Cherry Creek, high up toward the sources of the Platte and the western limit of Kansas Territory, defined, more or less, by the Continental Divide—and then others, around the high mountains south and southwest where, it was thought, the gold must flow from, and the whole area, ten thousand square miles of it, was loosely called Pikes Peak or, more carefully, the Gold Regions.

Fever: accurate enough in that the word put a name to the thousand varieties of human motive, otherwise unspecifiable, that united to strip whole populous villages in New England and New York of their people and leave behind, shipwrecked on bare village greens, only the church and a few houses of indestructible brick or stone, and, as the riverboats and railroads inched west, reached into like villages in every nation of Europe and became America fever, with like effect. And the word was true in another way too: the lands to which these fevers led were, rarely excepted, breeding grounds for actual fevers in countless forms, prostrating men, their women and babies, with heat and chill and agued limbs.

Abraham's personal variety of this fever had several sources. Land had its part: the remnant of two thousand Greenwich acres, divided, redivided, recombined through two centuries and seven generations of too numerous sons and their marriages until, though good land still, not enough was left but for one more inheritor, an elder brother likewise destined for the ministry and, so it was assumed, for the pulpit of the Congregational church built up the hill from the old home place; and so embedded and intermarried, these late generations, in the town, so narrowed and tribe-like in finding comfort only among their own kind, in common culture, speech, origins, descent, that the young men rarely made marriages except with cousins, and often Prides in name as well as lineage (and a result not easy to avoid in practice, apart from inclination, given the numbers in which the family had spread along both sides of Long Island Sound). Abraham's leaving had been, therefore, necessary, complete, and final: from Yale and seminary to a pulpit and marriage in a part of Vermont scarcely a generation from frontier. He was not allowed to rest there long. Farm products from cheap and better land in Ohio, Indiana—especially wool, a Vermont specialty, transportable by steamboat and canal barge—displaced Vermont's; there followed the disruption of money, credit, markets that became the Panic of 1837. Abraham's congregation, unable to keep up their minister's stipend, fearful for their own land and livelihood, grew quarrelsome. Abraham, casting about, with a twenty-year-old wife, a daughter and another coming, learned of land newly vacated by the Sac and Fox, along the Mississippi in the Iowa district of a new territory called Ouisconsin; and took necessity for vocation—to carry the Sabbath, as he put it, beyond the great river.

Abraham traveled out to look—three weeks by steamboat, canal packet, steamboat again, and finally on foot with winter coming and the Upper Mississippi closed by ice—and stayed to preach in the riverside taverns and make a choice: of steep land and wooded rising up the bluff to remind his wife of Vermont and home, he thought, but with no granite outcrops and a long view out over a great bend in the river and, being near the foot of the fifteen miles of the river's Upper Rapids, a capital spot, so its promoters argued, for a town and county seat; to secure which he staked corners, put up a cabin sixteen-foot square, and joined a club of neighbors contracted to protect each other's claims (the land, not yet surveyed, could not be bought nor title gotten). In the spring, commissioned by the Missionary Society, he went home to buy a team and wagon and bring out Mary and his two children, Lizzie and the newborn Isaac, dreaming of founding a church—a presbytery, a synod, a whole family of churches—and building a great city of the West.

Abraham's dream, like most dreams, most prophecies, turned out true in substance but deceptive in its particulars. The church indeed was built, on a corner of his land and with much of his labor, a square, white, spireless, long-windowed edifice, a meetinghouse, as in Vermont—but quarrels came, as there, incited by his very benevolence, and left him churchless, this time with the building but no congregation to fill it. The town too grew for a time but, with an adverse vote relocating the county seat, moved—taverns, hotels, steamboat landing, grist mill, narrow town lots and their shops and houses—four miles upriver toward the foot of the rapids and became the city backed by George Davenport and Antoine LeClaire. What remained, vacated, where Abraham had set his heart, was land too steep for prosperous farming, in time filled up by Rheinländer (Mary's Dutch, meaning German) coming upriver in boatloads, hundreds, with incomprehensible speech and diseases brought or caught en route, adjoining the county seat. History accelerated. In one generation Davenport surpassed what Greenwich had become in seven (or the towns of the Rheinpfalz in seventy): six thousand souls supported by a limitless hinterland, a railroad (built from Chicago, financed from Boston), a gas works and lighted streets, the first bridge across the Mississippi, a college, and New England public lecturers in season, among them Emerson.

Not only in appearance—set on steep slopes rising from navigable water—and in its transplanted institutions, was Isaac's Davenport like Abraham's Greenwich thirty years before: neither offered an obvious mold in which a young man lately turned twenty-one and brimming with undirected energy and intelligence might choose to cast his life. His father had made efforts, but these dreams too were thwarted. Year by year he enlarged the farm, ten acres, twenty, at a time, cut the trees to sell for firewood, grubbed out the stumps with chains and oxen, varied his crops from wheat for quick cash to corn and hogs (among the first to try this mix), sweet potatoes, small fruits, dairying, and built—a second, bigger barn with stone foundation, a carriage house, an icehouse, a shop, and added rooms and wings and gables, a second story, to the house, all built around and over the original cabin. Isaac worked well enough at the duties of the farm, but under direction and almost grudging, like a hired hand; a weakness his mother attributed sometimes to a delicate constitution, at other times to the dreadful fact of having made their life at the edge of wilderness, meaning the rolling prairies beyond the bluff, whence still came tales of Christian settlers killed or carried off by renegade Sioux acknowledging no treaties—but, dismayingly, the boy was apt at riding his horse, whole days at a time, across that country, at trapping coons for skins and snaring prairie chickens, and with his own gun or his father's, borrowed, at bringing back wild turkeys and an occasional deer. Not that the boy had been allowed to grow up unimproved by education. Abraham had led the committee that formed and chartered Iowa College and then through successive winters boarded his son in town that he might attend—the boy acquired sufficient mathematics to do surveying of new land out on the prairie (his father provided the instruments), a smattering of Latin, natural philosophy, literature, but no prizes and no degree.

Having turned his son toward farming, then scholarship, and finding neither to his taste and talents, Abraham considered trade and, using money earned from cutting wood and borrowed through relatives in Connecticut and Vermont at cheaper Eastern rates, bought a run-down sawmill across the river in the town of Rock Island. For a time—with the railroad building across Illinois, then west from Davenport, bringing people and money in—the business prospered. Isaac with filial diligence again took up the work his father set him—stayed the week over at the mill, coming home Saturday afternoons by the steam ferry or in winter daily walked or rode his horse across the ice —but without enthusiasm, was lonely, often tired and out of sorts. Whether in time he might have shaped his will to this life was left unanswered: another panic, that of 1857, intervened, money in the West was once more scarce, there was no sale for lumber, and the mill was closed and sold. Abraham, thankful to be shut of another failed dream and with his land intact, harbored no grudge.

But if not farming, teaching, running a mill, then what? Davenport might grow to ten or twenty times its size but it was established, set, closed in, and would not change much; there seemed nothing for a man to do but walk the paths already marked by others.

So for Isaac Pikes Peak and gold were not quite fever, but when the news had come and then in late summer of 1858 the first Peakers returned to the States with their tales, they had given form to the necessity of departure; and so he had announced and planned, and now would do; a trying out of himself, a testing, to learn what he was good for.

The motives of the others who would make up the party were variants on Isaac's. William Wood at twenty-five had for five years kept a store of general merchandise in town but since the panic showed more credit on his books than cash. He was freighting what remained of his goods to Kansas to trade at the frontier profit, meaning to get land, start a store, build a mill, and leave his clerk, Dave Kilbourn, in charge, while he came back to fetch his family—or, who knows, join a train bound for the Peak if that's how the chances looked; having a brother there already, farming corn near Lawrence, he had made the journey the summer past, knew the roads, and would lead. Andy McHarg, a neighbor boy whose family's farm adjoined the Prides', would partner Isaac in his wagon and was of the same age: a thick-set taciturn youth, given to obscure quarrels long maintained, for months now with his father over farming; and hence the resolve to join the party for the Peak; but—hunting and trapping together till Isaac started at the college, holding the surveyor's rod, working for a time on a railroad section gang and, when that gave out, briefly at the mill—always, surprisingly, on easy terms with Isaac Pride. Two other neighbor boys would make the third wagon in the train, John Saur and his younger brother Chris, who, having four ahead of them in the line of inheritance, had let Isaac persuade them that their share in the gold would buy the farm they otherwise had no prospect of getting. Although fifteen years already in Iowa, the whole family was German-born and remained so in their manners, speech, and flaxen looks.

Isaac with slow sips had finished his second cup of coffee when his father appeared in the doorway of the kitchen. Four inches taller than his son, but the difference seemed more: a strongly muscled man who held himself straight, shoulders back, and moved still, two months short of his fiftieth birthday, with athletic quickness, springing on the balls of his feet; but something contradictory in his look that made men uneasy with him, as if body and mind moved to discordant rhythms, lived different lives—a way of looking and not quite seeming to see or seeing more than was before his eyes, or looking elsewhere and inward, listening, a small smile of general benignity playing about his lips, as now, habitual and possibly ironic, creasing the folds around his deep-set, quiet eyes. A long face, strong-featured, surmounted by chestnut hair, gray-flecked, that formed a mass at his temples and above his ears; Isaac had his father's looks and color, lightened, his mother's lithe slightness, slenderness. Today Abraham had put on his long-tailed coat of ministerial black, with a black stock doubled around his neck that held the points of his collar tight against his jaw, and Mary, quick, remarked on his dress.

—Husband! You come before us in your Sabbath garments.

—Ah! He paused, eyes looking past them, taking in the swelling morning light beyond the kitchen window, the smile enlarging. Have I mistook the day? There was *something*, I had it in mind, unusual in store for us this day.

He lowered his eyes and appeared to consider, but Mary did not wait.—Shall we go in to prayers? I'll go call Lizzie.

—Perhaps, he suggested, holding up a hand, there was something important to her she felt obliged to finish, before coming down. She'll come.

He led the way along the hallway to the parlor: walls papered with a flowered print; a mahogany sofa tightly covered in shiny black horsehair, three similar chairs; a carpet, red and blue, with an emblematic eagle at the center, machine-made in Massachusetts, not yet taken up for summer; a Franklin stove fitted in the fireplace and, over the mantel, above the clock, an oval portrait, brought from Greenwich, of Abraham's grandfather, in uniform, white-haired and stern; and by a south-facing window a fretted mahogany stand where Lizzie kept a collection of small cactuses. It was not a room that encouraged mere sitting but sitting erect, in earnest discourse. Ozias waited in the room's other entrance that led to the family parlor, leaning against the doorframe, half in, half out, hat in hand. Abraham seated himself before the narrow table that held the two leather-bound volumes of his Bible, printed in London and elaborately illustrated with steel engravings that had been a delight of his children's childhood. Ceremoniously he produced his spectacles, a recent and unwanted necessity, and put them on.

As he opened the first volume and found his place, Lizzie with a whispering of silk-slippered feet came down the stairs and took a seat beside her mother on the sofa, in her hand two sheets of foolscap minutely written over in purple ink. She had her mother's darkness—hair, eye, brows—but freshened and amplified by youth: not pretty to most people's notions of prettiness in the year 1859—something too quick and knowing about her eyes and expression—but beautiful, perhaps, or, matured, might become so and be so acknowledged. This morning above her full black skirt she wore the new basquine she had sketched from *Godey's Lady's Book* and her mother had cut and sewed, around her shoulders a kind of long-fringed shawl she called a mantilla. She sat forward on the edge of the sofa, erect and attentive, eyes on her father's face.

—The lesson I have chosen for today is one you may recall—he inclined his head toward his wife—we read together on the day we prepared to depart from my father's house, exactly twenty-one years ago today. Mary opened her mouth to speak—it was in June they started, not *exactly* twenty-one years—but kept silent. From Deuteronomy, the twenty-seventh chapter.

Abraham read, deep-voiced, in the even-paced manner he had learned at seminary:

Moses with the elders of Israel commanded the people, saying, Keep all the commandments which I command you this day. And it shall be on the day when ye shall pass over Jordan unto the land which the Lord thy God giveth thee, that thou shalt set thee up great stones, and plaster them with plaster: And thou shalt write upon them all the words of this law, when thou art passed over, that thou mayest go in unto the land which the Lord thy God giveth thee, a land that floweth with milk and honey; as the Lord God of thy fathers hath promised thee.

Abraham lifted his eyes from the page and reverently closed the book.—As He does elsewhere in Holy Scripture, he began, so here God teaches us in figures. I shall not say much to interpret. The Church is our Moses, who led us forth from our own country and across a great river, to raise up altars to God in the land He promised us. We, therefore, on this continent are the Israel of God, chosen not through any merit of our own but solely for the fulfilling of His divine and inscrutable purposes. We know His Law: it has been written in our hearts, in characters each of us is best fitted to interpret and comprehend, according to the light of reason given us. By this Law were we commanded to go forth as warriors and seize the land promised us and abandoned by an alien people—not, I repeat, for our own sakes or through any merit of our own, but solely that God's will might be done—that thereby there might come peace in that land, and His people, as they are known to Him, might rejoice in the fruits thereof.

—All this we have done, according as the Lord led us. This lesson, therefore, for us, was prophecy. Let us each pray that it be so also for our son, whom this day we send forth to cross another great river and enter into another land of promise. And let us pray also that he carry there always God's Law written in his heart, and its strength, and its peace.

He ceased, and after a moment's silence opened the other volume of his Bible: the Psalm now, in their daily order of worship, which formerly they had often sung to one of the old tunes handed down in shape-notes of Massachusetts origin, and Lizzie accompanied on the harmonium. They gathered behind his chair to read the music of the words over his shoulder, together, as he pointed the place.

O Lord, thou has searched me and known me.
Thou knowest my downsitting and mine uprising, thou understandest my thought afar off.
Thou compassest my path and my lying down, and art acquainted with all my ways.
For there is not a word in my tongue, but, lo, O Lord, thou knowest it altogether.

Their reading was accompanied by rising squeals from the axles of a laden wagon climbing the bluff from the River Road, oxen lowing, whip cracking, shouts; then the concluding creak of a brake being set, silence, a booted step on the porch, a knock. Nervously bobbing her head, Treenie gathered her skirts up and ran out into the hall. The door swung open, a new voice came through, a name, and Mr Wood allowed as he would wait outside. The other voices fell away around him, but Abraham read on to the end, imperturbable, as if hearing only the Word of God. Concluding, he closed the book, rose, and knelt in the center of the carpet, and the others knelt facing him— except Ozias, who still slouched in the doorway, respectful, baptized, perhaps, at some time in remote childhood, but never yet churched. Abraham bent his head, eyes closed, lifted it again and looked up, clasping his hands. He prayed:

O Lord of heaven and earth, and of all that is, in heaven and in the earth. Lord of man's soul and mind and flesh. We know that if this Thy child goes forth to the ends of the earth, he goes only because Thou sendest him, and leadest him in his way. We pray Thee therefore that Thou, as heretofore, wouldst ever lead and guide him, and deliver him from all evil, as Thou hast most surely done since the day Thou broughtest him forth from his mother's womb and clothest him in flesh. And to his home return him at the last, for Thy own mercy's sake. Amen.

And the others answered: *Amen.*

Isaac sprang up and seized his father's hand to shake, man-fashion, and be gone, but Abraham's arms enclosed him in their strength, pressing his face against his shoulder: —Ah, my son, my son!

There came a rustling of papers behind them and Lizzie's voice, small.—Isaac, I have something for you.

Abraham released him, stepped back, and as Isaac gave a wide-eyed shake of his head, like a child caught in some inadvertent mischief, said—Son, I had most forgot, your sister has labored at a gift to send you on your way. Let us give her time to give it.

He turned, went back to his chair, and sat, face set in the look of glazed attention he reserved for poetry. Mary and Treenie returned to the sofa. Isaac, tight-lipped, half-sat on a chair arm near the door, one leg moving in short, impatient swings. Ozias, silently, had gone out front to inspect Wood's team.

Lizzie had taken a position by a window, one hand resting on the cactus stand, the other stiffly extended in front, holding the pages of her manuscript—a manner of delivery brought home from her two years at the female seminary at South Hadley, Massachusetts, from which, after the term of practice teaching, she had returned with a teacher's certificate, but the work seemed not to agree with her. For now she occupied herself with watercolors and occasional oils, though, despite lessons from a muralist who had opened a shop at Davenport, perspective remained for her an unplumbed mystery; and with writing poems, which she sent frequently to newspapers, where they were signed "from Ivy Nook," as she called the farm.

Lizzie made a little clearing sound in her throat and began to read, voice raised a note or two above its usual pitch:

To a Brother, Going West

I

Once more renewed by sweet, unconscious Spring,
The Forests deck themselves in leaves and flowers,
And nesting birds pause on the bough to sing,
Ere flitting to the woods' deep-shaded bowers.
  In celebration of your life's new birth,
  The heav'ns pour gladness upon all the Earth.

From far off down the ridge road came the sound of another wagon approaching, voices. Setting her face against distractions, Lizzie pressed on, voice rising:

II

As once our Fathers parted their old home,
And steer'd frail barks upon New England's shore,
Your wagon on the prairie seas of loam
You, Brother, launch today, as they, of yore.
  Go! Find your fortune in Pike's realms of gold!
  But be thou ever just, as thou are bold.

The sounds were getting closer, louder: those Saur boys coming, and their wagon. Out front, Ozias let out a whoop, as if for holiday.

III

And as your well-trained yoke of ox beside
You slowly march, and lead your noble horse,
'Mid wilderness of grass, keep high our Pride,
Rememb'ring Conscience is God's mightiest force.
  And, quaffing vintage sparkling streams afford,
  Know you are miss'd around the family board.

The mantel clock began to sound. Lizzie waited, hand trembling slightly with its tightly held papers, and on the eighth stroke resumed:

IV

'Til your return, our eyes yearn toward the West—
Oh! mighty West and noble, ever free!—
Where toiling trav'ler is by breeze caress'd,
And prairies billow endless as the sea.
  Will you write often to assuage our fears?
  Or will you build 'tween us a barrier of years?

At this point Lizzie paused to draw breath and turn over to the second leaf. Isaac leaped to his feet.—Lizzie, that was beautiful! he said, and, when her face contracted and that seemed not to have been the formula to please her and release him, he tried again: Really fine, Lizzie! Altogether the nicest poem of yours I've heard for—well, for weeks.

His father, standing, took the cue.—Yes indeed, daughter. It was a lovely poem. And now—

Lizzie's face crumpled, she clutched the pages of her poem to her breast.—But it's not finished! she cried. There's more—. With a shriek, gathering her skirts, she ran for the doorway and up the stairs.

Isaac bolted for the door. His parents followed, and Treenie, and stood on the porch, watching. There was Mr Wood with his clerk Kilbourn, their wagon wheeled in the road and set, ready to descend the hill. There was Andy McHarg coming along from his house farther up, a carpet satchel tucked under one arm with spare linen and other necessaries pressed on him by his mother, heavy feet scuffing the rutted dust and at every other step making a joyous skip. And there, a little farther back, came the two Saur boys, chattering to each other as they guided their single yoke of oxen and light wagon with little cries and cluckings of encouragement.

Mr Wood came through the gate, trotted across the grass to the porch railing and reached up to shake hands.—We've a fine day, Mister Pride, for starting out, he said. A prosperous day, a glorious day! I don't know but we'll get clear to Muscatine by nightfall—by dinnertime tomorrow, sure—

—Andy! Isaac cried. Andy, I'll race you to the barn! And set out down the slope, legs moving easily and fast until he seemed to float across the dew-wet, heavy-headed grass. The other boy under so many eyes hesitated a moment, then dropped his satchel in the road and set out after, fists tight, short arms pumping.

And then such confusion of arriving and departing, of shouts and laughs and whips cracking and oxen bellowing, of joy and sorrow all in one! The Saur boys guided their animals to the roadside, set the brake, and ran one at a time to pay respects to Mr and Mrs Pride, still surveying the scene from the porch, while the other stood by his nigh ox, stroking its flanks and talking gently in its ear. It seemed hardly a moment before Isaac and Andy came out from the barn, leading their team up the slope, already yoked, but the normally tractable oxen had caught the excitement and resisted hurrying with snorts and grunts, tossing their heads and pulling awry. Abraham watched till they were almost to the road and seemed about to bolt, then threw his coat off and ran to Isaac with the big wheelers, Jeroboam and Goliath. Mary gathered the coat up where he dropped it, dusted it with one hand, carefully folded it, and laid it over the railing.

Abraham got in front of the two animals, put his hands stiff-armed on the yoke and braced his feet, shouting.—Whoa, Jerry, whoa Golly! Whooaa! And as they slowed and stopped, put his hands on their foreheads, stroking and softly talking to them, gentling. He got around to the side, took the goad from his son, and prodded the nigh ox.—Now, get up, get up! Haw, Jerry, haw, Golly!—and they started forward again, slowly, swung to the left, and he led them along and halted them forward of the wagon-tongue, in position for chaining up. While Isaac hooked the heavy chain to the staple set in the yoke, Abraham ran back to help Andy bring the lead pair along, Caesar and Cicero, and get them in place for chaining to the wheelers' yoke. Isaac raced back down to the barn and returned with his dappled mare Regina on a long lead rope to tie behind the wagon.

Then it was done and nothing more remained. Abraham took his son's hand and for a long moment held it in both his.—Isaac! Our prayers go with you—go forward by the grace of God—remember us, remember us and this home of yours, always—

—Oh, Father!—Isaac began and discovered that there were no words sufficient to the moment of parting, that what he had thought to say had fled his mind, or his mind was too full, too pulled in opposing directions.

—Your *mother*, Isaac, Abraham said with a hunching of one shoulder toward the porch where she watched them. And Elizabeth—Sister I suppose will keep her room since we were so thoughtless—

Isaac flinched at the mild rebuke, pulled his hand free and ran. Mary leaned to him from the top step, both hands reaching from under the long gray shawl pulled close around her shoulders.

—You must write to us, every day if you can, she said, with news of your progress. And we—we shall be here, waiting for your return. And oh, Isaac—

What more was in her heart went beyond custom and discipline to speak, and the word trailed off to silence.

—Dear Mother! he said, looking her in the eyes, then saw the servant girl standing back by the door and, released, let go her soft, cool hands. And, Treenie! he cried. Remember what I told you of gold—beads and bracelets of gold, and gold combs for your hair, when I get my mines—

He was down the steps in one jump, running. His father held the gate for him, let it swing shut, and slowly returned to the porch. Isaac went around to the side of his nigh leader, Caesar, and stood waiting.

With a wave and a drawn-out cry—Git *uppp!*—and pistol crack from his long-handled whip, Mr Wood started his team, Kilbourn from his place behind eased off on the brake, and the wagon moved forward into the road and started slowly down the hill. The Saurs followed with their little wagon and undersized yoke, then Isaac—

Get up, get up! Gee, Caesar, gee, Cicero—and cracked his whip while Andy McHarg managed the brake, and the horse on her lead roused from tasting the grass beside the road and sedately followed. Ozias, leaning on the picket fence, noticed the boy's satchel still lying in the road, ran for it, stiff-legged and stumbling, caught up again and heaved it in the back of the wagon. For a moment he stood in the middle of the road, looking after them, then lifted his voice in a long hurrah and spun his hat high in the air.

Abraham and Mary stood by the open door to watch the little train down the hill. When no words came, he slipped his arm around her waist and drew her to him, and for a minute she let him, then edged away and took his thick-calloused hand in hers.

A bedroom window went up and Lizzie leaned out, waving a white handkerchief, and shouting her farewell.—Isaac! Brother Isaac! God bless you all the way!

Probably—the distance, the morning breeze blowing downhill, the squealing of brakes, the grunts of five yoke of oxen holding back—he could no longer hear the words, but he heard the voice, turned, waved, and gave a joyous leap in the air. And then at a turning of the road among the trees, they were gone.

II

The Chrysalis

A man's earliest memory is peculiarly important, less for the thing remembered than simply for being first, providing a reference point for the beginning and continuity of consciousness. Before it, there is nothing, a chaos of disconnected sensations, light and darkness alternating in no order, warmth, cold, insipid tastings, touchings, tales told after the fact by parents and relatives out of their own memories and taken on faith. Then abruptly come sharp images located in time and moving in time, one after the other, in order, and the child's life has become known and conscious, has been experienced, and has properly begun, like a merry-go-round starting up from motionless silence, bursting into whirling movement with its music, cries, and laughter. The memory's particular shape, which is that of the mind remembering, learning to remember, informs the memories that follow: a lens fixed in time, through which the mind looks forward into the memories that succeed it, but also back through the minds of all the fathers gone before in their generations of consciousness and life; a prism sorting the complex unity of experience into its parts, just as the precisely faceted crystal bends the invisible light to make it visible as bands and layers of color.

For Isaac, memory began with a walk down the road from the house, and finding the Indian chief. The year, perhaps, was 1844, maybe earlier, he had started school, anyhow: no fence yet separated the road in front of the house from the yard—or hardly that, an unused patch of rank prairie grass mixed with cornflowers and Indian paintbrush and at one side a bed his mother had dug for roses brought in pots from her parents' house in Vermont and worried through the winters wrapped in straw and burlap; they had built on a parlor along the side of the house, with real sash windows that went up and down and a bedroom over it, but the children—Isaac, his sister Lizzie, and colored Sally, (the orphan girl brought by his father in the fall on the boat from Louisville to learn sewing and cooking, butter-making, and reading too, from his mother) still slept in the low, slope-ceilinged attic up a ladder from the shed kitchen at the back.

It was early fall, bright days and hot, turning cool at night, leaves still thick on the trees but tattered, going brown around the edges, and the road out front was dry and ridged with soft dust. He had been wanting to go down that road, down the steep bluff to the river-bank, you could see it from the house, a line of trees and brush along the edge and across the way the break in the low mudbank where the Rock River came in from the east. He knew the way. In the winter his father and some other men went down to Credit Island to cut trees for wood to sell to the boats and make fence rails with and down at one end of the island they built a shanty for men to stay in all winter, cutting wood, and later they went to cut ice and haul it up in wagons. It was the dull time of afternoon between dinner and supper, no one around, and he squatted by the edge of the road with a handful of pebbles gathered in the lap of his roundabout and tossed them, one at a time, to see them splash and sink in the dust, and Lizzie was in the parlor doing sums in her copybook, his father was up the hill cradling wheat with Mr Garner, his mother gone up to rest before starting the evening meal, and Sally was supposed to be out back, scouring pots. He tossed the last pebble and got up, and started slowly along the edge of the road, kicking his sandals in the grass; not going anyplace special, just walking along by the side of the road.

After sauntering past the Garners' house and turning down the Buffalo Road toward the river, he took a running jump and got over a corner of the fence where the top rail was knocked down, pushed his way in among the rows of corn and continued at a trot, stumbling sometimes against the clods, hemmed in by the close-planted rows of ripe corn seasoning on the stalk but sure enough of his direction. He climbed another fence, ran along one side of a field of wheat, came out on the River Road, and crouched to look. It was where the slough came out from behind the island and joined the steamboat channel. Phil Garner had said there were Indians camped on the island and dared him to go look, he'd be afraid they'd carry him off or eat him; not that Isaac would take Phil's dare or any boy's, he knew that much —but he wanted to see for himself, and he knew the way well enough, he'd show that Phil who was scared or not. There was one house a little way along the road and then away off a man driving a wagon with an ox team toward town; and nothing, no one else, in sight.

Isaac darted across the road and in among the trees again and started up the slough. Along here somewhere when they first came out a man had taken the biggest catfish ever seen, long as a man is tall. There were still fish aplenty to be had if you knew where to go, but not any more like that. *A willful waste will make a woeful want:* that was one of his father's sayings, admonishing the children at table. The boy picking his way among the trees hummed the tune of it, a nursery hymn his mother had carried from her own childhood and sung them when little, and still, though rarely—

> *And willful waste, depend upon't,*
> *Brings, almost always, woeful want!*

and liked the sound well enough, though what it had to do with finishing your cabbage and potatoes he could not see.

The slough was getting narrow, maybe twenty feet across, and dark and cool, muddy like a swamp, on both sides, and vines hanging down thick as your arm, like snakes, and he came to a place where a little creek came in and wondered if he could wade or how he was going to get across, and the mud oozed in his sandals and up around his ankles and made a sucking sound when he shifted one foot; and maybe he *was* scared now, a little, and would like to be home again and sitting by the road waiting for his mother to call him in to supper. A little off to his left, under an arch of bushes, lay what looked like a log. He went to it, stepping high and slow like walking in snow, and gave it a kick, thinking maybe he could get it in the water and ride it across to the island: hollow, and he rolled it over, it was a little dugout some boy had made and hidden, forgotten, narrow and rounded like a log and smelling of pine and river-damp, pointed at both ends, and he shoved and lifted and got it half-floating and half-sloped up the bank of the creek. He unbuttoned his sandals, rolled his stockings down, and put one in each, in a ball, and left them. He lifted the end of the canoe, made a little stooping, running step, one foot in and holding the sides, and shoved off.

The canoe floated slow and straight out of the creek mouth and into the channel toward the island bank, slowing, no current that you could feel. He leaned forward, plunged his arms elbow-deep in the murky brown water, and dog-paddled with his hands, and slowly, very slowly, the canoe swung upstream and angled toward the other bank, and then all it was, he just had to keep it going straight, two hands paddling together, and not tip.

The canoe nosed against the bank and stopped. He grabbed for a vine trailing the water and pulled himself out and up, but the canoe was too heavy to get up, the bank was not high but sharp and his feet slithered in the mud when he tried to lift. He led it along, holding with one hand to vines and roots and tufts of grass, and got the bow into a little inlet among coils of tree-roots, and that would have to do.

He crouched and held his breath, listening: first nothing, then very softly the water in the slough moving like a whisper, licking at the bank, and high up in the treetops a crow calling and then farther off another, answering, and way up the river somewhere one blast from a steamboat whistle coming through the rapids, faint and deep and vibrating like the sound of snoring in another room. After a time smells came clear too, the sourness of wet and muck and wood-rot and something sweet and warm mixed in and very faint, woodsmoke; people—those Indians, maybe. The canoe had carried him halfway up the island and he started along toward the head. The trees were wide-spaced toward the north end, with scrub growth thick between, and he pushed through, ducking his head, hands out to shield his eyes. The island ended in a grassy clearing and a narrow, level point like the prow of a boat. A horse whinnied and he dropped behind a log at the edge of the clearing, then cautiously lifted his head to look: in the middle, a small smoky fire with a pole propped across it, run through the bodies of a row of birds, roasting, and a woman in a grimy buck-skin skirt that came to her knees, black hair in braids hanging down her back, stooped to put on wood and turn the spit—ducks maybe, ducks and geese and sometimes swans had been going over for a week, going south. Half a dozen men lay or crouched around the fire; one tilted a stone jug, lazily, and drank, and passed it to another. Woolly, slant-eyed Indian dogs lay off to one side, heads on forepaws, asleep. A boy no bigger than Isaac sat spread-legged on the grass, playing with a knife. The horses were beyond, a dozen scrawny po-nies staked along the beach where they could reach the water. He could smell them now, and the meat cooking. It made him want to eat.

A hand came over his eyes and face, clamping his mouth shut, and another squeezed both wrists together, and he felt himself jerked backward and held tight against a man's warm body. He held still, not struggling, and waited. The hand covering his nose smelled of earth and smoke and sweat. Then the hand came away and two hands held his wrists and turned him around, still squeezing hard, and he was looking into the face of a man crouching: dark-skinned and broad across the eyes, narrowing to a pointed chin, and black hair hanging lank to his shoulders around his face from under a broad-brimmed, high-crowned hat; long-tailed black wool coat buttoned across a bare chest, and coming through the coat skirts one knee and leg in buck-skin fringed with black hair and a moccasin beaded with blue and white and red. The eyes: dark, dark eyes like a dog's, all pupil, and something sad, alert, and laughing, all at once, looking right inside you. Isaac looked steadily back and did not blink, it seemed he had never looked so long and deep in anyone's eyes before. One hand let go his wrist and reached, and the fingers gently touched the boy's yellow-gold hair, and the thin, dark lips parted and softly said a word that sounded like "Sagonash," as if asking a question.

—You the Indian chief? said Isaac boldly, but with a tremor in his voice.

The man let go his other wrist and sat, cross-legged and straight-backed, drawing his shoulders back. Isaac sat back on the log. The man's hat had a pattern of porcupine quills, gray and white, going around it above the band.—Wasinton, he said, brows crimping in a momentary frown. Wasinton say Saukie people got no chief now but Keokuk. My father war chief. I be chief, sometime. I am Seoskuk.

Isaac tried it:—Sea-cook.

—*Se-os-kuk*, the man said, correcting, and waited, but the boy would not try again. Little Hawk, white men call me. My father Ma'ka-tai-me-she-kia'kiak—Black Hawk. Now, where you from, boy? You from house down other end island?

—My name is Isaac Aplon Pride, the boy said in a rush, and I live at Rockingham, Iowa Territory, and my father's a preacher, and he farms some too, and in winter he comes down to the island with men to cut wood, and he built the woodcutters' shanty—

Little Hawk raised a hand.—Maybe you come across steal my horse, swim him back?

—I don't steal horses! Isaac shrieked, hands making fists—or anything at all. Besides, I got a horse all my own.

—Then what you come for?

—My friend Phil says you eat boys, but Phil's an awful liar. I had to see—

The man leaned his face closer.—You fraid I eat you?

Isaac considered.—Not much, he said. Some. If you was hungry enough, maybe—

Little Hawk shrugged. He stood up.—Come, he said, and with a light leap cleared the log where Isaac sat and set off jogging across the clearing toward the head of the island. Isaac followed, running. Little Hawk slowed passing among the tethered horses and spoke and patted flanks and cheeks, and the horses quieted. The other Indian men lying around the cook fire did not look at them.

Little Hawk stood at the tip of the point, the toes of his moccasins almost wet. The river sloshed and rippled on the muddy beach as around the bow of a boat, going slow. The Indian raised his arm in a sweeping gesture to the right, taking in the Illinois shore: a wide grassy beach and behind, the bluff rising steeply, where the Rock River cut through.

—Saukenuk, great Saukie village, my father's village, mother make corn and beans there. I born over there. Then, abruptly:—Where you born, boy?

—I was born October third, eighteen hundred and thirty-seven, in

Greenwich, Connecticut, Isaac answered, as he had been taught. We came out the year after I was born. It was like talking to another boy, not a man.

—Now Wasinton say, we get off land, let white man take, go way off—he made another sweep of his arm, downriver, south and west—live in Konza land, beyond Pekatonoke Sepo, Whirlpool River, you call Missouri. We fight Shaw-hawk, Osage, Illini, sometime Menominee, Ioway, Potawatomi, Winnebago. Never have fight with Konza, not for long years. All Saukie people gone down Misse Sepo, live in Keokuk village—cept me and young men, wife and boy. We come visit home. Maybe next year go down, Konza land.

While he made this speech, deep-voiced, slow, and confidential, only partly understood—Isaac understood well enough that somehow these people had to go away, far off—Little Hawk crouched, resting his arms on his thighs, and the boy did likewise. The sun was getting down, cooling. The Indian thrust a hand in a kind of flat leather sack strapped around his waist and came out with a greasy lump of something, which he held out. Isaac took some and chewed, greedily—dried meat and fat with a taste of tartness mixed in, berries.

—We go out—another gesture, west—make summer hunt. Sometime—oh, whole village, thousand people, two thousand, hunt, thousands horses, kill thousands buffalo, get meat to go through winter, robes to trade. Now just us, and Shaw-hawk catch us, kill my daughter, chase us, and we don't get no meat at all. So now we go Konza land, hunt better, maybe.

Little Hawk held out another handful of pemmican and Isaac took it all and ate, wiping at the grease that ran from the corners of his mouth.

—You hungry, boy, the Indian said. Come eat. Then we got to get you home. Your father catch you, give you whipping, eh?

—My father doesn't whip me, Isaac answered. He just gets sad.

—White men *beat* their boys, Little Hawk insisted. Beat the badness in.

He stood up, led the way back to the fire, and cut a leg off one of the roasting birds, neatly at the joint. Isaac took it. The dogs roused and clustered around him, yelping and whining, jumping up, and he tore at the meat, hot and crisp and dripping with grease, chewy and half-cooked inside, and threw the bone in the fire. He wiped his hands on the sleeves of his roundabout.

Little Hawk swung around and with a few long strides returned to where the horses were staked. Isaac followed at a trot. The Indian pulled up the stake that held the smallest, a little piebald mare splotched with brown and white, untied the rope from its foreleg, and led it back toward the fire by its braided rawhide bridle. Halfway, he stopped, turned to the boy.—You ride that horse? he asked.

Isaac was speechless, uncertain what was offered.—Can I? Would you let me? he said, finding his voice. Father lets me bring in our mare Bessie, sometimes—

The Indian stooped, caught him by the chest and seat of his pants, swooped him up and set him on the pony's back. Isaac sat slumped forward, legs dangling, holding tight to the bridle. The horse stood patiently, waiting.

—You ride that horse, Little Hawk said, swim her across slough, go home that way, now. Name Pekatonoke, Whirlpool, good name for horse—I get her from Shaw-hawk, way out by river in Shaw-hawk buffalo country.

Realizing he was to ride this horse, get her over the slough some-how and home, Isaac for the first time felt scared. Ride! He gave the bridle a little shake. Gravely regarding him, Little Hawk gripped the pony's mane in one hand and with small clucking sounds guided it a few steps forward. Isaac, rigid, held the bridle tighter and pressed his knees against the pony's flanks.

—*Pe-ka-ton-oke*, the Indian said slowly and carefully. Her name.

—Pee-Kah—Isaac began.

There came a shriek and they looked to see Isaac's mother running from among the trees along the slough, stumbling in her skirts and long apron, and his father striding behind, still in his work shirt and vest.

—Isaac! Isaac!

His mother seized him around the waist, wrenched him down, and held him close. The boy squirmed loose and ran for his father, arms out and shouting.

—Father! Father! This is Seacooks and he's the chief, and his fa-ther's Black Hawk and he's a chief too, and he's giving me a horse to go home on—

Abraham dropped to one knee and held the boy's shoulders, silenc-ing him.—Isaac, your mother has been gravely concerned by your absence. We have hunted you for hours in the buggy, all through Rockingham and along the river. We feared you had drowned. . . .

The boy hung his head. Abraham took his son's hand and led him to where his mother stood. She put an arm across his shoulders and drew him close but after a moment stepped back to inspect him, and, discovering his bare feet and the drying mud caked to his shins— Isaac, she demanded with severity, what have you done with your stockings and new sandals? Have you lost them?

—I *left* them, he said, respectful but definite in the distinction. Over across the slough, where I—

Little Hawk dropped the bridle over the pony's head and came toward them.

—We are grateful for your kindness, Abraham began. In caring for our lost son—

Little Hawk was upon him, smiling, and seized his outstretched hand in both his.

—However, Abraham continued, drawing back, I cannot allow the boy to accept your horse. As the Indian stared at him, uncomprehending, he explained:—I mean, that pony would fetch ten dollars, gold, at Davenport. Until I sell my wheat, I have no money to pay. Besides, the boy has not yet learned to ride—not a wild Indian pony. It might do him harm.

—Oh, Father—! Isaac began, breaking away, and stopped himself. He looked down at his bare feet, scuffing the grass. His mother took one hand, his father the other.

Little Hawk pondered the white man; not a famous orator, as his father had been, but he could talk. Behind him, the young men were picking over the last of the roast ducks, tossing the frail bones among the clamoring dogs. One with a whoop stood up, let the empty jug fly at a tree, and sat down hard, rolling backward, and lay flat. The jug hit and smashed.

—Boy got to learn ride sometime, the Indian said. *Hunter* ride. Some boys warrior, some hunter—that boy *hunter*, come up so quiet my young men not even hear. And that horse—littlest in my herd, good for boy learn ride. Belong my daughter, killed by Shaw-hawk getting wood in creek bottom, out on buffalo hunt. Listen, I not sell that pony, not trade, I *give*—good boy and brave, tell true.

Mary came close, her back to the Indian, and in an emphatic whisper said—Husband, let Isaac take the horse. We must go. And Abraham, whispering also: But these people, this man himself, were at war with us, not ten years ago, are breaking treaty now by being here. And the horse, most probably, is stolen.

—Oh, pshaw!

—What of your boys? Abraham said aloud, pointing at the young men who lay around the dying fire, asleep. They need horses too.

The Indian snorted.—They go to sleep with skutah-wapo, crazy water. They *got* horses, get *more* horses, if they want.

—Whisky? Abraham said with indignation. You let your men get drunk on whisky?

Little Hawk shrugged.—Traders bring kegs whisky Saukenuk, my father, Black Hawk, smash them, pour out on ground. Long-knives at fort say that bad, ver bad, not do like that ever again. He not drink skutah-wapo, I not drink, but young men drink—make em feel brave and strong, then go sleep. Got to decide themselves—I not make em.

—But they must be *made* to understand, Abraham rejoined, that drink is an evil, ruinous to body and spirit, wasting man's substance—.

Little Hawk gave him a shrewd look, cocking his head to one side.
—Boy say you preacher, he observed.

—That is true, Abraham replied, drawing himself up. I am a minister of the Gospel, commissioned to Iowa Territory by the Board of Missions of the Presbyterian Church.

—Then you come preach my young men gainst skutah-wapo, do them good. For that I *pay* with that horse you take for boy!

Abraham pondered. It was a just proposal and for him, though not strictly within his commission, an opportunity to carry the Word of God among the heathen, as he took these to be. Take it, Husband, take it! Mary whispered. We must go.

So in the end, after further discussion and conditions, it was agreed, and again they shook hands. Abraham would return the next day with temperance leaflets furnished by the Tract Society in New York, would indeed preach, and Seoskuk would interpret his words in the Sac tongue. When his wheat was in and milled, he would deliver to the band at Mr LeClaire's house two sacks of flour in part payment for the pony, or, if they had departed, the equivalent in money for Mr LeClaire to keep for them or send somehow.

They went in procession to the place where Abraham had tied the skiff borrowed from Stephen Bawden, whose land came down to the edge of the slough. Seoskuk led, with the pony, and Isaac riding, sitting straight now and grinning as if to split his face, too happy to talk. His mother followed, lifting her skirts and stepping carefully from tuft of grass to tuft, avoiding the damp earth, then Abraham, slowly striding, reflective, looking around. Seoskuk's small son walked gravely beside them, wide-eyed and silent. Abraham pulled the boat in, steadied it, and handed his wife in to the bow seat, then set his son in the stern and got in. As he took the oars, Seoskuk stepped down into the water, handed the bridle to Isaac to hold, and gave the pony a smart slap on the rump. The animal stepped forward, following, and began to swim. The Indian watched them till they were across and Isaac had jumped out and led the little horse, splashing and shaking the water off, up the bank to where the buggy waited. Then he turned and in silence went back to his camp. It was almost dark and the fire was down. He shouted at the young men to rouse and make the fire up.

The pony was why Isaac met Andy McHarg. Isaac was the first boy at Rockingham to have a pony all his own. His father led him round the pasture, and Isaac sat with knees tight, holding the soft hairs along the ridge at the back of the mare's neck. Later they rode out together to look out a quarter-section on the prairie, and Isaac had a bridle of tanned leather straps and buckles that went around the horse's cheeks; he learned to get up with a running jump and a grab at her tail, a slide forward onto her back, and off! Uncle Theodore came out from Greenwich to look out land and up to the Falls of St Anthony by boat, for pleasure, and promised to send a proper saddle, but it did not come. Isaac called her Pee-ka, and she answered; sometimes Whirlpool, her American name, when others were about.

It was still early spring, toward the end of March, chill at night but almost warm by day when the rain held off, and on good days his father worked on the cleared land up the hill, plowing for barley, and Isaac walked beside the yoke of oxen, guiding them with a switch. The ice had gone out of the river the first week in February, but Black Hawk Creek had flooded twice and people said the bridge would be carried away again this year sure, if the rain kept up; the roads were deep in mud and his father drove double-teamed to town and still got stuck when the wagon sank to the axles and the oxen, steaming and quivering, could not pull through and he had to dig them out and throw in armloads of brush and come home again, exhausted and defeated and the day lost. Isaac had found an old clasp knife beside the road, must have lain there all winter, one blade broken off short and the other thick with rust, but he cleaned it and polished it on a piece of smooth rock and got it sharp till you could whittle a stick to a point. After dinner the sun darkened and his father said it would likely rain in the afternoon and no use yoking up to plow, and he intended to improve the afternoon indoors at a book. Isaac wandered down toward the barn.

—Pee-ka? he called through the dim light of the barn and the pony nickered an answer. He climbed the ladder to the loft and reached down a forkful of hay to her feed-box. There were still some oats in the bottom of a nearly empty sack at the foot of the ladder, and he took a handful and went and stood beside her and held it to her mouth to nuzzle, stroking her neck. Stretching, he pulled off the ragged piece of blanket he used to cover the pony's back when the weather was cool and laid it over the side of the stall. He took the brush down from its nail and started in, working back from the neck, stroking with one hand and brushing with the other, and felt the muscles under her skin twitch and flicker with pleasure under his hands. He was working down her stifle when he noticed something and stopped and turned, and there was a boy leaning in the door of the barn, watching.

The boy was towheaded and sturdily built but shorter than Isaac and barefoot. The family had come once or twice to meeting Sundays when Isaac's father preached, filled a whole row of benches, several older boys and a couple of girls. Had come out from Pennsylvania in the fall, Mr McHarg had owned land there, and good land too, but in Iowa would have twice as much and owe no debts to any man; Isaac had heard him talking after meeting.

—You're McHarg, Isaac said.

—And you're Zackie Pride the preacher's boy, the other answered pertly.

—How old are you? Isaac shot back.

—Eight in January.

—I'm eight in *October*, Isaac said. I go to school.

The other boy volunteered nothing more and Isaac went around to the pony's right and went on with the brushing. The boy edged closer, watching.

—Kilbourn says you got an Indian pony.

—Name's Whirlpool. Little Hawk, he's Black Hawk's son and he's a chief, he gave it to me.

McHarg was silent for a while, considering.—She's *little*, he said at length. Our Franklin's *twice* as tall.

Isaac paused and turned, hands on his hips.—She's not a horse to hitch to a plow or load up with wood. She's a *hunter*, and she can *run*. Having delivered himself of this important distinction, he went back to brushing.

He had finished and hung the brush up and was getting down the blanket when Lizzie appeared, stepping daintily in her polished button-boots. In her arms she cradled the new puppy Aunt Harriet gave from a December litter, a little, foolish ball of fluff with creamy ringlets all over its face till it could hardly see out, no bigger than a cat, and looked like some kind of cat, too, but wanted to play like a dog. She called it Fluffy.

—Father doesn't allow you to go riding alone, Lizzie volunteered. He doesn't!

Isaac gave thought.—I can ride, if I like—around the pasture, anyhow, he added, but not looking at her. He lets me. When she needs exercise.

—He doesn't. Doesn't!

—You want to ride? Isaac asked, turning to McHarg, and the boy nodded vigorously, eyes wide. You can get up behind. Only, just around the pasture, he added, with a ducking glance at his sister.

—*Isaac Pride*, Lizzie said, that's wicked. And I'll tell, I'll tell!

That did it. Isaac backed the pony out of the stall, got her bridle down, and standing tiptoe buckled it on.

—She sounds like my sisters, McHarg observed in an undertone, but Lizzie heard. She stood to one side, straight-backed and disapproving.

Isaac led the pony out, dropped the reins, and with a running jump got up. He walked her around to stand by the chopping block so McHarg could climb up. Lizzie followed at a distance, still carrying her puppy, but did not run for the house. Shaking the reins and clucking, pressing with his heels, Isaac turned the pony and started her in a slow walk up toward the road. The boy put his arms around Isaac's waist and held on tight.

They had completed a second slow circuit of the pasture when Isaac's father in his vest met them at the end of the barn and caught the reins. Lizzie had gone up by the house and stood watching.

—Father—Isaac began.

—We must not heat her, Isaac, while the weather's still cool, was all his father said, and lifted the McHarg boy down and then his son. Isaac was allowed to lead the pony back to her stall and rub her down and cover her with the blanket, and Andy helped. Then Abraham took the two boys by the hand and led them up to the house for fresh cookies and buttermilk.

It was on an afternoon a couple of weeks after that Isaac and Andy became keenly interested in dugouts. They had cut and peeled willow poles and gone down to the foot of the Credit Island slough to try for catfish along the bank; Andy had dug worms and Isaac had a pocketful of bits of bacon rind, but neither was getting anything, and they argued over whether the fish were still asleep down in the mud of the river bottom, as Isaac's father said they might be, or whether they should go farther up the slough to hunt a better spot, or what, a lazy kind of argument with no end to it, and they lay back in silence, waiting for something. Away off down the river came the whistle of a boat, faint but getting louder; coming up. Isaac's father came by up on the road in his buggy, stopped, and waved, and the boys jerked their lines in and ran. The boat might be coming in to the wood-yard on the island, he said, and would they like to go across to see?

A quarter-mile farther, where he kept a skiff pulled up on the bank, he pulled the buggy onto the roadside and tied the reins to a sapling. By the time they came opposite the tip of the island and got the skiff out, the boat was in sight, coming out from behind a low island over on the Illinois shore, white woodsmoke spouting in a steady spume from its tall chimneys. The woodcutters came out from the shanty and stood, shading their eyes to see. In a quarter-hour it had made the crossing and was coming in close, wheels slowing, then running backward, churning and shuddering, and they could read the name on the panel over the stairway up from the main deck: *War Eagle*, proudest name on the Upper River that spring. The big boat nosed its bow up on the beach like a skiff landing, holding back with the wheels, and men jumped and made fast to stumps, and others ran forward with the stage between them, got it across to solid ground and let it down.

The mud clerk came down the stage first, a little young man with a black moustache spreading under his nose, cap and short black jacket, behind him the gang of roustabouts—rousters for short, or roosters sometimes, in fun—all Irish, and they crouched on the mud beach beside the stage and took out pipes. Abraham left the boys standing and went to the clerk to shake his hand, and they walked beside the ranks of wood, bargaining. The mud clerk carried a pole for measuring by the cord, with marks for length and breadth and height; and offered thirty dollars a rank, twenty cords, and Abraham insisted it was mostly upland hardwood, brought down in winter across the ice from his own land, well seasoned too, and worth forty; and finally they agreed on four ranks and the money to be paid, some specie and the rest in notes of a St Louis bank, and they shook hands again. The clerk gave a wave and the roosters ran, gathering the wood in armloads and loading it on barrows, running up the stage, and the mud clerk shouting and swearing.

In the midst of the loading Captain Daniel Smith Harris came down from the pilot house and forward along the roof to lean on the railing, saying not a word: an ample man in a long-tailed coat, bushy black side-whiskers, and a long cigar puffing between his lips; twenty-two years on the Upper River since the keelboat days and had built and owned and captained more steamboats than most people could name and been up every stream that would float wood from St Louis to the Falls of St Anthony.

Two dugouts came down the slough and headed for the steamboat, boys paddling. The one in the lead stood up with his feet on the gunwales and leaned, paddling fast, skimming the water like a water bug, and the passengers on the boat's cabin deck crowded forward, clapping and shouting. (—That's Kilbourn, Zack, Andy whispered with a nudge.) The other dugout came cautiously and slow, John Saur paddling with his little brother Chris in the bow, no older than Isaac, and sidled into the beach. Chris stepped out in the water and then John, paddle gripped in one hand, took a running start, jumped over the end of the dugout and pushed off, like taking a flying start on a sled, and paddled like fury to catch up with Kilbourn. Instead of standing, as he came up even John lay forward, took a grip around the bottom of the dugout and rolled, right over, and came up on the other side, then paddled some and rolled again, and the crowd at *War Eagle*'s railing clapped and cheered. The two boys turned and headed back to the beach, paddling hard, dodging and zigzagging and slapping their paddles at each other, and grounded in the mud together.

From that day nothing would do but Isaac and Andy must each have a dugout canoe of his own.

They scouted the neighborhood but the best tree they could find for the purpose was a straight tall pine on McHarg's place, two feet and some inches across the butt. Mr McHarg after some discussion agreed they could cut it and take what they needed but would not take time off to help. Isaac's father came with his double-bitted falling ax and got the tree down, then squared the end with his long-blade

saw, cut ten feet from the bottom that would do for two dugouts, and
sawed the rest into four measured eight-foot lengths that would bring
money, he said, at the sawmill; it took a whole morning. The part
they would use, he thought, must weigh half a ton; he drove his oxen
over, chained up, and dragged it back beside the barn. The boys
helped at spudding the bark off, then levered and rolled with heavy
poles to find the spot to start the line of oak wedges, and driving them
in with his maul Isaac's father got it split from end to end.

Next morning, early, he shaped the outsides of the two half-logs
roughly with his broad-ax until they began to look something like a
pair of canoes, pointed at both ends, then got them over and chopped
the outlines of the inner shape with the ax; admitting he hadn't much
idea how to make a canoe and was just guessing, but he'd made bowls
and bread troughs and watering troughs and this wasn't much different, only bigger. In all their spare hours the next week the boys were
down at the barn, working with hand-adze and knife, chisels and
mallets, hands black with the pine tar, and at the end most of the
wood was converted to chips and splinters and they had a pair of
things that looked more like dugout canoes than the log they had been
and weighed not much over a hundred pounds each—between them
the boys could lift one end. Mr Pride helped with the final smoothing,
then produced planed boards of seasoned maple for the paddles, and
with a piece of charcoal sketched the outline of a blade and shaft and
grip, and showed them how to carve and shape with draw-knife and
chisel and sand the wood smooth.

The week ended, Saturday came, and nothing remained that they
could think to do. After breakfast Mr McHarg walked over with
Andy and helped load the dugouts on the back of the Prides' wagon
and chain up the oxen, and he walked beside them, guiding, while Mr
Pride managed the brake, down the bluff to the slough, and the boys
rode in the wagon-box with their canoes. At the bottom, they turned
left and drove up opposite the island, where the current was least.
Carefully the men slid and lifted the dugouts down, carried them to
the edge, and nosed them into the water till they floated. The boys
ran and held the gunwales and squatted down, studying how their
canoes sat the water: low and heavy, with possibly three inches of
freeboard, but evenly trimmed, lifting a little at their narrowing
bows. While they crouched there, Dave Kilbourn came drifting by,
steered in for the bank, and considered the new boats at length, trailing his paddle in the water. The boys waited.—Tolerable, he finally
pronounced them, very tolerable, and with a few quick strokes
headed on up into the deep shadow of the slough. The two fathers
held the dugouts while the boys stepped cautiously in, then pushed
them off and stood back to watch. It felt strange. You leaned a little to
put the paddle in and the canoe rocked over, you jerked back and it

tipped to the other side. Isaac sat with his paddle across the gunwales, holding on with both hands; leaned a little left and the canoe leaned with him, then to the right and it followed. Like a horse, it came to him, it was like riding the pony—it moved and you moved with it, opposite, shifting arms and shoulders, sitting solid and steady from the waist down. He tried it, reaching forward in a slow, careful stroke, and the dugout swung sharply right; dragged the paddle and it straightened out. He tried another stroke and another, getting the feel, and the canoe was moving along a narrowing zigzag out into the stream.

—Andy! Isaac shouted, Andy, I'll race you across!

At that point, however, the men concluded they had taken up enough of their morning and must get back to work, and they called the boys in. They swung the canoes around in a slow and wobbling arc toward the bank—No arguing now! Mr McHarg roughly cautioned, though neither had offered a word of complaint—and grounded. They got the boats up and rolled them over, shiny-wet, and the men worked the oxen around and headed back down the road. The boys followed, marching, paddles shouldered like muskets. They had dugouts of their own now!

For Isaac that was the beginning of the dugout summer. The two boys went up and down the slough and made the circuit of Credit Island several times, keeping in close, or sometimes they followed Isaac's father across to the wood-yard when a boat came in; often they just drifted with the easy current along the riverbank, trailing a fish line, sometimes as far as Horse Island two miles down, and then had hard paddling getting back. They learned currents, eddies, wind. They learned how the force of moving water shapes itself to the shape of bank and riverbottom, and how you feel the south wind coming up against the current, pressing your face and pressing the moving surface into waves, and all these forces cross and multiply for a boy in a dugout to sense and maneuver to. Not consciously: only that all the forces converge in movements of shoulders, arms, hands, paddle, and the canoe's bow follows and is right, and you get where you aim and, finally, to shore.

As they learned to manage their canoes—no tricks, no standing on the gunwales or rolling in the water for pennies and applause from the steamboat passengers—they were tolerated tagging along behind the older boys, Kilbourn and John Saur (sometimes with little Chris aboard) on longer expeditions, if they could paddle and keep up. Kilbourn knew places to fish at the foot of the rapids and how to get there—at the tip of Rock Island or over on the Iowa shore—and they drifted down to the head of Credit Island and roasted the fish on sticks over little driftwood fires in pits dug with paddles in the sand; and other places where you could get sweet grapes from vines thick as a boy's wrist or dig for roots that were sweet and white and crunched between your teeth. Isaac hid his shoes on the bank at the spot where he kept his dugout, sometimes his shirt too, and burned brown as an Indian.

So it came out that on the Fourth of July, 1845, the four boys and Chris too went over to Rock Island in their dugouts. Isaac had scruples; he was forbidden to go over the river. Kilbourn did not argue but said they would not go over, only across to the tip of the island as they often did, then up Rock Island slough for a look at Colonel Davenport's mansion—his gold, it was said, was buried out back. Late in the morning Isaac slipped away, jogged off down the road, and met the others with their dugouts on the bank at the head of Credit Island slough.

The boys paddled across and up to the tip of Rock Island and landed below the old fort to fish from the beach in the roiling currents coming out from the foot of the rapids. They took a couple of fair-sized pike among them and after an hour, getting nothing more, judged that would do, with the food Kilbourn had brought. They went slowly on up the slough to a place toward the upper end of the island where the trees opened out in a grassy meadow, headed in and got their dugouts up, and set to gathering sticks for a fire. Isaac said they should walk on up to Colonel Davenport's villa; if he was home he'd let them in, tell stories of the old times and the Indian fights; his father, he boasted, had known the colonel since he first came west. Already hungry, the boys debated. Kilbourn settled it by cutting slices from his sausage and passing them around with chunks of bread; the fish would keep for later. Isaac led the way up the island.

The colonel's house stood at a place where the island narrowed, facing out across the rapids toward the Iowa shore; even seen from one end, with its wings coming out from the two-story central block and its mass of chimneys and fresh white paint shining in the sun, it looked bigger than the courthouse at Davenport. In front was a long slope of trim grass down to the riverbank, and behind, a smaller patch of lawn with a well house in the middle, also painted white and a neat little shingle roof over it, and then a line of big trees around the rim of a shallow bay where the shore of the island turned in, a natural landing place for boats. A small keelboat was tied up there now, but there seemed to be no one about. The day was bright and turning sultry. Waves coming over the rock chains of the rapids tossed and sparkled in the sun. The sounds of a band playing came across the water from Davenport, not so you could make out any tune but only a kind of essence of music inhabiting the air, like magic. Apart from that faint and distant mingling of sound, the silence was absolute.

As they came out from among the trees and into the full, hot light again, the boys hung back, uneasy. Isaac went on around to the front of the house, but cautiously, catching their mood. A flagstone walk ran down from a square front porch to the river. Three marble steps led up to the porch, shaded by a heavy roof supported at the corners by circular white pillars. There were panels of glass on either side of the door and a half-circle fanlight above, but the door stood open now, carelessly, it seemed—or maybe to air the house from the midday heat; you could see down a spacious hall right through to a door at the other side of the house—halfway back, a curving staircase climbed to the second floor.

Isaac started up the walk with slow and hesitating steps. Abruptly the silence was broken by a short, sharp thump, something like a hammer clinching a nail home in hardwood—or a gunshot; so brief, so isolated, in the hot afternoon silence that a moment afterward he doubted what kind of sound it had been or if he had heard it at all. He stood rooted to the spot, shoulders hunching forward, hands up, as if to ward off a blow, for perhaps half a minute. Then from the open door came a roar of men's voices all shouting at once, thumping sounds and the crack of wood breaking; and then a drawn-out wail. He started backward, staggering, as if struck. From the right side of the house a pair of black-bearded, wool-hat roughs emerged into the hallway by the front door, dragging between them and shaking an old, white-haired man, feet trailing limp, head sagging forward. One of them was talking now, still loud and threatening, but the only word the boy made out was *gold!* several times over. The men shoved the old man along the hall and started him up the stairs. A third appeared at the door, following, swung the door shut with a slam, and Isaac heard no more. It was like a spell, from which by the closing of the door he was released. He spun and ran for the trees off at the side of the house where the others still waited, arms pumping, bare toes tearing at the grass, but it was like running in a dream—he ran and ran but the shadows under the trees and their safety seemed to come no closer, and he cringed and strained and sobbed, and any moment he would hear heavy boots following and hard hands seize him by the neck, and—

He dodged behind the tree where the boys waited and flung himself flat on the ground, panting and sobbing, and could not speak. They crouched around him, questioning.

—. . . coming? Isaac finally gasped out. Is he coming?

—*Coming?* Kilbourn demanded. *Who's* coming, Zackie?

—River pirates! They're murdering Colonel Davenport!

Kilbourn did not wait but jumped and turned, already running, and the others ran after; Isaac got himself up and followed, trying to run, staggering against trees, and fell with a crash in the dead winter leaves and brush, got up and ran; and came to a big fallen tree in the way and stopped, leaning across it and panting. Andy stood up, grabbed his arms and pulled, scraping him over, dropped him and pressed him flat.

Kilbourn lifted his head and looked. Nothing, no one coming, no sound from the house; silence, and only the serene afternoon light looked down on the grassy clearing and the silent house where something terrible was happening and was hidden from them.

They began to get their breath back and their courage. Kilbourn said they should light out for their dugouts and paddle down to the fort, hide there, or it might be they would find people come over from the town; John Saur said yes to the dugouts, but paddle for home and never stop or tell—tell anyone at all—or those pirates would find them and cut their hearts out as they'd done to old Davenport. Little Chris at this started to cry and his brother smacked him and clamped a hand over his mouth.

—That keelboat! Isaac said in a rasping whisper. It's the pirates' boat. And we can stop them.

The boat; the others had forgotten the boat tied up in the little bay behind the house. Isaac was for going and cutting it loose and they'd have those bandits trapped for sure, *then* go to their canoes and get help. They argued in whispers. At length Kilbourn said, whatever they did, they must keep together, and they should go and look at the boat, see who was about—do what we can, he suggested, vaguely— then back to the dugouts and they'd know what to do next; and it was agreed.

They went single-file, Kilbourn leading and John Saur behind, well back, with his brother by the hand: over to the Rock Island slough and up the riverbank through a thicket of willow-shrub, keeping down and inspecting every step before taking it. They reached the bay and clustered, looking. There in the middle was the boat with a thick rope looped around a tree, no name painted on the bow and a short mast with the sail dropped; water rippling against its sides and the boat lifted and swung and wanted to go, and no one about.

Andy McHarg sauntered out into the sunlight like a boy with nothing to do, going for a stroll; and stopped and looked at the boat; and went closer and looked again, shading his eyes. A man rose from a willow clump on the far side of the little bay and came toward him: a narrow, sallow young man with a beardless pointed face and blond hair coming out from under his hat, a blackened, dead clay pipe clamped upside down in his teeth; curving wooden handles of a brace of pistols stuck side by side from his belt and at his boot-top the butt of a big knife. The boys, watching, lay flat, holding their breath.

Andy looked up, seemed to see him for the first time, and ran for him, arms outstretched and babbling joyfully.—That's your boat and you're over for a picnic, and we're over for a picnic too, my pa and brothers—

The man caught him and pulled him close, pressing a hand over his mouth.—*Pic*-nic? he said in a trembling, high-pitched voice.

—Hey, Pa! Andy shrieked as the man's grip loosened. Hey, George and Henry and Garry and—

The man swung and threw him across the grass and ran for the house, shouting. Andy landed flat, with a thump, and lay still; Isaac scrambled out from his covert, grabbed Andy under the shoulders, and dragged him back.

Three men came out from the front of the house, running, one of them carrying a flower-pattern carpet satchel, and made for the boat and got in. The blond lookout followed, loosed the rope, and as the others poled off jumped, hit the water spread-eagle, grabbed, and pulled himself up and over the side. The man with the carpetbag got to the tiller, the boat swung around, someone got the sail up, and the boat departed, heading down the slough. Silence returned.

—Is there any more, Zackie? Kilbourn demanded in an urgent whisper as the boat slipped away.

—I only saw the three inside, Isaac answered. And the lookout. I don't think so.

Kilbourn was for going at once to the dugouts and getting away, but Isaac disputed him: there was old Colonel Davenport still inside and they had to know— No! Kilbourn said, there could be one of the robbers still in there, and John Saur said the pirates would catch them yet if they stayed around and kill them sure; but Isaac prevailed—he'd go back to the house and look and the others would wait, well hidden.

Isaac studied the blank windows all around, then took a deep breath and ran across the grass and along the side of the house to the porch, keeping down. In the doorway he paused—a splash of blood on the polished floor of the hall, still wet—and shuddered; then made himself go in, stepping on tiptoes over the spot and through an arch into the parlor to the right of the front door. By a window looking out on the riverfront an upholstered wing chair lay on its side, beside it an ivory-headed cane splintered in two; and on the soft blue of the Turkey carpet another blot of red. He turned and followed the trail along the hall and up the stairs, hanging on the banister with both hands and pulling himself up, one step at a time. A door stood open to a small room at the top: a tall dresser with the drawers pulled out and emptied on the floor, beside it an iron safe, door open. The old man lay on his back on the bed, eyes closed, face bruised, cut, bleeding, a gash in one trouser leg at the knee, oozing blood. A long-drawn moan came from the parted lips.

The boy could stand no more. He covered his face with his hands, trembling all over as with an ague, turned and ran down the stairs again, out the door and down the path to the riverside, shouting the whole way:—Help! Help! Help! Murder—they've murdered Colonel Davenport!

What he might have done next—jumped in and swam, perhaps, anything to get away—he never knew. Two men in a skiff came easing down the slow current close by the island, saw a small, towheaded, sunburned boy to his knees in the water, shouting and waving, and came on in. They listened, tied up, and leaving him behind went up the walk to the house at a run.

George Davenport died in the evening, but not before a doctor picnicking near Fort Armstrong had roused him sufficiently to talk and describe his three assailants; they had gotten away, it seemed, with seven or eight hundred dollars in gold and the old man's watch. He was buried next day in the lawn behind the house. The Episcopal missionary at Davenport came over to preach:—This know, that if the goodman of the house had known what hour the thief would come, he would have watched, and not have suffered his house to be broken through; the sermon, much admired, was judged as suited to the occasion as its text. The news traveled the river swiftly. The day after, Seoskuk with his young men came up from his customary camp on Credit Island and two Fox chiefs arrived with their band from farther up to perform ceremonies on behalf of Sagonash: around a tall cedar post set at the head of the grave the chiefs walked, haranguing the spirits of dead enemies, mostly Sioux, to serve the old man in the spirit land; afterward, the women set forth a feast so ample the leavings were carried away in basket-loads.

Isaac when he came home that late afternoon expressed surprise and indignation on hearing of the outrage—they had gone downriver, he said, to Horse Island for their picnic (when the men appeared, the other boys slipped away and Isaac followed). In his heart he wanted to go back to Rock Island for the Indian rites—and might, perhaps, have seen Seoskuk again—but dared speak of nothing connected with that afternoon. The other boys evidently felt the same; when by chance he met one, they did not speak or look at one another. Isaac stayed around the house now during the days and at night tried to hold himself awake, and when he dozed woke sweating and frightened from his dream. His mother, concluding he must be catching something, tried liberal doses of paregoric and camomile and promised a visit to the doctor if these did no good—and then the boy felt as desolate in body as he did in spirit. Everything—the murder and the murderers and feeling he'd somehow failed the old man, had been a coward, and not knowing then what was right to do, or now—pressed on him like a great weight, driving him down to hell, until finally he could bear it no longer. Saturday evening after supper, while his father sat at the kitchen table working at a sermon by the light of a tallow candle, Isaac went to him and began to tell all he had seen and felt, brokenly and with many hesitations, and as his father listened in silence Isaac began to cry—and cried and cried—and his father took him in his lap and held him close, comforting; but Isaac *had* done right, he said, as right as a boy could, and *all* he could; nor was it ever in life given to any man, save One, to do perfectly right, but only as best he could at any time, according as God led.

From that time the weight left him, and the dream with it. On Sunday after meeting, his father drove around and talked with the three other fathers; next day with their sons they met by arrangement at the sheriff's office at Davenport, and the boys told all they knew. *Heroes*, some people in the town said. Oh, scamps running after mischief with their tricks in those little dugouts, but heroes too. And that little Pride boy, the preacher's son—

Surprisingly, the crime's mysteries were unraveled in the course of that summer and fall, owing to a man calling himself Edward Bonney, who the previous winter had brought in—indicted, tried, hanged —the doers of a notable double murder of new immigrants on the river near Keokuk (and, some sourly said, knew more of the ways of stage robbers and river pirates than any honest man should). Bonney, self-deputized but supplied with blank warrants from the Illinois governor and a satchel of wildcat money, followed trails down the Mississippi, up the Ohio, and north from Cincinnati to Lake Erie. He came back with six men for indictment by the grand jury sitting at the village of Stephenson, or Rock Island City, as it was now named, across from Davenport on the Illinois shore: "Judge" Fox, the leader (but he got away in transit and never was heard of again); Bob Birch; John Long and his brother Aaron, the fox-faced lookout who panicked at Andy McHarg's lies; a young man named Granville Young from Mormon Nauvoo; and John Baxter, whom the colonel had befriended and who told Judge Fox too much about where money was kept in the house and where treasure might be buried. Isaac and Andy went over to the trial on the steam ferry with their fathers and made identifications (when the judge leaned forward and kindly asked at their swearings if they knew what happened to boys who told lies, Andy answered that his father would whip him when they got home, if not sooner; Isaac that he would go to hell). On a Friday at the end of October, three hangings followed: the two Long brothers, indubitably; Granville Young less certainly, for informing to Edward Bonney and boasting of horse-stealing. Birch was let off with a life sentence to prison—and after two years escaped and was never caught. John Baxter, the informant who started this mischief, went free, his conscious complicity unproved.

Abraham in an access of pride and thankfulness when the trial ended promised Isaac a gun. As a boy himself with his father and older brother, he had gone into marshes at the mouth of the Mianus or up Long Island Sound, harvesting migratory ducks and geese with bird shot. Mary disapproved. They were a learned people or anyway competent and resourceful farmers, transforming the land into capital; not hunters. But it was months before Abraham could keep his given word, and the unkept promise nagged at his conscience.

In early spring, soon after the ice went out and the river opened, Abraham traded John Burrows two sacks of wheat, four bushels saved from the fall in hope the price would rise, for a ten-year-old flintlock musket. Burrows at his general store at Davenport did so much of his trade in bartered wheat (or anything, such as this aging gun, that he could imagine turning a profit) that it overflowed his upstairs storeroom and filled several settlers' cabins abandoned at Rockingham when the village lost out to Davenport in the contest for county seat, and he talked grandly of building the town's first steam mill and setting up in the flour trade; and he did so much of the rest of his business on credit, given and taken, that his notes in small denominations passed locally for currency—there was as yet no local bank, money of any kind was scarce, and the many varieties of bank notes that circulated since Andrew Jackson's disastrous bank reforms were rightly distrusted (only gold coin—American but also British, Spanish, French—was sure, but there was never enough; and hence these expedients for the necessities of trade). Several times in the course of the winter when he went in, Abraham examined the gun: a thirty-inch barrel, its bore a fraction under half an inch; an elegantly shaped black-walnut stock; a strong spring, little rust, with a bullet mold that would cast ten balls at a time, and Mr Burrows as an inducement offered to throw in a neat small powder flask made of lead. The musket was well balanced and, at not over eight pounds—intended, perhaps, for cavalry officers or cadets—a quite possible first gun for a boy of under fifty inches tall and as many pounds; and loaded with small shot it would do very well for birds, while with its heavy ball rammed home it would bring down a deer at as much as a hundred yards—or so Mr Burrows insisted, and in the end it was agreed.

Weeks of teaching centered on this gun before Isaac was allowed to hunt: cleaning the barrel and lock with a rag soaked in sperm oil; molding bullets; priming the pan; exactly measuring the grains of powder for the charge; pounding the ball down on its paper wad. At one end of the pasture Abraham set a split maple log with a splotch of red paint to aim at and watched while his son practiced; up to a hundred yards the boy could hit more than half the time—the gun shot flat and straight, as Mr Burrows had said. Purposeful now, the boy explored the farm and in a thickly wooded corner half a mile from the house in twilight came upon the source of a throbbing sound in the air pitched almost too deep to hear, a bird strutting a rotting log, tail spread like a peacock's and beating its puffed-up breast with its wings—a ruffed grouse, called a pheasant according to the American custom of conferring exotic or literary names on native species; and led his father back to watch while he killed the cock and two of its hens with a palm-load of shot. A little later, alone, he started a flock of young turkeys, bunched together and running for the cover of the trees, and got two with one ball.

On a sunny Saturday afternoon in April Isaac rode out onto the prairie alone, sitting on an old flour sack for a blanket, with his powder flask and a sack of shot tied to his belt, his gun in a cloth bag slung around the pony's neck, to hunt prairie chickens; Mr Burrows had offered a dollar a gross for all the birds he brought in. He had tried a week earlier with Andy riding behind—had showed the boy how to prime and load as his father taught him and let him shoot, but Andy was too tense, too slow when the birds flew up, and between them they got only two, which Isaac's mother plucked and dressed and roasted for their supper. Now he meant to bring in a sackful to sell and, if his luck held, calculated to earn the price of a secondhand saddle—and his powder and shot too—before the spring was out.

The new grass had come up in knee-high tufts of pale green, with last year's matted down yellow and brown between. Occasionally he crossed a track where a wagon or a single horse had laid the grass flat, but there was no road, and he was beyond the last cabin, the last attempt at making a farm; though men in the fall came out to cut prairie hay, as did Isaac's own father, the several miles' distance was considered too far to haul wood for a house and fencing, the cost too much on top of the cost of the land, and no wood to be had except a little scrub along the stream banks. He came to the top of a rise and reined in to look: not flat but rolling—you could see into the far distance across endlessly repeated folds of grassy hills, but the contours of the country hid what was close except when you got on a hilltop or ridge; an occasional solitary tree made a landmark to steer by—otherwise there was only the sun for guide. Down below now in a crease where two slopes came together there was a little stream descending from a spring, marked by a wavering line of thicker, greener grass and a few misshapen elms and oaks. Isaac clucked to the pony and started down at an easy walk. At the bottom he sat for a minute, looking around, while she drank, then slid off and tied her by one foreleg. Patting her flanks reassuringly, he left her, took a wide step across the little stream, and started up the next rise. The constant wind from the west whispered through the grass as he walked.

Halfway up, remembering, he stopped, primed and charged the

musket, poured in shot and set the cock, but he flushed no birds. At the top, he halted again to look around, thinking out the course he would follow so as to find his way back; Pee-ka, placidly cropping a patch of new grass where she was tied, could not be above a hundred yards off in a straight line but looked small as a cat. The slope, which had seemed steep to climb, was very gentle from up here, almost flat. The top of the hill he had just crossed looked to be half a mile distant.

He started on up the ridge, holding the gun ready in both hands, leaning forward and watching the ground intently; up ahead where the two slopes met and the little stream began there might be birds. As he walked, from a few feet to his left off the ridge a prairie chicken sprang up with a whir, glided on outstretched wings just above the grass, then dropped and disappeared before he had time to shoot. Going down in a crouch, he advanced slowly toward the spot, and this time when the bird started got his gun up and brought it down. He tucked its legs under his belt and continued diagonally down the slope.

By the time he reached the bottom he had gotten five more and missed twice, and the dead birds were awkward to carry and heavy. Why hadn't he thought to bring the sack? He couldn't leave them— too hard to find again. Or maybe if he could get them back over the ridge there'd be a spot near the spring where he could, then go get the pony. Clumsily, two birds tucked in his belt, a brace in each hand dangling by their legs and his gun tucked under one arm, he started to climb.

He was breathing hard and sweating as he came over the top of the ridge. Where was the pony? Away off down the stream he picked out the twisted tree where he thought he'd left her, a little bigger than the rest—maybe she'd gotten behind it somehow so he couldn't see. As he scanned the horizon to the east, away off at the other end of the valley on the opposite ridge, he made out something dark moving through the grass, then another, another. Uneasily, he pondered what it might be. Bear cubs? There were still bears out here, it was said, but he'd never seen one or known of anyone who had. Wild horses? Young elk? But they weren't tall enough, didn't move right. The animals came on steadily, not fast, along the ridge, in file, heading into the wind, and now there was a fourth, and he realized and was afraid: wolves. When they got the scent they would come down the slope and go for his horse. He dropped the birds, started to run, stopped himself, remembering: had not reloaded the last time. He made himself do it, a double charge of powder and a handful of shot for what good it would do—he had brought no bullets in his pouch—and ran on. He was closer, it looked; but they could outrun him if they chose.

He kept to the ridge till he was opposite the place where he'd left the pony and could see her; and still ahead. His chest ached and he felt sick. He started down, calling the pony's name, and she whinnied back. It got easier. He stretched his legs, more jumping than running, and it was a feeling like flying, like dreaming of flying. As he came close, she trembled along her flanks and stamped her feet, watching and waiting for him, but did not try to break away. He dropped, panting, cut the rope short, and jumped on, swung her around facing up the hill. The wolves had caught his smell now too and lay down in a row along the top of the slope, watching: four pairs of up-pricked ears against the sky, four pairs of slanted eyes, four narrow gray muzzles tight-closed, keeping their counsel. The pony saw them, reared; Isaac felt himself sliding back, grabbed around her neck, and stayed on, holding her in.

—Now, Pee-ka, get up, easy now, get up, get up! he crooned in the pony's ears, leaning forward, and pressed his heels in her flanks. She started forward at an easy walk, and he swung her around and headed her down the bank of the stream. Holding the reins close, the cocked musket laid across his thighs, Isaac in a high sweet voice began to sing, loud as he could:

> *All people that on earth do dwell,*
> *Sing to the Lord with cheerful voice:*
> *Him serve with fear, His praise forth tell,*
> *Come ye before Him and rejoice.*

To keep courage up, certainly, his own and the pony's, but for defiance too. It was the only song he could think of just then and the only verse, and he sang it over and over; an old Psalm tune his father loved and hummed at his work.

The pony walked on, calmly, but glancing aside he saw that the pack was keeping pace and working gradually down the slope, heading him off. Then the big leader started to trot, speeded up, coming toward him in effortless floating leaps through the grass. He swung the pony around again, took the reins in his teeth and pulled her up short, gripping her flanks with his knees. The wolf veered, starting to circle in, and Isaac got his gun up, aimed, and fired, broadside at twenty yards. The pony jumped, danced, and he thought he was gone but held her, and she stood still, trembling, ears laid back; the lead wolf yelped and rolled, ran back, not much wounded but hurting, and the others stopped short, watching. With the double charge the gun had roared like a cannon and his shoulder hurt. He reloaded, raised the gun, and as the wolves warily drew back fired into their midst; too far off now for harm, but they felt the shot, at least, the noise scared them, and they ran in a bunch up the slope, the lead wolf lagging, trailing blood from his side as if he'd been whipped. Isaac turned and slapped the pony into a flat run.

He was an hour getting home. Twice he stopped, looked back, but was not followed. The stream widened out. He climbed, came to the Ridge Road, and followed it up at a walk, then down to the house and across the pasture to the barn. He led the pony to her stall, pungent with sweat, rubbed her down, fed and watered her. It was almost dark when he started the slow ascent to the house. He let himself in by the front door and went up the stairs to his room, a story to tell but not knowing how to tell it, and tired, and scared now more than when he faced the wolves; and disgusted too—his birds lying out on the prairie somewhere to be eaten, and no nearer than ever to earning his saddle.

He heard a high-pitched yipping, looked out and saw the pale shape of Lizzie's little fool of a dog Fluff running out from the back of the house and down the slope toward the barn; and there coming along the wall of the barn a dark form, big—one of those wolves must have followed him back after all! He grabbed a bullet from the buckskin sack beside the bed and ran, down the stairs, out the front door, and down the slope, loading as he went. Halfway down he got on one knee and aimed. The little dog danced and yipped, the intruder snarled. Isaac aimed and fired, and the animal dropped. Fluff ran to him, scared. He caught her up and carried her under one arm to the house.

Isaac's father in his shirt met him halfway, running from the kitchen door.—Isaac—

—I shot a wolf, Father. It was after Lizzie's dog.

—Dead?

—I think so. I couldn't see very well. I aimed for the head.

Abraham continued down the slope to look. Isaac set the dog down and followed, still carrying his gun. His father brought a lantern from the barn, lighted it, and held it close. Big dead brown eyes looked back. There was a leather collar around its neck studded with nails—a black, bad-tempered animal big as a wolf but a dog nonetheless and a neighbor's, the Saurs', known as Henny, for Heinrich, its German name. The shot had gone low and broken the dog's neck. Abraham in silence led the way back to the house. There was grave discussion in the kitchen while Isaac's mother and Sally finished preparing supper. His mother dryly doubted the dog would be much missed in the neighborhood; it had been a public nuisance since the Saurs settled, scaring horses, running the cattle. Abraham replied that that was not for them to judge, whatever the case, it did not justify their destroying a neighbor's property. Mary observed that she thought it right for a person to defend his own; Henny, it seemed, would have killed Lizzie's dog. When his father asked if Henny had attacked, however, Isaac could not surely say that it had. He would not explain or apologize, nor did he try to tell the story of his afternoon, the wolf scare, the loss of his half-dozen prairie chickens, and his parents and the two girls, pondering their dilemma, did not think to ask where he had been. Supper put an end to the talk. Isaac picked at his food in silence and went up to bed. Later, as he lay awake looking into the darkness, his mother came and tucked him in, smoothing the covers, as she had not since he was small, and told him not to worry, it would come right enough in the end; and softly sang, to help him sleep—*Twinkle, twinkle, little star*—but the charm had lost its power.

Next day when they drove home from meeting, several crows had settled on the carcass, tearing at the flesh with heavy beaks; Lizzie saw and with a shriek ran for the house. Abraham, waving his hat and shouting, drove them off, but they came back. After dinner, he dug a hole beside the barn, threw the dog in and covered it, first removing the collar, then drove to the Saurs'. The family spent the afternoon uncomfortably in the parlor, attempting to read in the ponderous, buckram-bound volumes—sermons, histories of the Reformation and the Protestant martyrs, Bible commentaries—of Abraham's library. The Sabbath precluded his discussing whatever words he had exchanged with Mr Saur; it was business of a sort.

After breakfast next morning Abraham took his son by the hand and in silence led him toward the barn. The awful weight came back, squeezing Isaac's chest like a great hand: *something bad coming, and you can't stop it*. Notions of punishment formed in the boy's mind: his father leading the pony away to sell; his father taking the gun to trade back to Mr Burrows.

—You wait here, his father commanded when they reached the door of the barn.

Isaac stood desolate, looking at nothing, but when his father returned with a switch of green willow, peeling the bark with his ivory-handled penknife, a little smile reshaped the boy's lips. Punishment: it was not going to be either of the worst things after all, only a whipping, and now when Andy and the other boys boasted of their fathers' tremendous lickings he would have something to answer; that had never been his father's way—oh, when he was little and reached for a hot stove lid, his father might slap his hand away, but that didn't count. And a licking was something real and definite and didn't go on forever, just over and done with. Abraham tested the switch's limberness, took a couple of whistling practice swipes through the air, and noticed his son's expression.

—Why are you smiling, Isaac? his father demanded with a severe look.

—I thought you were going to take Pee-ka.

—Er—no, I had not considered that. The pony, after all, has done no wrong. But—he thought further—you felt that the loss of the pony would be so great a loss that in comparison a mere whipping with a willow-switch is, er, comparatively nothing to fear?

The boy nodded vigorously.

—You must understand, Isaac, his father earnestly continued, that when we have done wrong, some harm, some punishment to ourselves, must invariably follow. That is the law of nature. It is most important for you to understand that now, while you are young. That is generally true even when the wrong is inadvertent or, er, unwilling, or unknowing.

The guileless round face looked up at him, pink-cheeked and golden-haired, with a smile of reassurance.—Father, the boy said sweetly, I know that you must do what is right.

Abraham looked away, clasping his hands behind his back.—On the other hand, he suggested after a moment's thought, perhaps you did not mean to kill the dog at all—that is to say, you believed you were defending yourself—and your family—against some wild beast that threatened your safety. Is that not possible?

—I *thought* it was a *wolf*, Isaac answered with a certain impatience, beginning to wonder what his father was working around to.

—Why *of course* you did! his father took him up. Why—it's what you said at the time—and believed it too, I'm sure.

And then Abraham argued the case through from the beginning on new premises until by a neatly connected chain of reasoning he was able to show not merely that it had not been wrong for Isaac to kill old Henny but that, in the circumstances, it would have been quite wrong for him *not* to have shot—and shot to kill, too, not merely to wound or frighten. Seeing how things were going, Isaac let him talk, only occasionally nodding assent, but resolved once more never to tell of that afternoon, his brush with the wolf pack, his fear, his escape. When it seemed he had exhausted the subject—and in any case he had not promised Mr Saur what form the punishment would take, only that *something* would be done, and by now, surely, the child had suffered enough, whatever the right or wrong of it—and never, on principle, had he believed in corporal punishment as a proper system for disciplining a boy—Abraham, although it was a working day, could think of nothing more but to suggest that they climb the bluff together to inspect the woodlot and, on the way, see how the newly planted wheat was coming on. Isaac assented.

Partway up, Abraham noticed that he still carried the willow-switch absently in his hand and offered it to his son as a riding crop, but the boy shook his head.—I've never beaten her with anything, he said, not even a little switch. Even when she was stupid, or bad. And I don't ever mean to.

—Ah! And twisting the switch in a double loop, Abraham threw it away and slipped one arm around Isaac's shoulders.

III

Father Abraham

Abraham's ten years in Iowa—he was not yet forty—had already taught him more about the ways of making a living on the frontier than he had meant to learn, but there was no helping it. The stipend provided by the Board of Missions was never more than three hundred dollars a year, about the pay for common labor which on a farm generally included room and board; the Board's intention, implicit in its frequent denunciations of missioners who like ignorant Baptists or Methodists turned to secular money-making, was to give its men strong motives for gathering a paying congregation, but in practice it rarely worked like that—the people were too pressed by the labor and cost of making farm and home from raw land remote from markets, the Western society as a whole too short of cash, to keep their ministers in unproductive piety; the preachers, by whatever means, made up the difference between their stipends and a living for their families. So in the fall of 1837 when he came west seeking a new vineyard in which to labor and leaving his wife, little daughter, and newborn son at his father's home in Greenwich, Abraham, like his neighbors, staked a quarter-section of the still-unsurveyed Black Hawk Purchase to claim by pre-emption when the Land Office finally put it up for sale. The land, up the bluff from the dozen houses, the hotel and grist mill, that constituted the promising village of Rockingham, was steep and wooded, chosen not with a view to farming but in the hope of selling it off in lots at a profit till the church was firmly founded. Through the winter he gathered the neighbor children for schooling and on Sundays conducted services in a cabin at Davenport or in the bar of Henry Higgins' Rockingham Hotel. In a corner of his claim he built a hewn-log cabin sixteen-feet square, with two sash windows, but otherwise indistinguishable from the other settlers' cabins, and undertook to make it over to the congregation if they would provide money and labor to rebuild it as a church. In the spring he went home to bring his family out.

The destiny of Rockingham and of Abraham's vision of a church down the bluff from his home was decided by elections in the course of organizing the county. Davenport won the first vote for territorial capital with the help of ten barrels of whisky and a boatload of lead miners brought down from Dubuque, the whole cost about three thousand dollars, but the territorial governor rejected the result. A few months later, Rockingham won by simple ballot-stuffing, but the election was again thrown out, and after two years—and the gift of land, a courthouse, a jail—the vote went to Davenport and was certified. The matter of Rockingham and its church was thus settled for good. The would-be townspeople drifted away to Davenport, or home, or farther west; the thin-spread farmers who remained on their quarter-sections did not contribute to a meetinghouse or a pastor's upkeep.

Abraham extended his efforts to West Point, Spring Creek, Mount Pleasant, Lynn Grove, a dozen other settlements where a congregation could be gathered in a barn or crossroads tavern within a day or two-day drive of his cabin. On a Friday afternoon or Saturday morning he harnessed up, left his wife to manage children, cows, chickens, pigs, and accepted the hospitality of meals and a bed along the way, returning Sunday night or Monday morning. Among such people, working his land was a pastoral as well as a human necessity; money and land, experiences shared, to be talked of, were their means to salvation. Following the pattern that had prevailed from Massachusetts and Virginia west to the edge of the grassland, he began by cutting wood, the most accessible commodity, for fuel, fence rails, rough-hewn planks (in new lands east and north the wood was burned and water-filtered to make potash, but here the land was found to have little need of fertilizer); he planted cabbages and potatoes close by the cabin, corn between the stumps, year by year and acre by acre grubbed out the stumps with chain and ox-team, plowed, and planted wheat, another quick and salable commodity.

Abraham, making his preaching circuit, successfully disguised his Eastern manners and the learned air acquired in the four years at Yale and three at Auburn Seminary, but not his wit or charity. When a neighbor questioned the carefully measured cordwood he brought for sale, he answered, with reflexive but unrecognized irony, that—a man can't seem to trust *anyone* here in the West—and next day brought another wagonload, dumped it, and departed without a word. When another, leaving church, complained of money and a land payment he could not make, Abraham, although it was the Sabbath, offered to lend him what he had. Tramps at his door, begging food, were taken

in, fed, clothed, and made to stay the night; a drunken raftsman put
ashore on Credit Island he carried home and hired for the rest of the
season. Although he counted himself a strict temperance man and
took the lead in the anti-whisky fervors of those years, he planted
grapes on a sunny slope behind the cabin and made various wines;
some years he diverted part of his grain to home-brewed beer. As
anti-slavery agitation mounted and Iowa and other Midwest states
nervously responded with laws inhibiting freedmen as well as
prohibiting slavery, he took up the uncomfortable middle ground:
conversion, education, gradual and compensated emancipation (as
carried out a generation earlier in New England), repatriation—"col-
onization"—to Africa; and tried to act on what he preached. Returning on the boat from Louisville where he had conferred with the
superintendent of the Western Missionary District, he brought an
orphaned black girl—Sally, no other name, about twelve years old: to
help his wife, certainly, but chiefly to train, educate, make free. This
acting out of principle was not a great success. Set to iron shirts, Sally
burned holes with overheated irons, spoiled the bread on baking day,
some days refused to work at all or ran off, angry, and reappeared
days later, hungry and bedraggled, skirt torn, shoes lost. Bad-tempered, when unobserved she pinched and cuffed the smaller Lizzie
and Isaac, and the children dared not tell for fear of worse. (After
nearly seven years, when Sally seemed full-grown, Abraham drove
her to the courthouse at Davenport, made out the legal document
certifying her freedom, and posted the bond required by state law,
lest any freedman, failing to find work, become a public charge. Some
weeks later when the circus boat tied up at Davenport, she disappeared for good; relatives downriver at Muscatine told of seeing her
there, doing a dance to a tambourine and riding a bareback horse in
flesh-toned tights.)

After nine years of this life, the pattern altered. Although Rockingham and its church had "exploded"—its people departed, their houses
moved, pulled down, or left to rot—Davenport now had a population
of fifteen hundred whites (and two Negroes), two thousand more in
the rest of Scott County, and its Presbyterians seemed ready to build
a church and support a settled pastor. As Abraham was beginning to
preach more regularly in town, a new presbyter arrived from Ohio
with a wife and daughter, rented a small house; the congregation,
presented with an unexpected choice, invited the two ministers to
preach alternate Sundays, and so they did, through the winter. Mr
Rea had taken a sixteen-year-old girl into his household in exchange
for housework and cooking. Abruptly in the spring the girl departed,
sought other lodging. When asked why, she told her story readily:
how at night Mr Rea in his underwear came to her bed, put his hand
on her breast, and offered to lie with her, which she indignantly

refused. The minister made angry denials, suggested that the girl had
dreamed, was hysterical, then that she was a habitual liar and a slut,
but the scandal persisted. Abraham, troubled, sought guidance in
prayer, discussed the problem with substantial laymen such as Mr
Burrows, the storekeeper turned grain dealer and flour miller, but
discovered no resolution. He also mentioned it in a letter to a college
classmate, who answered that he knew of Mr Rea: that he'd been
involved in similar scrapes more than once before; had indeed withdrawn from seminary because his intended was with child, though
that difficulty had been regularized by marriage and had not barred
his ordination.

Abraham kept this report to himself but at the April meeting of the
presbytery proposed that, in accordance with church law, they hold a
hearing on the girl's accusation, and one way or other resolve the
scandal; otherwise the prospects for the Gospel in Scott County (or
anyway its Presbyterian version) would be destroyed. The trial was
set for the October meeting.

Mr Rea in the course of the summer ranged up and down both
banks of the river gathering testimony against the girl; against Abraham; against any presbyter or layman who showed signs of siding
with Abraham or of feeling, at least, that there was any matter concerning himself that was worthy of judgment. A month before the
meeting, he collected this material in a pamphlet which he had
printed by the weekly *Gazette*, distributing five hundred copies free to
any who would take them.

Hence when the presbytery met, it presided over two trials, not
one. The proceedings lasted a week, most of the time taken up with
Mr Rea's charges against Abraham. The presbyters were not searching when they examined witnesses; Abraham was ineffectual in his
own testimony and in cross-examining those brought to testify
against him. His mind, it seemed, worked quickly but at a different
tempo from his tongue. The verdict was predictable. Mr Rea was
entirely exonerated. Abraham was censured: for Sabbath-breaking
(the offer of money after meeting); for unscrupulous business practices (the questioned sale of cordwood came up); for slave-keeping
(orphan Sally); for contumacy (discussing the girl's accusation with
Mr Burrows). One presbyter of the five voting dissented, a man who
like Abraham had been among the founding members and was accustomed to holding solitary opinions.

Mr Rea stayed through the winter but, when the congregation issued a formal call to another minister, returned to Ohio.

Abraham stayed. He continued to preach, but as a Congregational-
ist, less frequently and restricting his travel in favor of the work of
the farm. He did not attend another meeting of presbytery; but four
years later, when a new trial threatened (for failure to perform canon-

ical duties), he sent in a letter requesting separation; which was granted.

That same fall of 1848, two weeks after the trial ended, one of Abraham's old dreams came to fruition when the Preparatory Department of Iowa College opened in a small square building halfway up the bluff behind Davenport. Isaac, although small and young—he was just eleven—was allowed to enroll. He rode his pony the four miles each way and, when the weather turned cold, boarded in town with the professor of languages and moral philosophy, the Reverend Erastus Ripley, a Connecticut friend of his father's, and in later winters with the Reverend Daniel Lane, another connection, now principal of the Preparatory Department. Behind the six years of planning, talking, letter-writing, soliciting of funds that Abraham had already devoted to the college was another hope, unexpressed: that prepared in mind and spirit despite their remoteness from the established colleges of the East, his son might in the fullness of time, if he chose, succeed him in the ministry of a somewhere firmly established church. The boy still seemed more apt for riding out on the prairie, shooting or snaring pheasant or quail, than for books, and—after silently sharing his father's inarticulate humiliation—not at all for the ministry.

In the intervals of preaching Abraham had enlarged his farm with unused strips of neighbors' land, five or ten acres at a time paid off over years. The new land was level and south-facing, suitable, though not large, for cash crops: some years, strawberries by the hundreds of quarts, in others, sweet potatoes despite the risk and the excruciating labor the climate exacted. He turned more to corn and hogs, a new idea and a quick money-maker much talked of at the meetings of the county horticultural society, and at late-winter hog-killing time barreled up sides of bacon, hams, salt pork (and his wife saved head cheese and sausage meat for home use); a time Mary dreaded more every year, since, except for the actual killing and disjointing and, later, hanging the hams and bacon in the smokehouse, all of this heavy work fell to her and whatever hired girl was at hand. Gradually Abraham enlarged his herd till there were a dozen producing cows and, with the labor of Mary and a girl, forty or fifty pounds of butter a week—and milk, eggs—to carry through Davenport in his wagon, selling to the townsfolk. These efforts generated further labor. He built a second, bigger barn and kept the old one for a coach house; a new icehouse; rebuilt and enlarged the kitchen; clapboarded the original cabin, added wings, a porch, a full second story, under the new kitchen an ice-cooled storage room adjoining the root cellar.

When his energies still outran the available land and there was no more near to be bought, Abraham thought of a second farm that in time would come to his son—and found the means of getting it. Since there were others to inherit, Mary's younger brother John Aplon came out from Vermont, lived in the house, worked. Abraham conceived a scheme. They would take up unclaimed land, cooperate in breaking it, make a farm for each. They ventured onto the high prairie beyond the river bluff in the township called Blue Grass: two adjoining quarter-sections. By complicated borrowings, mutual indebtedness, they got title. Mary was anxious—not about money, notes, interest, familiar from childhood, but about the featureless, trackless land that produced only grass in its natural state—and went out only once, when the men went to view it.

Isaac on college half-days and Saturdays rode out to guide the ox-teams pulling the heavy breaking-plow driven by his father and uncle, tearing and laying back the mat of bluestem roots, an acre a day, three seasons, on the two farms, but showed no enthusiasm, no thought that one day half of this would be his own; left on the home farm, unguided, he slept, or took his pony riding, hunting, and Abraham worried again that his son lacked the constitution for a farmer. When the full three hundred acres of wheat was finally planted, John Aplon was of substance enough to marry a neighbor's daughter, and Abraham officiated. Abraham on his own quarter-section hauled out lumber and the stove from the old kitchen, built a house, and rented the land on half-shares to a German immigrant family.

The railroads altered the pattern again. The booming Western wheat crops, such as Abraham's on the Blue Grass farm—twenty, thirty, forty bushels an acre—were chimerical without ready transportation to the East and Europe. The need for connecting not merely the old frontier marked by the Mississippi but the new one on the Pacific was self-evident, but not the means. Between the Appalachians and the Mississippi the problem of distance and transportation had been eased by the great river's tributaries, above all the Ohio: first by boats built chiefly for one-way movement, floating with the current (because it was too costly in manpower to pole or tow back up), then by steamboats; and the rivers were fed by a network of state canal systems, financed by public bonds to be paid off, in time, by tolls—in New York, Pennsylvania, all the new states of the Old Northwest. The mule-powered canal barges and gradually the steamboats gave way to railroads—unrestricted as to where their routes could be laid (if there were traffic to support them); free of the low-water summers, the winter freeze-ups, the occasional floods, that closed the canals and rivers for parts of most years. Beyond the Mississippi, only the Missouri—shallow, winding, treacherous, but possible—lent itself to steam-powered freight, but it led nowhere; water on the Plains was too scarce and seasonal, in fact as well as in common opinion, to support canals, even if there were any practical way of carrying them through the Rockies to the Pacific Coast.

The remaining possibility, a railroad, was doubtful by reason of its construction and operating costs. The nine thousand miles of track in service by 1850 had been laid in relation to existing waterways—connecting, shortening, supplementing, paralleling. The railroad routes, nearly all privately financed, were designed to return, with profit, the capital invested in them; a line across the fifteen hundred empty miles to the Pacific was beyond the capacity and contrary to the logic of private capital. Public subsidy seemed precluded by Constitutional doubts and, in a practical way, by the political impossibility of imposing the cost of such a private venture on a population of twenty-three million spread continent-wide over three million square miles.

Gradually, the public domain—land—came to be seen as the solution for both difficulties. The experiment was first tried with waterways. A corporation with a scheme for improving the navigability of a river—by removing obstructions, dredging its channel, building dams and locks—could obtain, with the support of its state government, alternate square-mile sections of public land to a depth of five or ten miles on either side of the channel. The land thus granted was sold to finance the improvements (and the remaining land sold through the Land Office would in theory command a better price); no public money, apparently, was needed to pay for the project; that part of the public that actually bought the land (and thereby paid) received specific benefits in return—cheap transportation to connect its products with markets, and the rising land values that such a facility promoted.

Hence in the fall of 1850 it was but a short step to make the connection between railroads and the public domain. The immediate occasion was the Illinois Central Railroad, planned to parallel the Mississippi from Chicago to Mobile by means of revenues from public land in the states through which it would run. It was at this point that railroads began to affect the new state of Iowa, its growing port city, Davenport, and Abraham's own life.

While the Illinois Central scheme made its way through Congress, supported by an alliance of the Northern and Southern states it would serve, attention in Scott County was on a lesser project of more immediate import: the Rock Island and La Salle Railroad, to connect the Mississippi with the Illinois Central—and with Chicago and the East. Since the Rock Island and La Salle was not likely to benefit by the novel plan of subsidy with public land, the county in the spring of 1850 voted a cautious bond issue by way of support: its citizens, Abraham among them, bought the bonds, the county exchanged their cash for bonds of the railroad company, and the railroad used the money to promote further investment and start construction; a neat solution. With further and more generous bond issues, by late February of 1854 the railroad—by now renamed the Chicago and Rock Island—had reached the Mississippi, the first line to do so. In Davenport there were parades, bands; that night, at the foot of Rock Island on the site of old Fort Armstrong, a brilliant display of fireworks, and Abraham led his family up the bluff behind the house to watch. Work began on a wooden trestle railroad bridge—the first bridging of the Mississippi—and after two years the final span was in place and in September 1856 the first train rolled across from Illinois to the new Davenport depot.

Although the Mississippi had now been reached and other links would follow, the larger problem of the leap across the Plains to the Pacific remained unsolved. While the Rock Island line was still building, the energetic Secretary of War, Jefferson Davis, sent Army engineers to survey five possible routes for a railroad across the West. The choice among them would be weighted toward whatever line had already carried its track into the grassland. Hence in the summer of 1853, when an alliance of Boston businessmen proposed a railroad, the Mississippi and Missouri, to run west from Davenport, it found Scott County's citizens again receptive, and again a county bond issue provided seed money. In September, Antoine LeClaire presided over the speeches and band music and turned the first ceremonial shovelful of earth, but the work of grading and track-laying went slowly; it was two more years before the Mississippi and Missouri had enough track—two and a half miles actually completed—to justify ferrying a steam engine over (the *Antoine LeClaire*, the first to cross the river by any means). In 1856, a grant of public land came through the state government, which had already encouraged the new line with exemption from property taxes and the legal right to build across private land by the process of eminent domain.

From the mid-1840s on, the population of Scott County and its metropolis, Davenport, had been increasing at an accelerating rate—five hundred a year, then six hundred, a thousand, fifteen hundred. After 1845, to the double motive of cheap land and improving transportation was added another, more compelling: the ruin of farmers. The new lands of the West had made New England wheat, corn, and cattle increasingly uneconomic, but potatoes remained a staple crop —so successfully that for years the farmers suffered from overproduction, low prices and profits. Then in 1843 a disease—or a group of diseases, given various descriptive names, early and late blight, tuber rot, leaf-roll, black wart—appeared, reducing the harvest, and returned devastatingly over the next two years. Farmers already on the thin edge of survival sold out for what they could get or simply abandoned their land, and moved west. Potato exports seeded ruin throughout Europe, famously in Ireland but notably in Germany as well. At Davenport the stream of emigrants from New England (and from similarly failing hill-lands south of the Ohio) was swelled by boatloads of Germans traveling upriver from New Orleans, seeking familiar-looking land—many of them armed with gold from the sale of fifteen or twenty acres in the Rheinpfalz to exchange for a hundred and sixty—a quarter-section—of Iowa prairie, and the implements as well, to make it productive. Among the institutions transplanted from the East, the Germans introduced their own: churches, breweries, social clubs, newspapers.

At Davenport the effect of this double movement—of people, of railroad capital—was to compress into a generation developments that in the East were spread over two centuries: a tax-supported public school system; the town's first state-chartered banks; the telegraph line that followed the railroad from Chicago. In 1854, the weekly *Gazette* became a daily (besides the several continuing weeklies, in English and German) and added a steam-powered press. A year later, a gas plant was organized, using local coal as its raw material, and as lights appeared on the city's streets the Episcopal church became one of the company's first private subscribers.

Abraham's connection with these events was wood. It was something concrete, intelligible. With care, some skill, much labor, and a few of the farmer's basic tools, you harvested the natural increase of your land and exchanged it for cash, a simple transaction. He began by cutting trees on the scenic, steeply-wooded home farm, not good for much else anyway: first for logs for the original cabin, then for cordwood to sell to neighbors.

It was a short step from cutting wood for his own use and a few neighbors' to the venture on Credit Island. Through a complicated trade, with a little cash thrown in, John Burrows acquired the timber rights; Abraham went partners, supplying labor, oversight, and part of the money, borrowed from Connecticut relatives at less than Iowa rates. There was enough timber on the island—maple and elm mostly but oak and walnut too—to pay for three or four woodcutters working through the winters and a shanty for them to live in, a cook. The tops, trimmings, and young growth were salable to the steamboats as cordwood through the spring and summer; the biggest logs he hauled over the ice to Davenport to the mill. The winter following the presbytery trial, Abraham agreed with a barrel factory on the riverfront at Davenport to supply two hundred thousand board-feet of oak logs, enough for seventeen thousand barrels but representing no more than a hundred of the island's big first-growth trees. Business was good. The county was shipping barreled flour east by the boatload; the new German breweries needed barrels. The partners in the barrel works, Gilman Smith and John Marsh, paid fifteen dollars a thousand board-feet; Abraham, after paying the woodcutters and splitting with John Burrows, cleared more than a thousand dollars. Next year he renewed the contract and repeatedly in the six years that followed, as Isaac ascended the Preparatory Department of Iowa College and entered the college proper. Although many times renewed, it remained a simple transaction, no different from carrying around firewood to supply his neighbors.

In the summer of 1855, when Smith and Marsh paid off the last of that year's log contract, they made a proposal. There was a small sawmill over the Mississippi, on the Rock River at the lower end of Rock Island City (occupying, in fact, the former site of Black Hawk's Saukenuk): built ten years earlier at a cost of seventeen thousand dollars, it had been through three owners, and the present one, getting old, was desirous of selling out and open to an offer. The mill fronted an eddy below the slough, had its own dock and skidway, a boom to hold the log rafts floated down from the pineries on the Wisconsin and the Chippewa; a long, open-sided cutting shed with a circular saw and an upright sash saw, steam-powered, with equipment for cutting lath and splitting shingle, ten or twelve acres for storing the finished lumber. Samuel Wesley Van Sant's boatyard, adjoining, was already a steady customer for select hardwood planking and would doubtless improve. The mill as it stood could turn out a million and a half feet of lumber a year, double that if they put on a night shift. The retiring owner was asking eight thousand dollars but the property could be had, most likely, for six—Why, Mr Smith broke through his careful exposition, the way the country's growing, the land alone's worth that much! Tear the mill down, sell the land, and get your money back—and profit too! Money? Abraham wondered. Ah, well, yes, money—. Yes, money, precisely, was the difficulty and the reason for the partners' call. The barrel works had been producing full-time, selling all it made, but the wages—with the railroad coming and paying two dollars a day for common labor, workers were hard to get and dear, eating up profit; they were not making much, to be truthful, beyond expenses and a living for each, little enough to put aside for any new venture. If Mr Pride with his Eastern connections—if Mr Pride could see his way—: well, the truth of it was, Gilman Smith brought out, still doing the talking, they would split the profits on the mill for his share in the management. Smith, a machinist, would see to operating the steam engine and the saws; Mr Marsh would keep the accounts, as he had, very well, at the barrel works.

Abraham received this proposal with heaviness, but also with a kind of underlying lift, a feeling that Providence had searched his secret heart and reached out to his need. From the logging he had three thousand dollars put aside in Ebenezer Cook's bank and a feeling for once of ease about his life and prospects; but also a certain anxiety as to what was proper to do with so large a sum. On the other hand, there was Isaac—. Mr Smith was from Hartford, clever with machines, Mr Marsh an Irishman trained for the priesthood, learned, who had missed his calling in that Popish land but favored temperance and did not talk much; honest men. Abraham from his years of bargaining with mud clerks over wood—captains too, on occasion—knew enough to keep his feelings hidden. He agreed, however, to take the ferry across to Rock Island and look the mill over.

Through the weeks of summer Abraham reasoned about the mill's prospects and made calculations in a copybook, but although the heaviness persisted he could find nothing unfavorable about the plan. Davenport's population was eight thousand by now, according to the *Gazette*, with three hundred new houses being built, two million board-feet a year it might be, and only a couple of small mills to supply the lumber. Isaac, completing his second year in the College Department, knew enough trigonometry to join a surveyor's crew contracted to the approaching railroad (Abraham provided a transit and a set of surveyor's chains in a neatly made, velvet-padded wooden box); the railroad calculated its ties at twenty-four hundred per mile, oak by preference or whatever it could get, and was paying two dollars each; one third would have to be replaced every year. The wooden railroad bridge planned to link the Rock Island line with the new Mississippi and Missouri would require a huge quantity of heavy oak timbers at a very good price, if they could be supplied, besides all the little stream-crossings on the routes on both sides of the river. And finally, there was the boatyard with its winter repairs and orders in hand, said Mr Van Sant, for two new steamboats, to be completed in the spring.

Abraham sought advice from Mary's brother John Aplon. John, it seemed, had been doing well from his wheat and could spare three thousand dollars if the prospects were really so hopeful. The two men went across to look and took Isaac along. They spent a whole afternoon wandering through the lumberyard, trying to estimate the quantities of neatly stacked boards in a dozen widths, the boy doing the sums in his head till with his talk of ten thousand feet of clear pine in a stack, and scantlings, and lath, he began to sound like a lumber merchant bred to the trade. Wherever they walked they felt the pulse-throb of the engine; the tall brick smokestack rose beside the double-roofed cutting shed like the bell tower of a church, emitting a steady stream of gray-black smoke—the fuel for the engine, Isaac noted, was all bark slabs and other scraps and cost nothing, and the men were impressed. At seven o'clock the whistle sounded, the mill shut down for the night, and the three took the ferry back to

Davenport and drove home to supper much excited. Abraham honored the occasion by tapping a keg of last summer's wine.

So in the end it was agreed, because Abraham in his reasonings could find no argument against seizing the opportunity that had fallen to him; and Isaac's interest, perhaps, would flower into aptitude, a calling, a worthy station in life. (Mary expressed herself as uneasy at seeing all their cash go out at once but agreed that it seemed a proper step toward providing for their son and thereafter kept her doubts to herself.) The terms were set with handshakes all around, no complicating lawyer's writings: Abraham for finding the money was to take half the profits as well as bearing half the future costs; Smith and Marsh would have a quarter each. John Aplon would leave his three thousand in for at least four years at 10 percent. The mill owner accepted their offer, with three thousand down and the balance in six months and ten percent over for interest; the new firm of Pride, Smith, and Marsh would be left with three thousand in cash to work with. In December Smith and Marsh sold the barrel works to the railroad, which wanted the site for a freight yard, ferried their tools across on a flatboat, and took lodgings near the mill. For a rise of a few dollars a month they persuaded the sawyer, the fireman, and their helpers to stay on, hired a tallyman, laborers to stack the lumber, and from the deck crew of a boat putting up for the winter two brothers named Shaughnessy as teamsters. The firm had changed hands and was ready to start business.

The partners at once faced certain practical difficulties. The mill had a good stock of unsold lumber on hand but, except for the boatyard, few prospects for sales till spring—by then wages and interest would about eat up their cash; in the meantime they were out of logs and had to have more to saw through the winter for the spring trade. Then in mid-December Gilman Smith heard of a raft tied up at the village of LeClaire, above the rapids, and looking for a buyer, and the three partners drove up in Abraham's buggy—all boats by now were off the river, anticipating freeze-up. The raft pilot turned out to be a Frenchman from Stevens Point, far up the Wisconsin River, known up and down the Mississippi as Joe Blow, actual name forgotten, and somewhere had picked up the further nickname of Wild Penny. Wild Penny Joe Blow showed them over the raft with genial manners and in accents so strong they had to strain to make out his words. It was a raft of the usual size, ten strings of logs lashed together with birch saplings laid across and held tight by pegs driven into holes bored in the log-ends, four hundred feet long and a hundred and sixty wide, with a low cook-shanty in the middle surrounded by lean-tos of rough boards where the crew slept—a floating, flexible island as big as a large garden patch, a little unstable underfoot, water sloshing up between the logs as the lift of the current passed under. The logs, all pine, were of the eighteen-inch minimum through the butt or a bit better, as the partners judged them; half a million feet it would saw to, Wild Penny Joe insisted—half a million, if they knew their business.

The pilot led them back to the hotel bar to talk. It fell to Abraham to bargain, but there was not much of that to be done. Joe Blow would not settle for less than sixteen dollars a thousand board-feet—there were, positively, no more rafts coming down from Wisconsin this season, it would be spring, maybe April or May, before there were more, and by then, with no stock, the mill would be shut down before properly started. John Marsh did some hasty numbers with a pencil on a scrap of paper, glumly nodded, and Abraham agreed to the price. Then there were the terms. Captain Joe wanted two thousand dollars down, half in gold, the rest in notes of a St Louis bank, and the balance, six thousand, in a six months' note at twenty percent interest, signed by all three partners. The discussion became complicated—John Marsh was moved to raise his voice—they ordered supper and talked on. Eventually it was agreed: a thousand dollars—the minimum to cover the captain's commission from the loggers, wages and food for his crew, equipment, profit—and a fourteen percent note. Finally there was the matter of getting the raft from LeClaire to the mill. The captain wanted three hundred dollars, exorbitant, but he spoke somberly of the difficulties of reassembling his crew so late in the season, twenty men to buck the sweeps and a cook, the dangers of the rapids in low water and the new bridge with its stonework pylons already in place—they would have to tie up, break up the raft and take it through a string or two at a time, then work it across to the mill eddy and risk losing the lot. It was late; the partners wearily agreed, and Abraham counted out three hundred dollars in gold, half the charge for the passage through the rapids, the rest in earnest for the payment to be made when the raft was delivered to the mill; he had come prepared with four hundred dollars in gold in a leather purse tied around his waist, the coins prudently wrapped in handkerchiefs so as not to clink and advertise. The partners took a room for the night, where they uncomfortably shared a double bed; Smith was a snorer. The Frenchman, sipping brandy, remained alert to the end, enjoying himself, and seemed ready to sit there talking till spring came.

In the morning as they drove back to Davenport there was snow in the air, dusting the frozen ruts of the road. It occurred to Abraham, now the bargain was made and irrevocable, that Captain Blow was under as much necessity to sell as they to buy—the river would soon freeze and when it did the raft would break up and be lost; he could not hold it through the winter. All the talk and dickering for him had been only a kind of game, but for Abraham, uncomfortable, it was not

how his mind worked. The mill, with its payments to be made at
different times and its interest rates, wages to be met, was not going
to be simple, like selling wood to neighbors. He touched the almost-
empty purse at his belt, hunched over the reins, and pulled the buffalo robe closer to keep out the cold.

Four days later—it had taken two to collect his crew of Canucks
and their Irish cook—Wild Penny Joe brought the raft into the eddy
below the mill, the mill hands ran to close the boom and began
winching the logs up the skidway to the yard. Joe and his rafters had
had to make the whole raft fast to an outcrop of rock above the
bridge, take it through two strings at a time, tie up again at the foot of
Rock Island, and reassemble the strings for the tricky passage across
to the mill while the partners anxiously watched, passing a spyglass
among them; the pilot rode back and forth in the stern of the raft-boat
with two men at the oars. Captain Joe, when he came to John Marsh's
little office beside the engine house to settle, was expansive, no more
talk of the difficulty of the rapids at this season, and as for the bridge
—De bridge, he gave out, de bridge, she is *notting*—not for de pilot
dat know de river and her way! Abraham counted out the balance of
the gold and the St Louis bank notes from the strongbox, they put
their names to the promissory note, and the captain departed with his
carpet satchel.

The winter turned out fortunate. The river did not freeze solid till
the first week in January, and by then the logs were safely ashore and
stacked in the yard; it broke up in the middle of February and by
March building was active on both sides of the river—at the end of
the month they took on a second fireman and sawyer and ran through
the night, and Gilman Smith caught sleep as he could, on a blanket on
the floor of the office, and rarely got back to his boardinghouse. By
April they had gone through their stock of logs and acquired one of
the first rafts to come down the river at eighteen dollars a thousand,
bidding against the two Davenport mills. By June they had paid off
the note on the first raft, the balance on the mill, with its interest, and
John Marsh calculated they had cleared something over a thousand
dollars from the four hundred and thirty thousand feet actually cut
from their first raft; and in addition had made seven thousand from
the stock bought with the mill, much of it hardwood sold to the
railroad for bridge timbers and ties. By paying cash they were able to
get their third raft at the excellent price of fourteen dollars a thousand. When the night fireman quit for a railroad job, Isaac brought
around a likely young German who had worked with him as a rod-
man that spring, surveying a branch line to a bustling new farm
town, Coal Valley, ten miles south of Rock Island—tall, heavy-shouldered, a bushy black mustache and an air of seriousness; Friedrich

Weyerhaeuser, a pair of names only Isaac learned to pronounce with assurance, but he answered smilingly to "Fred" and was taken on.

By late summer the builders had taken nearly all the lumber they required to see them through the season, sales fell off, and the night shift was abandoned—Mr Smith at last got back to sleeping in his bed; Fred, however, when the crew was paid off was kept on as day tallyman at the same wage, forty dollars a month. When Mr Marsh closed his books at the end of September, he found that the firm had ten thousand dollars cash on hand and another four thousand owing on current accounts; and the same amount due on a twelve percent note for a final raft of logs, payable in March—ten thousand clear from the firm's first nine months. In addition, there was around a hundred thousand feet of lumber in the yard and nearly the entire raft of logs to be cut. Abraham offered a prayer of thankfulness, but his partners demurred: with sales at a trickle and no assurance of another easy winter like the last, their cash could melt away in wages and interest by spring. What they needed was an outlet to carry them through the winter. The railroad was still buying, but John Burrows was selling direct what remained of the Credit Island hardwood and there was no other ready source. Abraham talked of what the newspapers were saying of the new land opening on the prairie west of Davenport—surely the settlers would require lumber for houses, barns, fencing—and the established farmers, for that matter, would spend the winter mending fences and require wood; his partners agreed but pointed out that with the new railroad so slow in building they would be hard put to compete with the Davenport mills—rail freight across the river to the end of the line and then a yard to store the lumber and sell from. But it was a thought, they had the money to set up a branch on the Iowa side, and Abraham promised to investigate.

Isaac, who had come over for the day and been allowed to attend the meeting, leaning on a windowsill of the office in respectful silence, put in a word:—Coal Valley—if they wanted a place for a yard. . . . The town was growing, at the center of some of the last new prairie in the state, that was why the Rock Island had run the branch line. They could haul the stock direct by rail from the mill, there was no other source. . . .

The men were intrigued. A day later, Abraham and his son took the cars to Coal Valley, hired a buggy and drove around the country roads, came back to talk with the branch manager. Good land and settling up but treeless—lumber was brought from as far as Chicago, expensive, and the new settlers suffered for want of fencing. The railroad had land to sell along its right-of-way on the north side of the town, not cheap at two hundred dollars an acre, but the railroad would put in a siding. Isaac was wildly excited; the partners, soberly considering the next day, agreed that perhaps they had come on something. Within a week they had bought ten acres of the railroad land, hauled up five flatcars of overstock lumber, and started on a storage shed, with a little room partitioned at one end for an office. One of the Shaughnessys agreed to go up to drive the teams; they hired a helper at Coal Valley and a young lady schoolteacher to keep the books. Isaac was appointed to oversee the yard, starting at sixty dollars a month; he had just passed his nineteenth birthday.

The Coal Valley yard prospered through the fall. At three cents a foot, even three and a half, the firm was selling as much saw-wood as they could cut and haul from the mill, and no competition. Isaac took a room in the town and came home Saturday afternoons in time for supper, silent and exhausted; long hours, certainly, seven in the morning till dark—but the people, Germans mostly; the loneliness. In January the partners agreed on an exchange: Fred Weyerhaeuser would go up to Coal Valley to manage the yard; Isaac would come back to the mill. Fred, still formally a tallyman, had proved useful in other ways. A pair of Germans had come to the mill at noontime while he ate his dinner, talked, bought a wagonload of lumber for gold; others came, he could talk to them in their language, was trusted; was careful with money but not with his time. When the partners proposed that he go to Coal Valley, he bargained, quietly— not over money, but he planned to marry, buy a house at Rock Island; a girl born in his village he had met when he first came across and lived with relatives near Erie, Pennsylvania. John Marsh, usually silent except when explaining his trial balances and his monthly statements, said they could *build* him a house, in a corner of the yard, with lumber from the mill. It was agreed; in January the little house was built, Fred brought his Sarah out from Pennsylvania, and the exchange was made.

At the end of its first year, the firm of Pride, Smith, and Marsh had showed a profit of 2,690 dollars on a trade of more than 47,000 dollars; moreover, the mill was paid for, they had acquired the yard at Coal Valley and built and paid for the shed, office, and Fred's manager's house, and had on hand half a million feet in logs and lumber, including a hundred thousand board-feet stocked at the new yard. On the other hand, they were pinched for cash: most of it they set aside for the four-thousand-dollar balance due in March on the last raft; what was left, perhaps, would see them through the weekly wages and the interest of the slack season. Smith and Marsh agreed to take only three hundred dollars each from their share of the profit; Abraham, after much thought, decided he could manage well enough from the home farm and the rent from the new place on the prairie and left his half on the books. Nevertheless, the prospects for the new year seemed bright. Prices for all commodities were higher than for twenty years, and farmers in general, three fourths of the nation's people, seemed at last to have come out of the depression that had lasted since the Panic of 1837. With that incomprehensible war finally settled in southern Russia, a place called the Crimea, all trade was bound to pick up.

As it turned out, although sales at the mill started quietly indeed, receipts from Coal Valley came in steadily, the mill worked without a stop, building up stock for the summer, and the partners met their note in March with cash to spare; on days when the trade was quiet, Fred loaded a wagon with miscellaneous lumber and drove around the outlying farms—new emigrants, mostly, many of them German— getting acquainted, selling odds and ends as he could, leaving samples. Trade picked up at both yards. In April and again in May Abraham bought a log raft but the second time was obliged to pay the highest price yet, nineteen dollars a thousand; with sales on the rise, he was able to put down four thousand dollars on each, with the rest on the usual twelve percent six-month notes. These prices made him acutely uncomfortable—the thought of having to raise their charges to customers; an exaction, he called it, from neighbors, friends. John Marsh particularly was impatient with this line, and Abraham reluctantly gave in; the third week in May, a new price list was tacked to the office door, based on thirty-five dollars a thousand board-feet. Abraham was therefore alarmed when on a visit to Coal Valley he discovered that Fred had been getting forty a thousand since he took charge. The young German argued that the emigrants had the money, needed the wood, and would pay more to anyone else, but Abraham was unpersuaded, and remained so when Fred brought out his freight bills and showed that his forty dollars was really worth no more than thirty-five at the mill. At length, stolidly disapproving but holding his peace, he promised to take two dollars off and post a new set of official prices.

Sales at the mill slowed somewhat in June—Abraham was almost pleased, it had been one of his arguments against raising the price, but his partners would not relent; at the same time, the trade at the Coal Valley yard dropped alarmingly, despite the lowered price Abraham had insisted on. A certain uneasiness was abroad. Gold in the West was excessively scarce, reliable bank notes not much easier to come by; although at Davenport the banker Ebenezer Cook was making enemies by cautiously calling in merchants' commercial paper that for years he had renewed without question, much of the mill's business was done on credit, on personal notes of up to three months. Nevertheless, at the end of June John Marsh could show that they had sold half again as much lumber as in the first six months of 1856, and at better prices, and their profit on the books was over six thousand dollars, while they had nearly fourteen thousand on hand or in the bank and four hundred thousand board-feet of logs and lumber in stock. There were, however, difficulties ahead: large notes on the last rafts due in the fall; John Aplon's troubling three-thousand-dollar loan, though he as yet showed no sign of wanting his money; and three thousand dollars in unpaid accounts. Again, Smith and Marsh took out only what they needed to live, and Abraham left his profit to go on accruing.

What was beginning in June 1857 was a new direction in the arterial flow of the nation's money, a pulse, an impersonal heartbeat that had dislocated Abraham's life once before, in the events known as the Panic of 1837. In part, it had to do with land. In the past ten years a hundred and fifty million acres of the public domain had become private under a variety of schemes devised by Congress and the states, much of it bought with money borrowed at high interest, a debt of perhaps two hundred million dollars that touched every citizen in the West and stretched in a web of relationships and borrowings throughout the nation. New railroads like the Illinois Central, though endowed with public land, needed cash for construction and operating costs and got it by borrowing, nearly a billion dollars in debts secured by railroad bonds and stocks since they had nothing else so valuable to offer—and many of the banks based their circulating money on these securities, not unreasonably, since the stocks and bonds paid well and commanded good prices, so long as the railroads had freight to move and passengers to carry. And, finally, business at large was done largely on credit, notes given and taken, often several times over as an item passed from producer to final use, perhaps two and a half billion dollars' worth by 1857. (Abraham and his partners were both old-fashioned and naïve in doing most of their business in cash till pushed increasingly toward credit.) All this debt was money, though unrecognized as such and therefore beyond the control of the Treasury, the Congressmen and legislators, doctoring the national economic health. The swelling money-debt was one reason for the rising prices, the apparent good times and well-being of the 1850s.

The system worked well enough—the money pulsed at a healthy rate—so long as Europe, England above all, drew off rising American production as exports. The Crimean War diverted British and French gold from American trade and investment but compensated by shutting off Russian grain, and Americans were not much affected. When the war ended, Russian grain was again on the market and British gold continued to flow elsewhere, to new wars or rebellions, in Persia and India; the high interest rates that resulted sucked money back from American investments, such as railroads. By June of 1857 there was unsold American grain on the markets, a drop in rail freight and shipping, then in successive ripples a decline in sales and prices of other farm products, manufactured goods. In July mills all through New England began shutting down—fabrics made of high-priced cotton were backing up in their warehouses, unsold. The big-city bankers were nervous but remained confident: their deposits held up, money continued plentiful, they added no new restrictions to credit granted or extended.

Sales at both the firm's yards slowed in July. Abraham at length carried his point, took seven dollars off the price at the mill, and for a time sales improved, though nearly all on credit—and since by now they were well into cutting their costly latest raft of logs, it was not clear whether at that price they were actually making a profit. At both yards prices were cut twice again, and sales continued, but slowly; when Fred mentioned in passing that at Coal Valley he had restricted all sales to cash since the beginning of July, the partners diffidently followed suit but already had thirty-five hundred in recent credit on the books, besides another three thousand from the first half of the year.

In August a comparatively minor event set off a panic. The cashier of a New York bank absconded with enough money to shut its doors. Merchants who had kept their money there were ruined. Railroad stocks, the basis for much of the credit extended by all the leading banks, dropped on the stock market. What followed was panic in the literal sense—men in herds lining up at bank tellers' windows to take their deposits out in gold, the currency of stable and intrinsic value. The banks, with their assets in loans backed by declining railroad stocks and insufficient gold, suspended—offered depositors bank notes of doubtful value, not coin, and called in their loans; or stopped business. In consequence, more merchants, dependent on bank credit, were bankrupt. Besides refusing to pay in gold, many banks in the East no longer accepted the bank notes of Western banks, making them effectively worthless for trade—a merchant in Iowa, say, could not buy shovels from Massachusetts with the money of an Illinois bank.

By late fall twenty thousand men were jobless in Chicago, a hundred thousand in New York. Someone led a march on the Federal subtreasury in New York, with the idea of redistributing the public wealth; troops summoned by President Buchanan drove the men off.

Although its effects were real and personal enough, the panic's chief importance was symbolic: it marked the seismic shift in the American economic balance from New England and the Northeast generally toward the West—as such, the culmination of a long and complex interaction of ideas and events, within the national borders and beyond, but also a beginning. The widely held belief that labor, not land, is the ultimate source of all wealth had been confirmed by the opening of the West and had been acted on by the settlers wherever new land was brought into production: the belief that neither land nor any other material resource has value in itself. Most of those who made such land productive and profitable did so by a considerable investment of capital, hiring the clearing, fencing, and first plowing, the carpentering of house and barn, buying their basic equipment; but it was also possible, as the proponents of Western settlement tirelessly repeated, for the settler with little money to accomplish these initial tasks entirely by the labor he and his family could furnish in abundance—and must, or starve—and even his implements, many of them, were simple enough for a man of moderate skills to manufacture for himself.

If labor was the essential term in this equation of value, it was also in short supply for the work required, therefore comparatively high-priced when it had to be hired and became more so as the proliferation of railroads increased the demand; repeating on a grander scale the conditions that prevailed in the Atlantic coastal colonies through the 17th and 18th centuries. The effect was both to draw off labor from the Northeast and to increase its cost, sometimes to the point where a New England farmer could more profitably abandon his land and go west as a hired hand than maintain his independence. Like rising labor costs, improved transportation to the West also worked against the Northeast, reducing and then eliminating any cost advantage its products might have had in the great markets of the East as the competition of river and lake steamers with the canal networks, then of these with the railroads and the railroads with each other, worked a steady and drastic driving down of freight charges, until, for instance, Iowa flour could be profitably delivered in New York or Baltimore cheaper than that of Connecticut or the Shenandoah Valley. This competition between West and East served as a stimulus to development of machinery to increase production while reducing the requirements of high-priced farm labor—improved plows, horse-rakes, reapers, threshers, and so on, in hundreds of patented forms—but this too in the long run worked against the Northeast: increased the capital cost of farming there and, as the machines were adapted to Western conditions, the relative advantage of the West.

The effects of this new situation on Abraham's lumber firm were muted: their business was local, they could get along for now without importing equipment or supplies from the East, and Chicago or St Louis bank notes from sales—they saw no gold—were satisfactory for their needs; but scarce credit limited what they could buy and sell. By the end of September the mill had sawed the last of the logs bought in the spring, slow sales and scarce cash made it imprudent to buy another raft, and the fireman, sawyer, and their helpers were laid off; Isaac (still at the high wage of sixty dollars a month set when he went to manage the new yard) had been doing the tallying and parts of several other jobs around the mill—the Shaughnessy brother sent to drive the teams at Coal Valley had not been replaced. In spite of these difficulties, the firm at the end of the year had made a profit of more than fifteen thousand dollars on sales a little below those of the first year, the two rafts taken in the spring had been paid for, and the open accounts from the first half of the year were nearly all settled, with interest. Nevertheless, income for the second half had fallen below costs, they had no more than a hundred thousand board-feet of stock in the two yards, and thirty-five hundred dollars in credit sales outstanding. And as John Marsh somberly pointed out, their cash on hand exactly equaled the original cost of the mill and the three thousand dollars still owed Mr Aplon.

By March of 1858, things seemed to be improving. With the remaining stock all sold, they were able to take on another raft—at only fifteen dollars a thousand, with two thousand dollars down and the balance at ten percent. The production crew was rehired and for a few weeks the mill even worked nights again. A growing portion of the firm's income came from Coal Valley, and more profitably since the costs there were lower. By July, however, the partners faced a dilemma. They were running out of logs; no rafts had come down from Wisconsin since late spring. They could shut down the mill again, of course, but with no lumber to sell they would be out of business altogether, with idle property and money owing. Abraham spent all his days at Rock Island, leaving Mary and a hired man to see to the farm, and came home late to supper, worn and anxious, with sawdust in his hair and a smell of resin on his clothes. The firm's affairs occupied his evening prayers, not on his own account but for the sake of its employees, customers, Isaac, his wife and daughter, but no clear guidance came to him. His partners were no more helpful. Smith spent all his time tinkering with the aging steam engine and the saws and complained of the need for spare parts or, better yet, complete replacement, but there was no money for that—manufacturers even in Cincinnati would accept the bank notes in which the firm could pay only at ruinous discounts, if at all; money Gilman Smith now professed not to understand or have any interest in, only his machines. All through the month John Marsh was confined with the common disease of the season, a fever that rose till it seemed your head would fly off, followed by a chill and an ague that rattled the whole body so a man could hardly talk or write or think; a sequence variously attributed to the hot weather, low water in the river, a miasma rising from the sloughs and riverbanks. Abraham gravely missed the bookkeeper's calm, the certainties he called forth from his numbers and accounts.

At this point providence intervened in the person of a dapper, dark little man with a pointed chin-beard and a black whip-snake mustache waxed to long, sharp points in the style made fashionable by the French Emperor. He rapped briskly at the office door one steamy morning at the end of July, stepped in, and presented an elegantly printed card that identified him as Isaiah Purdy, Esquire, Owner, Proprietor & Gen'l Manager of the Purdy Steam Lumber Mill and Yard, Dubuque, Iowa. Abraham got up from the desk and greeted him warmly: Purdy, a numerous Greenwich family some of whom had married Prides—why, no doubt they were cousins of some kind, in a manner of speaking. Mr Purdy looked blank, then after a moment agreed that yes, that might be the case, his family *had* come from Connecticut, though he knew little enough of that himself—his father in the 1820s had emigrated to Ohio to take up military bounty land.

Mr Purdy took a chair and came to the point, leaning forward confidentially, hands resting on his cane. He had taken on rather more logs in the spring than he could dispose of in these unsettled times and was under necessity of taking steps now so as to meet his obligations in the fall; he was, he was free to admit, pinched for ready money. Abraham nodded gravely—cash, the merchant's daily anxiety —but, his mind still on Greenwich and home, relatives, youth, did not see where this talk was leading. Two full rafts in his booms, Mr Purdy continued, and paused—besides the stock of lumber in his yard. Pride's mill, with its two yards, was known to him by reputation, while from strolling through the yard just now he inferred that Mr Pride might be facing an opposite predicament, a shortage of stock; possibly there was some arrangement to be made to their mutual advantage. He paused again and waited.

—What arrangement might you have in mind? Abraham courteously inquired.

Mr Purdy—My friends call me Isaiah, and we're that, I'm sure, dear sir, seeing as we're likely cousins from the old times at Greenwitch—produced his cigar case and offered it expansively; Abraham accepted one and laid it absently among the pencils to one side of the desk. Between swirling puffs of smoke, the little man set forth his proposal. He was prepared to accommodate his colleague by selling him both rafts at the rock-bottom price of twelve dollars a thousand— not a penny more; a modest payment down—a thousand each, let us say, or more if you can see your way—and the balance in three months at six percent. He insisted on selling both rafts at once or not at all. So much stock, he admitted, was a good deal for one mill to take on at one time—but at such a price—

Abraham did not answer immediately but bowed his head slightly and clasped his hands before him on the desk.—Mister Purdy—er, *Isaiah*, he said at length, allow me to tell you that for this firm, at this time, your proposal is providential—yes, positively *providential*. . . .

Having made his point, Isaiah Purdy was urgent: the matter must be settled *at once* so that he could return to Dubuque and arrange for bringing the rafts down—why—he was almost rude—if he was to be niggled with dickering and shilly-shallying, after his handsome offer, he had only to take the boat on down to Keokuk or Hannibal or St Louis and he was certain of selling his logs on the instant—and on better terms too, very likely! Abraham by now, however, had so far recovered his native caution as to insist on viewing the rafts before concluding, and they compromised: there was a boat at the Rock Island landing; they would take it up overnight to Dubuque and in the morning, if Abraham found no objection, they would settle. Between them they wrote out a rather complicated agreement in two copies: the firm would pay a thousand dollars down on each raft, in St Louis bank notes, the balance within three months of delivery; the first raft would be shipped immediately, the second—since the mill could not handle so many logs at once—one month later, but the firm might cancel the shipment altogether before that time, only forfeiting the down payment; the firm was to arrange for shipping and bear the cost.

With a rare feeling of elation at his careful bargaining, Abraham went to find Isaac in the yard, asking him to carry home the message that he would not be back that night but probably the next night or the following morning. Gilman Smith was in the cutting shed, cursing a worn-out overhead belt that had broken again, shutting down the circular saw; he accepted his partner's news with a wordless shrug and went back to patching the belt.

The rafts were as Isaiah had described them and of acceptable quality. Abraham took dinner at his new friend's bachelor cottage behind the mill, signed both copies of the agreement and a note for the balance, and took the boat across the river to Galena. Dave Philumalee, an experienced and reliable raft pilot, had been idle for weeks and was eager to take the job on; Abraham paid him three hundred dollars on account, the balance to come when the second raft was delivered at the Rock Island mill, and took the cars back by way of the new Illinois Central line connecting with Galena.

A week later Abraham sent off a letter to Isaiah Purdy, Esquire, asking if the first raft had left, but received no answer. Another week passed and they laid off the production crew—there were no logs left to saw—but kept Shaughnessy and two laborers, although sales from their dwindling stock of lumber were hardly four thousand feet a week (and about the same at Coal Valley). Abraham wrote again, more urgently, and entrusted the letter to the captain of an up-bound steamboat for personal delivery, but no reply came. In the second week of August he took the cars back to Galena.

The ferry that carried Abraham over the Mississippi passed Purdy's mill coming in to the landing. He leaned on the guardrail, waiting while the deckhands brought the landing-stage forward for putting ashore. There was no sound or smoke from the mill's engine, no one about in the yard, though it was the start of a normal work-day; no stock that he could see in the yard, no sign of the two big rafts of logs that in July had been tied up along the riverbank. Even the mill's log boom, a floating structure of big logs placed end to end and strung together with chains, had disappeared.

Abraham was first down the stage and went on foot back along the dusty river road to the mill, trotting; and arrived out of breath, his hair plastered wet against his head, the sweat running in slow streams from his cuffs and down the backs of his hands. He made a circuit of the yard, mopping his face and hands with a handkerchief, but all was as he had already seen from the boat: except for a few bundles of shingles, a stack or two of lath and a decade of sawdust spread under-foot in a spongy carpet, the yard was empty, the rafts of logs departed as if he had only dreamed of walking them and counting, as if they had never existed; there were padlocks on the doors of the engine house and cutting sheds. Abraham hammered on the door of the little house where he had dined with Mr Purdy and signed the agreement, but it resounded like an empty cask, the curtains were drawn across the windows, the place smelled of dust and disuse. Abraham sat down on the step and covered his face with his hands: *My God, my God, my God, how have I betrayed my trust?* over and over in his mind like a verse from a psalm, but his mind could not get beyond it, he could not imagine what might have happened or what he must now do.

At length he walked back to the town. A shingle in front of an office on the main street—*Aaron Kohn, Esquire, Attorney-at-Law*—caught his eye and he went in with the thought that perhaps a local man of affairs could explain the mystery of Mr Purdy, the mill, and his two rafts of logs. The lawyer knew a little: that at the end of July Purdy had closed down, sold off his stock, and taken his logs down the river to sell; had not been back and had left no address—was variously said to have gone to California, Montreal, or Europe. Did Mr Pride possess a bill of sale or a receipt for his payment? From his pocketbook Abraham produced his worn and much-folded copy of the agreement, which did indeed acknowledge the two thousand dol-lars down. The lawyer gave his opinion that the money could be recovered—it would be necessary to prove that the logs had *not* been delivered—and offered, for a retainer of fifty dollars, to secure a judg-ment. It would be necessary also, of course, to find Mr Purdy; Dave Philumalee—the lawyer knew him by reputation—might be some help and would be needed as witness if the matter ever came to trial.

Abraham numbly counted out the money and put the contract away; Mr Kohn wrote out a receipt.

On the lawyer's advice, Abraham took the ferry back across to Galena, but the raft pilot's house was as empty as Purdy's cottage. Desperate, he knocked at the doors of all the neighboring houses and finally found a woman who would tell him something. Captain Dave had taken his family and gone to Minnesota, somewhere up the St Croix River north of St Paul, working for a logging company; she had an address. Abraham wrote a letter and took it to the post office. A month later he received a reply from Stillwater, Minnesota:

Dear Sir:

Yours of 10th ult. only just come to hand and contents noted, would say in reply: I started down with raft day after we talked, fierce headwind. We Tied up at Clinton, Iowa, two days, Gentleman offered to buy intire Raft @ 8$/thousand full cash, I explained Raft already disposed of, but Mister Purdy come on and told me he was accepting. I Protested I was paid by you to take Raft to your Premisses at Rock island and he showed me Tellygram signed by you saying it was alright to Sell. I don't know who got the second Raft, I am in hopes you got your money alright. I am rafting Saint Croy till freeze-up.

About the same time Squire Kohn reported that he had obtained judgment against Isaiah Purdy in the amount of $2,000 with simple interest at five percent; he would take steps to execute same whenever Purdy could be located but had as yet uncovered no trace of him despite several inquiries. He requested an additional fee and costs of $37.50.

IV

Downriver

By September 1858 the Coal Valley yard was out of stock; the employees there were paid off, except for Fred Weyerhaeuser, who agreed to bring his wife back to Rock Island, take lodgings, and do what he could around the mill until times improved. Sales at the mill yard were so slow that the remaining employees there too were let go—the partners, with Fred and Isaac, could do such work as there was. John Marsh, still feeble but coming to the office most days, calculated that by the end of September they would have just about enough cash to pay the note on the April raft due in October and cover John Aplon's loan—and, possibly, to get through to the spring when they could start fresh with a new raft. The firm's expenses had been so low that even with the trickle of sales they would have shown a profit—except for the two thousand dollars to that rascal Purdy and three hundred more to the raft pilot; as it was, their loss for the third quarter was around a thousand dollars. That loss, of course, would be more than made up by the fifteen hundred still owing from builders on both sides of the river, if they could get it, but the builders were mostly out of business and the firm's accounts far down on the lists of claims. Smith and Marsh did not blame Abraham, exactly—they might, they admitted, have done the same—but each was morose in his own way, Smith cursing his worn-out machines, Marsh silent over the books, and had little to say to him. All three were united in the single goal of somehow lasting through till spring but possessed no imagination for the intervening months. They still had something over a hundred and fifty thousand feet of lumber in the yard, if they could find any way of selling it.

One morning toward the middle of September Abraham and Marsh, glumly occupying the mill office, were visited by a tall, loose-limbed man who introduced himself as George Tromley, raft pilot. He was calling to inquire if there were any service in that line he might offer. Abraham told him shortly that he did not think so, the firm was not taking on any logs just then, but Captain Tromley did not take the hint and depart. He settled himself comfortably in a chair, one leg over the arm, an idle man passing the time with idle men. In a manner of polite conversation, he asked how their business was progressing.

—Rather slow, of late, Abraham admitted when Marsh said nothing. It seems that trade in every line is—slow—just now. The times are hard.

The captain ventured to observe that he thought businessmen were like mud turtles, floating away in the spring floods, then digging into the bank when the waters receded, the river sank, and the hot sun of summer beat down. But he was of the opinion that what most people called hard times were really times of opportunity—for a man who could see his way into the inwardness of things. For example—

John Marsh shut his ledger with a snap, announced that he was going home to his boardinghouse for dinner.

—For example, Captain Tromley amiably continued, ignoring the interruption, I know of firms holding logs up at Beef Slough by the millions that would gladly sell for six or seven dollars a thousand. A man could float them down, let us say, to Rock Island, saw them up to sell for twenty dollars a thousand—and come out better than a year ago at thirty. *That's* what I call opportunity, for a man that can see it. And all it takes is a little cash.

Abraham fleetingly considered the prospect but clamped his mind shut at the mention of money.—Our firm, he said, has uses for all its cash just now. It's an interesting thought, of course—.

Still the man did not go and Abraham did not know how to send him away. He talked on: of the railroad building west from Hannibal and high times there for trade, as at Davenport a few years back— fifteen years he'd been rafting, had seen all the bad times and the good on the Upper River. A man who knew the river and could recognize opportunity could take a raft of lumber down, sell it on commission— twelve percent, say—make his expenses and a profit too, and bring back thousands for the owners—.Captain Tromley broke off, excused himself, but said he would look in next morning; it had been pleasant talking.

When the raft pilot returned the next day, Abraham insisted that his partners at least hear him out. He seemed an honest man, though admittedly in these hard times no man's honesty was certain; he was, at least, what he said, an experienced raftsman well known on the Upper River. Through most of a sleepless night Abraham had tried to dismiss the idea as unlikely, risky, as once more trusting the mill's fate to a stranger's hands, but it nagged and would not leave him—if after all they could sell off their stock at St Louis, at a fair price— why, they'd have the cash to get through with ease and half to put into logs at those wonderful prices the captain talked of. They could start up the mill again, go back to building the business at Coal Valley —they'd be *saved!*

John Marsh was sufficiently impressed by the captain's proposal to point out that with the expenses of rafting, the lumber at twenty-five dollars a thousand would net little more than they were getting at the mill for twenty or twenty-one dollars—they would have to get at least twenty-eight or thirty dollars to make the venture worthwhile. George Tromley agreed but thought that was possible; and the lumber on hand would make only a small raft that could be managed with a small crew, eight men, say; and with any luck on the weather they'd make the 330 miles to St Louis in two weeks, which again would help cut the costs down.

Finally even Gilman Smith was persuaded there was something in the captain's proposition—worth trying, anyway, and it was agreed, though with a number of cautions and complications. For one thing, the partners were reluctant to trust the whole venture to George Tromley for a twelve percent commission on sales; they settled on a flat hundred dollars to him as pilot with five percent on whatever they took in beyond the current price at the mill, and he would supply Quincy boats and other equipment for the raft. The captain would hire the rafters but the firm would pay them—a dollar a day if possible, not over a dollar and a half—and provide food. To keep the crew down, Isaac Pride would go along and see to the firm's interest, and they would do without a cook; when Fred Weyerhaeuser heard of this, he expressed an interest in learning about rafting, and it was agreed that he too would go along, one less rafter to hire, and perhaps he could take charge of the cooking. Since none of the partners knew anything of building a lumber raft, Captain George would show them how and supervise.

They assembled the lumber in cribs sixteen feet wide, the standard length for rough lumber, and thirty-two feet long: boards of the same grade and size laid in crisscrossed layers; twelve layers high, framed with heavy grub planks two inches thick, a foot wide, held together with two-inch-square hardwood grub pins pounded through holes drilled in the planks. They built the cribs up on greased wooden rails laid in the mill's skidway; as each crib was completed, it slid down into the river when the retaining blocks were knocked away, as in launching a ship. It took them two days to make up all the lumber in the yard, working from first light till full dark. When they were finished, they had twenty-four cribs made up in four strings of six cribs each; and less than half a crib of miscellaneous leftover stock, which they piled loose in the middle of the raft to make a dry platform for cooking and sleeping. Although small on a river where lumber rafts of a hundred and twenty or a hundred and sixty cribs were common, this one was still as spacious as most steamboats, more than sixty feet wide and nearly two hundred long, but floated low and sluggish, creaking as the eddy currents lifted, straining one crib against another.

It took most of the third day to make the raft's eight sweeps, one at bow and stern of each string of cribs: huge oars made from young pine or spruce twenty feet long and a foot through the butt, the branches trimmed, the blades of two-inch lumber twelve feet long, fitted into slots in the thick ends of the stems and held in place by pegs. Isaac and Fred with difficulty lifted each sweep into place, but once balanced and settled on the tholepin stuck through the slot drilled in the thick end of the stem, it moved, they thought, almost as readily as the oars of a skiff.

George Tromley came back at daylight next day with his gear loaded on one of the mill's wagons, a small stove and cooking equipment in boxes, coils of rope, the two Quincies, a low tin-lined box to be filled with sand as a base for the stove; Abraham the night before had loaded the salt meat, lard, the sacks of potatoes, beans, flour, coffee, sugar. The sun was up by the time the crew straggled in, a couple of big Irishmen, four Canadians, Frenchmen really, squat, dark men with shoulders sloped and rounded with muscle, tasseled sashes at their waists, short pipes clamped in their teeth. The Irish joked about the size of the raft—no bigger'n a leaky little pismire of a horse-ferry to trust yourself to on the great river, Mother o God—but were glad enough of the work, having had none all summer and none in prospect till the logging camps hired on in Wisconsin in the winter. One of them, redheaded Sandy McCauley, wanted to know where the cook was—Or are we to go starvin to Saint Louie on cold grub and what we kin catch?—and Fred Weyerhaeuser stepped up to him, as tall and heavier through the shoulders, and said he'd do the cooking and man a sweep too, and they'd eat well enough, and in fine style once they'd sold their wood. Well, then, said Sandy, if yer the cuke, see that we've cakes and tarts and the coffee hot when a man wants it, and ye'll hear no complaints from me; and turned away.

Nothing remained. Abraham held his son in wordless embrace, gripped Fred's offered hand in both his, and ran with Gilman Smith to open the log boom. It was not like a steamboat moving out in the purposeful curve of rudder to current and the accelerating heart rhythm of paddle wheels. The raft lay against the bank, silent, held by the slow back-swirl of the eddy. Captain Tromley gave a shout— Stabbard at the bow!—and Sandy McCauley on the right front sweep

gave his oar a swing, dipped the blade, walked forward leaning into
the stem, and the other bowmen followed his rhythm, a little Frenchman, Largay, Isaac, and Sandy's partner Costello; then lifted the
blades clear, backed up, dropped, and pushed again. Fred ran forward
from the stern, grappled a loose plank from the stack at the center of
the raft, and braced it against the bank, heaving his strength into it.
The bowmen tramped back and forth with their sweeps, the
nailheads of their caulked boots thumping the boards in unison.
Slowly, excruciatingly, the raft moved away from the bank; the current caught, took hold with a tremor and creaking of crib against crib,
and pulled the raft out into the steamboat channel, and farther, carrying across toward the Iowa shore. The captain shouted, the eight
rafters marched, bow and stern opposite, aligning the raft with the
current, moving downstream.

The river below Rock Island runs nearly due west the thirty miles
to Muscatine before turning south again in a great bend. The whole
section is broken by low, narrow, sharp-pointed islands as much as
eight or ten miles long, hazards for steamboats and more so for floating rafts. By mid-afternoon with its late start the raft had come less
than ten miles and was passing the first of the islands. Captain
Tromley gave the commands that worked the raft in toward the bank
of the island and sent the four Frenchmen off in the two boats with
heavy lines to make fast for the night. With low water and the moon
not yet half, not to mention the two boys in his crew, he would not
risk running the islands by night; but it was his custom in any case to
make an easy first day at the start of a trip, feed the men up and give
them time to arrange their sleeping quarters—and then get an early
start.

Fred got the camp stove fired, started a mess of fat salt meat and
beans boiling in the big kettle, then rowed over to a farm on the Iowa
shore and came back with a dollar's worth—twenty pounds—of fresh-
killed beef and a peck of carrots to add to the stew. While they waited
for it to thicken, one of the Frenchmen—Pig-Eye, a name that was
Piégon once—on a bet stripped off his jeans and shirt, jumped in the
water and dived under the raft; and after minutes he popped up on
the island side, panting and crimson-faced, hands grabbed him, pulled
him on board and flopped him down like a big fish. "Soch leetle raff,"
Pig-Eye pronounced it, when he got his breath back, that he refused
Sandy's quarter. They lay around the cookshack eating in silence
from the heaped tin plates; Fred produced piles of biscuits. Sandy
wagged a spoon at him and pronounced him a middling cook, right
enough, for stew and biscuit—But ef ye can't fill a man up any better'n dat, we's be nothin but a crew of walkin skilitons before we
make Saint Louie—and brought up a tremendous, drawn-out belch,

winking one eyelid shut so that Fred understood it was his way of joking and answered with a small smile.

Afterward, while it was still light, the men arranged the loose planks around the shack, tent-fashion, like card houses. Largay brought a fiddle out from his satchel, tuned it, and softly and very slowly traced the melody of "Allouette," then other Canadian canoemen's songs, and the others hummed them with him. Isaac crouched near to listen, feeling sleepy and too full of stew, biscuit, sorghum, and coffee. He pointed across the river, up the Iowa bank: up there on the edge of the prairies was the village of Buffalo, in the township next to Rockingham, his home; he knew the river this far from paddling his dugout down, when he was little.

—Dat Buffalo, Largay said. Dat Buffalo where Buffalo gels at. You got you Buffalo gel, I bet.

Isaac blushed and turned away. The fiddle, mocking, sketched the tune. Costello stood up and began the verse, in a light, sweet tenor, a work-song now well known on the river, a bargeman's song on the canals, a chantey on the sailing ships.

> *As I was lumb'rin down de street,*
> *Down de street,*
> *Down de street,*
> *A beautiful gel I chance to meet—*
> *Oh! She was fair to view-O!*

He mimicked the story in little walking, waltzing dance steps, and the others joined in, shouting out the chorus:

> *Oh—Buffalo gels, won't ye come out tonight,*
> *Come out tonight,*
> *Won't ye come out tonight?*
> *Buffalo gels, won't ye come out tonight,*
> *An dance by de light o de moon?*

—with a thunderous clumping of caulked boots on the final note. And there were others, "Raftsman Jim," "One-Eyed Riley," songs to dance to, row to, all with rafters for heroes. The sun was down, it was getting chill, a clear night coming; they gathered closer around the cooling stove. Largay, saying his fingers were going to sleep, slid the fiddle back in its velvet bag. Costello produced a jug and hospitably passed it; Fred refused, but Isaac, curious, tried a swallow, coughed and spat. The captain spoke up—if they were going to sit up all night, they'd sleep till noon and never make it through the islands—and crawled into his plank tent. The others quieted and followed his lead into their shanties. With the creak of the ropes and the current whispering and bubbling under the raft, ceaselessly, sinuously, lifting and prying at the planks, it was like floating on a cloud. All, curled in their blankets, slept.

Fred and the captain were up in the dark and by the time the first rim of sun struck the water, lifting the mist in clouds, there were stacks of pancakes, slabs of fat-meat, keeping hot on the stove, gallons of coffee simmering. The men ate ravenously and wanted more but the captain said no—did they think they were off on some kind of pleasure cruise?

The Frenchmen went ashore to cast off and bring in the lines. The river this time eagerly caught at the raft, carrying it around toward the far bank. The captain shouted—Where'd ye learn yer raftin, ye sons of monkeys, in a tin washtub?—and all put their weight to the sweeps; slowly the raft swung and straightened, lining up with the current. From then till late afternoon, when they'd cleared the islands and were drifting past Muscatine, there was hardly a quarter-hour at a time to rest on the oars.

A little after noon Fred took time out to carry around chunks of double-baked bread and, later, mugs of coffee. By the time they were passing Muscatine, Isaac's hands, which he'd thought hard from the mill work, from handling plow and hay-rake on the farm, were painfully blistered and raw across the palms; Largay showed him how to wrap them in torn strips from an old shirt. As the river turned south and opened out in the long straight run toward Grand View—there is such a place, so named, on every great American river where Frenchmen have run their boats—Fred came forward and offered to take his oar if he would cook; and Isaac was too tired to argue.

They set lanterns at the corners of the raft and pushed on by night through this easy stretch, sleeping and steering by turns, and so through the next day. By evening, sixty miles out from Rock Island, the wind turned around, became wet, and rain enclosed them like a tent, beating the current into waves that washed the length of the raft. The raft lay motionless in the water as a grounded hulk, the wind strengthened and drifted it toward the bank, and the captain gave the orders to pull in and tie up behind a point, wait it out. By morning the rain had stopped, the wind was down, but a heavy fog closed the river in, silent and white as in a heavy winter snow: you could not see the opposite shore, or one end of the raft from the other. Captain George nevertheless gave the order to cast off—he could see far enough from the bow and read the river from the way the current moved, and anyhow they were starting another long straight stretch, no obstructions to speak of all the way to Burlington. Pig-Eye and André brought the lines aboard, the raft drifted off, and the fog closed around them, and they lay in it, silent and motionless, it seemed, as a raft of ghosts. When the scream of a steamboat whistle came through —no way of judging distance or direction, only somewhere behind, up the river—all jumped, the captain let out a whoop, grabbed the sweep from Isaac, and worked it frantically to help swing the raft in toward shore. Minutes after, the boat entered their closed-in world with a clatter and whistle and beating of spray, the pilot house hidden in the fog, and was as quickly gone.

As the weather cleared and the wind came around from behind, turning chill, they pushed on again through the night. The morning was Sunday. Over coffee the captain announced that—intending no disrespect for the practice of religion, in its place, but with the weather improving and a widening bend of the river ahead—they would not spend the day tied up; for the benefit, perhaps, of the preacher's son and his Lutheran friend, not that the rafters knew one day from another. By late afternoon they had floated to within a mile or so of the start of the Lower Rapids and tied up so as to see them through in daylight.

In the morning they crossed to the Illinois side at Nauvoo and kept to the bank down the rapids, with no serious scares but heavy work at the sweeps; and crossed to Keokuk to tie up above the steamboat landing. Captain Tromley had been saying as they passed the upriver towns that here surely they would sell some lumber, maybe a whole string and pay off the Irish and send them back. In the morning when he walked around to the mills with Isaac to talk, the owners all told the same story: the trade was slack; it was not worth their time to come down to the river and look.

The days ran together in a blur. Isaac and Fred traded off cooking and manning the sweep, sleeping by night two hours at a time. Isaac saw the smoke of a farmhouse far off, took a skiff and rowed ahead to buy a basket of eggs, six dozen for a quarter; and found the river empty when he came back from bargaining and rowed half the morning to catch up, his hands still tender through Largay's rags, pink and transparent with the new skin. At Quincy where the raft-boats were made he wasted another half-day with the captain while the crew idled and slept on the raft, but again sold nothing.

They made the run down to Hannibal by night, like Davenport now a railroad town as well as a river port, though its railroad, aimed at St Joseph on the Missouri, was no more advanced than Davenport's; but the beginning of the death of steamboating all the same. There was a steamboat at the landing and they tied the raft up behind it. As Isaac and the captain came ashore, a young fellow in a pilot's cap leaned on the rail near the stern, waved and shouted.

—Where you takin your matchwood?

—We're little so we travel fast, Isaac shouted back.

—I'll give a nickel a cord to fire my boilers, the man answered.

—We're a hundred and fifty thousand feet of seasoned, prime Wisconsin pine! Tie on behind and we'll *tow* you to St Louis—and if *that* aint fast enough to suit, we'll sell you the lot for fifty a thousand.

The pilot stepped over the railing, jumped, and landed lightly on the bank beside them. He introduced himself, shook hands: Sam Clemens, a year or two older than Isaac by his looks and making a start at a mustache; politely he asked how the Lower Rapids had been when they came through, and Captain Tromley told him—not that a licensed steamboat pilot had much use for a rafter's opinions but every bit of information concerning the river had its value. Sam, it seemed, had worked mostly the Lower River, below St Louis, where there were difficulties enough, God knows, but none in the shape of rapids; he was from Hannibal, home for a visit and going back as a passenger. The captain mentioned their idea of unloading a few cribs of lumber if they could connect with a buyer and wondered if Sam could suggest a likely prospect. The young man mentioned the town's lumberyards but thought the railroad a better bet—they had an engine now and were hauling west as far as Macon; and offered to take them along and introduce them to the manager, Miles Britt.

The railroad man was willing at least to walk down to the river to look—they had a plan to set up a winter tie-cutting camp and could use a few cribs of lumber for shanties and such, if it was cheap. Sam tactfully shook hands all around and returned to his boat, leaving them to dicker. The manager went over the raft, agreed it was good stock; and offered to take four cribs for two hundred dollars. "Two hundred *each*, I expect you meant," Isaac suggested, but the man gave a sharp, negative shake of his head. Isaac worked that out again and after a moment put on a smile and said that was a pretty good joke: about eight dollars a thousand. "I *meant* in *gold*," the man said in an aggrieved tone; George Tromley objected that anyway, gold or not, they couldn't afford to sell only part of the raft unless it was a full string at least and they could drop two men from the crew. They talked it back and forth, strolled back to Mr Britt's office; eventually they worked it around—the railroad would buy a string, six cribs, for six hundred dollars, still in gold and the grub-planks thrown in, and send its own gang to load the lumber on wagons. That, it seemed, was as high as he'd go, and he was looking bored and ready to see them out. Isaac and the captain stood apart to talk. It was still a poor price, not much over sixteen dollars a thousand, but getting it in gold and the prospect of two fewer men to pay and feed—. They gave in; with the sale they covered the expenses of the trip and something over, and in St Louis maybe could afford to wait out a better price. The manager opened his safe and counted out the coins.

The captain went back to the raft. Isaac found the post office and scrawled a letter home:

My dear Father,

Have found the lumber trade terrible slow all the way down til today, but have just concluded a pretty fair piece of Busyness, selling full string of one-by-twelve to Hanibal & St Jo RR for gold. Hoping to do some good at St Louis in few days.

I like rafters fine and we get on first rate. Fred and I both cook some but he does it better. About LaGrange, Missouri, I took the Quinsy ashore and got big eggs 4¢/doz., good cheap is what I say. Weather fine and cool excepting one night it rained all night & we rafted morning in thick fog.

We are paying off the two Paddys as with only three strings to manage we don't need them and can save their pay and keep.

Love to Mother and Lizzie.

In Haste,
Your Son.
Isaac A. Pride.

By the time Isaac returned to the landing, Sam and his boat had departed, the one string had been taken off, and the Frenchmen waited on the diminished raft with the lines loosely hitched, ready to let go. The captain stood with Sandy and Costello on the bank, counting out their pay in Illinois bank notes: fifteen dollars for the ten days' rafting and two-fifty over for deck passage back to Rock Island and meals. Shouldering their satchels, the men began the climb up toward the town to hunt, they said, a jug of good Missouri tanglefoot.

It took them four more days to reach St Louis; one night at sunset the captain cautiously tied up—islands more frequent now, there were jutting half-islands coming out from the banks, a growing traffic of boats, four or five in a day to watch out for. Below Alton they crossed to the Illinois shore, avoiding the swirling mouth of the Missouri; its yellow-brown flow ran side by side with the clear blue-green of the Upper River, two streams between one pair of banks. By St Louis, when they crossed again, the waters had mingled, murky when you dipped a bucket and after an hour or two of standing a fine brown sediment settled in the bottom.

It was getting dark as they came in and tied up at the upper end of the levee; below them, a shadowy forest of jack staffs and tall steamboat chimneys, and the lights of the town twinkling up the riverbank. After supper the captain counted out the Frenchmen's pay by lantern light and said they could sleep on the raft, take breakfast, if they liked.

In the morning Isaac and the captain strolled the levee while Fred stayed back to watch the raft. They made the rounds of the lumberyards together in a livery buggy. By close of day they had sold off half the remaining cribs, all at different prices, none good; the captain, openhanded, treated the boys to a venison supper in a smoky, candle-lit rafters' tavern beside the levee. Next day, they divided—box-makers, wagon works, furniture factories, any trade that might buy wood;

by the third day they had sold out. After all expenses, it seemed they
would clear something over nineteen hundred.

The captain had a room on a boat for Galena that would carry his
gear. In the afternoon, in the privacy of the cookshack on what remained of the raft, they sorted the money and counted out Tromley's
hundred dollars, no prices earning the five percent commission, but
he made no complaint; wanted part in the gold from Hannibal, but
Isaac held out. They shook hands, parted.

Isaac was determined on a night in a swell St Louis hotel—
Tromley had mentioned the Southern as one where the pilots stayed,
when flush—and Fred went along. Climbing Washington Street toward the town they passed Samuel Hawken's shop, one of two dozen
St Louis gunsmiths, this one known to any reader of stories of Kit
Carson, Jim Bridger, scouts, Indian fighters, mountain men. Isaac
stopped, looked, went back, went in, and Fred followed. There was
no one in the shop. From somewhere in back came the whining,
grinding sound of a lathe. There were rifles on racks, leaning against
the walls. One lying by itself on a rough table to one side drew him.
Isaac set his carpetbag down, leaned close to inspect it, hands clasped
across his back: an octagonal barrel, medium long, looked to be about
forty-five caliber, with an elegantly shaped maple stock finished in a
dark stain and a leather-covered half-stock; and a trigger guard big
enough for a gloved finger, ending in brass scrollwork finger grips,
with a patch-box on the side of the stock and a brass plate set into the
butt. The lock was a kind new to him—he used his father's small-
bore, flintlock Lancaster long-rifle for turkeys, small animals, the occasional wolf or deer, and for small birds he had still the old musket
he'd acquired as a boy: on this one the hammer came down on a little
metal tube sticking up like a nipple. Isaac lifted the gun carefully,
hefted it in his two hands, feeling the balance; not heavy, perhaps ten
pounds. He raised it, laid his cheek against the stock, sighted.

An old stooped man came out from the back-room workshop, a
wreath of white hair around his bald head, a blue apron hanging to
his ankles. He approached with a shambling, arthritic walk, watched
while Isaac swung the rifle first to one side, then the other, pointed,
fingered the trigger.

—You like that gun? the old man at length asked.

—It *feels* good, Isaac answered, cradling the gun in his arms. Does it
shoot straight?

—Look, I show you, the man said, reaching for the gun and
grounding it. He plugged the tip of his little finger into the mouth of
the barrel.—Feel! he commanded, and Isaac did so. I rifle barrel with
seven grooves and seven lands—nobody make guns like that. So the
ball spin, fly flat and straight. Now look again—he lifted the gun,
patted the breech. I make heavy here, to be strong—test with triple

charge—then thinner toward other end, for nice balance, and the whole gun don't have to be big heavy thing, a man can carry all day and not get tired. You hunter?

—I hunt some, up in Iowa, Isaac admitted. With an old Lancaster long-rifle.

—Ah, Lancaster! the old man said with a smile. I learn gunsmithing at Lancaster, long years ago. You from Lancaster? he asked, still smiling.

—I was born in Connecticut—just a baby when we came out to Iowa.

—Mr Carson has a rifle like this one, the old man said, coming back to his subject. Little neat man no biggern you, don't want no big heavy gun—I make it for him, oh, ten-twelve years ago—not *exactly* the same—I don't never make no two just exactly the same—but pretty close. He says, with his gun, long ball and double charge, he can kill bull buffalo at five hundred yard. What you say to that?

Isaac took the gun back, tried it again.—How much you want for it, Mister Hawken?

—Ah, you guess my name? He paused, considered. I sell you for seventy-five dollars. How's that?

Isaac frowned, returned the rifle to the table.—That's a lot of money, Mister Hawken. It's a beautiful gun, but—. Ready to go, he nodded to Fred, who had waited in silence, having no interest in such matters.

—You ever shoot caplock? Mr Hawken asked, bringing a small, copper percussion cap out from his apron pocket and holding it out between thumb and forefinger. Isaac shook his head but took the cap, turned it over, studying. Well, come on then, we go down by river, I let you try her out—don't have to buy or nothin, just for fun. You want do that?

Isaac nodded; it was too much money, but he wanted to try it. The gunsmith brought out a powder flask, swept a handful of balls into his apron pocket, shouted through the door to the workshop. They made a curious procession descending the hill to the riverfront: the stooped, slow old man with his flapping apron and painful gait, carrying the flask, Isaac with the gun in one hand and the carpetbag in the other, eyes on the ground, and Fred bringing up the rear, stolid and disapproving. The river, seven or eight hundred yards across, gave room enough to shoot, but at what? Fred squinted, pointed—a tree trunk halfway across, floating low. Isaac nodded, measured powder, set a ball in a patch, and rammed it home; Mr Hawken showed him how to place the cap. The sun was behind them, getting low, a light wind blowing from the flat Illinois shore, riffling the water, tossing up flecks of white as it broke the surface. Isaac straightened up, raised the gun, set the hammer, and fired in one easy, continuous motion and a dull *thck* echoed back, like the sound of an ax blow on a log, heard from a distance; there was no splash.

Isaac turned to the gunsmith.—Shoots flat all right, like you said. And I like the feel.

He reloaded. Far up the river, four or five hundred yards, another log was floating down with three gulls riding it, motionless in the slanting light; at the distance and in the late light the driftwood moved like a shadow and the birds seemed to be standing up straight on the water. Isaac pointed, waited for them to see.—The middle one, he said.

Again the gun came up to his shoulder in a rhythmic flow, fired. There was an explosion of feathers in the middle of the log; the two remaining birds leaped, skimmed off across the water with angry cries, lifting. The smoke drifted back in their faces.

Isaac glanced back. Above them on the levee a gentleman in a tall hat had paused to watch, beside him a trapper in buckskins and moccasins; on the decks of nearby boats passengers stood watching. A boy ran down with a bottle, offered to throw it for him to shoot at. Isaac ignored him.

—I came down to try your gun, Mister Hawken, Isaac said in a low voice, not to make a show of myself. But you make a fine gun, and that's a fact.

He handed the rifle back to the smith, turned, grabbed his satchel, and started up, walking fast. The others followed.

The Southern Hotel occupied a full block, with a wide porch all along one side and gentlemen lounging in rocking chairs while darkies in white coats carried tall drinks on little round trays. Fred hung back, awed, but Isaac pushed ahead, took the steps two at a time, and marched across the lobby to the desk. Behind it, to one side, a tall young man in a tailcoat and ruffle-front shirt, with curly black hair, sorted through a pile of papers.

—We want to take a room for the night, Isaac said, and waited. He said it again, louder.

The young man looked up, frowned, and approached with languid steps. After looking him over for a moment, taking in the worn carpetbag—The Southern does not take rafters, he said. There are taverns down by the levee—

—We're not rafters, Isaac answered, flushing, we're mill operators down to sell our stock—and we'll pay in gold! He brought the heavy buckskin purse out from his pocket, extracted a coin, and slapped it on the counter.

The perfumed clerk studied the gold piece—*Every*one seems to have gold just now, he observed, but he shoved the register across and Isaac wrote their names. The room was four dollars for one night.

The clerk produced a key, made change, and rang a little bell. A liveried darky came forward and tried to take their satchels but Isaac with a fierce shake of his head wrapped his in both arms. The porter shrugged, took the key, and led them toward the stairs.

The room was four flights up and small, with a double bed. The porter waited by the open door. Isaac thought, said they'd want a tub brought and water. The man shrugged, pointed vaguely along the hall, mumbling something, but did not go. Isaac thought again, produced a half-dime and laid it in his outstretched hand.

—Oh, *thank* you, young master, said the black man, rolling his eyes up in a parody of gratitude, thank you, thank you!

It was eight o'clock before they came down to take supper. Isaac had discovered that what the porter meant was a room down the hall for taking baths, with a long white tub standing on eagle-claw legs and spigots to let in hot and cold water; Fred had stayed in the room, guarding the packets of bills in Isaac's carpetbag, and contented himself with a cold-water sponge at the washstand.

The dining room was high-ceilinged, with dark oak paneling on the walls, lighted by glass-shaded gas jets; there were rows of long oval tables along the walls, covered in white linen, with mahogany armchairs and at each place the knife, fork, and spoon elegantly balanced on the upturned plate and a rolled napkin standing upright in the water goblet. The waiter seated them at a table with two older men, one bearded, the other with a puff of side-whiskers on his cheeks, each with a heavy gold watch chain across his chest. The menu, printed with the day's date, Friday, October 1, 1858, took some studying. When the waiter returned, Isaac chose a bowl of soup, venison pie, roast mutton with cranberry sauce, and grape pie. Fred cautiously said he'd take the same. The waiter asked what they'd drink. Fred would have liked beer but was scandalized by the price, a half-dollar a bottle, and firmly ordered a pitcher of plain water. At this the gentleman of the side-whiskers observed that—that sludge aint fit to wash your face with, and if you're set on drinkin it you better take something to wash it down—and called after the retreating waiter to bring the boys a couple of bottles of Alsop's East Indian Pale and put them on his bill.

Fred was still uneasy over the very high price of the Hawken rifle and the thought that Isaac might have been tempted to give the firm's money for it. Isaac reassured him: he had only meant to look and learn what the finest gunsmith in America could do, not buy. . . . They were on the mutton when the gentleman broke in again, waving his cigar.

—Allow me—Pomeroy's the name, he said, from Atchison City, up the Missouri in Kansas Territory—. Now, you're a likely looking pair

of young fellows, he continued. Bound west to make your fortunes in
the gold regions, are ye?

—Gold, sir? Isaac asked. You mean California?

The man told them of the great find at a place called Cherry Creek,
far out in the west of Kansas Territory, and then someone followed
the traces back into the mountains, looking for the mother lode, and
claimed to have found it around Pikes Peak. This was in the summer,
and a month ago a man turned up in Kansas City with a sack full of
gold dust, and now there were others, here in St Louis, and the stampede was on, fellows starting out on the desert with their tools in
wheelbarrows and others organizing wagon trains to go across in the
spring. It was all the talk of the town. Where had they been?

Isaac told how they'd brought a raft of lumber down from Rock
Island to sell and had had no news of anything for nearly three weeks
now.

—Mmmm, said the man, sucking reflectively at his cigar. Don't
find much trade for lumber here just now—not since those New York
rascals and their panic, ruining our money. Isaac made a non-committal nod. Now, the man continued expansively, you take that lumber
of yours out to Cherry Creek somehow and you'll do some good—ten
cents a *foot*, I'm told, and cheap at that—none to be had at any price.

—Yes, *sir!* said his companion, and flour and whisky and hardware
and salt pork and worn-out oxen and mules, and all other benefits of
civilization, all at the same rate. And very right and proper too, is
what *I* say. *Let* the poor buggers break their hearts beating mountains
into gold dust, as nature intended, and then let the others, as is men of
sense, trade off their gold for such things as they require and hasn't
thought to provide, also accordin to nature. Now *there's* the way of it
for an active man with some capital and his brains in his head and not
in his backside—*eh*, boys? he concluded, turning back to Isaac and
Fred.

Isaac mutely lifted his glass and drained his beer. The older men
paid their bill, thanked Isaac and Fred for the interesting conversation, and suggested they meet later to continue, in the billiard room.
Isaac was so inflamed by this talk of gold that he could hardly sit
through his pie; but cooled somewhat when the waiter brought their
bill and there was a dollar for ale added on to the dollar each for their
supper. The young men protested, the waiter said no, that was his
orders, somebody must pay, and Fred offered to fetch the gentlemen
from the billiard room and hold them to their word; but they ended
by paying all the same.

The way back to the levee in the morning took them again down
Washington Street, past Samuel Hawken's shop. Isaac slowed, looked

in the dusty window, but did not stop. They were fifty paces past when a shout turned them back.

—You! Young man! Come here!

It was the gunsmith, come out from his shop, waving his old arms. Isaac went back, slowly, feeling foolish, shouted at, and ducking his head; everyone in the street would be looking.

The old man gripped his arms, brought his face close.—Young fellow, what's your name?

—Isaac A. Pride, Isaac formally answered. I'm from Rockingham, Iowa.

—Listen, Isaac Pride, Mr Hawken said, leading him through the shop door, that gun—I been thinking about you, I like the way you shoot. I got a feeling. I make that gun, like the Carson gun, but it just lay around in the shop, nobody buy—I got a feeling you got to have that gun, but you think it too much money to pay. Now, how *much* you pay?

They were in the middle of the shop. Fred hung back, by the door. The old man lifted the gun, held it out. Isaac with a sharp catch of his breath straightened up.

—Mister Hawken, he said, I've a whole satchel full of money here, but it aint none of it mine—belongs to my father and my father's mill, from selling lumber. I don't have any money of my own to pay you anything at all. But that's the finest rifle I've ever put my hands to.

—Here, *here!* the old man cried, reaching his trembling arms. You *take* it—listen, this gun, you got to have it, understand? And when you can pay—you pay when you can pay—seventy-five dollars, like I said.

Isaac took the gun and set it down, reached out and shook the gunsmith's hand; it was agreed. He could not speak.

They had taken passage on the *Ocean Wave,* sailing north in midmorning; a day, a night, and another long day to Davenport. Their stateroom—a little closet with about room enough for the two bunks, one above the other, and a washstand—was on the larboard side forward of the paddle wheel, with a narrow, glass-paneled door opening out onto the covered cabin deck. Supper, served at long tables set up in the boat's grand saloon, was twenty-five cents and as ample and varied as at the Southern. Afterward, the gamblers set up their games in corners of the saloon, three-card monte, the shell game, dice at a half-dollar a throw, the running patter of their spiels mingling in restless counterpoint. Isaac and Fred watched for a while, nudging each other in amazement at the foolish simplicity of the games, the transparent deceptions of the gamblers, but were not tempted to try to beat them; and presently retired to their cabin, still keeping rafters' hours. Isaac for the novelty of it took the upper berth. Both mattresses were straw-filled and noisy but kept them from sleep no more than five minutes after Fred blew out the lamp.

They were startled awake some hours later: a thumping of boots on the deck overhead, men's voices, shouting. There was gray light, like dawn, at the cabin door. A man ran past, crying out—We're lost! We're lost! Fred and Isaac leaped from their bunks, seized their bags, and ran out on deck, barefoot in their nightshirts. Other doors banged open all along, ladies in nightgowns and robes thrust their turbaned heads out, gentlemen half-dressed stepped forth and leaned at the railing. What was it? Had the boat hit a snag, run aground, burst a boiler? But the *Ocean Wave* steamed steadily ahead, her paddles beat the water in their accustomed rhythm. Only, the light—.

The young men ran forward, climbed the stairway to the open upper deck. As they came out, the boat made a violent swing to starboard, heading toward the Illinois shore, and they grabbed at the railing to keep from being thrown down. In the growing light they could see through the windshield of the pilot house above them where the pilot in a frenzy pulled down on the great wheel, gibbering —The end! The end! Run er ashore!—till the bulky figure of the captain bear-hugged him from behind, pulled him off, and threw him down with a metallic clang of a spittoon sent flying. The captain grasped the spokes of the wheel, spun it around as the boat's spars and upper deck brushed among the branches overhanging the bank, and slowly the boat swung away, out toward the channel again, and straightened out. "By the living God," roared the captain, "you son of a Gyptian mummy! You'll steer my boat proper, in the channel where she belongs, and not up the bank—if it do be the end of the world! And the divil take you!" The signal bell to the engine deck sounded, the paddle wheels slacked off a little. The boat proceeded serenely up the middle of the river.

Isaac and Fred in their nightclothes became conscious of the carpetbags they both still carried, looked at one another and laughed; they walked back toward the ship's bell mounted on the raised skylight above the saloon, and sat down. The light was strange, not white like moonlight—the moon had waned as they neared St Louis, coming down, and was gone—nor yellow like the sun but gray, like a mist, surrounding, penetrating, making the trees along the riverbanks stand out in sharp outline. Its source: a small, glowing disk overhead that moved across the dull sky even as they watched, yet bright enough to hurt the eyes, and trailing two long, curving streaks of brightness—as if the sun, coming out by night, were shrunken and withdrawn, speeded up, departing.

—Isaac, said Fred after a time, dat ting up dere—wat you tink dat iss?

—*That is*, Isaac said—Fred, embarrassed by his greenhorn's English, had asked his friend to correct it. Some kind of comet, I guess, he continued.

—Comet? Wat's . . . *th*hat?

—Don't know exactly—maybe like a piece of a star that's gotten loose from where it belongs and falls toward the sun and goes on past. We studied them some in natural philosophy.

—Not goin to come smash on the earth?

—Not likely—it only looks close cause it's bright—might be, I don't know, a million miles off.

—Now that's *good*, said Fred with a broad smile, cause I didn't tink the Lord would spend all so much trouble on the earth and then jus knock it to pieces like that. Or if He do, got better ways, I expect.

They sat in silence for a time. The comet in a long arc was sloping toward the horizon.

—Fred, Isaac asked, is it after midnight, do you think?

—Muss be—seem like we slep already half the night before they woke us up.

—Why then, said Isaac with a wide grin, it's my birthday, I hadn't even thought. I'm *twenty-one* today.

Fred grinned back, reached out and shook his hand. Isaac was silent again, propped his cheek on his hand, thinking. Then, gloomily:— Twenty-one! And what have I done, what am I going to do? What's my life going to *be?*

—That's *easy*, Fred answered, clapping him on the back. We go back to your father tonight with maybe two tousan dollar, an he goin pay off the mill's debts, get another raft, open up and start sawing again— nex year we sell two million feet, year after three million, an—

—Maybe that's for you, Fred, what you're going to do. I don't know.

—Isaac! Fred remonstrated. Your father *own* that mill, or mostly own it. Who you think he's workin it for? He's buildin it for *you.*

—I *know* that. And Father's such a *good* man, such a kindly man. But I don't know. It's just, whatever he tries, it never seems to come out the way he means it, I don't know why. And me—maybe running that mill someday, same thing day after day, year after year—I just don't know. . . .

—*Isaac*, Fred cautioned, his sense of the fitting once more compromised.

—Fred, Isaac said. Those two men, you know, at supper at the hotel. What did you really think about them?

—Pair of damn liars! Can't trust a man about some little ting, some little fifty-cent bottle of beer, can't trust him about anyting.

—I meant—about Pikes Peak and the gold and all.

—I know what you mean, that's what I say. All just lies—Pikes Peak and Alsop Pale Ale and gold—all nothin but lies!

—But Fred, said Isaac, very earnest, wouldn't it be *grand* to go out there, see that country, find a mine, and come back *rich*, with sacks of gold?

—Like those fools down in the grand saloon, with their children games—maybe one man, one time, in tousan year!

—Fred! Isaac swung around, gripping the other's muscular shoulders. I'm going to do it. In the spring. Go out there and try—and you've got to come, go partners in everything—we can do it—

—Naahh! Fred cut him off with his braying negative, shaking his shoulders free. There's all the gold I need for my whole life, right there at Rock Island. All I got to do to get is work. Besides, he said, softening a little, I got Sarah, and the little new baby coming—first Weyerhaeuser born in America! I got to work for *them* like your father work for *you*.

The comet had faded, leaving a brief darkness, giving way now to dawn. There was no more to say. They rose, stretched, remembered their carpetbags; crossed the deck and went back to their cabin.

After dinner on that Saturday, Abraham had retired to the parlor, intending to read the *Meditations* of Marcus Aurelius through from the beginning, for the sake equally of the splendid language and the Stoic philosophy, something he had not found time for in more than twenty years and not properly since college. He went across to the mill now once or twice a week but did not stay long. Gilman Smith still puttered, lately using scrap lumber to frame in what he said would be an open-sided storage shed for select stock or, closed in later, a drying shed. Since the raft started down, Abraham had made the last cutting of hay for the season and harvested the wheat. A new blight had befallen the potatoes and when they went to dig they found them nearly all rotted in the ground—he had sorted not quite two bushels that appeared sound, worth storing through the winter for seed in the hope they were resistant; the apple harvest was hardly better, a few bushels for cider, the rest, wormy, rotten, undersized, for the pigs, none fit to sell—it certainly did save work, as Mary wryly observed. Saturday in times past had been his day for preparing a sermon, but though he attended the Congregational church at Davenport now, he rarely preached; the little outlying places had found pastors of their own, or died off.

There had been a letter from Isaac the day before, from St Louis—they expected to sell off the last of the lumber and be home Sunday night or Monday. The boy had not thought to mention what sort of prices he was getting, but Abraham could not help speculating. At say thirty-five dollars a thousand—not at all unreasonable, it seemed, from what people said of the trade coming in now from the gold regions, or expected—they would clear nearly five thousand dollars after all expenses and the commission to Captain Tromley; not perhaps quite the prudent arrangement it had seemed, but still—. Well, if they sold off at a good price, it was fair enough and no harm done. But then—ah, *then!* Well, they'd meet the note on the spring raft, pay off John Aplon's loan—not that he pressed for it, but in these times—and it was an anxiety, nagging, to have it outstanding, and the drain of the interest—and they'd be seven or eight thousand clear. He'd take the boat to Wisconsin, buy a raft, and hire George Tromley to bring it down at a normal rate, say two dollars a thousand, complete —and still be money ahead: they'd replace the worn-out saws—.

A delicate rapping at the front door interrupted Abraham's reverie. He laid his book aside and went to answer: Ebenezer Cook, who the previous spring had moved his bank to new quarters at Second and Main in Davenport and put up the town's first public clock on a cast-iron post out front; a small, gray, bespectacled man, face crimped in perpetual distrust. Abraham took his hat, led him to the parlor, and invited him to a seat on the sofa. He offered tea, but the banker declined.

—Then to what, Mister Cook, do I owe the honor of your visit to our country suburb? Is there some way I may be of service?

—I've come on business, Mister Pride, said the banker brusquely. Service—well, that's as may be. Abraham folded his hands and offered a look of expectant attention. To come to the point, Ebenezer Cook continued. I believe you had dealings this past summer with a certain Isaiah Purdy of Dubuque.

—Very bad dealings, I'm afraid, said Abraham with a faint smile. He contracted to sell us two rafts of logs, which the mill badly needed to keep operating and for which we paid a substantial sum on account —and then failed to deliver and departed the country. I have taken steps to recover, which I'm sure we shall, if we can ever find him—

—I know nothing of that, Mr Cook broke in. What I do know is that your firm owes this Purdy a very great sum of money.

—Mister Cook, said Abraham with a nervous tremor, you are entirely mistaken, as I've just told you—Mister Purdy owes *us* money through having defaulted on his agreement.

The banker waved him into silence, brought out his billfold, and produced a folded document which he held out for Abraham to see.— You are familiar, are you not, he said, with this promissory note?

He drew it back when Abraham reached to take it; but he knew it well enough—Purdy's copy of the note Abraham had put his name to in July on behalf of Pride, Smith, and Marsh.

—I am grateful to you, Mister Cook, said Abraham, sitting back, for returning that worthless bit of paper. I confess, in the circumstances, I had not given it much—

—I am *not* returning it, snapped Mr Cook—or not until such time as it is canceled in the customary manner, by payment in full. As for worthless—that, sir, may be your estimate of your credit, but I have paid money for this *paper*, as you call it, it is, I am assured, a valid obligation, and I mean to see that it is met. It is payable in ten days' time.

—Have the courtesy to allow me to examine it.

The banker stood up, spread the paper, face up, on the reading desk, and held it flat at the edges with both hands. Abraham leaned, peered.

—Turn it over, please.

The endorsements on the back told the story. Purdy, soon after taking the note, had discounted it to a Galena bank for cash, perhaps forty or fifty percent off; Cook, for whatever reasons, had bought it in at a modest increment about the time the raft floated downriver and now judged the time ripe to call it in and collect in full for a quite respectable profit. The banker returned the paper to his billfold. Abraham stood back, head hanging, hands clasped before him.

—Mister Cook, he said finally, I cannot think—I cannot *believe*, that you, a Christian gentleman—that on so flimsy a pretext—so transparently unjust—that you would *destroy our enterprise*—

—I cannot believe, sir, that you, a gentleman of the cloth, would deny a legal obligation. *Do* you deny it?

—It *appears* to be the note I signed. But, Mister Cook, its purpose—

—Do not equivocate with me, sir, the banker coldly cut in. All Davenport knew that was your way, when Presbytery dismissed you —careless in business—

—Do you dare carry those vile slanders into my own house?

Abraham straightened, flushed, stepped forward. The little man faced him up like a gamecock.

—I did not come to bandy words. I'll have my money. Ten thousand dollars, on October twelfth. I have taken steps.

—I'll see you out, said Abraham, and opened the parlor door, stood aside, then opened the wide front door of the house. As the banker crossed the porch: Mister Cook, he said, forgive me. If this note is according to law—if we are truly obligated—we shall meet it, even if we do not think it right. But we *must have time!* My son—

Ebenezer Cook at the foot of the steps swung around, looked smartly up.—Mister Pride, in these times, *everyone* wants time. I have obligations of my own to meet.

He turned, stepped briskly along the walk to the gate, where his horse and buggy were tied, climbed in, and gave the reins a shake. Abraham leaned on the porch railing and watched him out of sight.

Mary came out, touched his hand.—Ebenezer Cook? she asked, and he nodded. Husband, what was he raising his voice about, in our house? Old turtle-face.

Isaac's name for him—as a child going into town with his father to pay money—He looks like a turtle, he had said—of which Abraham conscientiously disapproved; he frowned.—Some business of the county, he said—er, Whigs and Democrats—and this new party, Frémont's party—Republicans. No matter. Isaac must be on the boat now, he continued, voice lifting—coming up from Saint Louis. Wife —when do you suppose he'll be home? Tomorrow, do you think? His birthday?

—Oh, the joy! Mary said in a firm, clear voice, and for a moment took her husband's hand. Her son's majority, his coming home, the panorama of his life stretching forward like an ill-drawn map viewed through clouded glass—she could not have said at what, or what more, she rejoiced.

It was dark when the *Ocean Wave* came in to the landing at Davenport and tied up. Fred and Isaac shook hands at the foot of the landing stage. Fred went off with a group of passengers to find the ferryman and persuade him to carry them across to Rock Island. Isaac, his bag in one hand, the Hawken rifle in the other, started on foot down the Rockingham Road. It was ten o'clock when he reached home. The house was dark, the front door locked. He set the bag down, rapped at the door, waited, hammered with the side of his fist, finally rattled the door with the gun butt. A tiny light appeared in the fanlight, the bolt snapped back—his father in his nightshirt, with a candle in his hand.

—Isaac! Isaac!—seizing him in a one-armed embrace.

His mother slowly descended the stairs in a long white robe, a cap pulled close around her head and ears, leaned forward and kissed him on the cheek, led them back through the house to the kitchen. There were hot coals in the stove still. Stooping, she threw in kindling, made the fire up, and heated milk and melted chocolate for cocoa. Isaac showed the gun and told of Samuel Hawken, how he'd gone in not meaning to buy, only wanting to see what his fine rifles were like —*wonders*—

—He *trusted* you? Abraham put in. A stranger, from a distant place, and not much past boyhood, and he trusted you for it?

—We shook hands on it, Isaac said. And I'll pay him too, when I can, somehow. But he just wanted me to have it, a gun that's the twin of Kit Carson's. I think he liked the way I shoot.

And then all in a rush and jumbled together Isaac began to tell all the things of their trip downriver: of the comet the last night that made midnight bright as day, almost (it had been bright over Rockingham also, Donati's Comet it was to be called, Abraham had read somewhere, perhaps in *Harper's* new weekly, for the Italian who discovered it through his telescope and calculated its orbit)—and how the people were frightened and ran about, saying the world was ending, and the pilot tried to run ashore; and Largay with his fiddle, and the songs and dancing—

—The *raft*, Abraham broke in. You sold the lumber?

—Every scrap, Father, and the grub-planks with holes drilled through the ends—

—*How much did it bring?*

—I'll *show* you, said Isaac, and brought out the purse clinking with coins and made neat stack of the gold—six hundred dollars less ten, and a handful of silver. He emptied his bag and laid the packets of bank notes on the table. Abraham sorted the bills—there were some on New York and Philadelphia banks, others from every bank of issue on the Mississippi, from New Orleans north—and made them into piles of equal value. Mary, tired, became impatient and went back to bed. Abraham counted the money twice over, but the sum came out the same: with the gold it made nineteen hundred and twenty-four dollars.

—Is that *all*, Isaac? Abraham asked at length. *All* you took in?

—Every last penny, Father, said Isaac, smiling. We kept expenses down by paying the Irishmen off at Hannibal. And we didn't have to pay any commission to Captain Tromley.

—Merciful God! I counted on three thousand anyway—we were getting that much at the mill, and no expense at all, twenty dollars or more a thousand. The captain said we might expect thirty, or thirty-five—

—He was mistaken, Father. We found no call for lumber all the way down, except Hannibal, and there the railroad man offered fifty dollars for a whole crib, and we bargained up to a hundred on six. And at Saint Louis we drove and walked over the whole town, every place that might take rough lumber, and the best we got anywhere was sixteen dollars a thousand, I think. We were lucky to sell. . . . Father? Father!

Abraham leaned heavily on the table, eyes closed. After a moment he straightened up, took his son's hands.—Isaac, he said, God bless you, you've done what you could. It's only—it's just—it's just *not enough*. . . . I had allowed myself to hope—oh, I had *so* hoped—

He took up the candle, blew out the lamp.—Come, he said, you are tired, you must rest. Tomorrow will be time enough to talk.

Isaac followed him toward the stairs. He had never thought of his father as old—such strength, so tireless in energy. Now in the wavering candlelight his face was deeply seamed with shadow, his thick brown hair flecked with gray, he walked slowly, stooping, had become somehow smaller.

The money Isaac had brought home lay in its neat piles all night on the kitchen table, forgotten. Abraham once more spent the night in sleeplessness and prayer.

In the morning Abraham went across to Rock Island to consult with his partners. They went together to deposit the cash, holding back the gold, which commanded a modest premium; allowing for discounted or worthless bank notes (none, at least, were outright counterfeit, so far as the teller knew), John Marsh calculated their cash assets at a little over fourteen thousand dollars. Without the note Ebenezer Cook had taken up, they could easily pay off the logs bought in April, make good on John Aplon's loan, if need be, and reopen early in the spring; might even think about bringing down a new raft of logs immediately, if it could be bought cheap, on long credit. With Cook's note, however—if it were enforced, if they were compelled to pay in full—they came out forty-five hundred dollars short. Possibly the logging company would extend its note, due in a few days, but they would have no cash to operate on and the interest still accruing, unless they could borrow somewhere. "Oh, tush!" said Gilman Smith with a bitter laugh. "Let the swine of a banker get his damnable judgment. We can't pay it if we've nothing to pay with, can we? *Can* we?" And still laughing he sauntered off to his boardinghouse to take his dinner.

In the afternoon Abraham consulted a Davenport lawyer, Stephen Eldridge, who after examining Abraham's copies took a very grave view of the note and the sales agreement: it was really too bad, too *very* bad, that Mr Pride had not seen fit to seek legal advice before signing—. And Abraham had no answer. The note, in short, was collectible. For a retainer of one hundred dollars, Mr Eldridge promised to use his best endeavors to mitigate the circumstances, but it did not seem that Mr Cook—or any sound banker just now, for that matter—was likely to extend.

Abraham wrote to the logging company at Prairie du Chien asking for a six months' extension—with the result that they put the note in the hands of a Rock Island lawyer for immediate collection; word of the firm's difficulties, it seemed, had traveled north to the Wisconsin River. He wrote also to relatives at Greenwich and New York, asking their help in borrowing working money "at more favorable Eastern rates," as he put it. Mary, when she discovered what so troubled him, sent off similar appeals to Vermont. The answers to both were slow in coming and uniformly negative.

By then, Mr Eldridge's arguments notwithstanding, Ebenezer Cook had secured his court order. The firm's remaining cash paid all but fifteen hundred dollars of the note, the balance to be collected from the partners' assets in proportion to their interest in the firm. Since neither Smith nor Marsh had any assets of value in the eyes of the court—and in any case, neither had been party to the documents on which the issue turned—the judgment fell entirely on Abraham.

Disposing of the mill itself would be a drawn-out, doubtful business and under a different court system, Ebenezer Cook evidently reasoned—he required his money without delay; the home farm was protected by the Iowa homestead statute, the rented farm at Blue Grass subject to a prior mortgage on which there had been no default. There remained personal property—the furnishings of the house; the purpose of the banker's visit had been to see for himself, and evidently he had liked what he saw. Accordingly, late in October the court ordered a sheriff's sale, the required legal notice appeared in the *Daily Gazette*, and the sheriff himself came out to tack the official poster to the front door of the house.

The sale was set for the last Saturday in October, a dry day and sunny, as it happened, cool. The sheriff came early, with Mr Cook, two men, and the auctioneer, and went through the house selecting and tagging the pieces of furniture estimated to meet the claim— tables, chests, chairs, the sofa, bookcases, bureaus, Abraham's desk, Lizzie's harmonium, the parlor carpet Abraham and Mary had brought back from a tour of the factory in Massachusetts, with the American eagle in the center, a smaller version of one woven for President Pierce. Mary, Lizzie, and the hired girl followed, emptying drawers, shelves. Ebenezer Cook drove back to Davenport.

The auctioneer's assistants carried the furniture out in front and the sale began at ten. It was not a large crowd, a dozen couples, nearly all friends. They worked together, spontaneously, at buying in— keeping the bidding down and, when it closed, returning the property to its owners; it was like the old days of the claim clubs, working the land auctions. Daniel Newcomb put up much of the cash, an older man who came out from New York a little after the Prides, bought largely in land below Rockingham, made a fortune in wheat and another in land speculation; retired to Davenport to live on rents and interest, and built a house as grand as Antoine LeClaire's though his worth was not reckoned at half. Patience Newcomb and Mary had been close friends from the start, their husbands got along for their sakes; as a Presbyterian who stood firm through Abraham's church troubles, he had often helped in small and personal money crises. When the sale ended, all furnishings of value or necessity had been bought in. Altogether, it had gone as the banker calculated: Abraham Pride in his predicament possessed personal property of some value, and he had friends; and the combination assured a prompt return, and profit. Abraham himself, shamed, stayed in an empty upstairs room, pacing, looking out at moments through the curtains, until it was over and the furniture carried back in.

One night a month after the sale a fire was set behind Ebenezer Cook's bank building—coal oil, wood scraps, rags—but the town fire marshal observed it, gave the alarm, and it was put out with no serious damage. No perpetrator was charged. It was not the first such attempt, nor the last; not many in the county who had had dealings with the bank were without motive.

For Abraham there remained the problem of Mary's brother John and his three thousand dollars. Except for that, the firm had paid all its debts, in the eyes of the law; its property—the mill, the yard at Coal Valley—was clear; but it had no cash, no stock, no employees, no credit. Fred Weyerhaeuser, making do by helping in his brother-in-law's grocery store, provided a solution: between them they could put together three thousand dollars for the mill and the Coal Valley yard. Abraham accepted—the money would pay back John Aplon; but at the same time with qualms on Fred's account—he would have, it seemed, even less money to work with than the firm had had, and cash and credit were equally scarce. Fred bought a raft for four dollars and a half a thousand. He agreed with a man to operate the mill and saw the logs at a flat rate of two dollars a thousand, complete, to be paid as the lumber was sold; and once more drove around the country in a wagon loaded with lumber, peddling. He set his rates at ten to twelve dollars a thousand, and the lumber sold, but not often for cash—he got hogs, hams, eggs, sides of beef, chickens, tinware, stoves, loads of corn; wheat in particular accumulated. Some of the produce stocked his brother-in-law's grocery; the meat and hardware he traded to rafters for additional logs. It did not seem a very promising enterprise, but Abraham had duly cautioned him when he made the proposal. His conscience was clear.

So at the age of forty-nine, when other men in the West might look forward to years of prosperity and ease from developed land lavishing its fruits on a settled, growing country, Abraham looked back on losses: of the mill and his entire savings; of the value of the land he had taken up—the home place, steep and intractable, chosen for the beauty of its situation, for sentiment, for his wife's sake and on the false premise of Rockingham's future greatness; loss too of his vocation as a minister of the Gospel; of credit, honor. The final loss came in December, not long after Fred Weyerhaeuser took over the mill. Isaac at supper announced that in the spring he would go west, to the land of gold everyone now vaguely referred to as Pikes Peak. It was all decided: two of the Saur boys and Andy McHarg were joining him; they would make up a train with Mr Wood, a Davenport merchant, as leader, who that summer had been as far as Leavenworth City and Lawrence in eastern Kansas, and his clerk Dave Kilbourn.

Although his father more than once assured him that the mill's failure was not his fault, he had done all anyone could, in the circumstances, Isaac had been more than commonly moody since returning from St Louis. Fred offered him a place in the mill, a chance to join with him in rebuilding the enterprise, and for some weeks Isaac went over every day but found he was not suited for jollying Germans into trading their bushels of wheat for a few rough boards: that was Fred's way and would always be; not his. He had bad dreams. He was enclosed in an infinite tunnel, dark and dripping, the only light a coin of brightness far off, and he ran toward it, stumbling, but it came no closer; he was an animal in a leg trap, struggling, crying out, but could not get free; he was a small child again, held in his mother's arms, and then she set him down, pushed him away, would have no more of him. It was necessary to break out or die, he was suffocating. The idea of gold, of getting away, going into the Far West, had stayed with him since St Louis, had grown, until it seemed the only way. That was the reason for his silence at home. It was not something he could talk of with his parents, and since it occupied all his thought, he had nothing to say. With his friends, however, he was eloquent. When they were persuaded and had agreed, he announced it as something decided, planned, and irreversible, not to be argued down or changed.

Abraham heard him in silence but with a sense of desolation pressing him down like a great weight: so many other losses, and now his only son. Yet he had no arguments to offer. All he found to say at the time was—Many others have the same thought now, my son, and you will be only one among them. It will be hard—all the harder—among so many. . . .

Mary's response was different but as sweeping. This quest into the desert, not for duty, or religion, or learning, or honor, but for mere self-interest, led by *gold*, the old temptation and root of evil—no, it was incomprehensible, but of a piece with what this country had made of him. She looked long in silence at him across the table: how could it be that flesh from her flesh should become a man so utterly distinct, so unconnected with anything she recognized as part of herself? Her feeling found a focus in anxiety: that her son, whatever he seemed or might become, should choose to plant himself among the barbarians thronging Kansas since that part of the Indian country was cleared for settlement hardly four years past, whose civil life, the newspapers said, was little better than civil war.

—Isaac, I should *hate* to think of you, she said—as if his decision, announced, were not truly final—it would give me great *pain* to think of you making your way among those terrible people, those murderous slave-catchers and border ruffians—

—Mother, he said, eyes steady on hers, we'll make a stout crew, I can tell you, and we'll watch out for such fellows. But let me tell you also: I've got me the finest rifle there is and know how to use it, well as any man. And what I say is, let *them* beware of *me!*

—Oh, Isaac—Isaac! she cried. *That is what I fear.*

V

Ho! for Kanzas

Late in the morning, leaving Carrolton, they came to a small stream, unnamed on their emigrants' map. Wood, in the lead, halted his team and went down the bank to inspect the crossing. West of Huntsville they had picked up the old main road from St Charles and St Louis to Fort Leavenworth, broad, worn deep, with ferries over big streams like the Grand the day before, bridges on the smaller ones. Here there was neither, it was fordable in the county road commissioner's view, but Wood cautiously took his time. Isaac walked forward to the top of the bank to look. There were three wagons behind, families with children they had camped with the night before, going to Kansas to take land, if they could, at the fall sale. The Saur boys, late starting again, were somewhere back.

—She looks to be mud bottom, Wood shouted up, but we'll get her across.

He plodded back up, kicking the toes of his boots in the dry red earth. Kilbourn eased off on the brake, Wood prodded his team forward, swung them a little to the left, and hung on to the side of the wagon-box as the oxen splashed into the water. The lead yoke had reached the far bank, but the wagon, axle-deep in mid-stream, stopped as if it had run against a log and seemed to pull back, settling.

—Looks like you found the mudhole! shouted Isaac, watching from the top of the bank.

Wood, still amiable after more than three weeks of travel, raised his arms in a gesture of resignation and jumped down, waded forward, the slow current eddying over his boot-tops. He shouted, prodded, the oxen jerked forward, panting, but the wagon did not quite pull free. The other boys knew what to do next; it was like the rainy week through Iowa when they had had to double-team half the crossings.

Andy set the brake. Isaac pulled off his boots and stockings, threw them in the wagon, rolled his jeans up to his knees. Releasing the chain, he led his team down to the stream, across, and up the far bank, stopped them and went back to attach the chain to Wood's lead yoke. Then, beside their teams, they prodded the oxen forward, shouting.

The oxen dug their hooves in the soft earth, straining ahead, grunting out breath, tongues lolling; the wagon rocked forward on its rear wheels, settled back, holding fast. There was one more thing to try before they begged another team from the emigrants.

—Hi, Kilbourn! Wood shouted to his partner, who still peacefully reclined in the front of the wagon, and he jumped down barefoot. They went around behind, one on each wheel, bracing, lifting, and this time when Isaac drove the oxen forward the wagon came free, rattled on through and up the slope to level ground.

Wood sat on the grass beside the road, emptying his boots.—You want my team? he asked.

—Let me try it first, Isaac said. I'm a little lighter than you, maybe. I'm going to take it a little more upstream.

Wood shrugged, lay back on one elbow, and dug his pipe and pouch from his coat pockets. Isaac released his team, drove it back across, and chained up. He went around in back, untied his mare, and rode her across for Kilbourn to hold, waded back.

—Now let her right off, Isaac called to Andy, and we'll give her a rush. He drove the oxen forward, swinging them around to the right, and the wagon followed with a rattling rush, swaying, lurching, pushing the beasts into a lumbering, groaning trot. The front wheels spun, hit the water with a splash, the wagon slowed but kept moving, the oxen were across, still pulling, and slowly the wagon came through and out, up the incline, and halted in the grass beside Wood.

—Thought for a minute there, Wood observed, puffing at his pipe— I thought you meant to *float* your load to Leavenworth.

—I got her across, didn't I? Isaac came back. Saved us time.

They moved their wagons forward and off the road, then watched while the three emigrant families brought theirs across. The road east was empty now, as far back as they could see. The sun was overhead, shadowed at moments by high puffs of cloud riding east on the wind. Wood decided they should take their nooning early in a grove half a mile ahead, turn the cattle out to feed and save what was left of their corn; Isaac would ride back to see what had become of their missing partners. The leader of the emigrant train, a Tennesseean by his looks and speech—long-legged, small-headed, with a greasy buckskin jacket over his hickory shirt—announced that he reckoned they would push on to make a tolerable distance before nightfall.

Isaac retrieved his boots, took the halter from Kilbourn, and vaulted onto Regina's back. He swung her around, walked her back across the ford, and kneed her into an easy trot, holding her in; after the morning of following the wagon she was ready for a run.

He found them a mile or so back, at the bottom of a little hill, pulled off to the side and their oxen, still yoked and chained, cropping the lush spring grass. Isaac let the mare out down the slope, then brought her up short, sitting back in a flurry of dust and pebbles beside the wagon. John Saur lay in the shade of the wagon-bed, hat over his face; Chris leaned against a wheel, sucking at a blade of grass. Neither looked up. In his clear tenor Isaac sang out in measured strain—

> *Ho! brothers, come, brothers,*
> *Hasten all with me;*
> *We'll sing upon the Kansas plain,*
> *A song of lib-er-tee—*

with an elaborate flourish on the final word. It was one of several new Free-State songs they had sung all across Missouri, usually with Isaac taking the lead.

—Aw, Isaac—said Chris. We don't feel like singing.

—We're just tired, said his older brother sleepily, lifting his hat.

—Our feet's sore—

—Cattle's foot-sore, I think they're sick, maybe—

—Well, praise be! said Isaac, sweeping his hat off in a low bow. I thought you must have broke an axle, anyhow.

John rolled over, crawled out from under the wagon, and stood up, stretching.—It's just—whynt we ever take a day off, rest, feed the cattle up—

—We *took* a day off, Sunday, before Huntsville, said Isaac, scowling.

When they said nothing, Isaac slid off and led the horse around to the rear of the wagon. John followed.—What you doing, Isaac? he asked.

—I'm tying her on behind. And then I'm going to drive till we catch up. You and Chris can get in and ride.

—You aint driving no wagon of ours, John said. He got in front, snatched the halter in both hands. Isaac jerked it free, stepped back, dropped the halter over the horse's head.

—Come on, then! Isaac said.

They faced each other, arms reaching, tense. John was older, taller, but slow-moving, clumsy, soft. After a moment he relaxed, shrugged, and turned away.—Chris! he called. I guess we've rested up long enough.

Isaac got on his horse and walked her to the front of the wagon. He looked down at them, slouching.—We'll wait another hour, he said. Help you across if you need it. Then we're going on—and you get stuck at the crossing, you can sit there till you *float* across!

He wheeled and walked the horse slowly up the rise. At the top he turned, looked back. The Saurs were moving again. He rode on, thinking of dinner.

The trouble with the Saurs began in Iowa, after they turned inland from the river at Muscatine and took the road southwest toward the Missouri line. It rained some every day. The stream crossings were bank-full with swirling brown water, the approaches ankle-deep in mud that was dark, fine-grained, and adhesive as axle grease; it was necessary to double-team every crossing; there were deep mudholes across the road, not yet filled and regraded from winter, where they threw in armloads of brush and as often as not one or other of the wagons still got stuck. The Saurs did not take to camping. Their little tent leaked; they neglected to ditch around it, and when it rained at night the runoff flowed under, soaking their blankets. Both caught cold, became morose and silent. They slept late, were last on the road, with the breakfast fire out and the others packed up, impatient to start.

Isaac for his part had never felt better. He took it in turns with Andy driving their team but on his days off walked beside the wagon or rode ahead to look out a pleasing stopping place. Most days they lay over two or three hours at mid-day, turning the oxen out to graze and getting out Isaac's little sheet-iron camp stove for their main meal, most often slabs of fried ham with bread—Andy discovered an unexpected talent for skillet biscuit, or at any rate, hot, with butter, honey, or sorghum, it tasted good, even the Saurs admitted—with eggs and fresh milk when they were near a farm; some days to save time they bought hay or fed the animals pails of shelled corn. They traveled on till dark and usually took a light supper of hard crackers and milk, sometimes with coffee. Even so, through Iowa on the terrible roads they made hardly ten miles a day, and Isaac took to waking himself in the cold murk before dawn, making the fire up, rousing the others. Weather and roads improved after they reached Missouri and turned due south—all the streams ran south to the Missouri River, and with few crossings to slow them they covered, some days, twenty miles. The road now was dry, packed paving-hard, the old ruts in places beaten to powder by the passage of heavy wagons. The grass, pale and fine in the wet Iowa spring when they set out, was here lank and summer-ripe, powdered with rust-brown Missouri dust at the edge of the road. From the hilltops the grass-green prairies spread before them patterned like a Turkey carpet with intense reds and blues that seemed to pulse in the sunlight.

The farther Isaac got from home, the better he felt; he was like a spring released. At night when they stopped he challenged the others to race to a mark or ran alone, for the mere pleasure of it, if none would compete. One evening he started a long-eared jack rabbit, dodged after it in its zigzag flight, dived and caught one kicking leg; broke its neck, he carried it triumphantly back to camp, cleaned it, and hung it from a branch to stew up in the morning for breakfast. "Runs like a regular prairie jack!" Wood exclaimed, and began calling him Jackrabbit, sometimes JR or simply Jack. In the twilight after supper, over John Saur's complaints at the noise, he practiced ten shots with his new five-shot Colt cap-and-ball pistols and then carefully reloaded for next day; in the tent by candlelight, while Andy curled in his blankets and snored, he dutifully worked at letters home —his mother had provided a neatly fitted box of paper, pens, ink; mornings when they had camped beside a stream he swam in the misty chill while Andy or Kilbourn made up breakfast, and came back steaming, fair hair plastered dark to his head and dripping under his hat. It was like being a boy again, but with the strength and competence of a man.

At night in the tent with the candle out, he soothed himself to sleep with familiar shapes of home—how the parts of the house fitted, his own room at the head of the stairs, the look out the window, the road across Black Hawk Creek, driving into Davenport. Were his memories changing? His parents were two dark-robed figures, silent and motionless on the porch, a long way off. Images came unbidden from a remote past: crouching small on the parlor floor over a picture in the illustrated Bible, his father massive and immobile in a pool of yellow light at the desk, writing, his mother on the sofa with a shirt to sew, silent and distant as on a mountaintop. None of these things touched what he was, had become, was becoming: a man, with a man's freedom to go and do and be whatever he willed. All that was vivid was ahead. In dreams he saw himself on horseback, the horse stretching out at full gallop across a treeless plain, and he lifted his arms and gave a great shout, guiding the horse with his knees—not the dappled Regina he had brought from home but another, sometimes a painted Indian pony, and no wagon to slow him, no stupidly plodding oxen to tend. Iowa—it came to him that he might never go back; that made it the more necessary to remember clearly, while he could.

All across Iowa the route Wood led them brought them to camp near friends or friends of parents, names at least mutually known. Once over into Missouri, he guided them by the direct roads to Weston, the river port opposite Fort Leavenworth and therefore—being protected by federal troops—unlikely to be closed, as others had been, by border ruffians hostile to emigrants recruited to the Free-State cause. From Missouri on, they were among strangers. All any of them knew of Missourians was what the Iowa papers for five years had been saying: of the border ruffians intent on conquering Kansas Ter-

ritory for the slave power, and all the West, if they could, crossing the
Missouri at night, in boatloads; of fraudulent elections and rival gov-
ernments, one slave, one free, and a vacillating President at Washington; of murders and massacres and the sack of Lawrence, the Free-
State stronghold; and, rarely, of violence on the other side, of
"Osawatomie" Brown, with his bloody nickname and his no less
bloody sons. Vauntingly, therefore, as they drove along the road or
lay around the stove after dinner, replete, they announced themselves
with Free-State songs—"Ho! for Kanzas" (there was as yet no general
agreement as to how the place should be spelled) or "Uncle Sam's
Farm," an old minstrel song recruited to the cause—and occasionally
a farmer resting on his plow near enough to hear the tune looked up
and waved; the people in that part of the state they traveled through
did not in fact differ much from Iowans in their feelings about what
was happening in Kansas or what should be done. One night after
supper when they had taken the trouble to cook, drinking coffee by
the flickering light from the stove door, Isaac started them out on
"The Kansas Emigrant," a new song from a New York Free-Stater
named Whittier that under various titles had been picked up by many
Northern newspapers:

> *We cross the prairie as of old*
> *Our fathers cross'd the sea,*
> *To make the West, as they the East,*
> *the homestead of the free.*

It was an easy tune, even the Saur boys this time joined in, hymn-
like and stately, with just the touch of syncopation to set a young
man's heart pulsing. Then it steadied to a march, steadfast and daunt-
less as the ox-team pace—

> *We come to rear a wall of men*
> *On Freedom's southern line*

and rose in the chorus to what each time leaped from their tranquil
young throats as a shout of defiance—

> *Hurrah!—The Kansas home and Liberty—*
> *Hurrah!—where-e'er our—*

There was a slither of dew-wet grass on boots and a tall figure stood
at the edge of the light, listening. Isaac was on his feet.

—Come on over, stranger, he called, and take some coffee while
we've got some. We've about eaten everything else.

Kilbourn laughed. The man came into the light, a long-nosed face
ending in a scraggly beard, broad-brimmed, high-crowned hat pulled
low on his forehead. Andy got a tin cup from the box, filled it, and
held it out steaming.

The man blew, took a cautious sip.—Where you from?

—Davenport, Iowa, Isaac answered. Been on the road nearly a week now—

—Then I reckon thet make *you* the strangers, he said. I *live* here, not half a mile along the road—. And having made his point he arced a glob of spit at the stove, and it ran slowly down the side plate, sizzling.

—Thet air song you was singin, the man said. Pretty tune. Kansas. You goin through to Kansas now?

—We're going through to the gold regions, Isaac said—maybe right through to California if Pikes Peak don't suit us.

The farmer sipped his coffee, ruminating.—Free-Staters, he concluded—you mought be Free-Staters, up that way. Thet air one a them Free-State songs.

Wood got up.—You can call us that if you like, he said sharply. We don't hold with people going across to another state and stealing people's elections. We think—

—Well, now—you know what *I* say? *Free land* and *free of* niggers is what *I* say—an them as wants free niggers, let em take em by they hand an put em in they cabins an in they beds—and feed em, too—and let *ever* man stay clear of *ever other* man's business. An I reckon thet make me a Free-Stater too, in a manner, same as you—now *don't* it, boys?

He grinned, spat again, emptied his cup, and set it down on the stove.—An I be bliged for your coffee, he said, and, swinging around, strode off in the dark.

They were four weeks out, the last day of May, when they reached Weston with its steam ferry over the Missouri: a single main street sloping down the bluff to the landing, with stores and warehouses built of brick at the bottom; a Davenport in the egg, waiting to hatch, but facing west. Fifty thousand people headed for Pikes Peak that summer, as many more for California and Oregon, and half of them by way of Weston and Leavenworth City. It was after mid-day when the boys came in, and a hundred wagons were lined up the slope and out on the prairie, brakes set and wheels turned in, oxen bellowing for food and some spans of mules and horses among them. They took their place at the end and Wood and Isaac walked down to hunt the ferry agent, thinking there had been a fire or the boat had sunk; but it was only the crush of people getting across. They lined up at the bottom to buy tickets, a dollar a wagon, and were given pasteboards with numbers to hand in when they went aboard; Isaac's was 127. The agent, unhurrying, said they might get across in the morning; the ferry did not run at night.

They fed their cattle the last of the corn, got in their wagons and tried to sleep. When the line moved and the wagon in front slid forward, brakes screeching, they woke and followed. Around midnight a boy came by with a jug, selling water for a half-dime a drink. Isaac paid and drank, and only then remembered his father's water kegs somewhere back in the wagon.

It took them all morning getting to the head of the line. Twice Isaac and Andy dug out a keg and filled a bucket to carry to the oxen to drink, and in consequence were occupied between-times in sorting and repacking the contents of the wagon. Isaac folded away in the bottom of his trunk the map that had seen them across Missouri and got out his Kansas map. It was the newest he'd found at Holmes's bookstore at Davenport, but two years old and already out of date, according to Wood. It showed a network of roads threaded across the eastern tier of counties, but there were new ones since, to be drawn in. The traders' road to Santa Fe and most of the military roads leading northwest and west from Fort Leavenworth had existed for forty or fifty years, but on these grasslands a road began wherever a man drove his wagon and cut his track across the native sod, and if the route were a good one others followed, the track cut deeper, wider, became a road, acquired a name and settlements to connect. Towns likewise, in this country with already too much history compressed in too few years: new ones proclaimed, organized, named, promoted, renamed, abandoned, their buildings dismantled and removed, according to their luck in the lottery of politics, roads, settlement, trade. On May 30, 1854, after months of sectional bickering over the issue of extending slavery into the Plains, the President signed his name to the Kansas-Nebraska Act, a deadly compromise that sealed the conflict with a stamp of agreement but resolved nothing—and opened the grasslands to settlers and a minimum of government; less than two weeks later—the time it took for the news to travel out from Washington by telegraph, railroad, stagecoach, steamboat—promoters crossed the Missouri to stake out and plat town sites. The towns of Lawrence, Leavenworth, Atchison, Manhattan and Topeka were established in quick succession following the Act.

Isaac's map was the kind called sectional: besides rivers, roads, and towns, it showed the boundaries of the counties, organized or prospective; was ruled off in Jefferson's thirty-six-square-mile townships, with their co-ordinates from the General Land Office; and was further subdivided in sections so far as the government surveyor teams had progressed at their contractual rate of one square-mile section a day—to be oriented, measured with surveyors' chains, their corners marked with stakes or mounds of earth. Lands of the emigrant Indians in process of accession—Iowa, Potawatomi, Delaware, Ottawa, Sac and Fox—were blank: unsurveyed, unmarked on the map. Lines in a vacuum to be filled: it meant land to be claimed, paid for at the minimum government price, and transformed to capital by the government patent. There were fifty million acres of such land, more or less, within the vaguely defined boundaries of Kansas Territory. Even for a young man passing through on the road to gold and quick fortune, it was matter to think about.

After the twenty-four-hour wait, the crossing was an anti-climax. The boat came in, three wagons rattled down the stage, and nine went aboard, all the deck would carry; a quarter of an hour. The boat backed out, caught the current and swung around, and dropped down the river and across, little more than a mile, and backed into a slough coming out from behind a big island, where a broad, deeply worn road came down to the water's edge. The road led along the top of the high Kansas bluff past Fort Leavenworth—ranges of two-story barracks built of creamy Kansas limestone and formed around three sides of an extensive parade ground, with porticos shading broad, paved walkways, the model for the lesser military posts to the west— and into the town of Leavenworth. Isaac had business to see to: the three barrels of flour shipped from Davenport; mining tools to select —his father had deemed it prudent to wait and see what was offered at this prime outfitting point. They left the wagons on Third Street at the edge of town and with John Saur Isaac went down to the landing to find the freight agent's warehouse.

Except on Delaware, the town's main street, there were no sidewalks—lumber for any but essential purposes was scarce. It had still not rained; the clay-colored earth was packed hard as macadam.

Isaac and John walked down Delaware to the freight warehouse, a brick building to one side of the landing. The barrels of flour—"Isaac A. Pride, Leavenworth City, K.T." brushed in black letters on the sides and tops—had arrived undamaged a week earlier. Isaac paid the two-dollar freight bill, took his receipt, and promised to call for the flour in a day or two. On the way back up they went into the post office to collect the mail. There was a letter each for Wood and Kilbourn; Isaac had four—from his sister and mother, two from his father—and three copies of the *Daily Gazette*, sent on by way of general news.

For his other business Isaac chose a store at the corner of Third and Cherokee, on the way back to where they'd left the wagons: Alex. Garrett & Co., Groceries Wholesale & Retail, Indian Goods, Hardware, Gen'l Merchandise—which seemed to cover the possibilities; the store, smaller than some and off the main street, had a dark and faintly shabby air of unimposing honesty. A bell tinkled as they pushed the door open and a man came toward them from the back with brisk, neat steps, a small, short-legged man with an open, earnest, round-eyed face, in a dapper suit that looked new and a size too big, trousers trailing the oiled floorboards.

—Mister Garrett? Isaac asked.

—Why no, gentlemen, I haven't that honor—E. H. Durfee! the little man volubly brought out and offered his hand. What can I do for you, gentlemen?

—We're bound for Pikes Peak—

—Ahh! the merchant let his breath out as if the very idea excited him and gazed expectantly, clasping his hands.

—We're bound for Pikes Peak and wanted an idea of the kinds of tools—

—Well, now, gentlemen, I can't tell you from *personal experience* what you might require—no, sir!—only been out here a week myself and hardly a mile to the west of the river. But I can show you the equipment as the boys has been buying that's going through with intention of prospecting—yes, *sir!* that I *can* do—and led them to a rack of tools along one wall toward the back of the store.

—Where'd you come out from, Mister Durfee? Isaac asked by way of politeness, but curious too—the man's way of talking.

—Why, from Marion, Wayne County, New York, to be sure—little place east of Rochester. I was doing some trade in buffalo robes through a commission man at Albany—wonderful winters we have up there—and thought to myself, I'll just take a flyer out to Kansas, where they come from, you see, and see for myself—and general merchandise being mighty slow, since the Panic, of course. Now let me just show you what—Mister—did you say your name was—?

—Pride, Isaac said. Jack Pride.

The implements the boys had been taking west were shovels, picks, several sizes of hoes and rakes; saws, adzes, hammers, kegs of nails; perhaps a little more heavily made, with thick wooden handles, but the common tools on any farm, except—

—Now this thing, said Mr Durfee, and he took up a shallow, wide-lipped metal pan shaped like an oversize soup plate, to demonstrate, this is the *gold pan*, and this is where you start. You take the sand from a likely looking creek bank, and you run water through, and you kind of swirl it around—he rocked the pan, to show them—and swirl it around, washing out the sand, you know—and when you get done, what's left and stays—it's *gold dust!* Fact!—seen it for myself, men coming back, pouches and sacks of—. And then they take all these other tools and dig the sands and run em through with water down a, what-do-you-call-em, flume—. Now—

The other novelty was a box, on rockers and about the size of a cradle, with a perforated tinware top for washing gold sands through and cleats at the bottom to catch the gold.

—How much for the lot? Isaac broke in. One outfit for one man
meaning to find gold?

Mr Durfee gave some thought.—Twenty-five dollars, he said
slowly, then: You won't do better at Leavenworth!

—Twenty-five dollars! John Saur exploded; he had stood back, silent but listening. Why, I could buy that mess for ten dollars at Davenport!

—You aint *at* Davenport, Isaac said, you're in *Kansas*. He turned
back to Durfee.—You sell flour, Mister Durfee?

—Oh yes indeed, by the sack or barrel—or lesser amounts. We—

—How do you sell it?

—Six dollars a hundred-weight, twelve dollars a barrel, or—

—Now, Mister Durfee, what would you *give?* For three barrels of
prime steam-milled Iowa flour down at the landing? That I had
shipped out here to sell—or carry out with me to Denver?

They had turned from the hardware display and drifted toward the
counter at the back of the store. Durfee rolled his eyes and threw up
his hands, called for Mr Garrett. The owner came out, ponderous and
white-haired. They talked at length of prices in Kansas and Iowa, of
the quality of the flour and whether it might have spoiled in transit;
Durfee from his years in the trade in New York spoke up for Davenport flour. It was at length agreed. Mr Garrett would take it for the
implements, throw in the cradle and ten dollars, gold; Isaac helped
himself to pen and ink, leaned on the counter and endorsed his
freight receipt, promising to come by with his wagon to load the
tools.

Durfee followed them out on the street.—That was sharp, he said,
very sharp, Mister Pride. Come back with your gold dust and we'll
trade some more.

He held out his hand to shake. Isaac accepted it.

In early evening they drove four miles out on the road leading west
from the town and made their camp by a little spring that fed into the
Stranger River to the south. Despite the boom talk that hummed
through Leavenworth, the land fever surrounding it like an aura,
there were no obvious signs of settlement even these few miles out:
the land was claimed, no doubt, if you looked you would find corner
stakes marked with dates and the pre-emptors' names, but there were
as yet no cabins built, no acres of the prairie grass turned over. So
they had it to themselves that night: land unlike any that any of them
but Wood had seen before, faintly contoured, almost level; deeply
shaded by immense trees, hickory and oak, wide-spaced, with no undergrowth but a carpet of lush spring grass. It seemed not a natural
growth but a landscape lovingly contrived by centuries of human
culture, like the noble parklands you read of in stories of old England.

After supper Isaac sat up till full dark, stars out among the treetops and the others all gone to bed. *Magical*—the only word he could think of for it. You wanted to run and run and somehow take it all in, possess it, yet—trees and grass and sky and earth's hands supporting all—it remained motionless and unpossessed, and you lay there unmoving, reaching out to it with your mind only, and that much it accepted, tolerated. Their cattle stirred, sighed, got up and pulled at tether, cropping the sweet spring grass. At moments, far off among the trees, an owl called, a small animal gave a shriek. Isaac went and lay face down beside the spring, lulled by the tinkle of water moving over gravel, caressed by the cool breath rising from it. At length, his wool shirt sprinkled with dew, he found his way to the tent, went in, and lay on top of his blanket. *Kansas:* what strange, drawn-out music in the two syllables! It sang in his mind, filling his thought with sweetness.

In the morning Isaac was up early, making the fire, slicing and frying bacon, boiling coffee in the big camp pot; Wood had bought a basket of eggs, and he fried four in the dripping. He was finishing, sipping a second mug of coffee, the others still in the tents, when a train of Army wagons came along from the direction of Leavenworth, heading west, with a squad of cavalry by way of escort—half a dozen heavy wagons painted bright blue, each drawn by four span of mules; ammunition, probably, for Fort Riley and beyond. A command rang out and the column halted. An officer rode over toward their camp, followed by a man in a buckskin hunting shirt. They pulled up beside the stove. Isaac set his mug down and stood.

—Would you gentlemen take some coffee? he offered. It's fresh-made.

The officer was gray-headed, stout, red-faced, forty-five or fifty, perhaps, but swung down nimbly as a cadet.—Captain Andrew Jackson Smith, U.S.A.! he introduced himself, in a parade-ground voice, formerly Chickasaw agent to the U.S. Indian office and before that, regular service, U.S. Cavalry, in the war with Mexico—and—yes, *sir!* —I'll take some coffee, if you please.

Isaac gave his own name, poured two more mugs, and held out the sugar tin. The man in buckskin was Dave Payne, a civilian scout—or means to be! the captain sternly interjected, meaning a joke, perhaps; a dark, silent, broad-shouldered, angular man, no older than Isaac but a head taller, with a bristly, close-trimmed black mustache and deep-set, staring eyes—eyes that seemed to drop on what they saw like a hawk, tear and consume, and move on. He wore a pair of pistols belted at his waist; a short cavalry carbine in a leather case hung from his saddle.

—That your horse, young fellow? the captain asked, pointing to where Regina placidly cropped the new grass on the stream bank below the spring, staked on a long line so as to reach the water. Isaac acknowledged that she was.

—Looks like she might be fast, he went on, setting his mug down and walking toward her. Ever race her?

—Not to count, Isaac said. I just keep her for hunting and pleasure —about a year now, and she's four years old. But she goes along well enough when she has to—only now she's out of condition, aint had anything but walking behind the wagon since we left Iowa, hardly— and, you notice, sun's fading her dapples, it's been nothing but hot sun clear across Missouri.

Captain Smith stroked the mare's forehead, gentling, and ran his hands along her flanks and down her hind leg, feeling her muscle.— Don't look in such terrible condition to *me*, he said. Say now, he continued, swinging around, it might be, while the men take break- fast, you're the one to settle a little dispute I've been having with my scout.

Dave Payne frowned, made a sweeping gesture with one hand as if brushing away a gnat. Isaac tactfully turned away and rubbed the mare's sides with his open hands, murmuring.

—Now the thing is, the captain said, we're under orders to Riley, take us five days and some, and I want Payne here to carry an express out to the commandant and meet me with an answer tomorrow night, coming back. And *he* says, can't get there in two days, hardly, nor back in five—which *just aint good enough*, nor what I understand a scout is expected, here on the Plains. Now what do you say to that, Mister Pride?

—It's a *hundred miles* from Leavenworth City! Dave Payne growled.

Isaac wanted not to answer but could not evade.—I rode Regina, he said, from Davenport to Iowa City and back before supper once— that's forty miles each way, more or less, and prairie country like this, good road, and only one stream to cross. I didn't let her out much.

—Now *that's* how I like to hear a young man talk, said the captain, swatting Isaac's back with his muscular hand. Why, when I was your age—or down in Mexico in the war—

Dave Payne snorted. The eyes swooped at Isaac.—Captain, he said, you weren't ridin no worn-out piece of three-legged Missouri horse- flesh that aint fit to haul a ambulance.

—*That's* what you say about every horse in the issue, Payne! Now—

Isaac looked at the scout's horse, not listening: a black, big-boned, straight-backed gelding with the USA brand gray on his rump, some Morgan in him—the kind that in Iowa would bring fifty dollars and be used for all work, riding out but pulling a buggy too and hitched to a plow if a man's oxen went sick; but strange-eyed and nervous, like Dave Payne.

—He looks well enough, Isaac broke in. I grew up on horses like that.

Captain Smith had an idea, wanted the two young men to change horses and race, just to see—. Isaac refused. Well then, on their *own* horses—.

Kilbourn, waked by the talk, came out from his tent, scratching and stretching, barefoot and his shirt open across his chest.—*Jack*rabbit! he shouted, laughing, I'll hold his horse and he can race you on foot. Fact! Coming through Missouri I saw him run a prairie jack down, didn't even need no horse!

Isaac flushed, started to explain, but was goaded by even such clumsy praise. The captain took over, commanding. He pointed out a tree a quarter-mile off, with a broken upper branch: they would take a standing start from the stream, ride to the mark, around and back; he would ride along—just to keep it honest. Isaac gave in since there seemed no refusing, but only, he said, to give his mare a little exercise she hadn't been getting. He would not saddle up.

Isaac untethered his horse, leaped on, walked her slowly up and down the stream bank, gave her a start, pulled her in, turned and came back to wait. Wood and Andy came sleepily from their tents to watch. Payne, scowling, unstrapped his gun belt and laid it by the stove. Kilbourn slowly counted down the start and set them off with a shout.

Isaac had a kind of picture of the race in his mind: if he let Regina go and won he would make an enemy forever—but equally if he held her in and lost; what he had to do was keep alongside the whole way and finish even—Payne's big Army horse, he figured, would go pretty fast running on the straight but slow and clumsy on the turn. That was how he started, sitting straight on the horse's back, legs hanging easy, a few feet to Payne's right. The mare kept pace at a steady, quick-step run, stretching her neck and enjoying it, smooth and rhythmic; behind them he heard the captain's horse panting, her hooves pounding the sod, but did not look back.

As they approached the mark, Payne moved in close, anticipating, then suddenly wheeled hard to the right across Isaac's path, swung in the saddle, and brought his crop down in a sharp cut on the mare's nose. She stumbled, veered off; Isaac lifted her head, slowing, fell forward and grabbed with both hands around her neck. Payne got his horse around the tree, slipping on the grass, straightened him out and drove him to a gallop, shouting and beating the horse's rump with his crop.

Isaac got her around, recovered. His picture of the race was gone; all he could see was the scout rising and falling to the heavy rhythm of the gallop and the distance widening between them. He brought his knees up tight on the mare's shoulders and lay forward, talking urgently in her ear. She answered with a great leap, stretching and flattening out, she seemed to float, and halfway back she caught and passed the other horse and drove on, effortlessly, still gaining speed. Isaac reached the stream, pulled her in and swung around. Payne was thirty feet back, heedlessly beating the horse's rump to the rhythm of the gallop, face contorted, the horse wild-eyed and tossing his head, mouth open and gasping, flecked with foam; the captain had not paced half the distance back, sitting stiff and straight in the saddle and coming on at a heavy canter as if leading a training exercise for new recruits. Isaac walked the mare slowly down the stream bank, patting her shoulder, swung her, walked back to where he had staked her and slipped down.

Payne crossed the stream, walked his trembling, winded mount over to the stove and dismounted. The captain came up beside him.— Payne! he said in his carrying voice. I *saw* how you did at that turn— don't think I didn't! Why—cut a little closer and you'd have *killed* the boy—

—Captain—Payne broke in, slowly buckling his gun belt.

—Don't you bandy words with me, sir! the captain said, swinging down, red-faced. I *saw*. And as for your mount—. He went around to look, pointing with his hand—thick welts raised along the horse's rump, blots of blood drying on his flanks where the scout had row-eled with his spurs. Disgraceful! he said. Any cavalryman that treats his horse in that barbarous fashion—

—Now you listen here, Captain, Payne shouted, his face darkening, I aint no cavalry horse jockey to be ordered around like a monkey on a string, but a civilian scout, under contract—

—Not in my command, sir, the captain roared back—or won't be when we get to Riley—no, *sir!*—if you last that—

—And I'll tell you another thing, Payne said, chest swelling—I didn't come wanting no horse race, nor quarrel neither—but you made that race and made me run it—and if I run, by God, I'm going to run to *win*, and the devil take the lot of you!

Insolently he turned his back, remounted his horse. Isaac had kept to one side, eyes cast down. Now the scout swung in his saddle and the hunting eyes found him, swooped and held—As for *you*, Mister Jackrabbit Pride, he said, voice vibrating deep in his throat—well, let me tell you, I'll remember that name and this morning and how you done me, oh, don't you think I won't!—his voice sinking to a crooning moan. He turned, straightened up, kicked at the horse's flanks with his spurs. The horse shied, danced sideward; he jerked savagely at the reins and struck with his crop. The horse moved back toward the road at a stiff trot.

Isaac watched him go, arms crossed on his chest, head hanging. The captain came over, put an arm gently across his shoulders.—Don't you let that loudmouth horse killer grieve you, son, he said. That's a beautiful horse you've got yourself—and oh, how you rode her, and bareback too—like an Indian!

—I didn't need any race to tell me my horse's good, Isaac said, or I can ride. I know that much.

The captain stepped back and looked him earnestly in the face.— Why, boy, he said, that's *life*, it's a testing, boy, day by day—the race comes and you got to run it and run to win, fair and square—and woe to faint of heart, as the Apostle says, don't any of you young folks study your Bible anymore? Now I saw, he went on after a moment—I *saw* what you were intending: hold your horse in and let the other fellow win. But he wouldn't *let* you, would he? That fool just wouldn't let you. And he gave a half grin, arching his brows, and clapped his hands together, pleased with his perception.

—That's *two* fools then, Captain, Isaac said, straightening up and looking him in the eye. For you fixed that race to make him look a fool, I don't know why—and you made a fool of me to do it. That wasn't right.

—Well, I've my reasons, Mister Pride, don't think I haven't. Try to *make* something of that young braggart, is what I want—comes out to Kansas two years, jayhawking around, and he swells himself like a Kit Carson and Natty Bumppo all in one, and thinks he's fit for a cavalry scout. Now, a young fellow like you, that knows a cavalry mount from a jackass, and has some sense and modesty besides—

Isaac gave his head a sharp shake. Captain Smith shrugged, turned to his horse, and mounted. He reached down to take Isaac's hand, let go and straightened up.—Well, anyhow, he concluded, just remember what I said. You get tired of washing gold out there and want some fun and a job too—why, come on back to Leavenworth and ask for Andrew Jackson Smith, and I'll take you on. You've got my word!

He swung his horse around and set off for the road at a trot. Isaac turned away. Wood, Kilbourn, and Andy were waiting in front of the tents.

—Well now, JR, said Kilbourn with a loud laugh, you lived up to your name that time, sure—showed the U.S. Cavalry how to ride!

—You shut up, Dave, Isaac said.

Isaac kept on walking, past them and in among the great trees, shoulders slumped, hands in his pockets. The Saurs had come out, he heard by their voices, all talking of breakfast, and the Army train on the road, moving on; banging pots and fresh wood clanging in the fire-box. Then he was over a little rise and the sounds were gone. The feeling that had waked him through the night like a glow of hot coals warming his breast: *joy* in this new land, *joy* in arrival, in the days of his life unfolding—it was gone now, gone as if it had not been or would ever come again; only a word, remembered, and he could not think what it had been, what he had felt or where the feeling had come from. And in its place, a terrible sadness, pressing him down, as if he had set his heart on the desire of his whole life, and lost it, and been deceived, not ever to attain to it again.

Ahead through the trees there came to him a mysterious, pulsing hum. Alert again, he stooped, went toward the sound in silence, stopped: fifty feet off on a fallen log a grouse cock puffed and strutted and drummed its wings, as on his father's farm, a boy with his first gun, hunting for something to shoot, he had seen that dance. He let himself down flat to watch.

It rained the second night they were camped west of Leavenworth. As they were finishing supper, the sky darkened, there came a roaring of wind through the treetops and a rolling explosion of thunder that seemed to shake the ground under them, and the rain came down as if the heavens like a giant's bucket had been upended. They left their pots and plates and cups and scattered to the tents. In minutes the carefully dug ditch around the tent was full and a flow of water came under the walls like an insect army passing through, swarming everything in its path.

In an hour it had passed over, the rain stopping as abruptly as it had begun. Heavy drops rapped the tent roof, falling from branches high overhead; thunder echoed from the east, charging on across the land. Isaac came out, then Andy, Wood, Kilbourn; the Saurs when they called would not answer. The stream still boiled. Where the wagon wheels had cut the grass there were ruts filled with water and clinging, yellow mud. Regina remained staked on the bank, head hanging, miserable and wet, faintly steaming in the damp air, but the cattle had wandered off among the trees; with the dark coming down, catching them would have to wait till morning. The blankets and the ground inside the tents were too wet for sleeping. Isaac climbed into his wagon, and after a time Andy followed.

It took them most of the next morning to catch the oxen and bring them in. They occupied the remainder of the day hanging out blankets to dry, airing the tents, washing the dirty clothes accumulated on the trip out, unloading and repacking the wagons. In the evening while they lay around the stove watching Andy cook, Wood suggested an early start for Lawrence in the morning: with a good, straight stage road on high ground all the way they could be at his brother's place by Saturday night. John Saur objected—he and his brother were still tired from the trip, no sleep the night before and their blankets not dry yet, the cattle had sore feet, and— Wood silenced him with a lifted hand.

—Now, we're not in that much hurry, are we, Dave? he said, turning to Kilbourn. Mights well wait another day and stick together for the company, till Lawrence anyway, eh boys?

And it was agreed without further argument.

In the morning Isaac woke early, the sadness that had dulled and oppressed him since the foolish race with Dave Payne entirely gone, impatient now to yoke up the team and start south; and remembered that to please the Saur boys they had settled on waiting another day. He dressed without waking Andy, saddled Regina, and rode into town. Thinking about breakfast as he came down Delaware Street, he reined in at the Planter's House, tied his horse, and went in. His expenses since leaving home had not been three dollars, and with the profit on the flour he could afford the luxury of a half-dollar hotel breakfast; if they got through to Denver, it might be, who knows, years, before he had another chance.

When he entered the dining room Mr Durfee was at a table by himself, recognized him, jumped up, and beckoned him over.

—I had supposed you must be halfway to Denver by now, Mister, er, Pride, the little man said with a smile.

—Some of the boys are a little tired from traveling, want to rest some, Isaac admitted, taking the offered chair. Mr Durfee pursed his lips sympathetically. I expect we'll be starting on in the morning.

The merchant gave him a nodding half-smile. The waiter came. Isaac ordered a beefsteak, fried, eggs, potatoes, biscuits, coffee. He looked around the room: not so large or grand as the Southern at St Louis, but handsome all the same.—You board here? he asked, turning back.

—Only temporarily and, er, for the time being, that is, until I can settle on suitable lodgings or perhaps a little house to rent. I don't know—why, bless you, sir, a cabin out on the prairie that a handyman could knock together in two or three days for fifty dollars rents for *eight dollars a month*, can you believe it?

Isaac in turn looked sympathetic. The waiter brought his breakfast.

—Or—I don't know—I may just decide that Wayne County, New York, wasn't so chancy after all—go back, you know. He frowned, sipping his coffee. Isaac looked up inquiringly, his mouth full of steak and eggs. Of course, Mr Durfee continued, there's still the emigrants and honest settlers coming through, but there's too many coming back, "go-backs," they're calling em, not a dime to spend and want it on credit besides, and the news from Denver so difficult to ascertain and find out for sure, one day you hear one thing and next day another—

Isaac raised a hand, interrupting. It seems to me, what you're worrying about is, whether there really is any gold out at Pikes Peak or not—and whether people will keep coming through going out there, making trade, or—

The merchant started over and explained. The great thing had never been the gold sands along the stream banks—why, he lifted a hand in a vague gesture, a man could no doubt find some specks of gold down by the Leavenworth landing, if he went on washing long enough—but where it came from, the vein or seam—the mother lode —up at the head of Cherry Creek and all the other little streams rising back in the mountains. Now since the news last summer, men, it seemed, had claimed all over the mountains—and broken rock and assayed it—but had found no source for the gold sands. And now for two or three weeks the go-backs had been coming, more and more; some had stayed all winter but others got halfway, met Peakers coming back, heard their stories, gave up and turned back—.

Mr Durfee brought out his watch, squinted, scowled, and shoved his chair back, saying he had the store to open. Isaac stood up.—Then you think I'm a fool to go hunting gold out there? he said.

—I don't say that, no, not at all, Mister Pride! Mr Durfee looked him in the eye. What I do say is, you've got land here for the taking, and people coming that'll make it valuable, and trade, and railroads going across—may go up, or down some like it is now, but always worth something. But gold—you work and break your heart and maybe find some—and dig it out, melt it down, ship it out—and it's gone, spent, and what have you got? But land—.

Isaac followed him out to the street. Mr Durfee complimented him on his mare (fast? he wondered, and Isaac scowled) and offered to sell her for him on commission, eighty or a hundred dollars, and he could get an Indian pony for half that, or less, more suited to the country he was going to—

—You collected the flour all right? Isaac broke in.

—Premium!—I always said, Davenport flour, when I could get it—not like some—

—My father grew the wheat and saw to the milling—

—Have him write me! Mr Durfee said. We can sell it.

He smiled, waved, spun on his heel, and stepped off smartly up Delaware Street.

Isaac visited the post office but no more mail had come. He went back, got his horse, and walked her slowly down the street to the landing. A steamboat had come in, whistles shrieking, and around him men were riding in the same direction, horses at a trot, or walking with hurrying steps, half-running; not that meeting a steamboat was anything novel for a young man grown up on the Mississippi, but it was something to fill a vacant morning in a strange town, and this one, it seemed—bound upstream for St Joseph, Omaha, and beyond—might be a little different from Davenport after all. A hundred or more passengers had gotten off, and as many had gathered around them, more still coming down from the town: hotel drummers with open carriages from the Planter's House and the lesser places; outfitters, among them E. H. Durfee, briskly seizing strangers by the hand and introducing himself; above all, the dealers in land in all its aspects —brokers with discounted land warrants and scrip to offer, others with money to lend, agents who for a fee promised to lead settlers or speculators to good unclaimed land in any organized county in the territory, town promoters with blank deeds and share certificates stuffed in their pockets, showing maps and plat plans to any who would look and, some of them, lumps of rock they claimed were coal or copper ore dug near their town sites. Gradually, while Isaac sat his horse, watching from the fringe, the crowd scattered. He turned and started back up Delaware Street. There was nothing to hold the attention of a young man with little money and no more than a vague prospect of getting some in the gold country six hundred miles to the west. The eagerness that woke him that morning and led him into town was gone. It was still early, not much past nine by the look of it, but nothing to do but go back to the camp and no prospect for the rest of the day but trying to argue the Saurs into packing up properly for a start in the morning.

He turned into Third Street and followed it north out of town, onto the road leading past the fort to the Weston ferry landing. Up ahead was a dust cloud rising, the end of a wagon with its cover drawn tight, a long line of wagons, ox-drawn and nondescript, in several sizes; not a military train for the fort but civilians on their way to the ferry, maybe a party of the go-backs Durfee had talked of over breakfast. Isaac slapped the mare into a trot, caught up, and rode on alongside. The oxen were unlike any he had seen—heavy, sharp-pointed horns so long it looked as if the tips of a yoked pair would clash when they swung their heads; tall as Iowa oxen but not half the weight, by their look—massive rib cage outlined tight through the skin, skin sagging loose over jutting hip bones, heavy heads hanging on their long necks—as if worked and starved through a month of dry weather and thin grass. Six, eight, twelve wagons he rode past and pulling up short called out to a driver in a ragged, broad-brimmed, sharp-peaked straw hat, walking painfully beside a three-yoke team of these starvelings.

—Hey there, mister! Where you coming from?

A dark young face swung around, lips shaped in a snarl; looked, eyes widening, and took on a smile of recognition.

—Isaac Pride! the young man called. You come to bleedin Kansas?

—George! Isaac said. I heard you were at Pikes Peak, digging out mountains of gold.

—Pikes Peak! God-damned humbug is what it is! And he spat a foaming gob in the dust, uncoiled his bullwhip and snapped it in a thunderous crack. The oxen lurched at the sound and let their heads down lower but continued at the same ambling, worn-out gait.

—George! Isaac cried, you got to tell me about it some—I'm on my way out now, leaving in the morning.

For answer George wheeled his wagon out of the line and into the grass at the side of the road. Isaac followed, jumped down. George produced a canteen and they sat back against a wheel in the shade of the wagon, passing the lukewarm water back and forth.

George McGranahan had come out to Kansas the previous summer alone, by boat from St Louis, with a hundred dollars saved, meaning to look around, pre-empt land, perhaps, if he found what looked right to him. And he was in no hurry—a year, at twenty, is an epoch, but there is no limit to the years ahead; and with fifty million acres of Kansas to pick from, and half a continent beyond, it seemed there would always be good land to choose, next year or next if not next week or month. So, meantime, he worked at what work he could find, making expenses and something over, and looked around: teamstering from Fort Leavenworth, west as far as Riley; odd jobs of carpentry; worked with a man plowing a few acres of prairie so he could swear at the Land Office at Kickapoo that the man was a bona-fide settler according to statute and bureau regulation, and accepted five dollars for his trouble in so swearing (and the man the same day sold his claim to a land agent for ten dollars an acre, or so he said). Twice George McGranahan staked out land on his own account, but neither claim proved up: on the first the Land Office records showed the land already patented to some man in Ohio, though there was no sign of it on the ground; the second turned out to be inside the Delaware reservation, unsurveyed and no assurance it ever would be open to settlement—there were squatters enough on the Indian land, a man could squat and make a farm, and a living too, and in the end have the land bought out from under.

So in late summer when rumors of gold came from Cherry Creek and his hundred dollars had grown to two hundred, George teamed with five others in two wagons and started for the mountains. They joined a train at Council Grove and went out by the most-traveled southern route to Pueblo and north to Denver City, Pikes Peak in sight all the last week and snow on the mountaintops, and arrived in late September. It was the Kansas game over again: you staked a stream bank or a mountain slope and took your description to the Land Office—and there was some other set of names already entered on the books; the object was to get a claim, take out some little chunks of rock that assayed at, oh, fifteen dollars a ton, and then sell out, take the profit, and start again. They got one of their own, it was on the records yet, but missed the vein. Winter settled. They sold the wagons, split up. George worked at building a flume, digging and timbering a tunnel, shoveling rock onto wagons. It paid three dollars a day but he couldn't live; flour was forty-five dollars a barrel and scarce, bacon fifty cents a pound, ditto. In January he was lucky, killed an elk and lived off it for a month or he would have starved; in the camp he learned to make a tea of pine bark and needles to keep off scurvy. By mid-April, with the snow melted from the high plains and the new grass coming and all his money gone, Iowa looked good again and he thought himself lucky to be taken on by a train of go-backs heading for the States, bull-whacking for his keep. For five weeks he had lived off moldy salt pork, biscuit, some fresh buffalo meat, and stringy beef from oxen that gave out along the way—it had been a dry spring, poor grass; his boots that had walked six hundred miles out and six hundred back were cracked and broken, worn through the soles, and his feet bled—he tore up an old wool shirt to wrap them. But once he crossed the Missouri again it seemed as if he could skip the whole way home.

The road north was empty now. In the distance there were dust and shouts and whips cracking, another train coming out from Leavenworth. George got over on his knees, took hold of the wheel spokes and hitched himself to his feet—Oh, God! in a whisper.

—I got to get these God-damned bone-bags moving again or they'll die where they stand, he said, catch up with the train. But, Isaac—he swung around, took Isaac's hand in both his—Isaac, it's really something, seeing a man from home out here. I could just kind of sit down here and cry like a God-damned girl—

George turned away. His team stood as if entranced. He prodded the nigh leader's bony rump with his whip handle. With a groan it took a step forward, leaned against the yoke, the chain went taut, and the others followed.

—Git *up*, ye staggering God-damned sons of rabbits, *git up!*—and he loosed the whip in a snapping pistol crack.

Isaac stepped along beside him.—Listen, George, he said, is what you say, there's no gold out there at all, and all the talk's just lies—?

—Oh, there's gold all right, I seen it, panned some for myself—and traded the dust for ten pounds of flour and a side of bacon. But no one's found the lode yet—or maybe they have, this spring, I reckon they will, sometime. It's just—it's just—his face twisted with rage and frustration as he struggled for the words—you break your back and freeze your butt digging rock—and then the big fellow comes along and buys you out for a hundred dollars, and a whole block of claims, a *mountain* of claims—or maybe he don't even buy but just comes in with surveyors and lawyers and shows how you aint never filed right and proper in the first place, there's been men killed, fighting over some empty piece of mountain. And then, see, he hires you back to do the nigger work, digging and tunneling, and you build him a flume

and a gravity railroad and a crusher plant—. And that's how it is—
you got money and no stinting, you going to find the gold and get it
for yourself. And if you aint—. Now that's the truth of it, and that's
all there is.

George turned back to his team. The whip whispered through the
air and cracked. The lead yoke jerked at the chain and the others
attempted a shambling trot.

—Git up! ye broken-back sons of torment! *Git up!*

Isaac stood, hands on his hips, and watched his old friend down the
road till the next train had nearly come up. He ran to catch his horse.

It was noon when Isaac rode into camp again. Kilbourn was up to
his waist in a pool a little way down the stream, taking a bath. Wood
sat cross-legged by the stove, rubbing grease on his boots. Andy lay in
front of their tent, asleep. The Saurs were off down the road, bringing the oxen back.

—Boys! he announced, I've had some more of my luck. Remember
George McGranahan, went out to Kansas bout a year ago? Well, he's
been to Pikes Peak—I met him going to the ferry, driving the sorriest
team of Texas bulls you ever saw.

And he slid off his horse and waited while the others came close to
listen, and finally the Saurs; and told them all McGranahan's story,
and what Durfee had said over breakfast of the news from Denver
and his worries and the trains of disappointed Peakers coming
through.

No one said much, each thoughtful in his own way. It was
Kilbourn's turn at cooking dinner and he made the fire. Andy stood
at a little distance, hands in his pockets, watching. The Saurs went
into their tent and closed the flap. Wood rolled his pants up and
barefoot went over to the spring to wash his feet. Isaac got a torn
scrap of blanket from his tent and set to rubbing Regina. Mc-
Granahan stayed in his mind; he was troubled as he had not been
while listening to his tale and strained to catch and hold the sense of
it: like a ghost come back and standing beside the river of the dead,
not dead exactly but not wholly flesh, and babbling to be heard; and
savage too, a wild man, desperate, with hurt feet and haunted eyes,
driving those broken animals that looked as if they'd not live to the
ferry crossing, much less back to Iowa—and those wagons with the
paint blistered to the bare wood and the wood cracked and shrunk by
the High Plains air and axles patched together with rawhide. . . .

After dinner, while they lay around the stove, drinking coffee and
putting off washing up, Wood brought it up again.—Well, now, JR! he
said in a challenging voice. You changed your thinking any about
Pikes Peak?

—Not much, Isaac said slowly. Maybe some. I don't say Mc-

Granahan's not a good man, but it don't sound sif he was well prepared or knew rightly what he was going into—like he thought the gold was just there lying on the ground like marbles to pick up. Now I know that much anyhow—and I aint afraid to work, and I know surveying and the ways of land claims, and I don't mean t'allow any man to sucker me like they did him. But he's been through something all right, and that's a fact.

—It don't scare *me*, Kilbourn put in. Why, you know, he said with a smile of discovering something, I'll go with you yet if things don't look good when we get to Lawrence. Remember what that preacher captain said about all life being a testing? Don't seem George did so well—took the test and just about got away with his skin.

—I'll not let it lay me low like that, Isaac said. I mean to pass.

—And what have the Saurs got to say for themselves? Wood asked. Still set on the Peak?

They looked at the two young men sitting side by side, Chris with eyes cast down, John looking off into distance, up at the cloudless blue of the afternoon sky. They waited.

—We talked it over before dinner, John said finally, in a low voice, hurrying over the words. We aint going. We're starting back, home to the farm. Tomorrow.

Chris, pink-cheeked and blond, nodded vigorously. Isaac stood up, set his cup down on the back of the stove, turned and faced them.— John Saur, he said, that's not *right*—we made an agreement: all the way and share and share alike—and anything decided, we decide together.

—Don't you shout at me, Isaac Pride! John answered him.

—But John—and Chris: you *gave your word!*

—We've made our minds up—wasn't no good all the way coming— and now the hard part's only just beginning—

Chris nodded again. Isaac turned away, clenching his fists.

—Isaac! Andy spoke up. Isaac pivoted, looking down at him. Isaac, he went on softly, I decided too. I'm going back with them.

—Andy!—Isaac began, and stopped himself. Andy, we must talk. That's fair. He beckoned. Andy got up and followed him slowly down the stream.

—Andy, Isaac said as they reached the road, you remember that first time, how you came to look at my Indian pony, and I let you ride her? They turned and walked along the road, side by side, into the glare of the afternoon sun, scuffing their boots in the dust.

—I remember. But you know what I remember? Andy stopped and turned, facing him. What I remember is, you taking me out on the prairie on that horse, trying to teach me to hunt, and me spoiling your hunt. That's what I remember.

They walked on in silence.—That's *nothing*, Andy, Isaac said at last.

We were like brothers, you know that? I never had a brother, but that's what they are: one's good at one thing, one at another, but together—why, together there's *nothing* they can't do.

—I thought it all out, Zackie. You're *smart*, going to do things, I don't know what, and me—well, I'm not, that's all—may do some things of my own yet—but they're not going to be together anymore, is all. I know that much.

For Isaac it was like a window that snapped open and shut; like looking through the lens of the camera portrait artist at Davenport and the scene you looked at was childhood, and Andy standing up stiff and straight in the middle of the group, and the shutter closed and that was over; and opened again, and the scene all different, yourself a man and great landscapes on the painted backdrop, but Andy was not there. Oh, they would meet again somewhere, sometime, and shake hands, smiling, and talk of their families and what they had made of their lives, but there would be nothing any more done together. Andy spoke true.

They stopped; turned and started back, following their long shadows back along the road. There was nothing more to say.

VI

On Freedom's Southern Line

Isaac, Wood, and Kilbourn started early Saturday morning, leaving the others in camp, still packing up, and reached the Stranger River crossing that night. They broke custom by traveling all Sunday across the Delaware reservation—none of them maintained any very decided Sabbatarian convictions, but it had been convenient so far, stopping over once a week to rest and feed the cattle, wash clothes; and they felt an urgency, now the decision was made, to get on. The Delaware country was a patchwork of clashing colors under the June sun: Indians with silver pendants in their ears, in voluminous deep blue hunting shirts dotted with white and red over buckskin trousers, long hair tied back in gaudy headcloths, passing on the road on little, trotting piebald ponies on their Sunday visitings, and in the tops of the big trees overhead the bright greens, yellows, and oranges of flocks of chattering parakeets, resting from their migration north. By evening they were still a mile or two short of the crossing to Lawrence and made camp in a dry, broad, shallow depression, by its look a cut-off former bed of the Kansas River, or the *Kaw*, as many seemed to call it. Once again they emptied one of Isaac's kegs, watering the oxen, cooking, washing up afterward.

The crossing to Lawrence was by rope ferry: a heavy rope anchored in the low bluffs on either bank, with ropes on pulleys attached to bow and stern of a flatboat; by pulling in or letting out on one or other of the connecting lines the ferryman angled the boat so as to let the current carry it across. The boat was big enough for one wagon and team, a few passengers or odds and ends of loose freight. Isaac let his partners go first, set his brake, and lay back on the bank to wait.

It was a bright morning, cloudless and dry. The town spread along the opposite bank like a painted panorama, its landmarks known at least by name to any reader of newspapers over the last four or five years: at the center, the sullen mass of the Free State Hotel, what was left of it, which three years earlier a pro-slave mob demolished with cannon, a keg of gunpowder, and fire. Behind it, to the west, the gentle, spreading slope grandly named Mount Oread, rising to treeless prairie back from the river, with the slow-turning, wood-slat sails of a large windmill at the north end and, to the right of it, pricked against the sky at the highest point, the walls of General Lane's sandstone fort pale in the sun, defending the town, and Governor Robinson's brick mansion. At this distance the town seemed random-scattered, like pieces in a half-played game of checkers, its two-hundred-odd structures—here a row of stores, there a new hotel of brick, a narrow, new-painted clapboard house in a style transplanted from New England, low, windowless bark-slab cabins, even still on the fringes a few of the famous prairie-hay tents such as the first settlers had hastily put up for temporary shelter—not yet drawn together in community or fitted to the gently sloping treeless landscape.

Once Isaac was across, Wood led them on a road that skirted the town center and climbed circuitously along the base of Mount Oread. They had not gone half a mile before he stopped, shouted, and waved his hat at a man in a light buggy coming down, a heavy, round-faced, balding man, thick side-whiskers and small, steel-framed glasses pressed tight against the flesh around his eyes; his brother Sam, looking perhaps twenty years older. Sam reined in his smartly stepping horse, climbed down, and ran in a lumbering trot to seize his brother in a bear hug; then stood back, shook hands all around.

—I couldn't think where you'd got to, little brother, Sam boomed, settled down to make a farm among the ruffians or—God knows what you'd be up to—took the wrong fork at Leavenworth and gone to Oregon. Where you *been?*

—We stopped some days after crossing the river, Wood said quietly, resting up. And then three of Mister Pride's party didn't like the news from the gold regions and fell homesick for Iowa. We left them starting back Saturday morning.

—Iowa! Sam repeated with a gasp of laughter. *Iowa*—that's good, that's wonderful! We don't need any more of *that* kind here—begging your pardon, Iowa boys—but you're here in time, anyway, gentlemen. It's our election tomorrow, Jim Lane's in town and going to speak—that's what I'm rigged up in my Sunday suit for, going to hear him.

The election that excited Sam Wood would be the fourteenth in a series begun a few months after the territory was opened to settlement, nearly all of them fraudulent, irregular, unsanctioned by law, or otherwise invalid. This one was for delegates to a convention charged with devising a Kansas constitution, another attempt by the territory to enter the Union as a state. Lane had passed through Davenport three years earlier, raising money and men to keep the Missourians from closing the river crossings into Kansas; he was some kind of cousin, apparently, of Isaac's father's reverend friend Daniel Lane, the Maine-born missionary and poet chosen principal of the Iowa College Preparatory Department. They followed Sam in his buggy the short distance to his house, staked the oxen in the pasture out back, and carried buckets of water for them to drink. Wood and Kilbourn crowded in beside Sam for the drive into town. Isaac saddled his horse and rode behind.

Men in buggies, wagons, on horseback and on foot, were converging on the center of town. Sam left his buggy in an empty lot and led them toward the front of the crowd. A bearded, soberly dressed man stood on the porch of the new Eldridge House, speaking in a quiet, high-pitched voice that carried only disconnected words—"duty," "Free-State," "legally constituted"—across the shuffle and whisper of his audience;—Doctor Charles Robinson, Sam explained, the governor. He seemed to have finished as they found a clear space a few yards from the porch. There was a scattering of polite applause. The governor turned away and took a seat on a bench at one end of the porch.

The hotel's front door flung open with a bang. After a moment a slender, angular figure stepped through and slouched toward the front of the porch, bareheaded, face cast down, hands in his pockets, and a patchy bearskin overcoat hanging from his shoulders, open down the front.—Jim Lane! Sam said in an excited whisper, nudging with his elbows—the general! Lane stopped, balancing on the edge of the step, waited; a narrow, scowling, sharp-chinned face—hawk-like, wolf-like, the face of a meat-tearing predator—with tufts of unkempt hair sticking up at odd points around his head, behind his ears. His head lifted, staring eyes moved slowly across the crowd, up the slope behind the town and gazed fixedly at the sky until heads turned in the crowd to look, to try to see whatever he saw behind them, coming. His hands came out of his pockets. He straightened, grew taller; a spring wound tight, a snake coiled to strike.

—Men of Kansas! he began in a low-pitched, grating voice. Men of Kansas, for five years you have labored—bared your backs to the blistering summer sun and stood against the bone-chilling blast of winter. And what have you got with all your labor? I ask you, *What have you got?* Some of you have secured a home where you may take your ease with wife and child, in this or other of the towns that rise across this bounteous land like the bluestem grass called forth by the gracious rains of spring. Some of you have claimed your land, possessed your quarter-section or your half-section, have turned the sod and brought forth crops of corn and wheat in abundance. Some of you—the voice sank lower, almost whispering—have left your sons or husbands, brothers, beneath that sod to fill a nameless grave, innocent victims of the hellish power that for five long years has sought to conquer what it could not take by right—to *rob* you, men of Kansas, of the just fruits of your labors.

An angry murmur swelled through the crowd. Lane waited, met it on the rise, voice still quiet, deep.—*Slaves* have what you have, men of Kansas—black nigra slaves consigned to the humblest quarter of the slavers' empire—a cabin to rest in when day's work is done—land to till—a place to lay their dead. You have not got, with all your labor, men of Kansas, the one true, glorious, necessary jewel of free men everywhere, of free *white* men—the voice rose to a trumpet blast, the measured words came faster; the bearskin slipped off his shoulders and lay in a heap on the floor, one arm shot out, stiffly measuring the tempo of his speech. You have not got a government of your own making, of your choosing—a government of free men to stand equal among the brother-states of this great Union. *There* is the purpose of all your labors, your final blessing and your recompense. For these five years, month after month and year by year, your labors have been frustrate by the hell-kites of Missouri—by the corrupted servants of the slave power—by weak and petty men debasing the just deliberations of Congress and our national government.

—How long—he flung both arms crosswise, wide, lifted his head and rose on the balls of his feet like a bow aimed at heaven—how long, great *God*, will You look down and tolerate the spurning of Your purposes for men? Another *year?*—scattered cries of *No!*—another *month?*—*No! No!*—another *day?*

The answer roared back like thunder breaking, rolling through the crowd, the guttural throbbing of men's voices from the depths of a thousand throats. Isaac found himself shouting with the rest, fists clenched in rage, his breathing short and quick.

Lane paced the porch, like an animal, caged; stopped and with sudden violence tore off his suit coat and flung it down, a man preparing for a fight, and stood before them in his carelessly half-buttoned shirt.

—Tomorrow is the day! the voice sang, rising, drawing the words out. The great day promised not merely from the opening of this territory but laid down and ordained and written in the book of the world at the birth of time. Tomorrow you shall cast your sacred ballot for delegates to the convention that will draft a constitution worthy for free men to live by in a glorious Free-State Kansas. Let us not

falter, men of Kansas! Let us go forth together—armored with courage—armed with the God-given strength of our bodies—and once
and for all—this one last time—drive the devils of slavery from this
good land—and back to hell and *Missouri* where they belong!

The last words rose to a high shriek. The graceless arms fell, he
stepped back, slumped beside the open hotel door, panting. The
crowd surged, shouting, cheering, laughing. If he had offered to lead
them out to conquer the enemy in the adjoining state, they would
have mounted up and followed without a dissenting thought. That he
wanted only their votes in the morning, on behalf of the new Republican Party, seemed not enough to have asked.

Sam Wood grasped his brother and Isaac each by an arm and propelled them onto the porch.—Got to meet him, boys, he shouted
through the clamor of the crowd. Oh, you've got to meet him!

Lane leaned against the doorpost, motionless, eyes wide and staring, the unruly hair pressed damp to his head. Recognizing Sam
Wood, he roused himself, stepped forward, the wide mouth opening
in a half-smile.

—Think we'll win this one, Sam? he asked.

—If we don't—Sam roared, why, Jim, by heaven—they try to rob
us of our rights again, they'll see such an uproar from fifty thousand
Free-State Kansans as'll make all's gone before seem nothing but a
children's game—. But here—my young friends, in this morning
from Iowa—

—Fresh recruits to the good cause! Lane proclaimed, his piercing
public voice returning. Every day they come, from every corner of
the Union, like the torrents of spring. Nothing can stop us!

—Jack Pride, Isaac said, stepping forward. The ungainly hand
clamped like a steel trap, the ferocious eyes gripped his. I heard you at
Davenport that time—three years ago it was, you were—

—I remember, Lane said, and released his hand. I remember the
occasion very well, sir. And now you've come to take up land. A wise
decision—no finer land anywhere in the national patrimony—or on
the face of God's earth.

—I was going farther west, Isaac said. Now—I don't know, my
plans—

—None better to be had than right here in Douglas County, Lane
broke in, sweeping his demurral aside with a gesture. They must vote
tomorrow, of course, he continued conversationally, turning to Sam
Wood. Sound young men. Kansas has need of such men.

—Now, *Jim*, Sam crooned, I hardly think—only just this day arrived—

—You're timid, Sam, Lane glared. I *wrote* that law—or helped write
it—get it passed too, God save my soul—and residence aint *in* it. But
if it'll suit you, we'll put em down for *prospective* residents—see, like

prospective pre-emptors—and give em their rights just the same. I'll see they're inscribed on the rolls.

And, nodding gravely to his three recruits, Jim Lane turned to other clients crowding the porch and led them through the doorway into the hotel.

Over supper that night at Sam's house the young men were much intrigued with Jim Lane's insistence on their voting in the election. Bill Wood was troubled in his conscience that the general—the principal leader of the Free-State settlers, of the just cause against the fraud and violence of the Missourians and their Slave-State allies—should offer to practice the same deception he had fought. Kilbourn, for his part, could see nothing wrong with voting, considering how often and how thoroughly every election held so far had been rigged by the Slave-Staters, with their voter lists copied out of hotel registers and old commercial directories—and this one too, no doubt.

Sam smilingly listened to their talk, the lamplight gleaming on his spectacles, but offered no opinion. As his wife dished up the blackberry pie, however, between mouthfuls he turned to Isaac, pointing with his fork.—I'll tell you one thing, Jack, he said. What old Jim told you about the land aint nothing but the God's truth, absolute one hundred percent. And it aint only what the land will produce once it's built up and developed—no, sir!—but what it's worth *right now*— why, they can't hardly survey and map it fast enough for all the people coming, and even since the panic, value goes on rising just about day by day. Now, here's the thing. You take and claim your quarter-section, pay the legal price, dollar and a quarter an acre—or take it with warrants, costs you maybe seventy-five or ninety cents— and the minute you walk out of the Land Office with your papers you can turn around and sell for ten or fifteen dollars—maybe even *twenty* an acre! Now I don't know much about mining gold, but that looks to me like a hundred, two hundred ounces' worth just for a little sense in looking out land, filing application, and putting money down. And I ask you straight: how many tons of rock you going to break—how many gravel beds you going to wash—to get *that much gold?* And nothing says you got to sell straight out, of course. You *keep* it, make a farm, a home, and if you're active you've got a livelihood for life—you can't go wrong.

Sam set his fork down and passed his plate back to his wife for another helping. Isaac gazed at him wide-eyed and forgot to eat.

—Supposing a man did want to *think* about land, he cautiously suggested. Where'd he best look?

—Now there's the thing, Sam rejoined, and I don't think Jim's quite in touch about *that*—but around here, all the land's worth taking's pretty well taken up already. But just a little west of here, Shaw-

nee County, say—. You set on going to the gold regions, take your
map and look up the records at the Land Office at Lecompton—aint
much out of your road anyway, and worth your while, I tell you—.

Isaac fell silent again and remained so till the meal was over and
they went to bed, the three of them in their blankets on the floor of
Sam's small parlor.

In the morning, according to scruple or indifference, Bill and Kilbourn stayed home, but Isaac, still curious, drove in with Sam to the
voting. It was a comparatively decorous proceeding. Although there
was a steady traffic in and out of the Eldridge House bar, there was
no whisky barrel set up in plain view with its top knocked in and a
tin dipper handy to all comers. The Republican candidates were lined
up on the hotel porch; above them, on the porch roof, a small brass
band held forth with marches and patriotic songs, Whittier's "Kansas
Emigrant" frequent among them. Altogether it was an occasion that
would not have been out of place on any New England village green.
The town had been from its beginning the chief object of the New
England Emigrant Aid Company in Kansas. The settlers, if not all
New Englanders, were at least like-minded, not many of them outright abolitionists but united in resisting the spread of slavery.

Isaac waited while Sam deposited his ballot, then asked the registrar if his name was on the list of voters. The man searched but found
no Pride. Isaac asked after William Wood and David Kilbourn, with
the same result. Sam stood by and laughed till his belly shook and he
started to wheeze and had to stop himself.

—I don't see anything funny about a man giving his word to something and not doing it, Isaac sourly remarked as they walked back to
where they had left the buggy. Even if he wasn't right to give it in the
first place.

—Oh, I guess it aint really funny, Sam agreed, only the first time
you see him do it to someone else. It's just Jim's way of doing.

—Doesn't sound like a kind of man I want to have much business
with, Isaac insisted, still peeved. We've got sharpers back in Iowa.

—It aint that, Sam said and stopped, put his hand on Isaac's arm.
Jim can be hard all right, an absolute devil if you get him wrong, but
he aint hard to like. It's just—he's got his eye on something grand,
away off down the road, and compared with that, individual people
and the little niceties about dealing with people don't count with him
for much. And I guess I ought to know, being in this thing with him
from the start and getting ready to go in with him now on a mill. And
that's another thing—Sam was laughing again—you ever have to do
with him again, as you may well, and he wants money—*don't you give
it to him* if you ever mean to see it back—but those two things apart,
and take him all in all . . .

They walked on in silence to the buggy.

Staying with Sam Wood at Lawrence, Isaac explored the vicinity on horseback, but it was as he had been told. Everywhere the first-choice land for farming had been corner-staked, there were men at work plowing the prairie grass under, hauling logs to make the foundations of cabins, first steps in establishing occupancy on land to be taken by pre-emption—in a few places near town there were already beginnings of productive farming made in the last year or two, forty or fifty acres at a stretch in corn or wheat, a cabin roofed, a shallow well dug, while the native bluestem, heavy-headed and belly-high to his mare—was ripening to a first cutting of hay for the cattle; land bearing no obvious signs of being claimed showed obvious defects to anyone grown up under the previous generation of Midwest farm-making, steeps that would gully if put to plow, thin soil with outcrops of pale sandstone thrusting from the slopes, no functioning watercourses wreathed in wood and scrub for fencing, the first settler's cabin. After a week Isaac and Kilbourn resolved to follow the universal advice and see what they could find in Shawnee County, the next one west and the limit of surveyed land.

Bill Wood stayed at Lawrence to help his brother finish his mill. Having looked around some on his own account, he talked of renting a quarter-section farm on shares with an option to buy in five years, say; he would have a place to bring his wife and child to in the fall.

Isaac and Kilbourn took the road south from Lawrence. In mid-afternoon they joined the Santa Fe Road and turned west. To anyone accustomed to the narrowly defined roads and the older forest trails of the woodland East, the magical name conveyed nothing of the reality: a hundred-yard-wide track of bare gray-brown earth, deeply rutted in this dry season and beaten hard, enclosed in a half-mile zone of close-cropped grass trampled sparse, its general course through eastern Kansas determined by a ridge dividing streams running northeast to the Kansas River from those flowing south to the Osage; therefore a route with few crossings to make, rarely impeded by wet weather. Now in mid-June, the high season of westward freighting, they were never out of sight of columns of wagons whose dust clouds hung in the air and spread across the country like a mist: huge freight wagons drawn by four and five yoke of oxen, loaded with two or three tons of goods from the river ports, Kansas City and Leavenworth, consigned to Santa Fe or Denver and beyond—distance made these cargoes precious and repaid their freight; at the Council Grove rendezvous the freighters would make up in trains of a hundred or more wagons for the passage across the Plains. And there were Army convoys carrying less bulky supplies—ammunition, guns, canned or dried food—to forts established for protection against the wild tribes;

emigrants' wagons, taking the southern route to California; an occasional mule cart or buggy traveling light and fast to the gold regions.

In the afternoon as they approached a place called Council City on the map, the wagon traffic ahead slowed and stopped, backed up. Isaac loosed Regina, climbed on, and rode forward to see what was blocking the way. A half-mile along he came to a steep, short slope down to a stream running deep between low bluffs, and a narrow bridge across, made of unpeeled cottonwood logs. The bridge-keeper stood beside a little gatehouse on the near side, collecting tolls, a dollar for a wagon and team, a half-dollar for a man on horseback. Back from the road at the top of the slope stood a substantial two-story frame house, broad porch across the front and a solid foundation of the local sandstone; beyond it, rising, several two-story houses built of the same stone, cabins, the open shed of a blacksmith's shop, a couple of frame stores, a mill of some kind, and the half-built brick walls of a structure big enough to be meant for a hotel—fifty or more buildings beginning to group themselves in the orderly huddle of a town. A voice hallooed. Isaac looked back at the white-painted house. A tall man leaned on the porch railing, waving.

—You, sir! the man shouted. Come on up here—I wish to speak with you.

Isaac wheeled the mare, climbed the slope, and held in a few feet short, looking up. The man wore a linen suit, a broad-brimmed panama hat pushed back on his head: tall, lean, muscular, holding himself straight, bushy white brows over narrowed eyes, a thick white mustache waxed to points, his expression and bearing both affable and commanding. In one hand he held a squat silver mug.

—Colonel Israel Titus, the man introduced himself in a melodious, slow-paced voice, sipping his drink. Late of the U.S. Cavalry. Unlike some in these parts, I earned my rank, in Mexico.

—Isaac A. Pride, Isaac formally answered, and waited.

—I like the look of your mare, sir, the colonel observed. Always ride her bareback, do you?

—Only when I'm in a hurry. I had to see what was blocking the road.

—Business *is* a little slow today—but I find it restful, sitting out here of an afternoon, watching my money come in. Attending to business, you see.

—You own that thing? Isaac asked with a backward toss of his head.

Colonel Titus nodded.—*And* fifty percent of the flourishing city of Burlingame.

—Isn't there a Council City somewhere about here? My map—

—Two years ago, that was. We bought it up, reorganized it with the new name. For the sake of the bridge, of course, not that the place doesn't have prospects—. But I was wondering, sir—would you consider seventy-five dollars, gold—

—I'd consider about a thousand maybe, Colonel, Isaac shot back. If I'd a mind to sell.

The colonel shrugged but returned his smile.—No offense taken at a friendly offer, I hope. I was thinking of a young relative, coming out from Saint Louis this summer to observe our curious ways—

—And you thought your—

—My *niece!* he said. But really—you've trained her beautifully, yet I can see she has her spirit—. See here, we can't stand talking here like this. Come up and join me in a toddy.

—My partner's back on the road with the wagon, Isaac said, but still easily sat his horse, returning the man's steady gaze. Behind him the wagons moved slowly forward, axles creaking, the teamsters shouting, firing off their whips.

—Going west, are you?

—Thinking of Denver City—that's what we planned anyhow, to start—but since we're coming through, we thought—

—You thought you'd see about land! And couldn't have hit on a better place for it—. Colonel Titus set down his mug and with long-limbed strides crossed the porch, leaped down the steps, and stood beside Isaac.—You'll be hours yet, getting over. Bring your wagon and your friend along and stay for supper—you can stake your team out behind the house, tell me the news from the East, and I'll tell you about Osage County land. Really, I insist.

Colonel Titus set a considerable table. There was wild turkey roasted by the freedwoman who did his cooking, served by her husband; green beans, lettuce, strawberries from the kitchen garden; a bottle of French claret, expensively hauled, like his staple groceries, the pine lumber for his house, the brick for the hotel, over the Santa Fe Road from dealers at Kansas City. The bridge alone was worth as much as a hundred dollars a day: he got the traffic going out and most of it coming back, though some returned east by other routes; the creek was among the few in the whole extent of the Santa Fe Road where a bridge was unavoidable—it had been Bridge Creek to the early traders, now Switzler Creek. His wife had died, childless, after he retired to Kentucky, about the time the territory opened, the occasion for his coming west to see what could be done. Isaac said something about the prospects for land in Shawnee County, and the colonel with a laugh corrected him: following the Santa Fe Road, they had crossed into Osage County, formerly Weller, of which Burlingame meant to be the seat, though for now most of the county land was still locked up in the Sac and Fox reservation.

Over the last of the wine, while Absalom cleared, Colonel Titus learned of Isaac and Kilbourn's connection with Sam Wood. The colonel's manner changed with that discovery. The young men were no longer passersby brought by chance to while a lonely man's evening but something like relatives, remote and undefinable cousins but kin all the same. He insisted on their staying the night. For the next two days Colonel Titus drove them through the gently rolling, trackless prairie hunting possible land. He had taken a half-section himself, seven miles southeast of Burlingame, using the warrant earned by his service in the Mexican War, and had pre-empted and paid for another quarter in his bridge-keeper's name; he expected the patent from the General Land Office within the year. Isaac was much taken with an adjoining quarter-section that still showed no sign of being claimed: divided from the colonel's land by a small stream flowing south into Switzler Creek, a source of water immediately and promising a shallow well for a house set back from the stream bank; no big timber but adequate small growth along the stream for fencing, with a hillside outcrop of stone, easily worked, which settlers in the area were already learning to use for building or, when there was enough, for fences. With his compass and a long rope, Isaac measured off the corners and set stakes with his name carved and the date and considered himself lucky in his find—for several miles around, the quarter-sections were all staked, in a few places pre-emptors had plowed a few acres or marked the borders of a claim with a single furrow, started a cabin, but this one had been left, perhaps under the impression Colonel Titus had taken the entire section. His land, as he already thought it: nearly level except for thirty or so acres along the creek, with a little rise that would be fine for a house. Kilbourn borrowed Isaac's horse and rode out by himself, looking, and came back saying he had something even better a few miles farther down the same stream. Isaac drove with him to it in the colonel's buggy and helped measure and stake the corners of the quarter-section.

—Of course, Colonel Titus remarked that evening over supper, you mustn't think it's only altruism makes me take such an interest in finding you land. No, *sir!* Naturally, gentlemen, I expect some benefit to myself.

The two young men together set their forks on their plates and turned sober and attentive faces. The colonel's notion of benefit was getting some of his land broken: he had the plow but no one to spare for the work and too much other business of his own; they had the ox team and their time. His offer was three dollars an acre, plowed both ways and the sod turned under so he could plant in the spring; or instead of cash they could take his own land acre for acre, up to eighty acres, from the unplowed quarter next to Isaac's, to keep or sell. Moreover, in the fall or whenever they had the money he would go with them to the Land Office at Lecompton and witness their claims. If they were short, he could perhaps lend them the difference at rates somewhat more attractive than usual in Kansas.

—You see, gentlemen, he concluded, what I really want is people settling this country up, bringing families and making homes and roads, bringing their trade to my town—active young folks like you, growing up with the country, as they say. But I don't mind telling you, if I can get some of that land of mine broken by the way, thout having to put my own sweat and shoulder to it, why—And the laughter gurgling in his throat completed the thought.

Isaac managed to contain himself till he and Kilbourn were in their room upstairs, but once they were alone could not stop talking. The luck of it, and paid by the acre besides! He had helped his father breaking the prairie farm west of Rockingham—three acres a day would not be too much with a proper plow and team, but say a hundred acres finished by the end of August, allowing for one thing and another—why that was a hundred and fifty dollars each, nearly all the money for their land and borrow the rest at, oh, one percent a month—. Now if they kept at it, working for other settlers around the county, into October or whenever the weather closed down—well! there was the rest of the money and the loans paid off and their own land clear and money besides, a quarter-section each for their summer's work and worth, say—

—Sounds worse'n digging gold, said Kilbourn with a snort. Like George McGranahan—cept we won't freeze our butts. I hear it's hot enough out here in summer to fry a nigger.

And ostentatiously rolled over to his side of the bed and closed his eyes. Isaac blew out the candle.

In the morning they drove the wagon to Isaac's land and made their camp on the stream bank with the tent set up to face the morning sun and the rim of trees behind for the afternoon shade, the water handy for cooking and its gossiping ripple to sleep to by night. Colonel Titus let them take logs from along Switzler Creek above the town-site. They spent two days cutting and hauling cottonwood logs, notching the ends, and laying them out in square cabin foundations, marks of claim and occupancy; Isaac placed his with care on the rise he had chosen, facing east, and was full of jokes about where his doors and windows would be, the addition to be built on and the barn, well back from the house and stream. The colonel advised them besides to plow an acre or two, but that could wait. On the second evening they loaded his big breaking plow, sent for from Kansas City in the spring, and brought it out. It was time for work.

The object of this work was grass. Where a city man sees only a mass, a yielding carpet covering earth's nakedness, a careful farm-maker a barrier to the riches of the soil to be released by plantings of wheat or corn, a botanist might recognize a hundred species of grasses and other plants in an undisturbed acre of prairie. On the colonel's section of Osage County, the form and color of the prairie grass was determined by several varieties of bluestem. Among these, big bluestem was dominant, a grass that grows individually in a tight-drawn bunch of stems and leaves that in turn forms massive clumps and colonies defending each other against competing plants. It was Isaac and Kilbourn's task to invade this kingdom: to break the prairie sod with their plow as a man breaks a wild horse to his will and service, as he breaks a seed pod to extract the edible fruit. Here and there on the Plains the bluestem would survive in isolated tracts kept for grazing and the cutting of hay, but its primordial and unchallenged reign was about to end, to be replaced by the tame grasses, corn and wheat and the others, whose culture men understood, yielding the obvious goods of food and income.

In the morning they ate a leisurely and abundant breakfast—a pot of oatmeal, eggs, ham, pancakes, a quart of coffee; the sun was well up, the light dew off the grass, when they brought in the oxen and drove the wagon to the quarter-section south of Isaac's where they were to start. They had stacked most of Isaac's load beside the tent to make room for the plow, a John Deere made at Moline across the river from Davenport—*luck,* Isaac considered it, coincidence being only luck in a long word pretending to allusions of science and philosophy: a twenty-inch share of polished steel angled to a knife-sharp point, welded on a cast-iron frame, with an eight-foot beam and a rolling colter toward the front of the beam—a sharp-edged wheel to cut the sod and control the depth of the furrow, a new idea since Isaac and his father had worked their farm on the prairie.

Isaac's plan was to run the furrows the full width of the quarter, defining his own land in the process. It started well. Kilbourn cracked the rump of the nigh leader with a stick and the team plunged forward into the grass as if pleased with the novelty of plowing after the days of fattening on hay from the colonel's barn and taking their ease on the prairie grass around the camp. The grass, months short of full growth but everywhere waist-high, fell with the turning of the furrow like a miniature forest laid flat by a cyclone; the beautiful sharpness of the plowshare sang through the tight-woven fabric of roots with a sound like silk tearing. It got harder as the sun rose higher and the day grew hot. The plow struck the heavy center of a clump of bluestem and instead of cutting through rode over, and they had to stop the team, back up, and try again; or it dived and stopped short with a muffled thud that shuddered through the plow handles, as if run against a tree root or boulder. Kilbourn tried riding the beam to steady the plow with his weight but it did not help much and the oxen wandered. By the time the sun was at mid-day they had turned six furrows and were back not far from where they had left the wagon beside the little south-flowing stream; a segment of plowed land half a mile long and ten feet wide that Isaac reckoned amounted to about half an acre. The oxen knelt in their yokes, panting, and stretched their necks to crop the tall grass. Kilbourn lay on his back in the grass, shirt open to the waist.

—Jackrabbit, he said, don't look to *me* like that colonel made us such an easy bargain. By damn—it's like plowing macadam! If we work all night we won't turn *two acres*. You reckon we'd kill ourselves any sooner digging rock out at Denver?

And he rolled on his side, pillowing his cheek on his hands.

—It's *all* work, Dave, Isaac answered, keeping his temper.

He unchained the oxen, got them up, and drove them, yoked, to the stream-side to drink and feed. He came back, wrestled the plow over on its side, and examined the share. The steel plate was still bright and clean, it scoured well, but the point, which had been knife-sharp, had blunted in the morning's work, with many little knicks along the edge. He left Kilbourn to make himself dinner and tend the team and trotted back to camp for his horse.

He rode the mare hard but was two hours getting to the town and back with a file borrowed from Colonel Titus. After that they pulled the plow out after every furrow and filed the share sharp, but with sunset coming they had finished only six more furrows, something over an acre, one way, for the day's work. They staked the oxen in reach of the stream, walked back to camp, and ate their fried meat in the dark, by the light from the stove.

The grasses with their interwoven mass of roots hidden below the surface were tenacious, but it was the earth itself that resisted the plow. There had been no rain to count since the downpour that caught them at their camp west of Leavenworth at the beginning of the month. Isaac in his letters home had several times remarked on the wonderful travel afforded by the dry Kansas road, to the dispraise of muddy Iowa, but what he had witnessed that spring was the start of an extended dry cycle, a *drouth* people were calling it, the first since the territory opened. Now the exposed earth between grass clumps had baked in hard, unyielding plates that when cut by the plow cracked up but did not pulverize; the earth held together, granular, compacted, dry, to plow-depth, a foot.

By the end of June they had succeeded in turning something over twelve acres of the colonel's land, a rate of not much over an acre a day even though most days they were up and at work by sunup and went on till dark. Kilbourn sourly figured they'd get on as well by hand, with shovel, mattock, pick, the mining tools Isaac had traded for at Leavenworth; or leaving the team in camp and hitching each other to the damnable plow—. He was joking and discouraged, but there was indeed something wrong with Isaac's oxen. In the ten days they had grown listless and heavy-headed, they did not relish the nourishing grass, and their ribs showed through. Isaac, remembering an epidemic that in his boyhood swept through the nation's horse population and as far west as frontier Iowa, wondered if the oxen weren't sick with something of the same. In any case, they were obviously not fit for the work, but if they could somehow get, say, two more yoke of healthy oxen, they might go on; since there were none to be had in the area, they resolved to go back to Lawrence. With borrowed scythes and rakes they cut a load of prairie hay and hauled it to Burlingame, left the team and wagon for Colonel Titus to keep. Titus gave Kilbourn the use of a little piebald Indian pony for his share of the plowing.

They rode back to Lawrence at a steady trot and reached Sam Wood's house by mid-afternoon on the fifth of July; they spent the next morning talking with a cattle dealer Sam recommended and came back discouraged. The only oxen the man stocked were scrawny, half-wild longhorns, not yet full-grown, for which he wanted fifty dollars a yoke. The longhorns had one advantage: they were immune to Texas fever, a disease often fatal to American breeds of cattle and from the sound of it—Isaac inquired discreetly—possibly what his oxen were suffering from; but the cost of two yoke of these beasts, with the yokes besides, would consume most of what they expected to make from plowing, and the animals would take months of training before they began to be useful.

Over supper that night, by way of conversation, Sam Wood mentioned a dilemma of his own. With a partner at Topeka he had been buying corn as agent for the Indian office, buying it on the ground since spring, and they now had two thousand bushels stored at Topeka, a little more at other towns along the Kansas River, and more coming as it was harvested. Now, the thing was, all they made on the corn itself was their commission, but where they figured to profit was on the freight contract, hauling the corn to the mouth of the Kansas, where it would be taken by steamboat to whatever tribes it was meant for—not very much less than the cost of the corn itself. Only, now it came to it, it seemed that Russell & Majors, the big Leavenworth freight company, had huge military contracts that had pretty well taken up all the wagons and oxen and teamsters in the territory, and those left were so high-priced it looked as if they'd lose money on the freight. Now, if they defaulted on the contract, they'd never get another—and who knows what troubles besides—

—You ever think about flatboating it? Isaac broke in and, when Sam looked blank, explained: You know, big, wide, square-end scow that you can knock together with rough lumber, like the emigrants used coming down the Ohio—and some still do use, from settlements up the Mississippi—haul just about anything, tons and tons, and you can't beat it for cheap. You take three or four men to steer and just kind of go with the current—

—You ever done any of that—flatboating?

—I took a lumber raft down the Mississippi, Rock Island to Saint Louis, three hundred and thirty miles—same idea, only about a hundred times as big. Father and I had a lumber business over the river from Davenport, next to the boatyard, till we got caught in the panic—

—They build these things at this boatyard?

—You don't hardly need a boatwright for such work—just stock lumber and ordinary carpentry, if you've got an idea what you're after—.

They sat at the table alone after the dishes were cleared away, talking. Sam wanted to know how big the boat would be, how much lumber it would take and how long to build, how big a crew, what kinds of tools and hardware—. Isaac penciled a sketch on a scrap of paper, made a list of the lumber, and gave him an answer of sorts, a couple of thousand feet, two tons, more or less, with the nails and hardware; depending on the quality of stock Mr Holliday, Sam's partner, had to offer at his mill at Topeka. Isaac, neither offered nor accepted, was taking it for granted that the flatboat would answer Sam's problem and that if it was built, he would take charge and pilot it down the river, and in the end Sam wrote a letter for him to take to Topeka in the morning, enclosing the sketch, and, well—if his partner agreed—if they could come to a mind as to wages—.

In the morning Kilbourn rode with Isaac to Lawrence, guarding his skepticism, but rafting this Kansas ditch, he granted, couldn't be any more fool's work than trying to plow the adobe at Burlingame. The river was generally reckoned navigable, meaning that there were men with hopes of running regular steamboats on it, but the evidence was inconclusive. The road as far as Lecompton ran close by the river. They rode down to look. From the water marks on the shelving, sandy banks the river seemed to be low by a foot or two. On the bends and at places halfway across there were long, dry, rounded mounds of sand and mud sticking up like dolphins' backs, with uprooted trees clustered high at the upstream ends but no grass or clumps of willow holding them together—not islands forming but sandbars exposed by low water. Kilbourn spat over his pony's rump.

—Jackrabbit, he said with a laugh, you reckon you could run a *row*boat down that puddle of lukewarm piss? Why, I believe I could skip across it and never dampen my boots, like the children of Israel with Pharaoh's army whooping at their heels.

—It don't look any worse for a flatboat than places on the Mississippi for a raft of logs, Isaac said. And don't blaspheme—it aint lucky.

—Now come on, Jack! said Kilbourn, irritated in turn. You can see that thing aint no more to the Mississippi than a catfish to a whale, and—

—Well, how *else* we going to get money for our land? Isaac shouted back, leaning close. Can't *plow* in this drouth—can't afford another *team* to help. *You* got some idea you're keeping back? And when Kilbourn answered nothing, he withdrew, turned, and kicked his horse into a fast trot.

They stopped again a few miles farther and descended the bank. Isaac waded his horse in to her knees to drink and, gripping the reins, leaned far over in his saddle to dip his hat.

—Listen, Jack, said Kilbourn seriously. You ever built one of these flatboats? D'you really know *how* to build one?

—No, and yes, Dave, said Isaac, smiling. I never built one, but I've studied some and I think I know. And anyhow, it's not like building a house or a real boat, you just make these things to go one way and knock to pieces when you get there, for the lumber.

It was late afternoon when they reached Topeka. Cyrus K. Holliday had his office in a small, white frame building that stood by itself on the packed bare earth of a street—there were no sidewalks—at the top of the riverbank half a mile back from the bridge. It was not hard to find. There were not yet more than a hundred buildings in the town, possibly a thousand people, scattered along the river; and the hotel and meeting hall that had been home to the Free-State legislature during the town's intermittent service as territorial capital. As much as Jim Lane, Holliday's circumstances had contrived to bring him west at an opportune moment for making himself useful; or so Sam had told it, as much as he knew of his partner, that morning over breakfast. Holliday had taken a hand in developing a small railroad in western Pennsylvania. When it was bought up by a Philadelphia company, he came away with twenty thousand dollars at about the time Kansas was opening to settlement and traveled out to see what could be done with his money; met Charles Robinson and became the active partner in founding Topeka as a counterweight to Slave-State towns a few miles distant on either side—chose the site, laid it out, served as its first mayor; and took, besides his shares and lots, a sizable tract adjoining the town, on the edge of which he put up his office building. His name, C. K. Holliday, was painted on a sign hung out front, and some of his business—land agent, loans, insurance—and, on the door: *Office. Atchison & Topeka Railroad.* That spring in the territory's Legislative Council—its appointive upper house—Holliday had put through the railroad's charter, so far without much result beyond a modest sale of stock to the incorporators. Isaac tied his horse and went in, Dave Kilbourn diffidently following.

The house on the ground floor was a single room of moderate size divided by a railing. A clerk sat at a small desk to one side at the front.

Two men were at a table behind the railing, talking. Both looked up as Isaac's boot-heels clumped across the bare floor. One was the man he and Fred shared the table with at the St Louis hotel, the fleshy curves of his face repeated in the globed contours of his balding skull, bushy side-whiskers getting gray, a gentle smile of practiced benignity but not of recognition; not a man to retain the memory of a young stranger's face unless connected with profit.

—Mister Holliday! Isaac addressed the other man, letting himself through the gate.

—Sir!

—I rode over this morning from Sam Wood at Lawrence.

Holliday's lips at the name crimped in a small smile, like a wink. The motionless eyes gazed steadily at Isaac's.

—He thought I could help you both out in your business. He's written you a letter—. Isaac brought it out, then held it, nodding at the other man. Is this gentleman interested in your business with Mister Wood?

The smile flickered again. Holliday's arms lay along the arms of the chair, his heavy body erect against the back, motionless yet suggesting force, a moment of utter repose between moments of violent, calculated movement.—This is my associate, Mister Pomeroy, he said.

—I believe I'd prefer to discuss Mister Wood's business in private. The steady gaze broke off from Isaac's. Pomeroy got up, still serenely smiling, excused himself, and glided toward a chair beside the clerk's desk. Isaac dropped the envelope on the table, sat down, and laid his hat politely on the floor.

Holliday gestured at Kilbourn, leaning on the railing, uninvited.—Who's that? he said.

—My partner Dave Kilbourn, Mister Holliday, Isaac said, come out from Iowa together. We're both in this.

Again the eyes clamped on his, lingered, broke off. He reached in a pocket for a cigar, bit the ends, spat, lighted up. He read the letter slowly, studied Isaac's sketch.

—I've got an interest in a steam mill down below the town, Holliday said at length. Oak and hickory mostly, some walnut—and the damned cottonwood. We cut it on the Kaw half-breed allotments over the river, don't cost us much, I can tell you—the smile flicked across his lower face. That do for this job?

—Hardwood's heavier, a little more trouble to work, but—sure, we can use it. Maybe we don't have to double-plank the bottom.

—All right. Holliday leaned forward, arms on the table. So what do *you* get?

—Why, said Isaac with a smile, I get your boat built for you and I get it piloted safe to Wyandotte and your corn delivered according to your contract—

—What do you *want?* the voice growled.

—I *want* money, Isaac said—to pay off my land at the Land Office—maybe something over to take us on to Denver and see what we can do about gold—

—You can *borrow* that, on the land, anyway.

—Not for me, sir. I'll pay cash and keep the interest in my pocket.

—Nobody pays cash, Holliday testily rejoined. If you got the money, get yourself a warrant. I could let you have a quarter-section warrant for, oh, say ninety cents an acre, a hundred forty-five dollars let's call it, do you the favor.

—I'll think about it—and I thank you—when the time comes. But I still got some money-getting to do first.

Holliday reflected for a time.—We had flatboats on the Allegheny when I was a boy. I know my way around a flatboat, I can tell you.

Isaac shrugged.—I expect you do, Mister Holliday, he said. But I expect you've got things to do with your time besides sawing lumber and pounding nails—

Holliday's fingers lifted from the table, thumped flat again.—All right! he said. How much?

—Well, now, Isaac said, thinking it out. You've got two thousand bushels, eleven hundred, twelve hundred hundredweight, say. And it's seventy-five or eighty miles by the river—say your contract is fifty cents a hundred. He paused but the steady eyes answered nothing. We'll do it for twelve percent of your contract, he said finally. And you supply the lumber, hardware, cordage, and such, and three helpers. And the grub for the trip down.

Holliday took his time working the numbers through his head.—I don't like your percentage, sir, he said at last. I'll give you each two dollars a day—and the rest as you said.

Isaac pondered in turn.—Make it three for me—my idea and the care of it, and I'll take it. *And* the stage fare back from Wyandotte at the end, of course.

The thought of paying the crew's fare back launched Holliday on a different tack: he wanted the boat returned to Topeka for the second load—it was agreed they would not try to carry more than a thousand bushels on the first trip. Isaac doggedly explained: the boat would be tricky enough taking downstream but the absolute devil to get up again, even against the placid late-summer current of the Kansas River, might take two weeks, more in labor than it would cost to build again, and besides, he planned to sell the lumber for him in the end, forty or fifty dollars' worth, it should be. And not only that—if he meant to reuse the boat they'd have to build it differently and stronger in the first place, more expense. Holliday sat immobile, eyes fixed, hardly listening; it was a point, having made it, that he was determined to win. Isaac at length let him have it.

—Mister Holliday, Isaac said, if a man hires my judgment, I'm bound to give it, but it aint for me, I guess, to tell you how to spend your money. And if you want that boat back at Topeka, why then, I'll tell you, I'll get it back here for you if we have to carry it along the bank on our backs. Fair enough? And stood up, reached his hand, and the older man took it in a quick shake, with another of his smiles, and it was done.

They built the flatboat at the sawmill Holliday had bought into on the riverbank, with three laborers from the mill to help with the carpentry and serve as crew. Isaac had planned it thirty-two feet long, sixteen wide, with four-foot sides, using full-length lumber, and an open-sided, roofed-over cabin cross the stern. They laid the heavy bottom planks out on cottonwood rollers and when the boat was finished levered it into the water, moored it to stakes driven into the bank, and left it overnight for the planks to swell tight. It had taken them five days to put together. Cyrus Holliday rode down every day to look, sitting his horse at a little distance, silent, for half an hour at a time, and departed without a word. They mounted a long steering oar at the rear of the cabin roof and sweeps on the forward gunwales made of hickory saplings with cottonwood boards for blades. With the sacks of corn loaded, Holliday came back, shook Isaac by the hand, offered his mechanical smile, and wished him luck. The river had dropped another half a foot since they started.

The corn made up in four hundred man-size sacks weighing a hundred and forty pounds each. They stopped at Lecompton and Lawrence and took on another hundred. Even so the boat drew hardly a foot—it seemed it was overbuilt; but they managed to run aground nearly every day and spent hours poling and levering the boat off the bars. They were six days getting to the warehouse at Wyandotte at the mouth of the river. They unloaded, lay over the rest of the day and night, and started back. They tried rowing, poling, but made little progress; as far as Lawrence they brought the flatboat up with a long rope run to the bank and Kilbourn and the mill hands towing, Isaac on the boat steering, and after that were able to row, but at a rate of painful slowness. It took them eleven days. Holliday wanted to know if they'd taken the corn to St Louis—or Memphis—*New Orleans*, for God's sake—and Isaac soberly answered him:—Mister Holliday, he said, I *told* you a flatboat aint made for going upriver, but you wanted it back, and I said I'd bring it back, and I did. You got what you wanted. Holliday instructed him to break the boat up and sell the lumber after delivering the second load; and brought out his purse and counted out the gold for the fare back.

A week later the stage deposited the crew in front of the Eldridge House. Isaac and Kilbourn, blanket rolls over shoulders, climbed the dusty road up the river bluff to Holliday's office to collect their pay. Isaac let himself through the wicket and laid the receipt for the corn on the table in front of Holliday, with forty dollars in bank notes from the sale of the rough lumber and hardware.

—There's the lot, Mister Holliday, he said. We're done.

Holliday studied the paper, then folded it carefully and placed it in his billfold. He went to a safe in an alcove at the back of the room, brought out his cash box, and counted out their money.

—I was thinking, Holliday said with a ducking glance from under his brows. Your first offer, doing the job for a percentage—

—But you made money all the same, said Isaac with a grin. Didn't you?

—Some, Holliday admitted. Didn't lose, anyway. But see, here's the thing—by October we've got another four thousand bushels, if it all comes in. What would you say to taking it on for sixty percent of our contract price and you bear all expenses—we let you have the lumber for the boats for, oh, twenty dollars a thousand—

—Contract still fifty cents a hundredweight?

—Fifty-*one*.

—I'd think about it, Isaac said slowly. Depends how my land turns out, partly. Thing is, the distance is so short, the stage fare just about swallows your profit. Now if we were taking this corn to Saint Louis, say, at a dollar a hundred and shipping the men back by the steamboat—

—There *aint* no market for Kansas corn at Saint Louis, said Holliday with a snort. But you wait. He stood up, towering, slapping one palm with his fist, agitated, for once, by indignation. You just *wait*—this dod-burned Congress gets down to business and gives us our land grant and we get our railroad—why, sir, we'll ship our corn—our wheat, our cattle—to every state in this Union. Now *there's* a future in Kansas for a young man that's got some grit and knows how to do things!

—We had our railroad in Iowa five years ago, Isaac said, I worked on a survey crew. And you're right, it brings money in, but it cuts both ways—in our lumber business we were up against big mills at Chicago, shipping in on the cars and cutting our prices. And then of course the panic—

—All the same, sir, you think about it, Holliday commanded. And one day, our railroad—.

And Isaac promised that he would think, and would write in a month or so when he knew his plans. The qualified promise, given, went into a part of his mind like money in a box, to be taken out again at need, but at twenty-one, with the world before you and the free-

dom of the world, every possibility that comes is only one in an
infinite series, and you do not know that every choice made or not
made, every act, sets a limit to all that follow; but Isaac was a keeper
of promises.

They were at Burlingame by noon the next day. Absalom had
taken it on himself to care for the oxen and they were fat again,
perhaps not sick with the fever after all, but not hearty, either; Isaac
gave him two silver dollars. In the afternoon they drove out to Isaac's
land and camped for a week. The land had changed in their five
weeks away. The grass had grown only a little, not much taller now
than a field of wheat, but in this dry season the seed heads were
already golden-ripe, curing on the stalk; they cut five loads of it and
hauled it to the colonel's barn to pay back the hay he had allowed
Absalom to feed the oxen. Isaac borrowed the colonel's breaking plow
again and for two days worked at breaking sod beside his homesite
where they had cut the bluestem, but after turning two acres the
team again showed signs of giving out and he gave it up. There was
still no rain. The earth turned over in heavy clods with the dry roots
intact. The sun burned day by day in a cloudless sky.

They drove back to Burlingame and for a week enjoyed the colonel's easy hospitality, settling into a routine. Mornings they slept till
the swelling heat in the little upstairs bedroom roused them, drank
coffee in the kitchen with Absalom and his wife Vinnie, and walked
to a pool they had found up Switzler Creek to swim and doze and
sun; in the afternoon they joined Colonel Titus on the porch, watching the Santa Fe traffic over the bridge, chatting, occasionally as suppertime approached joining him in a toddy, though by now his ice
was gone. So they were passing an aimless afternoon when a long-
legged man on a mule came along the road and purposefully up to the
house, tied the reins to a lower rail, and clumped up the steps with a
Colts pistol in his belt.

—Colonel Titus, the man said with a nod. My name's McKendrick.

And threw down a four-foot stake, rough-squared and pointed at
one end. The colonel turned it over with a reach of his boot-toe but
did not get up. The name cut in one side was legible: D. Kilbourn,
with a date in June.

—One of you Kilbourn? the man asked in accents of Tennessee. I
heard you was stoppin with the colonel.

Kilbourn blinked and gave a quick little nod.

—Now, the strange thing is, McKendrick continued—passing
strange—I come out in April, stake my land, file my papers, and come
home to fetch my wife—and when I get back, I find your name on my
corners. And what *I* want to know is, how it got there. Look like
claim-jumpin to *me*.

Kilbourn shuffled his chair backward. The man's hand touched the handle of his revolver.

—There *wasn't* any stakes! Kilbourn shouted. Nor any house or foundation or working of the ground—

—You took my land!

—You better have proof, McKendrick, said Colonel Titus, rocking back in his chair.

—I filed my statement, paid my fees. Here—

He brought out a paper from his shirt, handed it to the colonel, who examined it, passed it back.

—That description's Sac and Fox land, the colonel said. You can't pre-empt that land, Mister McKendrick—nor Mister Kilbourn neither. It's not up for sale. You both made a mistake.

—When I was home I heard they's goin to be a law you *can* pre-empt, McKendrick said. And—and they took my money at the Land Office and give receipt, it's *mine*—and—Colonel Titus, I aint no quarrel with you, but—any man try to take my claim, I'll *kill* him.

The colonel stood up.—That's no way to talk, Mister McKendrick, in my house, about my guest. He took a slow step forward; the Tennesseean backed toward the steps. Not before a justice of the peace, and witnesses, and the mayor and proprietor of this town—

—You heard me, Colonel, McKendrick said. I'll *do* it—and aint no jury in this county'd convict.

—Well! the colonel said. These gentlemen are going to Lecompton to see about their land. Your claim's what you show, you'll hear no word of complaint from them, or me, or any man.

Colonel Titus took McKendrick's hand and shook it. The Tennesseean nodded, slowly went down the steps, released his mule and rode away.

The colonel sat, banged his mug on the floor of the porch for Absalom to come and refill.—Mister Kilbourn, he said finally, it seems you've got a little difficulty about your land.

—Dave! Isaac said. Was that man's land marked, any way at all?

—It's what I said. I din't *find* any stakes.

Kilbourn got up and went into the house.

Over supper Colonel Titus proposed that they leave in the morning for the Land Office at Lecompton so that Isaac could file on his land. Isaac asked what he thought of Holliday's offer of a land warrant for a hundred and forty-five dollars. The colonel said it was fair, worth going out of the way to collect—I don't doubt he's got some reason, he observed, but when Cy Holliday offers a favor, you'd best take it and keep your questions to yourself. Afterward, sipping coffee, they conducted a little friendly dicker over Isaac's mare and settled on a hundred and twenty-five dollars. With that, the money earned in the summer, and what remained from his travel money, he could pay for the land in full, using Holliday's warrant, and would have enough over to equip his farm, build a cabin, and for forty or fifty dollars replace Regina with an Indian pony. Or, if he went flatboating for Holliday again in the fall, he would have money to put on another quarter-section somewhere as a speculation, or, say, go home for the winter and come back in spring to start real farming for himself—if he could manage to get the land broken without killing his cattle doing it; if the rain, finally, would come. Colonel Titus was expecting his niece early in September.

Lecompton was not much different in appearance from Lawrence or Topeka, except that the little frame stores and houses scattered over the site had mostly never seen paint and already had weathered silver; but with the feeling of urgency and purpose conferred by the presence of the Land Office—buggies and farm wagons lined the streets, horses clustered at the hitching rails, men walked in groups or gathered on the hotel porch, talking land and money, and half the stores seemed occupied by lawyers writing up pre-emptors' filing papers for land and loaning the money to pay for it—customarily in return for half the claim or, if the borrower could repay in cash, at the bargain rate of two percent a month. Colonel Titus advised Isaac to hire a lawyer for his business and recommended Bob Stevens, with his office in a twelve-foot-square building opposite the Land Office. The lawyer worked from an open window at the side of the house where a line of men waited in the sun for him to prepare certificates of location to be signed by the Land Office register (as the official was called), the first step toward claiming land. The colonel stepped to the head of the line, politely lifted his dusty silk hat, and invited Stevens to take supper with them. They drove to the hotel, took rooms, and settled on the porch to talk and wait.

Robert Smith Stevens had had the luck to be born the son of a minor Democratic politician in a town not far from Buffalo in the far northwest of New York. In the election of 1856 he joined his father in campaigning earnestly for Buchanan and Popular Sovereignty against the new Republican Party. In the course of that campaign, he met Wilson Shannon, lately forced out as governor of Kansas Territory, who persuaded him to come to Kansas and join him in a law partnership at Lecompton. As a Democrat on principle and a Free-Stater by inclination and his judgment of the territory's practical needs, he managed by affability, intelligence, and commanding good looks to make friends on both sides of the struggle. The people of Lecompton promptly elected him mayor; like Cyrus Holliday, he became an early railroad promoter, in alliance with Charles Robinson. Promptly at six Bob Stevens came striding down the crowded

street and led the way to a table in the dining room as if he, not
Colonel Titus, were the party's host. There was hump steak on the
menu, a novelty to Kilbourn and Isaac—fresh buffalo meat brought in
by Delaware hunters from herds that in this droughty summer were
no more than a long day's ride to the west—and all ordered it. Stevens briskly got down to what Isaac wanted but was skeptical when
he heard the land description; he had looked some in that part of the
county himself and had it in mind there wasn't an unclaimed section
to be had.

—Now, *Bob*, said Colonel Titus, I saw it myself—not a mark, not a
sign any man ever set foot.

—Colonel, said Stevens, you know that don't mean a thing.

—Maybe it just got overlooked somehow and young Pride here was
lucky.

—Possible, said Stevens with a frown. I'll tell you—just let me
search the records first, fee's ten dollars, save you time, trouble, and
expense in the long run, and if it's really clear—why then, you're a
lucky young man indeed. I'll get you your answer tomorrow.

Their business completed, Stevens listened politely while Isaac told
of what they'd done since arriving in Kansas but showed real interest
when he came to flatboating and that story led back to the Rock
Island lumber mill. Stevens had a new contract with the government
coming up in the spring, quite the biggest thing yet: the government
had a scheme for selling off Sac and Fox trust lands—new treaty,
going through for sure in the fall—and taking the money and building houses for the entire tribe on what was left. A whole town it
would be, five or six hundred houses, and schools no doubt, a town
hall or some such—haul in lumber and brick, hire carpenters and
masons—oh, a *very big thing indeed.*

—Now there's money to be made in this building business and no
mistake, Stevens continued. But the great thing, the *really* big thing, is
getting in first on this Indian land that's *not* up for sale—and quite
strict about it, too—*beautiful* land on the Osage River that the fool
Indians don't know what to do with. What do you say to that?

He held up a hand as Isaac started to answer and went on.—Now
here's the thing, Stevens said in some excitement. You and your partner here, you run this thing for me while I get on with my business,
and I'll let you in on a piece of the profit. But just remember, it's the
land—the land's the real start, make your fortune before you're done.

Isaac pushed his plate away and leaned back, thinking. Finally,
instead of answering—Mister Stevens, he said, it's a wonderful idea,
I'm grateful you'd think of me, but I just don't understand. Here I'm
not in Kansas three months yet and every man I meet's got some huge
job he wants me to take on, buckets of money in it. What is it? There

so much money around? Don't anyone here know how to *do* anything?

—Oh, there's money all right, Stevens said, dropping his voice as if to impart a secret. The *money's in the land*—no limit to that hardly, only most of them come out here don't know, no more than an Indian, how to get it out. They take their claim, they plant some corn, feed a pig or two, a cow, hunt a little, maybe, and sit there waiting for the land to make them rich—oh, they've got a *living*, but they've got no money. And town promoters—begging your pardon, Colonel— aint much better, take a square mile of prairie, stake it in lots and print some adver-*tize*ments, and think they're sitting on the next state capital, till another comes along and it goes flat as a dewberry in August. Yes, *sir*, Mister Pride, you're right about *that*. If you know how to do a thing, and you *will* do it, you've come to the place. And make your fortune while you're at it!

Afterward, Isaac went out alone and walked the streets, shoulders hunched, hands in his pockets. He passed half a dozen saloons or dance houses, yellow lamplight flooding out the open doors, pianos playing, sometimes with violins or cornets, tunes that were somehow bent out of shape and not quite recognizable; and girls' voices, waiter-girls in their short skirts, laughing, joining in the songs, the words lost. He made his way down toward the empty riverbank. Pigs grunted and snuffled in the darkness of the side streets. Dogs quarreled over garbage. A large black rat ran across his path, paused, looked up with glinting, insolent eyes, and ran on. The river here ran nearly straight, west to east, for six miles. The moon, half-full, was up, laying a track of hammered silver between the lightless banks. He found a sawed-off stump and sat.

Stevens had offered him another possibility. He tried to think it out. He'd done enough building so he knew he could, though this was different, a crew to hire and manage, get em to do it the way you wanted. But a whole town—five or six hundred houses, he'd said— exciting, no question, like God taking in hand to build the universe, even if it wasn't really yours and you never lived in it. Something more too: maybe he was obliged. The men in Congress and the government, talking so grand of the good of the Indian, and Bob Stevens and all the others out on the Plains doing the job: just talk, makes em feel good; never go to a real man like Seoskuk—Black Hawk's son, Isaac remembered him so earnestly hearing out his father's temperance lectures all those years ago—or even Keokuk, dead now and left a favorite son in the chief's job—never go and *ask*, or if they do, they don't listen for the answer. Isaac smiled. Maybe he'd have to try town-building after all, not for Stevens' sake but for the Indians'; and for his own, another note he could lock away safe in the strongbox of promises, to take out and collect on as need arose.

Yet he had not been able to ask the question he meant: what was it these men wanted in him, Sam Wood and Colonel Titus, Holliday and now Bob Stevens—and farther back, that cavalry captain, even Jim Lane in the moment of a handshake? And why did he resist? Why not just take it, let it go, do it, go on to the next? What did he want? Something in him was aimed like a bullet at a target, ready to shoot. He had no feeling where it aimed or what or who would pull the trigger. Then Dave Kilbourn, strange too: complaining, foul-mouthed, not quite to be trusted, maybe, when it counted—he had not asked again but there was something wrong about that Tennesseean and his land—yet they got on well enough, there was none of this feeling of misgiving and resistance he had for other, older men.

Isaac thought little about the land or the doubt Bob Stevens had meant to plant. He thought it his. It did not occur to him that he might not get it.

Stevens found him at the hotel a little after noon. Isaac was alone, Kilbourn and the colonel gone off severally to look around. They went into the bar and ordered bottled ale.

—It's like I thought, Stevens said. Your quarter's taken.

Isaac set his glass down hard.—That just can't be! he said. Mister Stevens, I swear—there wasn't a sign of anyone settling, boundary markers or a house or anything the law says—I put all those in myself, plowed some, cut some hay—

—I don't doubt you, but that don't count. This man's got affidavits says he's built a house—with *windows*, mind you—planted corn, and brought his family out. *That's* law. And paid by warrant, got preliminary title, and should have patent in four or five months.

—That's just wrong. Aint there something an honest man can *do?*

—Course there is. You get affidavits of your own, file suit, motions, cross-motions, discoveries, petitions to the court—meantime, this land's sold a hundred times over, and your own *grandchildren* won't live to see the end of it.

Isaac's fists collapsed on the table.

—Or, said Stevens, you can hunt through Kansas till you find this man and offer what the market's worth, say eight dollars an acre, and he takes you up, and you've got a deed you can take and record at the county seat—and the quarter's yours, and your heirs and assigns forever. Amen. . . . Or, finally, Mister Pride, Stevens continued, you can show some sense—you've got a military warrant, haven't you? Well, you go out twenty or fifty miles farther west, land as good as Osage County, better maybe, and roads and towns coming in a year or so and railroads—and you mark it out and plant your warrant same as this man did—. And that's all there is, it's yours. You know they've got a new law, just this summer? Says you don't have to wait till the land's surveyed or counties organized—you can pre-empt anywhere on the face of this territory, and no man or official say you nay.

Isaac took the rest of his beer in slow sips, finished.—Mister Stevens, he said, what's the name of this liar that's stolen my land? I'd like to remember it.

—Got it here somewhere. He riffled the leaves of his note pad, found the place with his finger. David L. Payne, he said. Ever hear of him?

VII

The Hunting Party

When Colonel Titus returned from Lecompton with Isaac and Kilbourn, he found a much-delayed letter from his niece waiting at the post office. By now she would already have taken the boat from St Louis to Kansas City and would come on to Lawrence by stage, was to be there in two days' time, on Friday, traveling with a cousin. Niece, the colonel explained, was a convenience for a vague and distant relationship—Marie Bisonnette, orphaned daughter of a cousin of his late wife's, not seen since she was a child, about whom he now felt a certain responsibility, but at least, at eighteen, she was about the right age for a niece. Her traveling companion was the son of a cousin of the colonel's, a young man making a start in his father's grain business—Leonard Eliot, known as Ned; musical, he remembered, but had not seen much of the young man either. The colonel left for Lawrence the next day.

During the summer, while Isaac and Kilbourn were floating corn down the Kansas, Colonel Titus had ordered a mowing machine and two simple horse-drawn rakes from Kansas City and had bought the horses to pull them. The machines were at last delivered and assembled, and the colonel made the young men a proposal: a dollar an acre for cutting prairie hay on his land and hauling it to his barn in Isaac's wagon; he would give them the use of his new team and the machines. Hence, on the morning the colonel left for Lawrence to collect his relatives, Isaac and Kilbourn loaded the implements and drove to the claim, leading the two horses. In a week they had cut something over sixty acres, as much, Isaac judged, as the mow of the colonel's small barn would hold, and were ready to start hauling to Burlingame—but with the distance from town they would be lucky if they moved two loads a day. They took the canvas top off the wagon, removed its frame of hickory bows, and built up the sides with cottonwood saplings cut along the creek.

The afternoon they drove in with their ponderous first load, Colonel Titus, sitting in his accustomed place in the shade of the porch, boots up on the railing, jumped up, waved his hat, and shouted to them to come on up. Isaac left Kilbourn with the oxen and climbed the steps. The colonel was calling through the open front door of the house.

A tall, languid young man came out, fair-haired, with bushy sidewhiskers of a reddish cast connecting with a mustache of the same indefinite color, and offered his hand; Ned Eliot. He wore a linen suit like the colonel's, but with a difference; on his lithe frame it hung creaseless and elegant.

—And this, said the colonel, is Marie, spreading his arms to take Isaac by one hand and the girl by the other as she stepped through the doorway, rustling in a gown of pale green silk.

Isaac tucked his hat under his arm, wiped his hand on his trouser leg, took hers and held it for a moment.—I'm all in a sweat, he said, apologizing, pitching hay on the wagon and then driving it in, in the heat of the day—Miss—

—Bisonnette, she supplied, slowly and distinctly. Marie Bisonnette —a soft voice, lifting and then dropping on the precise final syllable. A slender, oval face of the darkness women call olive, outlined by black hair drawn tight, wide eyes that looked back on a level with his own, unblinking: he dropped his eyes, released her hand, and took a step back.

—I've been telling the young folks about you, the colonel boomed. They'd enjoy riding out on the prairies, with you and your partner, show em land never touched by plow—not an old man like me—

—I have ridden your horse, only around the village, Marie said. She is lovely—*Regina*, a beautiful name, I should love to let her out and see her run. I am so sorry you had to give her up.

—You needn't feel sorry on my account, Miss—Bees-o-net—she smiled encouragement as he carefully repeated her name. The colonel did me a turn, buying when I needed money to get my land. And anyhow, I'd been thinking of getting an Indian pony.

—We should enjoy riding out together, she said. You could show us your camp, where you cut the hay.

—I'd enjoy that too, he said, but not on a borrowed horse. And not till we've got this hay in.

—Won't you sit and join us in a toddy? the colonel suggested. Absalom!

Isaac hastily excused himself, saying they had the wagon to unload, shook hands again, and darted down the steps. Kilbourn roused himself from the bank beside the road, prodded the oxen into movement, and they started up the lane to the barn.

—That this niece from Saint Louis? Kilbourn asked, and Isaac nodded. And her rich cousin?

—I guess so.

—Not what I call pretty. I like a bird with a little more meat on the bone.

—Someday—Isaac said. *Someday,* Dave, you're going to say more than I can put up with.

Kilbourn as usual ignored the rebuke.—What was all the talk?

—They wanted us to go out riding. I said we had to pitch hay.

—You can speak for yourself, Jack. I'm sick of hay-making already.

—How *else* we going to do what we promised and get our dollar an acre? Isaac said with a shake of his head and a snort.

The barn was built into the slope behind the house, with stalls for the horses and cattle below and the hay mow above, and a door at each level. They got the wagon backed onto the hay floor and Isaac climbed up and started pitching the hay down, and Kilbourn worked with his fork, moving the hay back along the walls of the barn. They worked easily together, to the same rhythm. And-bend-and-*push*-and-a-*toss*, ma-rie, ma-*rie*-bison-*nette*. Her voice sang the name while he worked, a musical phrase heard at a distance but lined out and complete, coming to a cadence, and the labor of his flesh was the chorus, answering: *Marie Bisonnette.*

—Hey there, Jack! Kilbourn broke in on him, leaning on his fork. You tryin to work yourself into a Kansas ague? Slow her down some before I melt away. . . .

Isaac woke in the tent before light the next day. He dressed in silence, feeling for the clothes piled on his boots by the tent flap, dropped a handful of hard biscuits in his coat pocket, and knelt beside Kilbourn.

—Dave! he said aloud, shaking him by the shoulder, but Kilbourn only rolled away, drawing the blanket tight. Dave, I'm taking the day off, going to find me a horse. You get some rest too.

He went out into the gray light. Both horses had pulled their stakes and wandered down the creek. He ran to catch them and led them back, restaking both with heavy blows of the mallet. He had already decided that the smaller one, a black with a lozenge of white on his forehead, would have to do, but neither of the colonel's drays was impressive even for the light work they had been doing, certainly not for riding. He had fitted the bit and bridle and tied the long reins short when Kilbourn came out of the tent in his undershorts and scuffed his bare feet across the trampled grass to stand beside him.

Kilbourn straightened up, yawned deeply, and spat.—Where'd you say you're going?

—Down into the Sac and Fox country—on the map the Agency's only about twenty-five miles down the river. I aim to get me a pony cheap.

—So what am I supposed to do, load that wagon by myself?

—You could comb your hair, go into town, and help the colonel entertain his kin, Isaac suggested with a smile.

—And hold their horses like a hostler? Go to hell. And Kilbourn turned and went back to the tent.

Three or four miles south, the little stream crossed the unmarked border of the Sac and Fox reservation and, cutting through the low bank, made its placid entrance into Switzler Creek. From there it was only a matter of following on down till it joined the Osage and a few miles farther, where the map showed the headquarters of the Indian agency.

In the course of the morning Isaac passed half a dozen, little windowless shanties hardly bigger than a pigpen, with low chimneys of sticks and mud, but set back from the creek bank on high ground with a long view upstream and down—the kind of camp a trapper would knock together for a winter hunt, all now with their roofs fallen in, doors hanging open, abandoned when the beaver—if it had been a beaver stream—and the other game gave out. He stopped and went into one: the human smell, must and decay and excrement, contained and concentrated, wrapped him like a ghost; mosquitoes, which outside the steady prairie wind kept off, rose singing from the bare mud floor and followed him out into the light.

Toward noon he came to a small stream entering from the west at a wide bend of Switzler Creek, still four or five miles, he reckoned, from where the agency was supposed to be. He waded the horse halfway across, pulled it up and let it drink. He took another of the biscuits from his pocket, crushed it between his palms, and picked at the fragments, looking around. A quarter-mile ahead, enclosed in an ox-bow of the creek, there seemed to be people living, the first he'd come to: a double cabin facing east, behind it on the flat bottomland a log barn, cows grazing an acre or two of prairie pasture outlined by a post-and-rail fence, a considerable field, ten acres perhaps, of corn golden-ripe for the cutting; a neat little picture of a farm in the making, prospering on someone's parlor wall. Isaac dug his heels and the horse splashed forward to the bank, kicking at the water with its clumsy feet.

As he passed in front of the cabin a man stepped out from the shadow of the breezeway, waving a straw hat. Isaac swung the horse and rode over to him. A small dark boy ran out from the door of the cabin, reached up and caught the bridle. Isaac vaulted down. The man came toward him, arms outstretched, smiling: hawk-nosed, skin burned dark by the prairie sun, hair that was still black falling to his shoulders from the hat; thick-bodied with age, moving his heavy legs arthritically across the hammered earth of the yard but holding his back straight. Isaac shook his hand.

—I was wondering, he said. I'm looking for the Indian agency. How far am I?

—Mister Fuller, Indian agent—got farm on Lawrence road. He stepped forward, pointing down the stream. Three miles down, you come to big creek coming in from west, Onion Creek. Go across, come to horse trail south, three more miles it come to road and Mister Fuller's farm. Why you go there?

—I was looking for someone to sell me a pony, figured he'd help.

—I got ponies, boy herding up on prairie—he gestured to the south. You like to buy?

—I'd like to look.

Isaac studied the old man for a moment. Except for the beaded moccasins on his feet he was dressed in citizen's clothes, denim trousers, blue flannel shirt, a sleeveless serge vest hanging open; something in the face stirred him—broad and dark, smooth-skinned but folded and fleshy with age, the straight black hair.—You Saukie? he asked, and the man nodded. I was wondering, Isaac continued, I expect you know a man named Seoskuk, came out here from Iowa, I was thinking, being down here, I'd try to find—

—*I am Seoskuk*, the man said, face unsmiling now.

—Seoskuk! I don't expect you'd remember me—

The old man took a step forward, head thrusting on his neck, eyes narrowed, intently examining.

—You were camped on the beach at the head of Credit Island, Isaac said in a rush, and I came and found you, you gave me a pony, wouldn't let my father pay you any money—Pekatonoke—

The old man wrapped him in his heavy arms, held him tight, and stepped back, hands on Isaac's shoulders, face close.—Little yellow-hair hunter boy, he said, grinning. Father preacher, come tell my young men, mustn't drink *skutah-wapo*.

—Seoskuk, I never thought—

Laughing, Seoskuk released him and strode to the cabin shouting. A young man Isaac's age came out, dressed like his father, a young woman less dark than the men, white perhaps or half-breed, with a little boy clutching at her skirt. The boy who had taken Isaac's horse came running from the barn.

—My son George Black Hawk, Seoskuk said, and the young man obediently stepped forward and took Isaac's hand. Remember little hunter boy, the old man continued, we camp on island—

—Jack Pride, Isaac said, and the young man nodded and withdrew.

—Coming back from hunt in Shaw-hawk country, Seoskuk said, you just little boy yourself, and I give your sister's pony. Got wife now, two boys his own, he said, turning back to Isaac, and he beckoned the young woman forward; she curtsied, and Isaac reached and shook her hand.—Marion Sarcoxie—Delaware woman, father John Sarcoxie, great hunter, live on Stranger River in Delaware country north of Lawrence—guide soldiers all over Plains, guide Frémont across mountains.

Blushing, the girl turned away, gathering the child in her arms.

Seoskuk insisted that Isaac stay and eat. The three men sat at the table in the kitchen half of the cabin, the two small boys crouching against the wall, silent and listening, Marion serving from the stove: a kind of stew of corn and beans, flour-thickened, white-flour biscuits with honey, salted buffalo tongue, sliced and skillet-cooked; the Indians dipped the stew from the pot with buffalo-horn spoons, picked the sliced meat from the plate, bit, and cut mouthfuls with their knives, and Isaac politely imitated them. Seoskuk talked while they ate, not like a white man, making conversation, but gravely giving and getting information, and his son listened, polite and shy. Keokuk, who came with the tribe when it removed to Kansas, was ten winters dead now, but the old rivalries persisted. His son Wunagisäa—like his father's, the name described a fox-like virtue, "leaps up quickly from his lair"—had become the chief recognized by the government, received the tribal annuities, and like his father distributed them to whom he chose while cultivating his reputation for generosity, eloquence, shrewd bargaining with the whites; to whom he was known as Moses Keokuk since turning Christian. Seoskuk, with no longer any followers of his own, had chosen to live at a distance from the agency. Unlike most of the other young men, his son George had attended the agency school for two years, learned to write his name and read, plow, and drive a wagon. The people no longer made big lodges as they had at Saukenuk; a few had built cabins near the agency and planted some, as in the old days, corn and beans and squash, but most had adopted the buffalo-hide tepee of the Plains and moved around, returning to the agency to collect their annuities. The tribe's great summer hunt was no more. Until this summer Seoskuk had still led a few men out after buffalo. Now his son, in fall or early winter when the farm work was done, with two or three others took a wagon to get hides and meat, traded some with the wild tribes. Five years earlier, Seoskuk had led a hundred men and some women far up the Smoky Hill River toward the mountains when they met a large party, maybe two thousand Kiowa, Comanche, Cheyenne, and some others, gathered to destroy all the Eastern tribes coming onto their hunting grounds. The Sac had good rifles, the others bows and a few old muskets and could not get close. The Sac killed two hundred and took scalps, drove the others off and chased them till they scattered; and came home with a herd of ponies to divide. The Sac were still the greatest of all fighters, but fewer every year. Many starved the first winter they came on the Plains, the agent promising rations that did not come, or not enough; then cholera, then smallpox; and whisky, always whisky.

Seoskuk pushed his chair back, finished, with words and with food. Something had been urging his son and now, hesitantly and indi-rectly, he brought it out. The agent said there was to be a council in a month—the whole tribe, commissioners from Washington. Each man was to take land from the reservation, where he wanted, a quarter-section, half-section; the rest would be sold. Those who would not take land in this way were to have a new reservation farther south, among the Creek.

Seoskuk snorted.—Each man on little piece land! All separate—no more tribe, no more Sac. . . .

George nodded politely but that was not what concerned him. A paper: the agent said, if a man was willing to take land, he would have a paper saying the land was his and could not be taken away. Could this be true?

—I expect he's talking about something called a patent, Isaac said. It's signed by the President, tells what the land is according to survey, and says it's yours until you give it to your children, sell it to some-one. It's supposed to keep anyone from coming along and just *taking* your land—unless you want him to have it. . . .

George pondered.—This *patent*, he said. It means I can live on this land forever?

—That's what it means. But it don't mean you can stay if you don't work the land. Look—Isaac stood up, went to the window, pointed out across the Indian's modest fields. You got a good start—got some cows for milk and meat, good field of corn even if there aint no rain. But you want to get it all fenced, then you can get pigs, turn em in when you're finished cutting and it's no work at all, hardly, feeding em—

—What do I want with pigs? George said, looking over his shoul-der.

—Smoke the bacon and hams, salt the meat, and it'll keep you through the winter.

—We *have* meat. When we don't, I hunt.

—Or ones you don't use yourselves, drive to Lawrence or Kansas City and sell—get money.

—What do we want with money? We got house to live in, food—

—You got to have money to build up your land—break more prai-rie every year, fence it, plant it. You don't work your land, people going to crowd in on you and your patent won't mean a thing, they'll take it just the same, somehow. Or you don't make money on your crops to pay your taxes, the state'll get it, sell it out from under. . . .

George frowned. The young white man was telling him more than he could take in.

—Come! Seoskuk said. We look at horses. *No one* going to take our little piece of land.

The old man led them slowly up along the sloping corn patch. At the top he stood still, breathing, swept the straw hat off and wiped at his sweat-rinsed hair. Spread across the grass half a mile off were a dozen dark figures, fifteen, twenty, Seoskuk's herd. A hundred yards off to the right a boy lay in the shade of a solitary tree, unmoving and apparently asleep, a little piebald pony staked nearby. Seoskuk waited, counting over his horses with his eyes, then shouted angrily at the boy. The boy leaped up, released the pony, got on, and rode off to bring the herd in. Seoskuk went on talking to his son.

—My father says, George politely translated, if we were Pawnee that boy be dead and we steal all the herd. The boy is orphan, lives at the agency. We bring him out, teach him to watch horses, but he is lazy, go to sleep.

The boy rode far out, circling, working back and forth, bunching the stragglers, bringing the herd toward them.

—Prairie chicken? Isaac asked, turning to George, and indicated the expanse of grassland. The Indian smiled and nodded. I spent a whole summer when I was little, hunting em to get money for a saddle—for Pekatonoke—country same as this, west of Davenport. Wolves too, black wolves. You get wolves?

George shook his head.—One old one, sometime. They stay west, follow the buffalo.

The boy had brought the horses to within fifty yards, a milling bunch of wild-eyed, tossing heads and flailing tails.

—I have one time hundred pony in my herd, Seoskuk said. Now I am poor—these are all.

Isaac trotted off, looking, trying to distinguish among the excited animals, but all at first sight looked the same, small and wiry, tough, white coats splashed with black or brown; one would do as well as another for what he wanted.

—They all been ridden? Isaac asked as Seoskuk and his son came up behind him.

—All ridden, yes. Not all trained to hunt. You hunt buffalo?

—I hadn't thought—maybe, since I'm so close. You hunt on horseback?

—In old times, George said, tribe hunt together, always on horseback. Now, when I hunt, two or three men only, I hunt on foot till I get meat and hides enough. My father—he smiled—thinks that bad way to get buffalo. For the last one, I ride and kill with pistol, but it scatters the herd. . . .

There was one horse different from the rest, taller, standing unmoved and observant at the back of the crowd, nostrils flaring the air: a creamy golden color all over, as much as Isaac could see, with a pale, silky mane.

—I wouldn't even ask if you'd sell the palomino, he said. But I'm going around for a closer look, if I can get it.

Seoskuk stayed him with a hand on his elbow, gave a nickering call with his lips. The horse, a mare, stepped forward, walked calmly through the circling throng of pintos, and stopped, facing the old man.

—Could I—he said—maybe I could just walk her around some—

Seoskuk gravely nodded. Isaac vaulted onto her back. A tremor went over the mare's body but she held still. With one hand he took a soft grip in her mane, pressed with his heels, and she started forward at a walk. He leaned, swung her in a slow turn, stepped her up to a trot. Behind him the ponies broke away, following, the herd-boy shouted, beat at his pony, but could not hold them. Isaac took his grip with both hands, leaned forward on the horse's neck, and let her out in a full gallop. The pony herd pounded behind him, strung out like a kite tail. He brought her around and started back, slowing to an easy, rhythmic canter, brought her up in front of Seoskuk and his son and slipped off.

—I'm sorry, Isaac said—didn't mean to run her. And your herd following—I should have known she's the leader.

Seoskuk put his arms around the horse's neck, laid his cheek against her velvet shoulder. He stood erect, turned, one hand still touching the mare's foreleg.—You got to have this horse, I think, he said. Great buffalo pony—you hunt, she do everything, you only got to shoot.

—I couldn't take her, Isaac said, too good for what I need. You pick out any of the others, I'll give you thirty dollars, gold.

—No, Seoskuk said, this is true. You goin to ride long ways, ride this horse. True! You call her Singing Bird, got Indian name, but her name now, forever. And I old man, never go to hunt again, never war. . . .

He started down the slope toward the cabin, clucked to the horse and she followed. Isaac and George came after together, slowly. Isaac stopped.—This isn't right, he said. He loves that horse, she's his—or, he can't use her anymore, by rights she's yours.

George shrugged.—You are to have the horse. He wants it, it is the right he sees.

They walked on, they were nearly to the cabin. Seoskuk had gone in. The mare stood facing the open door, head hanging. Isaac dug five gold coins from his pocket, pressed them in George's palm and closed the fingers over them.—That's fifty dollars, he said, he won't take money, but *you* take it, for something *for* him—in a whisper, brother sharing a secret with brother. Or—listen—take it and get you some young pigs to feed on your corn, get some wheat, like I said. It's a kind of fighting. You don't *fight* for your land, they won't let you keep it.

Darkness came before Isaac was halfway back, leading the colonel's plow horse by the reins. A young moon came out and stayed long enough to light him across Switzler Creek and along the stream bank toward camp. He was carried that far, exultant, but burdened too by the beauty of it, before the meaning of the mare's name came back to him. *Singing Bird:* that had been Black Hawk's beautiful wife; Seoskuk's mother.

In the next days, while they worked, Isaac now talked of going on a buffalo hunt when they had finished haying, somewhere farther west. Kilbourn was agreeable. Isaac's plan was for a month of hunting in the cooler weather of early fall, then home to Iowa for the winter. Although he had failed to get land, he had learned something of how it was done and would be money ahead from the summer's work, money by rights for doing something with, if he could think what: fifty dollars in gold and silver and another thirty coming from his share of the haying; and the new horse, worth a hundred in Iowa, maybe much more—not that he had any thought of selling her; and the land warrant bought from C. K. Holliday. At the same time, he had not given up on going to the gold regions, the reports were good again. Kilbourn was willing to talk about that too, if they got an earlier start in the spring, and this time with men they could count on. Just where they would find buffalo now was uncertain. From bullwhackers coming across the colonel's bridge at Burlingame, they heard that the buffalo had come farther in than they'd been seen for years—dry weather and poor grass out on the Plains—and were all around the Council Grove reservation of the Kansas Indians, hardly thirty miles west; others said the main herd was much farther out, at least a hundred miles, or that buffalo this year were scarce, had gone north of the Santa Fe Road—the drought again.

After a week, Isaac took another day off and in the morning rode Singing Bird into town. In the evenings after supper he had ridden her some, but cautiously, half expecting her to run home if given the chance. He had left her a whole day saddled but she had not objected, it seemed she was used to the saddle. He was still learning the things she was trained to. She came to him when he gave the nickering call, she followed him as she had followed the old Indian, waited docilely in place when he gave the command and dropped the reins over her head; she answered to her English name.

Colonel Titus, Ned Eliot, and Marie were still at the dining table, finishing a late breakfast, when Isaac arrived. He took a seat. Absalom brought fresh coffee from the kitchen.

—How're you coming with my hay? the colonel asked.

—First-rate! said Isaac. We'll be done in a week. Then we figure to go on a hunt.

—Buffalo? Just the two of you? And, when Isaac nodded: You'd do better to get up a party—safer. There's been trouble with the wild Indians this summer, emigrants and miners attacked.

Isaac shrugged.—We can look out for ourselves. But it might be fun with a few more. We had jolly times coming across Missouri in the spring, the six of us.

—I should like to join your hunt, Ned Eliot offered. There are others in town—young Schuyler. . . .

Isaac set his cup down. He stood up, grinning.—Listen! he said, I got me a buffalo pony. Come on—you've got to see. And led the way out on the porch. Singing Bird, cropping grass from the side of the road below the house where he'd left her, looked up. Isaac signaled and she came, stopped at the foot of the steps.

—Fine-looking animal, the colonel said. Where'd you find her?

—An old Indian chief I used to know, down in the Sac country. Last week I went down to look for him.

—Looks like an American horse to *me*, the colonel said, and stolen, I'll wager, from Texas—

—Not this one. I've known him since I was a little boy in knee-pants—Black Hawk's son, fine a man as there is—

—*Every* Indian steals horses, they think it's brave. And a man with a string of horses is a rich man in the tribe.

—Colonel Titus, said Isaac hotly, not meaning to be disputatious, sir, but she *aint stolen!* Come here—

The colonel descended the steps, frowning, and stood back. —You look her over, Isaac said. There isn't a mark of a brand anywhere on her hide. And now look at something else—he lifted the mare's foreleg, pointing to her hoof. No shoe, you see? Two or three years old and never been near a blacksmith—an Indian just don't use his horse that way—

—Perhaps I judged hastily, the colonel lamely admitted. And, trying to smile: Why, young man, you restore my faith, almost—the one honest Indian in Kansas!

Marie, who had kept silent, approached and placed one hand gently on the mare's shoulder.—She is very beautiful, she said. What is she called?

—She's got an Indian name, only I don't know what it is. But in English it's Singing Bird. It was—

—A *lovely* name, Marie said, the Indian name could not be more beautiful. Then with a broad smile, as if remembering something: And now you will come riding with us—it will be more interesting. Will you do that? I should like to see you ride her.

—I could ride out with you till dinnertime, till the day gets hot—if Mister Eliot's agreeable. Then I've got to get back to pitching hay.

Marie ran into the house to change, and Eliot sauntered after her. The colonel stumped around to the barn and shouted for Absalom to saddle the horses, Regina and his own big chestnut stallion. The lady's saddle, he observed while they watched the Negro work, had been his wife's, hadn't known what he kept it for—sentiment, of course, something of hers; and was silent, frowning.

—You *did* dispute my word, you know, young man, the colonel said severely. I do not know your Iowa, but there are societies in which that would not be tolerated. You would be challenged.

Isaac flushed but did not at once answer.—I'm sorry, Colonel, if I seemed pert, he said at length. But I only told you the plain truth, and I don't apologize for that. That's how I was brought up. I can't rightly do any other way.

The colonel paced a few steps, returned, hands clasped behind his back.—Perhaps you should learn, he said, bringing his face close, that there are times when a man, whatever he may think, had best say nothing. He turned and marched toward the house.

As Colonel Titus slammed the kitchen door, Marie came dancing around from the front of the house, almost running, with Eliot striding behind her. She had put on her riding habit: a loose-fitting black skirt that showed her ankles, a short jacket buttoned to the neck, a little feathered cap wedged on her forehead. Her cousin was in breeches, high polished boots, a white silk shirt with billowing sleeves. He had a leather riding crop under his arm.

—Is not Uncle Titus riding out with us? Marie asked.

—Seems not. He's peeved with me.

—He will get over it, I expect, said Marie with a complacent little shake of her head.

Absalom waited in front of the two horses, holding the reins. Eliot put his hands on his cousin's waist and lifted her lightly to the saddle, stronger than he looked; mounted.—Where shall we go?

—There's a pool up the creek, Isaac said, my partner and I used to go swimming—little grove of trees around it, cool in the heat of the day.

—Lead on!

They walked the horses abreast through the village, Marie in the middle, and onto the road leading north to Topeka. After a mile Isaac turned off, keeping to the stream bank. The mare stepped high through the belly-deep grass, trotting, wanted to run. For a time he held her in, glancing over his shoulder for the others, but they were keeping up and at length he let her go. The horse drove forward in soaring leaps and he hunched low, only guiding with the reins. Marie on Regina was a couple of lengths behind, moving gracefully but tense, the reins pulled tight. Eliot was far back, hanging on, tossing to the heavy gallop of the colonel's old cavalry plug. Isaac pulled his horse back to a walk and Marie came up beside him.

—Now *that* was exciting, she said, catching her breath.

Ned Eliot came up to them, erect in the saddle as a cavalryman.—I thought she'd run away with you.

Isaac laughed.—She's just fast, I don't know *how* fast. I've never really let her out. . . .

They had come to the grove. They dismounted, tied the horses. Isaac led them through the trees to the place where the creek swelled in a wide bend.—This is the pool, Miss Bisonnette, he said. Ten feet deep. We used to climb out on that branch over the water and drop— and let your breath out and go right to the bottom.

—It *is* lovely, she said. And cool, as you promised. She let herself down and settled with her back against a big oak, crossing her ankles. You must tell me next time you come, she continued. I shall follow, with Uncle's spyglass.

—Miss Bisonnette—Isaac began, and his face went crimson through his tan and he turned away.

—But I hardly think we need be quite so formal, she said. You may call me Marie. And Ned, of course, is Ned, nobody but his dear mother calls him *Leonard*. And she laughed.

—I've had lots of names since I was little, Isaac said, nicknames. But I guess Isaac is the one that sticks. He crouched and plucked a saw-edged blade of grass.

—It must be wonderful, Ned diplomatically suggested, traveling across this open country, camping where you like, going for a swim if you want, hunting.

—It aint really been like that for us yet—Ned—we've used up the whole summer, working at one thing or other, no time at all hardly, just for ourselves. That's why I want to get out on this hunt. Because you're right about the country, it aint *anything* like what you read in the schoolbooks—pretty streams every few miles, and timber, and all the game in the world, once you're past the frontier. Why, with a good horse and gun—

—When do you mean to start? Ned asked.

—Soon's we're done haying, a week or so. I've got a good tent and the team and wagon, food and such, nothing we need to do to get ready.

—Is it very dangerous, do you think, hunting buffalo, Marie asked.

—You read all kinds of things in magazines, Isaac said slowly—whole books, too—men riding after buffalo and the horse falls. Or a wounded bull and he turns and charges, hooks the horse. A lot of that's just stories, I expect, but I don't know, I'd like to see it for myself.

—Is that why? All the young men want to go on the Plains, kill buffalo. I do not understand.

—Marie—I've hunted everything there is, in a day's ride of Davenport—turkeys and all kinds of birds, coon and possum and once in a while a bobcat, and wolves out on the prairie, not that anyone, even Indians, eats em, but aint nothing to beat that fur in a hard winter—and white-tail deer, of course—used to be bear too but I've never seen one: but the buffalo's the biggest and grandest of all, on the whole continent—and the numbers of them, coming across the grassland in the spring like a tide coming up a river—. Oh, now, I think it's something a man's just got to see. . . .

—Oh, said Marie, I understand *that*. But I believe I should be content with looking.

—That's a part of it, all right, Isaac agreed. But see, if you don't do it—go on and hunt the game and take it—you'll never know if you can, if you're capable: don't find out anything about yourself and what you're up to. And then if there's a little risk to it, that's only fair, and another part of it. But once you've done it, maybe—I don't know that I care that much about it anymore, except to get something to eat and kind of keep my practice in—. No, wait, I won't say that either: it's always new, never the same, even if it's just a little catfish swimming along the bank, sucking mud off the bottom—I just *love* it somehow, any way at all—. He stopped himself again, embarrassed.

Marie had unpinned her cap and energetically fanned her face with it. The sun had come overhead, penetrating the big trees with direct light and heat. Ned produced his watch. It was after noon. They rode back at an easy walk, side by side, chatting as they went.

—I could see Uncle was angry, Marie said, but it never lasts. He is like that.

—He shouldn't say things about a man he's never even seen.

—He is really very fond of you, Isaac.

—Do you think so? I got the feeling he's always asking people in off the road—lonely, wants company. Or just curious, maybe.

—He does not bring them in his house or sit them at his table—or give them work or help them find land.

—He just wants me to help him build up his town. Seems like everyone in Kansas has something he wants from me.

—They must all see something special in you, Isaac.

—Then each one's got a different view of it—one wants me on his railroad and another wants me building a town for Indians. He pulled the reins tight, stopped. You know, all the time I was at home, I never had any idea about myself or what I could do. Now I've got a kind of glimmer that maybe I really can do something, but I still don't know what it is. But it's out there somewhere.

With her eyes she followed his gesture across the creek, along the rim of the grassland beyond, beaten smooth by the mid-day sun. Then, with a speculative smile and all the assurance of her eighteen years:—If it is there, I expect you will find it, Mister Pride.

Isaac and Kilbourn finished their haying, packed up their camp, and drove into town to occupy the colonel's spare room once more. Isaac's hunt grew to a party of six. There were Isaac, Kilbourn, and Ned; young Aaron Schuyler, with a wagon and team of his own, whose father had built a house big as the colonel's, using the pale stone quarried from the prairie hilltops, built and operated the grist-mill, and invested money and his name in the nearly finished hotel; Bill Shirley, a portly and dignified young man on his own, with ambitions of becoming a merchant; and Harry Cullum, coming down from Topeka, an accountant Cyrus Holliday had taken notice of and introduced to Colonel Titus. These arrangements took up time. Then the territory's election day was set for the first Tuesday in October, the referendum on the latest Free-State constitution, and the young Kansans had to wait to vote their yes or no or at least see the result. Then Colonel Titus determined on a ball honoring his relatives, the new state constitution, and the hunt, settling on the night before election day. He hired the Schuyler House dining room. The tables were removed, the chairs ranged against the walls. Mrs Schuyler's pianoforte was loaded on a wagon and carried into the hotel; Mr Schuyler could perform dance music on the fiddle. The colonel wrote out formal invitations which Absalom delivered to fourteen Burlingame families and their young people, riding the colonel's cavalry mount. Absalom's wife filled a tin-ware tub with punch; Colonel Titus outfitted him with a starched white mess-jacket to serve it.

After supper on the night of the ball the colonel led his party along the dark street to the Schuyler House, holding a lantern high; Absalom had been sent ahead. All the doors and windows of the hotel were open and the sounds of voices and laughter flooded into the street, then Mr Schuyler's violin overlaid on the thrumming of his wife's piano. Marie in layers of lacy white walked with little skipping, dancing steps as they came nearer and the music sounded clearly through the darkness; the lamplight glistened on her eyes.

Colonel Titus set his lantern on the porch by the front door and led Marie in on his arm. The long room was bright with a hundred candles in the wall brackets. There were pots of flowers, pink and purple and gold, on the table at the far end where Absalom dipped punch and on the wide sills of all the windows. As they came in, the couples swirled around the room to a lively waltz, with throbbing whisper of skirts and slippers on the bare waxed floor.

Isaac stayed by the door, watching. There were polkas, a mazurka, more waltzes, a galop, then something someone said was a new dance called the schottische that no one knew how to do. Marie and Ned started it out and others followed: something like a waltz, with many turns, but faster, and something like a polka, with much stamping of feet; joyous to see and yet with a terrible sadness hidden in the music. Isaac made his way along one wall of the room, keeping out of the way, and accepted a cup of punch. The colonel came over, took a punch, downed it, and held out his cup to be filled.

—Hot work, dancing, he said, wiping his brow. And here it's October already—Indian summer. Isaac absently nodded. I don't hold with these modern dances, really, too much excitement, too private. Give me the old longway dances, "Hunt the Squirrel" and "Down Went McGinty" and a fiddler who knows how to line out the tunes, a far more sociable style, to my way of thinking. Still, when it's the fashion—

The schottische had ended and Mr Schuyler was rapping his bow on his music stand. In a grating, high-pitched voice he announced the evening's first quadrille, Mr Eliot of St Louis having most kindly offered to perform a set based on songs from Italian opera, and the gentlemen might now choose their partners and take their places.

With a happy cry—Now *that's* something like!—the colonel set his cup down and hurried to offer himself to Mrs Schuyler. Marsh Murdock gave Marie his arm and led her to another group—a serious young man who wore his beard in bushy side-whiskers trimmed to points on either side of his chin; Isaac had liked him, had particularly invited him to join the hunt, but with a small press and three cases of type he was engaged in starting a weekly newspaper and could not spare the time. Ned sounded an elaborate introduction and with many runs and flourishes began. The music kept changing, and the figures of the dances with it. Isaac felt foolish, standing by the tub of punch, watching; even Absalom, with no one to serve drinks to now, moved to the rhythms of the music.

Isaac went along to the door and out on the broad front porch. He leaned with his hands on the railing, better out here, with the breeze blowing off the prairies, heavy with the smell of ripe grass and wildflowers. There was a new moon low in the western sky, a narrow arc of silver exactly curving like a shaving from a spoke: make your wish and never tell. The music and the dancing had made him sad—all that, he could make no connection with it. Or was it the hunt worrying him? Except possibly Kilbourn, none of the boys seemed to know anything of hunting or care, except as something to do because everyone talked of doing it. Wild Indians or no, he'd as soon go alone, with only his horse, rifle, and a blanket roll—oh, and a tin cup to drink from and a pistol in his belt, just in case. He stepped out of the light and leaned his back against the cool, gritty stone.

The music ended in a flourish of chords and the stamp of many feet thumping to a cadence; and laughter, prolonged applause. Two couples came out to take the air but did not see him in the shadow away from the window, then like a white cloud come down to earth Marie in her ball gown.

—Marie! he called in a low voice.

—Oh! She started, stopped, found him with her eyes, and came over. Isaac, she said, why are you not *dancing?* Too much *pride* to join with mere mortals?

Fact is, m'am, I don't know *how* to dance. My father doesn't hold with dancing.

—No dancing! Marie gasped. No balls and lovely Christmas parties—

—Doesn't hold with Christmas either. Considers it pagan, or—

—But Christmas, Isaac! It's about Christ—

—Or Popish, he concluded.

—Well! she said, facing him with hands planted on her slender hips. *I* am Popish, *Mist*er Pride—and giggled. But not a very good one, I confess, she went on soberly, since my father died. . . .

She followed him over to the porch railing and leaned against the corner post.—I'm only telling you how it is, he said. It's why I never learned to dance—or thought I wanted to.

—I could teach you, Isaac. The waltz—the basic step is so easy, and then a little half turn—and you turn and turn and turn. I let my partner lead me along wherever he likes, while the music plays, and shut my eyes. It's like flying—it makes me feel like a bird, high up in the sky. And talking on, she demonstrated, arms out and up, feet moving to unheard music: *step*-step slide, *step*-step slide, skirts swirling around her ankles as she turned. You see how easy it is? she concluded.

—It seemed like you knew all the dances in there, and—it's just beautiful, the way you do it. But maybe I'm too old to teach.

His seriousness teased her. She raised an arm to the setting moon— What did you wish for, Isaac?

—You know it won't happen if you tell.

—*I* know, she said with an arch look under her brows: you wished that you would kill a thousand buffalo—and all their little wives and babies weeping and wailing—

—I'll bring you back a buffalo tail.

—What would I want with anything so horrid?

—To shoo flies with.

—Besides, what makes you think I shall be here? Why, if *that* is what you mean, I shall go home tomorrow.

—I'll send it to you at Saint Louis. Then, as she answered nothing, face turned to the sliver of moon, thinking of something he said: Have you lived at Saint Louis always?

—*Ah, non! J'suis canadienne.*

—*Je suis,* he repeated. That's French. . . . And suddenly the words gave a name to the special music of her speech that he had been hearing for weeks now.

—I was born at Montreal, she said in a rush, but I was only six when we came to Saint Louis, so I speak French like a baby—there are French people at Saint Louis but I do not see them. My father was a winterer with the American Fur Company and they sent him to Fort Laramie, that is where he got sick. He had an uncle went out to the Western Ocean with Lewis and Clark—our people were always in the fur trade. . . .

In the ballroom old Mr Schuyler was announcing a Caledonian quadrille. The couples that had stepped out came hurrying back.

—What's your name mean, Marie? It's strange, I've never heard the like. Almost—almost—

—I do not know. It is only a name—a French name—. She took a step toward the door. They are starting again, she said. I promised Mister Shirley—

He seized her hand.—Of course you know. You just won't tell.

—No, I *will* not, she cried, stamping her foot, and pulled her hand free. It is my secret. And now I must fly.

There came a grand chord from the pianoforte and a preliminary flourish of the fiddle. Gathering her skirts, Marie ran toward the door, and the diaphanous fabric of her gown billowed against the light like a pair of great wings.

Four days out from Burlingame, southwest of the Cottonwood River, the Santa Fe Road left the broken country of the Flint Hills and entered a broad plain where all the streams ran south to the Arkansas: narrow ditches slashed through the tall grass, but clear, bedded in gravel and sand. The traffic now was mostly from the west, long trains of heavy freight wagons piled with bales of raw wool from New Mexico Territory, bound for Kansas City or Leavenworth, with sticks of driftwood and sacks of buffalo chips picked up along the way slung on rawhide ropes underneath, swinging to the slow rhythm of the wagons.

Isaac had spent the day of the election sorting and repacking his outfit, storing the stove, most of his tools, and four of his father's water kegs in Colonel Titus's barn. He had left the ball early and had seen Marie next day only at a distance; they had made an early start the day after the election, and she had not gotten up to see them off— just as well, considering the kind of fool he'd made of himself at the dance. The trip had been pleasant enough, clear streams to camp by every night and enough scrubwood to gather for cooking, with a little riding. Kilbourn had bought a wiry pony and an old cavalry carbine from the colonel. Ned Eliot had the colonel's borrowed horse tied beside Aaron Schuyler's behind Aaron's wagon; Shirley and Cullum had brought no horses, and whether Bill Shirley would ride after buffalo on an ox—or whether any of their oxen had the back for his weight—had become one of the fireside jokes, which he good-naturedly put up with. Not counting jack rabbits and a few prairie chickens, they had seen no game. Ned had brought in a rabbit with his uncle's deer rifle, and there had been a good deal of random shooting in the late afternoons while they made camp. Isaac had not yet taken a shot.

In the afternoon of the fifth day, a Sunday, they approached the Turkey Creek crossing a hundred miles west of Burlingame. Isaac was in the lead, driving his team, Kilbourn in the wagon asleep— silent anyhow; Ned had ridden north on the prairie, scouting, he said, Aaron with his wagon and the others were two hundred yards back. The road came to the crossing down a gentle slope perhaps two miles long. At the bottom a little back from the road was a low, sod-roofed cabin of cottonwood logs, behind it, dust-brown and wind-riven as an ant heap, containing a half dozen mules and ponies listless in the heat, a sod corral only a little smaller than the forts thrown up in and around Lawrence in the bleeding years: the kind of not-quite transient establishment they had found at nearly every crossing since they started, known in Kansas as a ranch. Inside, there would be an open barrel of tanglefoot to sell to the passing bullwhackers at twenty-five cents a drink; a box of stale cigars, possibly a sack or two of sugar and coffee, for sale or for trade with any Indians that chanced by. A pair of covered wagons was drawn up in front of the cabin, three span of mules each. For now there were no other wagons in sight on the road ahead. As his team's unhastening gait narrowed the distance a boy came out from the shadow of the lead wagon and waited, motionless, hands on his hips.

—Where you coming from? the boy called as Isaac brought his team to a stand. He was as tall as Isaac, blond hair grown long and brushed back behind his ears; slender and round-faced, with a transparent fuzz on his cheeks—a boy still, with some growing to do, but with a quietness and something hard in the set of his jaw that made it difficult to judge his age.

—We started from Burlingame Wednesday. My partner and I—

Isaac gestured toward the wagon behind him—came out from Iowa in May.

—I was born in Iowa, the boy said, only we emigrated when the territory opened, five years ago, so I don't hardly remember. I wasn't ten years old.

—Where in Iowa?

—Scott County, little place called LeClaire, on the Mississip.

—Why, we're from Rockingham, at the other end of the rapids! Isaac said, and shouted into the wagon for Kilbourn. What's your name?

—Bill Cody.

—Jack Pride, said Isaac, reaching his hand to shake. Kilbourn's face, sleepy-eyed, looked out from the wagon. Dave! Isaac said. Here's another Hawkeye.

—Well God *damn*, Jackrabbit, Kilbourn said, and spat a long spume into the dust. Way you was shouting, I thought it was Indians. He swiveled, hung his legs over, and began pulling on his boots.

—What you doing out here? Isaac asked, turning back to young Cody.

—Drivin for Mister Bill Mathewson, the boy said earnestly, he's got a ranch fifty miles west, on Walnut Creek at the Great Bend; he went out to the mountains trappin with Carson when he wasn't any older'n what I am now. Come here!—and he led Isaac to the back of the wagon, loosed the drawstring, and climbed up to open the canvas top, revealing the load of packs, neatly wrapped in deerskin, filling the wagon-box; Isaac got up beside him. We've got most four hundred robes in there, Indian-tanned buffalo robes traded from the Kiowa and Comanche, worth ten-fifteen-*twenty* dollars apiece at Leavenworth. And as many green hides in the other wagon that we hunted ourselves—course they aint worth as much, but they don't cost *us* anything, cept the work of killin and skinnin. Aint been to Leavenworth since April—. He jumped down.

—Where'd you get em? Isaac asked. We came out meaning a little hunting—just for sport, you know—but we aint seen a thing but jack rabbits in five days traveling.

—You talk to Mister Mathewson, the boy said, he's in there talkin. Bill the buffalo-killer they call him—in the winter when the Indians were pesky, settlers couldn't get anything to eat, he went out and sent em home with their wagons loaded with buffalo meat—. There he comes, he added, whispering.

The plank door of the cabin swung inward on its leather hinges and a man came out, stooping his head to the low-set lintel, followed by two smaller men. He was big, over six feet and heavy-boned, but moved with the delicacy of a dancer, as if deliberating each step; a long face lengthened by a pointed beard, the thin lips shaped by something less than a smile, an expression of benign and habitual attention. A man, you would say at first meeting, not easily moved or, once started, easily deflected. Dressed in unadorned moccasins, smoke-grimed buckskin trousers, and a blue flannel shirt, he had at perhaps thirty lived more than half his life in the West, by the boy's account; an old head in a new country.

—Mister Mathewson, Cody said, this here's Jack Pride from Iowa, and he's out to hunt buffalo and wants you to tell him where they're at—

The hunter's brows drew together in a slight frown that silenced him—the boy had not learned to say no more than enough—and made Isaac hold back from speaking. Mathewson turned his head, gravely taking in Isaac's team and wagon and Kilbourn leaning indolently against a front wheel, stubble-faced and his boots unlaced, and Schuyler turning off from the road toward the cabin, Shirley and Cullum walking beside him, talking among themselves, and the led horses, the empty road beyond to the east. He swung around and led them back behind the cabin, lifted one arm, pointing, northwest toward the unbroken rim of the horizon, and dropped it.

—Up toward the Smoky Hill, he said, easy day's drive with your outfit and you'll find what you're after. Or you could ride it in a hour or two. The bulls first, scattered all over the plain, then the cows and calves, beyond the river. In about five miles you cross the divide. He paused, reflecting: You don't find them close by the road now—too many hunters, they stay back. But with the drouth this summer . . .

—Thank you, Mister Mathewson, Isaac said. I figured we were getting close. We'll find them.

Mathewson nodded, waited, and when Isaac had nothing more to ask turned and strode to his wagon and climbed onto the driver's bench. Cody ran to get up beside him, and a third member of their party climbed into the other wagon. With a shake of the reins the hunter started his mules at a trot just as Schuyler and the others came up.

—Who was that? Aaron wanted to know.

—Indian trader named Mathewson, Isaac answered. Says we're about to our buffalo, another day's drive north.

—Why, you know who that was? Aaron said, staring after the retreating wagons. That was Buffalo Bill; folks last winter came out from as far east as Burlingame to get buffalo meat from him. And I didn't get hardly a look!

VIII

Buffalo Land

The hunting party made another mile up Turkey Creek after leaving the ranch and camped in mid-afternoon so as to get an early start next day. Each by the firelight cleaned and loaded his weapon, examined bullet pouch and powder horn, making ready for the hunt. In the morning they set their track northwest by the sun as Mathewson had pointed them. There was no sign of road now, no mark to show that ever wagon wheels had passed this way, but at intervals animal trails worn deep in the sod. After noon the land rose gradually toward the low divide and they entered a kind of shallow bowl, narrowing toward the north, as if once a stream had run here and gone dry. Kilbourn, walking ahead with his short carbine cradled in his arms, was the first to see: a quarter-mile ahead and off to the right toward the top of the slope a motionless shape black in the afternoon light against the autumnal green and gold of the cropped grass, the heavy head hanging.

—He's mine—I saw him, I get im! Kilbourn shouted and started at a run.

From behind came other shouts, the muffled quick-step of boots pounding the dry-packed sod: Ned Eliot stretching his long legs with easy strides, the colonel's long-rifle swinging in one hand like a spear; Harry Cullum a little back, then Bill Shirley, a large-bore horse-pistol in his belt, short arms pumping—stumbled, went flat, got up and ran on, audibly wheezing.

—Come back! You'll scare him off! Isaac shouted after, but it was if he had thrown his voice at the empty sky; silence came back.

Schuyler had stopped his team and crouched, peering, undecided. He ran around in back of the wagon, reappeared with a rifle, and followed after the others.

The bull stood as before, unmoving, facing them. When Kilbourn had come within two hundred yards, the heavy head lifted, winding something. Kilbourn went down on one knee, brought his rifle up, fired: a puff of smoke, then a sharp *thrmp* softened by the distance, as of an ax blade striking hard wood. Isaac prodded his oxen and drove on. Until he was over the ridge and coming down the other side he could hear, above the ox-chains and creaking axles and the slither of iron-tired wheels on sod, the crack and pop of the five guns, firing at intervals. He did not look back.

Fifty feet down from the crest of the divide, water seeped from a crease in the grassy slope, filling a sandy depression to a depth of a foot, the overflow blotted in the dry stream bed below; a very modest spring but clear, steady, and enough. Two or three miles off, at the foot of the long descent, a sparse belt of trees marked the convoluted course of the Smoky Hill River. Beyond, in the far distance, like towers of stone defending the sky in a medieval landscape, a group of steep-sided, flat-topped buttes marked the limit of the river valley, their outlines blurred and softened by the haze of fine dust or smoke carried on the slanting light: the Smoky Hills that gave the river its name. Isaac turned the wagon away from the pool, unchained the oxen and staked them with Kilbourn's pony, carried water in buckets for them to drink. Mounting Singing Bird, he rode down to the river to collect wood.

By the time Isaac returned, leading his loaded horse, Schuyler had come in with his wagon, the others following slowly on foot and Bill Shirley last over the ridge, footsore and shambling. Isaac threw down his bundle of sticks beside the spring.

—What kind of camp is this, Jack? Kilbourn said, coming up to him. Aint hardly water enough to spit in.

—I liked the view, Isaac said. You get us some hump steak for supper, Dave?

Kilbourn turned away, went over to the wagon and threw his gun in the back. He sat down cross-legged, resting his chin on his hands.

—I believe the salt pork would be very satisfactory tonight after all, Ned Eliot suggested, and the others nodded in silence.

Isaac laid wood for a fire, filled the coffeepot from the spring, and hung it on a crossbar.—You didn't get him?

—It seems there's more to killing a buffalo than we supposed, Aaron Schuyler said after a time.

—Simply *amazing*, Harry Cullum agreed, the weight of lead the brute could carry. I believe he got away with twenty pounds.

Isaac had the fire lighted. Shirley sat down heavily near it, mopping his face with his handkerchief, and cautiously worked his boots off, then his socks, wriggling his toes.—I believe I'll put in for the mineral rights when we get back, he said. That whole hillside—why, dig it up and you'll have a regular lead mine!

The story came out in rueful fragments while they cooked and ate. Mindful of the wounded buffalo's reputation for ferocity, they had gone no nearer than a hundred yards, all firing, but the animal had not seemed to take much notice. Finally it stirred, turned, and moved off slowly over the hill and out of sight. There was some argument as to how many hits they had actually made, the thickness and toughness of a buffalo's skull and hide to turn a bullet—Schuyler recalled that the Indians made their shields of buffalo hide; or whether there was something wrong with their guns, their powder. . . .

They were finishing the last of the coffee. Bird, staked with the other horses a little way up the ridge, whinnied. Isaac stood up. There was still light on the tops of the Smoky Hills. The shallow valley between had filled up with darkness that flowed and rose like an incoming tide. There was something moving up the slope toward them, a shape solidifying as it entered the half-light fifty yards down; one man, afoot.

—Who's there? Isaac called.

No answer; the man came on, slowly. Kilbourn crouched, put another piece of wood on the fire and stirred it up with a stick. Shirley held his pistol toward the light to see. He had not thought to reload the cylinders when he came in from the hunt.

Twenty yards off, the man stopped, open hands raised shoulder-high: light blue trousers tucked into high wool socks, a long-tailed hunting shirt belted at the waist, face hidden under a broad-brimmed hat.

—I'm alone, the man called in a high, hoarse voice. Unarmed.

Isaac stood facing him. The others had backed away from the firelight toward the two wagons.—Come on over where we can see you, Isaac commanded.

The man took another ten slow steps toward them.—That's close enough, Ned Eliot called. Ned had gotten his gun out and held it in both hands, ready.

Isaac spun around, saw.—Oh, put that thing *away*, he said. He turned, went over to the man, gave his hand a shake, and led him to the fire. It's just, he added in apology, the boys are a little jumpy, didn't have any luck with their buffalo today.

—Buffalo! the man muttered. Who are you?

—Just some boys out from the settlements for a little sociable hunt, Kilbourn said. He had pushed up close. The man did not move: half a head shorter, straight-backed, hard-muscled, dark eyes staring out from under heavy brows; a long scar grooved one black-whiskered cheek. Kilbourn took a step backward. You tell us about yourself, mister, he said in a hard voice.

Isaac threw more wood on. The man crouched, looking into the leaping fire.—Name's Farris, Harry Farris. My brother and me, we're starting a hunt up the Saline, meaning to stay the winter, only our cattle come sick with the Texas fever, can't work none at all, and I concluded to come down to the road, see if I couldn't find someone'd stake me to a yoke or two till ours is better. My brother's staying with the cattle and the outfit.

—You're about twelve miles still, Isaac said, little ranch at the Turkey Creek crossing, we were there—

Farris nodded.—I started in the dark this morning—thirty miles, the way I come. I was going to get up a tree by the river for the night when I seen your fire. . . . The buffalo, he added after a moment—thick on the ground in among the buttes and the gray wolves following. Makes a man feel a little careful.

—Without a gun? Ned put in. You came through thirty miles of this wild country on foot without a gun?

—Wild! Farris came back in his rasping voice. He lifted his head, looked long, until Ned dropped his eyes. I've been in country's a whole lot wilder'n what this—. He broke off, seemed about to tell more, but did not.

—You had anything to eat? Isaac asked.

—Some hard bread. I was travelin light.

Isaac brought a slice of pork from the keg in his wagon, threw it in the pan to fry. Bill Shirley mixed up batter for pancakes, Cullum made a fresh pot of coffee. They watched in silence, drinking coffee, while the stranger ate.

—I was thinking, Isaac said at last. He tossed the last of the wood on the fire, raising a column of sparks. I was thinking, maybe we could give this man a hand. We're going that way anyhow, it's where the buffalo are, it seems—.

—What could we do? Aaron said quickly. We've no cattle to give him.

—We haven't enough horses for ourselves, Ned added.

—They could get the fever too, Aaron said. Then where would we be?

—I thought we just wanted a little peaceable hunt, Cullum said. Not—.

Farris looked at the circle of faces one by one, a half-smile on his lips; shrugged. He had asked nothing.

Kilbourn got up, ostentatiously stretched and yawned.—I'm going to sleep, he said. Tomorrow—

—Tomorrow, Shirley said, we get our buffalo.

In the morning Farris was still there, asleep by the dead fire. Isaac rode down to the river to get more wood and Aaron with him, rifle in its case slung from his saddle.

—I don't like this Farris, Aaron said.

—If there was something wrong about him, Isaac said, he'd've run off in the night. Or—I don't know, if he's got a gang out there or whatever it is you think—they'd have come in, run off the horses, maybe.

—Too many things he's not telling. I don't like it.

—I don't think any man tells more of himself than he has to, Isaac said.

They rode on in silence.—I wanted you to know, Aaron said after a time. Whatever his story, I'm not taking my team anywhere near wherever he says he's got his camp. I don't trust him.

—He aint asked *anything* yet. Isaac turned in his saddle. Aaron sat erect, face set, staring straight ahead. Let's just get on with our hunt, Isaac finally said, we're going that way anyhow. He wants to come along, let him, I say. We've got plenty of food with us.

—I'll be watching him, Aaron concluded.

After breakfast the hunting party crossed the river and entered its Great Bend, a narrowing plain enclosed on the west and north by the Smoky Hills, defined on the east by the river's long northward run to join the Saline. Farris had eaten their pork and flapjacks, drunk their coffee, but had offered nothing except to say that as they were going north he would travel along with them, no one objecting; and, when he put it that way, none did. He walked beside Isaac with his oxen, silent. Kilbourn that morning had saddled his pony and kept a quarter-mile ahead, loaded carbine across his thighs, determined on getting the first shot. Toward noon he came back at a trot, swung around, stopped, and pointed. A mile or two ahead, the steep slopes of the hills to right and left were patchy with dark clumps. Farris looked but said nothing. Isaac stopped his team, dropped to a crouch, steadying his head in his hands, and squinted.

—They're moving, he announced. They look like trees off there, but they're moving.

Aaron Schuyler came up beside him with his wagon. Isaac stood up.

—What have you seen? Aaron called.

—They're buffalo—the herd, we've come to them, couple miles off still, I reckon.

—I saw them first, Kilbourn said. I'm riding ahead.

—Dave! Isaac pleaded. You don't have to hurry now, they don't look to be going anywhere. They'll keep for us. . . .

Kilbourn rode off at a trot. Ned got his saddle from Schuyler's wagon and threw it on his horse, followed at a heavy gallop. Cullum and Shirley climbed in to ready their guns. Schuyler cracked his whip and drove his team forward.

After another hour the flat land narrowed to a little over a mile across, walled by steep, grassy hills rising three or four hundred feet on either side, then opened out again in generally rising ground to the north. Isaac and Farris came up to Schuyler and the others beside a spring that ran in a ditch-like groove down the center of the valley. There were buffalo all around them on the slopes, within a quarter of a mile: not a herd in the sense of sheep or cattle penned behind fences but scattered individuals, heads down and grazing. Aaron had his team unchained and staked and was cinching the saddle on his horse.

—We figured to camp here, Aaron called, go out and get us a buffalo.

—Suits me, Isaac answered.

—You coming along?

—Go on. I'll take my time.

The three young men rode off, Shirley and Cullum following on foot. Farris raised one arm and Isaac with his eyes climbed the western slope where his hand pointed: half a dozen animals spaced along the ridge, sentineled against the sky, goat-square, spike-legged, motionless.

—Antelope, Farris said, seems like they follow the herd. When they move, the herd moves.

Isaac looked after the retreating hunters, the two on foot already small in the distance. The wind was coming up the valley against them. The buffalo grazed placidly as before. Methodically he loosed his team, led the oxen down the minuscule stream to feed and drink. He got his rifle out, powder, balls, slipped a box of caps into his shirt pocket. He hesitated over Bird, still tied behind the wagon, rubbing her flank with his open hand.

—Any of them—Farris gave a nod down the valley—ever hunt buffalo?

—Don't look like it, Isaac said. Nor much of anything else. I'm worried they'll run them off before I get a shot.

—You can't make no sense of why they go. Sometimes they'll just up and clear the country, miles around, no good reason you can figure. You ever hunt em?

—Fact is, I never *saw* a buffalo till yesterday, cept in pictures. But I've hunted every other kind of thing we've got in Iowa. How about you?

—Some, Farris said. Up in the Platte Country, only going out with the meat hunters—. But you learn things.

Isaac decided about the mare and led her over by the stream, knocked in a stake.—She's a real buffalo pony, he explained, maybe as good as there is, seems a shame not to take her out, but I don't know much about that—don't even know if I *want* to hunt, just kind of look for a while. You coming?

Farris nodded and followed him across the creek. Isaac led the way

up a low hill that circled around to the west. After a mile the bench
fell away sharply. He went down on his knees, crawled forward,
pulling the rifle along behind him, and lay flat. Fifty feet below and
two hundred yards off there was another tiny stream, running north,
and twenty buffalo strung along it, grazing, young bulls. Isaac took
his hat off, spread his elbows and rested his chin on his hands, looking. What you read of buffalo was all about their great size, the massive hump rising from the neck, their reddish color. These animals
were not like that. From this distance it was impossible to judge actual size, but the range was considerable, from two or three young
ones, a light red-brown about the color of a Hereford cow, to others
twice as big, presumably full-grown, that looked pure black; most
were in-between, in color as in size, a chocolaty dark brown like
beaver fur. With their heads down, grazing, their backs sloped upward from rump to neck; only when one raised his head to test the
wind was the hump apparent. Their light hindquarters looked no
bigger than domestic cattle, their forequarters disproportionately
heavy, deep-chested, thick-legged, culminating in a huge head set on a
short neck, all sense of their size and proportions confused and exaggerated by the thick coat of woolly fur covering head and forequarters. Feeding, they seemed to call to one another with deep-voiced,
pig-like grunts. They stood facing into the wind blowing up the valley, broadside to the slope where he watched.

Isaac rolled over and with deliberation measured his powder,
poured it down the rifle barrel, patched a ball, and rammed it home.
He set a cap on the nipple of his gunlock.

—You're giving yourself a hard shot, Farris said. You could get
closer.

—I don't want to run them off.

—They haven't got the wind of you. Keep down and they won't see
you—don't seem they see too good.

—I don't like the slope—have to go too far down to get another
good place to shoot from.

Isaac brought the rifle around, sighted, let it down again, and lifted
one hand to feel the wind.

—The heart's the best shot, Farris said. Pick one turned away some,
so you go in behind the foreleg and low down, toward the brisket.

Isaac raised the gun again, steadied.—How low?—the whisper of
his words blown away like spit on the wind.

—Bout two thirds down from the top of the hump.

He had his buffalo picked, the biggest of the bunch, pure black in
the afternoon light, enormous hairy member hanging like a hawser
from its belly, it seemed—steady the barrel a little more, hold the
breath half in—he could count the hairs on the end of it. He brought
the gunsights forward and up, thinking about the wind. His finger

caressed the trigger inside the Hawken's oversize guard: *Now: do it now:* his finger drew back on the trigger.

He felt the baritone *thrkk* of the report, the slap of the gun butt against his shoulder. A moment, a heartbeat, and the echo touched his forehead, coming back. He eased the gun down, let out his interrupted breath.

The heads came up together from the grass, the band of animals moved a dozen rocking-horse paces down the slope, stopped, heads up, hunting the scent, the enemy; except his bull, it stood there, motionless, head down, as before.

—Did I miss him? he said in a low voice.

—Wait—a hand cautioning on his elbow.

Isaac sat up, hunched, brought his powder horn around and reloaded, watching. The bull's forelegs flexed at the knees, immense head went lower, pulling the whole body after and over on one side, legs out.

—Looks like the heart shot all right, Farris said.

Isaac started down the slope, keeping low, carrying his hat.

—Wait a little! Farris said sharply, behind him. He could get up.

—Let him.

Halfway down Isaac started to run, waving his hat and shouting, toward the remainder of the band. The heads came up again, the near animals shied, turned. When he was within fifty yards the nearest raised its tail stiff up, pivoted on its hind legs and started down the valley, drawing the rest in tossing, galloping panic. Half a mile off they vanished down a slope, reappeared, slowing, and came to a stand. Isaac walked back toward his bull.

—Looks tolable dead, Farris said as he came up. But why in the devil'd you run em off? You could've had the lot.

—That's how my father taught me. Take what you need—but save the rest for another day.

—I'd starve to death, hunting like that. Besides, God-damn buffs bout as scarce as grasshoppers on the Plains.

—I didn't come out here to make a living at it—just come for a little fun, get me a buffalo and see what it's like.

—Well, by God, said Farris, scowling still, you try that in midsummer rutting time and you won't do it twice—one of them big bulls comes hooking after you with his horns—.

Isaac did not answer. He laid his gun down, walked slowly around the bull, crouched finally looking into the great dark eyes: eight feet from rump to nose, man-tall or more at shoulder; hard to judge from the shape, the light hindquarters, but it might go two thousand pounds, nearly twice the weight of his biggest oxen, but no more to killing it than a prairie chicken with bird shot and his first gun, one dead as the other.

The sun was getting down, the steep hills to the west shadowing the valley, cooling the air. He roused himself, hungry; took out his knife and with some advice from Farris cut a square of hide from the flank to wrap the meat in, removed the tongue, cut deep along the spine to get at the tenderloin, and folded it up in the piece of woolly skin, as much as he felt like carrying; and last the hairy tip of the tail, and stuffed it in the pocket of his jeans.

They returned circuitously to camp, hiking to the head of the valley and up over a steep hill that rose three hundred feet above the surrounding plain. From the top they could see across the whole country, five miles east to the winding, northward course of the Smoky Hill, far to the north where the up-sloping land met the sky in the blue-gray afternoon haze, and everywhere the low ground was dotted with the dark shapes of feeding buffalo.

Descending the east slope of the hill, they walked along the rim of a narrow canyon where another small stream ran down toward the Smoky Hill. There were a dozen buffalo grazing along its banks not a hundred yards off. Isaac went down on one knee, studying them. It wouldn't be right—and yet—and yet, one more among so many, millions of them, people said—. He brought the rifle up, pressed a cap on. There was one facing him, head up; it would make a different shot.

—I thought you didn't like to take more'n you could use, Farris said in a low voice.

—Shut up or you'll spoil my shot.

Again the explosion racketed back off the canyon walls and the band, alarmed but discerning no threat it was equipped to meet, moved off a little distance, stopped, and stupidly went back to feeding; and the bull he had chosen stayed on its feet for a minute or two, then slowly went down on its belly and rolled on one side. Isaac had his gun reloaded and went down the slope in running leaps. Farris followed, carrying the package of meat.

He had cut the tail when Farris came up.—I just had to see, you know, if I could get him from the front, he said—where you'd have to put the bullet in to find the heart. Maybe that first one was just luck.

—Looks like you found the spot, Farris said, crouching to look. But you could take the tongue anyway, about the sweetest, tenderest meat of all. I'll take turns with you carrying.

—Say, you want to hear something funny? Isaac said as they left the canyon, the band of buffalo moving off and scattering ahead of them. Farris watched him. Last week was my birthday, Isaac continued, twenty-two and I didn't even notice. Farris shrugged but said nothing.

A mile before they came in sight of the camp they could see a faint haze of blue smoke clinging to the grass on the slope above the stream bed. As they came nearer a rank smell infused the air, like bacon kept through the hot summer and gone rancid. The five young men were gathered dubiously around the fire when Isaac and Farris came in. Isaac laid his pack of meat down and went over. They had the big iron skillet on the coals. A slab of something dark sputtered in the fat, curling up around the edges, smelling strong.

—What you got there, boys? Isaac cheerily asked.

—Buffalo meat, Kilbourn came back. What'd you think it was?

—Where'd you find it?

—Two miles off, Schuyler said. And listen, we didn't *find* him, we *hunted* him—came on him off by himself, ran him down and headed him off. Dave here got in the killing shot.

—Well, you get tired of chewing on that thing, I brought in some *meat*, Isaac said. He knelt and opened up his piece of buffalo hide to show.

Kilbourn came over to see.—Looks like a piece of beef from the butcher shop. And a couple of beef tongues. Your friend do the shooting for you?

Isaac flushed but said nothing.

—Listen here, Farris put in, your friend here picked the choice young bulls out'n two different herds and killed em both with just one shot each, two different shots—first one from two hundred yards. Now that's *shootin*. Why, he could've loaded both your wagons up with prime buffalo meat, only—

—Now you listen yourself, said Kilbourn hotly, pushing up against him, you don't have to come in here with your sick ox tale and eating up our grub and telling us off about Mister High-and-Mighty Isaac Pride—

—Boys! Isaac said. What's the matter with you? I had a little luck, brought in some meat for supper, and you're mad about it—

—He hadn't ought to talk so much, Kilbourn said. Nor you neither, Jackrabbit. He turned away and threw himself down on the upwind side of the fire.

Keeping his temper, Farris explained, choosing his words with care. What they had gotten was a solitary old bull, driven out from the herd to die, meat so tough and foul in the first place no one who knew anything would ever touch it except in desperation; and besides, he brought out, the piece they'd chosen was not hump steak, as they supposed, from the ribs, but a thin slab of gristle and stringy muscle under the thick skin at the top of the hump, meat rather less edible than a piece of shoe leather.

Schuyler heard him out and silently upturned the skillet and dropped the unpalatable slab sizzling on the coals. Bill Shirley roused himself, brought an armload of sticks, broke them up and laid them one by one on the fire. Isaac knelt and cut his tenderloin and one of the tongues into inch-thick slices. Cullum carried the coffeepot down to the stream to fill.

The penetrating sweetness of the frying buffalo meat stilled their rancors, and for a time there was no sound but the click and rasp of knives and forks on tinware plates, the hiss of fresh wood on the fire, and the gurgle of coffee poured out from the big enamel pot. The meat was up to reputation, the loin in particular: crusty-brown on the outside, pink and marbled inside with streaks of fat, tender enough, almost, to cut with a fork—it made the hump steak served at the Lecompton hotel taste like ordinary beef, and not the best at that; Isaac ended by slicing up and cooking the second tongue he'd thought to save and boil for breakfast.

While they finished their coffee Isaac put on a few more sticks and set a pail of water to heat for washing.—Well, boys, he said across the leaping firelight, what do you say? We starting for the Saline country tomorrow? Sounds like the buffalo's plenty on the ground as flies. And maybe along the way we can help Farris here and his brother out of their fix. . . .

No one answered. At length, politely, Ned Eliot broke the silence. —I shouldn't like to stretch it out too long, he said, ought to be starting back to Saint Louis by the end of the month. But of course if the others—

—I already told you, Isaac, Schuyler irritably broke in. I'm not taking my team that way. I haven't changed my mind.

Cullum and Shirley sat together, turned sideways to the fire, looking out across the plain; no use asking them. The sky was changing from purple to dark gray, the light fading while they watched. Isaac waited. Kilbourn lay on his side, legs outstretched, propped on an elbow and taking the last of his coffee in small sips, looking into the fire.

—Dave! Isaac said. You're coming, aren't you? New country up there, and oh the game to be had—you've just got to—

—No I don't! he said harshly. He set his mug down and sat up. You want to go, go on, but I aint going with you. You can go with—with Farris here, if that's how you want it.

Kilbourn stared back, defiant, still angry, though exactly why there was no way of telling: half a lifetime of knowing each other and the whole summer traveling together, living together, and now the look he gave was the look of a stranger; no, of an enemy, wishing hurt.

—I didn't come here to make trouble for you, Farris said. I can go on down to the road like I started. I'll find something.

—No, Isaac said. He stood up. I said I'll go and I'll do it. I'll manage my team well enough without any help, if that's what I have to.

Besides, I've come this far, I want to see all there is. We'll start in the morning, early as we can. . . .

Aaron poured off the fat from the skillet and the fire flared. They washed up in silence. Isaac sorted the things that were his, carried them to the wagon and put them in back, feeling for the places in the dark. Someone was sitting with his back to the front wheel.

—Dave! Isaac called in a low voice. That you? A grunt answered. I've got to talk to you.

—What was it you wanted?

Isaac hesitated: wanted? what did he *want?* And finally:—I just don't understand, Dave. How you could let me down—

—*Let you down!* Kilbourn said, raising his voice. Seems like you're the one, going off God knows where with a stranger walks into camp with some cock-and-bull story—

—Listen, he may not talk much but he aint told any lies that I know. You talk like young Schuyler and those others, town boys scared to trust a man cause they don't know his whole life story—

—Don't you call me scared, Jackrabbit, Kilbourn said, his voice grating. You push me and I'll make you run yet.

Isaac hesitated but ignored the challenge.—You never looked scared to me, Dave, he said, when we were boys running back and forth on the river in our dugouts. And that's the thing I don't understand. Why, the two of us together, I figure we can stand up to any other two there is.

—The two of us! Kilbourn said scornfully. That aint how it's been since Leavenworth. It's been you thinking up things and me doing the nigger work.

—Dave, Isaac said, that's just dumb. We did all that together, partners all the way, and you know it. A little more luck and we'd both have our land, worth ten dollars an acre.

When Kilbourn did not answer Isaac turned away and started slowly down the valley.

—Where you going? Kilbourn called out.

—I want to be by myself now, Isaac answered without looking back. I've talked enough. And kept on moving till he seemed to fade away into the hazy light.

He went only far enough to get beyond the sounds of the camp, the horses, oxen, far enough to feel alone. He sat down, gathered his knees in his arms, resting his head. Kilbourn had taken him by surprise, but looking back now he could see all the times he should have recognized the same feelings, building up, getting stronger, and ignored them: times he put down to laziness, bad temper, that he tried to jolly him out of, it seemed you could only push him so far before he dug in his feet, started kicking and biting. A human jackass! He sat up, clenched his hands thinking about it, made him mad enough to want to fight. No use in that, though—couldn't argue him into it, you couldn't fight him either. It was the first of the species he'd come up against. Why? *Why?* Wasn't any kind of answer to say that's how he is, that kind of man, born that way, though that's maybe all the answer there is. Then what? Resentment, envy? Because there were things he was good at doing, quicker, because he had a way of kind of pushing people along? It wasn't right, fair, it was only the way he was, never thought much about it, recognized it, whatever it was. But envy: you saw something and not having it made you feel small and mean inside, and that's how you acted. The hunting was what it all came to—he'd succeeded and Dave, the others, hadn't, and they hated him for it. He'd have tried to show them something about stalking an animal and how to shoot, but it wasn't likely they'd have stood for it. No, whooping and clamoring around, they'd have spoiled it for him too, and then been twice as mad. So he was back where he started: there *was* no answer. Or he hadn't found it, anyhow.

He got up, feeling tired with the effort of thought, and walked back toward the camp. The moon was high now, still bright. The fire had fallen to embers glowing like animal eyes in the dark, what seemed to be Farris sleeping beside it, still with no blanket. He could not see Kilbourn and the others; over by Schuyler's wagon, perhaps. Isaac found his blankets in the wagon, carried one over and spread it over Farris; a hand reached out, touched his, smoothed the blanket down, and the man rolled over. Isaac got under his wagon, pulled off his boots and trousers, and wrapped the blanket around him; still too dry to make much dew, but getting cool.

Sleep did not come. He turned on his back, supporting his head with his hands. The truth of it was, he was nervous about going off by himself with this Farris. Schuyler was that far right—a man to approach with caution. Oh, a man of his word, he felt sure of that, but all the more dangerous if you went wrong with him. And then what was he really going to do? His team could be dead by now, anyhow not fit to work. He could haul their outfit to their winter camp or back to one of the towns. And then? Start home? Go back to Burlingame? Whatever he did, it would be a long, dull journey and alone, probably too late by now to team up with any go-backs from Denver, and the hard winter settling in. Yet he had to go. Duty, giving help where it was needed, was the least of it. Something called him that way, led him, providence his father would perhaps interpret it, but he thought of it as his luck: take it when it comes or cease to be a man. The first thing was to recognize it. . . .

He stared long and long into the great round eyes of the buffalo, so dark he could not distinguish the pupils. The black skin of the long eyelids and flaring nostrils was delicately grained, the whole head thickly grown with soft dark hair, lightly curled, that covered cheeks and mouth and hung in a beard below—a face bespeaking innocent sunlit days of animal browsing, nuzzling and caress of kind to kind. Short black horns curved upward to sharp points from beside the eyes: a brute face too, armed for red-eyed combat with its own or any alien that challenged, carried by rage to its inescapable conclusion and one or other of you maimed or driven off or dead; and therefore not the face of an enemy, an antagonist, but a kind of partner, offering its innocence and rage to the necessary combat which is life. It had happened too soon, too fast, he had been pushed himself, he had only begun to see and know this particular beast. It should have been like love, unhurried, savored through months of gradual knowing to its climax. It was the process itself, the sense of knowledge growing, that mattered.

He woke with a feeling of terrible longing and, simultaneously, canceling it, desolation: the thing he wanted most was gone, irretrievable. It came to him finally that he had made his first buffalo kill in that hour or two of afternoon; it was over, done with, and if he lived a thousand years and killed a million others, it was a thing he could never do again. If a man only could take one moment in his hands, wriggling and alive, and hold it tight, forever. Memory is too pale and fragile, like the ash left when the wood is burned, falling to less than dust; but all you have.

It would have been better alone. He would not have hurried.

He was awake. The moon was gone, the stars dimming; the darkest time, hours yet till dawn. Far off a wolf howled in a rising tremolo and a chorus of others answered. There was someone coming toward him, a solid shape in the darkness, keeping low, steps whispering across the grass.

—Farris?

A hand rested for a moment on his shoulder.—You sleep like an Indian, Farris said in a low voice.

—I just didn't sleep very well.

—Thanks for the blanket. It cooled off some.

—You thinking of starting? Isaac asked, propping himself on one elbow.

—It'll take us till dark anyway, might not make it at all today. We could walk it faster.

—You wait till you see my team! Isaac said and, throwing his blanket off, reached for his trousers.

They had made a small fire and boiled half a pot of coffee when Kilbourn came toward them, fully dressed, an odd little smile on his lips, and crouched down facing Isaac. The sky in the east had turned gray, silhouetting the hills. The valley below was still filled with darkness.

—I was thinking over what you said last night, Kilbourn said. I've changed my mind. I'm going with you.

The smile enlarged, meaning to ingratiate. Isaac studied him for a long moment, drank off his coffee and set the mug down.

—I'd have respected you better if you stood by what you said, Dave.

—What do you mean?

Isaac stood up.—I mean you're not going. I won't have you.

—After everything, just because a man talks a little out of turn? I don't have to put up with that. He was on his feet, fists clenched.

—You've been talking too much the whole summer long, Isaac said quietly. Now, put up with it or not, it's my team, my wagon, and my outfit, and I'll say who goes with me and who doesn't. And you don't.

—Then I'll give you something to take along, Kilbourn snarled.

He kicked through the fire, knocking over the coffeepot. Isaac faced him, hands raised. Before Kilbourn could do whatever he meant, Farris was around behind him, gripping his upper arms, pulling him back against his upraised knee.

—Mister, he said, I've listened to you enough. Now, one more word and you take a broken back home with you.

—Let him go, Isaac said.

Farris with a shake pushed him away and he fell heavily to the ground and lay there, looking up at them. Isaac stooped, got his hands under his shoulders and heaved him on his feet.

—Dave, Isaac said, I'm sorry, we've been friends a long while, but I was thinking too last night, and the way you are now, I'd never be able to count on you when it matters.

—Jackrabbit, I promise you—

—What'd I tell you, mister? Farris rasped.

Isaac looked up. Schuyler had emerged from the gray light barefoot and in his drawers, balancing his rifle in both hands.

—It's just us, Isaac said. You can put that thing away.

—I thought it was Indians, stealing the horses, like you hear about.

—No, Aaron, Isaac said with a laugh, just a little discussion about good manners.

Schuyler shrugged, turned, and wandered back to his wagon, and Kilbourn followed him.

—Come on! Isaac said. It'll be light and we haven't got the cattle in.

He ran off toward the oxen with floating strides, and Farris followed.

They were all day traveling to the place where Farris had left his brother, walking side by side with the team, talking a little. It was not long till they were calling each other by first names, Harry and Isaac; Isaac, hearing his nickname too often from Kilbourn, was tired of it.

Harry was twenty-four, his brother Irwin a couple of years younger; from somewhere in southern Ohio, had been in the West almost a year, north of Kansas on the Platte, had had some practice skinning and butchering buffalo and a little hunting, but what else they had done in that time Harry did not say and Isaac did not ask. They came to an agreement. If the buffalo continued plentiful, Isaac would join them in making a winter camp and stay to hunt. Each would hunt and skin for himself and take the price of his own hides when they hauled them to Leavenworth in the spring to sell; other work they would share. There was nothing else Isaac could think of to do through the winter that would get money so readily, and when the spring came there would be other possibilities to help him get land. The alternative was to go home, spend the winter helping his father around the farm, but there would not be much to do till pig-killing time, times were still hard; and it would be too much like giving up.

Farris led the way north down the creek where they had camped the night before and around noon they stopped long enough to rest the cattle, make a pot of coffee and eat some hard-bread, but did not cook dinner. They turned northwest and climbed into broken country. Several times in an hour they passed small herds of buffalo, more cows and this year's calves now than bulls, scattered among the folds of the hills. Isaac kept his team stepping along smartly all day, but it was nearly dark before they reached the river. Harry took his time considering and concluded that they should turn upstream.

The Saline here was forty feet across, slow and meandering, and looked shallow. The bank was gullied earth ten feet high and steep.

—Your brother's camped on the other side? Isaac asked.

—Was when I left him.

—Is there a crossing?

—I expect so. We just hadn't found it yet. Fact is, it's better game country over there anyway, all the way to the Solomon, we figured to make our camp there. But we was *looking* for a crossing when the team took sick—

—Harry! Isaac said. Farris turned to face him. The oxen shambled ahead. Harry, you mean you got me up here and there's no way to get my team across?

—I said we didn't *find* it. But we will. And I didn't ask. You came.

—Well, sure I came—because you needed help and I wanted to come. But don't you fool me like that again if you mean to be partners.

Harry shrugged.—We'll manage it in the morning. But we got to find my brother while it's still some light.

He went on ahead, hallooing now, calling his brother's name at the top of his voice. They had gone half a mile like this when they heard a babble of yips and snarls from the opposite bank, so loud and numerous the sounds seemed all around them; then a prolonged inarticulate cry. Bird whinnied and shied at her lead, rattling the tailgate with her hooves. Harry pushed through the brush to the top of the riverbank, calling out. Isaac stopped his team, went back to quiet the horse, and got out his rifle, hastily loading in the dwindling light.

He was standing beside Harry, watching, when a figure appeared among the scrub on the other bank.

—Harry! the man called across. That you?

—It's me, Harry shouted back. I got help.

The man ran forward, stumbled, and fell flat entering the water, got up, wading. Halfway across, shoulder-deep, he pushed off, thrashing his arms wildly. A small dark face came through behind him, low down, eyes glinting. Isaac raised his gun.

—Don't shoot, Harry said. It's Watch, our dog.

Isaac laid the gun down, braced himself to a sapling, and offered Harry his free hand. Irwin waded through the shallow, his brother let himself down, hanging on, grabbed his upreached hand and pulled him up, panting, onto the level ground. The dog, running up and down opposite, barking frantically, ran forward, plunged in, and swam toward them. As it scrambled up the bank, another dog-face appeared, looking out, then another. Isaac retrieved his gun.

—You aint got another dog, have you?

—Only the one.

Fire gushed from the gun barrel, answered by an animal scream, then a tearing and crashing of retreat through the brush. They got Irwin's arms over their shoulders and half carried him back to the wagon, set him down, and gathered a heap of deadwood for the fire. Isaac staked the oxen and his horse in close. Irwin came over while they fried pork and lay by the fire drinking coffee.

—They were all around me, Irwin said in a low voice. He lay back. I thought you wouldn't get here.

—We heard, Isaac said. I taught one of them some manners, anyhow.

—I was fine the day you left, Harry, Irwin said, only lonesome with nothing but old Watch for company. Kept busy chopping wood and greasing my boots, one thing and other—tried fishing some in the river but didn't get nothing, too muddy, I guess. And slept in the tent like a babe that night. They started in the next morning. Terrific to-do and the cattle yelling—I thought it was Indians. I loaded a gun, snaked along through the grass on my belly, and there was a wolf pack, had gotten one down already and the others backed off and swinging their horns and bellowing, only they hadn't much fight, being sick.

—You use your gun? Isaac asked.

Irwin nodded.—I shot some, but it was like swatting flies. They'd
go off a little and come right back.

Harry forked his brother a slice of meat on a plate.

—I brought the rest of the cattle in close, Irwin went on, chewing,
the fat running from the corners of his mouth. Bout fifty feet from
the tent, kind of did guard duty on them all the rest of the day, but
the wolves were all along the riverbank and around me, I could hear
em, see em too sometimes and I'd take a shot—must've got some too, I
don't know. I brought in wood for the night but daren't go far, you
know, I was afraid they'd get behind me, cut me off. . . .

He reached his plate for more. Isaac cut another slice, dropped it in
the pan, and poured himself a mug of coffee.

—I kept the fire up all night, Irwin continued, but toward morning
I dozed, just seemed I couldn't keep my eyes open any more if you'd
held a gun to my head. Woke up again with the cattle bawling and the
wolves snapping and fighting over them. When the light come those
three bulls was about half gone so you couldn't tell what they'd been,
and by nightfall those wolves hadn't only the bones left, cracking em
and breaking em up and scrabbling around on the ground after more.
I got in more wood but not enough to last the night, it just didn't
seem safe. I always heard a wolf wouldn't go for a man, but maybe
this lot didn't know that or went by different rules. Getting too familiar to suit *me*, anyway—one of em came right into camp, astonished
me so I shot without aiming and missed im by about ten yards, and he
run off, kind of grinning over his shoulder at me. So most of the day I
just stayed with the dog in the wagon and all that night, figured they
couldn't get at me there or wouldn't try, or I could fight em off easier,
but I don't know—sat there chewing on hard-bread and watching,
never tried to make a fire or cook or nothing. Next day—that's today
—they'd moved off some but tracks everywhere, and when the sun
started down they come back, and I could hear em, moving in and
kind of talking back and forth about how to proceed. I figured if I
lasted another night we'd get across the river, me and the dog, and
start south, see if we could find you—didn't seem I could be any
worse off'n what I was. And then I heard you hollerin over on the
other bank. Oh my! . . .

He set his plate down and lay on his back, eyes closed. Harry and
Isaac talked in low voices about how to manage the night. It was
likely the wolves would cross the river, or some of them; they agreed
to take turns sleeping and standing guard, keeping the fire up. Isaac
made a place in the wagon for Irwin and the dog, helped them in;
Harry was already asleep underneath. Isaac built up the fire, moved
the animals closer where he could see them by the light; rummaged in
the back of the wagon till he found his revolvers, and sat down by the
fire to the tedious task of loading the ten chambers. Bird was nervous

but not frightened, smelling the wolf smells and the blood, whatever else was left, at a remove. From the sounds, the wolves had gone north into the hills beyond the river and scattered. He put on more wood. The horse would give the alarm if the wolves came back in numbers. . . .

He was looking at a pair of bare legs covered with curly black hair. He kicked out, rolled backward, and landed squatting on his feet, a gun in each hand, pointed. Harry grinned down at him.

—I wasn't asleep! Isaac said.

—I'll give you a dollar if you have to wake *me* up when it's your turn, Harry said, still smiling.

Isaac stood up, handed Harry a pistol, and stuffed the other in his belt.—You startle a man like that, you could get yourself shot.

Isaac started to show him about the revolver.—I've used em before, Harry said. You get to bed. He laid the gun down and stood by the dwindling fire to pull on his jeans.

By daylight Isaac could see that the difficulty in crossing was not the steep bank but the depth of the river. The Farrises had made their camp on low bottomland on the inside of a long curve, with a steep high bank only on the south side; moving a mile downstream to where the river straightened out, they had easy approaches on both banks. The river, however, was too deep to ford and mud-bottom besides. Isaac and Harry cut cottonwood logs and chained up the oxen to haul them to the place; lashed them with ropes to make a crude raft; unloaded the wagon and removed the wagon-box and wheels. They stripped to their drawers. Isaac swam across with a rope and Harry guided and pushed from behind as far out as he could stand, floating the box over, then the wheels and running gear. The green cottonwood sat low in the water. For the powder kegs, flour, meat, and other perishables, it was necessary to cut more logs and lay them crosswise on the raft, and as a further precaution they wrapped these goods in the wagon top. Last, they drove the oxen into the river and forced them to swim; and Isaac rode Singing Bird across, the sluggish flow licking at his thighs. Irwin, still exhausted from his wolf scare and sleepless nights, was allowed to rest up, watching the animals, and was towed across in royal style, fully dressed, on the raft's final trip.

It was dusk when they drove into the Farrises' camp. The tent and wagon were undisturbed; of the four oxen nothing remained but the fleshless skulls and half a dozen unidentifiable large bones too heavy for wolf jaws to crack. To pay back his easy day Irwin was elected cook and wood collector.

Isaac woke under his wagon with the first light; after the tedious crossing it had not seemed worth the effort to get the tent out. Harry and Irwin slept on in their tent. He dressed, got his rifle, powder horn, and bullet pouch, brought in Bird, saddled her, led her silently across the grassy bottomland of the campsite, and rode north up the gradual rise back from the river. To the soaring eye of an eagle, to anyone looking down from a mountaintop, a tower, the country would be flat. It was not like that on the ground but rolling, creased by stream beds of a lost age, dried up and mantled in grass but capable of running like mountain torrents when the spring rains poured off the slopes. Below the crest of each hill smooth slabs of limestone jutted, scraped clean of earth and grass. At one he stopped, climbed down to look, scratched with his knife point, verifying, and it came to him; he was riding where a sea had been; its folds were the channels of a sea, retreating, and under the millennial layers of loam it had left beds of salt which sometimes a stream bed found, probed, dissolved. Saline, the Saline River: not salt to taste but muddy, only at moments the wind carried a faint whiff of salt air.

He had not run the horse since starting from Burlingame but held her to an easy canter, slowing to a walk as he came over each rise, watchful; hunting, perhaps. After five miles he came out on a broad, open ridge dividing the Saline from the converging valley of the Solomon. Below, to the east, a creek descended a grassy hollow and lost itself in the flood-plain. There were buffalo grazing along the bank, hundreds or thousands more dotted and clumped across the valley. Isaac drew his rifle from its case, dismounted, and ran toward the edge of the hollow, keeping down, and lay flat. The animals by the stream were small, cows with their calves, fifty or more; half a dozen bulls had stationed themselves on either slope as if standing guard, the nearest two hundred and fifty yards off. He had thought to make a quick kill, return to camp with fresh meat for all of them for breakfast. That seemed bravado now. He felt no hunger yet, this time would not be hurried, would fill his eyes with looking; nevertheless, methodically, he loaded, it was well to be ready, and laid the rifle in the grass beside him. He had no sense of time passing while he watched, his mind flowing to the rhythm of the animals, heads down, feeding, moving a few steps at a time down the hollow, and at intervals he moved with them. Then there was a change. The near bull lifted his head, faced around up the creek toward the top of the divide, motionless; other heads lifted below him. Isaac looked but could see nothing back there to disturb them, could feel no wind behind him—a current of air, perhaps, flowing down the slope, contaminated with man-smell, horse-smell, the scent of enemies. The bull dug at the sod with his hooves, grunted, tail switching. Behind him the band began to move, the cows herding their young in, the other bulls came down the slope. A worn track ran along one bank down into the valley, leading most likely to a crossing of the river. The animals converged on it, trotting, and last the bull that by whatever means had given the alarm and turned and followed. A mile off, where the ground leveled out, they slowed, spread out again, and went back to feeding. Isaac got up and returned to his horse.

He varied his route back to the Saline, circling to the west, seeing the country differently; until he turned south and left the divide he could see buffalo spread across the valley of the Solomon to the limits of sight. He reached the Saline again at a point where it was masked in a dense growth of trees, the usual cottonwoods but with oak and walnut mixed in. From within it came a crashing sound of something big breaking through, then silence. He slipped down, dropped the reins over Bird's head and, taking his rifle, followed through an opening in the trees. He came out in a natural meadow, with a few trees rising solitary from the deep grass. Fifty yards off a buffalo cow faced him, head up, a calf at her flank, strays somehow separated from the herd and scared off as he rode up. He went down on one knee, brought his gun up, placed a cap, and fired. The cow's head jerked, she swung around, moved off, driving the calf before her, and turned to face him, head down and moaning, blood running from her mouth and wetting her beard; shot low, it seemed, hurt her some but had not killed. He measured out the drams of powder, reloaded, and aimed higher up, between the horns. The cow dropped. He stood and walked toward them. The calf pushed at its mother's face with its muzzle, drew back bleating as he approached, made a defiant rush at him, stopped, veered, and ran off. He followed at a trot. The calf turned and ran at him and, dropping his gun, he made a diving leap. He got it around the neck and threw it down, knelt on its shoulder, and pulling out his knife cut its throat. The blood gushed, no different from killing a pig.

Isaac got up and walked on, at his ease, gun over one arm. The meadow occupied a kind of peninsula formed by a sharp ox-bow of the river, half a mile long, looking almost due south, four hundred yards across at the widest, eight or ten acres altogether. From the point, there was a long view up and down the river and into the broken country to the south: any game crossing the bottomland for miles in the three directions, coming down to drink, would be seen and easily taken, you had only to sit there and wait. It occurred to him that the buffalo cow had led him to the spot for their winter camp. The heavy timber would shelter them from the north and be handy for logs for a cabin, rails for fencing; at that end the peninsula narrowed to two hundred yards or less where in time the river would cut through and straighten its channel. A fence across that neck would convert the meadow to a pasture for the oxen—the bank all around was too high and steep for cattle to get down.

Pleased with his discovery, he sauntered back to the calf, wondering what he could save from it so as not entirely to waste it; *a willful waste will make a woeful want.* It was the whole spirit of his growing up: never really lacking, yet never an abundance of money or anything else, a pinching carefulness in everything. And now, suddenly as if waking from long sleep, he found himself in abundance, where free land, untouched by men, invited in all directions, meat wandered through for the taking, and the timber for a house and fuel grew on the doorstep. He stood up, looking around with a feeling of dazzlement: good land, wonderful land, better than Osage County, already taken up anyway by the colonel and the Schuylers and the rest of the speculators, bringing their money in—better than Iowa!—and it struck him that, whatever the others intended, he wanted something more than a little low-roofed trapper's cabin knocked together for a winter's hunt. No, he wanted a double cabin with lofts and a big stone fireplace, a corral out back for the horses, a barn, a smokehouse, an icehouse maybe, they could cut the ice on the river, yes, and in front a vegetable garden neatly fenced, he'd get his father to send seeds in the spring. Home: he would not soon go back there; he had found a place to live; a home, his own.

Hunger broke through this flow of revery and calculation. No breakfast; the sun was high, getting toward dinnertime. He crouched by the calf again. He had only killed it because it would not live, probably, without its mother, or would make a meal for the first wolves that chanced along and caught its scent, but what could he take now to save it from wasting? They never ate veal at home or much beef of any kind, their cattle had to grow up useful, to give milk, to work, be sold. He ran his hand along the animal's velvet flank, still warm; not much meat there; made a slit between the bones of the lower jaw, thrust his fingers in and felt, but the tongue was too small and thin to be worth cutting out. He lifted a hind leg and worked it on the joint, meaty, it would roast like fresh ham, and not too heavy to carry; and began a careful cut all around, found the joint, forced it open, and got the leg off. He walked back to the cow, carrying the leg by its small, dark hoof, and from her took the tongue and a section of rib steaks from below the hump. He wrapped his meat in a piece of the hide, made slits along the edges, and pinned it up with green twigs, but even so it made an awkward bundle. His hands were sticky with drying blood. He rubbed them together and the blood came off in flakes and scattered in the grass.

Isaac rode slowly back to camp, balancing his pack of meat on the pommel of his saddle. It was four miles but bottomland and level the whole way; it must have been twenty-five miles he'd ridden since starting at daybreak.

The Farrises had packed up the camp, made a new fire to cook dinner, and lay beside it with the air of men who had waited a good while now and could think of nothing more to take up the time except eat.

—We figured you'd run off to join the Indians, Harry said.

Isaac reached his bundle down and dismounted.—I brought in some fresh meat for dinner anyhow. It'll be a while before we have to eat salt pork again. Irwin roused and brought the big skillet, set it on the coals, cut off three thick steaks, and threw them in to fry.

—Where'd you get it? Harry said.

—I just rode out for a little look around, Isaac said, and kept on riding and looking—but oh, the buffalo! Looks like the whole herd up there, just over the divide and all along the Solomon—some this side too, I got this cow and her calf right by the river, a little ways west. And say, *didn't* I find the spot for our winter camp! She led me right to it. . . .

It was the middle of the last week of October when the hunting party returned to Burlingame. Marie was sitting in a rocking chair on the porch of her uncle's house, taking the afternoon sun and trying to read. There had been no frost but it was chilly at night now and cool in the mornings, the trees along Switzler Creek all bare; she had taken to wearing a dark wool skirt woven with a tiny pattern of flowers and birds and a knitted shawl over her shoulders. Uncle Titus had driven off somewhere for the day. The book was a story by Irving about traveling with a company of dragoons through the cross-timbers country in the Indian Territory to the south. There was a Frenchman who ate a skunk. Horrid! Also, a buffalo hunt. The men rode alongside the buffalo and shot them with horse pistols. It sounded dangerous. Isaac had said something about that style of hunting and she wondered if he had read the same book. He had said that he had never personally hunted buffalo.

There was not much traffic on the road now. She could see the single wagon coming a long way off. Aaron Schuyler drove the oxen, walking slow and footsore. Mr Shirley and, what was the man's name from Topeka, Mr Cullum, sat up at the front of the wagon-box. Ned was a little behind, swinging his long legs and whistling, walking along as if out for a Sunday stroll along the levee at St Louis. Mr Kilbourn was far back, his legs hanging down from his little pony, he sat it like a donkey. Where was the other wagon? Marie dropped her book and ran down to meet them as they came across the bridge. Aaron stopped in front of the house.

Marie looked at him, the others, hesitated, but Aaron only nodded, politely enough, waiting for her to speak, and at length she asked.

—Where is Isaac? And when he looked away, not answering: Has something happened to him?

—He didn't come back with us—went off with his outfit headed for the Saline.

—He didn't think much of our way of hunting, Ned added, coming up to them. Fact is, I don't think much of it myself, seeing as all we got among us, the whole time out, was a couple of superannuated old buffalo bulls just about fit to make into shoe leather.

Marie smiled, then made her face serious again.—Then he is—you are all—*all right?*

—A man came along into our camp, claimed to be a buffalo hunter, Aaron continued. Isaac went off with him.

—That was up in the Great Bend of the Smoky Hill, Ned explained. We stayed around most of a week, expecting he'd come back, but he didn't. . . .

Mr Cullum climbed cautiously down from the wagon and turned to reach Mr Shirley a hand. Mr Kilbourn arrived and stayed on his horse, scowling down at her—angry about something and at her too, somehow, by his looks, the boys had had some kind of quarrel. Curious but uneasy too, she refrained from asking more.

—Well! Marie said. After your journey, you must all, I am sure, be tired and thirsty. Will you come in and have some tea? She thought for a moment: And Mister Kilbourn—Mister Cullum—Uncle is out for the day, but I am sure he would wish you to stay the night.

She ran up the steps and into the house, calling for Absalom.

Toward the end of the month Isaac started for Burlingame alone, on horseback, with his gun, a rolled blanket tied behind his saddle, and a buffalo tongue and a skillet in his saddlebags.

The brothers had liked his choice of land and the building of the camp was pretty well finished. Irwin turned out to know something of rough carpentry and had with him the several kinds of saws, a good quality broad-ax, a large auger, a hand-adze, a shingle knife. They worked carefully together, as Isaac insisted, taking their time. They made the cabin twelve-by-sixteen, of squared logs notched at the corners and chinked with a plaster of mud, clay, and dry grass, leveled on a foundation of limestone slabs Isaac dug and hauled from the hilltops to the north; with a wide hearth and fireplace also of limestone, topped by a log chimney plastered inside with fine clay. The one window was closed with a curtain of buffalo hide; in the spring when they drove their hides to Leavenworth they would bring back a mill-made sash, and they talked of adding a front porch with a roof. Isaac had learned enough of broad-ax and adze to make the rough boards for a low table and three-legged stools; their beds were sprung with rawhide woven across the frame. They had made besides a stable the same size, with room enough for the four oxen and the horse in bad weather, but having no scythe or sickle had cut no hay;

and had run a worm fence seven rails high across the narrow neck of the peninsula, with gateposts set in the ground but as yet no gate, the opening closed with rails set on slanting pegs. The Farrises were agreeable to Isaac's plan for a smokehouse, perhaps the icehouse too, but there seemed no hurry about building a corral with only one horse among them to hold, though it was a small enough job compared with what they had already got through.

They took off a day at a time to hunt. The season was cooling but the weather held clear and dry, there was no urgency about finishing their building. They hunted apart, the brothers together, with the wagon and team to haul back meat and hides, Isaac alone. In the two days they went out, Isaac, experimenting with different shots, killed twenty buffalo, as many as Harry and Irwin between them—they did not seem to be practiced or very lucky hunters—but did not keep up with the skinning; several of his animals, left overnight, were destroyed by wolves. With a carcass for bait he waited one evening till full dark for them to come but killed only one—and took the pelt, worth two dollars or so; they were wary and did their work at night. He thought of traps, or poison such as his father used in the barn for coons and rats. There were deer around, turkeys, other game, ducks and geese in passage to the south, but for now they hunted only buffalo. They saved much of the meat, tongues, hams, loins, whole sides of ribs; the fat too from along the spine and paunch, rendered and stored in kegs, purer and clearer than beef lard or pork grease, light as butter, they spread it on their biscuits and pan bread, and Isaac had a notion it would bring money, was worth storing in quantity. The hams they hung from the rafters in the stable, the other meat stored in an empty flour barrel, in the cool weather it would keep for a time. They consumed meat at a huge rate but worked also to get ahead for the winter. It was necessary, therefore, to get a smokehouse built, perhaps in the meantime rig up one of the tents for smoking; between them they had enough salt for the purpose. The hides had different requirements no less logical and necessary. Isaac as a boy had trapped some for muskrat along the Mississippi and knew what the buyers wanted: skins pegged out, scraped clean, dried, made up in uniform packs wrapped in deer hide; buffalo would be the same, only bigger—they would have to build a press to reduce the bulky hides to compact bundles. Each marked his own with a hot iron from the fire; for now they stored the hides, unfolded, in the loft over the cabin.

Isaac hunted for meat, of course, and in the hope of eventual profit from the hides; but chiefly from the complex of motives he summed up to himself as sport—the geometry and calculation of the hunt that made every kill different from all others, drawn in by the land itself, taking this part in the economy of its life. The hunt—the things that

surrounded it, made it possible, followed from it—had not yet become work, a means to livelihood.

Isaac had announced over supper that he was leaving for Burlingame in the morning. There would be mail from home; he needed to
answer, let his parents know of his plans. He would buy a couple of
scythe blades—they could whittle the handles for themselves, make
the rakes—so they could get in hay for the winter. He wanted to see
what could be done about the wolves; and he would try to hire a boy
for the winter, to help with the skinning, save time with the cooking
and washing up. Irwin offered to build the smokehouse; Isaac on a
piece of the writing paper his mother had provided sketched the kind
of structure his father used for smoking ham. He figured to be back in
a week.

Isaac rode east from the camp, following the north bank of the
Saline. After an hour and a half he ran into a wagon track and three
miles farther joined what was evidently the road from Fort Riley he
and Harry had met coming north. The road here crossed the river
and went on to the southwest; a small flatboat rigged up as a rope
ferry was tied to a stump on the bank. He got down, knocked at the
door of the ferryman's cabin, and roused a white-bearded old man
made talkative by solitude and a late-season scarcity of passengers.
There was a new town, Salina, two miles south, within the junction
of the Saline and the Smoky Hill; from there a road led pretty directly to Burlingame, ninety miles more or less, and Topeka. Isaac
paid his quarter and was floated across. Strange: Harry had been so
vague about what lay to the east; had left his brother to the wolves
and started for the Santa Fe Road to get help when this Salina was not
half that distance. It was the one direction Isaac had not explored in
the two weeks since coming to the Saline.

The first house he came to was a low, square, wide-eaved cabin, its
bark-slab roof weighted with poles, smoke rising from the chimney, a
flapping buffalo hide half-covering the low doorway; beyond, the scattering of houses—two of them substantial frame dwellings, one of
which was perhaps a hotel, a blacksmith's open shed, half a dozen
cabins—that constituted the town. Several horses were tied to a rail
in front of the cabin. Isaac looped his reins and, stooping, put his head
in the doorway.

—Come on in! a reedy voice called. You're a hunter, come on in and
share my meat and drink.

Isaac peered. A little, old, potbellied, bush-bearded man stood at the
back of the cabin, bald head rimmed with gray hair, arms spread in
welcome. Two or three others sat on stools or upturned kegs, another
helped himself from a tin dipper in an open keg of whisky. A haunch
of buffalo hung from a bracket, roasting over the smoky fire, half cut

away and dripping with juices, and where the drops of fat fell the fire flared spurts of flame.

—I'm a hunter, Isaac said, pushing the hide back and going in. My partners and me, we're making a camp up the Saline, mean to stay the winter.

—Tommy Thorn! the little man introduced himself. You'll be smack in the middle of the Pawnee road, aint that right, boys? You'll have yourselves some company.

—Pawnee! a man said in a rumbling basso. Aint never bothered me none, less'n they hungry goin through, help theyselfs to a ox or mule. Now them *Sioux*—

—Now *me*, Tommy Thorn said, I always hunts alone, built my cabin out alone too, ere ever they was road coming through, till the town come and built around me—and now I've got company every day. He sat back heavily on a stool. Go on now, help yourself, don't wait to be invited twice, young fellow. What you say your name was?

—Isaac Pride. Some call me Jack.

He got out his knife, cut himself a thin slice of pink meat, rolled it up, and crouched by the fireplace, chewing. He stayed for an hour, listening to the desultory hunters' talk while the men helped themselves to Tommy Thorn's meat and whisky. Antelope were getting scarce now, elk too; catamount on occasion; one claimed to have killed a Plains grizzly the previous spring but would not say just where—and "all gone from that place by now anyway," he reckoned. Isaac ventured to ask what they did about the wolves and his idea of trapping them was dismissed all around. Poison was the thing. The big, bristle-voiced hunter called Rasmus Horn who had talked of the Sioux produced from a pocket a little cork-stoppered glass bottle containing a fine white powder: a dram of strychnine, enough for thirty baits that would each kill a wolf dead as dead; all used it, though each according to his own method, which he was chary of describing in particular; none had any to spare or sell. Isaac excused himself and left with a wave of hands all around, promising Tommy to visit again when he came back.

Riding on through the town, Isaac stopped at the blacksmith's to order the two scythe blades, to be ready in a week, for a dollar apiece; and agreed to take the handles at another twenty-five cents each. While he was transacting this business, a gentleman came over dressed in a dark suit, tie, and broad-brimmed black hat and introduced himself as William A. Phillips; and in a few minutes elicited Isaac's recent history, in outline—that he was from Iowa, had come to Kansas in June, had built a ranch on the Saline with the Farris brothers, and was on his way now to Burlingame for, among other things, his mail.

—Now, Phillips said, I don't know what a man wants with riding a

hundred miles for his *mail* when we've a post office right here at
Salina—. And furthermore, Colonel Phillips continued, warming, he
couldn't see what an active young man could want in a backwater
place like Burlingame when here was Salina, on the crossroads of the
center of the state and with the new constitution approved in the
referendum would be the capital too, before they were done.

—Why, young man, he said, you happen along at a turning point in
history! Take a share in the town, turn it into lots, build yourself a
house, and then sit back and take your ease. Your hundred dollars—
take your lots along one of our two magnificent rivers—will grow to
thousands before your very eyes! Now, if you'll just step over to my
house and let me show you the plat—

Isaac thanked him again and promised to think about investing in
the company if ever he had the money to spare.—But he said, just
now I've got me a hundred-mile frontage on the Saline—stocked with
a million head of cattle—didn't cost me a cent—and I believe for now
that will be enough.

And, smiling and pleased with himself and the image of his prospects, he shook the colonel's hand, mounted, and rode off.

Colonel Titus presided at his supper table with rudimentary courtesy. He had come home late that afternoon and in ill humor, something about money or land, no doubt, but with the consequence that
he scarcely greeted the boys Marie had received in his name and now
passed few words other than to offer another slice of Vinnie's roast
turkey, another glass of claret. Ned had taken on the duty of conversation, bantering about bullwhackers met along the road, the famous
hunter Buffalo Bill Mathewson, their own ineptitude as hunters.
Marie herself, sitting opposite her uncle, contributed only an occasional word, a look of inquiry or mild astonishment. In the afternoon
while she walked Mr Kilbourn to the barn with his pony, he had put
both hands on her waist, slid them up till they cupped her breasts,
and brought his bristly face close to hers as if to kiss her on the
mouth. She wriggled free, ran into the house and up to her room, and
did not come down again until her uncle returned. She had not mentioned this to Ned, least of all to her uncle; now it seemed so strange
and momentary, she wondered if she had possibly imagined it,
dreamed it. She had exchanged hardly half a dozen words of politeness with Mr Kilbourn since coming to Kansas; knew no more of him
than that he was a childhood friend of Isaac's from Iowa. Uncle Titus
would be driving Ned in the morning to Topeka to take the stage for
Kansas City. Mr Kilbourn, offered no renewal of hospitality, had announced he would ride to Lawrence to stay with friends. Marie intended to lock her door that night with the key. Could she properly, if
Uncle and Ned started early, stay there till she was certain Mr Kil-

bourn had left? She was not traveling back with Ned. She would stay the winter, in charge of the household, her uncle would pay her something, though just what he had not said.

Isaac appeared in none of Ned's little stories. The little the boys had told when they arrived had both worried and reassured. He had gone off, they knew not where, with someone they knew nothing of and did not trust. It was inconsiderate of him, selfish. He set his heart on something and went for it with never a thought or feeling for anyone else who might be affected. She felt again as she had that morning they rode out along the creek and he let his new horse run and Regina raced after, she could only hang on: heart-deep unease, anger, fear—not chiefly that she would fall and hurt herself, make a fool of herself, though that was something; but that he cared *nothing* about the others galloping along behind. She had ridden out four times this past month to the swimming pool, not to swim, of course, but to look; once she persuaded her uncle to ride along but he complained going and coming about not having his good horse, loaned to Ned for the hunt. The leaves had turned yellow, dried brown as if pressed in a book, and had fallen early. There was still no rain.

Marie, smiling to one side and the other at her guests, then down the table at her uncle, willed them to say something more about Isaac, but Ned desperately chattered, Mr Kilbourn, shaved now, kept his sullen silence, and Uncle restricted himself to remote formalities. Absalom came in and carried out the plates, the platter, serving bowls, and set a pork and apple pie, a vessel of hard sauce, before her.

—This man, Colonel Titus said, clamping his severe gaze on Kilbourn, and Kilbourn looked down. This man just came into your camp in the dark, no horse or gun or wagon? Kilbourn nodded. And your friend Pride went off with him, took his team and wagon and went off with him the *very next morning?*

—It was the day after, Ned corrected. Next day they hunted together. Isaac shot two buffalo.

—But what sort of man *was* he? the colonel brought out, leaning forward and resting his elbows on the table.

—A hard sort, Kilbourn said, dangerous—a man that would kill. If we were back in Iowa, I'd have taken him for a river pirate.

—A deserter, that's what he sounds like. A *deserter!*

—His trousers were light blue, tucked into his boots. And a dark tunic of some kind.

—You see? the colonel declared. Some of the regiments aren't half strength. But we had a way with that kind, when I had a hand in it, in the war. He looked from one face to the other around the table. Know how we did? Pegged em out on the prairie in the sun, forty lashes on a bare back. *That* taught em something about deserting in the face of the enemy.

There was a silence.—Isaac is not in the Cavalry, Uncle, Marie said. Therefore he has not deserted in the face of anything.

—Left his friends out on the prairie, the colonel said, didn't know east from west, the way Ned tells it.

The colonel stirred his pie and hard sauce with his fork; let the fork drop with a click on his plate and emptied the decanter into his glass.

Leaving Salina late in the morning, Isaac followed the road east at an easy pace and toward sunset camped by a stream not far from where the road from Topeka came across, going to Burlingame. He might still have done it in a day by pushing his horse; or might have continued in the moonless dark and arrived late. He made a small fire, cooked slices of the tongue, and slept in his blanket. It was around eleven the next morning, the first of November, when he rode into the village. He stopped at the store to collect his mail, two letters from his father, one each from his mother and Lizzie, and a roll of Davenport papers tied up in brown paper; and put it in the saddlebag with the skillet to look at later. There seemed to be no one around at the colonel's house. Leaving Bird, he climbed the steps and rapped at the front door. A minute passed. He was knocking again when the colonel himself opened.

—Isaac! You're the last person I looked for.

—Thought the Indians got me? Isaac answered, laughing. I rode down from Salina yesterday, new town Colonel Phillips has started— camped the night on the road. . . .

Colonel Titus gazed at him, silent and unsmiling. What was it? Still angry because he'd contradicted the silly things the colonel said about Seoskuk? Such foolishness in a grown man!

—I suppose you'll stay to dinner? the colonel finally suggested, pursing his lips.

Isaac was on the point of saying he supposed nothing of the kind if he wasn't welcome, when Marie came down the stairs and stood at her uncle's side.

—*Of course* he'll stay, Marie said, laughing, and taking Isaac by the hand brought him into the house.

—Marie! the colonel said. Tell Vinnie we'll be three at dinner.

With a submissive bow of her head she turned and went off to the kitchen. The colonel led the way to the parlor and Isaac followed, carrying his hat and feeling suddenly frayed and dirty, in need of a bath and a change of clothes, though while they were building their camp he had swum nearly every day in the Saline, and used soap too at times. Colonel Titus sat at one end of the sofa and motioned Isaac to the armchair opposite, and he sat forward on its edge as for a formal interview.

—Isaac, the colonel began, I believe I know you well enough to tell

you when I am—disappointed in you. You seemed to me a sound
young man, but I am mightily displeased by what I have heard of this
hunt—leaving your friends and going off with some riffraff—

Isaac stood up, flushing. There he was again, making his hard judgment about matters he knew nothing of. Or was it only his clumsy
way of trying to express a fatherly concern? He sat down again.

—Colonel, Isaac said, I appreciate your concern, but I do what's
right the way it looks at the time, or try to, anyhow, and I don't have
to justify myself to you or any man. And the other boys—well, they
don't need *me* nurse-maiding em. Fact is, they didn't—

Marie came in.—Vinnie and Absalom say welcome, she said, and
we're having fried chicken for dinner. That, I expect, is something
you see little of on the Plains.

—Well, there's *prairie* chicken—.

The colonel, silent on the sofa, was a constraint. Marie asked questions and Isaac made brief answers, feeling hopeless of finding words
by which they could grasp the wonder he had been living the past
month. But he told them in this parsimonious fashion of learning to
hunt buffalo and only once taking two shots to kill; and of finding the
beautiful place for the winter camp and how they would spend the
winter hunting and take the hides to Leavenworth to sell in the
spring; and of building the camp, which people out there called a
ranch, and the snug cabin finished with its great fireplace, and the
stable for his team and horse, and the prairie hay still to cut before
snow came, and the smokehouse planned, the icehouse, the corral;
and go-ahead Colonel Phillips and his town, which he meant to make
the capital of Kansas.

Colonel Titus had kept silent and severe while Isaac talked but
became attentive as he told of his plans for hunting and the money to
be made from buffalo hides. Now—capital indeed! he snorted. Why,
sir, if the speculators had their way, every little prairie bubble in the
territory would be a state capital—one for every day in the year and
two on Sundays.

—It's fine land, anyhow, Isaac said, speaking to Marie, and no per-
juring claim-stakers to spoil it—didn't see anybody else the whole
time, and it don't seem there's a settler or anybody but wild Indians
west of my ranch clear to the mountains. When it's open to sale, I
believe I'll buy where I've built. And the town too—good land all
around, two established roads and two pretty rivers—capital or no, it
looks like the spot for a town.

—Kansas has room for many a town within her borders, the colonel remarked, puffing at his cigar.

—The other reason is, Isaac went on, turning to the colonel, I'm
looking to hire a boy for the winter, help with the camp chores, teach
him skinning—it's a lot easier killing the animals than keeping up

with the skinning and cutting up, why, I could keep *two* of them working full-time if I had the money to pay em both. He paused, but Colonel Titus gazed sternly back and offered no suggestions. With a grin Isaac said: Now of course if you'd let Absalom come out with me —and Vinnie to do the cooking—

The colonel let his breath out in a rush like air from a bellows. Before he could construct a reply, Absalom himself put his head in to say that dinner was on the table.

The talk over the meal continued at cross purposes, the colonel silent and cool, Isaac speaking in bursts as Marie prompted him and breaking off. She tried to turn the conversation to general matters— Isaac, for instance, knew nothing of the event that had excited the nation since mid-October, Brown's raid on the government arsenal at Harpers Ferry in western Virginia—but the colonel, flushed and thumping the table with his fist, declared that Brown and all his followers must be remanded to a military court and promptly hung. By the time they reached the bread pudding, however, Marie had hinted her uncle around to inviting Isaac to stay the night, and Isaac accepted. Afterward she went with him to lead Singing Bird to the barn and a stall beside Regina's; waited while he took off the saddle-bags, gun case, saddle, fed and watered her, rubbed her down, and covered her with his blanket.

—You ride her much? Isaac asked as they walked back.

—A few times up Switzler Creek—to your swimming place.

—She's a strong horse, needs exercise.

He set the saddlebags and gun case on the porch by the front door. Marie lifted the gun case, feeling its weight.

—It seems very heavy.

—Something over ten pounds. It's a good weight for me. They can go a lot heavier.

She sat in one of the chairs, looking out to the west.—I spend the afternoons here, she said, taking the sun, now the fall has come. He brought a chair over.

She made no move. They sat in silence.

—You know, it *beats me,* he said, frowning—the colonel. What's he mad about this time? Didn't he ever hear of "Judge not, that ye be not judged"?

—I think he was—worried, she said in a low voice. We were *both* worried—about you.

—What about? he said with a quick glance. Some foolish story of Indians running off our stock or such? We never even *saw* an Indian.

—It was *not* a foolish story! she said indignantly. It was this man you went off with—in the middle of a wilderness—sounded no better than a cut-throat and desperado. Uncle says he must be an Army deserter.

—Harry Farris may have things to hide—I don't know but what everyone has something he'd best keep to himself. But he's an honest man in what I've had to do with him, and a pretty fair hunter, and he's had some experience of the Plains—his brother too. They're my partners now.

—But Aaron and Mister Kilbourn said—

—Kilbourn! He was almost my oldest friend, but he sure didn't measure up.

—What was it, Isaac? Please tell me.

He hesitated. She looked in his eyes, wide-eyed and earnest.—I don't like talking of such things, he said. But I don't like him worrying you—or the colonel either. All it was—this man walked into camp in the dark, Harry Farris, and his oxen were sick, and he'd left his brother and his outfit and come looking for help. And I figured I'd better give him help—but the others—oh no, they made every kind of excuse, just plain *scared*, if you want to know—Kilbourn too, worst of the lot, for all his bragging and his bullying ways. What kind of way is that to treat a man? So I took my team and went off by myself—not but what I'd have liked company and someone I knew, just in case. . . .

—Isaac—I am so sorry—I did not understand—

—Don't you be sorry, he said quickly, reaching and touching her hand as if patting the head of a restive puppy. It didn't seem like taking any big chance, and I wanted to see the country for myself—

—You will stay the winter then?

—That's the plan. A month ago I didn't know what I was going to do, seemed like I'd tried every kind of thing and nothing came out the way I wanted. And now I've got a living for the winter at something I like—and something more. Yes, he continued, his words coming slower, I've got the chance for my land now too—worked for it the whole summer and just couldn't do it, but this time—I'll tell you, it was *luck* when Farris walked in with his trouble. A man has to take it as it comes. . . .

Marie, thoughtful in her turn, said nothing. Isaac blushed and looked away.—I must sound an awful fool, running on about myself. . . . I expect you'll be starting home soon, before the weather turns. . . .

—No, she said with a faint smile, this is *my* ranch, you see, I am staying the winter also—Uncle asked me to take charge of his house. But *your* ranch, Isaac—will that not belong to your partners?

—Well, we're agreed, share all the way, that's right. But if the hide business is what they say—and I find me a boy to help out—why, in the spring I can buy them out—or, I don't know, trade them somehow. Thing is, I *found* that spot, I planned the camp the way I want it, and I believe I'd be happy living there and *never* go back to Iowa.

—That seems sad, not having a home to go back to. I have had none since Father died—staying with relatives, being helpful. Uncle Titus is very kind, but—

—I think you have to make your home for yourself. And Iowa wasn't such a go-ahead place for me that there's any special place to go back to—oh, to visit my family, a few friends, maybe—

—And then the life of a hunter in such a place—wild men and savages for company, killing those great animals for their hides. It seems cruel—and wasteful. . . .

He was startled again, as when she had spoken of worrying about him: now she was pondering the life he was choosing. What could he answer?—Is it any different from taking the heads off those chickens for dinner? he said finally. Or at home when we kill our pigs, we make something of all of it, right down to the trotters, get money for the hide and bristles too, most years. Isn't any waste to it, anyhow, and I don't see that buffalo's any different, such fine meat, folks'll buy that too if I can get it to em. And the men—well, if they're rough, it don't mean *I* have to be. Let em watch out for *me*, is what I say. . . .

He stopped himself and leaned back in the chair, again with the feeling of talking too much and all about himself; but also that she somehow made him talk, drew him out. He folded his hands tightly in his lap.

A shiver went through her. She looked away. Nothing had moved in the landscape he watched out there, only the sun, getting lower, cooling the earth. She drew her shawl close around her.

IX

Pride's Ranch

My Dear Son,

. . . You have not told us your plans for the winter. When will you start for home? Do you intend to sell your team and wagon and return by boat? Now that the railway is completed to St Joseph I understand that it is possible to take the cars from there to Hannibal, avoiding St Louis. But you would do well not to leave the journey too late in the season as the Upper River this year will likely be closed to navigation by early December, and the journey from Hannibal by coach is tiresome and expensive. I have no doubt your Buffalo hunt will have been both interesting and entertaining, but one cannot prolong the pleasures of youth indefinitely. At your time of Life, your chief care should be for electing the course which you will run. . . .

. . . Fred with Mrs Weyerhaeuser called after dinner on the Sabbath and stayed to tea. Altho' he still drives around the country selling lumber as he can, there has been considerable emigration despite the hard times and he has built a number of Houses for the New Settlers, supplying the lumber of course, also cottages on the town lots attached to the Mill property; Coal Valley is such a go-ahead place he says, and so built up you would scarce know it. He expects to clear 5,000$ this year, much of it in wheat, however, taken in trade which he must then dispose of in order to realize his profit—he talks of building a mill at Coal Valley and making flour! also a good vein of coal on the property there which he intends to mine. Well, he is a shrewd and resourceful man for business but honest too, and I am thankful that he has been the means of making good to your uncle John and our other creditors. . . .

Mrs W's brother, Mr Denkmann, operates the machines. It seems that he put in very little money of his own beyond a wagon or two and teams, Fred loaned him his half of the Capital out of his earnings at Coal Valley but shares the profits equally. I have no doubt but that he would take you in also on *advantageous terms, of course the more you could bring from your savings during the past Summer, the better the terms would be. . . .*

Isaac lay in the stiff autumnal grass, studying the band of buffalo on the slope below him, thinking about how he would take them; twenty, all cows, and a dozen calves. Lonnie, waiting with the wagon back of the ridge, would be wondering why he heard no shooting, but his eyes blurred, remembering, the gun sights wavered and would not line up, and he lowered the rifle and relaxed.

Parts of his father's last letter stayed in his mind as if he could see it before his eyes: the angular, flowing, emphatic script—it looked the way his sermons sounded. He had not answered the letter yet; or rather, had written one short note responding to the four he'd picked up at Burlingame, telling a little of buffalo and the hunt, mentioning Kilbourn's betrayal but not the circumstances, and saying he was minded to see more of the buffalo country and they could write for now at Salina—telling, too, where it was located, since probably it did not appear yet by name on any maps they had. He signed it, as usual, "in haste," which was true enough—haste to be up from the colonel's writing desk and talking again with Marie, making his peace, if he could, with Colonel Titus, *doing* something. He had not anyhow answered his father's questions, or the others that went unasked: *why have you not come home to us? why? why?* That was ever his father's way, more so now he was grown: not advise, ask, urge, certainly not command; only set out the alternatives and leave you to choose, but so the choice would be obvious to reason. Isaac had not mentioned the Farrises or his plans, only told them that when he went out again it would be with friends, not alone; his father and mother both would disapprove of trying to make a living hunting buffalo, they would think it no better than woodcutting or the landless labor taken on at harvest time. He had to tell them what he was doing, what he intended, but he was not so sure now himself.

Fred was a proper, dutiful young fellow—probably would take him in, and make enough from the mill for the three of them. However they put it, he would be working for Fred; eventually there would be the farm to inherit, perhaps the land on the prairie, if they kept up the taxes, got it clear of the mortgage; his father was fifty now, he surely would not go on working like that many years longer. Was that what he wanted? A year of plowing, seeding, cultivating, and when the harvest comes in there's no market and you'd as well burn your crop in the stove instead of wood? A lifetime of paying interest and an Ebenezer Cook buys your note at a discount and takes you to court to collect in full? No, hunting buffalo was a simpler matter: shoot and kill and skin it out, take the best of the meat, and it's yours and clear, no questions, no complications. In the spring it might be he'd have five hundred hides to sell at Leavenworth at two dollars apiece, say, a wagonload of meat and rendered fat at five or ten cents a pound; it might make fifteen hundred dollars altogether, all expenses paid and only the boy's wage to come out—not the five thousand Fred had already made in his year of operating the mill but not bad for a winter's work.

The band of buffalo moved a few yards at a time down the cleft between the ridges and resumed their feeding. Isaac kept pace along the crest, bent double, loaded rifle in one hand, studying them, in no haste to begin. One cow, staying a little back—no calf following, perhaps an old one, bigger than the rest—lifted her head, tested the light breeze, and moved, and the others followed. Isaac sat for comfort, hunched forward, knees raised to steady his elbows, and swung the rifle on the old leader, finding the heart shot in his sights. His finger caressed the trigger, the *brroum* of the shot echoed back, the gun butt pressed his shoulder. He did not move, watching. The black-powder smoke drifted along the slope, dispersing, heads raised among the band, uncomprehending. The leader sank, went on her side. Isaac lay back, reloaded without haste, drams of powder, patched ball, ramrod shoving down the barrel, sat forward, fired; again, again. . . .

The rifle barrel with its half stock was hotter than he wanted to handle and he laid it aside. Nine cows lay around the first, in a radius of thirty yards; it would take the rest of the afternoon to skin them, with the boy helping; he kept trying new shots and some were slow to kill, the animals, dying, moved off. He was learning, consciously teaching himself to do better, yet the joy remained through these first weeks of serious hunting. Sport: the numbers of the kill, the animals' passivity in accepting death—it was like netting a boatload of fish, like killing cattle in a slaughterhouse without walls—would be beyond all experience for his father, beyond believing, but not the feelings or his son's careful and deliberate style, the excitement barely contained by concentrating his mind and all sense on the one object, throat tightening, heart quickening, palms moist with something not very different from fear. Isaac had learned anyhow that the kill left overnight would be torn apart by the wolves, but had learned how to deal with them, using the vials of strychnine carried back from Topeka—a single animal would do, you skinned it, opened the carcass, sprinkled the poison, and left it overnight; sometimes he cut out small chunks of meat, poisoned them too, and scattered them across the plain, making trails leading to the baited animal. The first time, he had made these preparations by daylight, in the afternoon, and in the morning the grass was thick with the ravens that followed the herds as purposefully as the wolf packs. Wolves, it seemed, would hunt or feed only by night. It was not a lesson he needed to be taught twice.

Isaac stood now, ran partway down the slope, waving his hat and shouting, and the remaining cows ran off, crowding the calves in among them. He watched them out of sight, then turned, climbed, and started back to where he had left Lonnie Parker and the wagon concealed behind the ridge, but already he could hear the boy calling, the wagon wheels creaking on their axles, coming to meet him—he had kept quiet while the shooting continued, waited out the silence when it stopped, and come on, not needing to be told; still slow at skinning and not much with a gun, though Isaac let him practice a little with targets, but serious, and he too was learning. He had been a helper at the Topeka mill since spring, about to be let off for the winter, and C. K. Holliday had recommended him; Isaac promised him fifty dollars and his keep for the season and traded his revolvers for a pair of ponies, one for the boy and a spare.

The team crested the ridge and started down, Bird on a lead behind the wagon—Lonnie had figured the direction from the sound—and Isaac ran to manage the brake. At the bottom they left the oxen yoked and chained up and worked together: rolled the first cow on her back, Lonnie spreading the legs while Isaac with his rounded skinning knife made the first cut from neck to vent. Harry Farris would not by choice kill a buffalo cow—the hide, he said, would bring less than a bull—but you took the herd as it came or wasted the day. The cow hide was smaller, thinner; once dried, they wore blanket-soft with use, and Isaac had ideas for selling them—at Leavenworth he meant to save out a couple of cow hides, have a tailor cut them and make them up in a winter overcoat, to wear but also to show. There was still an hour of daylight left when they finished, the hides folded and laid out in the wagon-bed with those from the morning's kill, a tongue and a long strip of tenderloin for supper and breakfast. Isaac started the boy the two miles back to their camp to peg out the hides for drying. With his horse staked, he sat down to wait for sunset.

Isaac knew enough of the buffalo already for his purposes—getting hides to sell, meat for immediate use—and would go on learning, yet the sum of all such knowledge was and has remained incomplete, leaving obvious and fundamental questions unanswered. The race of buffalo was as various in its physiology, behavior, and adaptation as the race of man. No observer in the buffalo years—the explorers, the hunters, for sport or profit, the traders, soldiers, the occasional naturalist pursuing his curiosity systematically according to the scientific standards of his time—knew the race in all its variety.

They were peculiarly creatures of the central grasslands, yet in seasons or places of poor grass would live like deer or moose on leaves, shoots, and bark of willow and cottonwood, sustenance Indians and plainsmen knew to provide their horses and draft animals in like circumstances or in winter. Their range was very nearly continental, from subarctic forest sixty degrees north to the Gulf of Mexico; the earliest white explorers, Spanish and English, found them also in the valleys enclosed by the Rockies and the Appalachians and on or near the southern coasts of both oceans, though on neither did they stay long after the beginning of European settlement. At these western and eastern extremes of range their appearance was recent, probably no earlier than the 15th century. Why they came is among the unanswered questions: whether driven or led by climatic changes on the Plains and beyond its borders; or forced to seek new habitat by the pressure of their own numbers and their success as the dominant and characteristic species of the grassland.

How to describe their relation to their habitat provides a similar conundrum: whether they were not creatures of the grassland but rather agents in its creation, eating out treelets as they sprouted (except in narrow belts along the eastern drainage of the principal rivers), tilling the grasses with their hooves, broadcasting and fertilizing their seed by means of their dung; or whether the characteristic prairie fires which kept out tree sprouts but tolerated and encouraged deep-rooted grasses with hard seed cases, besides being natural, lightning-caused events, were purposefully set by Indians to preserve and enlarge the buffalo range. The buffalo's heavy winter coat suggests an origin in the far north, and they regularly survived blizzards and extreme cold—facing into the wind, nosing and pawing through snow to reach buried fodder—in which domestic cattle would perish; yet they were never known in the Arctic (unless they share a common ancestry with the musk ox), and they reached probably their greatest numbers in the comparatively mild climate of the Central and Southern Plains where a coat of fur was for half the year a disadvantage to be shed by rubbing up against riverbank tree trunks, by rolling and pawing in the prairie earth, producing, besides more natural tillage, the shallow, circular depressions, ten or twelve feet across, that travelers called buffalo wallows—the dry soil, stripped of cover, loosened and pulverized, blew away, and when rain came the basin so formed filled with mud. The buffalo gave form to the grasslands in other ways as well. Unlike ordinary cattle, they cropped the prairie grasses sheep-short before moving on to fresh range, thereby at the same time determining which of the native grasses adapted to the climate would survive and dominate. The effect was the one observers meant when they described the Plains as park-like.

Travelers crossing the buffalo range, their seasons coinciding with the mysterious seasons of the buffalo, created myths: of a single great herd that occupied the Plains in uncountable millions, moving north with the spring grass. The facts of observation are incontestable: the springtimes when the Central Plains to a width of a hundred or two hundred miles were covered with buffalo all moving urgently northward in parallel columns along deeply worn trails; the times in spring or fall when the animals, teeming one day across the whole of a hunter's range, had mysteriously vanished the next. The realities—of numbers, behavior, migration, range—are more complicated than the myths by which men at the time sought to explain them.

Working backward from fragmentary records of the trade in buffalo hides, one arrives at a total population in the 1850s—when young men like Isaac Pride were finding their way into the business of hunting—of around twenty million. With small changes in assumptions—about the hide trade, the ratio of hides to total kill, rates of reproduction—the total can as reasonably be worked out to fifteen million or thirty million.

Within fewer than four centuries, it appears that the buffalo at least doubled their range, to the limits of the continent, and then contracted again. Almost nothing is known of the part played by rhythmically changing climate in this vast movement, or of the effect of the entrance of waves of Indians upon the Plains, a movement that seems to have coincided with the movement of the buffalo. Regardless of differences in language and culture, every tribe that succeeded in adapting to the Plains preserved similar legends of its relations with the buffalo: of a time when the buffalo were not and the people starved and were cold; and of the appearance of a buffalo-god or demigod, rescuer, savior, bringing the herds to the people and the people to the herds, teaching the uses of buffalo in forms that were first of all self-giving, sacrificial—tales that suggest actual and simultaneous movements, of tribal migration and discovery but also of the buffalo entering the habitat of men.

In the late afternoon Harry Farris and his brother carried their stools out to the south end of the cabin and sat, leaning back, to take the last of the sun. They had come in early, pegged out their five buffalo hides to dry, fried steaks, and as a treat stewed a pot of dried apples sweetened with sorghum. Their hunting had not prospered. In the month since building the cabin they had taken between them about fifty buffalo, nearly all old bulls, the hides marked, folded, and stacked in the loft; Isaac had brought in more than that from his first week-long hunt after returning from Topeka and now had been out again for five days. The difficulty was, they still had no team for their wagon, and without a wagon they were restricted to day-hunting within five or ten miles of the ranch, and no more hides than they could pack home on their backs or, now, Isaac's spare pony. Harry had wanted a yoke of Isaac's oxen to use with his own wagon, had offered fifty dollars for them when they took their hides to sell, but Isaac had refused, reasonably enough—the animals were trained to work as a team, and besides, one yoke hadn't the strength, with even a

light load it would give out; and then where would they be?—and
Harry was not a man to ask a thing twice. Isaac at least had made no
difficulty about offering them the use of one pony, though he insisted
on taking the other for his boy.

—You could take the hides you've got and trade, he had said. Salina,
just a little place yet, but not much over twenty miles, you'd find
someone to give you a yoke for em, Colonel Phillips, say, the proprietor. Or go on to Junction City, there's a real town, with the fort and
all, another fifty miles. I'd lend you my team for a week anyhow, to
help. . . .

Harry gazed at him in silence but did not say that he would not go
to the settlements. He stirred the fire and put on another piece of
wood.

—What you got against going to Salina anyhow? Isaac said. And
that first time, too—well, it's all worked out, but I just don't understand. Here's Irwin with his cattle dying on him, and the wolves
gobbling em up and nipping at his heels—and a town that aint hardly
a good day's walk, and a road, or wagon track anyhow, ten miles
along—and you start out pointing for the Santa Fe Road, which is
twice as far—

Harry answered with his slanted, broken-toothed smile.—Just
dumb, I reckon, he said, voice rasping. Didn't *know* there was any
settlement closer'n a hundred miles—but the road—well, I had an
idea about where, and how far. . . .

The day after Isaac came in from his first hunt on his own, he had
his hides pegged out all over the pasture, drum-tight and drying, and
him and the boy with draw-knives down on their knees working like
monkeys to scrape the bits of fat and flesh clean—good clean hides, he
figured, would bring more—and he had a kind of press rigged up,
four-inch cottonwood poles in a framework tied together with wire
and rawhide, smooth, squared slabs of wood top and bottom and a
long lever held down with a length of chain, and him and the boy
folding the green hides and pressing them tight, making them up in
packs, ten hides to a pack, a hundred and fifty pounds, and every one
with his cipher, IP, branded in a corner with a hot poker, and the
packs wrapped in deerskin and tied with rawhide—there were blacktail deer up in the hills toward the divide, a few down in the woods
along the Saline, the Farrises had shot some themselves when they
couldn't get buffalo, by way of practice, not that the skins were worth
hauling to sell, hardly, but useful anyway, and the meat made a
change—and half a load of fresh buffalo meat still on the wagon that
he hadn't seen to yet, a thousand pounds and some. Well, and into
camp come a party of greenhorns, nesting somewhere east of Salina,
and a heavy cart with a hard-favored mule between the thills, carrying their guns and footsore from walking—out to get some meat for

the winter and hadn't no luck. And Isaac stopped what he was doing, ran to meet them, introduced himself, shaking hands all around, and he made them bring the cart over and loaded them with hams and tongues and slabs of tenderloin and one whole hump of buffalo steaks, and sent them on their way rejoicing, as he said. They carried the word, it seemed. It was not a week before a pair of long-boned, scrag-bearded, coon-capped Tennesseeans rode in, long-rifles tall as they were, and asking if they'd come to Pride's Ranch and where was Mr Pride, the famous hunter, they wanted to meet him, have some talk. Harry told them Pride was out on a hunt, pointing the way he had started, but told nothing more and did not ask them into the cabin to visit. This was two days ago and it rankled still.

Harry drew a tin of cut plug from a vest pocket, worked a curl of tobacco between his palms, and with deliberation loaded his stubby pipe. Holding the flare of a match to the bowl, he got it going and puffed reflectively for a time, rubbing his fingers through his beard—he had let it go, a good inch long by now, coarse, thick-grown, and blue-black, covering the jagged scar on his cheek, and when he ate the meat juices and fat caught and congealed in the ends of his mustache.

—So how do you like it, little brother? Harry said. Working for Mister Pride.

—Pride's Ranch! Irwin glanced at him, pink-faced and downy-cheeked, and let out a snort. It don't seem we'll get along till we're on our own—go on west some and find us a place that's all ours.

—And lose our labor? Building this cabin and the barn, and every kind of thing, the way he wants—

—It aint that much that we can't build again to suit ourselves, in a week or two. There's timber along the big rivers, and we've got the tools.

—No, you listen, little brother, Harry said, that aint the way. I've been thinking. We stay the winter like we planned, hunt as best we can, and then spring comes, we let him carry the hides along to market and bring us back a team out of our share. And *then*—we sell out. Our claim's good as his, worth two dollars an acre with improvements, and he wants to stay, he can buy us in, both of us. There! New team and our outfit, and two or three hundred dollars clear from the winter's work, and we start in again. *That's* how to do it.

Harry leaned back, puffing contentedly at his pipe. His brother gazed at him a moment in admiration and smiled, rehearsing the plan in his mind.

The dog, lying at Harry's feet apparently asleep, snuffling and whimpering in dreams, roused, ran a few steps to the front of the cabin and stood barking and jumping, tearing at the beaten earth with his nails: someone coming through the woods. Irwin went inside and came out with a rifle. They heard the thump of rails thrown

down from the gateway, wagon wheels creaking, voices, and Isaac
emerged from among the trees on horseback, coming toward them,
and Lonnie behind, driving the team.

—Speak of the Devil and he shall appear! Harry said.

—He's got you quoting Scripture, brother.

—The Devil can quote Scripture when he's a mind. I know that
much.

Isaac came up, reined in, and looked down at them, smiling. He
reached a hand to Harry to shake.

—You have any luck this time? Harry asked.

—Some. Isaac swung down, clapped the horse on the rump,
clucked, and started her for the barn. I've got seventy-five hides in the
wagon, more cows than bulls—I didn't bother with calves. And a
hundred wolf skins, more or less. And meat from the last two days—
cooling down now, I figured it'd keep to haul back. You finish that
smokehouse?

—We worked at it some, Irwin said. We was out hunting too.

—Ought to finish it off. I figure that meat'll be worth something, if
we can get it cured and hauled to market. Or use it ourselves. Better
than leaving it to the wolves and ravens, or the coyotes.

Isaac regarded them soberly, looking from one to the other. His
right hand came up, the index finger pressed the golden hairs on his
upper lip, stroking, smoothing them flat. He turned and followed
after his horse with long strides. Lonnie came up, stopped the team,
and came around to take a dipper of water from the barrel beside the
door of the cabin. Watch jumped, pawing at his waist, and he stooped
to pet the dog. Isaac, halfway to the barn, swung around and stopped,
waving.

—Come on there, boy, Isaac shouted. We've got work to do before
we can play.

The Indians came the day after Isaac got back. The Farrises had
borrowed his team and gone out for a three-day hunt. Isaac calculated
something over two days more to dry, clean, and pack his hides and
pelts, another day to finish the smokehouse. He had not decided
whether to stay on and smoke the meat or leave it salted and go out
again as soon as the brothers returned.

It was late morning. He and Lonnie had the green hides pegged out
in the pasture beyond the stable and were working on them with the
draw-knives when he looked up and saw two men on horseback in
front of the cabin, three more horses with Indian saddles, and the
cabin door standing open. He had heard and seen nothing. Dropping
the tool, he started at a run, calling to the boy to follow.

Isaac passed the horsemen without looking and entered the cabin at
a jump. There were three Indians inside, all with brightly colored

breechcloths hanging over buckskin leggins, short vests open on bare chests, heads plucked of hair except for a patch at the back left long and braided down the neck. One sat on a bed examining the edge of a butcher knife and saying something that sounded like "wiskee-wiskee" over and over. Another had found the sack of crushed white sugar and stood over it with a double handful held to his lips, sucking it in.

—Get out of that! Isaac shouted and knocked his hands away, scattering the white crystals across the puncheon floor like snow.

The other was bent double in the flour barrel. Isaac made a grab at his waistband, pulled him over backward, and a dust storm billowed through the room. A wordless screech came from outside, Lonnie's voice, pitched high with fear. Isaac spun, caught up his rifle from a corner by the fireplace, and bolted out the door.

One of the men still outside had dismounted and was amusing himself with the boy: had him backed against the cabin wall with a long, sharp-pointed, double-edged dag held an inch from his chest and with playful little passes cut the boy's buttons and the shirt sagged open. Isaac with a dive laid the gun flat, caught the Indian's wrist and jerked the knife back, then with a twist sent it spinning off into the grass. Catching up his rifle, he backed away, pushing the boy behind him.

The remaining horseman looked older than the others: a narrow-faced, sharp-cheeked, dark-skinned man who sat motionless on his horse, surveying the scene with benign disinterest; he wore a black serge tailcoat open on a breastplate of elongated, light blue beads, a bear-claw necklace, a single pendant hanging from the lobe of each ear, an eagle feather stuck in the knot of hair that fell to his waist; breechcloth of dark blue fabric with a horizontal red stripe, leggins, moccasins. The other had retrieved his knife and drew a short-barreled carbine from the buckskin case hanging from the pommel on one of the horses. Isaac felt for a cap in his breast pocket, popped it on the nipple of his gunlock, and set the hammer.

—Shinga-wassa, the chief said with great distinctness. *Konza.*

—We don't keep shiggy-water at this camp, Isaac said hotly. Have to get your shiggy-water someplace else.

One of the braves emerged from the doorway, floured white as a ghost from plucked scalp to moccasins, carrying the big iron kettle in both arms.

—Shinga-*wassa*, the chief patiently corrected, smiling faintly.

Isaac swung his rifle in a rapid arc from the flour man past the one with the gun and took aim at the chief's breast.—You tell your boys to lay their hands off my property, mister, he said, or I'm going to have to kill you dead, and the devil take you.

The chief gravely considered, then spoke in a loud voice, emphatically and at length. His assistant returned the carbine to its sheath. The flour man set the kettle by the door. Another came out, still with the butcher knife in his hand; the chief spoke again and he threw it clattering on the floor inside. The last appeared, carrying what seemed to be a cotton sack of Harry's tobacco. Isaac did not move.

The chief dismounted with stiff deliberation. One of the Indians produced a blanket and spread it on the grass before his horse. The chief sat, cross-legged, draped his tails across his lap, and drew his pipe tomahawk from a loop at his belt. Another filled the bowl from Harry's sack, returned it, held a match while the chief puffed to light it, and stood back. The chief with a courtly gesture invited Isaac to be seated, and Isaac, remembering things he had read about the peace pipe and Indian notions of decorum, sat down facing the man, his rifle on his thighs, still cocked. The chief blew a jet of smoke to the south, then to the other directions, and offered the pipe. Isaac took a short puff and blew it out, feeling light-headed. The chief took the pipe back and laid it aside.

—Shinga-wassa, the chief said again, tapping his breast with the fingertips of his right hand, and Isaac understood.

—Isaac Pride, he said. My name's *Isaac Pride*, and I'm pleased to meet you, Mister Shin-woss.

—Ice-prad, Shinga-wassa repeated, smiling broadly. He clasped both hands in front of him, then reached his right hand to shake. From his tail pocket he produced a grimy sheet of paper, carefully folded, and held it out. Isaac opened it out and read, in a florid official hand:

> *To Whom It May Concern:*
>
> *This will identify the Bearer—To wit, Shinga-Wassa—as chief of the Kanzas tribe or Nation, He is leading his people on their annual winter Hunt for the buffalo, in the Saline Country. He is a peaceable and intelligent Indian, and he and his Tribe are under protection, according to law and Treaty, of the US Indian Office, neither he nor any of them to be hindered or molested by White Citizens so long as they behave themselves. Also it is a crime punishable by fine or imprisonment, or both, for any Trader to have dealings with any Indian, wild or tame, for Whiskey.*

The document was signed with a flourish by Milton C. Dickey, styling himself "US Ag't, Kanzas Agency." Isaac folded it and handed it back. Shinga-wassa shook his hand again, smiling.

The chief now adopted a serious mien, getting down to business, and holding himself erect launched into an extended discourse, speaking slowly and distinctly, accompanying his words with graceful, dancing gestures that employed both hands and arms. Finished, the chief gazed expectantly, but Isaac could only shrug his shoulders and stare back uncomprehendingly. Perplexed, Shinga-wassa frowned, thought for a while, and resolved to try again. He placed one hand on his breast: *Shinga-wassa*, he said loudly. Isaac nodded. The chief pointed at him: *Ice-prad*, loudly again, and smiled as Isaac nodded assent. Then, abandoning words and gestures, he acted his meaning out with his whole body, still sitting—riding horseback, faster, galloping, shooting with a bow and arrow, something falling dead—.

Isaac, getting in the spirit of this game, raised his rifle and took imaginary aim at something off to the northeast, over the chief's shoulder. Shinga-wassa watched him, puzzled but imperturbable, but his four braves jumped back with angry mutterings and brought out knives and hand-axes from their waistbands.

Before Isaac could think of something to make them understand that he was only showing his own way of killing buffalo, two riders came through the woods and along the path toward the cabins, each leading a loaded packhorse: in the lead, a stocky, broad-shouldered man with his hands clasped in front of him and raised above his horse's head, a dark blue military tunic buttoned to his neck, a broad-brimmed campaign hat on his head, an eagle feather sticking up from the band, and his hair in two tight braids hanging to his shoulders. Isaac jumped up, gun ready, the braves spun around; Shinga-wassa raised himself with dignity and turned to see.

The chief stood erect, arms outstretched, waiting. The blue-jacketed horseman came up, stopped, facing him, then his follower.

—Take their bridles, Lonnie! Isaac shouted without turning away, and the boy ran to do it.

The leader got down, went to Shinga-wassa and embraced him, speaking his name; stepped back and clasped the chief's two hands in his, then went to the four braves one by one, repeating the handclasps. His follower—taller and as stoutly made, with a blue-and-white polka-dot shirt hanging loose over his buckskins, the end of a red-striped sash trailing down one leg and a band of the same material tied around his head—dismounted and made the same round of courtesies. Lonnie stood wide-eyed and rigid between the two horses, gripping the bridles tightly. The leader approached Shinga-wassa again and questioned him at length, using a few words and a complex sequence of gestures, and stood back while the chief answered. He turned to Isaac.

—You must be Pride, the man said, and Isaac nodded. They told me at Salina of a new camp along the river, Pride's Ranch, and as I was coming this way to trap I thought to visit. I did not know that you would have company.

—Thieving Indians! said Isaac indignantly. I thought I'd have to fight em.

—These Kaw—

—I know they're Kaw—the old man showed me a paper from his agent.

The man looked sympathetic.—They are mostly no-account—a poor people. But the chief is a good man. I have known him as long as I have lived in Kansas. I am John Sarcoxie.

—Say! Isaac said. I know about you—got a daughter married to Seoskuk's son—

—George, Sarcoxie supplied. You know Seoskuk?

—Since I was a little boy—and this summer went down to see him at the reservation. He made me take his horse, Singing Bird.

Sarcoxie embraced him, clasped his hands, and called his partner over to be introduced: Ashapenak, another Delaware, his nephew; they were headed for a stream two days west where they meant to camp for the winter, trapping beaver.

Shinga-wassa spoke up and Sarcoxie turned, watching the fluid movements of his hands. He turned back to Isaac.

—He says he is puzzled, Sarcoxie translated. The white man is wise like the spider and knows all things. But you, when he explains things to you, are like a baby and understand no more than a baby. He smiled. He says also, the Delaware continued, that his people mean you no harm. They wish to trade, if you will agree on just prices—they have buffalo robes and other furs, will have more—

—That wasn't how it looked to me! You tell him, John—tell him if he don't keep his boys out of my goods I'll punch em full of holes like a soup strainer.

Sarcoxie, with a deprecating downward glance, turned back to the chief and went through an extended explanation. At the end, Shinga-wassa came over to Isaac, smiling and shaking his hand, nodding emphatically. With a gesture of farewell, he called his men, one gathered up the blanket, and they mounted their horses.

—What'd you tell him? Isaac asked as the five Indians rode off, single-file, with the chief in the lead.

—I told him, Sarcoxie said with a grin, that you are a poor man and regret having little that you can offer in trade. Also, you are much occupied in preparing your hides. However, if Shinga-wassa will return with his people in a week and bring robes of good quality, you will be happy to trade with him for such of your goods as you can spare—sugar and flour, coffee, tobacco, perhaps powder and lead if you have more than you can use, or tools of iron, which can be cut up to make arrow points. . . .

—I'm a hunter, not a trader, Isaac protested. And I aint got more of anything than I need to last the winter—

—You can get more. They are camped twenty miles west, on the south bank, the whole tribe, and will stay the winter. It is better to know them as friends. You will see. . . .

Sarcoxie and Ashapenak stayed three days at the ranch, relishing Isaac's fresh meat, sleeping at night on the cabin floor by the fireplace in their blankets; both rose early in the frosty mornings and went to the steep, muddy banks of the Saline to bathe, and once Isaac joined them and came back with teeth chattering to warm himself for an hour before the fire, wrapped in his blanket. The younger man was taciturn, keeping to himself, cleaning and repairing the harness, oiling their guns, sharpening knives, molding bullets; or stayed in the cabin and slept. Sarcoxie sat out with Isaac while he worked at the hides with Lonnie and finished the smokehouse, sucking at his pipe and chatting sociably. He had been born in western Ohio, on land given by the Miami tribe—his family, he said, had been slow movers, slow to leave Pennsylvania, slow to go on to Kansas. He had taken title to a quarter-section on the Stranger, farmed it some, sold timber, went out sometimes scouting with the Army and knew Captain Smith at Leavenworth—they gave you a horse, gun, ammunition, food, and twenty dollars a month besides; he had been a scout and hunter on Fremont's last expedition. Mostly he got his living by trapping in the fall and spring, did not like the cold but this winter, he said, would be mild and he might stay through. Now that part of the tribal land had been sold to settlers, there was talk of moving the tribe again, what was left of it, farther south. He had not decided if he would go; a slow mover still.

This personal history was by way of persuading Isaac to master the sign language; they were both of them strangers in this country. There were dozens of languages on the Plains, no man knew more than a few words of any but his own—Sarcoxie had known Shingawassa twenty-five years, more or less, but could say no more than fifty words of Konza. The people also used the signs among themselves while they talked, they emphasized things, made your meaning clear. After supper by firelight, in the intervals of work in the day, Sarcoxie taught him the rudiments. It was not hard once you got the principle. The signs looked like what they meant—"buffalo" was two fingers pointing the horns, "robe" or "blanket" the gesture of putting it over the shoulders, "trade" something passing from hand to hand; you expressed numbers with the fingers, each finger of each hand having its own value. Isaac learned to say the things he would trade in when the chief returned, sugar, coffee, flour.

The Farrises came back from hunting, their luck unchanged—thirty hides between them and a dozen tongues they had bothered to cut out; and grumbled about the crowd in the cabin. The two Delaware left the next morning. Isaac rode with them a short day's journey, camped with them in mid-afternoon, and stayed the night. There were beaver on the stream where they stopped, Sarcoxie said, but farther up, bank beaver—dug burrows into the stream bank but made dams like others and lived on green cottonwood bark. He got a trap from one of the packs and led Isaac a mile up to show him how it was set. Stripping, he waded in, fixed the trap with a stake of dry wood driven through a link of the trap chain into the stream bed, and stuck a green stick in the bank above the trap for bait. He gave Isaac a smell from the little bottle in which he carried the scent for his bait, a mixture of castoreum, roots, herbs. Slapping the water from his body, he reflected on the trap and decided to leave it overnight; it was not far enough up the stream, he was only showing how it was done.

Isaac had brought buffalo steaks in his saddlebags. Afterward, they sat by the fire and went on talking.

—That Shinga-wassa, Sarcoxie said, he'll come back, like he said—maybe miss a day, he forgets one day in a week, but he'll come. You give him coffee to drink, roast some meat, smoke the pipe with him, and agree on prices. Most say ten cups of sugar, one buffalo robe, but some robes worth more, some less.

—I've only got about a sack of sugar, Isaac said, maybe half a barrel of flour I brought from Iowa—

—You trade like I say. You don't trade, the young men come to the ranch at night, run off your stock, and he won't stop them—

—What you mean is, I've got to trade with him whether I like it or not, said Isaac indignantly.

—You'll see. They don't do bad things to traders. They want traders for their friends.

The people whose name sounds something like *Konza* were known to most white Kansans as *Kaw*, as is the river along which they settled. They have not had much history nor have they ever been numerous. Always they were pressed in and subjected by all other surrounding tribes—Kiowa, Arapaho, Pawnee, Comanche, Sioux. In the 18th century the Iowa and then the Sac and Fox came to fight, reducing the growing Konza population to around fifteen hundred, the level at which it remained in the late 1850s when Isaac Pride first encountered this people.

In 1815 the tribe made a treaty of peace and friendship with the United States, an undertaking thereafter prudently kept. Ten years later, they gave up their claims, if any, to land in Missouri and the territories that became northeast Kansas and southeast Nebraska, retaining a tract of nearly three and a half million acres extending west along the Kansas River and into the High Plains. In 1846 by a further treaty they exchanged that land for a reservation twenty miles square, centered on Council Grove on the Santa Fe Road. The tribe abandoned its traditional plantings but persisted in the annual hunt. The

trade in buffalo robes tanned by the women—and government annuities, the products of the demonstration farm—provided a living.

This was the tribe that would give Isaac his first tentative experience as a trader: a generally peaceable and upright people clinging to
a tradition and an identity it had never had the force to make eminent; habitually treated with condescension by whites, by other tribes
of the Plains, and by such defeated and dwindling but still proud
emigrants as the Delaware.

Shinga-wassa returned at the end of a week, as he had promised,
with four men who may have been the same who made the first visit
and, leading pinto packhorses, two women, thick and shapeless in
cloth skirts and blankets over their shoulders, hair hanging loose.
Isaac in anticipation had loaned the Farrises his team for another
extended hunt and occupied the remaining days in setting his meat to
smoke. He had the big pot of coffee hung up in the cabin fireplace
when the Indians appeared, wood and a spit ready outside; and sent
Lonnie running to the smokehouse for a half-cured buffalo ham to
roast.

Isaac made the peace sign with his hands. The boy brought a buffalo hide from one of the beds, spread it in front of the door; tin cups,
the coffee, sugar. The pipe went around, there was talk, painfully
slow, the chief smiling encouragement, the boy brought plates and
peeled slices from the outside of the roasting meat, carried out the
sack of sugar, the flour barrel, coffee beans, cups for measuring; the
women unloaded their horses and spread their robes to show.

Isaac knew nothing of the grading of buffalo robes in the trade, not
much more about their value. For most he gave ten cups, half that for
a few that were obviously inferior, imperfectly tanned and stiff, worn
thin by use as clothing or bedding; for two the men insisted were
especially fine by reason of their unusual color and softness he gave
the equivalent of fifteen cups in flour and coffee. He tried to proceed
with deliberation, but the trade, the computation of prices, was a
game, its fever seized him. At the end he had measured all his sugar,
flour, and coffee into the Indians' envelope-shaped, buffalo-hide parfleches and had bought thirty robes, ten coonskins for a cup each,
four buckskins for three cups each, and two that looked like skunk.
The women still had two packs of robes. Shinga-wassa offered to
leave them—they could agree on a price, he could pay when he had
restocked—but Isaac refused. He promised to get more flour, sugar,
coffee—and cornmeal, cloth, bar iron, powder, lead—and bring them
in three weeks to the Konza camp to trade. The chief smoothed the
bare earth in front of the cabin door and drew a map with his knife
point, the shape of the river, the places where its side streams came
in; the camp was on the south bank, where the Saline came out from
high bluffs. The men would float his goods across somehow in what

Isaac understood as bull hides. He gave the chief a buffalo ham to take away, an old skinning knife, a double handful of Harry's tobacco, and refilled his powder horn. The chief could see that he had no other presents to offer; the white hunter was a poor man, as Sarcoxie had said.

Isaac and Lonnie worked the next day loading the wagon. The Indians' robes and miscellaneous furs made up in two packs. From the loft they carried down twenty packs of his own buffalo hides and three hundred wolf pelts. The Farrises were back in the evening. Harry was skeptical of Isaac's notion of trading, annoyed at the Indians' making free with his tobacco; but agreed to let Isaac take fifty hides to Leavenworth to sell. Isaac offered to buy him a yoke of oxen from the proceeds, make up the difference as a loan if it wasn't enough, but Harry stupidly refused—he would get the cash in his hands and pick out his stock for himself. No use arguing with him, and Isaac started the reluctant boy east at dawn the next morning. It was something under two hundred miles to Leavenworth, more than a week for the heavily loaded, ox-drawn wagon. Isaac would stay to finish smoking the meat, ride through and join him there. It would take him, he figured, two good days.

Going through Salina, Isaac stopped at Tommy Thorn's cabin. The old hunter lay on his back, asleep, in front of a smoldering fire, a buffalo robe pulled up to his chin. There was no one else in the cabin.

—Tommy! Tommy Thorn—

The eyes opened, blinking.—Come on—come on in, boy, help yourself to meat and drink.

He sat up stiffly, pushed the robe aside, knelt on the hearth, and reached a piece of wood onto the embers. There were still scrapings of meat to be had from the leg bone hanging from the bracket over the fire. Lazy, he said, getting old; the others were all out at their winter camps by now, about time for him to be getting out too for the long-haired winter hides and his whisky about drunk up anyway; still some meat hanging up outside, and pushing himself up he hobbled to the doorway to bring a piece in. Isaac, hungry at the smell of the fire-dried meat, cut slivers from one end and sat on an empty keg, chewing, stirring up the fire with a charred stick.

—You having any luck out there? Tommy asked as he dropped the empty bone on the fire and replaced it with a fresh haunch.

—Some—

—Some! Tommy wheezed. Way I hear it—the boys in town here—you're cleaning up the whole dod-burned range till there won't be nothing left for an old man like me. Pride's Ranch—see, I remember —*Jack* Pride—like you had the whole herd fenced in for your private preserve. . . .

—Well then, it *is* luck, I guess, Isaac admitted. They're thick on the ground right enough, some days the stragglers come right down to the woods back of the cabin—but mostly I go up toward the Solomon with my wagon. . . .

Tommy brought the keg over and set it between them. There was still whisky sloshing in the bottom. He lifted it in his arms, careful as with a baby, and filled two tin cups—for sipping while we wait for that meat to cook some.

—You seen anything of them Pawnee yet, Jack? Tommy asked, setting his cup down. You're about on their road.

Isaac shook his head, coughing.—We've got some Kaw camped twenty miles up the river, might be the whole tribe, for all I know. The chief came over with some people to trade their robes—

—Kaw! Tommy said. I wouldn't take any Kaw robe, not if I had the choice. Now Kiowa—or Comanche, which used to go all over the Plains, trading—. But a Kaw just aint first-rate at anything, fighting or hunting or trading or—

—Well, I traded off all my staples to them, that's why I'm going through to Leavenworth, get more and go on trading.

—I used to trade some, had a place out beyond the Great Bend of the Ar-kansas till the Kiowa got mad about something and burned me out. Before that, working for Colonel Bent at his fort. Why, I was younger'n what you are when I first went out to the mountains, trapping. See, the big fur companies, they'd send their goods up the Missouri on their steamboats, first thing in the spring, and then haul em or pack em to the place where all the trappers agreed on a get-together, which we called the rendezvous. And then, oh the times we had! Two hundred of us packed in from all over the mountains—and the feasting and the drinking, fighting, and running races and shooting at the mark. Only—here's the thing—you'd come in with your whole winter's take, maybe six hundred pelts—well, this was thirty years ago, and there wasn't any call for anything but beaver. But you'd think: now I've done it, I'm rich when I sell my beaver. But warn't never like that. Comes time to settle up, the merchant counts up your skins and writes em in his book, puts on a long face—times is hard, he says, can't give you what I paid last year! And you come to pay for your whisky, your powder and lead, your flour and such, and —oh, *times is hard*, and everything you want cost twice as much. And when you get through, isn't hardly anything left from all that work, running up and down the mountains and chopping through the ice to set your traps—and some half-wit Indian boy takes a shot cause he fancies your hair ornamentin his shield—. Ha! At least I'm no temptation that way anymore. . . .

He smoothed his palm approvingly across his hairless scalp.

—They say the beaver are all gone now from the mountains, Isaac suggested.

—I was done with it before that. There was good times all right, but it wasn't such a life, take it all in all. Now I've just only myself to look out for, and I kill enough buffalo to get my keep—and a keg of best Kentucky once a year when I go in to the States—and that's all I want. But the dod-gummed merchants! They aint changed none. Now your average robe, Kaw or anyone, that's worth five dollars' gold at any port on the Missouri, fifteen or twenty when they carry it east—and a first-class robe, why that's three times as much, all along the line. But your merchant! He'll offer two maybe three dollars, and you'd think he was doing you a kindness. And same with your hides and your wolf skins and everything else. And if you're a young fool like I was, you'll take it and thank him, at least the first few times. . . .

—I took special pains with my hides, Isaac said. Dried em and scraped em clean with a draw knife—

—*That* don't make no difference. They buy by the pound, sell em to cover saddles and such. A half-dime a pound—maybe six or seven cents if you bargain em up. You can save your trouble. . . .

Tommy added wood to the fire and leaned over to give his meat a turn.

—You ever come across a trader named Bisonnette? Isaac asked after a silence.

Tommy thought.—There was a André Bisonnette, kept accounts at Laramie till he took sick, neat little man, family at Montreal or Saint Louis or someplace. Frenchman same as me—bet you wouldn't know that, would you?—or my daddy, anyway. Our name was *Thon*, which is a kind of fish, means we were fishermen sometime, or sailors. I changed it into something Americans can say.

—It's a strange name. What do you think it means?

—Some kind of fish, I *told* you. Big. I don't know *what* kind.

—I mean Bisonnette.

—Ah, *bisonnette!* I thought anybody knows that. Why, boy, *bison*, that's just what you call a buffalo. And *bisonne*—that's a cow, that's how you say it, and *bisonnette* is a little one, a calf. Only—.

Tommy emptied the last of his whisky into his cup, turned up the keg and arranged his back against it, feet stretched toward the fire.

—Here, he said. I'll tell you a story to pass the time while the meat cooks, and sweeten the sippin.

—*Bisonnette*—that's what a Frenchman calls a buffalo cow, but what it really means is, buffalo-*woman*, and that's something strange: between a goddess and the mother of God. Every tribe hunts buffalo has stories about her, I reckon I've heard a dozen—in the lodge at night, and they go around the circle telling tales, and you pick out the words you know, and the fellow if he likes you and means to be polite, he talks with his hands so you can understand.

—Now this story happens way long ago, before the people had bows or guns or anything to get meat with, fact is, they didn't *eat* any meat but they dug roots out of the ground like a bear. And the buffalo, they was different too—lived in villages and traveled around the Plains, and when the spring come, which is the time for fighting, the young bulls would go out together, ranging around till they come to a village of people. And then they'd go in and kill em all, women and men and the little babies, and have a feast. The buffalo, see, ate the people then, not the other way around.

—Well now, in one of the people villages there's a exceeding handsome young man, son of the chief, all the girls come around his lodge and say how handsome he is, and strong, and brave—cause, see, they'd all like to marry him—but isn't one of these girls suits him. But then one day comes along a strange girl no one's ever seen before, very dark but very beautiful, and that's the one: he picks her out and takes her into his lodge, and he's married to her, that's how they do. Well, everything's fine, and his wife has a little baby boy. But then he wakes up one morning and his wife and boy are gone, can't find em anyplace in the village, and oh, he's sad, but he says: I love my wife and child, and I will find them and bring them back—and makes up a set of moccasins to travel with and away he goes.

—He picks up the trail soon enough, young woman and little boy, and keeps following along till away off on the horizon he sees one tepee all by itself, and it's where his wife and boy is camped. Now she comes out to meet him, says: Don't follow us anymore, I must go to my people far away in a country where men cannot live, and my people will be angry, they will kill you and eat you, and I do not want for you to die. But he says: No, I love you and my son, and I will follow you wherever you go. Well, she doesn't argue, it seems, but lets him come into the lodge and stay the night, cause he's her husband after all. But in the morning he wakes up and they're gone.

—You think that stops him, maybe? No, *sir*, he's a very stick-to-it young man. He hunts around and he finds their trail and starts in to follow—but pretty soon it's not a human trail anymore but buffalo tracks, a cow and a little calf, going along together. But that don't stop him, of course, cause like I say . . .

—Well, same thing happens day after day, night after night: follows this trail, catches up and finds his wife and child, and stays the night —and in the morning they're gone, and the tepee's gone, and he's following a buffalo trail again. Finally he comes to the great buffalo village, whole herd gathered together and his wife and boy in among them, but he doesn't know how he's going to get them back. So he kind of stays around the buffalo village, keeping out of sight, but the buffalo chief, he knows there's a man out there right enough, sends out the criers and calls a council, says: Buffalo! What we going to do about this man has found our village and is hiding out there? Well now, the biggest and bravest of the bulls stands up: I'll find him and kill him—what's there to killing a man, anyway?—and bring him in so's we can have a feast.

—So in the morning this buffalo brave goes out hunting the young man—raging and pawing the ground and tearing up with his horns, like they do—and finds him, too, and makes his run, meaning to trample him, stab him, tear him to pieces. But the young man, he just stands there facing him, looking him in the eye, and he don't move no more'n a big stone stuck in the ground. Well, sir, the buffalo *he* don't know what to do with that, cause he figures the man to give him a run or try to fight, or *something*, and he pulls up short and kind of hunches back on his hindquarters, looking. Finally he says, You're too many for *me*, young man—and turns and trots back to his village, tells the chief and the other bulls all about how brave this young man is and his wonderful powers, that you can't kill him.

—Well, in the stories this happens lots—other bulls go out, and Buffalo-Woman's father and brother—but, every time, the young man acts the same and they can't kill him. . . .

—Now in the night while the young man's lying out on the grass, trying to hide and sleep, or maybe he's dug into a cave somewhere, *I* don't know—but he has a dream, and in his dream here's his wife, real as life, and she's the beautiful dark young woman he picked out of all the others to marry, but also and at the same time somehow she's a buffalo: Buffalo-Woman. And telling him: Young man, my husband, I cannot come back to you now or bring our son, but because you are brave and for love have followed us to buffalo-land, I must teach you. She says, It is not right for the buffalo to kill men and eat them, and men starve on roots and tree-ears. Says, Men got to learn that buffalo is good for all their food, got to learn how to fight them and kill—. Then Buffalo-Woman shows him what a bow is and how to make one, and arrows, and how to put the points on and the feathers.

—Now the young man wakes up and goes and does like she told him—makes his bow and his arrows, practices till he can shoot and hit the mark every time. Then when a big old bull comes out to kill him, the young man just lets him come, and then he shoots him dead. And he cuts a little piece out to taste, and it's true, like Buffalo-Woman told him—good, and what he needs.

—The young man starts back toward his own country, and his village, but along the way he comes to a strange village—and here's a band of buffalo bulls attacking, and the people down behind a wall of earth, beating them off with clubs, but the buffalo just come on charging through and carrying them off. So up he comes with his bow and starts in shooting—and the buffalo falling over dead and all in confusion, and pretty soon they've had enough and they're running off, or what's left of em. And then he goes in and teaches the people to cut up buffalo and that it's good to eat. And that's how the Indians learned about buffalo.

—There now, Tommy Thorn said and sat up. My whisky's done and so's the meat, like I said—or done enough. You got your appetite?

—Did the young man ever get his wife back? Isaac asked.

—There's stories about that too—in some he does, and some he doesn't. But when times is hard and the game scarce, or it's winter and the people starving, a man goes out from the village and waits for his dream—and in the dream, it's Buffalo-Woman, leading him to the herd. . . .

—And the young man—doesn't he have a name?

—Some, he's Sun-Boy, some he's Stone-Man—but those is a different bunch of stories again. But always it's a young man does the business, whether he's called by name or not—something special about him that sets him apart from everybody else. And a beautiful young woman that helps him do it. . . .

Mr Alexander Garrett stooped over an open pack of buffalo robes, shaking them out one by one on the floor, examining. Besides the store on Cherokee St, it turned out he had a frame warehouse three blocks over where he kept his goods in bulk and stored his hides and furs, goods of every kind stacked to the rafters along both walls and space between to drive in two freight wagons and their teams. E. H. Durfee, still associated, as he put it, with Garrett & Co., had come along from the store but took no part in the proceeding and stood off to one side, chatting with Isaac. There were no other customers in the store when Isaac came in, and Durfee put on a smile and acted pleased to see him—remembered his name too and wanted to know if he was back from the mountains already with his gold or possibly bringing in another shipment of that excellent, top-drawer Iowa flour; but no, Isaac said, only a load of furs he'd brought from the buffalo country to sell so he could take back goods for trading with the Indians.

—Good *as* gold, though a mite heavier, the little man assured him. Mr Durfee excused himself, brought a stepladder over, climbed up, and lighted a big brass lamp hanging from a chain overhead.

Isaac had caught up with Lonnie and the wagon that morning, ten miles out, and led him on in with only a brief stop to rest the team. He was hungry and becoming impatient, Mr Garrett had been at it for an hour already, and what was so difficult? The buffalo hides he'd scraped were clean and soft, as good almost as a robe, compared with the Farrises', anyhow. And the Kaw women's robes!—whatever

Tommy Thorn said, they were better than anything his family ever owned in Iowa. But old Garrett—taking his time about it and no way to hurry him, first he had half the buffalo hides off the wagon and weighed the packs on a big scale, then with his jackknife he cut the rawhide thongs on two of them, opened them up and spread them out —as if he couldn't take a man's word and you'd fill the pack up with slabs of wood. And going through the wolf pelts, and now the robes, one by one—

Isaac went over to him.—You mean to buy or not? he said, his voice tight.

The man went on looking, imperturbably fingering over the robes, and did not answer; turned over the last and very slowly stood up, his face expressionless.

—Sure, I'll buy, he said. Tell you what: two hundred for the lot. And, he added with a hint of concession, I'll make that gold.

Isaac took a few moments to run the offer through his mind.— Mister Garrett, he said, maybe you could tell me how you arrive at that—I've got robes and hides and wolf skins. Maybe I'll just sell you part, and take the rest somewhere else.

—Why, I don't mind. I figure sixty for the robes—

—That's *thirty robes!*

—and seventy-five for the hides, and same for the wolf and the odds and ends—

—That makes two-ten!—

—Does it now?

—and more than twenty-five hundred weight of first-rate hides— why, that's practically two hundred dollars right there, everyone says—

—*I* don't say, Garrett said, taking his time still. *I* say, two hundred for the lot.

Isaac looked down, clapping his hands softly together as if counting.—Mister Garrett, he said finally, I came straight to you with my wagon, cause we did some business in the spring—haven't talked to anyone else in Leavenworth. I'll have to give your offer some thought.

—You do that, boy. And if you're done thinking in the spring, and haven't sold—why, bring em back and we'll talk some more! And now—he straightened up with unexpected vigor—I'll be getting back to my store—and turned and swung off with long strides toward the door.

They were a time, Isaac and the boy, remaking the packs and getting everything back neat in the wagon. Durfee waited, not hurrying them.—I'll walk along with you, if I may, he said as Isaac started after the wagon, leading his horse. Isaac, thoughtful, nodded. Have you made arrangements, the little man continued, coming up to him, for lodgings, and a place to stay?

—We came straight to the store, Isaac said. We can camp out on the prairie somewhere—done that before. Or sleep in the wagon.

—Perhaps you would accept the shelter of my roof and a blanket on the sofa. There's hay in the barn for your animals. It isn't far.

—That would save me some trouble.

They walked another block in silence. Durfee had something on his mind and was working around to it.—I believe you did right, refusing Mister Garrett's offer. I don't know a great deal about furs—

—I surely don't, Isaac said, except how to get em.

—but I believe I know *something*, Durfee continued, I've traded myself, and your hides—very acceptable. And the robes, with one or two exceptions—. Lump them together and I'd say they're worth *double*, even four-fifty, perhaps.

—Not from him they're not. Who else in Leavenworth?

—Oh, there are houses—not that I wish to trade against the firm, you understand, but still—. But if I were you, I'd consign them down to Saint Louis—season's late, but the river's still open, boats running. The great time for the trade, and height of activity, is the spring of the year, but just now, whatever Mister Garrett lets on by way of bargaining . . .

Durfee's idea was for Isaac to ship his load to W. C. Lobenstein & Co., St Louis, who would take it for cash, less the freight. He would want ten percent commission himself for making the arrangements and collecting. But Isaac would come out with four hundred clear, double what Mr Garrett would give.

—That'll take a month, Isaac objected. What do I do for cash? Those Indians are waiting to trade, I promised—and I haven't even got coffee, or flour for flapjacks.

—You could take what you need on credit. Everyone does.

—What credit? I've never done business in Kansas, except bringing you my father's flour in the spring.

—Say thirty days net at two percent, that's nothing much. I'll talk to Mister Garrett. . . .

In the evening after he came back from the store—Isaac for supper fried up the last of the meat he had brought from the ranch, on the stove in the shed kitchen at the back of the tiny rented cottage—Mr Durfee wrote out in duplicate an inventory of the hides and furs to be shipped to St Louis in the morning. Isaac gave him the list from memory, noting the two robes he judged to be premium-quality as well as the two he thought less good, and the merchant took him at his word; and signed a receipt attached to Isaac's copy—Good as money, he commented in passing, if you're short and take it to a bank to discount, just like a grain receipt.

Isaac did not sleep much that night on the sofa in the narrow front room of Durfee's cottage, with the cold stove in one corner. The furs out there in the wagon beside the house were real and substantial, they had heft, a hundred pounds to a pack in their deerskin wrappings, he had figured to trade them off pack by pack for Garrett's goods to fill it up again—well, and take those out to trade and bring them in for *two* wagonloads. What he had was a piece of paper—and in the morning another paper, promising to pay in full, in a month. Thirty days: any snow and they'd be ten days hauling out, then straight out to find the Indian camp—suppose they'd moved or had nothing to offer or the weather got worse?—and just about get back in time to meet the note; or miss the date and never have credit in Kansas again. A lot to promise for a piece of paper. Or Durfee—take the money from the consignment and light out for New York or San Francisco, like that what's-his-name, the scoundrel his father trusted and ruined the mill over two rafts of logs. Still: Durfee was there in the spring and hadn't run yet. It might be he was what he seemed and said, and would keep his word. . . .

Durfee was up with the light and came through to the kitchen, knocking up a very small fire in last night's ashes for coffee and porridge. He led them down to the freight agent's warehouse on the levee to unload and arrange for shipment to St Louis, advancing the tariff with his own money and taking Isaac's receipt for the charge. At Garrett's warehouse he brought out the key for the padlock, swung the door open, and led them in; Mr Garrett, it seemed, was leaving this business to his clerk. Isaac and Lonnie went down the aisles, carrying out sacks and heaving them on the back of the wagon while Durfee kept count on a printed billhead: sugar, Isaac decided, was the big item, but almost as much flour, twenty bushels of meal, a hundred pounds of green coffee beans, fifty pounds of tobacco. Durfee did his extensions and added them up. The bill so far came to under three hundred dollars. Isaac and the boy went on—kegs of powder, pigs of lead, a few lengths of bar iron; the wagon was full but not piled high. On a shelf at the far end of the building Isaac spied a bolt of blue polka-dot cloth like Ashapenak's shirt, pulled it out, carried it over to the wagon, and threw it on, for luck. It was enough.

At a rough table near the door Durfee wrote up the bill in full and copied it out. Isaac read it through and did the addition for himself: $374.50—for forty-three hundredweight in goods, a pretty good load. He signed it in full, his three names and the date. Durfee showed him the note: with the interest it came to $381.99, to be paid not later than January 20, 1860. Isaac handed it back.

—The figures look right. But why's it made out to you?

—Mister Garrett is a very conservative and, I might say, old-fashioned man of business. He—

—What you mean is, Isaac said, he'll trust you for this stuff but not me. And if somehow I don't get back here on the twentieth, then—

Durfee nodded glumly, then brightened a little.—But I'm sure you *will*, Mister Pride, he said. And if—well, there's your consignment to Lobenstein to cover, which I'm sure it will—and *more* than cover—. And then if all comes to a prosperous conclusion, and works itself out, as you might say, why, I have a different way of going at things from what Mister Garrett has, let me tell you, if you take my meaning—

Isaac studied the little man's guileless face for a moment.—I just wanted to understand what I was putting my name to, he said; and signed the note with a flourish and put his copy and the copy of the bill away with Durfee's receipt.

Isaac rode beside Lonnie as far as the crossing of the Stranger River. The morning was still early, frost on the grass beside the road. Maybe it was that, being up and traveling west, or the work of loading the wagon, getting the blood moving, and his own wagon going out with a bigger load than he brought in: whatever had worried him in the night was gone, he could no longer imagine it. Why, that note —seventy-five robes would cover that, and he could buy that many with five hundred pounds of sugar—and there was *sixteen hundred* pounds of sugar in the wagon, and everything else. Or say the Kaw had three hundred hunters in their camp and he traded *just one robe* for each, that was fifteen hundred dollars right there, and the cash still to come from Lobenstein at St Louis. And just beginning—hides of his own at the ranch and more to get, fast as he could shoot and skin them out. . . .

Isaac had thought to stay with the boy all the way back, heavier load now and all depending on getting it safe to the ranch. It seemed more urgent to ride on through and get back to hunting. Coming up from the crossing, he decided and told the boy: he was riding on ahead—don't kill the cattle but push right along and there's a five-dollar bonus waiting for you at the ranch to start the new year. Isaac slapped his horse to a run. However things came out for him, he still had money to pay the boy for honest work.

—What do you mean, you didn't get paid? Harry Farris said again. What'd you go to Leavenworth for if it wasn't to get money?

—I *told* you, Isaac said.

He had ridden through, stopping at Salina only long enough to ask for his mail, and reached the ranch the second day out. The brothers were finishing a supper of meat from the smokehouse. It did not seem they had hunted that day or the day before. The argument was starting over.

—I told you, Isaac said. The merchant at Leavenworth just

wouldn't give a fair price—if I took his offer, your share wouldn't have come to fifteen dollars, about half what it should have been. So I sent the lot on consignment to a firm at Saint Louis, then they sell and—

—Consignment! Harry said, rubbing his fingers across his whiskered cheek. I don't know about consignment. I just want my money.

—I'll have it when I get it from Mister Durfee—maybe in a month. I could pay you in goods, Isaac continued after a pause, when Lonnie comes in with my wagon. Sugar say, I'll have plenty of sugar. What would you say to three sacks of sugar? And take em to the Kaw camp to trade for robes—forty or forty-five robes, in the spring when you take em to sell they'll be worth over two hundred dollars. Aint that worth waiting for?

—I don't want no sugar, or trading with Indians neither, Harry said. I want to kill my buffalo and get my hides and take em to sell. And I want to *get paid.* Aint that right, Brother? he concluded, turning to Irwin.

Isaac made no answer.

Ned Eliot came to Burlingame for Christmas and stayed till New Year's, his brass-bound leather trunk half-filled with presents—a bottle of old Bourbon whisky for Colonel Titus, fine French linen handkerchiefs trimmed with lace for Mrs Schuyler, cigars for her husband and Aaron, a tin of peppermint candies for Bill Shirley, and a book for Marie. He had not forgotten Vinnie and Absalom: a large, brightly printed bandanna for her, a pair of serviceable black leather gloves for her husband. One day he rode out with Marie up Switzler Creek and another they drove east along the road in the colonel's buggy, wrapped together in a buffalo robe. In the evenings they read Marie's book, a new one with engraved illustrations, *The Courtship of Miles Standish,* taking turns reading aloud while the colonel lay back in his chair, listening and dozing; and afterward talked earnestly of the rights and wrongs of Longfellow's story. Ned could see only that John Alden had betrayed his friend.

—Why, Ned? Why? Marie warmly answered. He carried the message well enough, even though it went against his own heart. Priscilla simply did not like it.

—He had no right to speak to her, when he knew his friend's feelings.

—I do not see that at *all,* Marie said—foolish man, too shy or stupid to speak for himself. And where would they all have ended if John had *not* spoken up?

—Because Miles *loved* her, Ned said with a blush. And John knew he did.

—Well, it was not as if he had put his brand on her, Marie said with a laugh—or tied her to a stake like a naughty puppy. I do not know how she was expected to know a thing like that.

—A woman just knows such things. She knew well enough how John Alden felt.

—Oh, that was *different*, Marie triumphantly concluded. Besides, when it is over, and they are married, Miles even *admits* he was wrong to take it badly, and then they all are friends again.

Nevertheless, the story did not seem quite as clear to Marie as she had made it out to Ned. She read it through again that night by the wavering yellow light of the bedside candle. What *was* this feeling, and was it really true that a woman knew more about it than a man? But how was she to recognize it in someone else unless she knew it first in herself? And such different things said of it—sometimes it sounded like a kind of warm peacefulness, like sitting by the fire on a cold night, and again, as if the fire was inside you, burning, and heating your mind to delirium till you could no longer know what you were doing or think two sensible thoughts together—no, she did not think she would like that feeling at all. Ned, now, if they were performing the story on the stage, would do very well as John Alden, graceful and handsome and gentle, always tactful and polite, never mean-tempered, it seemed. And Isaac Pride, of course, would be Miles Standish, gruff and shy, going off somewhere to fight the Indians. She had written to him at Salina, as he seemed to want, but only once. He had not answered, too busy no doubt building up his ranch and hunting. Or suppose like Miles Standish in the story he was—but no, they only *thought* he was killed in the war, gone so long, and in the end, on their wedding day, he came back. She did not feel at all like Priscilla, so beautiful and sweet she was supposed to be. Sometimes in the mirror, with her hair new-brushed and smooth under the little feathered riding cap, her face did not displease her.

In the night she dreamed in snatches. She was sitting in a chair, sewing, and a man came up to her in a heavy steel breastplate, with a wide-mouth blunderbuss over his shoulder and a helmet that hid his face, telling her of John Alden and his love for her, his wish to marry —and it was Isaac speaking, but in a fluent, singing voice that was like music. And—Isaac, she said, Isaac Pride! I don't want you talking to me like that, about someone loving me and marrying. Not now— not yet. . . .

For the last day of the year Mr and Mrs Schuyler invited a few friends for an evening of musical entertainment. There was a bowl of punch on a table in the parlor, a fire of soft Kansas coal in the grate, a luxury hauled in a hundred miles by wagon. Mrs Schuyler seated herself at the piano and the guests gathered behind her. She began with "Chesterfield," then "Montague," "New Jordan"—old psalm tunes everyone knew, though not all the same words, but it was the music, not the words, that mattered, the chords resolving one to another in the necessary sequence leading to conclusion and the voices densely following, expounding and sweetening that logic, then returning, restating, insisting, beseeching, at each succeeding verse. Mrs Schuyler stood up—enough, she said, for her stiff old fingers, and would Mr Eliot, perhaps, care to offer something for the young people?

Ned struck up with a dance tune, the "Louisville Quickstep," then "Frankfort Belle." When he came to "Old Rosin the Bow" Mr Schuyler said that was a fiddler's tune if there ever was and got out his violin to join in, and made him play it four times over. Colonel Titus, smiling again, set down his cup, seized Mrs Schuyler, and danced her around the room till she made him stop—she was out of breath, and if he didn't stop he'd smash her crystal and burn the house down.

Ned was starting back on January 2. Mail came in on the stage from Topeka in the morning, with several pieces for Colonel Titus and a letter for Marie, which Ned brought and handed to her.

—It must be from Isaac, Marie said. It is from Salina.

—Salina? Where's that?

—It is a settlement on the Saline River, right out on the frontier about two hundred miles west from Leavenworth City. And he has a ranch somewhere out beyond, in the Indian country, hunting buffalo. Did Uncle not tell you when he wrote?

Ned shook his head.—Hunting buffalo? That sounds a rough occupation for an educated young man. I mean—oh, I expect it's well enough for a lark, but really—when a man has his way to make—

—Ned! Marie said with a little laugh. You sound just like Uncle.

There were two pages, closely written on both sides in Isaac's sprawling hand. She skimmed through, conscious of Ned standing over her at attention, hands clasped behind his back, and refolded the letter and put it away for later reading.

—He wrote this on Christmas Day, she said, with a turkey in the Dutch oven in the fireplace, waiting for it to cook. Turkey by the hundreds roosting all around in the trees, but the buffalo and deer and all the other game so plenty they mostly do not bother—except now and then, for variety. And what do you think? He says he has turned Indian trader—the whole Kaw nation camped nearby for their winter hunt, and he has a wagonload of goods coming from Leavenworth to trade with them. *Ten times* the profit, trading for Indian robes, that there is in hunting, he says. Now is *that* not an interesting occupation for an educated young man?

. . . *It was, I am told by Mr Burrows who was present, as sordid a spectacle as any Davenport has witnessed since its founding. Cook & Sargent suspended in September, as I may have written—have not paid out a dollar in specie on deposits*

but only bank notes and have been taking in "wild-cat" money that they spon-
sored, pretty heavy, so all knew they were in difficulties. Then on Friday morning
16th December Mr Ebenezer Cook announced by printed notice in the window,
they would not open and went home. All quiet enough 'til round about supper time
along Front St comes a column of men marching some hundreds it seems, and
carrying clubs and torches and no shouting or singing but entirely silent, formed
up like troops. Mr Burrows says he felt some concern they were making for the
bank building or possibly his mill and warehouse as he has been pretty active in
currency himself, and runs along to shut up his windows with iron shutters, and
all the other merchants too. But no, up Perry St they turned and went along to Mr
Cook's new house in very good order and took up positions all around. And then it
seems the word went among them and they gathered stones from the roadway and
begun to throw by light of their torches, and did not desist 'til every window in the
house was broke, and then went in and carried off the furnishings among them, but
did not offer, Thank God, any molestation to Mr Cook or his wife and little ones,
who were up in the attic all the while. . . . For my part I feel as much sorrow for
the assailants as for Mr Cook and his family. To the losses they have suffered
through him either now or in times past, not to mention sharp practice and Inso-
lence, they have added the Sin of Violence.

It was thus with some heaviness that we received word of your venture. Surely
the troubles of Cook & Sargent are a sign and warning set up on the way for our
instruction. When once you lay out your credit at interest—and in an enterprise so
uncertain as trading with the Indians—you know not where it may end. There are
twenty other Iowa banks broke up since the Panic, I am told, and hundreds more
across the country. . . .

Isaac, seated at the writing table in the small bedroom upstairs at
the back of the Planter's House, pushed his father's letter to one side.
Ever anxious over money and credit: he wanted to tell his father as
plainly as he could that there was nothing wrong with his credit in
Kansas now, he was good for all the stock he could load his wagon
with, and money over to his account besides—but not too boldly, not
boastfully; and there had been worries enough, getting to Leavenworth, and then the morning hunting up Mr Durfee at his new premises. When the business was done, he concluded to stop the night at
the hotel, and realizing that Lonnie would be sharing the bed—the
boy, when asked, thought his last bath to count had been in the river
at Topeka, sometime in September—had taken him along to the clothing store and bought him trousers and a wool shirt, a union suit,
socks, sheepskin gloves, and left the boy's former clothes with the
storekeeper to throw out; and for himself a suit of heavy black broadcloth such as his father wore for Sundays, with a silk vest patterned
with tiny pink flowers worked in the cloth. Arrived in the room, he
sent the boy with soap and towel along to the bathroom for a soak and
extracted from his satchel the thin sheaf of letters he meant to answer
before supper.

The weather had turned cold, with a little fresh snow, when Lonnie arrived at the ranch, two days before New Year's. Isaac gave him a day's rest and did the unloading himself, leaving a stock of staples on the wagon; Harry was not pleased with the sacks of sugar, flour, and meal piled up at one end of the cabin, but until they could build a proper storehouse there was nowhere else. Isaac reached the Kaw camp on January 2. The chief gave him the use of a large buffalo-skin tepee to sleep in and lay out his goods; the family that owned it supplied meat, but it was understood that Isaac would furnish what they wanted of flour, sugar, and coffee.

Isaac stayed a week at the camp and was two days at the ranch, sorting the buffalo robes and making them up in packs. The time was getting uncomfortably close to the due date for his note. He had not hunted much since returning from Leavenworth but still had five packs of hides from before, with as many of the Farrises', a hundred wolf skins; and ten packs of robes. It was necessary for him this time to travel east with Lonnie and the wagon. They started before light on the twelfth and were on the move every day from dark to dark, sleeping most nights with settlers along the way—for a dollar a man would move his family onto the floor of his cabin and give the strangers the bed—and buying hay for the team to save time. Isaac did most of the driving and let the boy stay in the wagon, wrapped in a spare robe. Bird followed, a blanket over her back. At nooning time, while Lonnie cooked, Isaac rode her a little, bareback, for the exercise. They had made it through to the outskirts of Leavenworth by the night of the nineteenth; the note was due the next day. Isaac still had sixty-two dollars left from his summer earnings, most of it in coin.

Mr Garrett had just opened up when they arrived in front of the store in the morning. Mr Durfee, he said, had left his employ, but he was uncommunicative as to where he would be found or what he was doing. "You'd know well enough if he still owed you money!" Isaac hotly told him. "That's as may be but none of your affair, I don't think," Garrett answered and turned away to fire up his stove. Isaac left Lonnie with the wagon and went through the town inquiring till he came to the freight agent on the levee, who remembered him and told him plainly: Durfee had started the new year with his own business, little place rented over on the south end of town. It was late morning before they found it: a two-story frame building with empty lots on either side and a new sign nailed up over the doorway, *E. H. Durfee & Company*, unadorned black lettering on a white ground. The little man himself came out as they pulled up and shook Isaac by the hand, apologizing for not having written him at Salina.

The store was stacked like a warehouse with goods hauled in from St Louis, no shelving or counters in yet; Durfee meant to concentrate on the Indian trade, dealing with traders and hunters like Isaac, and it did not matter for now, not being in the center of town, he did not expect to carry general hardware and other merchandise as Mr Garrett did. Isaac sent Lonnie to bring in coal for the stove—the merchant having as yet no boy of his own—and sat down with him at a table to go over his accounts. The consignment of furs came to over four hundred dollars with all expenses paid, which Durfee had already credited against the note. Together they brought in several packs of robes and hides to weigh and examine. Durfee reckoned he could pay at least eight hundred dollars when he sold them and offered an advance of a hundred dollars if Isaac would leave the balance on deposit at one percent a month—Makes it a little easier for me, you understand, getting started, he explained; and two months' credit on goods taken by the wagonload. That was when Isaac decided on the new suit for himself and a night at the Planter's House before starting back: a hundred and fifty dollars in gold and St Louis bank notes in his pocket and seven hundred dollars or more in prospect. The new lot of robes had cost him sixty dollars in trade, he figured, and most of the tobacco given out in presents to Shinga-wassa and his chiefs, with a little powder and lead. The Konza had wanted salt and matches which he did not have to spare; otherwise he reckoned his stock at the ranch would pretty well last through till spring, and there was not much he needed to take back this trip. He picked out two bolts of striped cotton cloth to try out. The Indians had shown little interest in the polka-dot fabric he carried to their camp; a few of the men had accepted strips of it as presents, to braid in their hair. As a final afterthought, he selected a cheap, light carbine for Lonnie. The boy would be more useful if he learned to handle a gun.

Isaac cleaned the nib of his pen on a piece of blotting paper, dipped ink, and began slowly to write on a sheet of the Planter's House letterhead, forming his words for once with care:

My Dear Father, Mother, and Sister Lizzie—

As you will see by this, I have put up at a hotel, my first since leaving home. From which, if you conclude my circumstances are a good sight sounder than you have feared you will not be far off. I have this day disposed of my first large lot of Furs, also another lot of hides of my own and partners, and cleared my note in full —quite the reverse now in fact—as the Merchant is now in my debt to the amount of 700$ on his books—on which I take one percent so long as I choose to leave it— also credit freely offered for all the Goods I can carry. The merchant is newly set up in the trade, I believe he has as feeling an interest in my prosperity as I in his. Davenport seems a very slow place compared with this, I venture to say, they do as much in trade any day as Davenport in a week. If fur prices hold I see no reason why I might not clear 2000$ from my winter's work—stock on hand at the Ranch is worth that much in robes—

I start my helper back in the morning but will go myself by way of Lawrence stopping with friends. I have been a good long while out of the World and feel need for society. . . .

Coming into Burlingame, Isaac dismounted, wet his handkerchief in the creek, and made an effort to clean the mud off his boots and trousers. Putting on his new suit and a fresh shirt in the morning, he had ridden slowly, keeping to the edge of the road, but a thaw had come, the thin snow was gone and the road slick with mud, no way to avoid it. In Lawrence the evening before he thought he saw Kilbourn coming out of a saloon—a tall man, roughly dressed and unshaven, with his arms around a pair of drunken, undersized half-breed girls and drunk himself—but did not get close enough to be sure before the trio lurched around a corner. Bill Wood thought he had been driving for a Kansas City freight company. Sam recalled that Kilbourn, after a noisy dispute with a saloonkeeper, had been invited by the sheriff to make his abode in another town—quite enough of our own riffraff already, Sam vehemently concluded, without letting in new ones.

Absalom answered his knock and went to lead the horse around to the barn. Marie had been drinking tea by the fire in the parlor, reading a month-old copy of Harper's *Weekly*. Dropping the magazine, she ran to the hall to welcome Isaac.

—You have grown a mustache! Marie said, standing back to survey him. Her eyes took in the new suit too, but she thought it not proper to comment.

—It's been growing awhile, Isaac said with a faint smile, one forefinger self-consciously touching the blond spike on his upper lip. It seems it's beginning to show.

—Your letter came right after New Year's, Marie said, settling herself in her chair. Isaac sat stiff and upright on the edge of the sofa. You didn't say you were planning a visit.

—I didn't know if I'd get here. I had business two days ago at Leavenworth, that's all I've thought of for a month now. If it didn't—work out right—I wouldn't have felt like showing my face anywhere in Kansas.

—It must have been something very terrible, she said with a teasing smile, but it was lost on him, he looked back obliquely, his thoughts on himself.

—Just something I promised, and was trusted for, and had to do, and didn't know if I *could* do. But it's all right now.

—I have meant to write to you, but nothing happens to make an interesting letter. This morning I made cookies with Vinnie—here. She stood, held out the plate—sugar cookies, lemon cookies, small and pale, shiny egg-glaze cookies cut in shapes of birds, fish, flowers. He selected a star and took a cautious bite. Marie nodded and poured him a cup of tea.

—I mightn't have got it anyhow, Isaac said, balancing the cup. I left the ranch ten days ago. Before that, I was out at the Indian camp, trading. These are just Kaw, he added when she looked concerned—

pretty tame, I guess. First time I met them though, I thought they'd come to rob me or I don't know what, but they only wanted to trade. We didn't know how to talk to each other. Now I've learned a little of their sign language.

—Oh! she said, clapping her hands. Say something in signs!

—I don't know so many yet—wait!

Slowly, concentrating, he sketched a sequence of gestures for her.

—Lovely! Marie said—like dancing. What does it mean?

He repeated, matching the words to their signs:—I—trade—ten—cup—sugar—one—buffalo—blanket.

—Oh, she said, pursing her lips in mock disappointment. Is that all you talk of with your Indians?

—I'm still learning. It's about the only kind of thing I know to say yet.

—Still, she said, smiling, it is like a fairy tale, is it not? Magic—turning sugar into a woolly warm buffalo robe.

—Isn't that *any* trading—turning something somebody else wants into something you want? It's—

—Uncle Titus, Marie said. What does he want from his magic with the bridge?

—Whisky! Isaac answered without hesitation. And if that's not magic—.

They both laughed. Marie refilled their cups.

—Here's one, Isaac said. Horn-pointing his index fingers above his ears, he made the buffalo sign, then, fingers of both hands spread, the combing gesture down the sides of his head that means woman and her long hair.

—What is that?

—It's *you*, Isaac grinned. I found out your secret!

Her questioning look changed to alarm.

—*Buffalo*-woman, he said, repeating the signs—that's *bisonnette*, it's what it means. But that's all right, *I'll* never tell. It's *our* secret now.

Before Marie could answer there came a heavy tread on the stairs and her uncle entered, roused from his afterdinner nap.—Afternoon, Isaac, he said, holding out a hand, I thought I heard voices. Is there still some tea?

X

Paradise Valley

The earth was black. Between fall and the ending of this mild and almost snowless winter, the golden-ripe grass had burned to its matted roots, charring the slopes and hills and stream banks to the limits of sight. Soot stained boots and trousers, wagon wheels and spokes, the heavy bellies and plodding legs of the oxen. By day you marched sooty legs beside the team, eyes on the ground, noticing perhaps that the blackness was flecked with brown of seared grass stems, and when you looked up it dulled your sight and the pure Plains light, altering and blurring landmarks; by night it absorbed the light of moon and stars, smudging the faint line of horizon between earth and sky, and you hated it. Prairie fire: it was a particular hazard Kansas newcomers were warned of, Isaac's first experience of it and now only at a remove, not the roaring menace of leaping, racing flames but its desolate aftermath; yet as needful to the life and renewal of the grasslands as rain and sun, the tillage of buffalo herd and prairie dog. It had, however, an immediate and practical consequence for the hunters traveling through: the burned-over land was empty of game, for meat or hides, and would remain so until spring sun and rain, if finally the drought would break, brought forth the grass again.

The partners had tried hunting together and separately, but whatever they did was limited by transportation; the Farrises, although Isaac had paid them their share from the hides, still had not ventured east to replace their team. However they paired, with only two yoke of oxen their hide-hunting was restricted to what they could haul back in a single wagon.

Returning from Burlingame, Isaac had waited a week at the ranch for Lonnie to get back from Leavenworth with the wagon, trading a little with the Konza who came down from their camp, but the Indians had already traded off most of what they had to spare and were occupied in readying meat and robes for their own use when they returned to the tribal village at Council Grove. The herds of buffalo had moved off somewhere and were no longer near the ranch. Isaac proposed to Harry that they make a hunt together up the Smoky Hill, taking the boy when he came and leaving Irwin in charge of the ranch, of Singing Bird and the two ponies—they had already hunted several days' travel up the Saline and the Solomon; in his journeyings back and forth on the roads to Leavenworth and Burlingame, Isaac had not ventured into the Smoky Hills since his first hunt in the fall. Diplomatically, in preparation, he had informed Shinga-wassa that Harry's brother would do no trading while they were out, accompanying the warning with a present of a pound of cut plug. He had also ridden to Salina to send a letter asking Mr Durfee to apply his credit in buying a wagon and a team trained to the yoke, if they could be had for two hundred and fifty dollars.

It was early February when Isaac and Harry started, the day after Lonnie's return from Leavenworth. The boy grumbled at going out again, and Isaac let him ride in the wagon and sleep. They crossed the river on the ferry west of Salina and followed the course of the Smoky Hill. The fire had evidently started somewhere to the west and carried on the prevailing winds as far as the easternmost buttes before light snow or a counter-wind stopped it. How far west or how wide a swath they could not tell—three days now they had traveled without sight of buffalo or wolf or any animal but the survivors of a prairie-dog town where Isaac amused himself by shooting half a dozen and sent Lonnie to collect them for the evening's stew; and an occasional eagle soaring against the cloudless pale blue of the sky in a direction that seemed to be north and west. Another evening was coming. Their cured meat brought from the ranch was nearly gone— they had expected to get fresh along the way. They had found an occasional patch of untouched grass by the river but had fed the cattle mainly on bark of young cottonwood branches cut along its bank.

Harry brought the team up with a clanking of chains and waved his hat. Isaac, who had been scouting along a rise two hundred yards off to the right, jogged down the slope toward him.

—Something wrong?

—Just thinking about camping, Harry said, cutting feed for the cattle. Don't matter much where—it's all bad. He gave the nigh leader a slap on the rump with his whip handle and turned the team toward the river.

—We'll get out of it, Isaac cheerfully insisted.

—When? When we're starved out for want of fresh meat? Where in the hell has the boogers got to?

—I figure back up toward the Saline, Isaac said, keeping pace beside him, we ought to start that way tomorrow—if we'd known the fire had come through we'd've gone straight from the ranch and saved a day's drive. But we're seeing the country anyhow. In the spring, when the grass—

—Won't *be* no grass in the spring, Harry rasped, way it's burned out. And why you figure to go north again? Why not keep on the way we're headed? We got to be most through it. Or south, toward the Ar-Kansas—they say there's always buffalo winters there.

The reasons were more complicated than Isaac could explain. He offered one.—The big birds, Harry, he said, aint you been watching? That's the direction they're hunting, small game and scraps of killed meat—it's what they live by, smell it or see it miles off, and there'll be buffalo too. And, he grinned when Harry looked skeptical, you don't trust the eagles, you can trust my luck to get us through! And with a whoop he ran ahead toward the river to settle on the campsite.

In the morning they crossed the divide separating the Smoky Hill and Saline rivers, and laid their course north by the sun. Isaac left the wagon to Harry and the boy and kept ahead, waving, pointing, leading them on from high ground to one side or other of their route. By mid-afternoon they had left the track of the prairie fire and Isaac was looking down on the winding, winter-shrunk, mud-brown shallows of the Saline, two hundred feet below. He ran back, shouting down to where Harry followed with the wagon, making damping motions with his arms to stop and wait, and Harry understood, halted in the cold shade of the hills, and sent Lonnie running to fetch wood for a fire and coffee. Isaac returned to his lookout and sat down to study.

Straight across, the riverbank sagged in what looked like a stream mouth, twenty feet wide, dry now, but perhaps in spring there would be a flow swamping its banks on either side. The dry creek came out from between steep hills, treeless but glowing red-brown in the south light of afternoon. His eyes followed it back, to where it swung around to northwest, paralleling the course of the Saline, folded among successive ridges like those they had crossed in the morning, coming north. The farthest of these ridges appeared to wear a dark fringe along its back: trees. Isaac hunched forward, squinting, resting his chin on his hands, holding his eyes steady on that black line penciled across the northern horizon. The trees were moving. For another minute he held himself still, all muscles tensed: moving!—animals, in such mass, such numbers, they could only be buffalo.

He leaped up, went back, and ran vaulting down the slope to where Harry and Lonnie crouched beside their small fire, warming their hands with their tin mugs of coffee.

—We found them! Isaac shouted, we found them!—a big herd, maybe five miles ahead and moving northwest. There's a dry creek comes in across the river. All we got to do is follow it up and it'll take us to them. . . .

Harry jumped up, threw out the last of his coffee, and stamped out the fire. They started the team, crossed the river, and entered the creek bed, smooth, firm, and unobstructed as a highway. Isaac stayed close now, urging them forward, and the others caught his excitement. After an hour they came to the reason for the creek's dryness, a tight beaver dam built across, only a trickle of water seeping through from the pond behind and sinking into the stream bed. They turned out and followed the bank, and from here on the creek was full, kept slack by two more dams farther up. Smaller streams entered from the right, through steep-sided, narrow-cut canyons, their banks guarded by savory cedar and massive oak. It was as if enchantment had admitted them to a world from which all others were excluded, or led them backward in time to a land set apart and readied for man but not yet inhabited. This was not only the young man's illusion, that in a world where everything is novel to his experience all must be equally so to all men.

Along the creek bank the beaver had downed cottonwoods, some nearly a foot through the butt, to get at the tender bark of the upper branches, clear a trail, but there was no cut anywhere of a steel-edged ax. Toward sunset the creek turned more to the west and the country around it rose and opened out in steep grassy hills. Isaac, still in the lead, stopped and pointed ahead and up.—Look, he called back. Boys, look! Along the top of a ridge a mile off, in silhouette against the golden light, a file of buffalo made south toward a watering place, shaggy heads hanging. Isaac turned and ran back, exultant, clapped Harry on the shoulder, seized his hand and pumped it.—Boys! he cried. Didn't I tell you last night? We've found our way to paradise.

Harry surveyed the scene in silence for a moment, hands on his hips.—I aint ready to go that far *yet*, he said. But it looks to be money-making country right enough—and good camping too, for once.

—You *wait*, Isaac said, it's fresh buffalo meat for breakfast in the morning—and my luck's only just getting warm. . . .

After supper they built up a huge fire and sat close, faces reddening in the warmth as if sunburned; Isaac opened his wool shirt to the waist. They did not talk much. Even Harry, usually with an answer for everything, though generally sour of late, had become thoughtful. Isaac threw a log on and the fire leaped. Far off to the north a wolf howled, scattered yips answered, and then the pack in concert. Lonnie shivered and leaned closer.

—You reckon there's—anyone out there? the boy asked in a low voice, with a wide gesture to the circle of darkness around the camp.

—That's what the fire's for, Isaac said aloud. Any hunters around—they'll see it and come visiting, wouldn't that be something? Or wild

Indians—big fire, they'll know no one's sneaking up and won't bother.

—Or know where to find us easy, Harry said.

—Let em, said Isaac carelessly. My gun's loaded. He stood up, started for the tent, stopped, and turned back. Lonnie! he called. Since you're anxious about company, you can sit up. Mind you keep the fire up. You run short of wood, you know where there's more. . . .

The boy looked him in the eyes: smiling but hard-eyed, making a joke of him but serious too. He got up and followed after the hunter. —I'll get me a blanket anyway, he asserted. To keep the cold off my back, while I watch.

Isaac was up in the morning before light and came out stealthily, carrying his rifle, powder horn, bullet pouch. The boy had built the fire up and come in around midnight, and he let him, pretending sleep. He set the things down, stirred the ashes with a stick, and stooped to warm his hands at the coals. The light was coming in the sky over the hills at his back. In half an hour, an hour, the sun would be high enough to feel. The stick flickered in the ashes. There was a rind of transparent ice on the water in the bucket. He sank a cup through it, drank; frost fuzzy-white on the blades of grass, beyond, the dark bulk of the four oxen tethered and asleep along the stream-bank. Isaac raised himself and started up the creek, stepping lightly, the rifle swinging his arm as he walked.

He had not gone a hundred yards when he heard the trampling of a band of buffalo bulls coming toward him from a gulch off to the right. The rifle came up—not fifty yards off but coming head-on, tricky in the half-light—aimed for the back of the leader's neck, break the spine, boomed, the sound snapped back from the hillside. He crouched, reloaded; two more dead before the rest took fright and retreated up the canyon. He walked on for another half-hour, slowly, looking around, climbing the valley. Ahead through the trees there was something moving toward him. He backed off to one side, knelt: another small herd, half a dozen cows this time, coming to drink, unmindful of any threat. He let them come even with him, not fifty yards off, and killed two before driving them off; an easy shot both times, broadside, at the heart. The sky was bright now, the sun just coming over the rim of hills to the southeast; feeling the first warmth, he realized he was hungry—cow meat, sweetest of all. He went over, opened one of the cows along the belly, pawed the guts out steaming on the ground—and as he did so, a sac of fluid burst, spilled, and disclosed an unborn calf, small, pink, and hairless as a newborn pig. Laying the cowhide back, he cut out the tenderloin, thought for a moment and took the tongue as well, and, wrapping the meat in a piece of the hide, stuffed it into the chest cavity to keep, collect on his way back to camp. The country still drew him on.

Its contours, the growth of trees and underbrush, had led him east, away from the stream. There was an opening to the left, a worn path —the watering trail the cows had been making for—and he turned off to follow it. Something small and gray, narrow-faced, was coming toward him, a coyote returning at a twinkling trot from a morning drink, unconcerned as any boy out for a stroll. It was close enough to reach with his rifle barrel before it stopped: dead still, wide-eyed, meditating the unfamiliar scent—and, tucking its tail, ran off among the trees to the north. Isaac walked on. The trail opened out as it neared the creek, bare and pounded soft by buffalo hooves. He knelt, recognized among the hoofprints the neat doglike foot of the coyote, others, hooves and paws he could only guess at, and among them the broad, manlike print, high-arched, long nails incising the mud, that could only be bear, though not recent. He washed his hands in the creek, rubbed them together, drying. Blood from the cow had spattered his shirt sleeves to the elbows, still sticky-wet.

A few yards up the creek a massive cottonwood, roots undermined, had fallen, bridging the two banks. Isaac went to it, pulled himself up, and started across. The bank on the other side sloped upward to a hundred-foot cliff of creamy sandstone. In front of it the sandy earth was bare of trees and brush, the worn grass was dotted with small hillocks: a prairie-dog town. Isaac lay down to watch.

From off to the right a pair of turkey cocks came running across the dog-town, heedless of his presence, intent on their private dispute— spring coming, beginning to be that time of year, contesting over hens. Abruptly the lead bird stopped, spun, and faced its pursuer, threatening with its wings, made a fluttering leap to spur the enemy, and the other bird dodged back and began to circle. Isaac dropped, got his gun up, and waited till they were lined up, curious if he could get both with one ball, but when he fired only one fell. The remaining cock stepped back, feathers smoothing, then slowly walked around its rival, nudging with its beak, but could not get it up and, still puzzled, walked away. Isaac, unhurrying, followed after it.

The cliff was shaped to the westward-curving course of the creek. He climbed to its base, feet slipping in the sandy soil eroded from the soft rock, looked up: overhanging at the top, a mat of grass and roots, shadowing the spot where he stood, cavelike and cool against the rising sun. He reached out and touched: gritty as sandpaper, soft as new pine, flesh-colored and alive, it invited inscription; scraped with his thumbnail and made a faint mark. He stood back, looked up again. Others had answered the same invitation farther up the rock face when the yielding earth lay higher against it or climbed to leave their marks with flint knife, bone auger, point of buffalo horn, whatever hard, sharp tool came to hand: a turtle-shape that might be emblem of a band or tribe; a buffalo, recording a hunt or homage to the buffalo-power's pity for the hunter; a horseback man, hunter or warrior; among these, many that were mysterious: sun shapes, star shapes, some with man-faces. He walked backward, neck bent back, and at length found one word off to the right and apart: VERITE; and numbers below it, a date, very dim—he ran to it, reached up, felt with fingertips—1786. Below the word and date Isaac began to scrape with his knife point—his initials, IP, in the form of a cipher, a brand, taking pains to cut deep, square, and true, that the sign might endure in this perishable stone; under it, the year, 1860, and around both, for whatever meaning, a many-pointed sunburst like those left by the Indians among their records of hunt, war, worship, of their presence, passing through this land.

Wolves were swarming his two cows when he returned. It took him a moment to make out what they were: not the gray-black he had encountered in the fall but white, or nearly so, as snowshoe rabbits. The rifle came up, fired. He went on shooting into the pack, not aiming, until half a dozen lay dead and the others had run off. Mr Durfee had not been generous in his pay for wolf pelts, but these now, white—a dollar, maybe even two dollars apiece? Of the meat he had cut out and hidden, enough remained for their breakfast. He retrieved it and followed his trail back. Another wolf pack, also white, had about demolished the three bulls. Again he shot and kept on shooting till all were dead or driven off; he had not thought to bring a vial of strychnine when he set off on his morning stroll. From down the valley rolled the sound of a rifle shot, then at an interval another. Out looking for him, signaling? Two hours, perhaps. He had not been gone long.

Harry and Lonnie were up when Isaac came into camp, had remade the fire and had coffee boiling. He dropped the bloody skin of meat beside them, stooped, and washed his hands again in the bucket.

—There's meat for breakfast, he said, like I promised—what's left of it, anyhow, we're sharing with the wolves. When you've eaten you can take the wagon up along the creek and skin them out. There's about a dozen won't steal any more of my meat. . . .

They stayed a week at that camp, working methodically to fill the wagon—buffalo hides, wolf skins, gray and white, but also elk, blacktail deer; in a pond a mile downstream Isaac shot two large beaver. He did most of the hunting and at length agreed with Harry on skinning for a share in the take. He told the others only in general of what he had found in that first morning's exploration and did not mention the cavelike cliff with its record of past men.

Among themselves they adopted the name Isaac had given: out for a day's hunt among the hills to the north and the night coming, "Aint it about time we was heading back to Paradise?" Harry would say, not without his usual irony, and the name stuck; it had become a place, a known mark on a land still largely nameless, and they had to call it something. Returning to the ranch, they told others of their find, and when the few hunters traveled that way, Tommy Thorn's friends, it was Pride's Paradise they steered for. (Later still, when the survey contractor came through in the process of organizing the counties west of Salina, marking off the land for sale, he put the name on the map sent in to Washington, with some others Isaac had given to tributaries of the Saline. Records of priority: so far as government was concerned, he had been there first.)

Around the middle of February Mr David Kilbourn called on Marie and her uncle, took tea and then supper at the colonel's hospitable invitation, but politely declined to stay the night, explaining that he had taken a room at the Schuyler House and would be riding on early to Topeka—meeting with Mr Pomeroy, he said, and Colonel Titus nodded, impressed. Marie did not recognize him at first. Since the fall he had grown a mustache and beard that covered his mouth and chin, pointed and very black, making him somehow taller, more purposeful, as well as older; his cheeks were newly shaved. He had also in that time, at Kansas City, he said, acquired a ready-made suit of a brown-and-white checked material, a white shirt with a high, stiff collar that concealed the back of his neck, and a brown silk tie with drooping ends that formed a cross on the starched white triangle of his shirtfront. Marie nevertheless remained uneasy with him and contrived to have her uncle present, or at least Absalom, when Kilbourn was with her.

Over supper the colonel prompted him to explain his new prosperity. Vaguely or modestly, Kilbourn talked of establishing a freight line, Lawrence to Lecompton and Topeka for a start, but if it took with the public, they would carry to Burlingame (the colonel nodded approval), Emporia, right on through to Denver City, and be on the spot for the Pacific railway, when it came—. He spoke more freely of the sufferings of Kansans in the drought, the settlers starving in their cabins, wives and little ones, abandoning their homesteads and going back to hardfisted landlords in the States: there was a relief committee organizing at Topeka, meant to send agents all through the North, that was the purpose of his meeting. Much moved, Colonel Titus listened intently, cupping one ear and nodding repeatedly.

Afterward in the parlor Kilbourn accepted one of the colonel's cigars, bit the end with long, fierce teeth, then delicately removed the shred of tobacco and flicked it at the cuspidor. What was it about him? He was very polite, choosing his words. That grab at her in the summer, she had never told anyone, no longer even certain it had happened, or if it did, perhaps it was only a boy's folly, over and done with, and Mr Kilbourn was not a boy anymore either, that much was plain; that was the Kansas way with its young men. He went on chatting, but his eyes were on her, hard and appraising, unsmiling. At a decorous hour he drew his watch from a vest pocket, opened the case, and excused himself, promising to call again when his business brought him this way.

—A fine young man! the colonel pronounced him over a final toddy. Come right along since I first saw him walking beside a wagon and dreaming of Pikes Peak. And active!—freight lines and relief committees and railways—.

Marie frowned. His vehemence sounded like a rebuke. What did he mean to say to her? Of Mr Kilbourn—of—

—Do you truly think so, Uncle? Mister *Kilbourn?*

He straightened up, set his cup down, and frowned in turn.— Would I say what I *don't* think, Marie? he said. *Would* I?

Isaac, Harry, and the boy were five days returning to the ranch. Isaac left Harry and Lonnie to manage the wagon and hunted on ahead, taking off the hides himself and leaving them folded, marking the route, for the others to collect as they came along, rejoining them for the mid-day nooning and at night. On the morning of the final day, not far northwest of the ranch, he had been out for several hours in this manner without finding any game and circled back. Misjudged the distance, it seemed—he crossed the wagon track and started after it at a trot. Coming over the top of a hill he heard voices ahead but could make out no words. He dropped down, crawled forward. Down the slope, beside a narrow creek, the wagon was stopped, a bunch of Indians all around it and Harry and Lonnie in the midst, back to back. One of the Indians had taken off a bundle of wolf skins and was handing them around. Pawnee, recognizable by the peculiar, horn-like roach running along the top of the head, smoothed and held in place by grease and paint, eyebrows and the rest of the scalp plucked bald. No horses in sight, they were starting out for a season of horse-stealing among the southern tribes, each with a pack of pemmican and spare moccasins on his back, bow and arrows, they would travel clear to Mexico if they had to, John Sarcoxie had said, to make up their herd. Pawnee in English, *pariki* in most other languages of the Plains, a horn, for the tribal topknot, *wolf* in the sign language, the usual two-edged Indian epithet, meaning both the wiliness of the wolf and its rapacity. Universally hated for their thieving ways, the Pawnee were fair game for any band seeking proofs of valor in useful warfare but generally and officially at peace with the whites through successive treaties by which they relinquished their homeland along the Platte and finally, in 1857, accepted a reservation of four hundred and fifty square miles on a Platte tributary.

Isaac counted: thirty of them and what looked to be an older man, a red blanket wrapped around his shoulders, most likely the expedition's leader.

Isaac circled around to the left, running, got down into the creek bottom, and followed it along until he was opposite the wagon. Parting the thicket, he stood up abruptly in the midst of the band, a few steps from the chief; went up to him, hand out, but the man scowled, kept his arms folded close under his blanket, and would not shake. Isaac swung around. One of them had Harry's rifle, another Lonnie's light carbine, their knives. There were a dozen wolf skins scattered on the ground. A brave had stripped the boy of his shirt. Lonnie leaned against Harry as if paralyzed, face white, teeth chattering.

—Damned ignorant fools! Isaac shouted. You squittering pair of babies, you! How in the nation you get yourselves in such a fix?

—They came up around us, acted friendly, Harry answered, voice low and tremulous. One of them talks some English, said he wanted to look at Lonnie's gun—. I figure they mean to kill us.

—By God in heaven! Isaac roared back. You two don't get humping, gather up my skins, I'll kill you first myself. Get on now, get *moving!*

He took a step forward, jerking the gun barrel at them. Very slowly, reluctantly, Harry stepped away, stooped, picked up a skin, then another. The Indians, silent, did not interfere. Isaac went over to the one who held Lonnie's carbine: short, slender, hardly past boyhood, hiding his anxiety under a bold face.

—You the one talks English? Isaac demanded, and the young man nodded. Then you tell your friends, anyone wants to take what's mine, he's going to have to fight me for it first, understand? And you don't give me that gun back, I'll start on you.

He reached out, seized the gun, and jerked it free, and the Indian let him. He handed it over to Lonnie. A collective gasp of indrawn breath escaped the band; they drew back, eyes on their chief, but the old man watched in silence, face expressionless. Isaac went around the circle, talking steadily, while the youth spoke in Pawnee, commenting, perhaps translating: the rifle, two skinning knives in their cases, Lonnie's shirt—he took them, threw them on the pile of furs. The last was a big hunting knife taken by a young man, face streaked with red finger marks, who looked determined. Isaac made a grab. The man jerked the knife back, would not let go. Isaac backed away until he had the chief alone between himself and the half-circle of doubtful Indians. He cocked his rifle, brought it up, pointed at the chief's breast. Instantly his men dropped their packs, strung their bows, fitted arrows. Isaac faced them but kept his rifle on the chief, finger on the trigger. The old man spoke at length, sober and authoritative, from the young man's grimaces and angry negatives he seemed to be telling them a hunting knife, however fine, was not worth a Pawnee death—this white hunter was crazy, maybe, but looked as if he would kill for the knife, more than one before he was finished—. The young man stood with his face set, gripping the knife with both hands, and would not answer. The chief brought his arm out and pointed at him, commanding; the others took a step back, still with their bows up.

Isaac waited.—Lonnie! he shouted. Get over there and get that knife!

Hesitantly Lonnie went to him, reached out, and the Indian let him take it; then brought his bow up and gave the boy a thumping crack on the head, a gesture of challenge and contempt. Lonnie backed away, rubbing his head with his free hand. Isaac brought his rifle around, aimed at the brave, and held it thus a long moment staring him down, thinking hard. The Indian dropped his eyes.

—All right, sonny, he said quietly, this time—all your friends around you with their bows—this time I'll let you. But I've got your ugly face in my mind now, let me tell you—you ever come around my camp again, or anything that's mine—.

It was over but the two sides were not yet extricated. Isaac ordered Harry to take his rifle, keep it on the chief, while he approached the old man with his hands clasped in the peace sign. The Indian this time smiled and offered his hand, the white man's sign. Using his hands slowly and carefully, eyes on the chief's eyes, Isaac explained: they were hunters on the way home, no doubt the chief knew of his ranch and would be welcome to trade there; they had no quarrel with the Wolf people, known everywhere as friends to the white men, and wished them well in their raid—provided they molested no other whites or hunters. Isaac ordered Lonnie to bring a wolf pelt, the chief accepted it, and, calling out to his men, led them off, single-file, down the creek at a jogging trot. The three whites watched them out of sight, repacked the skins, and started on their way. Isaac stayed with them and ordered that they keep all their guns handy and loaded.

—Bout one more minute, Harry said as they climbed the slope from the creek, and I figured that bunch'd have you pricked full of arrows like a pincushion. The three of us, he added after a moment.

Isaac's face blazed again, his breath came fast, he bounced on the balls of his feet, stabbing with his fists. At length, containing himself —Then I reckon it's a good thing I wasn't thinking about that, he said. No, he went on, calming, I could see the whole thing right through, when I came in sight and saw the fix you were in—let em take your weapons and they'll finish by killing you just for the fun of it. But stand up, let em see there'll be killing both ways—well, now!

that puts the game in a whole new light. *Don't* it now? he concluded, turning abruptly to Lonnie and smiling. Bet you learned something this morning, eh, boy?

—Yes, *sir!* Lonnie answered him, round-faced and guileless. *Stay away from wild Indians*, is what I say.

—Well, God *damn!* said Isaac, slapping his knee. Aint you learned *anything*, boy? And walked on ahead.

There was no more talk among them all the rest of that last day. Isaac, keeping ahead but in sight, watchful, frequently turning to look back, scan the hills on both sides, reflected that for the first time in his life he had blasphemed aloud, not once but twice. *There is not a word in my tongue but, Lord, thou knowest it.* The Bible, why did that verse stay in his mind? And remembered. Anger too, his father would count that as big a sin, rage, pumping right through your body like a galvanic current and your mind running at double speed—oh, feeling peevish or quarrelsome sometimes, afraid, or sunk right down and hating yourself. But real anger: it was something he never in his life had known.

Irwin had spent an uneventful three weeks at the ranch, had meant to hunt some, nearby, but became nervous, alone. Twice parties of Indians had come to the fence gate, calling out, but he waved them away and they went, might have been Konza—he could not, he admitted, tell one Indian from another, let alone which tribe. He stayed close—went out to feed the horses, bring in wood and water, but only in daylight, and when he went gave a careful look all around before stepping through the doorway. All this he told readily, satisfied with his precaution. His partners' brush with the Pawnee seemed to confirm that he had been right to watch out.

For a week after their return they were occupied with the hides and pelts, curing the meat. Harry worked at this along with his brother and Lonnie. Isaac insisted: part of their agreement for his share in the hunt. Several days three or four women rode over from the Konza camp. They brought nothing to trade, they came only to watch while the men worked, followed them into the cabin while they made dinner, watching, and politely squatted on the floor, accepting fried meat, biscuit, coffee. They were curious about the white men's implements, their ways of doing, picked up tools and examined them but did not try to steal; observed with frowns and clucks of disapproval while Isaac experimented with packing a barrel with buffalo tongues and brine, meaning to pickle it like salt pork—and were right, it seemed; the meat did not spoil but came out tough, unappetizing, and gray. The women rode astride, an Indian custom invariably mentioned with leering distaste by writers of polite literature, but decorously, their deerskin skirts covering their thighs. In the confinement of the cabin they exuded a kind of smoky, fleshy muskiness like the smell of an Indian-tanned buffalo robe that was not unpleasant.

Isaac was not sure it was each time the same women. They looked alike to him: broad, dark faces, expressionless except rarely, when talking among themselves; black hair slicked flat with grease and drawn back in two braids, the parting streaked with vermillion.

One was different: younger, perhaps, less dark, heavy; animated in gesture and expression, often smiling, frowning, laughing aloud. Her name in signs seemed to be a sentence describing the south. He called her Southwind and she repeated the word accurately the first time she heard it and seemed pleased when he explained it back to her in signs; she called him Japprey. The name made her giggle and cover her mouth with her hand in polite embarrassment, but she would not tell him why. It was Southwind who told Isaac how the wild tribes were again allying themselves—Comanche, Kiowa, Cheyenne, Arapaho, Sioux—to drive the whites and the reservation Indians from the Plains. The war was planned for the summer. The Konza, having got wind of these plans, would be returning early to Council Grove, in a week or two.

On her last visit, Southwind brought him a buckskin hunting shirt, soft as flannel, neatly sinew-sewed, with long fringes covering the seams. Isaac was nervous about accepting it—Sarcoxie had mentioned by way of caution that the Konza had the reputation of being careful about their wives and daughters, he could not guess what she expected in return. At length he offered her a double handful of tobacco and her choice among the buffalo hides drying in the pasture, and she seemed satisfied when she understood these things were meant as gifts, not trade.

The blockhouse, as they called it, was Harry's idea, when Isaac gave an unsensational summary of Southwind's warnings. Isaac pointed out that they were hardly into March, the war, if it happened, was not planned till summer, the preferred season for Indian fighting, but consented, since the others wanted it; it was a change from the routine of hunting. Harry, who seemed to know about such things, took charge. They dug a trench forty feet square around the cabin, set cottonwood logs in it bound tight with rawhide and pointed at the top; made platforms at the corners, with notched-log ladders, set up a massive log gate on the east side, cut sod to fireproof the roof, having heard of fire arrows. At the north end of the cabin they dug a well, finding water at eight feet even in this dry time, and covered it with hewed planks; brought in a load of hay for the animals and then worried about fire and covered it with green hides staked tight.

It was around the middle of March before the stockade was finished. Isaac, with Lonnie, started the next day on a hunt. They went out the Saline as far as the Konza camp, but the Indians had already departed, leaving the ashes of their fires, middens of buffalo bones and broken tools, and the earth of their village worn bare of grass for a mile along the south bank of the river. They turned north, making for the Solomon along a marshy creek Isaac had found and named in the fall, Spillman's, for a young surveyor working out of Salina who had described it to him. Toward the end of the second day they still had seen no game—the buffalo had been through in the fall, eating the grass off short—and were looking for a place to camp when they came to a grove of oak and elm mixed in with the usual cottonwood. A putrid smell struck them as they drove in under the trees, as if someone had brought carcasses in to butcher and then left the meat to rot. Up ahead a pale shape bulked in the shadows. The ox-team stopped and would not go on. Isaac with his rifle walked warily forward, looking all around: a light wagon with a canvas cover, beside it a few hides, slashed with knives, a broken sack of flour, its contents scattered. The pair of oxen lay in front, still yoked and chained up, bellies bloated, it seemed they had been stuck through with a spear or large knife and their throats cut for good measure; birds had torn at their flesh in places but the wolves, off wherever the buffalo had gone, had not yet found them.

He came on the wagon's owner fifty feet farther along, propped against a large tree, head hanging forward and his arms twisted back and tied around the trunk. There were a dozen arrows in his breast. The man's rifle lay to one side, its stock broken. Isaac went around behind and cut the strip of rawhide that bound his wrists; they had bled before he died. He tried one arm—the joints worked, stiffened and gone limp again, maybe dead a week. He knelt close, lifted the gray-bearded chin: his nose had been cut off with a knife, birds, perhaps, had gouged out his eyes, gashed his cheeks. The ears—he had no ears, from the mat of dried blood it looked as if the top of his head had been taken off; the smell made him feel sick. Isaac stood up, closed his eyes, remembered: it had to be Tommy Thorn. Whoever did it wanted a scalp and he had none, had taken ears and all to get the fringe of hair that would give him something to show off, boasting his valor around the campfire—for a little old feeble potbellied man, never did anything but hunt a little, enjoy his whisky and telling tales, hold open house in his cabin for his friends! Rage came again, his vision trembled as if he had been struck in the head. He held on tight, gripping the rifle, made himself breathe deep.

Isaac dropped on his knees, crawled around on the trampled earth, looking. Moccasin tracks of course, only two individuals, as near as he could make out; not the Pawnee party they had run up against, any-

how, though it might be two off on their own, or that bad-tempered
one who took the knife, with a friend—no, the Pawnee were out for
horses, not white scalps, not an old, feeble—. Every tribe had its own
pattern of foot gear, Sarcoxie had said, its own style of arrow. Silently
he cursed himself for his ignorance. He could no more tell one tribe
from another by its tracks than Irwin Farris.

There was a clatter of dry leaves behind him, footstep, animal moving. He jumped up, rifle at his shoulder, searching.

—Lonnie! Where are you, Lonnie? Come on over here!—as if calling a dog—.

Movement, the boy moving among the tree trunks, slowly, stopping by the wagon, mouth open, eyes wide.

—You, Lonnie! Come here, boy!

Lonnie came a few more steps, saw, stopped: the body with its
arrows bristling in the chest. A long wail came forth. Isaac went to
him, hit him a rattling open-handed blow on the side of the head,
slapped the other side. The boy quieted.

—Shut that squalling and take a good look. That's what you got us
into with those Pawnee the other day, if I hadn't come along. And
then talking like a fool afterward—.

The boy covered his eyes with his hands. Isaac gave him a shake.

—He's only dead—Tommy Thorn, I knew him, he was my friend!
But death—that's nothing, we're up against it every day to make our
living. It's how you do it, and Tommy—he let them get the jump.

He was talking too much, loudly, and doing no good. He put an
arm over Lonnie's shoulders, turned him, guided him back toward
the wagon and the restive oxen.

—And don't be mad at Indians on account of Tommy, it's only two
—can't even tell which tribe. If we're going to be hunters, we got to
go among them, tell good from bad, and take our chances and trust
our luck. . . .

They drove out of the grove again and camped on open ground,
though it meant carrying wood and water: the smells of death. Isaac
put up the tent, made the fire, cooked; sent the boy to bed and sat up,
watching, his loaded rifle cradled in his arms. Lonnie, sleepless, came
out and sat beside him in silence, holding his light gun.

In daylight Isaac made the boy come back. They were Christians,
Tommy too, no doubt, they owed him a burying. They dug a shallow
grave in front of the trees with knives and fingers. Isaac wrapped the
body in what was left of two buffalo hides and they rolled it in. They
scraped the earth over it, carried stones from Spillman's Creek to
cover it against wolves. When they were finished, Isaac discovered
that he had no words to offer, no prayer—in a lifetime in his father's
house there had been no funerals, they were young people in Iowa,
his parents' age, coming to few deaths; another part of life he had not

learned. He found a stump of a dead tree, solid, squared one side, cut an inscription with his knife, and set it at the head of the grave. He wrote:

> T THORN
> 1860
> HE HUNTED
> ALONE

It was mid-day when this work was completed. Isaac gave thought to the wagon, no benefit to Tommy to leave it here to rot, but even empty and with their light load it would slow them. Still, it would be a waste. Between them, with the oxen pulling, they got it around, chained it behind their own. Isaac cut the yoke free and threw it in back, worth something too. What else? He stood for a time in thought, then returned to the grave, gathered up the arrows and the broken shafts, Tommy's useless rifle—still loaded, with the cap on the nipple—and placed them carefully in the back of his wagon.

Isaac took the most direct route he could figure but they were two long days getting back to the ranch. The boy remained badly rattled and spoke scarcely five words the whole way. The Farrises, when Isaac told them, without embellishment or rhetoric, what had happened, were for getting out immediately. They argued about it all through supper: between them they had probably two wagonloads of hides and furs, besides the remainder of Isaac's trading stock, none of which he was prepared to leave for roving redskins or anyone else, and they still had only the one team for what was now three wagons. Isaac was on the point of telling the brothers they could clear out tomorrow, so far as he cared, if that was the kind of men they wanted to be taken for; but refrained. Finally:—You shut your yap, brother, Harry growled. Can't just run off and leave the stuff we've worked all winter for. Let the bastards come and try us, is what *I* say—we're ready for em. But got to get us a team of cattle somewhere, and that's a fact. It was settled, then. Isaac would be riding to Salina in the morning to let the people know about Tommy's death. He promised to hunt for someone willing to trade a team of oxen for the Farrises' hides.

There was smoke from the chimney of Tommy Thorn's cabin when Isaac rode by in the morning. A deep voice answered when he shouted through the buffalo hide covering the doorway and, taking it for invitation, he went in. A big man in buckskins knelt on the hearth, feeding sticks to the fire, head wreathed in spiky black hair; Rasmus Horn, the bristle-voiced hunter Isaac had met there in the fall.

—Thought you was Tommy, the man said, glancing around. Got in last night, folks say he's been out a month. Been by your place?

—Tommy's dead.

—Go to hell.

—I buried him three days ago at Spillman's Creek—that's what I call it.

—Where's that?

Rasmus swung around, sat, his back to the flickering fire. Isaac described the creek, the grove. Rasmus recognized it, had camped there.

—That's the Pawnee Road, he said.

—I ran into thirty of em and a chief—oh, three weeks ago, ten miles west of there, going south after horses. This was just two. They tied him to a tree and used him for a target. Wait—.

Isaac went out and brought in one of the arrows, handed it to the man.—Which tribe is that?

Rasmus examined the arrow, held it to the firelight.—Cheyenne, he said, handing it back.

—How do you tell?

—Turkey feathers and the way they flitched. Way the shaft is grooved and the grooves filled with paint. Cheyenne. . . .

—The Kaw say all the wild tribes are getting ready for a war, in the summer.

—Kaw! I heard it was just Cheyenne and the others holding back. Looks like they started in with Tommy.

—Any idea why?

—Wasn't Tommy picking no fight. Could be a thousand things—some Indian in a scrape with a soldier, his brother kills the first white man he comes on, that makes it square, cause they figure we're all the same tribe—cept Texans, they as different to redskin as Dakota and Wichita. And they can *kill* Texans, most of em I know, for all I care. . . .

—He owe you anything, Rasmus?

—Not one thing. Rasmus got up, leaning back against the chimney. Not one blessed thing!—drank his whisky, ate his meat, and slept on his floor, and he didn't owe me a thing.

—I brought his wagon back. They killed his cattle, spoiled his hides and flour, broke his rifle—anything else he had, they took. But his wagon—anyone thinks it's owed, it's at my place. . . .

Isaac went on into Salina to tell Colonel Phillips of Tommy's death and the Kaw rumors. The report of these depredations—the menacing official term—would no doubt appear in his next letter to the New York *Tribune;* whatever immediate good the settlers got from Isaac's warning, they would profit in the long run—Saline County, threatened by Indian wars, would be cleared of savages and organized, and Salina would be its seat. The colonel had two letters for him that had lain weeks at Campbell's store and post office. Isaac opened the one from Mr Durfee, wrote an answer, paid money for the postage, and started back.

Lonnie did not come out to take his horse when Isaac returned; the stockade gate stood open. He rode all around it and to the end of the pasture, rifle at the ready, but found nothing amiss, only carelessness. He put the horse away, closed the gate, and went into the cabin, frowning. The boy was huddled by the fire and did not look up.

Isaac gripped his shoulder.—You're dreaming, boy, need a change of scene. How'd you like to go on a trip? The boy's face looked around, questioning. Leavenworth, Isaac said. I'm buying a team and wagon from Mister Durfee at Leavenworth. You got to ride through and bring them back.

Lonnie stood up, a cautious smile on his face.—And stay at a hotel?

Isaac looked grave.—All right, he said after a moment, and the boy grinned, triumphant. A night at the Planter's House. *And* supper and breakfast. Just you step along, going and coming.

Isaac started him east in the morning with ten dollars to travel on; and reassurance—a traveled road and settlers all the way from Salina, in two weeks he would ride out to meet him and bring him back, about Junction City it should be if the boy made reasonable time.

Harry over supper wanted to know about oxen at Salina. Isaac told him he had not found any, if he wanted to buy oxen he could go look for himself. Harry answered nothing.

While Lonnie was away, Isaac persuaded Irwin to come out with him as skinner for a share in the hides. Harry stayed at the ranch on guard—feeding and exercising the horses, sleeping. They hunted toward the Solomon, two days at a time, standing watches at night; not time enough to fill the wagon, but after the Indian rumors Isaac was nervous of staying long in one camp. By early April when he started east to meet Lonnie, he had seen no sign of Indians nearby, but he remained watchful.

Mr Durfee had produced an Army freight wagon, its blue paint and red trim chipped and faded with hard use, but serviceable; and the three yoke of oxen Isaac had asked for in his last letter, which if not up to Iowa standards had pulled well enough on the road from Leavenworth with the empty wagon. Harry considered the extra yoke of oxen in silence when Isaac returned to the ranch and finally, with an air of authority, pronounced the wagon too heavy for a team that size, if fully loaded—what it needed was mules, about six span. Isaac offered the Farrises the use of his old team for a share in the hides they took. For a month they went on hunting, usually together, making short trips within a cautious day's drive of the ranch. Isaac on these hunts now led Singing Bird and the two ponies behind the wagon. They could not leave the horses alone at the ranch, of course, but they would be a means of escape if they ran into hostile Indians again.

The buffalo herds had moved off. They were finding only stragglers, old bulls and wary, worthless for meat, except the tongues, though the hides, being thick and heavy, might bring a somewhat better price than usual. For want of other game, Isaac tracked and killed a dozen deer and took the skins; and the meat was preferable. Returning to the ranch one day, they fell in with two hunters going east for supplies with a wagonload of hides from far up the Solomon. The herds were back, they said, but farther west this spring. Isaac resolved on an extended hunt in that direction, following Paradise Creek up to the Solomon. Harry and Irwin found excuses. They would stay behind to look after their hides.

Coming over a ridge a few miles above the mouth of Spillman's Creek on the second morning out, Isaac saw smoke rising from the valley ahead. He stopped the team, ordered Lonnie to get out his carbine, and ran forward with his rifle, keeping down. Half a mile off, straggling along the wooded creek bank, there was a village of buffalo-skin tepees, perhaps a hundred of them, and a large herd of ponies spread across the open bottomland between the village and the ridge, Indian boys riding among them, keeping them together. And something strange: in the middle of the village, a large, white canvas wall-tent with a small American flag fluttering from a pole in front, a light open wagon drawn up beside it and a pair of mules staked nearby. Isaac ran back, saddled Bird, and, leaving Lonnie to guard the wagon, rode slowly down the slope and through the herd, steering for the flag, his loaded rifle across his thighs.

A white man had taken a seat on a folding campstool beside the door when Isaac rode up: a long, soft face, clean-shaven, perhaps fifty, half-military in dress—cavalryman's blue tunic, unbuttoned, a campaign hat, buckskin leggings and moccasins. He stood up and introduced himself as Captain William Dennison, U.S. agent to the Otoe tribe. Isaac dismounted, gave his name and mentioned the ranch on the Saline. The captain, three years with the tribe, thought he had heard of the place, a new one on the frontier west of Salina.

—I never heard of Otoe. Where're they from?

—Small tribe—they got a reservation on the Big Blue, just over into Nebraska Territory. This is their summer hunt. I come along to keep em out of mischief.

The captain sat again, slow-spoken, sad-voiced, sleepy-eyed. Isaac stood, looking down at him.

—You heard anything about Indian troubles coming this summer? Cheyenne, maybe?

The captain sighed.—We always got troubles when we come down here, but the Otoe, *they* say this is where they always hunt. And the Cheyenne, *they* say this country is theirs and the buffalo too, anyone takes em, they'll chase em out. And then the Pawnee—. But the Otoe can look out for themselves—they send scouts out in the hills around the village, watching for buffalo, or strange Indians—

—There wasn't any scout when I came up with my wagon, not half a mile off. Isaac turned, pointed up the slope to the east, beyond the tribe's grazing herd.

Captain Dennison looked, pondered, frowned.—They figure Cheyenne to come from the west, if they come—off there now somewhere, most likely, in their winter camp, western Dakotas, or maybe up the South Platte. They're a big tribe.

—You ever hear of Tommy Thorn?

The captain nodded. They had found the fresh grave with its inscription, the dead oxen, as they traveled down the creek.

—That was early this spring—I was the one found him, gave him burial. It was Cheyenne arrows that killed him, two men. They could have been scouts for the main bunch.

The captain sighed again, heaved himself up.—I reckon you better tell the chief yourself. I can talk their language some. He knows a little English.

—I'm learning the sign language, Isaac said.

The chief's tepee was the biggest in the village, by itself at the upper end of the encampment. It was painted in black and red with stick-figures recognizable as men, horses, buffalo; records of warfare and hunting. The agent called him Redtail. He stooped, scratched with his fingernails at the hide covering the doorway, and a deep voice answered. Isaac followed him in and laid his rifle by the entrance. After the brightness of the morning, it seemed dark inside; the tanned hides of the tent covering had been thinned to translucence; the center was lighted from the smoke hole above. To the left of the doorway at the back the chief reclined on layers of buffalo robes, supported by a basketry backrest, a pair of revolvers and a caplock carbine at his side. He got up, shook their hands, sat cross-legged under the smoke hole and produced a pipe and a pouch of tobacco. The two white men sat facing him. It was necessary to smoke before they could talk.

The ceremony completed, Captain Dennison spoke at some length in Otoe. Redtail looked expectant. Isaac wanted to tell him everything exactly as he had seen and heard it: how Tommy's oxen had been killed, the contents of his wagon scattered; how the hunter had been tied and killed, his unfired rifle broken; the way the arrows were made and the shapes of the moccasin prints he had found; the Konza woman's warnings of a general war and what Horn had said of the Cheyenne leading it; how the east side of the Otoe camp was left unguarded—no, he had come within half a mile and had *seen* no guard, but he had ridden through the tribe's herd unchallenged. It was difficult, in parts of three languages. He did not know enough signs. Redtail's English was half a dozen words; the agent's Otoe sounded fluent but was limited. The chief was gravely observant, once or twice putting questions directly in signs slow and emphatic as if addressed to a child. When Isaac had nothing more to tell, Redtail spoke at length in Otoe, eyes still on the young hunter.—He's saying you do pretty good as a scout, Captain Dennison translated. Straight tongue—for a white man, that is. The chief excused himself and went outside. They could hear him calling out, a shuffling of moccasined feet in the dust of the village street, other voices, answering.

—These Otoe interested in trading? Isaac asked. I don't want anything but robes, though, or maybe wolf. The other furs aint worth the bother.

—They're only starting their hunt, took their rations the week they come off the reservation. You could ask Redtail.

—I've got flour, sugar, meal, tobacco at my ranch, some cotton cloth. I could bring a load out if they've got robes.

—*Say*, the agent said. You got a license to trade with the Otoe? You don't have a license, I'd have to arrest you. His weary face crumpled in a faint smile.

—I don't know about any license. But I'm not really a trader anyhow. It's just—the Kaw camped near my place in the fall, came over and traded off all my winter supplies, so I had to go to Leavenworth for more. I've still got stock to use up, if—

—You get yourself a proper license all the same, the agent admonished. You apply at the Superintendency at Saint Joseph, make bond. I'm supposed to sign something says you're all right. . . .

When the chief came back, Isaac addressed him on the subject of trading but understood only part of the answer.—He saying he don't want to trade? he asked, turning to Captain Dennison.

The chief repeated himself in Otoe. He says, the agent explained, time enough to talk trading tomorrow. You can sleep in the strangers' lodge tonight. That's a compliment.

The chief lay back on his bed. A woman brought in an iron kettle of stewed meat. Redtail invited his guests to eat. Isaac was uncomfortable. Lonnie had been alone on the hilltop for more than an hour.

—I don't want him misliking my manners when he's offering me meat, he said, speaking to Captain Dennison, but I've left my boy out there with my outfit. You reckon he'd take it wrong if I went and brought them in? And then I could sit down and eat with him long as he likes.

The chief looked from one to the other, questioning. With a weary shrug, Captain Dennison set about explaining the difficulty.

Shouts came from outside the tepee, a rifle shot, then another. Redtail leaped up, belting a revolver on, and ran out the doorway. Isaac followed, grabbing his rifle.

Out on the plain east of the village there were Indians among the horses, flapping buffalo robes and shouting. Two of the herders lay on the ground, arrows in their backs. The whole herd, a thousand horses or more, was bunched together, starting to move down the valley, animals on the outskirts of the mob rearing and screaming. Men from the village were running toward the herd, the chief in the lead, others loading their rifles and firing at the intruders. The camp dogs ran in circles, barking, women ran, calling out for their children.

—God-damn Cheyenne! the captain bellowed. They're running off the herd.

Isaac started at a run back through the village toward the agent's tent. He had released Singing Bird and mounted when the captain came up to him, darted into the tent, and came out with a Colt repeater carbine, faster than he looked, for all his lethargy and age. He made a grab for the reins and stood there panting, unable to speak.

—Let go! Isaac shouted.

—Don't you run off now! the captain gasped. That's—just a skirmish out there—with the horses, draw the fools off. What they're out for is the camp—got to stay and defend—

—Only camp I care for's my own—got to save my team and wagon—

The horse trembled all over with excitement. Isaac slipped the rifle into its case, jerked the reins free, and nudged his heels in her flanks. Bird gave a leap and started across the valley at a run. Isaac lay forward on her neck, watching the movement of the herd off to his right. Redtail had caught a horse, was racing along the far side of the herd. Two other Otoe followed. Four of the Cheyenne were mounted, crowded in at the rear of the stampede. The chief got his pistol out, fired. A Cheyenne loosed an arrow at him, nicked the upper part of his bare left arm, and the chief without slowing pushed the head through, broke the shaft, and threw it aside. He drove his mount faster, keeping in close, shouting to hold the frightened horses together, working along toward the front of the herd: he meant to head them off.

Isaac turned and started down the valley on the other side of the herd. Redtail was still ahead of him, out in front now. Isaac was getting there, crowding in close, shouting. The leaders were spreading out. Bird brought him up beside a big stallion, slowing a little, keeping pace, till he could make a grab for the horse's mane, pulling back hard, and the horse screamed, leaped, they were all around him, bucking, pawing. He let go, gave the mare a kick, she leaped forward, pushing, dodging, they were clear and out in front. There was a shot, the chief had downed one of the leaders, a dozen horses crashed around it, piling up. Redtail fired again. Isaac dodged off to the left of the herd, pivoted, rode straight at them and at the last moment veered off, rode ahead, and repeated the maneuver. The stampede was slowing, the horses farther back were bunching up, beginning to mill. Three other Otoe came up to the chief now, shouting, firing their guns in the air, lashing out with whips. The leaders were turning, the herd followed, swinging around in a close-packed column, starting back. The Cheyenne who started the rout had vanished, shot, perhaps, and trampled, more likely escaped among the trees along the creek. Isaac rode along the side toward the front, keeping the horses in, an Otoe brave fifty yards behind him. When they came opposite the village again, he waved and started up the slope to where he had left Lonnie.

The boy lay in the grass at the top, holding his loaded carbine. He had saddled the pony and staked it beside the wagon a little way back.

—I was ready to run, he said, sitting up.

—Good thing you didn't. They could be all around us.

—What's happening? Is it the Indian war starting up?

—Could be just horse-stealing. The village is Otoe, whole tribe, I guess, down from Nebraska Territory. The horse thieves are Cheyenne, don't like the Otoe much or anyone else comes into their country, including us. The Otoe have their agent with them—that's the army tent and flag—an old cavalryman, and he thinks there's going to be a fight.

Isaac dismounted, led his lathered horse over to the wagon and tied her.

—We could get back to the ranch tonight, riding, Lonnie said.

—We might. I aint ready to give up on my team and wagon till I see what's happening.

The Otoe had brought their horses in among the tepees. Men had run out to carry in the bodies of the dead herders. The women and children were out of sight, the warriors spaced around the village, waiting. Captain Dennison was up on his wagon, waving with his carbine and shouting. Lonnie lifted one arm and pointed across the valley. Beyond the creek to the west the hills rose steeply. Along the top of the highest bluff, more than a mile off and outlined against the afternoon light, there was a group of dark forms that might have been small trees, buffalo, or other game. A bigger shape lifted against the sky like the wings of a great bird flapping; disappeared, rose again.

—Good boy! Isaac said. Getting better—must be the blanket signal you hear about, the Cheyenne captains watching the village from over there, same as we're watching. So their people are down there and we're going to see some fun.

—D'you think they've seen us?

—I reckon. But it's the Otoe they're after—won't bother us till they've settled with them.

Isaac, less confident than he meant to sound, sent the boy to the wagon, had him raise the cover all around and keep watch while he waited for the fight. It was not long in coming. Suddenly the whole valley was filled with whoops and screams as horsemen swarmed from the trees to north and south of the village, converging on it at full gallop, each group an apparently leaderless mass—their leaders watched from the buttes on the other side of the valley, signaling with blankets. There were a few riders out front, pulling away, as in a race. Flights of arrows arced toward the village, the defenders answered with rifle fire, and within each group men slipped from their horses, horses fell and rolled. The two columns rode through each other without slackening and along the valley in opposite directions, out of rifle range, wheeled and halted. The dead and wounded had been gathered up, double-mounted; only the downed horses remained. It did not appear that any of the Otoe had been hurt. Now from each group of Cheyenne half a dozen braves rode out singly toward the camp, dodging and shouting, taunting, but the Otoe took their time reloading and held their fire. The Cheyenne hung on their horses' flanks, working closer, shooting under the horses' necks. An Otoe took an arrow in his shoulder and cried out. Another caught Captain Dennison in the thigh as he stood up in his wagon to shoot; bellowed, fell. Shots rolled from the village and the Cheyenne champions raced off, leaving two men on the field. There were perhaps a hundred Otoe warriors, four times as many Cheyenne. The Otoe made up for their numbers by being well armed with rifles and a few revolvers. For the Cheyenne, a bow and a quiver of arrows were still more effective in horseback warfare (or hunting) than a single-shot rifle or musket.

—You could pick em off, Lonnie said softly, crouching at Isaac's side. They're easy shots.

—Sure I could—and they'd be on us like hornets! Aint my fight anyhow. Isaac turned and looked severely at the boy. Didn't I tell you to stay in the wagon? Get on back there—you're supposed to be watching out for Cheyenne scouts sneaking up—and keep yourself out of the way of an arrow. . . .

Down below, the Cheyenne made another breakneck charge and were driven off. Again a few warriors rode toward the village, daring the Otoe to fight. In a rush a single Otoe came forth at a gallop toward the Cheyenne in the lead. The two men rode toward each other, arrows flying, came together, grappled, stabbing with knives, their horses rearing; fell, locked arm to arm, both dead. The sun was getting down toward the western hills. Abruptly Isaac stood and went back to the wagon.

—Lonnie! he called. Looks like they'll occupy each other for a time. We'd best get started for the ranch. But I do wish I hadn't traded off my pistols. I thought I had no need for a man-killer. . . .

—We're starting east, Isaac announced when he walked into the cabin the next afternoon. Tomorrow or next day—soon's we can get packed up.

It had been a clear night with a bright half moon. They traveled till midnight, Lonnie dozing in the wagon, slept three hours, and came on, stopping only an hour at noon to make coffee and chew on chunks of cold smoked meat. While the daylight lasted, Isaac left the boy to drive the team and rode along the ridges above their wagon track but could not discover that they were followed.

—You aint been out long, Harry observed. Run into trouble, did you?

—Looks like this war we've been hearing about is starting up after all—Cheyenne end of it, anyhow. It's going to be something too lively for hunting this summer, out where the buffalo are. And he began to tell what he had seen of the fight at the Otoe village.

After supper that night, leaving Irwin and Lonnie to scour the pots, Isaac invited Harry to come out and look things over; Harry carried his loaded rifle. Walking slowly, side by side, in silence, they inspected the fence across the neck of land, the barred gateway, returned and spoke to the horses in the corral, went into the stable to see to the oxen. All was in order. Isaac led the way over to the river-bank and along it to the point of land where the river made its sharp bend and swung around to the north.

—Harry, Isaac said, I've been thinking. I'm buying you out.

—Who says we're selling?

—Way I see it, Isaac continued, ignoring the challenge, if I'm going to have a partner in this thing, he's got to go shares in everything. Now you and Irwin between you—you aint half pulled your weight at hunting, just aint cut out for it, it seems, and aint lifted a finger at trading when opportunity comes. And then for doing business at Leavenworth or even Salina—why, every time it comes up, you've got some reason—

—Just aint my style. I come out here to hunt.

—Maybe you did, but the way I see it, a man can't more'n just scrape along, hunting. Trading's the thing, and if you can't help with it, or won't help, we can't stay partners together. Making me send that boy alone with the wagonload to Leavenworth!—and then again to bring out the new wagon and team—well, Lonnie's a good enough

boy and learning, but that's *man's* work, Harry, I can't do it all myself, and hunt and trade and build up the ranch besides—
    —What're you offering?
    —Let me finish! Isaac said, raising his voice. Because there's some-
thing more'n all the rest—I don't know what you're hiding from, but
you owed it to be straight.
    —Listen, Jack, Harry growled.
    —I never asked you, never pried around, but I've got a guess. Say
you were a teamster for the Army up at Laramie, got yourself in a
scrape and they put you in the punishment detail, whatever they call
it, demote you and cut your pay, and somehow you run off. And now
you're scared to show your face in any town in the territory for fear
some officer or some soldier will recognize you for a deserter and
bring you in for trial and prison. That's what it looks like, anyhow—
you aint here to hunt or *anything*—just hide. . . .
    Harry gripped the rifle in both hands.—So now you mean to turn
us in, he said at last.
    —Harry! Don't you know me after all these months? I don't have
any personal quarrel with you or Irwin either—nor mean to do the
Army's work for them, if it comes to that. But you got to see, we can't
be partners anymore. It just aint equal. . . .
    —All right.
    They started back toward the blockhouse.—You can take your pick
of any yoke from my new team of oxen, Isaac said—not the old team,
they've worked together too long to break up. Seventy-five dollars
they cost me at Leavenworth, they'll do for the light load you've got,
and you've got the cash I paid you from the first load of hides—you
can buy yourselves another yoke or trade with the hides you've got on
hand. Now aint that fair? I found this land in the first place, picked it
out—I could've *hired* the work you've done, building, for that much
cash. . . .
    Harry admitted it was fair and became almost cheerful; he was not,
after all, in a position to argue. Isaac offered, besides, five packs of his
own hides for the brothers' work in skinning and made no mention of
what they owed for the use of his team. They shook hands on it and
walked back to the cabin to sleep. It was settled.
    Talking vaguely of going to Kansas City, the Farrises left at noon
the next day, Watch looking wistfully out the back of the wagon.
With the hides Isaac had paid them, they had ten packs altogether,
worth at least fifty dollars. Isaac suggested shipping on consignment
to Lobenstein at St Louis and wrote the address on a scrap of paper;
and because they were low on all supplies, filled their powder horns
for them, gave them ten pounds of bar lead, flour, sugar, and coffee,
and their pick of the smoked meat.
    Isaac and Lonnie were two full days sorting and packing up. The

hides and furs filled one wagon and part of the second, with the remainder of his trading stock and the meat. They managed to work Tommy's old wagon into the stable and braced the door tight with a log. In the cabin he was leaving the few pieces of furniture but taking everything else. Late in the third morning he sat at the rough table writing letters to leave at Salina—to Colonel Titus, telling of the Indian troubles coming in the summer and offering to plow again or cut hay, anything that would pay, till fall; to his parents, of his large harvest of hides and his hope for a good price at Leavenworth, but mentioning his encounters with Indians only in passing—when he heard a trampling of horses' hooves in the yard outside, then a hammering at the cabin door.

Isaac leaped up, seized his rifle, and jerked the door open. A young Indian stood on the step, hands clasped in the peace sign, naked in the soft May morning except for a breechcloth, moccasins; under one arm he carried a short-barreled rifle, its butt ornamented with copper nails in a starburst pattern. Isaac stood his gun aside, shook his hand, and followed him out. There were four others at the stockade gate: Otoe scouts. The rest of the tribe was half a day behind, meaning to camp on the Saline a mile or two below the ranch. The fight with the Cheyenne had lasted three days while the Otoe retreated down the creek, ending in victory: the stripe-arrows had ridden off to the west, leaving twenty dead; the Otoe had lost four and some wounded, among them the agent. The scout had a message: the chief wished to have talk with the golden-hair hunter. Isaac told him he was traveling east but would put off starting till afternoon.

Isaac finished his letters, wrote jokingly to his sister about the Konza squaw and the buckskin hunting shirt, and to Marie Bisonnette. When he tried to write to Marie his mind swirled with volumes of things done since he saw her last—travels, hunts, Indians, the break with the Farrises—and he ended by putting down two stiff sentences:

> I am sumoned from my Ranche to the presence of one Red Tail, the great Chief of the Oto a small tribe returning from war with the Shyan. In one months time I should like to take tea in your presence, when I have disposed of my Hides at L'worth City, and other busyness.

He addressed an envelope for Marie, made a last fire on the hearth and boiled a chunk of the unpalatable salt buffalo tongue for himself and Lonnie, and lay on the stripped bed to sleep. He woke to a confusion of sounds: horses neighing, his own answering, human voices calling, singing—the Otoe passing down the river. He sat up, pulled on his boots, and shouted for Lonnie.

—Come on, boy! We're camping with the Otoe tonight.

The women had half the tepees up by the time Isaac and Lonnie drove into the Otoe camp. Some of the men rode in with trophies of the fight tied to their lance tips—long-braided Cheyenne scalps stretched on hoops of willow; fingers, ears. With shouts all around and a jingling of harness, Captain Dennison's wagon rumbled in, the mules wild-eyed, kicking, jerking from side to side, each ridden by an Indian, no Otoe having yet mastered the art of driving a team. Isaac ran over. The agent lay in the wagon bed on a mat of buffalo robes, his trouser leg slit and his wound bound with a torn-up shirt, swollen and painful, feverish.

—We are going through to Fort Riley, the agent announced, propping himself on one elbow, eyes bright, stubble-bearded face glistening with sweat. I shall make a personal complaint to the commandant. I shall demand an expedition, sir!

The two braves had dismounted and walked away. Isaac shouted for Lonnie to come and unhitch the mules.

—It is an outrage, sir! the captain continued, rehearsing his protest. Why are the Cheyenne permitted to perpetrate their depredations on peaceable dependents who have placed themselves under the protection of the United States? Why are they not punished?

—Do you think they'll go on with the hunt?

—Not this year—not in Kansas, I hope. Redtail maintains that after their thrashing the Cheyenne will think twice before making another attack on the Otoe—insists they will return next year if not sooner. Great God! I shall resign. The service has made an old man of me. . . .

He seemed to doze. Isaac got the agent's tent out, set it up, carried in the folding bed, stool, table, helped the captain down and half-carried him in, laying him on the bed and covering him with blankets.

The tribe had chosen for their camp a wide bend of the river enclosing a grassy plain, roughly circular and two miles across, defensively, perhaps, but providing good grazing and easy herding for the horses. Redtail this time had placed his lodge at the center of the half-circle of tepees set up along the riverbank. Isaac found him sitting cross-legged in front on a pile of buffalo robes while two of his women crumbled jerked buffalo meat into a large pot and a third with a Bowie knife sliced a yellow root the size of a man's forearm; manroot. The chief leaped up, smiling, and drew him close in a muscular embrace.

—Good man—brave, the chief said, and, exhausting his English, went on in Otoe.

Stepping back, Redtail explained in signs that the robes were for Isaac, that was why they were spread outside. Isaac attempted to make excuses, but it was apparent from the chief's expression that he could not refuse, and with a slight bow he assented. Next, he asked if

Redtail had meat. Apologetically, the chief said no, the tribe had only just made camp, had not begun their hunt. . . . Signing to him to follow, Isaac led him to his wagons, opened the tailgate of the new one, and showed him his meat—a nearly full barrel of tongues and four hundred pounds of smoked hams, tenderloin, ribs. Climbing up, he cut a slice from a ham and offered it to Redtail to taste: he wanted the chief to accept half his meat; and apologized for the quality of the tongues. He pulled out a buffalo hide, spread it on the ground, and with Lonnie helping made a pile of the meat. With some cutting, there was a piece for every lodge in the village.

The robes Redtail had set out would make up as a full pack, not new but worn soft as fine wool with use; two, painted on the flesh side with scenes of hunting and war in the manner of the chief's tepee, would bring double the usual price. Redtail was determined to lead the tribe back the next spring for the hunt. He promised to trade and would send a messenger to the ranch when the people were ready.

—Very well, Mister Pride, Durfee said with a faint smile, six hundred dollars for the lot. He rocked back on his heels, thumbs hanging from his vest pockets, at ease. It's really quite *all* I can offer and leave anything over for my profit. . . .

They had been two full weeks coming from the Otoe camp. The weather continued clear and dry, but the spring grass seemed thin and lacking in nourishment. With the heavily loaded wagons, Isaac dared not push his oxen too hard; apart from the land warrant, he had something over ten dollars left in cash and could not waste it buying hay, if there was any to be had. Dennison, lucid again after a sick night, had been eloquent in urging the hunter to drive him to Fort Riley or at least make a place for him in one of the wagons and lead the mules with his horses, but Isaac resisted. He had done enough; it would have cost him a week. He had camped with Lonnie the night before beside the road on the prairie west of Leavenworth and then again had trouble finding Durfee's establishment. The store at the south end of town was empty and locked up. The merchant seemed to have gone into partnership with Mr Garrett. Garrett kept on with the store on Cherokee St; Durfee operated the warehouse.

Isaac worked the offer through in his mind. Mr Durfee had been effusive about the white wolf skins, most unusual in the trade, in his experience, and complimentary about the quality of the hides and robes; and offered five hundred dollars. Isaac answered that for that he would take his goods on a boat to St Louis and sell them direct.

—All right, Isaac said to the merchant's renewed offer. Six hundred and I'll keep the painted robes.

Durfee's eyes narrowed.—Really, Mister Pride, he said, I rather fancied those two, and their story—the, what was he, Otoe chief. But after all—.

They compromised the difference: Isaac kept one of the pair and let Durfee have the other, for another fifteen dollars. Mr Durfee seated himself at his desk and reckoned it up. The wagon and team had come to twenty-five dollars beyond Isaac's remaining credit, there was a ten-dollar commission for arranging the purchase, one dollar and fifty cents in interest: the net came to five hundred and seventy-eight dollars and fifty cents. Promising to be back to stock up for trading in the fall, Isaac insisted on being paid in gold and silver; and then counted back seventy-five dollars to cover a draft on Lobenstein payable to Samuel Hawken, gunsmith, 33 Washington St, St Louis.

They finished unloading the wagons and backed them out into the street. Isaac, with more than five hundred dollars still in his purse, was thinking of driving down to the landing to take dinner at the Planter's House before starting south, when Lonnie came up to him, his face set.

—Now you've got your money, Mister Pride, the boy said, I want mine.

—*Of course* you'll have your money, Lonnie. But right now, right here in the street, and people passing by and looking?

—I want my pay, the boy insisted.

Isaac studied the boy: round-faced and plump, greasy black hair spilling from under the ragged hat brim, smudges on his cheeks and nose—he would grow into one of those big, fleshy men working at nondescript common labor, reliable enough; not stupid but with a way of masking thought and feeling that was on the whole a virtue in anyone a man had to live with day after day. All the way from the ranch he had been more than usually silent and morose. Isaac had attributed this moodiness to growing up and had not inquired.

—Well, all right, Isaac said, you'll *have* your pay. But you're coming on to Burlingame, aint you?

—No, I *aint*. Going to Topeka, see if they'll take me on at the mill again. Late as it is, they might be done hiring—.

Isaac flushed.—Why, boy, you aint *thinking*—Burlingame's right on the *way* to Topeka, practically, you'll be there in a week. How in the nation you expect me to drive two wagons single-handed?

—I hired for the winter, Lonnie said, fists clenched. Fifty dollars for the *winter*—and here it is coming into June. You want me to drive for you, you can pay a teamster's wage, dollar a day.

Isaac thought back—paid the boy a bonus and bought him a suit of clothes, never asked for change from the travel money for the second trip to Leavenworth—and fifty dollars was what they agreed; but was too angry to argue. He took out his purse and counted the boy's pay.

Lonnie dropped the coins in his pocket, turned without a word, and started down the street. Isaac went back into the warehouse.

—It would perhaps have been politic, and indeed convenient all around, Mr Durfee observed when Isaac had explained his difficulty, if you had offered something extra for the drive to Burlingame.

—I reckon, Isaac said. It just made me mad—here I've treated the boy square right along, is what *I* think, and now—. I just can't manage it alone. You know anyone I could hire for the week? I could pay his stage fare back.

Mr Durfee leaned his elbows on the desk and arched his fingertips thoughtfully together.—It is no easy task, finding casual labor in Kansas. Those who have work in these uncertain times, or have taken up land, are fully occupied. The rest, for now, have returned to the States. . . . On the other hand, if you would consider a man of color—

—I don't care what color he is, Isaac said, if he can drive one of my teams without breaking their necks.

—I cannot speak for that, Mr Durfee cautioned. I have employed him myself on occasion and found no complaint. Mostly he holds the gentlemen's horses at the Planter's House and is permitted, I believe, to sleep over the stables—after the years of controversy on the subject, not to say violence, the good people of Kansas do not clasp the black man to their bosom. Cornelius Smith—a freedman who was body servant to an officer at Fort Leavenworth and took his name—

—Captain Andrew Jackson Smith! said Isaac with a grin. I met the old rascal the second day I was in Kansas.

—Quite well spoken, Mr Durfee continued. From being around the officers, I expect.

—Don't sound like a man for a hard day's work—not what I call work, anyhow.

Mr Durfee suggested they take dinner together at the Planter's House—he would introduce Isaac if he liked the look of the man. Isaac drove his wagons back into the warehouse and tied the horses. They walked over to Cherokee St and started down toward the hotel.

There was a kind of throbbing in the air, sound more felt than heard, beginning sometime after they crossed the Osage River on the road from Lawrence: like cicadas on a summer night, frog song, birds in their dawn chorus, herd animals in stampede—repetitive and unrhythmic, living, impersonal, coming to them from the remote limits of perception. Isaac halted the wagons, spied all around for minutes but could find nothing to connect it with. The road was empty in both directions. The rolling grasslands of the Sac and Fox Reservation circled them to the horizon, serene and golden-green in the soft June light.

They came to the top of another of the gentle hills and the answer was spread out before them. Below, not half a mile distant, were the neat structures of the Agency—the substantial, two-story clapboard house that must be the Indian agent's, gleaming white in the noon light, barns, workshops, a somewhat less imposing farmhouse and the sprouting fields of the demonstration farm, a hundred brown-and-white cattle peacefully grazing in a fenced pasture; and all around this island of American order the hundred random cottages of a made-to-order Indian village in the making—stacks of lumber and brick, little houses at every stage of completion, open wagons, carpenters hammering at timbers, beams, siding, shingles.

—That's where we're going, Isaac said, lifting his arm. Mind your team, going downhill. And if the wagon starts to push em, run for the brake.

Cornelius Smith had said he could ride a horse or mule, drive a one-horse buggy tolerably well, but knew nothing of managing an ox-team and freight wagon. That truthful modesty had persuaded Isaac —and the prospect of wasting perhaps days at Leavenworth, hunting an experienced teamster. He offered Cornie, as he began to call him, seven dollars for the trip to Burlingame, about a week, out of which the black man was to find his own way home. Isaac put him on the empty wagon, and he did well enough on the flat; Isaac took both wagons down steep hills himself, across streams and the rope ferry at Lawrence, with Cornie on the brakes. Isaac one evening tried him on one of the ponies. He rode stiffly erect as a cavalryman, as he had learned from Captain Smith. His feet had blistered the first day, nearly hobbled him the second, but he kept on, dogged and silent except when answering a question, and was hardening; a town boy, raised at Louisville, about twenty-five—he did not know his birth date; could write his name very presentably and had taught himself to spell out the New Testament he carried in his coat pocket and get the sense—there had been a Presbyterian missionary at Louisville, preaching to the black people on Sunday afternoons. If not much with a wagon, he was an adept cook, producing biscuits that Isaac pronounced as light as his mother's. The night before, camping at the crossing of Appenoose Creek, Isaac to vary their diet shot half a dozen prairie chickens and Cornie deftly cleaned and plucked them and roasted them gold-brown on a spit, basting with bacon fat and syrup.

As they drove toward the agent's house, a man came out from behind it in a light buggy with the top down, dark suit, white shirt, high-crowned black hat. He was nearly past when he waved, shouted, and reined his horse in.

—Mister Isaac Pride, to be sure! An unexpected pleasure!

It was Bob Stevens. Isaac walked over to him, reached up and shook his hand.

—I wrote to you at Burlingame, Stevens said. Didn't you get my letter?

Isaac shook his head.—Aint been back there since January, Mister Stevens. I'm going there now.

Stevens set his reins and stepped down from the buggy, smiling broadly.—You see I got my contract, he said, taking in the little houses and the gang of workmen with a sweep of his arm. But finding someone I can count on to manage the job—well, that's another matter. I'm having to stay down here and do it myself, and neglect my business at Lecompton just when the emigrants are starting up again —more to do up there than Mister Shannon and a clerk can keep up with. That's why I got to thinking about you again—

Cornelius came up to them, stepping tenderly in the soft dust of the road.—Shall I turn the cattle out to feed, Mister Pride? he said.

—Go ahead, Cornie, but leave them in the yokes—and better stake them. We can take our dinner here, after a while.

Stevens took in the deferential black man, the two wagons, the sleek oxen.—Seems Kansas agrees with you, Mister Pride, you're maybe too occupied to take on this job of mine. Setting up as a freighter, are you?

—I've been hunting through the winter, trading some, but it looks to be a little hot for a white man on the Plains this summer. How long do you figure it to run?

—Supposed to finish before winter—depends if I can keep the men and materials moving, the lumber and such. We've got ninety of these things started. The contract is three hundred and fifty-three. . . .

They left the road and walked slowly toward the nearest of the cottages, framed in on a foundation of freestone, with its subfloor, fireplace, chimney, awaiting roof beams, siding, windows, doors.

—Of course the really big thing, Stevens was saying, is the new treaty. See, the Indians are supposed to take their land in severalty now, eighty acres to a family, and we build em these houses, and the government sells off the rest of the reservation to pay for the improvements. Three hundred thousand acres, Mister Pride! The last big tract of first-rate untouched land in eastern Kansas. Now here's the thing—a man on the ground, with money and a chance to look things over—why, he can pick up all he's got money for at a dollar an acre, sell it in the fall—or next spring, anyway—at ten or fifteen—. Or hang on, if that's his mind. But either way—

—I've still got that quarter-section military warrant I could lay out, Isaac said thoughtfully.

—Why, of course, of *course!* Stevens said with enthusiasm. The Indian department hasn't laid out all its rules yet, but it'll go through the Land Office, and I don't doubt but they'll take warrants. I could look after it for you.

—I've got a ranch out beyond Salina that I'm building up—mean to claim around it when the county's organized and up for sale.

—Of *course*, Stevens repeated—spread your bets, there's the way. . . .

They stepped through the empty doorframe of the cottage. Isaac's eyes found a stud marred by a large knot halfway up. He went to it, flexed it.

—Your men should have thrown that piece out, he said. One good knock with a hammer and it'll break in the middle.

—It won't show, will it? Stevens anxiously asked. Once the walls are finished, I mean. The contract calls for plaster, if I can find the men to do it. Tongue-and-groove pine would do as well for an Indian, so far as I can see, and cost a whole lot less—and a darn sight less bother than—

Isaac knelt. The ends of the floor joists showed under the rough boards of the subfloor and were carelessly fitted to the notches in the sill; one of the joists was short, supported only by the boards nailed to it. Isaac stood, rocked his weight on it, and the floor sagged, the joist creaked, rubbing its end against the sill.

Mr Stevens sighed.—That's the kind of detail I need a competent manager for, he said. Got to be fixed, I suppose, does it?

—Go right through when you get some weight on it, if you don't. To do it right, you practically got to take the floor up—unless you could get under there with a post somehow.

Mr Stevens took out a pocket memorandum book and wrote himself a note. Isaac went over to the fireplace in the end wall of the house, got down on his knees and looked up the chimney. The fireplace was small and shallow, hardly a foot deep, with a narrow stone hearth. He stood up.

—I don't think any more of your masons than I do of your carpenters, he said. First time you make a fire in that thing, you'll burn the house down.

Mr Stevens looked pained.—I'm not sure you understand my difficulties, Mister Pride. Despite the things you may have seen in the Republican papers—

—I aint seen a paper of any kind, cept maybe once or twice, since November. Been out beyond the frontier, hunting—

—All the same—it's a neat round sum, right enough, but it's also three hundred and fifty-three houses. It only foots up to around six hundred each, and—

—Six hundred dollars! Isaac said. Why, in Iowa for that—what is it, twelve by eighteen feet?—we built houses bigger than that, and two full stories, and good materials and workmanship all through, for six hundred dollars—

—Of *course* you could, Stevens said indignantly. And didn't have to hire your carpenters and masons at Kansas City or Saint Louis, and haul in every stick of lumber, every nail and brick, and window sash and door, and food to feed em, and a cook, and tents—*and* show a profit in the end. . . .

They walked slowly back toward the wagons, Isaac silent and abstracted, intrigued by the arithmetic of the project: the number of houses still to be built, all the same, and how you could calculate the number of feet of each kind of lumber needed for each, cut it to fit, and haul it to the site. They stood in the road beside the buggy, facing each other. Isaac explained his difficulty in giving an answer about the job. He had meant to spend the summer at his ranch, and when that changed had offered to help Colonel Titus with his farm, it was a kind of promise; now if the colonel wanted him, he would have to do it. Stevens went back to Lecompton at least every week. Isaac would write to him there and let him know.

—Say, Isaac said as Stevens started to climb into his buggy. I bet you know Seoskuk—an older man, old Black Hawk's son that started the war in Illinois, Little Hawk they call him in English. I came this way on purpose to see him, wanted to give him something cause I figured I owed him.

Stevens seated himself, smiled.—They don't come around much where we're working, he said, but I don't know one from the other anyway, cept old Moses Keokuk, their chief. The agent could tell you, only he's gone to Kansas City with his family.

But Seoskuk, Isaac said—he'd know this one; and he described the place, six or seven miles up the Osage from the Agency, his son George who had gone to school and could read and write, George's wife, the children.

—Oh, *that* one, Stevens said, the troublemaker—everyone else in the tribe put their names down for allotments except him. He wouldn't take any land.

—Wouldn't any man trade what *he* had for eighty acres—four times as much, and corn and some cattle and horses, and a neat double cabin down by the river: a pretty little farm in the making.

Stevens shrugged.—The other thing was, he said, we got a railway right-of-way in the new treaty, and the engineer says the best route is through this place of his. I don't know where he's gone, but he's gone. Just wouldn't see reason.

He took the reins, shook them and drove off.

Marie had remembered what Isaac wrote about taking tea with her and was waiting for him in the parlor when he came down from taking a bath and changing into his suit. The colonel had taken it for granted that Isaac would stay, and Cornie too—Vinnie had made up a bed in the storeroom next to her own room in the attic. Isaac had driven through slowly from the Sac and Fox Agency, arriving after dinner on the third day. He had stopped at Seoskuk's place, meaning to give the Indian the rest of his smoked buffalo meat—that was his purpose in this roundabout route to Burlingame—but it was as Stevens had said: the old man and his family were gone, with their cattle and horses, leaving their fields unplowed and unplanted. Isaac thought of taking the meat back to Mr Stevens to sell, but it hardly seemed worth the time for four or five cents a pound. He had also taken thought for the lawyer's suggestion about locating land in the reservation, do him the favor of managing his builders and he would make sure your claim went through, legal and proper, and no nonsense this time about absentee claimants.

Absalom carried in the steaming teapot on a large silver tray, with plates of cookies and fresh toast, a pot of jam, and set it on the table beside Marie's chair.

—Did you enjoy your interview with, what was his name, Redtail? Marie asked as she filled the cups. Such a funny name for an Indian chief. She laughed.

—I expect it sounds better in his own language, Isaac said, but Redtail's all I know. But he's a real chief all the same—got the whole weight and worry of his tribe on his shoulders—just a little tribe, the Otoe, hardly a hundred men that can fight when they have to, and up against all the wild tribes with their thousands of braves, that wouldn't think twice about killing them all, if they could. But the Indians seem just like a herd of buffalo—get set on going someplace, and not killing or anything'll turn em back. . . .

And he told her the story of finding the Otoe camp and the Cheyenne attack. Marie listened attentively and looked properly concerned when he touched on the stampeding horses and his part in saving them.

—You do seem to be out among the Indians, she said when he had finished. I expect you have a pretty little squaw in every camp, do you not, Isaac?

He hesitated. She looked serious enough but, he concluded, was really joking with him.—Oh, I expect I would, he said, if ever I found any pretty enough. Some are jolly and intelligent and kind—but I wouldn't call em pretty. There was one, a Kaw, gave me a beautiful buckskin hunting shirt, and it worried me, I thought her father'd be along next with his scalping knife, inquiring after my intentions, but it seems she only meant to be kind. Generous, that's how they are, like to give you things—and then it's only polite, of course, to give something in return.

—What would you give me if I made *you* a shirt, Isaac?

—I could give you a hide and a smoked buffalo steak, same as I gave Southwind, that was the girl's name, now that's pretty enough, aint it? Or say, that buffalo tail I promised and keep forgetting, to switch flies with—

—It is still horrid! Marie said, making a face. He held out his cup and she filled it. Your friend Mister Kilbourn made us a visit, she continued in a different voice, smiling again but watching him closely. When was it now, February sometime, after you were here? And then he came again only last month, coming through from Topeka.

—I'm sorry to hear that.

—Mister Kilbourn is starting a freight line—and is engaged with Mister Pomeroy in Kansas relief—and has grown a most *elegant* little pointed black beard—

—Marie! Don't you know *anything?* Why do you let him come around?

—Why not? Uncle gives him an excellent dinner, and port and a cigar afterward, and *so* enjoys his conversation.

—Oh, Marie, can't you see it's not your uncle he's after, it's *you?* And you don't know the way Kilbourn's been carrying on, Marie— drinking, and Indian girls—and once almost started a riot, and the sheriff at Lawrence made him clear out—

—Ah! said Marie gaily, the little squaws again, how romantic. But that is only hearsay, Isaac—or a different Mister Kilbourn. *Our* Mister Kilbourn is most gentlemanly and polite.

—You're only teasing, Marie, but you oughtn't. It's serious.

—*Am* I, Isaac? said Marie, eyes wide. Well, I think *you* are jealous— of poor Mister Kilbourn.

—Marie! He flushed, stood up, and took a step toward her, almost threatening. Marie, it's not that. It's only—you're gentle, innocent, Marie, and Kilbourn—well, the kind of man he's turning out, he could do you terrible harm, and I'm just not going to stand for it. I won't have him near you. . . .

—*Really*, Isaac, she said after a pause, her voice very cool, though her hand trembled slightly as she set the cup down. Really, I do not see that it is any affair of yours, who calls on me and who does not—if it truly is me Mister Kilbourn comes to see. I am quite capable of deciding such things for myself. And if not—if I should have so little sense as you take me to have—why, it is *still* not your affair but my uncle's—or my cousin Ned's—

She looked him steadily in the face, but his expression had changed again.

—Say, Marie, Isaac said, so pleasant coming back here, and talking,

I nearly forgot—but I brought you something, from right out on the Plains, and not any buffalo tail, neither. Wait—.

He strode briskly from the parlor and out the front door, to bring in the beautiful painted robe Redtail had given him, neatly wrapped in a piece of buckskin and left in the wagon. Marie shook her head, frowning, rose, and went to the window. Isaac passed below, heading toward the back of the house with rapid steps, delight and anticipation on his face and no more mindful of the rebuke she had intended than of the buzzing of a fly.

XI

Sun-Boy

Bill Mathewson's principal establishment was a stockaded trading post at the Walnut Creek crossing of the Santa Fe Road, near the northernmost reach of that part of the Arkansas River known as the Great Bend. He employed four men there as hunters, skinners, teamsters, with a boy to help, while himself attending to the more profitable trading with the tribes. On a summery night late in the spring of 1860, all five were in the bunkhouse, the gate of the stockade closed and barred, when a commotion in the unguarded corral out back disturbed their lamplit repose: horses milling, clattering against the cottonwood rails, frightened whinnies, mules braying. A man ran out, mounted the firewalk, saw a dark shape on the corral fence, raised his revolver and fired. A scream answered, the shape dropped back into the darkness, there came a whisper of footsteps in the dust, cries, the muffled drumbeat of unshod hooves, one horse, double-mounted, going south. Mathewson came out, stayed an hour, and called young Cody to keep watch for the rest of the night with a brace of pistols, but there was no further attempt at horse-stealing. In the morning he examined the moccasin prints beside the corral, judged it had been two men, Kiowa, and warned his men against going out alone. If the wounded brave died, a relative or friend would feel obliged to kill one of them.

Mathewson at thirty was already seventeen years in the West: started by running away from a drunken stepfather in backwoods New York; worked his way west, logging, hunting, trapping; ranged the Rockies while the beaver lasted; joined with Kit Carson at the Bent brothers' fort on the upper Arkansas, and, when Carson went home to Taos in 1853 to set up the Utah Agency for the Indian department, went into trading for himself, establishing his post at the

Great Bend, two hundred and seventy-five miles down the Santa Fe Road from its base at Independence. He was a big man, an inch over six feet tall, weighing more than two hundred pounds and heavy-boned, with a long beard trimmed to a point; known to the Indians as generous and just, to his men as disliking liquor and profane speech, a man of few words, exchanging information, Indian-fashion, but not given to conversation.

A year earlier, in 1859, when the War Department determined on a cavalry post to guard the route to the gold regions, Mathewson advised on the location of Fort Larned, forty miles up the Arkansas from his own place. It was his luck that, in consequence of this decision, his trading post became a junction: the Army surveyed a road running west from Fort Riley past the new town of Salina, then southwest through the Smoky Hills toward the Great Bend. Officers posted to the area found it prudent to obtain Mathewson's advice in exploring the country or settling disputes with the Indians. That same year the Kiowa had followed the herds north and held their mid-summer Sun-Dance near the Great Bend—the tribe's chief festival, focusing every kind of religious and social aspiration, among which the hunting of the buffalo was central. Their unaccustomed presence in country claimed by the Arapaho and Cheyenne and disputed by the Pawnee, in combination with that summer's drought, provided Mathewson with the opportunity to help settlers venturing west after meat and earned him the nickname Buffalo Bill which elicited a disapproving frown when used in his hearing. Others were to use the nickname Buffalo Bill. But when Bill Cody adopted the name years later, Mathewson wrote him ". . . you have no right to call yourself 'Buffalo Bill' and you know you haven't."

A week passed with no further attempt at robbing the corral, or at vengeance, if indeed there was a life to avenge. Mathewson opened the gate by day, as usual. Bullwhackers, going or coming, stopped to buy tobacco, flour, coffee, one or other of the canned luxuries, and exchange information on the part of the road they had come; Indians came in to trade. Mathewson started Cody and two of the men east with two loads of winter robes and hides, in the company of a returning military train. The next day he sent the other two up the Walnut with a wagon to cut firewood and bring it in; and was therefore alone in the store when the five horsemen galloped through the gate and reined up at the cabin door, ponies rearing above the trailing dust cloud.

The leader entered the cabin with an exuberant leap, grinning, his four young men cautiously following, sober-faced: Set-t'ain'te, a name simplified to Satanta in English, leader of one band of the Kiowa; a big man, nearly as tall as Mathewson and as heavy, everything about him made large as if to be obvious at a distance, in a crowd—wide-mouthed face broad across the cheeks and dark as shoe-blacking, dominated by a thick wedge of nose under heavy brows, massive shoulders, arms, and chest swelling through his knitted shirt, wrestler's legs bulging the buckskin of his trousers. Mathewson turned his head slightly, seeking and holding the eyes; nodded, spoke the name, Satanta—he had known him since the summer before and the Sun-Dance, longer by reputation; and looked away.

Satanta came up, leaned, brought his face close, still smiling but with eyes raging: he had come to kill the trader, clear the goods from his shelves and storehouse, burn the post. Assisting his words with the habitual signs, he spoke Comanche, the language of trade among the dozen of the South Plains, imposed by the tribe's numbers and arrogant sagacity.

—I was expecting you, Satanta, Mathewson answered in the same language, still without moving, but you were a time coming. I thought you'd given up caring what happened to your horse-stealing young bucks.

Satanta straightened up, the forced smile vanished, he struck his thighs with clenched fists. Very slowly Mathewson drew himself to his full height. Satanta took a step back.

—Or maybe your man just took his time dying, Mathewson continued, his voice still quiet. Didn't know he was Kiowa till I went out in the light and looked. Now, he'd come in the day and trade for a horse, fair and honest—or down on his luck and he didn't have no horse—. But he ought to've knowed, come to my ranch in the dark of night and try to take what's mine, he'll go home hurt—Kiowa or any Indian, or white man too—or runaway soldier from the camp, trying to run off my stock—

Satanta with a harsh laugh turned to his men: the trader could kill white men or soldiers any time he wanted and welcome; not one Kiowa. He swung around, thumping his chest: Time for the white man to die. They had come to kill him and clean out his goods.

Of course, Mathewson courteously answered, but it would be a mistake to kill him without first letting him show his goods, there were things in the store Satanta did not know about—coffee mills and corn mills, a tool for opening the canned goods without spoiling a knife, a new kind of pistol that fired a ready-made metal cartridge so a man needn't waste time loading with cap and powder and ball—

With a long-legged stride Mathewson was behind the counter, reached, and brought out one of the Smith & Wessons he had described, swinging the barrel in a slow arc from chest to chest: the Indians would be advised to go out and get on their ponies. There was a ball for each in the gun and one over for any who was slow killing. The four young men backed toward the open door, eyes wide. Satanta stood immobilized across the counter, one hand clenching the grip of his belt knife. Mathewson took a slow and deliberate step around the end of the counter, laid the gun aside, and held up his empty hands. The Indian stared back but did not move. Mathewson took another step, struck an openhanded blow to one side of the Indian's head, then the other, moved in close, bringing one knee up hard in the man's belly and at the same time giving a straight-arm shove to his shoulders with both hands. Satanta went over backward, head toward the door, and hit with a thump. Before he could move—roll away, draw the knife—the trader with a flying leap landed heavily astride and began pounding Satanta's face with closed fists, one side, then the other, slow and rhythmic, not hard enough to kill.

Mathewson stood up, wiped his sweating hands on his trousers—mid-afternoon, getting warm now, the sun through the doorway veiling the Indian's motionless form in a pall of brightness. The empty eyes stared back, seeing nothing. Mathewson stooped, got his hands under Satanta's shoulders, and dragged him out into the yard. The four young men sat slumped on their ponies, undecided, neither retreating nor attacking. With a final heave Mathewson sent the Indian toward the fifth horse.

—You can ride him back to camp now, Mathewson told them. And you come back, any of you, any time you're ready to do honest trade for anything I've got. But you come after trouble, trying to steal my horses or anything that's mine—why, let me tell you, boys, there's a whole lot more where that came from.

Mathewson turned and went back into the store, leaving the door open.

Isaac spent the summer of 1860 at Burlingame. Colonel Titus offered him fifty dollars a month to work at improving his land, out of which Isaac paid Cornie a third for staying on as helper to the end of August, with the understanding that if he proved himself the black man would come on to the ranch in the fall as cook and skinner. Between them they built a rough cabin suitable for a tenant and lived in it when on the land, eating Isaac's smoked buffalo meat until it became too tainted with mold, too foul to nose and palate, to trust and they were reduced to the salt tongues and such small game—prairie chicken, an occasional turkey, fox squirrel and coon, and once a skunk—as Isaac could get with his gun. Cornie became competent with the broad-ax, though slow, and learned to manage a team of oxen but not the colonel's heavy breaking plow. Together they turned another eighty acres, working the oxen, double-teamed, on alternate days, and the animals this summer stayed healthy, but it seemed to Isaac work thrown away. Not counting the thin and short-lived snow of the winter, there was still no rain. The land plowed the previous summer had turned to dust and remained barren. The heat was intense. One afternoon the thermometer on the porch of the colonel's house measured a hundred and fifteen degrees. The wind blew constantly and hard from the southwest. A hand held to an unchinked crack in the cabin wall came away red and sore as if scorched by a blast from an oven. In early August they cut the sparse prairie hay and hauled it to the colonel's barn.

Isaac was conscientious about earning his pay but there was not work enough to occupy him, and fully half his time he spent at Burlingame, visiting Marie or riding out with her. Once they took a saddlebag picnic and rode down Switzler Creek to the Osage and as far east as the Sac and Fox Agency, on the excuse of inspecting land soon to come up for sale. Isaac had written promptly to Bob Stevens, declining his offer, but had had no reply. By now the lawyer had other things on his mind. The mutterings about his contract in the papers from Topeka and Leavenworth had become a scandal. Two hundred thousand dollars, it was said, had been sunk in the project, although, since it was not public but Indian money, to be recovered from the sale of undistributed reservation land, the exact sum was of little consequence. Work on the cottages had, at any rate, been stopped. The Indians returned and made such use as they could of the construction, stabling horses in the little houses; settlers came down and removed the doors and windows, offering whisky in payment, if they could find a tribesman to accept it. Seoskuk's homestead remained empty. A young son of Moses Keokuk answered vaguely and indifferently when Isaac asked after him. The people did not know where Little Hawk and his family had gone.

After dinner on a day in August Colonel Titus summoned Isaac to the parlor to "have some talk." Marie with Absalom had driven out the Topeka road in an unpromising search for a farmer with fresh vegetables to sell. Isaac took a seat on the sofa, erect and alert, expecting some question about further plowing or starting work on a barn. He had a scheme of his own for running a ditch from the creek along the north line of the colonel's land so as to turn water on it for planting in the spring and had taken the trouble to write his father about it, asking advice. The creek was spring-fed and ever-flowing even in this dry time.

—You'll be starting back to this—ranch of yours, I expect, Colonel Titus suggested. Now that summer's getting past.

Isaac agreed that he would, in a month or so maybe, if the colonel could think of nothing more that wanted doing. It seemed a devious opening, like an invitation to depart, but then the colonel—

—Don't seem much of a life, Colonel Titus continued—hunting—for an active young man that's had some education, and wants to make something of his life, and has his opportunities all before him—

—It's not just hunting, Isaac objected, it's trading too—fact is, I mean to do more trading than hunting this year, if I can, more money in it. Why, look at the Chouteaus, at Saint Louis and all through the Indian nations—or the Bents with their big place out toward the mountains on the upper Arkansas, living like kings in a palace—

—Oh, the Bents! With their Indian wives and their half-blood children—.

—Besides, Isaac insisted, I don't see any better way of getting a sure claim on good land, when the time comes—and all built up besides, or will be.

—And there's the thing, the colonel said, pursuing his own thought. What kind of life would that be for any lady, out beyond the frontier, and no proper feminine society to count on, for hundreds of miles? And wild Indians sneaking around, or you going out to them and maybe getting yourself killed—

—A *lady*, Colonel? Isaac gasped. Why, Colonel Titus, we *never*—. And he broke off, blushing crimson.

—Come now, young man, the colonel said with severity. I'm talking about Marie. You've seen a great deal of her, these past months. As her nearest relative, I have the right—and the duty too—to satisfy myself that you're—well, that your intentions are—serious. . . .

It was as if the plow had opened a chasm across the prairie and he stood on the edge and felt the earth crumbling and his feet slipping and dared not look to the bottom.—Colonel Titus, we go riding, and we take tea, and we talk—and enjoy it, I think—but truly, I never thought—I mean, one day perhaps, far off—

—Then it's time you *did* think, Isaac, the colonel said, softening a little. It's all very romantic, I've no doubt, going out to hunt, and trading with Indians—. But for a serious man that means to make a place for himself in life—

—Well now, Colonel, Isaac said, finding himself on firm ground again. I'm better than five hundred dollars clear this spring and paid all my debts. *And* two good wagons and the teams to pull em. And land and improvements, and still got a warrant to put down when the time's right, and goods to trade with that'll bring *ten times* what they cost me—

—Five hundred dollars! the colonel broke in, and the lordly sum withered away to nothing. When I was speaking for Missus Titus, I worked and saved to get *two thousand* dollars, out of my lieutenant's pay, and one thing or other, and long it took me. But little enough it is, when it comes to setting up and furnishing a household. I won't hear of you coming to Marie with anything less. . . .

—Two thousand dollars! Isaac said at last. Why don't you say *twenty* thousand and be done with it, if that's where you're headed?

The effect of the colonel's talk was to confer definite purpose, an order and shape, on the random action and reaction of Isaac's life; which was perhaps what the older man intended. As Isaac thought about it, the sum Colonel Titus had set him no longer seemed unattainable. He would have to trade more, that was obvious, enlarge and vary his stock, go out and seek the tribes in their villages. There was more too to be made from hunting than just the hides and a little of the meat for personal use—the Indians found uses for every part of the animal, and why not learn from them and turn their practices to profit, selling to white people in Kansas and beyond? One thing though, he would not get far, trading or hunting, with just Cornie to help; he would have to hire another skinner, maybe someone besides to see to the ranch when he was out, but what he needed was an experienced partner. He considered the men that had hung around Tommy Thorn's place, but all seemed too rough, too wild, to have around with—. Marie? A wife, married? It did not seem possible, he was getting ahead of himself, and the thought shivered his flesh like a cold blast. There was Mr Durfee now, setting up to do business with hunters and men in the Indian trade, he would know of someone—.

The ranch, which had seemed snug and welcoming, all built with his own hands, became small, mean and dirty in contemplation, not a place a man would feel proud to bring his bride to. It needed a proper house, with real windows and doors and more than just the one room, and planed boards for a floor. And then of course a warehouse for his goods and hides, not just everything piled up in the cabin or the loft. And a garden, a woman wanted fresh things for the kitchen, peas and beans and berries and lettuce, melons maybe.

There was much to be thought of and done. Isaac was impatient to get away, get started, and now, when he was with Marie, silent and preoccupied, and when she noticed the new mood and kindly asked what troubled him, he did not know what to answer. Was that all there was to what people talked of love, wanting to be with someone, wanting her to be with you? It seemed so simple. What was complicated was the long series of things you had to do to make that possible. He ought to be starting immediately for Leavenworth City, to stock up, see who he could find to go partners with before they all went out for the winter, but going that way would add two weeks at least to the trip.

In all of this Isaac did not consider giving up either hunting or trading for the several forms of tame living that had been offered him in Kansas, as Colonel Titus, and perhaps Marie as well, seemed to want, but as it became purposeful, the hunting in particular came to seem like work, a means, not an end, no different from any other work, and the delight, the anticipation of delight, faded.

It did not occur to Isaac till later that neither he nor the colonel had considered Marie's wishes in the matter. Both assumed that a properly brought up young lady, having no family behind her and possessed of no fortune, must be in want of a husband; and if the candidate was young and strong and kind and by some might be judged handsome, and showed promise of making his way in the world, why so much the better. But what if she would not have him? Oh, God! What if she would not have him?

Late in August, while Isaac still pondered, and his objectives became clearer in his mind and the means of attaining them, but not yet precisely what he must do next—and next, and after that—he had another piece of luck. He was sitting in the shade of the porch at Burlingame one afternoon, talking with Marie, when a wagon went by on the road below, bound west by the colonel's bridge: two yoke of big, sleek oxen driven by a plodding, thick-bodied, gray-headed man, behind it two wiry pinto ponies with Indian saddles and a tall man, dressed in buckskins, with a dark, flat-crowned, broad-brimmed hat, walking beside them. Something in the look of the man—his tireless, elastic, tight-muscled stride, the alert movements of his head, left, right, then straight ahead, scanning the horizon, missing nothing and imprinting everything he saw on memory—seemed to call to Isaac, and hailing him, he ran down to the road to talk. The man turned, shouted to his driver, pulled to the side of the road, stopped, and came toward Isaac smiling, hand outstretched. Abraham Bos the man called himself: a head taller than Isaac, narrow, bony face softened by a shiny-black full beard, trimmed short, deep-set eyes shadowed under heavy brows. A revolver hung on his left hip, balanced by a leather case holding a long hunting knife, a skinning knife, a sharpening steel.

—You look to be a hunter, Isaac said. That's why I came down to borrow a little of your time.

—Some, the man admitted. Out north of the Great Bend, last winter. I figured on going back to my old camp, if the buffalo's still around.

Isaac told him about the ranch and how you could hunt from there up all the valleys west of the falls of the Kansas, as far as the mountains, if you wanted, and how the Kaw and the Otoe came to trade their robes and pelts, and his partners giving out and his boy quitting on him, and now he had only just the one black man for a helper, apt enough but you had to teach him everything, that he aimed to make a skinner of, but what he really was looking for was a partner to go shares—

Bos considered.—Sounds like you and me could team up, he said. When're you headed out?

—I've got the two wagons, but there aint that much—I could be packed up tonight. Figured to go back to Leavenworth where I trade, for supplies and trading stock, but I've enough to get through for a while—I can bring more out when I go in with the first load of hides. . . .

Bos promised to camp the night on Dragoon Creek, the next crossing west of Burlingame, and wait for Isaac in the morning. They shook hands.

Isaac took a hasty supper that night in the kitchen with Cornie and Absalom and went on with packing the wagon. Colonel Titus stood in the door of the barn, watching by lamplight while he worked, putting in an occasional skeptical question about Abraham Bos, but Isaac could only tell him that he looked like a seasoned hunter and the kind of man he had been wanting for a partner. As he finished, the colonel took him aside to explain that he would send a draft for his summer's pay to Salina, not having the cash in the house at the moment. Isaac answered that he could afford to wait and take the money in gold around Christmastime, passing through on his way to or from Leavenworth—with one percent a month for waiting, it would come to six dollars, about half what money was worth most places in Kansas. The colonel for a moment looked pained, then smiled at his shrewdness and clapped him on the shoulder, and the bargain was made.

Isaac was up in the morning with the light and then waited in the kitchen for Vinnie to come down, impatient to start and hungry too, but knowing enough of women and their kitchens not to interfere by helping himself. By the time he and Cornie had the oxen hitched and had guided the wagons over the colonel's bridge, the sun lay full athwart the eastern reach of the road, an enormous globe copper-red in the rising heat haze. Isaac walked beside the loaded second wagon, looking back at the blank-eyed house, and as he looked a window winked up, a tiny, white-gowned figure leaned out, and a handkerchief fluttered at the end of a bare arm. He lifted his hat and waved.

They reached Council Grove a little after noon the next day, made camp, and Isaac and Bos rode over to the Konza village to smoke a pipe with Shinga-wassa, Isaac getting out his fringed hunting shirt for the occasion; depending on where the herds wintered, the chief intended to make the tribe's winter camp again somewhere up the Saline from the ranch and promised to send his people to trade. The rest of the journey was uneventful. They saw no buffalo till west of Salina when, riding into the hills north of the Smoky Hill, Bos sighted several old stragglers. The herds would be along the Solomon again, but whether they would winter there or go farther south it was too soon to tell. First week in September now: the killing heat was past, the grass turning sere on the hilltops back from the streams.

Abraham Bos was a year older than Isaac, had started west in 1858

after turning twenty-one; grew up in Franklin, the earliest of the
Missouri River ports that in its time had served as a base for the Santa
Fe trade—Kit Carson was from there, still had family around and
came back occasionally to visit. Like him, Bos had been apprenticed
young to a harness-maker but had kept at it long enough to master the
skill—along with the frontiersman's rough-and-ready farm-making,
carpentry, blacksmithing, hunting, trapping—and brought his tools
when he came to Kansas, meaning to use his trade to get land; but in
the hard times found more profit in hunting. His skinner, Ambrose
Willard—Bru—was from the same county in Missouri but had come
to Kansas when the territory opened and lived through the troubles
as a Free-Soiler whose strongest conviction was a home-bred dislike
of Negroes—in his laconic way he did not address Cornie by name or
at all if he could avoid it, but tolerated his sleeping under the same
wagon at night when they camped; had been in his fifty-odd years a
farm laborer, deckhand, mule-skinner, bullwhacker; had tried hunting, not successfully, and settled for the steady twenty dollars a
month Bos paid him for skinning buffalo.

They were all cheerful as they neared the ranch, stopping at noon
only long enough to make coffee and fry some pork—Isaac had been
extolling his pasture, and besides there was still hay for the oxen in
the stable, left over from the spring. Bos was almost voluble, praising
the rich bottomland, the neat rail fence across the neck of land to hold
the cattle. The gateway, however, stood open, the rails that had closed
it carelessly flung to one side, some of them broken. They stopped,
examined the ground, found a fresh wagon track.

—I never left it that way, Isaac said. It was all shut up, every gate
and door.

—Then it looks like you've got company, Bos observed. Aint Indians anyway, with a wagon.

—God-damn claim-jumpers is what you mean. Man goes off and
leaves his place, two or three months, and—

Isaac ran to get his rifle from the wagon. Bos drew his revolver,
examined the cylinders. They advanced along the trail through the
trees, leaving Cornie and Bru to bring the wagons on. A thin smoke
rose from the cabin chimney. The gate stood open in the stockade,
before it a clumsy-looking, two-wheeled covered cart with a sorrow-
ful mule between the shafts, its nose in a pile of yellow prairie hay.

—Looks like they helped themselves to that hay the cattle was
lookin forward to feastin on.

—And my cabin and woodpile too, by the look of it, Isaac said with
a grimace.

They entered cautiously but there was no one around. Isaac went
over to the open cabin door, rapped on the doorpost with his gun
barrel, and stepped in. A bulky black-gowned woman, hair in a tight

gray bun on her neck, crouched on the hearth, feeding wood and muttering to herself. A large kettle hung from the bracket.

—I'm sorry to trouble you, ma'am, Isaac began, but—

The woman leaped up, spun, gasped, and let out a piercing, drawn-out shriek.

—Please, ma'am, we don't mean to upset you, it's just—

—Santa Maria! The woman looked from one to the other, open-mouthed, wide-eyed, and gathering her long starched apron bolted for the door.

Isaac and Bos sauntered after her as far as the gate, but she was already past the stable and corral, running down the pasture toward the point, gasping and screaming still, and the words floated back in a despairing wail—*Soccorso! Soccorso! O sposo mio, ci son banditi, ban-dii-tii!*

—What's all the skritchin'n jabber? Bru wanted to know.

—Like Bos said, Isaac answered him. We've got company we weren't expecting.

He pointed down the meadow at a small procession coming toward them: in the lead, at a stumbling, broken-winded run, a big-bellied man with enormous mustaches and a red sash wound around his middle, waving an antique cavalry pistol of large bore, then two graceful, long-limbed dark young men, one with a pair of fishing poles and a string of catfish, the other self-consciously carrying, stiff-armed as if holding a poisonous snake, a little six-barreled pepperbox pistol, butt of numberless Western jokes; and last the old woman, stepping high through the rough brown grass, still gasping accusations about *banditi*.

—*Basta!* the big-mustache roared. *Evidentemente, non son banditi, son galantuomi americani ed emigranti, come noi, a questo bellissimo paese. . . .*

Drawing himself up, he stepped forward, beaming with seignorial welcome. Isaac did not accept his offered hand.

—Mister, he said patiently, I can understand—you're a foreigner of some kind, don't know our customs and our laws—and you come along to my ranch and figure to move in. But that's just your mistake —you can't do that, cause I found it and claimed it and built it up and it's mine. Understand? Here you are, sleeping in my beds and cooking in my fireplace, making free with my hay and wood, and you haven't any right. . . . Now, I'll give you till tomorrow to get packed up and out, but—.

Isaac's voice rose and fell as the man looked blankly back, frozen in his patronal gesture, and Isaac tried both to make himself understood and restrain his indignation. The young man with the fishing poles spoke at length in their language. Big-mustache went red, swelled his chest, and stood on tiptoes.

—*Ah no, no, no!* he shouted. *Questo podere, l'abbiamo trovato ab-*

bandonato, l'ho scoperto, e tocca a me! Abbandonato! É il mio, mio! Glowering, he smote his chest with his fist.

Isaac grabbed the mule by its halter, jerked the animal's head out of the hay, and with a slap on the rump started it turning toward the trail through the trees.

—Now, you get *out* of here, you hay-robbing thief, he shouted. And take your friends along with you!

The mule took a few tentative steps, felt the tug of the cart, and stopped. The big man came resolutely forward, jerked its head around, and pulling hard, leaning, led it inside the stockade. The old woman and the two boys followed, the one with the pepperbox drawing the gate to behind them. The bar thumped into place. After a moment the older man showed his mustached face above the stockade, waving his pistol and shouting defiance.

—*Now* what we going to do? Bos said. You want to burn em out?

—And have to cut all that timber and rebuild? No, Isaac said with a smile, they want to stay in there, let em stay awhile, is what I say. They've got my well but they can't have a whole lot of food unless they want to eat their mule. When they get hungry enough. . . .

They blocked the gate with Isaac's empty wagon and led the oxen off to feed. All the hay was gone from the stable—and Tommy Thorn's light wagon. Isaac put his tent up facing the stockade. Cornie gathered a woodpile and made a fire. Bos still had a sack of jerked buffalo meat left from the spring, and they poured it into a kettle with a pail of water and set it bubbling to make a flour-thickened stew.

One of the young men climbed over the stockade, came, and stood in silence a few feet off, watching while Cornie ladled the steaming meat onto their plates, picking catfish bones from between his teeth with a splinter of wood.

—You speak English, young fellow? Isaac asked after a time, looking up from his plate. The young man nodded. What's your name?

—Giovanni Volterra, signore.

—Well, listen here, Giovanni, Isaac continued, we aint got any objection to sharing what we've got with a man that's hungry, or a stranger that needs a bed for a night or two. Aint that right, boys? he asked, looking around, and the others nodded. Giovanni took a hopeful step toward the fire. But we don't give a thing to any man that comes along and tries to take what's ours. Now, he said, pointing at the young man with his fork, you get your people out of my stockade and my cabin, and we'll all be friends, everything fine. But if it's trouble you're after—well, by God—. Leaving the threat unfinished, Isaac reached his plate to Cornie to refill.

Giovanni hung his head but did not leave. He came closer and crouched down, wanting to talk; he began to speak, hesitantly, stumbling over words, snapping his fingers and frowning when the English eluded him, but intelligibly enough. The *padrone* was the young men's uncle, Signor Da Costa, had been a landowner and innkeeper in Tuscany, and when the troubles started in the fall, and then the new government this past spring, he had sold all he had and come to America with his wife and the two boys to make a new start: took the *piroscafo* from Genova to New Orleans, then another up the Mississippi to St Louis, changed again and came on as far as Leavenworth City, where Signor Da Costa bought the cart and mule and started west. And so they had voyaged ever westward to the final settlement where, *purtroppo*, there was already *un albergo* operated by some American or German, though not in the least *di lusso;* and so to the end of the traveled road and beyond, where lo! they had come upon this vestige of habitation in the *deserto*—Giovanni indicated Isaac's buildings with a sweep of his arm—and the *signore*, judging that providence had led them here for purposes of its own, had resolved to settle until something more opportune presented itself. Perhaps the road would extend, a town be built, and he would be its innkeeper after all. Giovanni's younger brother was called Luciano.

—That makes a pretty good story, Isaac said, mouth muffled by biscuit, but it *still* don't get you any of our meat, or biscuit either. Starting up a hotel out here! He laughed, sputtering half-chewed bread into the fire.

Giovanni, mocked, got up and in dejection walked back to the stockade. Isaac set his plate down and followed.

—You tell this Da Costa, he said, he's making a bad start in a new country if he starts out stealing a man's land. I'll let him stay one more night, but I want him out of my cabin and off my property in the morning.

He looked up. The Italian had been watching them, leaning his arms on the top of the stockade. Giovanni spoke to him and Da Costa answered at length.

—He says, Giovanni translated, if you will show him your papers proving you are *proprietario*, he will beg your apology and depart peaceable. If not, he will stay.

—Hell! said Isaac. This land's not offered for sale yet and there *aint* any papers. But when it is, I get to buy it by pre-emption. That's the law.

The boy shrugged, climbed on the wagon, and reached to pull himself over the gate.

—You tell him, Isaac shouted. We'll be watching, and aint none of you coming out again till you all come peaceably. And if you don't, you can stay and starve till the rivers of hell run dry, the lot of you.

Giovanni gave a jump, got a leg over, and dropped down inside. Da Costa stared down at Isaac, scowling his incomprehension.

The sun was getting down. Isaac and Bos sat by the fire, sipping coffee and talking lazily of their first hunt, whenever they had settled with the Italians. Isaac was for going north to the Solomon to see what they could find, then working west. Bru walked back and forth between fire and tent, around and around, stamping his feet, swinging clenched fists. Finally—What in the nation's eating on you, Bru Willard? Bos said. You buzzing around like you got a hornet up your ass, makes me tired just watching.

Bru stopped short, face set, arms clasped across his chest.—It's just —he said. It's just—. And the words burst forth: It's just, I aint sleepin in no tent with no nigger, is all.

Cornie clattered his pots and plates indignantly. Bos stood up.— Why, Bru, he said soothingly, you've slept with oxen and horses and jackasses and Missouri mules—dead buffalo and Indian squaws, and I don't know what all. What's so special about a nigger?

—Nigger's got a smell like nothing else on God's green earth. You get it on you once, and—

—Cornie, Isaac said, is that a fact? *Do* you smell different?

The black man stared back, round-eyed, and ostentatiously lifted his shirtfront, sniffing.—*I* don't smell anything special, he answered.

—When'd you last take a bath?

—Down in the river at Leavenworth, place we used to go, before we started for Burlingame—

—And washed the mud off after you came out? Wait—Isaac said and ran to the wagon, climbed in, rummaged, and came out with a towel and a cake of his mother's brown soap, little used, which he tossed to Cornie. Get along now, before it's dark, and you can sweeten yourself to suit Mister Willard. I'll finish your pots.

Bos produced another towel and a sliver of soap and put them in Bru's hands—I know *you* aint washed since we left camp and started for Kansas City, he said. You have your bath now and you can start even with the nigger. And you don't smell right when you're done, we'll let you *both* sleep outside. And with a shove started him at his stolid gait down the point after the Negro.

They were wakened, all four in the tent, at first light the next morning by a drawn-out metallic scream, insistent as cock-crow and as punctual but louder and more penetrating. Isaac sat upright and grabbed for his rifle.

—It's only that God-damn mule, askin for his breakfast, Bru said from his side of the tent, and rolled over with a whistling grunt.

There followed a babble of Italian voices—Da Costa's, deep and emphatic, his wife screeching complicated curses, the two boys, polite, reasonable, and insistent—and over all the bellowing chorus of the mule. Isaac dressed, saddled Bird, and started for Salina without waiting for breakfast. There was still no smoke from the chimney of his cabin.

—Well, that don't sound to *me* like any big problem, Colonel Phillips said as Isaac sat in the straight chair beside his desk two hours later, explaining his difficulty with the Italians. Everybody in town knows the place is Pride's Ranch.

—But the thing is, Colonel, Isaac insisted, this Da Costa don't understand English. And even if he did, he's the kind that's jackass-stubborn once he's got an idea in his head, says he aint moving, near as I can understand, till he sees the papers proving the place belongs to me. And you know there *aint* any papers till the Land Office offers the land for sale. So what am I going to do, Colonel? I don't want to hurt em, I just want em out so we can get on with our business. . . .

—Papers, is it? Colonel Phillips said thoughtfully. Well then, we'll *give* him papers. And with a wink he took a fresh sheet of lightly lined paper, dipped his pen, and wrote:

BE IT KNOWN THAT:

Isaac A. Pride of Saline County, Kansas Territory, is the acknowledged claimant of a certain tract of land known as Pride's Ranch, situate on north bank of Saline river twenty miles up-river, more or less, from Town of Salina, and surrounded three sides by the same river; together with all buildings structures improvements and appurtenances belonging thereto;

TO HAVE AND TO HOLD, by Right of Pre-emption, until such time as he shall be enabled to take valid title to such tract according to law pertaining and the rules and regulations of U.S. Land Office for Territory or State of Kansas, as the case may be, then prevailing.

AND BE IT FURTHER KNOWN, that any Person or Persons attempting to deprive said Isaac A. Pride of his just Rights in said tract by force or Fraud or any means whatsoever, shall be subject to full Penilties and Reprobation as shall be determined by the Settlers Association of Saline County.

Colonel Phillips wrote his name with a flourish at the foot of this imposing document and, below it, his titles—Mayor, Proprietor, and, for good measure, President (of the settlers' claim club). From a drawer he brought out the seal of the Salina Town Company, embossed the signature, and handed the sheet to Isaac.

—There now, Colonel Phillips said. Your man wants to see a paper, he shall *have* a paper, and if that don't fetch him, why—

Isaac read it through, smiling, then laid it down and considered for a moment.—Colonel Phillips, he said, that's just beautiful. But suppose—well, suppose this Da Costa don't *read* English any more'n he speaks it—

—I was thinking of that, Mister Pride, the colonel said, and if he is not moved by documents written out in full and proper legal form, why then, he shall be moved by the force and majesty of the law itself. Here now—. He turned over papers in another drawer and brought out a stationer's form for the appointment of a deputy sheriff, elegantly printed in engraver's script, and filled in the blanks: Isaac's name and the date, the town, county, and territory, and signed it in his capacity as mayor. He shoved the paper across to Isaac and placed on top of it a silvery star. Isaac took the badge, examined it, polished it on his sleeve, and, beaming, pinned it to his vest.

—Colonel Phillips—he stammered, why, Colonel—that's just—

—Just don't arrest him, the colonel cautioned. If you can possibly avoid it. We haven't got ourselves a jail yet—or a sheriff either, till we hold our election in the fall. You bring the rascal in, we'd have to put him up at Jones's hotel—a dollar a day, and board besides—. And speaking of money, Colonel Phillips smoothly continued, that badge —well, I don't mind writing up papers and being neighborly, but that badge now, that's genuine nickel plate. I've got to have a dollar for that.

Isaac reached in his pocket, found the coin, and laid it on the desk, expectant. The colonel had more to say.

—Now, neighborly, Mister Pride, he continued, well, neighborly goes both ways. Man wants to be neighborly in return—and lay out proof he's serious and means to be a bona-fidey settler, as pre-emption law requires, when time comes for *that*—why, he'll take a share in the town that's destined to be the seat of this county. You given thought to that offer I made you when you were through here, when was it, last fall?

—Indeed I have, Colonel, Isaac politely answered. I just don't know as I could afford a full share.

—We've made provision for that—don't mean to restrict ourselves to the large speculator—no, sir! This town—he gestured at the hand-drawn plan tacked to the wall behind his chair—it's two quarter-sections and we've got it platted in fifty-six blocks of forty-eight lots each, two blocks to a share. So you see it's easy to divide up—man doesn't have to take a full share if he can't afford it, he can have a half, a quarter—

—I've got a quarter-section military warrant, Colonel. What would you give for that?

Phillips thought it over.—Why, he said, I think we could let you have a *full sixteenth* for that. Six lots—I could write em up for you along the river, that's choice property, and they'll bring seventy-five dollars *apiece*, maybe a hundred. Double or triple your money!

Isaac sat in silence for a time, deciding, and at length, standing up —All right, he said, I'll take it—bring the warrant in next time I come to town, you've got my word. Largely smiling, Phillips pumped his hand. That is, Isaac concluded, stepping back, if I can get these Italians off my place. If I don't, it doesn't seem there'd be much point putting money in the future county seat. Now would there?

The colonel's smile slackened perceptibly.

The drought finally broke with a heavy snow around the middle of November. There came a week of gray days while the storm ripened and the weather chilled, and you woke in the morning to find a skin of ice on the water pail till the fire made up and a rime of frost on the threadbare grass by the cabin doorstep and the velvety touch of cool moist air on your hands and face and the smell of snow coming, and at night went to bed, expectant, wrapped in your buffalo robes, but it did not come. Isaac and Bos drove to the Solomon to hunt, with a wagon and two yoke of oxen, leaving Bru at the ranch in charge of Cornie and the two boys, finishing an ambitious double cabin Isaac had insisted on building between the stockade and the corral, facing south. They woke in the morning, cold, with the tent roof sagging and the sides pressing in, damp coming through the canvas and running in streams down the walls; crawled forward, dragging their robes like snails in their shells, forced the flaps open, and stuck their heads out in a roiling, luminous haze, a foot of snow on the ground already and still coming down, swirling and whistling around the tent, and down the creek where they were camped four snowy hummocks that were the tethered oxen, pawing at the ground and bellowing.

They took their time dressing, talking soberly. Neither had been through a Kansas snow nor ever caught out in such weather at home. No use, obviously, in traveling or trying to hunt till it stopped, then they would have to wait and see how the weather turned; the snow was wet and heavy, the kind that packs an animal's hooves in frozen lumps till it can hardly walk, the cold penetrating, dispiriting, but not yet extreme, wrapped in their robes—. At least by the creek they had the shelter of trees, but here too the snow had piled up two or three feet deep to one side of the wagon, and once they started over the ridges to the south there would be drifts they could not get through. Their immediate concern was the four hungry oxen and Isaac's mare: bring them in close, tramp down or clear somehow an area where they could get at the grass; Isaac knew of feeding willow sprigs and bark in winters of scarce grass, there was willow along the creek. They had made a point of bringing in wood the night before. They had possibly half a ton of choice fresh meat in the wagon.

Commonsense precautions, easier thought of than applied, once they left the tent. It was like the beginning of blindness. There was no horizon to measure the boundaries of travel by, no sun to mark direction, only the eddying onslaught of snow. Familiar landmarks, taken for granted, had removed beyond sight or came through blurred, softened, enlarged, as if shrouded in gauze. Isaac found Bird, head hanging, uncomplaining, and wiped the snow from her back and flanks till his gloves were sodden, then freezing stiff, and combed the ice from her mane and tail with his fingers, hands red and painful, turning numb; and brought a robe from the tent to cover her, led her along the creek to load with willow cut with his hunting knife. Bos, when he came back, had brought in the oxen and made a fire.

By evening the storm had passed over, leaving perhaps a foot and a half of snow on the flat. They spent the day by the fire, wrapped in their robes, with a buffalo ham hung from a propped pole to roast, cutting off outer layers of meat as it cooked, as Tommy Thorn had done in his cabin; got up at intervals to feed the animals or carry snow-water for them to drink.

The next day was clear and cold, bright sun burnishing a milk-blue sky, dust of snow dancing across the crackling snow crust. They started south in stages, a few miles a day, taking turns: one drove while the other rode ahead till he found a band of buffalo huddled in the shelter of a creek bed, then went on shooting until his partner came up with the wagon and joined in the skinning and cutting out the meat. In this manner they succeeded in filling the wagon by the time they reached the ranch.

It was the start of a winter of extreme cold. There was not another big snow, but what fell stayed and accumulated, packing hard in a rutted glaze of polished ice along the traveled roads. Dogs left out froze in their huts, there were tales of cattle lost between pasture and barn, of whole families—the man injured or sick, unable to get food or any help—starved and frozen in their fireless cabins. The hard winter came on top of nearly two years of drought, the lingering effects of the Panic of 1857, scarce money and costly credit in combination with the years of land speculation and unacknowledged civil war. The warping of national land policy by sectional rivalry added a further difficulty. Bowing to Southern opposition to settling the territories with Free-Soil farmers who in time would upset the balance between the sections, President Buchanan, like his predecessors since the 1830s, vetoed the latest Homestead Act intended to turn the public domain into family farms at nominal cost; and at the same time opened large tracts of Kansas to sale—with the consequence of dispossessing squatters who had occupied land in the hope of earning the money to pay for it, eventually, under existing pre-emption law, or getting it more or less free by the newer Homestead principle. All these causes worked to change former emigrants into go-backs, perhaps thirty thousand in the course of 1860.

The hunters, on the other hand, were not much affected by these troubles; and they were few in number. All through the winter, there were buffalo to be had wherever the convolutions of the land or a shallow valley provided minimal shelter or a narrow growth of scrub-wood and the snow lay not too thick or crusty to nose through to grass, and their coats this year were thick and silky, promising a good price. (As the winter progressed, however, Isaac and Bos ranged ever farther up the rivers to the west, but except for the several species of deerskin and the occasional wildcat or antelope, the best hunting simply for numbers of hides was reported to be along the Arkansas and on south.)

There were as usual men who prospered from the hard times: those, naturally, who had taken settlers' land in pledge for loans and now foreclosed, provided they could afford to wait and take their profit on the next season's wave of emigrants; and Sam Pomeroy's relief committee. Sam and his committeemen followed Northern railroads and steamboat lines as far as New York and Boston, wherever a church or meeting hall could be found to accommodate the pious and the public-spirited in numbers. Sam's Sunday-school eloquence in particular, his humble and sorrowing benignity, as he retailed the new sufferings of Kansas, produced wonderful outpourings of generosity. Donations were addressed simply to "S. C. POMEROY KANSAS AID," and frugal farmers whose wives remade the empty sacks of seed-grain into gowns for their daughters, shirts and trousers for sons and husbands, wore daily reminders of his organized charity stenciled on their garments; but none of the cash raised was actually distributed in Kansas. Naturally, therefore, when a few skeptical Kansas newspapers raised awkward questions about where the cash had gone, they addressed them to the chairman of the relief committee. Mr Pomeroy expressed pain at these insinuations and let out that the moneys collected had all been "absorbed" by travel costs, freight charges, and other "necessary expenses," but refused to dignify his accusers by making a detailed accounting. It was noted, however, that beginning that spring he was able to make his way as a gentleman of independent means and, in time, to invest largely in Kansas land, railroads, politics, and other useful enterprise. His assistants also prospered. Isaac's father went to hear Dave Kilbourn at the Congregational church at Davenport and wrote feelingly of what a well-spoken and substantial-looking young man he was turning out, but also greatly alarmed at the terrible times in Kansas, and would it not be wise for Isaac to give up on the place and make his way home before its misfortunes overwhelmed him?

When Isaac and Bos got back to the ranch from their November hunt, they found the roof on the new cabin but nothing more done. Cornie and the boys since the big snow had stayed inside the stockade, keeping the fire up and eating, and Bru, knowing better but inarticulate, had let them; and when the animals clamored tramped through the snow himself to feed them from the new cutting of hay stacked by the stable. The Salina proprietor's papers and deputy's badge had settled one Italian problem but created another. The mule still raged when Isaac returned. Signor Da Costa had made one frantic attempt at breaking the gate open and driving the animal out but desisted when Bos placed a pistol ball a foot or two over his head; and thereafter stayed "tolerable quiet" until Isaac's return. After his trying and foodless day, the *signore* deferred to the symbols of American authority which Isaac produced and within an hour, after turning the mule out to pasture, had the cart packed up and ready to start east. The two boys assisted this activity with languorous, doe-eyed reluctance. Isaac offered to take them on as skinners—at ten dollars a month and five cents a hide, in view of their inexperience—and, once they understood that they had been asked to stay, was accepted; their uncle wasted thirty minutes of his eloquence, trying to dissuade them. Isaac naturalized them as Joe and Luke.

Even at their modest wage the Italians were unprofitable. The one time Isaac took them on a hunt they managed no more than two hides a day between them—neatly done, admittedly, nearly fleshless; and not much better when he took the time to stand over them, advising and demonstrating. Thereafter he judged it more satisfactory to find work for the boys at the ranch and hunt with Bos and, usually, Bru, doing his own skinning and hurrying to keep up.

Isaac's new plan for enhancing the profit in hunting increased the work at the ranch. There were not only the hides to be dried, cleaned, marked, pressed in packs, and wrapped. He was saving and smoking most of the meat now and had learned from the Konza a satisfactory method of preserving the tongues. He also had an idea that the fat—rendered and packed in deerskin boxes formed in a frame of willow—would be salable; and the horns, to be made into buttons; the long hair from the buffalo's head and shoulders, to stuff mattresses or possibly to be spun into yarn.

The Italians, Isaac found, could be trusted to keep a green fire going in the smokehouse once it was properly started, or to render lard without spilling much. On the other hand, they objected to sleeping on the floor by the fireplace (and Bru had grumbled at the crowding—filling the camp up with foreigners)—that had been one reason for starting immediately on the new cabin. Here too, however, they felt themselves ill-used, when finally the roof was on: the half they slept in was dark, Isaac not wanting to cut out the windows till he brought the sashes for them in the spring; with the doorway hung with buffalo hides, they complained of the cold. As the winter deepened, Isaac provided them with robes, which they slit and wore over their heads like ponchos, and later cut in strips to stuff in the chinking and stop drafts, not being handy at cutting and hauling wood or keeping up effectual fires in the new stone fireplace Isaac had built.

The Konza came back in late October, camped farther west this year, on a tributary of the Smoky Hill. Four of the men rode in with a

pack of last year's robes to trade, and Isaac loaded the remainder of
his stock on a wagon and, borrowing Bru, followed them back; and,
when he had emptied the wagon, promised to bring out a fresh supply by the start of the new year. He had luck hunting on the way
home and named the stream Buffalo Creek.

By early December the other half of the new cabin held more than
enough hides in packs to fill a wagon, besides Isaac's Konza robes and
the various products of his experiments. There was no difficulty
about starting Bru and the black man for Leavenworth with the two
wagonloads. Cornie went on improving as a driver. The two men had
developed a guarded mutual tolerance. Bru had twice remarked that
Cornie did not *smell* like a nigger and made the lightest biscuits in
Kansas. Cornie observed that the skinner's manners were as good as a
white man could have who lacked the advantage of a military education. The difficulty with the Italians was solved by a letter to Joe from
Topeka, which Isaac carried back from Salina. Signor Da Costa had
established a *taverna* dispensing the finest *uischio di Kentucky* and
looked to have his hotel in the spring. After their season in the wilderness, the boys were eager for a visit with their uncle. Isaac worked
it out on the map that they could travel with the wagons as far as
Indianola, where they would be close enough to walk to Topeka or
beg a ride; and paid them off with thirty-five dollars each for their
time on the ranch. They closed up and started east on December 17.
Bos and Isaac rode with them as far as Salina, then took the road to
Burlingame, where Bos went on to Kansas City for a Christmas visit
with relatives. It was agreed that they would meet again at Leavenworth on the last day of the year.

That Christmas, Marie's second in Kansas, was not jolly as her first
had been. Early in the month Ned Eliot wrote Uncle Titus that he
was to be married in April, to a young lady whose father owned a
music store, known to Marie by name. Ned married! It made her feel
old. She was nearly twenty. Her own birthday came in April. Mr
Kilbourn wrote on the printed letterhead of the Topeka and South
West Freight Co.—listing Samuel C. Pomeroy as proprietor and himself as general manager—apologizing for being unable to visit Burlingame, he had been traveling all fall, in Iowa and elsewhere, on behalf
of Kansas relief. Marie did not answer. None of his wagons had yet
come down the road from Topeka.

Isaac Pride arrived a week before Christmas, expecting to stay, and
her uncle duly invited him. He came with his new partner, Abraham
Bos, tall and dark, with a threatening black beard, who stayed half an
hour without passing three words, departed without apology, and
rode off at a gallop, meaning to make Lawrence by dark; but a first-
rate hunter, Isaac said, and a man to be trusted when it counted.

Her uncle gave a ball. Isaac attempted some of the dances, but it was like a dog walking on its hind legs and he preferred to sit out, watch and talk, and Marie was torn between her joy in dancing and her duty to her guest. At the Schuylers' musical at-home he sang well enough, provided he chose what to sing, but knew none of the new songs. The night before he was to leave, he made up the fire in the parlor after supper and they made popcorn and afterward sat up, talking.

Finally—Why is it, Isaac? Marie said. You never talk about your home in Iowa, your mother and father, your sister—I know you *have* a sister.

He had been running on till it made her tired, about the ranch and the new cabin and how many buffalo he had killed since September and the money he expected to make when he got to Leavenworth.

—I expect, she said, you tell *them*—do you ever write letters home? —no more of *us* than you tell of them.

Marie was gratified to see that he blushed. She was right, of course. Very likely he had never even mentioned her name in his letters home.

He nodded.—That's true, you know, he said, and strange—I never thought about it. They write—oh, every week, anyhow, telling about people at home and what they're doing—and asking about me, and when am I coming home. And you see, I tell them, but then all the people here—they don't know any of them and wouldn't know what to make of them if they did, and it's just too complicated, and never time. . . . But that's strange too, Marie. You looked right through me and saw thoughts I didn't know I had.

—Tell me about your parents, Isaac, Marie said, and the irritation that had been gathering since he came softened and evaporated, leaving tenderness in its place. You never talk of them. Would I—like them?

—I don't see how you could help it, he said, and smiled helplessly, it was like all the letters never written, too much to tell and no way of beginning. They're kind, and educated—Father graduated at Yale College and then three years at seminary, he can read Latin same as most people read a newspaper, and Greek too—and always thinking not just what they *want* to do, but what's *right*. But not everybody *does* like them, and I expect that's why. They'd have been happier living where they came from, I know Mother would—everybody at Greenwich a cousin practically or some kind of relative, and knowing everybody and their parents and grandparents—why, when they're back there they can travel from New York City right through Connecticut and never stay the night with strangers, and then in Massachusetts my mother's people take up, clear to the British line. Only, you see, there wasn't any place for my father when the time came, in Connecticut or Vermont. . . .

He tried to tell her how this had come about: how seven generations of Prides had lived on the home place at Greenwich and worked it and built it up, kept it together, some of the land bought first from the Indians, each of them named Ebenezer, one after the other, and the last his father's older brother, educated too for a minister, meant to have the land, of course, and hoped to have the church in his time, but married too young, a sickly wife and then children that died—. There was a story handed down, a dark tale from the old time, a prophecy, how an Ebenezer Pride would keep the land through seven generations and then no more—but it was still in the family anyhow, only his father's brother wore his health out with his sick wife, and preaching, and disappointment, and died untimely, and the place went to a younger brother still at home and his father let it go, said his brother Theodore had the greater need.

Marie listened as he talked on, not understanding all he said of his family and its past, its place in the New England way of things, but this much: that he both admired and rejected it—it was part of him but had no place for him, his father, he said, had *let it go.* The sorrow, the feeling of having lost forever something never to be replaced was his mother's and came to him from her.

—Would you have liked it, living there, in Connecticut?

—My parents went on a long visit there when I was little and took us along, steamboat to Pittsburgh, then the canal packet and the cars, the stage to New York, and finally another boat from New York— raising money for the Iowa mission and settling about the inheritance —this was after his brother died—and I don't know what all other business. I remember a meadow big as my father's whole farm, ran right down to the Sound, and beautiful horses in the stable, and little ponies for Lizzie and me to go riding across the meadow and along by the side of the sea—and off to one side at the foot of a steep, rocky hill the family plot with a white fence around it, all the generations of Prides lying there and in the middle my great-grandfather that was in the Revolution and made a general when the War of 1812 came. I don't expect it was land up to what we've got in Iowa, or Kansas either, but there was still a lot of it then and my! it was beautiful for a boy to run around and explore. And then they had real servants—not just an ignorant hired girl and a broken-down farmhand or two, brought in at harvest—to do everything, and a fine-looking old black man with a uniform, to drive the carriage when you went to town or visiting—and it seemed it was every day visiting, or people coming, aunts and uncles and cousins and every kind of kin—at least, when Father was home and not off traveling to beg some congregation for money. . . .

He paused, eyes lost in remembering. She waited. Then he was looking at her again.

—That's kind of a long way around to an answer, he said, smiling—you started me thinking again. But what I wanted to say—oh, it was so beautiful—but all kind of settled beforehand, over and done with, and all there'd be to enjoying it, you just had to settle in and *be* the current Pride—oh, well, and keep the house up, keep the land together, keep it making money, and raise your children to keep it all going, which aint small things either, I don't mean. . . . I've got to *do* things, can't just settle back and accept—got to take hold with my own hands, settle on a thing in my mind and go after it, so it really *is* mine when I'm done. . . . I expect that sounds selfish or hard or mean—Marie shook her head, watching him intently—but I know it's true now. My father, you know, he continued, had all kinds of plans —wanted me to have his land and farm it, then he sent me to college, thought I'd make a teacher, I guess, maybe even a minister like him—. Isaac laughed. I just went through the motions, half asleep, like someone in a fairy tale, with a spell on him—and Mother worrying I was delicate and my health giving out on me! He laughed again. I never in my life felt so live or wide awake as I have out here. And if I'd stayed —why, I'd've just drifted my whole life away and ended with nothing —been nothing, and done nothing. . . .

—And that is why, Marie groped—why you do not write, or—

—Oh, I write home regular enough, Isaac said. It's just—I don't know how to tell them about my life here, what it's truly like. And Iowa—oh, happy enough times we had, I guess, mostly, but I look back and it's all like something happened a thousand years ago, to someone else, or in a dream—.

He caught himself, stopped.—I expect that sounds like romantic foolishness, he said. And here I am, running on about myself, more than a man should. Marie, he concluded with a grin, you do have a way of setting me talking. Maybe you're the one in the fairy tale, casting the spell. . . .

—No, Isaac, she said, I like it, and I believe I should like your parents, too. And do you know, Isaac? It is the first time you have talked of what you feel, and not only of things done. . . .

He was thoughtful again.—I expect that's because I don't think a man's feelings matter much, he said. I mean—he can have all the fine feelings in the world and it don't mean a thing. It's what he does, and doing it well, the best he can, that counts. . . .

Bos was waiting in the lobby of the Planter's House when Isaac came in from Lawrence late on the afternoon of the appointed day. They rode together to Mr Durfee's warehouse. Finding him alarmed by reports that reached Leavenworth daily by telegraph Mr Durfee was more than usually anxious, voluble, and unquiet: the news from South Carolina, in particular, hadn't they heard, the legislature had voted the state out of the Union, effective Christmas Day. Bos had heard some of this at Kansas City but had not thought it important enough to mention—South Carolina and some others had talked secession for years and passed their fool resolutions. Well, let em go and good riddance! was his sentiment. It was the first Isaac had heard of most of this. Sensitive to his new responsibility as a shareholder in the town company and honorary deputy sheriff, he had taken the trouble to ride into Salina and vote Republican on election day, immediately before they started their last hunt, but it was not till he arrived at Burlingame for Christmas that he learned the result, transmitted three weeks earlier by leisurely mail from the East.

After his cautionary preamble, Mr Durfee agreed on the quality of their cold-weather hides and was prepared to go six cents a pound without opening more than half a dozen packs to inspect. Robes and wolf were flat—he could pay no more than he paid in the spring. He came to the products of Isaac's new plan with alarm and much drumming of fingers on his desk: horns and sacks of buffalo wool and fifty bails of rendered buffalo tallow! Very enterprising, of course, to have thought of such things and collected and gathered them together and transported them two hundred miles across the prairie, but he had *no idea* where to dispose of them in these uncertain times. In short, he offered nothing but was at length persuaded to take them on consignment, and if he found buyers, well and good, Isaac would have a fair price—and if not, why, Mr Durfee lost the value of warehousing them till spring but would not do it twice.

After taking off for five hundred dollars in new trading stock, paying Cornie a month's advance on his wage and settling his share in the travel expenses, Isaac came out of this transaction with something under three hundred dollars. Bos had done nearly as well from his hides and wolf pelts, with no expense for trade goods. The merchant called Isaac back as he was leaving, had nearly forgotten an item carried on the books for months: his draft to St Louis had come back unpaid, Hawken's shop was closed and no doubt the old gunsmith had died. The return was seventy-five dollars. Isaac chose to take it in cash rather than leave it any longer on account at interest.

It was still early afternoon when they finished. They started the wagons back immediately. Isaac was for going with them but Bos, feeling expansive after counting the profit from his furs, insisted on another night at the Planter's House. Morning would be soon enough for starting back, they would catch up with Bru and Cornie, travel with them a day or two, and ride on through to the ranch. There would still be time for a short hunt on horseback before the wagons came in.

Bos slept the afternoon out in his half of the hotel bed while Isaac occupied himself with writing letters; Bos woke up lively, took a leisurely bath, and after supper wanted to go out somewhere for a drink. He meant a saloon. Isaac had no scruples about a glass of beer or wine at the hotel bar—his father made both and served them at his table on festive occasions, they fell within his careful meaning of temperance and he could cite Scripture to prove it—but after the years of his father's temperance campaigns, the sermons preached, the tracts given out, a saloon was precisely what he understood by intemperance.

They were half an hour walking the town before they came to a place that suited Bos: back from the empty steamboat landing, its front windows steaming in the cold, warm and inviting with lamplight. Bos led the way to a table by the stove. A waiter-girl came over, gotten up in a ballooning short skirt that showed her plump knees as she walked and a length of fleshy, white-stockinged calf above high-top button boots. She leaned on the edge of the table, pale breasts thrusting melon-ripe at the top of her low-cut, long-sleeved blouse, face blank and self-absorbed as a young heifer's, and addressed them in the flat accents of Bos's own Missouri. Isaac asked for a bottle of export ale. Bos ordered whisky, specifying a fresh bottle brought to the table, and slapped a gold eagle down, but the girl was unimpressed.

Isaac, finishing a second bottle of ale, with the stove glowing at his back and the drafts swirling under the table when the saloon door opened and closed, felt sleepy and dull and excused himself to go back to the hotel.

He was nearly there, hands deep in his coat pockets, thoughtful, looking down, when he became aware of a tall figure coming toward him, swinging strides hammering the boards of the sidewalk: long cloak thrown back over one shoulder to show a red silk lining, high-crowned hat with a velvety sheen to its nap, and a full black beard. Something in the swing of the man's walk, the set of head on shoulders—a tingling went through Isaac's body as if waking suddenly from sleep, not fear but an electric alertness, ready for action, rage, and the blood pumping faster in his veins. He was almost past when Isaac stopped, remembered—he had grown a beard now—and called out:—Dave Kilbourn!

The man turned, squinting in the light from the hotel porch, and came toward him, smiling, pulling off a pale kid glove.—Isaac! This *is* a surprise. He stepped back. I wouldn't have known you with the mustache—and looking fat as a pig, Kansas suits you, eh? Say, you stopping here? he said with a wave at the spacious entrance to the Planter's House. Isaac nodded. Well now, I'm on my way to—an appointment—his right eye clamped down in a prolonged wink, the smile enlarging—but hang it all, here we are, two sons of Iowa, met on Kansas shore. Come on in and we'll have a drink.

Isaac resisted the guiding hand on his elbow—a new way of talking to match the new clothes. Kilbourn faced him again, frowning.

—What is it, Isaac? You don't bear a grudge about that business last fall?

Isaac considered.—No, I don't, he said. Fact is, way it's turned out, you gave me a push when I needed it. But you didn't *mean* good, I remember that well enough. No, what I've been hearing about Pomeroy and you, and relief—well now—

—Now, Isaac, Kilbourn smoothly broke in, I'm disappointed—you *know* there's never good work done that doesn't stir up envy and malice, and bring enemies creeping out from under every privy, writing lies in the papers—

—That's how old Pomeroy talks, aint it? And maybe true, in a general way—but out on my ranch, I don't *see* the papers or hear any news from one week to the next. I'm talking what I know for myself, Dave—you going home to Iowa and singing your song of sorrow in Kansas till there wasn't hardly a dry eye and the money filling up the collection boxes—*your own people*, Dave!

—Mister Pomeroy, Kilbourn said, drawing himself up, can account for every penny.

—Maybe he can, but he aint done it, has he? And I've seen that stuff, came clear out to Salina—castoffs from people's attics that wouldn't make a respectable rag rug, scraps of food aint fit to feed a goat, but never one cent of all that money. Now where'd it *go*, Dave? Who got it?

—I'm sure it hasn't lined *my* pockets, Kilbourn declared, looking honestly pained—other than necessary expenses, of course, all correct and accounted for, and very modest they were, I can assure you—. Why, if you *think*—

—I don't know what to think, Dave, knowing you all these years, but I know times aint any harder in Kansas than anyplace else—meat and drink for any man that'll work, and good land for the taking. And I heard about that time at Lawrence too, sheriff rode you out of town, told you never to come back—

—Truly, Isaac, Kilbourn said, pulling his gloves back on, elaborately smoothing them—well, you know, a man goes a little wild sometimes, when the luck goes against him, but truly, that wasn't hardly anything, just a mistake mostly—and the sheriff took it back, and apologized too.

—Maybe he did, but I saw for myself one time, traveling through— you drunk till you could hardly see and a brace of Indian sluts leading you along the street like a trained bear. That aint the man I used to know, or would trust my charity to—

—Listen, Isaac, Kilbourn said, his voice taking an edge of menace. Kansas aint such a big place but word gets around. Now, you go carrying tales about *me*—well, I heard what goes on at this ranch of yours, the squaws coming through every day in platoons, and I can think of a certain charming young lady at Burlingame that would—

—God damn your eyes, Dave Kilbourn, Isaac shouted, his face flaming, if you ever again—if you go *near* Miss Bisonnette—

—You'll what? Kilbourn snarled. He brought his face close, seized Isaac roughly by the lapels. I thought we'd be friends, he said, but if it's enemies you want—

Isaac knocked the hands away, shoved, and Kilbourn stumbled backward, stooped, and came up with a snub-nosed pistol from under his cloak. Isaac kicked out, caught the pointing hand a sharp blow like a mallet striking wood, and the Derringer flew and landed softly in the snowy, rutted street.

—God damn you, Kilbourn! Isaac shouted. Coming at me with that mean little peashooter—why, don't you know, I've killed a thousand buffalo since I came on the Plains, and one skin-and-bones liar in a fancy cloak, why—

He burst out laughing. Kilbourn faced him, clenching his fists. Then they heard steps approaching and the watchman came into the light, deputy's badge glinting on his breast, revolver belted over his long winter overcoat.

—Evenin, gentlemen, the man said with a lazy salute, and paused, looking slowly from one to the other. You experiencin some difficulty here?

—Nothing at all, Sheriff, Kilbourn promptly answered in his platform voice. Just two old friends, haven't met in a long year, talking of the old times. *You* know how it is. He touched a finger to his hat brim, drew his cloak close. Good evening, Sheriff, he concluded with a little bow of his head, and, swirling his cloak skirts, turned and with stiff-legged dignity retreated down the sidewalk.

Around the middle of March Mathewson received a dispatch from Fort Riley signed by Lieutenant Colonel Andrew J. Smith: in five days' time the Army would be starting a train of ten wagons for Fort Larned; besides powder, lead, and other usual supplies, the train was transporting in one of its wagons one hundred of the new Henry repeating carbines, which Mr Mathewson had tried and recommended as a cavalry weapon the year before, with twenty thousand rounds of ammunition in patent metal cartridges. Personnel detailed would consist of the ten mule drivers and five other men—scout, hunter, cook, helpers—with a lieutenant in command, on the supposition that a larger force would be more likely to excite the enmity of the wild tribes. However, if Mr Mathewson had intelligence of hostile activity, the commanding officer was prepared to assign a detachment of cavalry as escort, but in that case it would be necessary to postpone the shipment for a month. His advice was therefore earnestly solicited.

Mathewson gave the rider coffee and a bowl of stew from the kettle simmering on the stove and sent him to lie down for an hour on his own bed while he composed his answer. Since the Texas vote for secession a month earlier, he had heard of agents stirring the tribes to the south against the Union, threats to the traders and peaceable tribes in the Indian Territory, dissensions among the civilized nations farther east, slaveholders favoring secession against the majority who owned no slaves; after the hard winter the wild tribes were still in their winter villages and the buffalo herds were not yet coming north in numbers. The Kansas Plains remained at peace: he ventured the opinion that the train would get through without grave risk and that avoiding an ostentatious display of force was indeed the course of prudence.

It was the next afternoon that Satanta rode through the open stockade gate, rearing his horse as he pulled up short, raising a dust cloud. He came alone, showing himself for the first time since the previous spring. Mathewson had all his men outside working on hides, packing them up to ship east. Calling young Cody to take the Indian's horse, he went to him, open-armed, sleeves rolled up, wrapped him in a hug, took him by the arm and led him inside. Seated in Mathewson's chair, Satanta accepted coffee, heaping in the sugar; shared a pipe. The trader leaned back, waiting.

Sin-pah-zil-ba and his men, Satanta said, were taking too many buffalo, making the hunt less profitable. The Comanche had determined to stop this: kill all the pedal-pa-go, hairy-mouths, white men, now they were at war with the Texans, and burn the post. It was not one chief and a few young men doing their duty on behalf of a tribesman killed by accident—the Indian smiled; it was a decision of the council. Some Kiowa would join, but not Satanta or any of his band—the trader was a brave and generous man, he did not wish him dead.

That was too bad, Mathewson gravely answered, he had no quarrel with the Comanche, no wish to kill their young men. They sat for a time in silence, smoked another pipe. At length Mathewson thanked the Indian for his advice and gave him a double-handful of tobacco in a sack to take away. They went out together. Mathewson called for the Indian's horse and his own and rode with him as far as Walnut Creek. As an afterthought, looking him in the eye, he said that if Satanta encountered any Comanche, he should tell them Mathewson did not want to kill them but would protect his men, both those at the trading post and those out on the hunt. The Indian agreed to carry that message, if he could, and slapped his horse into a trot.

Again Mathewson took precautions: ordered a watch on the fire walk through the night and by day as well; brought the horses and oxen into the stockade at night; kept the gate barred during the day, no Indians to be allowed inside unless known to him as friends and then singly only, but none came. He cleaned his guns and kept them loaded. Besides a pair of Colt revolvers, he relied on one of Samuel Hawken's rifles and a heavy, big-bore Sharps of somewhat greater range and nearly as accurate; the experimental Henry he had returned to Colonel Smith when he made his report the previous summer. His men were similarly but less expensively armed.

For three days after Satanta's visit the men not on watch were occupied in loading the wagons due to start for Kansas City. Mathewson spent long hours pacing the fire walk, watching, but except for the outpost with its four men and the boy Cody, the surrounding plain as empty of human movement as if no man had ever yet intruded. Late in the afternoon of the third day the man on watch called out a dust cloud miles off to the west and all ran to look, Mathewson for two long minutes studying the movement through his telescope, elbows braced between sharp-pointed pickets; and concluded it was only a fair-sized herd of buffalo trotting urgently north, no Indians he could see on horseback, hunting, among them—might be the beginning of the spring migration, a little early, though possibly Indians to the south—he knew of no other hunters in that direction—had started them. The military train by now should have left Fort Riley, according to the dispatch. Mathewson considered sending someone to meet it with a message, young Cody, for instance, but the risks when he counted them up outweighed the little good it might do, and the teamsters, though few in number, would have the new repeating rifles, if needed—stand off a thousand Indians and come out even. So Mathewson would only go on waiting. Maybe too Satanta had carried his warning to the chiefs and the Comanche had changed their minds.

The attack came the next morning. The boy had taken the watch after midnight. As the blood-red sun breasted the low ridge to the east, a column of horsemen galloped in tight formation out of the brightness; at first look you took them for cavalry, so silent and disciplined, pennants fluttering from their lance tips, then they opened out, four abreast, the long war bonnets whipping out behind now, an army of dragons riding the dawn light—. The boy waited, three hundred yards, let em come on, two hundred, the column divided; hunched his hat brim low to shade his eyes, picked one in the lead, brought his rifle up—steady, don't rush it—

The growl of the buffalo gun rolled across the plain, the horse turned a broken-necked somersault, lay flat, rider leaped clear, two steps, running, horses behind arc-lifting over the fallen one, the man up behind another, hanging on—whoops, yells, rage creasing the

morning air, *po-po-pop* of light Indian carbines answering, antique
musketoons—.

Mathewson was standing beside him in his trousers, a revolver in
each hand. Mathewson shouting—Get on down there, Bill, you got to
load for us—and with a spring-steel, openhanded swat on the behind
sent him running for the ladder.

—To the corners now, Mathewson shouting again, keep your heads
down, let em close and use your pistols, save the rifles till they back
off.

The two columns of Indians circled the stockade in opposite directions, keeping up their fire, three hundred of them perhaps, they
came closer at each pass, a hundred yards, wary still, getting bolder—
seventy-five yards, waiting, one would start the rush at the stockade
and the short and easy journey to the land of the glorious dead, eter-
nal spring and good hunting always, and the others following, up and
over, dropping down, from all sides, and—

—Now's your time, boys! the trader cried. Knock em down!

Twenty-four shots in as many seconds, aimed, unhurried, deliberate from the four corners of the stockade, each insect lead ball *whng*
seeking a particular enemy: the spinning carousel of horses and men
exploded outward like an incoming wave striking a reef, the ordered
mass of disciplined men and mounts became a riot of individuals
riding off, shouldering, falling, men leaping up, running, leaving
weapons, shields, running—a dozen horses downed, screaming, men
fallen and unmoving, riderless horses, running—. The men on the
wall turned, each in a floating toss sent his hot revolver down to Cody
to catch, lay carefully down for reloading.

—Use your rifles now, Mathewson called out. Show em how you
can shoot. And finally the raised left hand dropped and smacked the
wall.

Five shots from the buffalo guns, carefully placed, at men, not
horses, killing: when he judged the distance at three hundred yards,
Mathewson ordered a halt and reloading. The attackers stayed off,
resting, disputing tactics, until the sun stood at mid-day. Cody had
time to fire the stove up in the cabin, boil a gallon of coffee; carried
the pot out, reached it up, ran to fetch the cups, the sack of sugar.
Abruptly the Indians were coming in again, spread out this time,
riding in from all four sides, and again Mathewson let them come
within sporting range for the revolvers before giving the order to fire.
Another volley, like a broadside—horses leaping, falling over backward, riders pinned, screams of horses, men: one standing on his
saddle got under the wall, gave a leap, gripped picket points, screaming, and took a ball from Mathewson's pistol full in the mouth; fell
flat, face mashed, with a *thrmp* like a log striking the pounded earth,
skull cracking like a melon, and the riderless horse ran after the re-

treating horsemen, a buffalo pony, dodging still as it was trained. Rifle balls followed, and again the trader pulled his fire before the Indians were out of range.

The Comanche stayed in sight, scouts on high ground, watching from horses, the rest farther off, but did not attempt another run that day. The boy carried out a sack of jerked meat and the men ate in handfuls, stuffing their mouths, chewing and slowly chewing, calling for the water jug, and spent the night on the fire walk. From the Indian camp to the east, beyond the gentle escarpment of Walnut Creek, came the glow of a big fire and the resonating thump of hand drums beaten in chorus until the dance-fire dimmed in the light of the returning sun. None apparently had come close in darkness. When full light came, the fallen bodies lay as they had fallen, unrescued.

The Indians kept their distance all the rest of that day. When one or two ventured within five hundred yards, a shot came from the stockade and as often as not found its mark. At intervals the attackers wasted their powder in a return volley, but the range was too great for their light guns and the spent balls rattled off the pickets like pebbles; but they showed no signs of departing. The darkness passed in silence, no fire, no drums, no dancing.

The morning of the third day—light turning gray in the eastern sky, the west still night-dark, starless, from that side of the stockade a man watching from the fire walk called out: a darker mass in the darkness not a hundred yards off, the Indians, some of them, a picked few, self-chosen, in the night had led horses around, hooves padded with shoes of hide. A spurt of flame from the revolver barrel, a scream, whoops, more screams, muffled hooves pounding: Mathewson left it to the four, kept his place on the fire walk opposite, over the gate, watching for the other half of the attack. No light: the men fired into the dense-ranked horsemen, not aiming. The boy ran from the bunkhouse with a flaming stick of tallow-dipped stovewood in one hand, revolver in the other, climbed the ladder, ducking along the fire walk, holding his torch up—leaned out, shooting down—. A pair of hands clasping the pickets, a face, clubbed back with the pistol butt— light by moments swelling across the sky, sun coming—another face, shoulders, pulling over, Mathewson raised his revolver, fired; gone— then another, Cody jabbing with his torch, a long shriek, falling, cut off by a thud as of an ax blade sinking home—.

There was a red rim of sun in the east now, light, deep shadows pocking the ground, mantling the human and animal dead—visible now, the remainder of the Comanche force, two hundred maybe, waiting at limit of rifle shot while the attackers circled close under the wall, shooting up, the men on the fire walk following, running, ducking, to shoot back, Cody on the ground again, reloading the guns—. A long shout came from the main force, the circling riders turned off, galloping east toward their comrades. . . .

The men came over, crowded close, the boy. Mathewson pointed: on the ridge above the creek, in silhouette against the rising sun, an Indian with a blanket, flapping—up, down, to the side; a scout, signaling a report.

—There's a train coming along the road from the east, Mathewson said—could be the one from Fort Riley the colonel wrote about. Maybe they figure they've had enough of us for now, but they go after *those* boys, well—.

The Comanche force, regrouped, rode in a slow column toward the higher ground where the scout had showed himself, splashed over the creek crossing, climbed the low bluff girding the valley. Three miles off, the Indians dismounted, made their horses lie, and crouched beside them, motionless: a row of dots, a wind-plowed furrowing of the ridge line, even with the long glass you might guess a moderate buffalo herd digesting their browse in the morning sun. Mathewson sent the men back to their places to resume the watch. He would keep his post over the gateway, looking east.

An hour went by. Mathewson rested his hands, stiff-armed, on the stockade, watching the brown receding track of the road till neck and back ached; straightened up, stretched, searched the arc of the plain, took up the telescope. The Indians were still there, had not moved. Then to the northeast, at the far limit of sight, between horizon and sky, rose a ballooning dust ball, a mountain moving, becoming firmer, more defined, a giant, hump-backed buffalo-shape: mirage. He closed his eyes, rubbed them, looked again, squinting, raised the telescope again: coming along the military road to the junction a white-covered, blue-bodied freight wagon, mule team pulling, behind it another, another; out front a uniformed man on horseback, outriders a hundred yards off on either side.

—Here comes the train, boys, Mathewson called. Come over here and watch the fun.

Clatter of boots on rough boards, the men pressing around him, Cody leaping up the ladder to watch. Mathewson pointed, explaining:—Aint many of them in that train, ten wagons and their drivers, an officer, a couple of scouts—don't like how he's got his scouts, though, too close to tell anything, but—. But the thing is, they're hauling a new kind of rifle to Larned, shoots sixteen shots without reloading, think of that! One man with that gun, he's good as twenty! Now, those Indians decide they want to take that train—Oh, my! They think they've had it hot with us and our little trading post—. I just want to see. . . .

The train came down the slope, onto the level leading to the crossing, three miles off, mules stepping smartly, two miles, yellow dust misting to either side, following, each wagon distinct now, clink of harness audible as distant birdsong.

—What they waitin for? a man said softly, as if to himself. Maybe them Indians—

Suddenly the ridge behind the train began to move, bristling with men mounting up: a great shout, a line of horsemen swarming down the slope, spreading out. A shot fired in the air, shouts coming faint across the distance, the outriders spurring horses, galloping in: the officer had his saber out, glinting in the sun, waving, shouting— cracking of mule-drivers' whips, wagons wheeling—. The Indians came on at full gallop now, a few racing out in front of the line, to get inside before—mules rearing in the traces, kicking, circle of wagons forming up end to end, the teams turned in, men inside, running, throwing themselves flat to shoot between the wagon wheels—.

The riders in the lead veered off, leading the others in a single line circling the wagons a hundred yards out, men lying on their horses' necks, firing into the circle: firecracker popping of answering fire from the wagons, sporadic. . . .

The trader watched in silence, frowning; lifted his telescope, adjusted the eyepiece, held it steady—

—God Almighty! Don't look like they're using anything but some old one-shot pistols, a few revolvers—lieutenant's got a cavalry carbine. . . . He cupped his chin in one hand, pondering: Why, God in heaven! Poor devils don't know what they're hauling. Billy!—he turned to young Cody—You bring my horse over!

The boy ran, slid down the ladder. The others followed Mathewson down.

Cody came at a trot, leading Bess, the saddle thrown over the horse's back; he stooped, struggling with the cinch. Mathewson pushed him aside, jerked the strap tight, buckled it up. He straightened, grinning, shook hands all around.

—Just bar the gate good after I'm out, he said. And get back to your watch, or some fool Indian'll take a notion he can whip us yet. . . .

Bos and Isaac, with Bru and two wagons, had started up the Saline on March 17—as Isaac worked it out afterward, it was the day before Mathewson received Colonel Smith's request for intelligence—on what would probably be their last extended hunt of the season, though they still debated whether it would be profitable to spend the summer at the ranch. Four days out, finding the game scarce, they turned south, crossed the river, and set their course for the Great Bend country, familiar to Bos from the year before. Four nights later, skirting the eastern rim of the marshy basin known as the Cheyenne Bottoms, which divides the drainage of the Smoky Hill from the Arkansas—a geological relic, perhaps, of the shallow sea that once

drowned the Central Plains—they climbed to the high ground above
Walnut Creek and made camp a few miles short of Mathewson's post.
Finding the game still not plentiful, they determined to go there in
the morning to learn what the trader could tell them about where he
was finding the large herds.

They had driven hardly an hour next day when they heard a burst
of gunfire in the distance ahead. Leaving Bru to see to their weapons
and guard the wagons, Isaac and Bos threw saddles on their horses
and set off at a gallop down the ridge. The shots came louder, more
frequent, they were in sight of the roofs of Mathewson's buildings,
his stockade walls. Isaac drove his horse faster, racing ahead, then
abruptly pulled her up short, leaped off, raising one arm in warning,
threw himself prone, and pulled Bird down. Bos came up and got
down beside him.

Below them a mile off, like a panoramic painting of Indian warfare,
lay the little train of government freighters drawn up for defense
beside the military road, the milling, howling swirl of attacking
horsemen.

—God *damn!* Bos said in a low voice, panting. We've run ourselves
into a God-damn Indian war. Come on! Must be two hundred redskins down there—

—Wait! Isaac said, gripping his arm. We can't outrun em with the
wagons—

—Hang the wagons, they won't catch our horses. Jesus, Isaac! *Leave*
the wagons and the cattle too—*that's* the way, and we'll get half a
day's start while they tear em up—

—Look! The boys in the fort—they're coming at em from behind—.

Isaac raised his arm, pointing. West of the Walnut crossing the
stockade gate gapped inward, a man came forth on horseback, lying
forward in the saddle, already moving at a flat run. The gate clapped
shut.

—Name of holiness! Bos groaned. It aint but one man. Others
maybe is all dead by now, he's getting away—

—No he aint.

The horseman had gained the broad track of the road, splashed
through the shallow stream crossing, heading straight for the embat-
tled wagon train. The Indians had seen him now, were turning off
from their attack, riding toward him, firing. The man hung to one
side of his horse, shooting back with his revolver from under her
head, dodging; a brave rode at him head on, he saw, swerved, hit him
point-blank. In a moment half the warriors had converged, like bees
swarming—shots, animal howls, horses rearing, plunging—

—Great God! Isaac cried. He's getting through.

He stood up, drew his rifle from the saddle sheath. The gray horse

—no, the man on her still, hanging to one side—emerged from the mob, pulled himself back up in the saddle. Men inside the circle shoved at a wagon, making a narrow opening, the horse leaped, entering.

Bos grabbed at the rifle with both hands.—God damn you, Isaac! he shouted. You shoot and they'll be after us next. Come on!

Isaac jerked the gun free, slapped Bird on the rump, mounted as she rose, and started down the slope. He lay forward, slipped the rifle back in its case. As he came erect again a tug of wind caught at his hat and floated it off.

Mathewson stood in the middle of the wagon circle, shouting for a hatchet, crowbar, for the wagon that carried the heavy wooden cases, the guns. A man reached him the tools, another pointed—long-legged heavy running strides, slashing at white wagon cover, tearing, leaping in—coffin-shaped crates, stenciled *New Haven Arms Co*, the Henrys, the square boxes of cartridges, smaller—. Desperate, he hacked at the stout boards of the cases, chips scattering, calling out for the lieutenant, again, again—prying lids up, rending of wood, nails creaking resistance—sudden whine of musket ball, wagon hoop splintering—

—Lieutenant! Quick, get in here. Quick!—These rifles, didn't they tell you?

Young officer's white face showing scared through torn canvas, pulled at too young from too many sides, death watching over all—. Mathewson grabbed a hand, pulled him up and in, very quiet now, demonstrating the loading mechanism of the strange rifle, the lever action that ejects the spent cartridge and places the next shot in the breach—watching while the soldier loads, clumsily, carefully, hands tense, trembling with concentration—Hurry! Got to hurry—but do it right, for pity's sake, get it right—

Shots all around them, singed-linen smell, bullet holes popping the canvas—screams, Indian yells, pounding of hoofbeats, stronger, getting closer—

Four rifles loaded, ready to fire—bench-tested at the factory, they must work—

—Carry them around now, man, run—show your men. All they got to do—aim and fire and pump that lever, keep on firing—I'll load some more—.

Shoving, Mathewson huddled the officer over the wagon side, reached the four rifles down to upreached arms—

Silence, eddying among the wagons, moving outward, a cyclone of silence, circling, as of earth yawning, swallowing all enemies and their violence—. Carrying a loaded rifle, Mathewson leaped from the wagon, running, shouting—What is it? What's happened?—stopped short, staring with the others where a man pointed, up the high ground to the north.

Toward them a man races on a creamy-pale horse at full gallop, silky tail and mane outstretched on the wind, sitting straight, arms raised, guiding the horse with his knees, golden hair streaming from bare head, fringed Indian hunting shirt rippling. The line of Indians parts, the horsemen draw back, silent, watching, firing no shot.

Mathewson ran to a wagon, shoulder to the front gate, shoving—Come on there, push her back—let him through!

Out there a single Indian voice cried a word, others repeated, taking it up in chorus, a cheer.

The blond horse without breaking stride lifts, soars, over the wagon tongue, lands four-footed, pulls up, rears, men shove the gap shut, the golden-haired boy slips down, rifle out, running—

The circle of attacking horsemen was moving again, dividing, riding west, away from the wagons, retreating, double-file, like liquid bubbling from an opened bung. Isaac leaned against a wagon, brought his rifle up, fired—horse stumbling, rolling, rider leaping clear, taken up behind another—. Others with the new rifles around him, shooting after—he measures powder, reloads—

—Hold your fire, men! Mathewson roared. Stop that shooting! They're going now. Let em go. . . .

The Comanche force rode west along the road at an easy canter, like a regiment of cavalry on parade, a mile off now, down to the Walnut crossing, splashing through, past the stockade, unswerving, two miles, a dust cloud, sun-gilded, diminishing, settling. Within the wagon circle a man started up a cheer, others joined: cheering, prolonged, filling the silence.

In the late afternoon, light turning blue with approaching dusk, Isaac and Mathewson rode down to the Arkansas together, behind them, ringing the stockade, the herd of hobbled mules, wagons drawn up, white tents, men gathered by cook fires smoking with broiling buffalo meat carried out from the storehouse. Neither felt hunger. Mathewson, man of few words, had something that needed saying. They sat their horses by the riverbank, letting them drink.

—What'd you do that for? he demanded.

—I don't know. I saw you riding and the Indians closing in—I just had to do it. I lost my hat. . . .

Mathewson scowled him into silence.—Should've got your head blown off.

—It was like something set me on Bird and set her running, I don't know, I figured—. He shrugged, thinking. You got through, didn't you?

—That's different, I was dodging, I know some things—been in

Indian fights, you haven't. An Indian, he can't shoot much anyway, mostly, in the first place, and you get a man running at him, a battle, why, he gets so excited—

—I wasn't thinking that, I didn't see anything, only a little space between wagons and my horse going for it, and I had to get in there, and—. What was it they shouted as I went through, Pie—Pa—?

—*Pai-tal-ye*, Mathewson said, that's Kiowa—there was some Kiowa in there, besides mostly Comanche, they run together. Then, to Isaac's questioning look: It means Sun-Boy, Mathewson explained, that's a kind of hero, way in the old time, all kind of stories about him —. That's what I want to tell you, two things. First is—don't you think, cause they let you go through this one time, they'll do it again. That was just crazy—but an Indian, crazy—that's mystery, that's power—stand back and let's see what it's good for, and is it dangerous —. He's just a kind of little boy, and a fight—well, that's another kind of game, and if he gets killed, that's part of it, and a short and easy ride to the happy valley—. But next time he's got a different notion, pulls you off your horse and holds you down, and the others gather round to stick knives in you, keep it up and keep it up, cutting and cutting, to see what this power is good for and how much you can stand. . . .

—What's the second thing?

—The other is, I saw you shoot and didn't interfere, and you shot for the horse, not the man—

—I brought him down, didn't I?

—No, you didn't! The man, you didn't kill him, he's up and gone, got spare horses off somewhere, and one day maybe he'll be back—. But that aint my meaning. You can shoot, I see that, so you had a choice but you wouldn't do it. Now me—I don't go looking to kill anything on God's earth. But—well, I got to eat, I'll kill me a buffalo. Or a man comes trying to kill me, hurt me, take what's mine—why, I'll kill him too if he don't get me first, don't make no more to me than squashing a fly under my thumb—. But you, Isaac—well, you're the other kind—aint nothing to do with courage or being scared of getting hurt when you do what you got to do. You just aint a man-killer, and you better know the kind you are. That's what I had to say. . . .

XII

Sun and Moon, Earth and Heaven

Crazy-Knife, Southwind said, making the Kiowa sign. Isaac had asked what she knew of the tribe and, glad of an excuse to gossip, she dropped the pounding stick in the wooden bowl where she was crumbling dried meat for pemmican and sat back on her heels to talk. Know all kind of thing about Crazy-Knife—when little girl, only ten years old, man comes to Konza village, steals horses, two girls, herself and one other, ties to horses, leads them back to his village, keeps her and gives other girl away. His wife jealous he make her second wife, beat and pinch when slow bringing wood or water, not make moccasins right Crazy-Knife way, make mistakes talking their language. Tried to run away but man tracked her, caught her, cut her feet with knife, for one moon she could not walk. Her father loved her very much, after one year came to Crazy-Knife village with horses and bought her back. Now no Konza man will marry her, they think she is Crazy-Knife—Southwind laughed. She does not care, she will find a Konza who is not afraid to have her.

Konza men, she explained when Isaac responded with a look of conventional sympathy, believe Crazy-Knife women have teeth inside: when a man goes into her, she bites him off. They do not do this, of course, to men of their own tribe.

Isaac frowned, but there was no mistaking the sign she had used: thumb and fingers of one hand forming a ring, stiffly pointed index finger of the other thrusting insistently into the receptive opening. He felt a pink warmth flooding his face, tingling in the roots of his hair. Southwind stared back, puzzled in turn: did the white man suppose that she would bite *him* off? She shrugged. Such an intelligent, polite young man, but like all other whites—when you think you understand them, you discover that you do not know what is in their minds. Strange. . . .

—Pai-tal-ye, Isaac said aloud, did she know—

Southwind made the signs, sun, young man, and repeated the word —great power, Kiowa tell many stories of Sun-Boy, in the winter, sitting around the fire in the tepee and the smoke going up the smoke hole, wind moaning around the tent poles.

What power? What stories?

She looked down, folded her hands in her lap, thinking. She would tell him one story. Then she would use her hands to finish her work. There was talk in the village that the winter camp would soon be over, the Konza would return to Council Grove. Her father would need his meat packed in the parfleches.

Once in the time long ago, before the people had horses, a young woman lay in her family's tepee at night but could not sleep. It was summer. The skins were rolled up all around to let the breeze through. She lay on her robes at the outer edge of the tent and looked up at the stars, some bright as torches, some dim, some faint as coals of a dying fire seen at a distance through the darkness. She was a most beautiful young woman, all the young men in the village came to her lodge to sing to her, but none pleased her—none was handsome enough, or strong, or brave enough to please her. As she lay on her robes in the dark, she thought how the stars were men, and those that were faint were old and weak, and the bright ones young and strong. And she thought of the sun, brightest of all the lights in the heavens, that puts out the light of the stars till it goes to its rest, so bright no one can look at it long without pain: that is the one I will have for my husband, most handsome, and strong, and brave of all. The wind bellowed across the grassland and rattled the lodgepoles.

She woke alone in a strange tent and went out into a land she had never seen, where it is always spring, and the grass grows thick and tall, and the cool streams flow across the plain, and the animals wander, grazing, and come into the villages to offer themselves for meat. And there a young man came, the handsomest, the strongest, bravest, she had ever seen, and took her hands in his, looked in her eyes, and said: I am Sun-Boy. He was fierce and bright as the sun on a summer morning, yet now she stood beside him, she could look him in the eyes and feel no pain, only great joy, warming her whole being. You wanted me to be your husband, he told her. I have brought you to my home, and you will live with me and be my wife, you will be always young and beautiful, and never grow old. All the animals that graze and plants that grow are for your pleasure and to feed and serve you. Only one plant of all you must not touch, and he showed her soapweed—which is poison, Southwind explained, you chew it up and eat it and it makes you sick.

A long time the young woman lived with this Sun-Boy, and it was all as he said, and she did not grow old. In the daytime he went out to hunt, and in the evening he came back to his tent, and she brought him meat, and roots which she had dug from the earth. But all the time she was thinking about this plant he had told her not to touch. It grows tall and strong, she thought, and has beautiful pink flowers. It may be, if the plant is bad, the root is good. She went and found the plant and took it by the stem and pulled—pulled and pulled—and it came out, root and all, and there was a great hole where it had been. She lay down and looked through the hole, and there far below was her own village, and the lodge where she lay in the dark and could not sleep, looking at the stars and thinking how they were handsome young men, and there inside her father and mother, alone.

Now the beautiful young woman wanted to go back there. She took the stalk of the soapweed and pulled it apart, and took the fibers and braided them together till she had made a long rope strong enough to hold her. She tied one end around a rock, let the other end down through the hole and began to climb down. Climbed and climbed, going down toward the earth, but came to the end and still she hung high above the earth and could not get back there.

In the evening Sun-Boy returned to his lodge, looked all around and could not find her; came to the hole, lay down and looked, and saw his wife hanging there far below, between earth and heaven. Are you still alive? he called. I am still alive, she answered. You wished to be my wife, he said, and I brought you to my home. You cannot go back to earth again, but you are my wife still. In the evenings when I have finished hunting I will bring you meat that you shall not starve, and you will live forever and not grow old, as I have said.

The moon is that beautiful young woman, hanging between earth and heaven, and cannot go back to Sun-Boy or return to her first home. And that is why the Kiowa young women do not wish to be married to a star, or the sun, and are content if the young men who come for them are not handsome or brave or strong. We, Southwind concluded with a laugh, have different stories.

Sitting forward, she gripped the pounding stick in both hands and resumed her task.

Isaac and Bos had agreed that it would be folly to continue their hunt. The buffalo were indeed coming north, but three or four days' travel west, beyond Fort Larned. Although the Comanche and their allies, in attacking Mathewson's post, had left their usual range to the south, it was probable that the entire tribe was gathered somewhere west of the Great Bend, pursuing the herds. The day after the wagon-train fight, the two hunters turned north again, taking their time, hunting, killing a few buffalo stragglers along the way. They went by way of Buffalo Creek and camped for a day with the Konza. The Indians had robes to trade; Shinga-wassa was vague about when they would start back to their reservation except that it would be soon. Isaac promised to return with a stock of goods before they left.

They drove from there straight back to the ranch. Isaac reloaded a wagon and started the next day for the Konza camp with Cornie, leaving Bos and his man to hunt nearby, between the Saline and the Solomon. Isaac stayed four days with the Konza, with his goods spread out in a guest lodge designated by the chief. The trading was only moderately successful. The Indians had been hampered in their hunting by the winter cold and the prolonged snow. The buffalo robes they were prepared to trade amounted to no more than five packs, and of these most had been taken since the return of warm weather, summer-thin or carelessly and imperfectly tanned. Isaac completed his business by accepting a barrel of cured tongues and half a dozen packs of tallow which the Indians were accustomed to keep for their own use and had not expected to trade. Since these products had not cost him much in goods and he still had half the stock he had brought out, he determined to return to the ranch by a long circuit north to Redtail's Otoe village in Nebraska Territory, hunting on the way. It was early May before he got back. Bos and Bru had come in two days earlier and were working on hides.

They were three days loading the wagons. Isaac had taken to keeping a record of his trading stock and its costs in an account book, along with his receipts of furs and what he had given for them in trade. His shipment this time counted up to fifty packs of hides, ten of robes, nearly a thousand wolf skins and miscellaneous furs, a ton each of tallow in deerskin packs and cured meat—tongues bought from the Konza and Otoe, his own smoked buffalo hams and steaks; and five hundredweight of buffalo wool and horns packed in old flour sacks. Going down the final list, he calculated it should come to four thousand dollars anyhow, quite possibly a good deal more, depending on just what Mr Durfee would give for the meat, tallow, horns, and so on. Now, say, if he could get teams of men out hunting for him, pay so much per animal brought in and take everything, the way the Indians did, and a proper warehouse for his trading goods, why, the ranch would grow up like a town—of course, then a lot of his business would in fact be the haulage back and forth to Leavenworth, he could hire a clerk or two to look after things but would have to stay around, managing, couldn't get out much to hunt himself, except a little just for sport, or training up the new hands in his way of things, well—.

He could hardly wait to see the look on Colonel Titus's face when he heard that Isaac had met his end of the bargain and gone him some better, too. Why, in less than half a year he had more than doubled the amount the colonel had set, good as married. He thought how he might joke him about it—Yes, sir! Ought to give *two* pretty little nieces to marry, if he was a man of his word—

—What you smilin to yourself about? Bos broke in.

—Just looking over my accounts and thinking how it's going to be when we get to town and sell out.

They started east on May 7 and two days later, camped near Fort Riley, got their first connected news since January of events in the nation. Cornie had politely insisted on calling on Colonel Smith, and Isaac rode over with him. The black man was increasingly at his ease, almost expansive: nearly a year now in Isaac's employ, with the prospect of continuing, his first regular job since the colonel provided his freedom papers two years earlier; he had become a competent if not lightning skinner and had learned to drive a team of oxen with nearly the offhand confidence of Bru, accomplishments to be certified by the balance of his winter's pay due when they reached Leavenworth, one hundred and seventy dollars. They found the colonel in his quarters, off-duty but occupied with the sheaves of papers on his desk, dispatches to be answered, reports to be commented on, extracted, circulated; moderately interested when Isaac mentioned his brush with the Comanche raid on the Fort Larned train, but that was old news by now. He was scandalized by their ignorance of events,—like men dropped from the moon, as he said. Since the new President Lincoln took office—knew something of war, it was said, though it was a ragtag scramble of militia and Indians, nearly thirty years ago—the seceding states had held a convention, elected a president of their own, and constituted themselves the Confederacy; had collected a force and attacked a fort in South Carolina, and it had surrendered. *Secession!* A word for politicians and lawyers. It was rebellion—war, *civil* war. Lincoln at least had responded like a soldier, so far as he could with a dithering Congress—put out a call for volunteers to fight and proclaimed a blockade of the South. Now Virginia had gone over and the Confederates had moved their capital to Richmond, scarcely a hundred miles from Washington City. Besides all this, there were prospects for a rebel government in Missouri and Indian troubles on the Plains. Mail and the newspapers from eastern Kansas and St Louis came regularly to Salina every week. Isaac had known something of the progress of Secession but nothing of Fort Sumter and what had happened since. They stayed ten minutes, excused themselves, and left the colonel to his papers.

The preparations for war were more obvious at Leavenworth than at Fort Riley—at a military post, after all, you expected to see troops drilling, hear the spatter of gunfire from the firing range. There were printed broadsheets tacked up all over town, advertising the various regiments in process of organizing, recruits drilling on the steamboat landing under sergeants sent over from Fort Leavenworth, most not yet provided with uniforms and carrying a motley assortment of weapons—antique muskets, short-barreled sporting carbines, flint-lock long-rifles; one regiment had already gone down the Missouri to St Louis. Jim Lane had been elected to the Senate, along with Sam Pomeroy, when the new state legislature met at Topeka in March and already was making a stir: going east to claim his seat (dressed up to the occasion in sober broadcloth, with embroidered vest, clean white shirt, tie, all furnished, naturally, by borrowed money), he had stood off a secessionist Washington mob by the sole power of his oratory. He had formed a Frontier Guard—Kansans and others from the West —to defend the capital during the days of uncertainty while the Army took up positions on the city's outskirts; and now he was back in Kansas with a brigadier-general's commission from his old friend Lincoln, to organize the defense, meaning not merely to guard the new state's borders but to carry the fight once more against the Missouri ruffians.

Mr Durfee, when they found him at his warehouse, greeted the hunters with a torrent of contradictory anxieties: very pleased and gratified, of *course*, at their success on the Plains, *three* wagonloads; on the other hand, his reports from St Louis were very doubtful—markets disrupted, prices of all goods extremely chancy, and even if Missouri could finally, somehow, be saved for the Union—. Already there was a shortage of ordinary money, people naturally hoarding specie as it came to them, and, Kansas having as yet no banks of issue, dependent on the St Louis banks for circulating banknotes, well—

Mr Durfee was not pleased to learn that one of Isaac's wagons carried another *ton* of buffalo meat. He had kept the last lot till April, applied himself diligently, but had found no buyers. When it began to spoil and the smell threatened to infect and contaminate his entire stock, he would have to fumigate the warehouse, he had ordered his men to load the barrels on a wagon and carry them away; they had, he believed, sent them drifting down the Missouri, and a most suitable end it would be if the meat fell into the hands of rebels marching off to support the Confederacy. As for the buffalo wool and horns and such—no doubt in normal times they might have been considered a valuable addition to the trade, but now—well, there simply was no call. . . .

After this doleful preamble, Isaac for his part expected the worst— to be told finally that the merchant would buy nothing, that there was no market anywhere; that his hopeful winter's labor had been wasted. When it came down to actual business, however, Mr Durfee's actions were less pessimistic than his words, and the result, though half what Isaac had expected was a grand success in comparison to what Mr Durfee had seemed to be leading up to. In the end, Mr Durfee bought—with many deep-drawn sighs and much anxious wringing of hands, to be sure, but shrewdly and decisively all the same—all Isaac's hides and wolf skins, at prices no lower than he had offered in January. The buffalo robes were down, admittedly an inferior lot, but still brought a sizable amount. The tallow came as a happy surprise. Mr Durfee had promptly disposed of the previous consignment—two hundred dollars on the books to Isaac's credit, hadn't he written? so difficult finding a competent clerk, and now with a war coming—and would be happy to take all he cared to bring in, at seven cents a pound.

The total came to over two thousand dollars. Counting his two-hundred-dollar credit, Isaac had made fully three thousand dollars since the fall, with all expenses paid, including the rest of Cornie's pay. Putting down five hundred dollars to renew his stock of trade goods—in view of the uncertainties of future supply and the likely disruption of prices, Mr Durfee advised him not to delay—and leaving another three hundred dollars on deposit at two percent a month, Isaac came away with two thousand dollars clear, which the merchant made no difficulty about paying in cash, half gold and the balance in reputable bank notes. Such a neat round sum, so much more satisfying than a ledger entry to have the heft of it in your pocketbook, a picture came into his mind of himself laying it out before Colonel Titus, the sheaf of crisp notes and the stacks of gold eagles, half-eagles, double eagles—more than five pounds troy in gold!—And now aint we as good as married? he would say, daring the colonel to contradict.

Bos would be taking the boat to Franklin for a visit with his family but would be back at the ranch later in the summer. Isaac meantime had agreed to take Bru on, to help with his building. With Cornie, they would drive the three wagons home by way of Burlingame. Isaac found a mattress-maker at Leavenworth who would make a sack of buffalo wool up in a mattress for his father and arrange for shipment. At the freight office, he deposited a barrel of tongues, consigned to his parents. He also kept a barrel of smoked buffalo hams to take to Burlingame as a present. The rest of the leftovers—the barrels of meat and horns, sacks of wool—they rolled quietly into the Missouri to follow the others down the river.

Isaac's bravado over his good fortune in meeting the colonel's condition evaporated when they were again face to face, and his money stayed locked, unshown, in the small tin trunk he had carried since Iowa and now reserved for valuables. He could not find words in which to talk of the matter, and Colonel Titus allowed him no occasion to bring up anything so private; and the colonel's consent was in any case the least of the difficulty. The afternoon of his arrival, through supper and on into the evening till bedtime, the colonel interrogated him about the news from Leavenworth, but Isaac had nothing more to tell him than he was getting in the newspapers that came through the mail from Topeka, Lawrence, Kansas City, and St Louis. At Christmas, when South Carolina's secession, in the slow reports that reached Burlingame, still seemed the irrational threat of a few romantics, sure to be patched over yet again by reason and compromise, the colonel had blustered over his whisky like a fire-eating young subaltern about leading his old regiment south to teach the politicians respect for the sacred compact of Union. Now that the unthinkable had come to pass and reached beyond the possibilities of imagining—not one or even several states proclaiming their separation but a renegade government formed, gathering an army and challenging the nation to fight—he was glum. The disappearance of the Whigs had left him without a political voice and turned him into an old man, though he was still some years short of sixty: outlived his time, he gloomily proclaimed, and woke up like Rip Van Winkle in a world run mad, the secessionist lunatics as incomprehensible to him as the raving abolitionists of the North.

Colonel Titus appeared for an early breakfast next morning and insisted that Isaac drive out with him to look over his land. It was that kind of day, a day for a man to be going somewhere, setting his hand to new business: bright, neither hot nor chill, the sun riding across the sky escorted by crisp white clouds. After the winter-long mulch of snow and the spring rains, the grass was already knee-high and not yet June. That, really, was what the colonel wanted to talk about: country looking like wheat country again, corn country—money country! Maybe the Union *was* breaking apart, spurning under foot the good old ways of its founders, but a man still had to get on with his business, do what he could, day by day, as it came to him. Just now he was looking out for a tenant that had some work in him: let him plant the plowed land and finish breaking the rest and forgive him his first year's share, or two years', or there were other ways of working it, give enough of the land to make a reasonable farm in return for the prairie-breaking. That was a good enough cabin already, for a start, wasn't it?

Isaac had put it on the spot where he would have liked a house and built as if he meant to live in it. Get a barn up, add on to the cabin, weatherboard it, nail on clapboard, and you'd have a place fit to found a dynasty on. That was how his father did it twenty years ago, in Iowa, no limit to how far you can go if you build right to start.

Talking on—of the cabin, the land, the crops it would carry—Isaac ignored the colonel's bait.

Then—I expect you'll be heeding the President's call, Colonel Titus cautiously suggested, by way of understanding why Isaac showed no inclination to tenant his land. Going off with the other young men to put down this rebellion. They say it can't last long, I don't know. In my time the best and most of the officers were all from the South, and if they conclude to put their home states above the Union. . . .

Isaac had thought about it certainly, talked it over with Bos. Both for different reasons had come to one conclusion: wait a while and see, too serious a matter to go heedlessly running like a pack of dogs yelping after a rabbit, but if you were truly needed—if it seemed there was no other way—. The one thing he was clear about—and more and more so as the months lengthened from his home-leaving—was that he would submit to no man's judgment as to what was good for him or where his duty lay.

—I've been thinking about it, Isaac said guardedly. What I'm thinking, though, is, I can do a lot more good out on the frontier, where I know my way around, keeping the wild Indians off the settlements—or anyone else takes a notion that way—than I could on a parade ground, drilling for some flunky that wouldn't in a long year know what I know in one day about riding a horse and shooting.

—Well, *of course* you've got to do some of that—parade-ground drill, Colonel Titus agreed, couldn't have an army without it—but—. What you mean is, he continued with a sideways glance, you're staying out at Salina, mean to keep on with the hunting, is that it?

Yes, Isaac said firmly, that was what he was going to do—the summer too, finishing off the big new cabin at the ranch, to make it, well, more suitable—more homey. He hurried on, embarrassed. He needed to add on to the stable, really ought to have a cabin separate from the others, just for trading, storing his trade goods, and he was thinking about building a proper house in town—at Salina. It would mean hauling the lumber from Junction City, seventy miles, but—well—

—I can afford it, Isaac said quietly. I've done as you said I should.

—Oh? said the colonel, hunching over the reins, his eyes on the jogging horse's back, the faint wagon track receding through the tall grass. What was that?

—Why, Colonel! Isaac said, his voice rising. The *two thousand dollars* —you said a man thinking of marrying ought to have two thousand dollars put by or keep his thought to himself. I didn't see how I'd do it, but I worked, and saved, and—well, it's worked out—.

They had come to the edge of the colonel's land, the small, square tenant's cabin over by the stream in the distance. He pulled the horse up.—Did I really say that? he asked in the silence, turning on Isaac a look of blue-eyed innocence. Not that it isn't good advice, what with all the expense, I just—. I suppose it's Marie you're thinking of, he said, turning away.

Isaac nodded. What could he say? *I haven't anyone else to think of.* Or: *I don't think of anyone else.* . . .

—I couldn't tell you what *she* thinks, Colonel Titus continued. Didn't like it much, I can tell you, when Ned Eliot wrote he was getting married, but I don't put much store in that—like a boy with his eye on the last piece of cake on the tray, don't want it for himself, but he don't want some other boy to get it, neither—. He laughed. And then there's Mister Kilbourn—I know *you* don't think much of him, he said as Isaac scowled, I know he's a little wild still, but—well, I think he'll come out all right for some young lady. . . . I expect you know that freighting scheme he had didn't come to anything. Isaac looked at him sharply and could not help smiling; he had not known. No, the colonel said, he's gone to Washington City, Senator Pomeroy's confidential secretary. I reckon that's the place to be in these times, if a man wants to get his feet in the trough. . . .

They sat in silence, contemplating the burgeoning land. Finally— You won't find *me* standing in your way, Colonel Titus said with a nudge and a wink. But it's what *she* wants that matters now.

Isaac stayed only three days at Burlingame. On the last, he and Marie took a picnic lunch and rode up Switzler Creek to the little grove beside the swimming place. Vinnie had provided cold fried chicken, jars of potato salad and slaw with her special egg-and-vinegar dressing, generous cuts of chocolate cake in a tin; they had a bottle of claret from the colonel's cellar. Isaac sickled the sweet grass short with his hunting knife and Marie spread a tablecloth and knelt at its edge, serving the food onto plates. The ride from town had left Isaac thirsty, and he helped himself to three glasses of the wine. Mingling with the gentle afternoon warmth and the delicate tastes of Vinnie's cookery, it made him sleepy. He lay on his back, resting his head on clasped hands, looking up through the branches; it was the first day in months when nothing whatever called to be done, he had only to lie there and ponder his own feelings, and Marie's.

—I wish I could give you a dinner like we have out on our hunting trips, Isaac said dreamily. Steak from a fresh-killed buffalo broiling in the pan and some of Cornie's biscuits. . . .

—You seem in a terrible hurry to get back there, Marie said teasingly. Three days—that hardly counts for a visit.

—There's a lot to do this summer. Got to finish that new double cabin, it's just rough—put in the windows and doors and a proper floor, and the stable aint big enough for three teams of oxen now, and I need a place to store my goods and show em, when the Indians come in to trade. And—Marie, did I tell you? I gave my warrant for a share in the town company—well, only a part share, really, but I get six lots from it, and I figure to build a neat little house on one or two of them and still come out ahead when I sell the rest. Then when we're married and I'm off on a hunt—

—Isaac Pride! said Marie indignantly. What are you talking of? *Married?* Who is it you mean to marry?

Isaac jerked upright, blushing crimson. What had he said?—Why, *you*, of course, Marie, he burst out. Who else would I think of?

She gazed steadily back, then, throwing up her hands, lines of laughter crinkling lips and eyes, dissolved in silvery giggles until silenced by the shamefaced look that sealed his face.—Really—my dear Isaac, she said gently, folding her hands. Is it not customary for a gentleman to ask a lady first, *before* he talks of marrying her? It would seem only sense to get these things in their proper order.

Her laughter made it easier, even if it was at him. He blundered ahead, telling how her uncle had challenged him, if he was serious, to earn the sum he would need to be married on, how it hadn't seemed possible but he set to work, and saved, and his luck had stayed with him, and—well, it became a kind of habit of thinking that it really *would* happen, but—oh, he hadn't *meant*—

—Really, Isaac, Marie said severely, Uncle and you—you make it sound like two farmers dickering over a prize heifer. Two thousand dollars indeed! I suppose I should feel flattered.

—Oh, Marie! he cried, reaching clumsily across the tablecloth and taking her hand in his. You know that wasn't it, it was just your uncle, thinking ahead and wanting me to be practical. I only wish it was *ten* times that much—or a hundred times—if it would help me give you a home you'd be happy in. . . .

She let him hold her hand for a time, then gently withdrew it and, folding her hands in her lap again, sat very erect.—It is not only marrying, she said, eyes blinking, it is so many things to think of— furnishing a house, and clothes and linens—and if I *were* to marry, would it matter if there were no priest? or would you care if there were? Not that I have been serious about it, for a long time, but if we had a church, perhaps I would go sometimes—and then, of course, marriage—that *is* serious, and—oh, Isaac, I *do* enjoy your company, I do look forward to your visits, and talking with you and hearing you talk. But—my life is so dull here, yet am I ready to change it, so utterly, Isaac? I do not know. It—it frightens me. . . .

He listened, not looking at her, while she groped to discover and express what she felt. He did not hear or remember her words or the reasons behind them; only that she was not refusing him.

—You know, Marie, he said slowly, the first time ever I saw you a kind of trembling went right through me—not falling in love the way people write of it in stories or thinking, maybe here's the one I'd like to marry, nothing so definite but—just wonderfully happy, never so happy before in my life: here's someone come into my life, I don't know what's coming, what's going to happen, but she's going to stay there and be important—more important than anyone else. . . . And then later, something else, it was this past winter and I was off by myself, hunting I guess, I had a kind of waking dream: I could see myself, there I was, getting old, and children around me, other people, and some woman that might have been my wife, only that I'd never seen or thought of. And I looked, and there I saw you, afar off, alone, and old, walking across the lonely, silent places of the moon—a little old, dried-up, withered woman—as if we'd never met and somehow none of our life together had ever come to pass. It made me feel so *sad*, Marie! I wanted to reach out and take your hand and bring you back, and I couldn't. I couldn't reach across to you. . . .

The terrible sadness came back as he spoke, and he hung his head. With in-caught breath Marie shivered in the soft warmth of the afternoon as if touched by a cold wind, a momentary tremor that shook her shoulders and coursed down her body.

—What is it people say? she said, trying to smile. Someone walking across your grave. . . . I had a bad dream too, Isaac, she said. I saw you, far in the distance, young and strong as I see you at this moment —sunlight golden in your hair—. You were all alone, Isaac. I was not there—I was not anywhere. I did not exist. . . .

—Marie! He took a step, knelt down facing her and brought his face close; he did not touch her. Marie, he said, I would not let any harm come to you. Do you know that? All the strength of my body and skill of my hands, whatever quickness there is in my mind—I want to stand between you and the world like a shield, to keep you safe, forever and ever. I don't want anything else ever in this world. . . .

—Are you not afraid of things, Isaac? Marie asked. People grow old and lose their strength, they die. . . . Are you afraid of death?

—I don't know. I think if you meditate on a thing, look on it all around, you can get to be afraid, but when it comes to doing—well, I don't seem to scare easy. And death—you know, my sister in some of her poems writes as if it's lovely, something you wait all your life for, wanting. I don't think that, I don't think that idea's good for anything but poetry—it's ugly, and horrible. But when it comes to doing something. . . . I don't go looking for it, but I'll do what's right. No. I'm not afraid. . . .

—I think I am afraid of many things, she said. Of growing old and dull, staying out here with Uncle Titus, and of *not* staying here, of his dying and leaving me with no home. Of marrying and of not marrying. Sometimes, Isaac, she said, her eyes flickering across his, I am afraid of you. . . .

He stood up.—Marie, he said, it seems there's a question here between us. I didn't ask it very well, but it's there. He raised one hand as she seemed about to speak. I don't want you to answer till you're ready, but I want you to know: I'll wait for you as long as you like. If it's the rest of my life, I'll wait for you to answer.

The ranch when Isaac got back two days later seemed different. Nothing had been broken into this time, nothing taken, so far as he could see. It was an absence, not a presence, that had changed it. He tried to look at it as Marie might and was uneasy. The log buildings that before had seemed so snug and workmanly had become, in the few weeks since he left, rough, unfinished, dirty, meagre; well enough no doubt for a gang of young hunters or a backwoods farmer of small ambition, hardly a place to fill a young lady's heart with joy at the prospect of turning it into a home. He remembered the matter-of-fact grief with which his mother spoke sometimes of her first sight of Iowa in that long-ago fall after the summer's travel over the dusty emigrants' roads—New York, Ohio, Indiana, Illinois—from her home in Vermont. At least, Isaac reminded himself, his own place was farther along than his father's had been. But there was much to do.

There was a garden for a start. With his mail at Salina he had collected a neatly made box of seeds, wax-paper-lined, that his parents had made up: beans, peas, lettuce, two kinds of melons, corn, cabbage, all sealed in tins labeled in his father's flowing hand; and hollyhock, petunia, pansy, snapdragon, poppy, put in by his mother, with a note on starting some in a cold frame if the season was not too far along— the box had been a month coming, and she could not, she admitted, imagine his Kansas weather. Along the front of the new double cabin, facing south, he turned a garden forty feet square, cut and split cottonwood rails for a fence. He used a planting stick, Indian-fashion, for the corn, and as he stepped the seeds down thought for a little of bringing out a pair of pigs to feed, but what did they want with pork when they had buffalo and every other wild meat in limitless supply? The corn would be for eating. Cornie talked knowledgeably of the varieties of cornbread he would make in the fall when it was dry and pounded into meal.

And there was building. They doubled the stable with a second log structure of the same size adjoining the first, but with a full loft above for hay and a long roof-tree sticking out to carry a block and tackle for lifting the hay in. They built a third cabin, double like the last, facing the stockade gate; hewed joists to floor the previous one, which Isaac now regarded as his own, though he still lived inside the stockade with Bru and Cornie. The new cabin he intended as a storehouse for trade goods and hides, but if he hired more people half would do for them, and he therefore built a fireplace at one end.

It was late July before Isaac thought again about the house in Salina and drew sketches in the back of his account book. There was not much to planning a house on a twenty-five-foot town lot: twelve by twenty-four, it would make two good square rooms, one for cooking, eating, sitting, the other a bedroom, with a gabled attic, fully floored, reached by a ladder, a small porch at the front door. In time he could add a shed on one side for a kitchen, another bedroom, raise the roof for more rooms above, all things his father had done with his house over the years. He would put it at the front of the lot, leaving room behind for a garden, a stable, perhaps a couple of apple trees; some-time too he would have to dig a cellar to store vegetables and meat. A stove would have to do for cooking and heat—he did not know of a source for stone near Salina, and there was no brick. He calculated his lumber and, leaving Cornie to cut hay and care for the animals, started for Junction City with Bru and two wagons.

In this manner Isaac occupied the summer. He did not hunt except when meat was running low and then rode out alone. The buffalo were near again, though deer were scarce. He saved the hides. No word came from Abraham Bos. At Salina on the way to Junction City he got the news of a battle south of Washington, a Union rout whose only consolation was that the rebels had lacked the wit and courage—maybe just the teamsters and the wagons and mules for supplies, Colonel Phillips suggested—to complete it by taking the capital; pos-sibly in the aftermath Bos had joined up, like so many others.

At the end of August, in a long letter home in which he wrote of his summer's activity, Isaac mentioned in passing that he was think-ing seriously of being married in the fall. Of the young lady he said only that she was not a great beauty and not rich but he thought she would suit him; he did not mention her name. This vagueness was now deliberate, Marie having made him aware of it and his reasons: by not courting his parents' approval, he took no risk that it might be withheld. The name alone—and borne by a young woman of un-known and probably dubious antecedents, French-Canadian and Catholic, if not devout, quite possibly spliced with Indian. No, he could hardly expect them to hear the music that he heard in that name. His mother looked uneasily upon the lumpish peasant Irish, the more numerous and purposeful Germans that crossed her path when she could not avoid them. What could she possibly make of Marie? On the other hand, suppose his father accepted his choice in its undisguised reality—entirely possible, what his father made of things was far from predictable—and arrived in Kansas intent on performing the ceremony, bestowing his blessing on the bride. Might not Marie like a young doe take alarm at such enthusiasm, vanish, unreachable, into the nearest thicket?

More to the point, when he looked at his situation carefully and all in all, Isaac felt no assurance that there would be a ceremony or any bride to bless. Marie had not merely put off and avoided making up her mind, giving him his answer, she had sent him away into this exile of uncertainty. He had said he would wait till her fears had passed and her mind was clear, having faith that finally her answer would be yes. *Forever* and *always:* a boy's words, lacking all sense of how time lengthens with waiting or how warily a man must give his word to anything. But he had promised her. He could only wait. Yes, because you go on working as long as you must, as long as it takes, as if the end you strive for you will finally attain in fact. That was what his father meant by faith: the substance of things hoped for.

So Isaac meantime occupied himself with work as he could and when that failed wrote lists of things still to be done, mostly matters on which he would have liked to consult Marie but dared not presume the right to do so. He would have to dig another well near the new cabin—*their* cabin, as he meant it to be—he certainly could not have her carrying water in a bucket from the river or having to go into the stockade for it. The house in Salina too, of course, could he hire someone to dig a well? And furniture there—the stove, a table and chairs, a chest of some kind, a bed—what else did a house need? His parents had had separate beds as long as he could remember, and now, since the last addition, separate bedrooms. What would—? And would she be content with an extra-fine buffalo robe on her bed, worth fifteen dollars wholesale, or insist on blankets? All things to be bought at Leavenworth and brought out, a long trip, going and coming, and how much would it cost him? Colonel Titus had been right about money, it took a good deal of it for a man to set up a household, and he was set on having two—because there was the ranch to think of also. . . .

At least every week Isaac rode the twenty miles to Salina to look for mail, and usually there was a letter from Marie, but her letters were brief, formal, and impersonal, granting no relief. His mind ran in circles. He could only wait. He had promised. That is love.

Colonel Titus did not find his niece very entertaining that summer. She was listless and silent at meals. She complained, which was unlike her—of having nothing to do, but when Vinnie suggested she bake the week's bread or make a cake or a meat pie she stood at the kitchen work table with the ingredients spread around her, staring into space as if forgetting what she was there for; of the heat, although compared with the summer before the weather was mild and agreeable. Much of the time she sat on the porch in a billowing gown of white chambray, fluttering a fan, looking out along the road to the west, and attempting to read one of her uncle's improving books.

Colonel Titus gloomily followed the war news in the papers that arrived nearly every day. General McClellan, who had done lively work earlier in the summer, clearing the Rebs from the mountains of western Virginia, had been put in command of the Union armies after the disaster at Bull Run and had done nothing since: much hauling in of supplies, marching and drilling—two hundred thousand volunteers now, it was said, in the camps around Washington City— and months of talk and speculation about strategy, but no real action, and every little skirmish and picket's challenge made out to be a battle. And of course the Confederates positioning their armies around Richmond, digging trenches and building forts till they'd never be pried loose, and going where they pleased up and down the Shenandoah Valley west of the Capital. And now Douglas had gone home to die at Chicago, the man that to the colonel's thinking had seemed to have some chance of saving the Union, certainly compared with this back-country lawyer the Republicans had put in—. Closer to home, Lane's ragtag Brigade of Kansans was marching up and down western Missouri, saving the state for the Union—and saving Missouri horses, mules, cattle, chickens, one time a whole warehouse full of whisky, for themselves. They were ready enough to turn their field guns on some little Missouri town, abandoned and undefended, and knock it flat, but if the Rebel army came within fifty miles that brigade marched off in the other direction as fast as stolen horses would carry them. Not that the colonel retained any tender feelings for Missourians, it was just no way to conduct a war. Lane's head had swelled from hearing himself called general too often, but that didn't make him more than what he was, an amateur soldier and a thoroughgoing politician; and the Confederates when the time came, if they wanted, could get at Kansas from every direction but north.

The colonel in late September proposed that Marie join him on a short trip, the change of scene and her company for his benefit, not hers. She acquiesced, viewing it as a duty. They took the stage to Topeka and on to Leavenworth and stayed five days at the Planter's House, avoiding Kansas City. It was not clear from the news that came to Burlingame whether western Missouri was quiet again, but if it were, it was unlikely that Kansans would be welcome after Lane's summer of filibustering. They employed the time in outfitting Marie. She had turned twenty in April, her uncle pointed out—if she had no particular thought of marrying just yet, she soon would, no doubt; it was a provision a self-respecting young lady was obliged to make. She accepted his reasoning and let him take her around the shops, glad of his silent guidance when it came to the dressmakers; it was not St Louis, but her uncle would no more take the boat across the state in these times than he would venture into Kansas City. While he looked on she chose dresses, skirts, lingerie, hats; boots, a pair of pretty but impractical silk slippers; sheeting and blankets; printed yard goods that could make up, she said, as curtains or as skirts or dresses. He gave her, finally, a large square leather trunk with brass fittings, to carry her trousseau back to Burlingame. On the last afternoon, spying a watch with a hunter case that he fancied in a jeweler's window, he rushed in and bought it, with a suitable chain and penknife, and came out smiling to himself but did not explain. She knew he already owned a watch.

Marie came home to Burlingame—she thought of it as home now, her uncle's house, the slowly growing town—with feelings of energy and purpose she had not known since the spring. The first morning she laid her new things out on her bed for Vinnie to admire; she invited Mrs Schuyler and Miss Shirley to tea to show them and answered with a demure smile when the older woman boldly asked when she was planning to marry, and whom; and after supper she folded everything carefully away in the trunk.

She sat at the little writing table in her room, hands folded on the sheets of writing paper, the pen and inkpot waiting. The hooded lamplight shone silvery on the windowpanes; it was necessary to lean forward, press your nose against the glass, shield your eyes, merely to see out, and then you saw nothing, only the darkness receding across the empty prairie. If only she could fix her eyes in exactly the right direction, it seemed to her she could see through that darkness to the place where he had his ranch and look inside—what was he doing now? sitting at a table of rough planks and writing a letter by the light of a thick tallow candle?—they had no lamps, he said, made their own candles from buffalo fat—or sleepy already, tired from his work and thinking of bed, and the others already snoring under their heavy buffalo robes? They kept farmer's hours, he had said, at the ranch.

It was four months now, she owed him his answer, but what was it after all to be? It was cruel to make him wait so, as if he had offered her something terrible, shaming, when all he meant and wanted for her was kindness—to put his life between hers and the world like a shield, he had said. It seemed, when she thought back over what she knew, that he had arranged his whole life in Kansas for that purpose. But could any man promise that? It was herself she waited for and still the answer had not come. When she had closed her eyes that time and looked into herself, she saw only Isaac, living out his life alone, and herself not with him, how could that be? or was it only a foolish, girlish fancy? That picture remained, of fear for herself and her very existence, but smaller now and sunk deep within; she had grown used to it. But for that, she wanted him and wanted him to want her: the choice truly was not between telling him, yes or no, and all the long chain of events set in motion by that answer, it was between wanting and not wanting, being wanted by him, or not. Dear, sweet God! If after all he tired of waiting, wore his feelings out, and no longer wanted her!—it was like a knife entering her heart, she felt cold, she shivered, and a panic as of imminent death settled over her. Marie turned her head to look at the trunk of beautiful things her uncle had given her, standing at the foot of her bed—if they should stay there, never used, the emblems of an old maid's folly!—and her eyes blurred, she wiped at them with her handkerchief. And there was something more: if Isaac wanted her, it was that, however strong and quick he was, sufficient to himself, and however weak and silly and unworthy she knew herself to be, he was incomplete without her: he *needed* her. How then could she keep herself apart? So the two fears balanced, like weights on a scale, and if the old one was still present, she would no longer heed it.

Dipping the pen, Marie in her small round hand wrote slowly and carefully the place and date in the upper corner of the sheet, as she had been taught at school: *Sunday, October 6, 1861.* And then *My dear Isaac,* and stopped and laid the pen down—so cool and formal. She put the sheet aside and began again. If only she could get the first words right, the rest would follow.

> *My truly dearest Isaac,*
>   *In the Spring when you visited you asked me a question*

She smiled, staring into the mirroring window. It was not a question at all but a statement! He *assumed* they would be married, and his mind was already on the practical things that would have to be done in consequence.

> *of the most serious kind, and for which I found myself ill-prepared—O my Dear, I know you must wonder at that, seeing we have known one another more than two years now—yet I can but tell you truly what was in my Heart—I was content to live my life day by day, enjoying your visits when your Busyness brought you to my Uncle's house—with no thought for what lies ahead—*
>   *I needed time to consider—to determine in my mind what was right—you kindly granted me that time. It seemed so complicated to me—so many things to consider, so many consequences, extending all the rest of life. But now after long and earnest consideration, I see that the question is not complicated, but simple, and not a question at all—it is that*

Dear heaven! How was she to say it? So bold, it made her tremble at the thought of setting it down in words, and yet she must—press on, not falter—

> *you wish to share your life with me and have me for your wife—and I want nothing more from life than to have the right to call you Husband.*

Therefore, Dear Isaac, if that is still your wish you have your answer, yes, at last, and all my Heart—

There! She had said it, but what next? He was so practical, she must think it through, be sensible. . . .

There are many things a sensible woman must consider in planning for her household and the Home in which she means her Husband to find Happiness—This past week my dear Uncle Titus took me a journey by stage to Topeka and Leavenworth City—he was fearful of going into Missouri because of this horrible War—there he outfitted me with garments in which I shall be proud to appear as your Bride, and you proud to see me too—also linens and fabrics, I shall be busy with my needle, I can tell you, I shall ask Vinnie's help—

The date, silly! that was the point, what does he care for your sewing? She took the spoiled sheet of paper on which she had begun, reckoned the weeks, and hurried on.

I am sure I can be finished—will be ready for you—by the end of next month. Would you like your marriage to be held on the first day of December, I should like that myself—to start our new life with the month in which our Savior came into the world, I remember you told me, in your family you do not care much for Christmas. It is a Sunday, we have a preacher now Rev Mr Appleyard, he comes Sundays and holds his services in the dining room at the Schuyler House—a Methodist I believe, he seems a good man, I shall speak to him next week—

Oh, dear! He might be off on a long winter hunt, perhaps had already left—he had to hunt, of course, to get his living—*their* living. Not knowing how to express this new difficulty, she left it to Isaac to think of.

Do write soon, dear Isaac, and tell me if that will be satisfactory—and when will you come to stay?

Until which time, my Dear, I am—your loving wife that is to be—if you will have me—

Marie Bisonnette

Isaac received Marie's letter five days later at Salina, along with one from his father and a bundle of Davenport newspapers. Leading Bird, he carried his mail to the hotel, asked Mrs Jones to bring him coffee and a piece of her raisin pie, and sat down to read. He had a feeling that Marie's would be important, would settle things—looked and felt no different from her others in the course of the summer, and yet the feeling would not leave him—; and therefore put off opening it. The burden of his father's letter was the death of Antoine LeClaire, by apoplexy, two weeks ago, and his funeral at St Anthony's, which his parents attended along with most of Davenport (Lizzie had taken the boat to St Paul in the hope of a job teaching school—no word yet how she had succeeded). Isaac's father quoted St Paul on marriage, that it

is better to marry than to burn, but refrained from demanding more
particulars than his son had volunteered; and expressed the hope that
his morals had not suffered by his life among worldly men on the
frontier. . . . Isaac refolded the letter in its envelope and put it in the
pocket of his coat. The copy of the *Democrat* his father had sent was
largely devoted to LeClaire's life, works, and funeral: the biggest
thing at Davenport since the coming of the Rock Island Rail Road, in
which, of course, he had played a considerable part; he had been three
months short of sixty-four. So old LeClaire was gone and Ebenezer
Cook no longer meddled in money, but there was still George Davenport—what was he, the nephew of the one the river pirates killed? It
was still no more a country for a young man that meant to put his
mark on life than when he put it behind him.

Finally Isaac slit the envelope of his other letter, drew it out,
opened it with trembling fingers, and as his eyes fell on the salutation
the held breath burst from his lips like a jet of air from a bellows: it
had happened, she would have him!—the words could have no other
meaning. Pushing aside the plate and the saucerless cup, he laid the
letter flat on the table and hunched forward to read, shielding the
sheet of paper with his arms. His eyes flew across the lines, he flipped
the page over with a snap and read to the end—*your loving wife that is
to be*. It was going to happen, on the first day of December he would
be a married man—man and wife, Mr and Mrs Isaac A. Pride—Mrs
Isaac Pride, Mrs Pride—Marie Bisonnette Pride. . . . He found a
stub of pencil in his pocket, tried the name in its several forms on the
back of the envelope, sounded them over to himself and liked the
sound—a grand sound, an invincible sound!

He was reading the letter through for the third time—but already,
it seemed, he had the words by heart, familiar as a prayer learned in
childhood—when it struck him that if Marie—*his own Marie*, with a
quick in-catch of breath—if she felt the six weeks' burden of preparation for their wedding, he had at least as much still to do himself. He
ought—he closed the letter, slipped it in beside his father's, shoved
the chair back—ought to be starting this minute for Leavenworth! He
was up, the chair somehow went over backward—saw himself riding,
past the little towns, Junction City, Manhattan, Louisville, St Mary's
and the empty Potawatomi land, Indianola, Pleasant Hill—not yet
noon, if the weather stayed clear he'd be there tomorrow night—. He
stooped, set the chair up, started for the door, remembered—the untouched piece of pie, the cooling half-drunk coffee—went back and
clinked a coin on the table; turned, moving with long strides, almost
running now, hand on the doorknob, and stopped, frozen. He had no
money with him, a few silver dollars in his purse, it was all in the tin
trunk at the ranch: he would need money, a hundred, two hundred—
if he bought at Leavenworth he could perhaps pay by draft against

his credit with Mr Durfee, but suppose there were things at Junction City that would suit—and save time besides—And should he take a wagon from the ranch? or have the furniture shipped by freight? Expensive, of course, but that too would save time—if it got to Salina by—when, mid-November?

Mrs Jones came from the kitchen to investigate the clatter in her dining room and stood staring at him, wiping her hands on her apron.

—I'm getting married! Isaac cried, as if that explained everything, and jerking the door back, he darted through, across the porch, and took the steps in one flying leap.

At the beginning of the last week of November Abraham Bos rode through the gate of the stockade at Pride's Ranch, unannounced; he heard without comment Isaac's news and noted the changes since the spring as Isaac led him around—the addition to the stable, the new cabin opposite the gate, now with Romulus Tripp and his wife Malvina living in it to manage things when the hunters were absent; and agreed to ride to Burlingame with Isaac to bring the horses back, Isaac meaning to take his bride to Salina by stage. Bos had stayed on for the wheat harvest and then helping his father rebuild his barn; no trouble around Franklin, and the Missouri government was still Union. He had thought some of joining up for the sake of the two-hundred-dollar enlistment bounty but had calculated to make a sight more profit by hunting.

Isaac when asked how the hunting had been admitted he had not done much—busy all summer and into the fall with building, then with buying his furniture from Leavenworth and making more for the new cabins at the ranch. Riding into town to collect the shipment from the freight office, he had noticed smoke from Tommy Thorn's old cabin and found it occupied by a couple of recent emigrants, the Tripps, childless and in their forties; he was a long-limbed, stooping, lethargic scarecrow of a man who looked and sounded like Tennessee —had come from ten years of scratching corn and tobacco from a hill-country farm west of Nashville, where he had met his wife—but was in fact born and raised in southeast Connecticut and for all either of them knew could be one of Isaac's numberless family connections there. With a lopsided smile Tripp declared that he had given up his cabin and brought his wife west because he did not mean to meddle with the dod-burn slavers and abolitionists and their fight—let the bastards kill each other off, and the sooner the better—. Malvina hushed this rude talk, told him plainly he'd be off soon enough if the Army could find any use for him, and Isaac liked her at once—a little, plump, motherly woman whose insistent cheerfulness and energy belied her barrenness; she got them money by doing laundry for Colonel Phillips and his family and a few others, helping out with cooking and washing up at the hotel, while old Rom hunted enough to put meat on the table and very occasionally took a turn at driving freight to Junction City or Topeka, meaning to put out money when he had some, he said, on land farther west, maybe in the spring. Isaac gave him two dollars to help move his furniture with his little two-wheeled cart, and when they were finished offered them thirty a month to come out together and stay at the ranch. Malvina accepted with hardly a glance at her husband and within an hour had their few possessions loaded on the cart and started. Malvina, Isaac concluded, would provide the womanly company Marie would want in her new home and get enough work out of Rom to earn their wage.

Isaac and Bos started for Burlingame early in the morning of November 27. The weather had turned cold, the air smelled damp, and sun and sky were masked in gray cloud. As they left the ferry after crossing the Saline, the first specks of snow drifted down, collecting as they watched, swirling among the brown stalks of grass. Bos, slouched in the saddle, turned his collar up, drew a knitted scarf from inside his coat—provision of his mother's forethought—and tied it around his neck. He looked around, scowling. It was coming from the northwest.

—It's starting like that big one last winter, he said. We could hole up in this house of yours till we see what it's going to do.

—It aint like we're out in wild country, Isaac said, it's a road you can follow from here on, settlers and cabins every mile or two the whole way. Besides—look at it—it aint going to last. But if it does, well, we better make time while we can. Come *on*, Abe! he shouted. Don't you know I've got to be married on Sunday? Come on, I'll race you into town.

And grinning, Isaac kicked Bird into a run. Glumly Bos followed at an easy trot, not a man to kill his smaller pony with running when there was no need.

> *May the grace of Christ our Savior,*
> *And the Father's boundless love,*
> *With the Holy Spirit's favor,*
> *Rest upon them from above.*

Isaac stood self-consciously at one end of the Schuyler House dining room, facing Reverend Appleyard while the minister led the singing, and refrained from looking around. Behind him Mrs Schuyler rolled the chords on her piano. The rhythm was measured and like a waltz, but taken a little slow for dancing.

> *Thus may they abide in union*
> *With each other and the Lord,*

> *And possess, in sweet communion,*
> *Joys which earth cannot afford.*

Marie stood beside him now, close enough to touch, one hand resting in her uncle's arm. With a lift of her chin she turned her full face to him, smiling. The blue silk dress she had brought from Leavenworth, a pattern of flowers when closely looked at, blue and red and white, minutely twined, had become her wedding gown. She had been nearly frantic when they rode in from the darkness the night before, wet and cold and the horses' tails crusted with ice. The snow had kept up. They were four days coming through to Burlingame, a day and a night coiled in their buffalo robes, asleep, on the bank of what was probably Clark's Creek, halfway to Council Grove, while the snow boiled across the land and there was no road to follow, no sun, no direction, and they had not attempted to dig out fallen wood for a fire. Marie had been watching from a parlor window and threw the door open, weeping, as they came stamping across the porch. For minutes he held her close, lips caressing her cheeks, wet with the salt of her tears.

The *Amen* wound back into the piano and there was a clatter of chair legs scraping the floor as the people sat. The minister cleared his throat, surveyed the room, and held the open book out stiff-armed before him.

> *Dearly beloved, we are gathered here*
> *in the sight of God, and in the face of this congregation,*
> *to join together this Man and this Woman in holy Matrimony;*
> *which is an honorable estate,*
> *instituted of God in the time of man's innocency,*
> *signifying unto us the mystical union*
> *that is between Christ and His Church.*

The words came fitfully to Isaac's mind. It was the wine, no doubt. He had to concentrate all his attention to follow what the preacher was saying.

> *First, It was ordained for the procreation of children. . . .*
> *Secondly, It was ordained for a remedy against sin. . . .*
> *Thirdly, . . . for the mutual society, help, and comfort,*
> *that the one ought to have of the other. . . .*

They had attended Mr Appleyard's morning service, Isaac and Marie together, Colonel Titus, even Abraham Bos, uncomfortable in tight new pants and clean shirt, and come home to dinner. Marie took up the afternoon packing and repacking her things, sitting patiently on the chair in her room while Vinnie brushed and plaited her hair and pinned the braids close to show off the shape of her head, with blue ribbons tied in bows; but found an hour to show Isaac the service she had chosen, in a prayer book borrowed from Miss Shirley. The minister was liberal in such matters; Marie had wanted the Episcopal wedding because it was most like what she remembered of the two marriages she had attended at St Louis. Her uncle had provided an early supper and honored the occasion by opening two bottles of his best claret. The wine had made Isaac not sleepy but excessively alert: each sensation came through the crystalline shell of consciousness hard and vivid as a diamond—the light touch of Marie's gloved hand on his arm as they walked to the hotel, the crunch and squeak of his boots on the packed snow, the cold wind off the Plains burnishing his cheeks—.

He started, hearing his name. Frowning, the minister repeated it—

Isaac. Will thou have this Woman to thy wedded wife,
to live together after God's ordinance
in the holy state of Matrimony?
Will thou love her, comfort her, honor and keep her
in sickness and in health;
and, forsaking all others, keep thee only unto her,
so long as you both shall live?

The silence lengthened while Isaac smilingly contemplated these grave questions, looking steadily into the minister's sober blue eyes. Behind him a boot scraped the floor, a woman suppressed a titter—evidently something was expected of him at this point in the proceeding. Mr Appleyard leaned forward, frowning again, as he mouthed the words: *I will.*

Everything seemed to speed up now, Marie, head high, shoulders thrown back, had given her own answer in her clear, sweet voice, the minister seized Isaac's right hand and placed it in hers, he was rehearsing the vow a few words at a time

I Isaac take thee Marie
I Isaac take thee Marie
to my wedded wife
to my wedded wife

The minister was asking for the ring. The *ring?* Isaac felt in one pants pocket, then the other, vest pockets, coat—found it, held it tight between thumb and forefinger—it slipped out, clinked to the floor, he was on his knees, retrieving it—. Marie held out her hand, fingers spread, Mr Appleyard pointed to the ring finger and Isaac placed the circlet of gold on it, held it there, repeating—

With this Ring I thee wed,
With my body I thee worship,

> *And with all my worldly goods I thee endow:*
> *In the name of God.*
> *Amen.*

Now Reverend Appleyard had them kneel side by side while he read a lengthy prayer over them—*as Isaac and Rebecca lived faithfully together*, and the rest left no more track across Isaac's mind than a fish passing down a moving stream; and startled him to attention by bending down and joining their two right hands again, which he held tight with both his own while, gazing on the assembled witnesses, he pronounced the solemn admonition:

> *Those whom God hath joined together*
> *let no man put asunder.*

And then as they knelt, hands still clasped, he lifted up his arms in blessing:

> *O God of Abraham, God of Isaac, God of Jacob,*
> *bless these thy servants,*
> *and sow the seed of eternal life in their hearts;*
> *that whatsoever in thy holy Word they shall profitably learn,*
> *they may in deed fulfill the same.*
> *Look, O Lord, mercifully upon them from heaven,*
> *and bless them.   Amen.*

Isaac looked up as he ceased—a nod, a lifting motion with his hands—and, still holding Marie's right hand, placed his other on her waist and brought her to her feet, and so led her to the side of the room to stand beside her uncle. Mrs Schuyler's hands were poised above the keyboard, there was another drum roll of shifting chairs and feet, but the minister was not finished. Having bowed thus far to custom, the sentiments of the bride, and his own forebearing nature, and seeing likewise a number of unfamiliar faces within hearing, he could not let slip the opportunity for edification.

—Brothers and sisters, we are gathered here this evening to rejoice in the marriage of our dear friends Isaac and Marie. Right and good, brothers and sisters, right and good: as our Savior Himself rejoiced in the marriage at Cana of Galilee, honoring it with His first miracle, turning water into wine—and no ordinary wine neither, but *good* wine—so gather we here tonight, brothers and sisters, right and good. Yet do not think that the Lord in His Providence has brought us here only for amusement and pastime. No!

Isaac with a nod guided his wife to an empty chair and sat beside her, still holding her hand. There were sounds of a general settling into seats.

—As He does ever, the preacher continued, finding the rhythm of his homily, the Lord takes the rawhide of our delight and braids it in a rope to wind us up to heaven—opens to our minds the common happenings of man's life and lights them with the light of salvation. For some of us here tonight *are* married—others of us *will be* married —yet salvation is for all, and marriage is the figure and means and emblem of salvation. We look *into* marriage and we see how the delight with which man cherishes his wife—and woman her husband— opens the gateway to a new soul coming into life and starting its journey up the long trail to heaven. Again, we look *out from* marriage and we see how the unity of man with woman is also the unity of mankind in God's Church—and the union of His Church with Christ. What says the Apostle in our text? *We are members of His body, of flesh, of His bones—one flesh.* How is this wonderful unity to be, this miracle planted in the midst of our sinful, erring, ignorant race? It is by *giving*, brothers and sisters, as Christ gave His very life for the salvation of mankind and His Church. Go and sell all that thou has, and *give*—so Christ commanded the rich young man who asked Him, What must I do to be saved? Give *freely*, as you give the food to nourish your own flesh, says the Apostle.

Warming, waving his arms and jogging the pages of his Bible, Mr Appleyard showed how St Paul taught the duty of man to wife, and elsewhere of wife to husband; how St Peter—himself a married man, as he said—likewise taught; what the four Evangelists in order had set down; and, from the slips marking his texts, seemed of a mind to work his way back through all God's instructions on the subject— Isaac and Rebecca, Abraham and Sarah—to the first parents of mankind, when he paused to draw breath. Mrs Schuyler seized the opportunity to sound a commanding chord on her piano and in her reedy, aging voice started over on the wedding hymn. With a thunderous shoving back of chairs the congregation rose and joined her.

> *May the grace of Christ our Savior,*
> *And the Father's boundless love,*
> *With the Holy Spirit's favor,*
> *Rest upon them from above.*
>
> *Thus may they abide in union*
> *With each other and the Lord,*
> *And possess, in sweet communion,*
> *Joys which earth cannot afford. Amen.*

Isaac looked Marie in the eyes as they finished, saw tears, and drawing her gently to him pressed her cool forehead with his lips. Bill Shirley let out a whoop. Cheers and laughter echoed from the walls.

Abruptly Marie and Isaac found themselves grinning arm in arm at the center of a milling throng of friends pressing forward to shake hands, offer congratulations—there was stout, red-faced Bill Shirley, with his sister Martha on his arm, young Aaron Schuyler, and Harry Cullum, ridden down from Topeka for the occasion, Marsh Murdock back in his uniform for a visit, the only one so far among Marie's young Burlingame friends to answer the Presidential call, Abraham Bos, tall and silent among well-dressed strangers—. The men withdrew, leaving the women to admire Marie's gown, her stylish silk slippers. There was a clatter of chairs being carried and shoved back against the walls, and Isaac, releasing Marie's hand, ran to help. Absalom came in with a wooden tub of punch, sloshing with chunks of ice floating on the top, slices of orange and lemon, Vinnie following with a tray of cups. Mrs Schuyler had returned to the piano, her husband beside her with his violin under his arm and rubbing his bow with rosin.

Colonel Titus had taken his stand by the punch table, had one of the filled cups in his hand, tasted it, considered, smiled his approval at Absalom, and drank it off. Rattling the empty cup on the side of the tub, he called out for silence and invited his guests to help themselves so they could have a proper toast.

—The bride and groom! the colonel boomed in his parade-ground voice. May they have all the joys of this earth—*as well as* the joys of heaven the preacher has been wishing em! And bowing gravely to Mr Appleyard he rolled his head back and drained his cup. Shouts and laughter, cups clinking—the colonel raised his hand again for silence, he had something more to say: Now I've given this young man a bride—well, I reckon *someone* had to give her, isn't that right? he demanded with a solemn look around the smiling faces. But you see, he continued, now I've done it anyhow, I feel responsible—I remember myself how a young man with a new young wife kind of *loses track of time.* So—with a flourish he brought from his pocket the new gold watch, with its chain and the penknife dangling from the other end, and held them up—I went and did something about it. There now! He handed the watch to Isaac. You may not know what day it is—or night from day—but at least you'll know the time. All you got to do is keep it wound—and look!

The first dance was a waltz, the "Prima Donna." Isaac astonished his bride and everyone else by asking her to dance it with him and leading her out in proper form; and even more by carrying it off— stiff as a cavalry recruit on his first mount, Colonel Titus remarked, but with vigor and dash all the same. The others watched while they whirled around the room to the first strain, and joined in when the Schuylers started it through the second time. When Marie, signaling the turns with movements of her shoulders, sweetly asked why suddenly he was so silent, Isaac answered with a tight-lipped smile, eyes set in numerical concentration, and she threw back her head and laughed. When it was over, loud enough for all to hear, he declared that he meant to have every dance with his wife—so long as the musicians kept up the waltzes; and they obliged with another. Later, when the Schuylers turned to polkas, mazurkas, then a schottische, and finally a galopade, the "Victoria," Isaac did his best to waltz them too, until Marie, feverish between trying to follow the mixed rhythms and not wanting to lead, suggested they rest and watch and drink some punch. (It was long afterward that Isaac told her his secret: that waltzing was among the graces Cornie had acquired by keeping his eyes open around the officers' quarters at Fort Leavenworth; and the hours in the privacy of the new double cabin while he learned to dance—Cornie humming the tune and taking the lady's part, and Isaac counting. He had found a moment before Reverend Appleyard got down to business in which to beg Mrs Schuyler to start off with a waltz and go on with as many as she had music for.)

The Schuylers ran out of waltzes, repeated. Bos, dancing with Marie after several visits to the punch table, revealed an unexpected vigor in the stamps and turns of the polka. Colonel Titus stood by while Absalom replenished the punch with white wine, the juices of several fruits, a double-handful of milled sugar, whisky from a jug, ice from the icehouse spilled from a gunnysack; and commanding the center of the room clapped his hands for attention and announced a complicated series of longway dances, Mr Schuyler to call. It went on for twenty minutes. Isaac, watching from the punch table while Marie in her dark blue gown whirled through the figures, took out his watch and opened it: eleven o'clock. With two fresh cups of punch and a look of determination, he went over to the piano and spoke a word in Mrs Schuyler's ear.

The music became the "Prima Donna" once more, played with dreamy slowness. Isaac hunted through the crowd of dancers, found his wife, and took her in his arms. Her hand was moist in his, her head thrown back in the whirl and turning of the dance. The skin of her face and neck and arms had turned Indian-dark with the blood coursing under it, pulsing to the pulse of the music, the dance. Her gray-green eyes looked out at him through half-closed lids as from a mask, the face almost of a stranger's, no longer perfectly familiar as he had thought it, carrying it these months in memory; or only now beginning to be known.

—My dearest, said Isaac softly. You must be tired. You know we mean to start early, in the morning.

—I am *not* tired, Marie answered with alarming clarity. I should like to dance all night. I shall see the dawn.

He danced them purposefully toward the archway entrance to the dining room. Vinnie waited with a candle, her uncle. Isaac released her, Colonel Titus leaned, placed his lips on her forehead, the black

woman took her hand and led her to the stairs. Mrs Schuyler modu-
lated into a waltz from the *Sonnambula.*

—Here! the colonel said, holding out a pint flask. His face was
flushed, his hair sweated flat to his skull.

Isaac took the bottle, held it up, swirled it against the light, dark
and heavy in appearance as molasses.—I don't need that, he said.

—Go on, drink some. I was married once myself.

A single tear ran down the colonel's cheek, broke in the folds
around his mouth. Politely Isaac drew the cork, tipped the bottle, for
a moment let it pour—not fire, a sour, heavy taste like a fist in the
belly; and let the flask slide into a pocket of his coat. Vinnie was
coming down again. He started up the stairs.

The best room in the house he had said he wanted, but they were
all the same. A number—he found the door, a room facing the back;
leaned on the doorframe, tired as if back from a month of hunting and
had not slept. A cheer came up the stairs, their absence was discovered. Mrs Schuyler struck up the "Flying Cloud," the violin followed.
Isaac rapped the door and when no voice answered tried the knob.

Marie lay propped in the bed facing him, her hair loosed on the
pillows, the coverlet tucked tight across her breast. The short single
candle stood on the night table beside her head. Isaac turned the key
in the lock, went to her, knelt. Her fingers found their way among his
hair like mice, caressing. He knelt with his head pillowed on her
breasts and let her fingers contemplate his hair. His ear felt the alternating pressure of a heartbeat throbbing its endlessly repeated tune,
hers or his own, or both in their now joined consent.

—My dear, Marie said, the day I first saw you, I wanted to put my
hands in your hair. Was that wicked? Now I can.

The candle guttered. Mr Schuyler's violin came through the bare
floor in the "Jenny Lind," feet thumped the polka.

—Isaac, she said, you are not afraid of things. I mean to be like you
now, Isaac—never afraid of things ever again.

He roused himself, rose, cupped one hand around the candle and
blew it out. His hands were under her shoulders. His lips lay long
and long against her lips.

—My king—my sun—my husband! Hold me. Never let me go.

XIII

A New Life

Isaac had been out more than three weeks on his second hunt of the winter, only two days longer than he said—she had made a calendar on a sheet of writing paper and marked off the days—but Marie was anxious. In the weeks since coming to the ranch she had found occupation enough to leave little time for worrying. From the first day she had taken charge of the cooking, and Malvina was content to just help; most days they took dinner and supper together at a long table Isaac had made, with rough benches, in the old cabin inside the stockade. She had made curtains of brightly flowered cloth for the windows in both rooms of their own cabin. Putting Isaac's clothes in order, washing, mending, patching, sewing new shirts and underthings, had taken a whole week; she had a sack of scraps saved for a rag rug for their bedroom. Mrs Pride had written kindly, inviting her to visit, and they were sending a box of seeds for the garden. The only Indians they had seen were half a dozen Kaw men who rode in from their camp somewhere west while Isaac was on his first hunt, with buffalo robes and wolf skins to trade for coffee, sugar, and tobacco; squat men on wiry little pinto ponies, dressed in citizens' clothes and moccasins. Mr Tripp let them into the stockade and sat on the floor with them around the big fireplace in the cabin, smoking and drinking coffee, before he took them out to the storeroom to do their trading.

Marie quite liked Mr Tripp. There were whole days while Isaac was gone that he spent with his pipe on a stool propped by the door of his cabin, but he was active when started at something and ceremoniously polite to Marie—Missus Pride, ma'am, with a touch of two fingers to the brim of his hat. When she asked he had cut a rawhide rope from a deerskin for a clothesline and rigged it on hooks between the stockade and their cabin.

On that morning, the first bright one after a week of misty rain mixed with sleet, Marie had been hanging out wash. Malvina was baking. The yeasty sweetness of fresh bread hung faintly in the air mingled with woodsmoke and the smell of slowly cooking meat from the smokehouse—still early in the day but it made her hungry for dinner. There came a clamor of voices, whoops, shouts, from the fence across the neck of land at the front of the property. Marie ran to look—Isaac coming home, what was it?

A pounding of hooves along the worn wagon track and a dozen Indians came galloping at the stockade, naked to the waist in the winter sun, faces hideous with streaks of red and black; at the end, at a walk, came an older man heavy in the saddle, a chief, and Cornie with a rawhide rope around his neck, led like a heifer, black skin showing through the ribbon slashes in his shirt and his eyes rolling up white when the chief prodded his lance tip at his backside. The stockade gate slammed to, the bar thumped into place. The Indians let out a great cry, rearing their horses.

Marie screamed, her voice rising through and over them all. The cabin, get behind its heavy plank door, safe—she ran, pointed toes of her boots caught in the hem of her petticoat, fell face forward, flat, in the mud with a smack of palms wrist-deep—. Heaved herself up, running, skirts gathered in mud-wet hands, running—got through, door slammed, panting, heaved at the trunk and dragged it screeching across the board floor, thump against the latchless door, and stop—. Lay across it, breath heaving her chest and whistling through her throat—pain, death pangs, death coming, sweet Christ, *Notre père, qui es aux cieux, que ton nom soit sanctifié.* Sweet Christ, deliver me—

Laughter, whoops, from the east end of the cabin. Marie got herself up, went to the window, peeked, drawing the curtains close around her face. The men had dismounted, were clustered around Cornie like bees at spilled syrup. One of them lined his brown forearm beside Cornie's black one, pinched the Negro's bare belly in the fingers of his other hand like a man looking a horse over he was thinking of dickering for, till the black man cried out in pain and fear; brought his face nose to nose and when Cornie flinched jerked him back with a pull on the lariat and, looking around at the others, grinning horribly, said something in a loud voice and let out a long-drawn, coughing laugh. Trembling, Marie snapped the curtains shut, took two unsteady steps, and threw herself face down on the bed.

After a time the sounds changed: the Indians' voices united in a droning chant on two or three slow, deep notes. Marie roused herself, went back to the window. Two of the devils had taken her sheets from the line, slit them in the middle and pulled them over their heads. Others had gotten into Malvina's dresses and petticoats and draped them over their shoulders—the storeroom, at least, in the other half of the Tripps's cabin was closed with a padlock, but they could break the door in. They had formed a circle, bent forward one behind the other, circling in a shuffling dance. Cornie stood in the middle, paralyzed. The chief sat his horse, clapping the slow measure of the dance, the end of the rope tied to his pommel—an ugly man with a prominent hooked nose, the bone protruding as if sometime it had been broken. *Where was Mr Tripp?* There were guns in plenty inside the stockade, kegs of powder, bullets ready-molded for all. Marie went back to the bed and lay, arms folded across her breast, looking up at the unpeeled log rafters. She tried to calm herself by praying.

Silence. She held her breath, listening, but could hear no sound, what was it? She ran to the window—Indians halted, motionless, staring toward the stockade—. She drew the curtains wide, jerked the window up, leaned out, craning—Isaac walking slowly toward them with a smile on his face, talking in a low voice, gesturing with both hands—and there behind him Bru and Mr Bos, revolvers out, pointing, and the wagon, the oxen faintly steaming in the winter air—

Isaac went up to one that had taken a sheet, frowning now, face red with anger, took hold, tore it off with a ripping sound down the middle and threw it on the trampled, muddy grass, shouting for Mr Tripp—Tripp! Rom Tripp! You get on out here, you lazy son of a Tennessee polecat!—pointing around the circle of silent Indians. Cornie slumped to his knees, head bowed. Two of the Indians had their bows up and strung, quiver of arrows held close, each with an arrow nocked and pointed at Isaac's breast, and—

—Stop it! Stop!—her own voice crying, she dived through the open window, jarred stiff-armed on her hands, hurt, rolled in a somersault onto her back—up, running toward them, hair streaming, crying out and sobbing—

—Isaac! Isaac!

Bos and Bru were coming toward them, pistols raised. Isaac caught her with one arm around her waist and held her close, and she knew nothing more.

—I know you were upset, Isaac said gently as they sat their horses waiting for the ferryman to cross, but you shouldn't ever startle a bunch of Indians like that—could have gotten us all killed, starting with yourself. They had ridden this far without a word. Even the tame ones, he continued, that are getting civilized—it's like hunting bear, or maybe a sow-bear with her cubs. Come on her unexpected and set her off, you can't tell which way she'll jump, but it's going to be quick, and you aint ready for her, she'll have you down, and tearing at you with her paws, and chewing you up, before you know what's happened. But you go at em open-handed, face em and talk em down, don't look afraid or try to run, and most times they're peaceable and you'll come through fine and friendly. Or that's how I figure it, anyhow. . . .

They had taken a week for their wedding trip. Isaac had planned nothing, it had not occurred to him, but Marie assumed they would do something, and her uncle offered the use of his buggy and his handsome pair of black horses, and Isaac improvised a circuit of the Kansas River towns, up to Topeka, on to Tecumseh, Washington, Lecompton, Lawrence, and so back through Bloomington to Burlingame. They stayed a night in a hotel at each place. Isaac took his wife to call on the solid men of his acquaintance—Cy Holliday, Bob Stevens, Sam Wood, even Jim Lane. Marie grew accustomed to hearing herself referred to as Mrs Pride and was no longer startled or vague when the men used the expression. Everywhere the talk was of railroads and the war, somehow connected: iron hoops to bind the Union in one, Senator Lane called them, and with the Southerners no longer in Congress to set road blocks, they would have to go the central route, through Kansas, with grants of public land just as for the Illinois Central. Slapping his hands together, Mr Holliday roundly declared that he did not care how many roads the general government paid for, the more the better—so long as one of them was his Atchison & Topeka.

There was still a cover of melting snow on the ground as they drove north from Burlingame at the start of this journey. Marie sat close, a buffalo robe across their laps, tucked under on both sides. It made Isaac think of his parents' wedding trip, a tale much told in the family. Winter then too but not much of a trip, only the twenty or so miles from the Vermont village where his mother was born and they were married, to the one where his father had his first church. There was deep snow but a warm spell had come—it was January—and it had worn thin on the road, down to muddy ruts in places, and the sleigh did not go right, so his father drove off the road to get better snow, and pretty soon the sleigh ran into a hole and turned over, spilling them both out, breaking open his mother's trunk—and the old horse broke its harness, ran away, an iron runner snapped on the sleigh—. They had to walk back to the village, stiff and limping, and get the blacksmith to haul the sleigh on his wagon and mend the runner, a fearful expense for a young preacher new-married. A farmer along the road caught the horse for them. No doubt they had been wrapped in a buffalo robe too, Isaac concluded, holding the reins in his left hand and patting his wife's knee with the other, but he did not know. Sleighing was still among his mother's great delights; when the Iowa snow fell and the river froze hard and the time came to get the cutter out again, her eyes sparkled like a girl's and she danced through the house humming while his father hitched up for the first ride of the season.

Marie treasured such revelations but was unable to draw out the tales that enclosed them, they merely happened when something reminded him. It was strange her, more than two years you knew someone, you concluded there was no choice but to give your life to him, and you discovered that really you knew nothing of him—or rather, in comparison with your accumulated ignorance your little knowledge is as nothing, which a lifetime of learning will scarce fill up: the particular way, for instance, a man stands at the washstand of a morning, and bends and splashes his face with cold water from the basin and combs and brushes his hair, and the look of concentration as he strops the razor and prepares to shave; and when he pulled the night shirt over his head to dress, she modestly drew the bedclothes over her face and caught hardly a glimpse; and dressed, he tactfully removed himself and went down to the hotel parlor to wait while she got up and washed and put on her clothes.

He knew, of course, no more of her than she of him, in all these ways. Their ignorance was opposite but shared, two halves of one knowing. She lay against him flank to flank and felt the muscles of his cradling arm flex and tense under her neck, and so slept, and woke to the touch of his fingertips delicate as butterfly's wings, his lips touching her lips, her eyes, his pink face moon-bright and close, enormous, in the curtained light, and thought that if God gave her a thousand years to live, her life would contain no greater sweetness than this moment, this day, this week.

They rode up to Topeka on the stage alone, with Marie's precious trunk thumping in the boot behind, and from there west to Salina shared the coach with two men and a sack of mail and sat primly apart facing them on the opposite bench: a smart young lieutenant posted to Fort Larned and a stolid, long-faced, bearded German named Greiffenstein who said he was a trader too, with a place not far from Mathewson's at the Great Bend.

They stayed two days in the new little house at Salina till Mr Tripp drove in with his cart to take them out to the ranch.

In early July Isaac and Bos determined on an extended joint hunt toward the Great Bend. Cornie was left at the ranch, and Isaac made do with Tripp in his place as skinner. After some thought, he also left his mules to fatten on the ripe grass in the pasture and took oxen instead, so as to keep pace with his partner's team and wagon.

They followed Isaac's Buffalo Creek down past the old Konza camp and found the herds after a week's travel, on the other side of the Smoky Hill. While the others made camp and staked out the oxen, Bos took his pony, rode up a dry gulch that cut this high, broken country, and came back with the tongue and steaks from a single buffalo cow, so as to have fresh meat for supper and breakfast. A hot wind blew hard in the night from the west and they lay on their robes in the wagons to get out of it but did not sleep: the oxen, staked by the spring, were restless, moaning and tugging at their ropes; then in the dark of moonset all around their camp came the snorts and belling grunts of buffalo signaling band to band, the trampling of many hooves in purposeful movement, and when the light came back the valley, which at sunset had been dotted thick with peacefully browsing buffalo, was empty of game. They walked out from camp; Bos took his horse and rode to the place where he killed the cow, but it was so—the carcass lay untouched, even the wolves had cleared out.

—It don't hardly seem you could have scared em off with just one shot, Isaac said, puzzling over his partner's news.

—Could be they've concluded they've eaten up all the grass and gone looking for fresh, Bos said as he got down. The thing is, where?

—I reckon they'll be clear to the Whitewater country by now, Tripp said, and when the others turned on him drew himself up with importance at having something to tell.

—Where's this Whitewater country? Isaac wanted to know.

—Pretty little stream runs into the Ar-kansas, bout a hundred miles down from the Great Bend. I drove a freighter there once before we come to Salina. They've got a county organized, runs right across southern Kansas, but no government to speak of and no taxes. And a county seat started they call El Dorado, which means place of gold, only they aint none, nor people neither, I've heard, since the war and rebel whites and Indians raiding from the Territory and scaring em off. And them as is left aint no account—just a few horse thieves and half-breeds and runaway niggers that plants a little corn and sits in their cabins—and when they hungry enough, they hunt some. *That's* the Whitewater, he concluded.

—Sounds like your kind of country, Isaac said when he had taken this in. Why didn't you stay there, Tripp? And the others laughed with him.

The war, although remote, was unsettling even in Saline County. The news from the West had been mostly good since early spring. The Confederate move to invade Missouri had been turned back before it got out of Arkansas; Grant since Shiloh had about cleared the Southerners from Tennessee, was into northern Mississippi, and Farragut and his fleet had made New Orleans Union again; in Salina people rejoiced at the fall of Memphis in June, which could not help but be good for Western trade and land. In the East, on the other hand, and perhaps more important in the long run, things had gone less well: the iron-clad fight in the James River was written up in

Republican papers as a Union victory but seemed not to have settled anything; McClellan's long-prepared campaign against Richmond had started promisingly but broken down in a series of bloody battles and once more there was alarm that the way was open to Washington. In August, pondering these events, Bos, in his usual decided tone that brooked no argument, announced that he was taking his hides to Leavenworth and going through to Missouri for a visit; and maybe now, seeing how things were going, he would join up after all, not Lane's men certainly, but if they'd take him into a company of sharp-shooters he'd heard of, where he'd do some good, and the state still paid the enlistment bounty—. Isaac mildly answered that the war news had not changed his opinion: that keeping up his ranch out on the frontier between the wild tribes and the settlements was worth a regiment of troops, though if the Rebs came raiding into Kansas as they had in Missouri and Ohio—but besides, now with a wife to look out for. . . .

Bos left the third week in August, with Bru. Isaac started with them but took his mules to try, drove on ahead, and met them on his way back from Leavenworth. The mules were a success—he made the trip in fourteen days—but business was decidedly unsettled since his last visit nearly a year earlier. On the one hand, good robes were running fifteen dollars each, while green buffalo hides were bringing six cents a pound—there was a large trade in hides, it seemed, for saddle coverings to fill government contracts—and tallow was seven cents; every buffalo Isaac killed was now worth something over a dollar. But on the other hand, the prices of trading staples such as sugar had doubled; and the prices Mr Durfee quoted were all in a new paper currency—if a man wanted gold, he took a twenty percent discount, and gold was scarce. Mr Durfee was deeply regretful as well as sorry he could not allow Isaac more than one fourth of his money in gold and that only as a favor, he would prefer to do all his trade in paper and hang onto such gold as came his way. Paper money of fluctuating value and scarce gold were, of course, nothing new to anyone bred in the West. Bank notes, however, promised to pay in gold or silver on demand, and except in the worst panics the solid banks could generally be counted on. The new greenbacks issued by the general government made no such promise—only that for ordi-nary debts they were to be accepted as legal tender (and were there-fore so called), in the East, men of finance pointed out that the new currency was in reality an unsecured, interest-free loan by the people to their government, though others, less critical, already argued that eventually it would have to be redeemed in specie like all other notes —if the Union endured.

Isaac did not weigh these arguments closely but concluded he had as well trust the government's legal tenders as the notes of a St Louis or New York bank; and took what the merchant was prepared to offer. At that he came out rather better than he had expected, considering the hunting that summer had been disappointing; but his trade in robes had held up, and the prices were excellent, as long as he settled for greenbacks. In view of the uncertain times and his doubts about his partner's plans, he decided to take back only supplies enough to meet the needs of the ranch to the end of the year. Mr Durfee seemed to favor this plan, but from his own perspective. He had bought out Alex Garrett and was trying to enter the trade on the upper Missouri. Now, if Mr Pride had money to invest, ordinary interest was higher than ever, and however the war went, the chances for large profits in the trade seemed very promising. Isaac promised to consider, when he knew what to do about his trading stock.

On the way to Leavenworth, Cornie had said he meant to visit friends for a while, perhaps see if an officer at the fort would take him on again as body-servant or, who knows, since he could read and write and had his free papers, he might have a chance in one of the new regiments for colored. Isaac heard him without comment and when he finished with Mr Durfee paid him off, in greenbacks. Cornie promised a letter to Salina when he knew his plans, if Mr Pride wanted him back as a skinner.

Two alarming pieces of news reached Leavenworth the day Isaac started back. There had been a second great battle at Bull Run, and again the Union force was routed and driven back on Washington; Pope, the commander, had resigned in disgrace. The Confederates had now regained nearly all of Virginia and Lee was said to be leading his army toward western Maryland, meaning either to invade the North or to get around behind the capital. Worse in its way, the Santee Sioux, no longer respecting the reduced garrisons, had come off their reservation in southwest Minnesota, had driven out thousands of settlers, slaughtering hundreds. There seemed no reason why the uprising should not spread farther into the border country, Kansas, Nebraska, the Dakotas, where there were already troubles enough with casual raiding against hunters and isolated settlers. With his lightly loaded wagon, Isaac drove his team hard the whole way and made it back to the ranch in five long days.—As good as an express wagon, he boasted, to cheer Marie and cover his own worry, when she wondered at his coming in empty and alone, and his mules worn thin; next trip, he said, he would put in for a freight contract.

The ranch, which all summer had been a center of life and purposeful activity, now seemed lonely and inert. Isaac and Tripp by unspoken agreement abandoned the stockade cabin and took their meals apart in their cabins with their wives, well enough so far as Isaac was concerned, but he missed the habitual fragmentary talk with Abraham, Bru, even Cornie, fool-headed as he could be—fragmentary, it came to him, because they had lived and worked so long together that in most things they did, each knew his part with no need to talk it through. With Rom Tripp you had to explain any ordinary chore, such as cutting hay to keep the stock through the winter, before you started him, then watch while he did it and go back afterward to see that he'd done it right. When he finished with the hay, Isaac saddled Bird and rode out on a long day's circuit of scouting, west, then north to the Solomon and down to the Saline again. He could find no sign of Indians, but the buffalo were back in thousands, within an hour's ride of Salina itself, and the next morning Isaac started for a two-day hunt, taking Tripp to do the skinning and leaving the ladies to keep each other company in the old cabin inside the stockade. The scattered bands seemed to be coming together, anticipating the end of the good grass and the great move south—cows and their spring calves, yearling bulls, and old ones in numbers, mixed in. Tripp seemed more than usually slow and listless. Isaac killed twenty bulls the first day, then had to do half the skinning and still lost two hides to wolves overnight when darkness overtook him; and twelve more before they started back the next afternoon, of which he had to skin out six himself. The work was further vexed by something wrong with the Hawken rifle—spring getting weak apparently, half the time the hammer did not strike hard enough to set the cap off and fire the charge, and he wondered if Charlie Cresson, the gunsmith at Salina, knew enough to set it right or make a replacement, or if he'd have to take it farther east; and what he could do for a gun in the meantime.

Isaac returned to the ranch not angry at Tripp or irritated over the failure of his rifle but generally morose, his mind divided as to which of the necessary steps had best be taken next; and went straight to his cabin, leaving Tripp to see to the mules—time enough to unload in the morning, by daylight. As he opened the door, a sound stopped him for a moment, the honking cries of the first flight of geese, high overhead in a ragged V wavering like a kite tail, moving southwest toward the Cheyenne Bottoms and the setting sun. Time to be moving: could a man follow them, load his wagon and follow the buffalo south to wherever they wintered? Down through the Indian Territory, Bos said he heard once, into Texas and clear to the Gulf—but not now, not with this war, anyhow. Moodily he pushed the door to and went and lay on the bed to wait for Marie to come and cook supper.

Afterward, while she stood at the table, washing up in the tin wash pan, Isaac, hands in pockets, scuffed his boots on the floorboards, talked of making up a fire for the light and cheer, though it was not cold, but did nothing, and finally carried his chair to the hearth and leaned back against the chimney, silent, watching her.

—What *is* the matter, Isaac? Marie asked with a glance over her shoulder. Was the hunt not successful?

—It was well enough—would've been a whole lot better if old Tripp knew his business.

—I *like* Mister Tripp. He makes me laugh.

—I'd like him better if he wasn't taking up more of my time than I can afford. No, Isaac said, letting the chair down on its front legs with a thump, I've about made my mind up. I'm paying him off—both of them. I'll tell him we're closing down awhile, going into town—

—*Are* we going into town?

—I don't know what else we can do—can't do it all myself, and can't leave you here alone when I'm on a hunt or going down to the Missouri. Why, Marie, I need a clerk I can count on and a skinner that aint afraid of work—leastways a boy or two I can train up, cause it looks like I can make work enough for two. And a teamster running back and forth with the mule team to Leavenworth, I figure we could do some business freighting, along with our own goods. And I'd like it better if I could get another experienced hunter, hire him for forty a month, say, or go shares—but I can't start on that till I know what Abraham's up to—. I'd hire Bru back if he'd come, he's worth his pay—

—*I* have a reason for going into town, Isaac, Marie said very quietly.

—You didn't get another Indian scare while I was gone, did you? She straightened up, brushed a wisp of hair back with her wrist, shook the wet from her hands, and began to dry them in her apron, slowly and elaborately. He went over to her, touched his hands to her drooping shoulders.

—What *is* it, Marie?

She pulled away, turned and faced him.—I am going to have—she began—*we* are having—and broke off, frowning, shook her head in vexation, all the phrases she had thought of coming out wrong. She drew herself up, regarding him squarely. *I am with child*, she said firmly. I am carrying our child. . . .

—Marie! He reached out his arms, held her with his hands, looking her in the face.

—I was not sure, but I have talked of it with Malvina, Marie said—now the important thing was out, the rest was easy. It will come in January sometime, I think—early January. . . .

Isaac felt foolish. He had indeed noticed a certain thickening around the middle but if he thought of it at all put it down to hard work at the ranch and a heavy diet of fresh buffalo meat. *Pregnant:* not a word to say out loud, a painful word, like the prick of a knife point, so much softer and gentler the way she put it—*with child*—

Isaac took his wife's hand, led her cautiously to the table, and made her sit. Taking up the dishpan, he carried it high to the door and with a flourish flung the soapy water out; he came back, set it down, seized the dish towel, and began polishing furiously at the plates, pots, tableware. Marie watched for a time and began to laugh. Isaac, holding a fork up critically to the lamplight, froze and gave her a severe look.

—I'm sure *I* don't see anything funny, he said.

—My dear husband! You might think I had told you of some terrible disease, It is not. She giggled again. I feel—wonderful! And it will not be for four months—five months, yet. . . .

Isaac dropped the towel, brought the chair over, and sat down facing her.—We'll go in to the house at Salina, he said briskly, close up here and I'll take the wagons and the stock—the buffalo's all around there now, I can get a living hunting on my own and come home to you every night—. Only—there's no doctor—Marie, there's no doctor for you nearer than the military surgeons at Fort Riley—whatever good they'd be to you—

—Isaac! she said, and reached for his hand, covered it with both of hers, caressing. I have no need of a doctor, I shall bear our child as easily as an Indian woman. But when my time comes, I should like to have some good woman by me—Malvina, perhaps—

—There's Missus Phillips, the colonel's wife—two little ones of her own, you liked her, Marie, that time you met. She's kind. . . .

On the afternoon of September 15 a column of horsemen cautiously approached the Saline, coming cross-country from the northwest, and halted before the gate of Pride's Ranch, closed with a strap of rawhide: Indians, you might have judged, seeing them at a distance in their nondescript denims and greasy buckskins, mounted on undersized spotted ponies, warriors of a half-wild tribe ambiguously armed—with rifles, shotguns, long-barreled revolvers, antique horse pistols, Bowie knives—for hunting or raiding; and only coming closer known them, from the brimmed hats, the unshaved faces, the pink skin showing through the week's grime of campfire smoke and dust, for the white men they were in fact. Thirty of them, perhaps, coming at a walk, in single-file, and at the end, a little way back, two mule-drawn wagons guarded by outriders on either side: the man in the lead—a big man distinguished by a fur hat with the earflaps tied over the top of his head, a long blue overcoat that might once have been military, a thick bush of black beard that represented a season's purposeful growth, not a week's neglect, and the narrowed, unyielding, wrinkle-rimmed eyes of one who has spent too many years in the mountains pursuing furs or gold—lifted one gloved hand and the column halted; he turned in the saddle and signaled two men to open the gate and ride on through to investigate.

The men stealthily advanced, leading their horses, revolvers drawn; circled the buildings but saw no smoke from the chimneys, no people; looked in at the cabin facing the stockade; hammered at the gate, which was barred somehow from inside, hallooed; and at length, satisfied, called out for the others to come in. They stayed the night and the next day, leaving guards posted along the fence. One man climbed the stockade, lifted the bar, but found only furniture and bedding, cookware—nothing worth taking—in the cabin; another, intrigued by the padlock on the barn, chopped the door in with an ax, threw down the seasoned hay from the loft for the horses and mules, but got nothing more for his trouble; half a dozen buffalo hams hung in the smokehouse covered with green mold but proved edible when well scraped and sliced up for frying, and the company feasted.

After midnight on the night of the sixteenth they rode out along the track to Salina, finding their way by starlight with weapons and harness muffled by strips cut from buffalo robes in one of the cabins; there was no moon. Before they left, the captain went around closing doors, seeing no reason for leaving a stranger's outfit to spoil in the weather.

Isaac was up before light, meaning to get in a full day hunting while the game lasted. He dressed in silence, but when he bent over to leave a kiss on Marie's brow it seemed she was only pretending sleep; she stirred, her eyes opened, and she insisted on dressing and making him breakfast before he left. After sending the Tripps away, they had stayed on a week at the ranch, alone, while Isaac loaded the wagons and Marie cleaned out the remains of her garden to take in— melons, cabbages, the last of the green beans, a bushel of half-ripe tomatoes. Isaac had arranged with Bill Bean, a settler making a farm two miles north of town, to store his wagons and board the oxen, mules, and horses, keeping only the one pony so as to save on feed in town—his plan was to ride out there and take a team and wagon to the buffalo ground, still within an hour or two of Salina, and hunt by the day; all Bean asked in return was to be kept in fresh meat, and glad enough to have it. When the buffalo gave out within reach of town, as they surely would soon enough, Isaac figured to work seriously at surveying and see if the fees would not keep them and let him stay close till the baby came: at the last election, as one of the duties owed the dignity of householder in the county seat and owner of record of a sixteenth share in the town company—not to mention his unrescinded appointment as sheriff's deputy—he had allowed Colonel Phillips to put him up for county surveyor, since someone had to fill the office; and his father had shipped his instruments and chains.

As it happened, when Isaac brought Marie in, three days since, Colonel Phillips had been on the point of starting for St Louis on business, was to be gone at least three weeks, and insisted that the young people share his house while he was away, to keep his wife and children company. The two ladies, it seemed, were going to like each other. Marie admired the babies, sat with Amanda, reading aloud, while she nursed, and was allowed to bathe and dress the children. Mrs Phillips overflowed with solicitous advice when she learned that Marie was to be a mother herself in the new year.

Marie fried a buffalo steak in the big skillet, cooked pancakes in the grease, boiled coffee; she took her husband's cup, refilled it, and sat down by him at the end of the table. The light was coming at the window beside the stove but he lingered, sipping at the coffee, too hot to drink still, and added milk from the pitcher, a luxury supplied by Bill Bean, who had brought cows out when he took his claim.

—We could keep cows at the *ranch*, he said. You could have chickens if you like. I can't let my time go, making a farm, like my father, but if I could get a man to look after things—. I ought to be starting, he went on, indicating the light spreading in the yard behind the house, but still made no move to rise and took another slow sip. I aim to get me ten buffalo today—that's fifteen dollars for the hides and tallow, I couldn't make that by any farming I know of. . . .

—I do not like your hunting alone, Isaac.

—It's all right—settled country around here, practically, now, just since I came three years ago. When it's all broken up in farms, the buffalo'll be gone and we'll have to go farther out, if there's still money in it—. But it's true, I got to write Abraham—he aint much for letters, but I ought to know if he's coming back. I could hire me a skinner, team up with someone—it works better, that way—

There was a single shot, then a volley, a pounding of hooves past the front of the house. Isaac leaped up, ran to the front room, and pushed a curtain aside. A band of rough-looking men rode by at a gallop, four abreast, and pulled up in front of the hotel fifty yards to the east, raising a dust cloud. Marie, behind him, caught his hand and held it tight.

—They don't look like soldiers anyhow, Isaac said, but they're shooting their pistols in the air. I reckon they just mean folks to wake up and pay attention.

The men had dismounted, some going into the hotel, others in groups of two or three walking purposefully back along the street, knocking at doors. Four were coming toward the house, heavily armed, carrying rifles or shotguns, led by a big, bearded man wearing a fur cap.

—I'll see what they're after, Isaac said, going to the door. And as

Marie stared at him, openmouthed, but did not venture to speak: It'll be all right. You just stay in the house.

Pulling the door to behind him, Isaac stepped briskly along the street and stopped, facing the men, blocking their way.

—What do you mean? he demanded, holding the black-bearded man's eyes with his own. Riding into our little town here by the dawn light, shooting off your guns—

—Jeremiah Blackthorn, the man said, offering his hand, and all we're after is guns and horses—don't mean you any harm, but you try to make a fight of it and we'll burn you out—

—Now why in the nation'd you do a thing like that? Isaac said, his face reddening. We're peaceable people, never done you any wrong—

—Well, I don't know about that—we're all from Texas mostly, been out along the mountains in the Green River country and heard how the war's going. We mean to go back and help—. Now—he nodded to one of the men—take him along to the hotel with the others—and edging past Isaac strode off toward the house where Marie watched from the doorway.

—You heard the captain, the man said, nudging his back with the shotgun.

—You just wait a little! Isaac said, gripping the gun barrel and pushing it aside. That's my wife there—and my friend's wife and babies inside. . . .

Isaac had left the Hawken with Charlie Cresson but there was a new, cheap rifle standing in the kitchen, loaded, that he had meant to try on the day's hunt—and what else? the old musket Cornie half-killed himself with, a little spoiled Indian rifle he had picked up one time beside Beaver Creek as a curiosity, barrel full of sand, the broken stock patched with rawhide—now if the captain and his men went pushing in, looking for guns, how would Marie take it? go wild with fear, and rage too, the way she did with those Cheyenne?

Isaac let a slow breath out: looked as if it was going to be all right. Marie faced the men demurely, hands clasped across the small, round bulge of her stomach under her apron. Captain Blackthorn took note and with a slight bow doffed his cap, spoke. Marie nodded, went in, leaving the door open, and came back with the musket, which she handed to one of the men; went again and brought the Indian rifle; and stood square in the door with a cool little smile of apology—very sorry, she seemed to be saying, but that was all she knew of in the house, they were not rich folk—. The captain smiled back, thanked her, replaced his hat, and led his men off down the street.

—All right, Isaac said, now that's settled, I'll go along to the hotel with you. And as long as it's your party, I'll let *you* buy the drinks!

There were not forty men in the town at the time, and they were soon collected in Mrs Jones's dining room, among them Romulus

Tripp, rousted blear-eyed and querulous from Tommy Thorn's old cabin, where he had once more settled in with Malvina. They clustered uneasily at the room's front windows under the careless eye of two of the raiders set to guard them, with double-barreled shotguns loaded, they said, with deer shot. The town's rifles and a few revolvers, old-style pistols, made no better show, gathered and thrown down in a heap in the dust below the hotel porch. The raiders did a little better with horses, collecting a herd of at least fifty (with the little wild-eyed hired-man's pony Isaac had left picketed behind Colonel Phillips's house), along with eight big-boned mules from the stage barn across from the hotel. The only violence came when Charlie Cresson locked himself in the back of his shop and refused to come out, and someone smashed his front window with a gun butt, broke the door in, and dragged him, scared and loudly protesting, to the hotel to tie up in a chair, with a bandanna stuffed in his mouth to shut him up. The guns from his shop fell last on the heap of weapons. Isaac saw his Hawken and kept an eye on it.

The raiders picked through the pile of guns, each taking what suited him, and threw the rest in one of the wagons. The captain called out for his men to take their mounts and prepare to depart. The Salina men, except Charlie Cresson, followed their guards out the door of the hotel and stood uncertainly on the porch, watching. It was not yet eight o'clock. The raid had lasted scarcely an hour.

A long-haired, dark young man, standing beside his horse behind the captain toward the head of the column, had the Hawken, hefting it in his two hands, taking it to his shoulder and sighting. Isaac leaped down from the porch and marched up the street with long, stiff strides. There was a stir among the horsemen, mutterings, but Captain Blackthorn, watching, gave no order, and Isaac looked neither right nor left. The young man turned and faced him, a head taller, rosy-cheeked.

—You a gunsmith? Isaac demanded, his breath coming quick as if he had been running.

—What's that to you? the young man answered in a loud voice, but looked down, gripping the gun hard, and took a step back against his horse.

—Cause that rifle's no good to you if you aint! Isaac said. Here!— and stepping close grabbed the rifle, jerked it free, and backed away. I'll show you!

He took a cap from his shirt pocket, fitted it, set the hammer, and raised the barrel pointing at the man's breast, all in one motion. Down the line of riders there was a prolonged clicking of gun hammers pulled back; silence. Isaac smiled; his finger found the trigger, eased back—dull knock of metal on metal, harmless, no fire, no explosion, no shot. Someone on the hotel porch let out a cheer.

—You see? Spring's no good. That's my rifle, I'm a hunter, get my living by it, but that gun's no use to me or anyone, the way it is. That's why I left it with the gunsmith.

Well now! Captain Blackthorn said, coming over to them. Well now, Lieutenant, don't take it hard. That's a clever young man, and I reckon he's done you a good turn. Where'd you be now if we get in a fight, going down to Texas, and your gun won't go? I reckon you better pick you a gun that'll shoot. . . .

The young lieutenant blushed crimson but did not answer. Swinging the rifle from one hand, Isaac walked back to the porch, stepped up among the others. The captain mounted and followed, turned and faced them. Looking to right and left along the line of horsemen, he raised an arm for silence.

—Folks! I can see you're wondering what we're doin here, and before we set spur to horse and take our departure for the South, I'm goin to tell you, the captain declaimed in a loud voice, in accents that might once have been Missouri or Arkansas, if not Texas. We've enjoyed your hospitality—can see you're gentlemen, and we wish we could know you better before we go. Well, now! you say. Why you treat us so damn rough, runnin off our guns and horses, if that's your sentiments? And I'll tell you. Reason is, we've been done the same ourselves, and weren't nothin for it but we had to find others to get even on. And the best thing you can do, and my advice is, go and find others to get even on yourselves! And when you do, we aint got nothin gainst you, cause you've been square with us, but we wish you luck—. And if you're ever down Texas-way and happen around where we are, y'all come'n see us, and we'll treat you white. Good day!

With a bow and a sweep of his fur hat Captain Blackthorn turned his horse and rode off down the line at a gallop, and the others fell in behind him, returning the way they had come, taking the military road west.

A few miles out from Salina the road to Fort Larned, linking at the Great Bend with the old road to Santa Fe, was joined by another coming west from Topeka. Late that same morning, as a rolling, rattling stagecoach drawn by two span of big gray mules slowed for the Elkhorn Creek crossing, a party of men rode out from behind one of the buttes that rises, castle-like, north of the Smoky Hill, wheeled across the track in front, and, before the astonished driver or his conductor could get their guns up—*Pull up there, driver, pull up!*—ordered a halt with pistols drawn and aimed. The driver reined in his team. Shouts for all to get down and stand aside, emphasized by a shot in the air, and after a deliberate minute one door of the stage swung out and the passengers complied. There were four of them:

Dutch Bill Greiffenstein with his Cheyenne wife Jennie, returning to their trading post from a visit to Topeka; Colonel Jesse Leavenworth, aging son of the famous soldier for whom the fort and town were named, himself a graduate of West Point, retired and lately recalled by a commission in the Colorado infantry, traveling now to take up a command at Fort Larned; and Lizzie Inman, a blue-eyed, downright woman who since Topeka had talked steadily, in accents of Great Britain, of her impending visit to Bill Mathewson at his post, of how he meant her to marry him and whether or not she would accept him and the tiresome life of an Indian trader.

As they watched, the raiders gathered around the mules, holding their heads, hastily cutting through the harness, while others disarmed the driver and his partner, promising no harm if they gave no trouble. A tall, rosy-cheeked young man came over to the passengers and demanded their guns, if they had any, and their money.

—Now just you listen to *me*, my man! cried Miss Inman, face flaming, voice rising in fury. My name's Elizabeth Inman, and I've come out to this godforsaken country to marry Mister Bill Mathewson. And if you take anything that's mine or touch one hair of my head— or any of my friends here—you'll answer to Mister Mathewson for it —and you'll wish you'd never been born!

A big, black-bearded man, watching from his horse at a little distance, called out—Lieutenant! You can leave these people be!—and coming toward them at a walk removed his hat and reached down to offer the young woman his hand. Captain Jeremiah Blackthorn, Miss Inman, ma'am! he said. I could wish to have met you in happier circumstances, ma'am, for I know Bill Mathewson of old, in the mountains, before folks called him Buffalo Bill, and you have my word we mean you no harm. I'll be pleased if you give Bill my respects when you see him—

—I should like to know what you call harm, Captain! she loftily answered. Leaving us stranded in this desert with no team for our coach—

—An accident of war, Miss Inman, the captain assured her. We require these mules for the service of our country. But—he raised one hand before she could break in—you are not twenty miles out from the little town of Salina, and if you can ride—

—I can ride, sir! she said with undiminished vehemence.

—If you can ride, ma'am, the captain mildly continued, you shall have the pick of the horses in our cavayard, and a saddle too, to convey you there—I regret we have no sidesaddle to offer—

—You may bring them over, Lizzie Inman commanded, and we shall see!

—I do not believe I've had a better day's luck since I come out to Kansas, said Isaac sententiously as he sat on the edge of the bed, talking by the light of the single candle. Except, of course, the day I met you, my dear, he added with a smiling nod to Marie, who lay propped against the headboard.

—Oh, of course! said Marie with wifely tolerance as she heard his story through again.

—Not that I put much store by getting that runty little Indian pony back, he continued. No, I'd about concluded I was well rid of him and I'd get something better—for a man is known by the stock he keeps. But there we are, getting up runners to go to Fort Riley—and here comes my pony down the street, rearing and steaming and kicking out his heels, twenty miles an hour—and this beautiful young lady on his back, pumping along like a cavalry trooper, golden hair streaming in the breeze, and singing out like an Indian!—Oh, my—.

—She was surely a sight, Marie prompted.

—And here I am, the only man in Salina that's still *got* all his horses and his mules—and oxen too. And the only two working guns—

—I think, said Marie seriously, sitting forward, arms around her knees—I think, Isaac, we should give our thanks to God.

—Oh, but I *do*, he quickly agreed. But I thank my luck too—*our* luck. And hope it stays good.

Isaac had been out in Salina's one street with the other men when Miss Inman came riding in the previous afternoon—the raiders had neglected to tell her they had cleaned the town out in the morning; had recognized the pony, caught the bridle, and helped her down. He rode out to Bill Bean's, brought in Bird and Regina and his mule team, and started immediately to relieve the travelers; the young lady, winded but undaunted, refreshed by tea with Marie and Mrs Phillips, had insisted on going along and accepted the loan of Marie's horse and saddle. When the stagecoach came in that evening, hauled with patched and improvised harness, Mrs Phillips offered Miss Inman the hospitality of her front room and sofa, while the other travelers put up at the hotel to wait for the fresh team of mules sent for from Junction City. They would be starting on to Fort Larned probably the next afternoon.

—I've a mind to go on with them, Isaac resumed. Not that they need *me* along, he added with a laugh, when they've Miss Lizzie Inman for company—. But the thing is—I know Bill Mathewson, like him, I'd like to see him again, and it might be we could do some business together. And it wouldn't *cost* anything. The stage agent wanted to give me a pass when I wouldn't take money for use of my mules. And it's not like I'd be gone long—two or three days and come back on the next stage east. . . .

—Oh, you must *go*, dear Isaac, Marie assured him as he waited for her consent. If you think you can do some good.

—*Still*, he reflected, now she had conceded, I don't want to press my luck too far or fast. And I oughtn't to leave you here alone. . . . You know, I've been thinking—I promised Colonel Phillips I'd keep his family safe, but when he's back—Marie, we've got to get you away from here, and our little one—and at the thought he reached out, pulled her to him, and for a long minute held her close.

—If I had parents of my own, she said, looking him in the eyes when he released her, I should go home to them, for my lying-in.

—We'll go to Burlingame, he said as if the idea had just come to him. You can be with your uncle—and there's people you know in the town, and Vinnie—you'll be safe.

—There are your parents in Iowa, Marie said, sitting forward, I should like to know them, and your sister. Your mother has been most kind when she has written, she seems to want us to come. Do we not owe it them?

He considered in silence.—It's a long way, he said. Two hundred miles by stage, and the boat—down to Saint Louis and up the Mississippi—

—I am not afraid, Isaac.

He stood up, suddenly tired; bent down to kiss her again, resettle the pillows.

—Let's talk of it in the morning, he said.

With a puff of breath he blew out the light and began to unbutton his shirt.

Marie sent a letter off to Burlingame by the next stage east, and in a week a cordial invitation came back from her uncle. Isaac after all dissuaded himself from visiting Mathewson's place and made do with a message carried by Miss Inman. Just what business they could do together was anyhow not yet clear in his mind. Despite his reputation, Mathewson, it seemed, no longer hunted much on his own account except, perhaps, for sport and occasionally to supply meat for his two trading posts; his main business was trading, and the post at the Great Bend was well placed for it. His own place on the Saline, however he admired it, however convenient as a base for hunting, wasn't worth half one of Mathewson's on the Santa Fe Road, and only the Kaw came in regularly, sometimes the Otoe, but the others were only war parties passing through and went elsewhere for their trading—to Mathewson, probably, or the posts of the big fur companies up on the Platte and the Missouri. If he wanted to trade with the Sioux and Cheyenne and the others, it meant loading the goods and going out to their villages, maybe hundreds of miles. But now with his own place on the Saline, and Mathewson's, another up the Solomon, and maybe out somewhere, in the Indian Territory—they'd have an arc of trading posts right across the Central Plains, pull all the tribes in, and Mathewson in charge of the trading for all of them, known and respected, feared too, from his half a lifetime in the West, and Isaac could manage the supplies and selling off the robes and furs as they came in.

He did not for that matter yet see clearly what he wanted himself: to be a great trader, perhaps, somewhere out on the Plains, living behind adobe walls of his fort like a prince in his castle, or maybe a merchant in an office at St Louis, buying and selling and managing others. But land—it seemed it was land he wanted, and not just to sit on or break his heart over, working it, but land to make money from. Speculating, they called it, but no different from speculating in the cups of sugar or the yard goods you traded an Indian for a buffalo robe—it was what every man who came to Kansas was up to, if he could, if he had the knack for it: get your name on some land and let those who come after pay you for it.

Isaac and Marie started for Burlingame three days later. For the first time since the raid he drove to the ranch, cleaned up, secured doors and windows; harreled up the last of the smoked meat so as to have something of his own to offer in Colonel Titus' house; and loaded the remaining flour and sugar, some bars of lead, a keg of powder, to store in the relative safety of the little house at Salina. The horses—Singing Bird, Marie's Regina, and the two ponies meant for hired men's use—made an awkward string behind the wagon, slowing them even if Isaac had not become dutifully careful of his wife's comfort.

They were three days on the road. Isaac had brought his tent but did not use it. He had made a place for their bed near the front of the wagon, and a chair with a back for Marie to sit in, made fast with rawhide to staples set in the wagon sides, but mostly she sat beside him on the rough seat he had put across the front since buying the mules, while he drove. She laughed at his solicitude but was becoming noticeably heavy with the child; on the rough ground where they camped she moved with arms out for balance, feeling the weight of the life growing in her, and let him carry the water for cooking and washing; once at a rocky stream crossing he insisted on stripping off his trousers and carrying her over.

Isaac within a week had tired of the colonel's easy hospitality. He was idle, superfluous; activity in the household lapped in silvery rings outward from Marie, and the babe swelling her belly was its center. She stayed in bed mornings, reading, and Vinnie carried up tea; came down to dinner leaning carefully on the stair rail and afterward used the time in sewing and knitting with nearly the energy she had spent on household furnishings and her own clothes in the weeks before their wedding; and in the late afternoons the ladies of the town came in for tea, and their hushed voices and delicate laughter filtered through the firmly closed door of the parlor.

Isaac wrote to Bos at Franklin proposing a winter hunt, but no answer came; Bos was not much for letters. He wrote again, extolling the upper Solomon and its two forks, new country to both of them, and still heard nothing. And finally, as the days turned to December, he set out his terms: take the wagon and the team boarded at Salina, since the winter would be hard on mules, and he would hire a boy, if he could find one, to keep the camp and help with skinning, and they would go halves on whatever they took. After a week Bos's letter came, written in pencil and smudged, on a lined half-sheet:

Say Pardner—
   Yor Hunt sounds good—Wil meet you at Saleena about 15th of Month—Misora has throwed off some on inlistment Bonty—

That night, lying beside him, not moving and her breath coming slow, simulating sleep, Marie took his right hand and held it to her belly. Except for a brotherly kiss at rising and retiring, and other such impersonal gestures, he had kept himself from her since they left Salina. He let the hand stay, but tense and hardly touching, fearful that the least careless pressure would crack it, burst it open like a great egg and spill its contents, wet and thick and warm, across the bed, and—. Through the flannel of her nightdress he felt the hard lump of her navel protruding from the tight-stretched skin and muscle of her belly. Then: something firm and purposeful thrust at his palm as if in protest, no mistake about it, he felt it distinctly.

—God in heaven, Marie! he said aloud, and jerked his hand away as if it had been burned.

—It is all right, Isaac, Marie said in a low, grave voice. She found his hand again in the dark, stroking, soothing. He has been doing that for weeks. Sometimes in the mornings, lying abed, I feel it, and I can look and see—like he is waking up, and thinking *It is time to come out now*—or only lying there dreaming of paradise and rolling over in his sleep. . . . Missus Schuyler says his heartbeat should be heard now —it is hardly a month yet—

—Is that a fact? said Isaac, suddenly interested and alert, his caution forgotten. *Can* you?

—I do not hear it, I can *feel* it—for weeks now, I do not know when it began—as constant as my own, but different and apart—

—Say now, I've got to hear that! he said, and setting the springs jangling he threw the bedclothes back, sat up, knelt on the mattress, and cocked his ear lightly to the bulging round of her stomach; for what seemed long minutes nothing came, the scratch and rustle of her garment, magnified, something, faintly heard or felt, her own heart, the unhastening pulse of her blood—. He held his breath, expelled all other sound, became all ear, listening with his whole being: the ear of God laid to the skin of the universe. And yes, at last, something else, a kind of liquid stirring there, a turning, like a great fish that rises lazy and effortless from the muddy river depths, you see an eye and a flash of white belly rolling in the sunlight, tail fin for an instant riving and surface—and gone, no more, as if it had not been; but something there had been for a moment, submerged but alive and making itself known, and a pulse or beat distinct from hers, as she had said, it skirred across his mind like a voltaic current.

—Oh my dear God!

He brought his head up, lay full length again, his head beside hers on the pillow, body rigid. After minutes, she stirred, raised herself on one elbow; fingertips touched his cheekbones, tight-closed eyes, and came away wet.

—I'm going on a hunt, leaving tomorrow on the stage. We'll take the team and wagon from Salina. I promised. . . .

—I know.

—How do you know? he demanded. I didn't know myself, till—

—Your letter from Mister Bos, what else would he write of? But I knew you had to go.

—Can't just sit here idle, can I? Got to get a living—for all of us.

—It is *all right*, Isaac. I shall be all right—and when you come back, I shall introduce you to our son.

Awkwardly she slipped her arm under his shoulders, turned him to her, held him, caressing. Released and comforted, he roused himself.

—What makes you so sure it's a boy? he said, grinning into the darkness.

—Missus Schuyler says it moves like a man, but I knew already. I shall call him Isaac. Your name.

—And Bisonnette for a second name! he said with finality. And if you're wrong—if it turns out a girl, we'll call her Marie—Little Marie. . . .

They lay long together, his arm across her ripe small breasts, his cheek pillowed on her shoulder. At length—Isaac, I'm cold, she said. Pull up the covers. . . .

XIV

Whitewater

Senator Samuel C. Pomeroy was seated at the writing table in his room at the Chase Hotel when he heard the heavy tread approaching along the hall that was most likely Cyrus Holliday. Laying his pen aside, he drew his watch out: nearly eleven o'clock; a discreet and punctual man. Returning the watch to his vest pocket, he closed the leather-bound journal reserved for his most private memoranda, stood up, and placed the book under the pillows of his bed, smoothing back the coverlet; although in public he cultivated an air of principled detachment from the mundane concerns of ordinary men, he was in practice a methodical man who had long since mastered the successful rogue's first axiom—keep accurate records of your business and never lie to yourself. It most decidedly would not do for that record to fall into another's hands, and the best way of guarding against that distressing possibility was to make sure no one else knew of its existence; but the record itself must be kept.

The Senator's nearly two years in the seat of power had fleshed him out considerably around the middle and under the chin, had polished the last thin hairs from his deep-browed skull and grayed his abundant side whiskers, but these changes only enhanced the appearance of benign well-being he presented to the public. He had not been long in mastering the mechanics of government: finding the point at which the local interests of one's constituents intersect with the national interest. Once a man has that fulcrum under his hands, he can lever his colleagues along to suit his purposes, and if a little private benefit falls by the way—*Why, sir, I ask you: Is not the laborer worthy of his hire?* For all its dignity and power, the Senate of the United States was no different in its principles from the Kansas Territorial Relief Commission.

Just now the fulcrum, the meeting point of divergent forces, was railroads and public land, and if the war was in many ways a nuisance, it offered the great benefit that after twenty years of argument the Southerners were no longer present to stand in the way of a central route, and the Northerners were not disposed to place the supposed rights of a handful of savages on the Western prairies ahead of the national interest. Working with purpose and therefore persuasively, Senator Pomeroy had made a nice division of the choice riverfront lands of the Kaw half-bloods around Topeka; had himself written the new treaty by which his own Atchison and Pikes Peak Railroad would acquire the Kickapoo reserve lands and laid it before the Senate; and this past summer had helped set in place the Pacific Railroad Act, the keystone in the great arch of a transcontinental system of transportation. Altogether, Mr Pomeroy could look back with satisfaction on his labors in the vineyard, and forward in anticipation to grander works to come—not, he fancied, the sort of feelings entertained by the other Senator from Kansas. Jim Lane had no sense of purpose: up to the White House instructing the President how to conduct the war, out to Missouri raising an army, back to Kansas to arrange the elections; like a Roman candle shooting off fire in all directions—and might hit something too, but a man never knew where he was aiming.

Lane was the main reason Pomeroy had elected to spend a few days of the Christmas recess at Topeka. Back at the time of statehood they had pooled their votes in the legislature to elect each other, but Lane had not proved a satisfactory partner in the Senate. He had had it all his own way in the fight with Governor Robinson—Robinson had chosen not to stand in the November election, was judged to be finished with politics, and Lane's man was succeeding him, or one thought to be Lane's man. Pomeroy was inclined to a longer view, and therefore had stopped at Leavenworth to call on the new governor, and now had spent an afternoon in serious and private conversation with Charles Robinson. This was the matter he had been committing to his journal.

The heavy steps were marching nearer the door. The Senator turned down the light on the writing table, leaving the others bright, took up a book, and seated himself in an armchair in the corner. It was a satisfactory room, on the third floor near a back stairway that enabled visitors to come and go without passing through the lobby.

The steps ceased. A silence, and then two peremptory raps on the door. The Senator waited a moment.

—Come in! he sang. The door is open.

The door swung inward and Cyrus Holliday stepped in, a big, thin-haired, bearded man who moved with threatening abruptness, an air of violence barely contained.

—Cyrus! Mr Pomeroy said, smiling gently but without getting up. So good of you to take time from your many affairs. There's some excellent old Bourbon whisky in the wardrobe if you'd like—

The courtesy was wasted. Turning his back, Holliday closed the door with silent firmness, stooped and turned the key in the lock, then tried the knob to make sure.

—Or there's brandy, of course. . . . The Senator's smooth voice trailed off. Holliday straightened up, turned, and leaned back against the locked door, glaring down at him. Mr Pomeroy politely closed his book and put it aside.

—Now you look here, Sam! Holliday said with scowling harshness. I didn't come up here in the dead of night for chitchat. And if it's whisky I wanted, I'd as soon buy it in the public bar. The Senator gazed mildly back but answered nothing. Holliday seized a straight chair, jerked it across the room, and sat, knees nearly touching the other man's. Mr Pomeroy pressed himself a little deeper in the easy chair and folded his hands across his belly, offering a look of innocent attention. No, Sam, Holliday continued, what I want to know is, how d'you keep so busy down there with railroad business and none of it comes the way of my Atchison and Topeka? Now answer me that!

—Really, Cyrus! said Pomeroy in an aggrieved tone. I thought I deserved better of you, after the way I put my shoulder to the wheel to push that Pacific Railroad Act—

—Oh, come now! You know that was my convention here at Topeka started that—and the citizens petitioning for railroad routes across Kansas. But it don't do a thing for the Atchison and Topeka.

—We take our oath to serve the general good, Pomeroy coolly reminded him.

—General good, my ass, Sam! Holliday growled. No, you look here. I didn't say a word about that half-blood land of yours, though it's right where we've got to run our road if we ever get building—and when we do, your land'll be worth fifty an acre if it's worth a dollar. And I stood still for the Delaware business and this Potawatomi swindle. But this Kickapoo business now—by God, that's another matter.

—Ah! said Pomeroy, lifting his eyes piously to heaven. I'm sorry, Cyrus, but that matter is before the Senate. I really cannot—

—The Kickapoo Fraud! Holliday said, punching his palm with his bony fist. That's what the papers are calling it. The Kickapoo *Fraud!*

The Senator sighed.—No man in public life is immune to the calumnies of enemies.

—Taking that land and handing it over to your miserable Pikes Peak Road, Sam! A hundred and thirty-five thousand acres of prime land at a dollar an acre, and not one quarter-section for the Atchison and Topeka!

—Cyrus, I'm shocked, said Pomeroy in a low voice. The contents of that treaty are privileged. It has been presented to the committee only in executive session.

—Would you like to hear more, Sam? Holliday asked with a hard smile, and leaned back in his chair, folding his arms across his massive chest. About what your share's supposed to be? and your brother-in-law's?

The Senator considered for a time.—No, I don't believe I do, he said finally. But I do think it hard. It's not as if you'd been forgotten. There's still the Osage land, right across southern Kansas, ten or—I don't know, *twenty* times the quantity of that Kickapoo reserve, and hardly a squatter's yet set foot, as I hear it—

—Osage is a long way off, way I figure it, Holliday broke in, but let me tell you. We aint hardly started on that Kickapoo business, and you don't think of something better for us, and quick, your treaty's going to sit in committee till it turns to dust—and not just the Kickapoo Fraud, neither, but *Pomeroy's* Kickapoo Fraud to every woman and child in the nation. And when we're finished you won't find ten citizens of Kansas to vote you into the county poor farm. . . .

Mr Pomeroy frowned, knitting his untroubled brow, clasped his hands tight, and finally looked the other straight in the eyes with an agreeable smile.—What can I say, Cyrus? he said. Blood is thicker than water. I've made no secret of my interest in the Pikes Peak Road.

—You've got an interest in the Atchison and Topeka, Holliday came back. In the state records as one of the incorporators. And the stock you took aint never cost you one cent—

—But, *Cyrus*, Pomeroy pleaded. I am not *president* of the Atchison and Topeka. . . .

—Well, God *damn!* said Holliday, awed in his turn.

—*Please*, Cyrus, said the Senator, raising one plump hand and putting on his Sunday-school teacher's expression.

Holliday slumped in his chair, chin resting in his palm, eyes blank. He fumbled a cigar from an inner pocket of his coat, bit the end, spat, struck a match, puffed; and in afterthought offered the case. Senator Pomeroy shook his head.

—Look here, Sam, Holliday said finally. I'm as ready a hand as you are for making money—land or railroads or stocks, or anything that's going. But there's a difference—that's all you want—or, well, give you your due—power maybe, and hold your head high in the United States Senate and among the folks in Kansas, and maybe someday a great fine house somewhere, sit on the porch and look out and all the land out there, as far as you can see, belongs to you—. But me, I don't give a God *damn* about any of that—there aint one thing on this earth that I really want except to get this railroad built—and running, clear across the Plains—and knock these other bastards flat, that think they can run against me. And I'll tell you, if it would help me get that done

—why, I'd put the devil himself in the president's chair and never think twice—. He stopped himself, gave a quick upward glance at the other's face, and looked away. No offense, Sam—

—Please, Cyrus. I take it as a compliment, from you.

—But you understand, I can't hand the office over, and the things that go with it, on just promises—no, I need something more material than that. And what I need is land, right-of-way and a decent slice out of the public domain, and then—why then I can take my bonds and stocks to the money-men at Boston and New York with something to back em up, and we're off and running. . . .

—There *is* that Osage tract, Pomeroy said thoughtfully.

—No, Sam, Holliday said with an emphatic shake of his head, I've looked into that. Too big even for you and me to bring off—it aint ten times or twenty times the Kickapoo tract, like you said, it's fifty miles wide and near three hundred long, according to treaty, nine and a half million acres, more or less. And too chancy—these Osage, they aint like these other little emigrant tribes, and it'll take more than a barrel of tanglefoot and a bushel of beads to pry em loose from their land. Besides, it's too far south for the route we mean to go—

—Then what *do* you want, Cyrus?

—I just want as good as Congress gave the Illinois Central, Holliday said, blowing an emphatic jet of smoke, and sat back, smiling.

The Senator reflected.—Six square miles of public land for every mile of track? As I recall.

—Let's say ten—aint got the population yet, and everything costs more, out here, besides something over for profit. You get us that, Holliday pursued, rubbing his hands together, and we'll be laying track within a year—start south from Topeka, way I figure it, and pick up the old Santa Fe Road and follow it out—been proving fifty years and still the best—no high mountains or snowed-in winter passes, and we capture the southern route to the Pacific and Old Mexico. And you'll be elected the day Lincoln puts his name to the bill. That's a promise. . . .

—It's a large undertaking, far more than putting through some Indian treaty—both houses of Congress, and the President—

—Of *course* it's big, Sam. Two thousand miles of right-of-way—and you with your hand on every mile, and every little town site mushrooming up, and every citizen of Kansas calling you benefactor. Aint anything worth doing that isn't big.

—I can try, the Senator said. Put it before my colleagues, show them the advantages—

—You'll do better than that, Sam, Holliday said, very hard. I made you a promise. I'll have your word on it.

—Yes, he said, I'll do it, on my honor—whatever is possible, yes!—

—*Well* then, said Holliday, smiling again and standing up, let's have

a drink on it, is what I say. Where'd you say you hide this fancy
whisky of yours?

Isaac and Bos had been about two weeks in their winter camp on
the North Fork of the Solomon when a heavy snow came—started in
the night soft as a whisper, kept up all the next day, a billowing mat
of cotton laid across the earth, and departed the morning of the second day, bright sun rising on cloudless blue and the snow devils
whirling across the surface, leaving the tent sagging like the udder of
an old dried-up cow and two feet of snow on the level, as Isaac measured when he went out, weightless and fine as double-milled flour.
Something about the camp misgave him that morning: too open and
not enough timber for shelter, firewood, browse for the cattle, he
could not say what; but made up his mind to move.

It was toward the end of January, but he was no longer certain of
the date, one day was like another. Isaac had reached Salina on the
appointed day by the stage from Topeka, bringing with him Titus
Sexton as camp helper and apprentice skinner, another out-of-work
mill hand recommended by Cyrus Holliday's foreman; a tall, well-
made youth of eighteen who showed signs of intelligence and humor,
and who, heeding the talk of a coming Union conscription, judged
he'd rather take his chances on buffalo and Indians out beyond the
frontier.

They were a week reaching the hunting ground: out the Saline to
the mouth of Paradise Creek, up that to its source and over the divide
to the waters of the Solomon, across its South and Middle forks to the
main stream known at that point as the North Fork—farther than
Isaac or his partner had yet carried a hunt. They traveled at an easy
pace, hunting on the way with an eye out for elk. Bos had stopped
through Leavenworth coming west: elk hides were in demand, bringing five dollars apiece, common gray wolf two-fifty or better, in
greenbacks; buffalo were still plentiful and bought by the pound
seven or eight cents. Until the blizzard came, there were only patches
of desiccated snow that had lain a month under thick timber and on
north slopes, none fresh. At night and in the mornings till the sun
came warming over the eastern hills, the cold felt like an Iowa winter,
or nearly so, down around zero. They chose the North Fork camp in
part for its shallow but constant water, in part for the several small
creeks converging, the broken ridge land walling the river bottom
north and south, promising country for game. They announced their
presence with a huge fire the first night, but no visitors presented
themselves. No one else, it seemed, Indian or white hunter, was in
that country then. Bos said nothing of Bru Willard's absence, maybe
only saving the wage, since Isaac had offered to provide his own skinner, and Isaac thought it none of his business to ask.

There were, it turned out, small bands of buffalo wintering up the canyons, nosing through the patchy snow to get at the short-grass, with their following of wolves in plenty; elk, two or three to a bunch, on the high ground; a few antelope. The hunters fell into a daily routine, by unspoken consent: hiked out singly in the mornings, taking different directions, till they found something to kill; did their own skinning, and in the afternoon bundled the hides in packs to carry back to the camp. On days when they took more than they could skin or carry, they opened the carcasses to save the hides from the wolves, set strychnine baits, and next day brought a wagon to haul back the take. Titus, most days keeping camp alone, was much occupied but cheerful: boiling the coffee and frying the meat for breakfast and supper, scraping and drying the hides, rendering tallow in Isaac's big iron kettle when the hunters took time to bring it in. The oxen, in constant appetite, took half his time—leading them to drink, cutting cottonwood or elm and lopping the top branches to feed them. Occasionally Isaac let him drive a wagon out and watched critically while he finished the skinning.

—We got to move camp, Isaac said. He kicked the snow off the woodpile, pulled a log out and set it on the fire. We've about cleaned out, everywhere we can reach from here, he added, as if he needed to explain.

Bos, squatting by the fire, spooned sugar into his coffee.—Where d'you figure to find better?

—There's a creek comes in about four miles west, steep ridges both sides, and up at the head a grove of big cottonwoods—good shelter, it's where I got those bull elk that time. We can make a real winter camp in there, won't have to move again till spring. Bos stirred the coffee, blew the steam away, but said nothing; could hunt as well up there, he figured, as down along the river, and if Pride was set on moving—. I'm going to chain up and take my wagon on ahead. I'll leave you and Titus to load the hides and you can follow my track when you're done. . . .

—You're in a tearing hurry, partner, was all Bos answered.

—I aim to get the new camp built so we can get back to work.

Once he had brought his oxen in and yoked them, Isaac hesitated, picturing the route in his mind: four miles or so up the frozen riverbank, then turn south and follow the creek up to the grove, another four miles maybe, easy going all the way except for the deep snow the team would have to pull through; or climb the west wall of the creek valley and follow the ridge top where most likely the snow had blown clear by now or never settled, a hard climb for the cattle and a sharp descent at the end, but more direct than the other way, one side of the triangle instead of two. He prodded the nigh lead ox with a stick and started toward the slope.

They got no more hunting that day. Isaac found a level place in among the trees, cleared the snow, dragged fallen logs and notched them with his ax, and began setting them in place to make a low, open-front, slope-roofed shed. The outlook suited him: he faced the cabin west to catch the sun till it went behind the opposite ridge; you looked out now through the trees into morning brightness as if from within the walls of an immense, shadowy, silent church. From a little distance, hardly ten yards in any direction, you could not tell that a camp was there, only a random-fallen heap of deadwood, unless signaled by the light from a fire, the blue smoke eddying among the treetops. The creek was frozen tight below the camp and hidden under the new snow, but the spring it fell from ran free, collecting in a bucket-deep pool before its outflow vanished beneath the crust of ice.

Bos and Titus came in around noon and helped him finish, windproofing the cabin with green buffalo hides weighted with slabs of wood. It was mid-afternoon before they were through dinner, taking their time over it. Leaving the boy to tend the oxen and make up the woodpile, Isaac and Bos took their guns and, together for once, climbed the ridge behind the camp and worked their way back along the way they had come. Isaac wanted to look out likely directions for the next day's hunt, and if they came on any game, there was still time to get it and bring the hides in before dark—.

—Get down! Isaac said in an urgent whisper and laid himself flat in the snow, pointing ahead and down the slope—three quarters of a mile off something dark roiled the snow along the track they had left coming from the old camp, tossing spumes of snow in the air as if a wounded animal floundered in a drift.

The movement ceased and the dark shape revealed itself as a party of Indians, twenty or thirty of them, Arapaho or possibly Sioux, tightly bunched and on foot; a hunting party most likely, out for meat but alert for any other game that presented, and they would have found the other camp, coming down the river, the carcasses of their two weeks' kill. Several were down on hands and knees now in the snow, examining the trail sharply etched in the afternoon light, others peering in all directions, up the slope where Bos and Isaac lay watching.

—They're tracking us, Bos said.

—Your rifle loaded?

—Sure it is. But I left the pistol back in camp.

—It aint likely they'd come charging uphill, on foot in the snow and no good cover, but a careful shot or two'd change their mind quick enough—we'd have time to reload.

—Pears they're havin some discussion bout what they're findin. Might be they can't read our track too good and think we're more'n we are.

—They can see the wagon wheels fresh in the snow and the ox tracks, that's white hunters. And a big party, the extra men'd be walking along behind, you'd see the boot prints clear enough.

—You reckon they got a notion of our cook fire?

—We're low down on the other side of the ridge and the trees hold the smoke. Aint much wind, but it's coming the wrong way to smell it—*I* can't smell it anyhow, Isaac concluded, lifting his head slightly to test the air.

The Indians seemed to be arguing among themselves, as Bos had said, some pointing south or up the ridge, others back toward the river, but the light wind carried no sound of their voices. At length, decided, they turned and started back the way they had come, in single file, moving at a jogging trot. Isaac and Bos lay in the snow, watching, till they were out of sight.

They made no fire that night but chewed at strips of frozen jerky brought for emergency and afterward sat up in the cabin, wrapped in their buffalo robes, loaded rifles across their laps and talking in whispers to spell each other awake. When the light came, still cautious of making a fire, they left the oxen securely tied and all three climbed the ridge again with loaded rifles, Bos with his revolver in his belt, and followed it down till they were above the first camp. Isaac and Bos spread out and watchfully descended, guns raised, leaving the boy at the top to cover them, but the Indians had merely passed through—scratching at the bare earth where the tent had been but finding nothing, only that they had three men to deal with, three different sizes and shapes of boot—and continued down the river; twenty or thirty miles off by now, Isaac judged with relief, and signaled Titus to come down.

—You know what it was? Isaac said as the boy came toward them. They're hunters, don't like folks interfering with their game any more'n we do, but they followed our trail till it looked like we were going south, right out of their country and wouldn't bother them any more. So now they can get on with their hunt. . . .

Still cautious, he led them back along the Indians' trail, guns ready, keeping watch on the high ground that rose on both sides of the frozen river, stopping frequently to examine the tracks. After two hours they reached the place where the creek came in, a narrow trickle sheathed in ice, and there the Indians had camped one night— a circle of trampled snow on the riverbank, a broken arrow with its steel head removed, a pair of worn-out moccasins, a half-dozen small fires scattered Indian-fashion around the site, a few broken buffalo ribs that wolves had already been at; the same creek whose source a few miles up the valley Isaac had picked for their new camp. A snow-shoe rabbit, hiding motionless against the whiteness of the snow, started as they came near, and lifting his rifle he dropped it with a shot to the head.

—Now how's *that* for luck? he shouted, laughing, and ran to retrieve it.

The echo rolled back from the hills to the north, fading; died.—Wouldn't be no luck if them bastards heard that and come lookin to see what did it, Bos said.

—No, they've cleared out, Isaac said with assurance. He threw the rabbit down, knelt beside it, knife out. And there's our dinner, he said, or the appetizer to it anyhow. And I'll tell you something else, he continued. I was thinking of coming this way to the new camp, it just seemed the natural way and easier on the team—I'd have run right into them. Or if we never moved camp at all—

—How'd you know to do it? Titus asked, round-eyed.

—I didn't! Isaac looked up, grinning. It's just, I had a kind of feeling about camping along this river. Like a great highway, in winter, every passerby looks in and knows your business better'n you know it yourself.

Later, his share of the hot meat finished, the thin bones broken, sucked, discarded, Bos wiped his sleeve across his lips and stood up, still doubtful.—I'd as soon we was startin back, in the morning, he said.

—What *for?* Isaac demanded. The hunting's good. It'll last till spring.

—So I don't have some redskin ripping my belly up, some night.

—I *told* you—they won't come back this way. And if they did—they'd go right by our camp and never know anyone was in there.

—That sounds like Pride ridin for his fall, to *me*, Bos said.

Isaac gave him a sharp look but had no answer. Nevertheless, sobered but still elated, he insisted on scouting back to their camp along the western rim of the creek. They climbed laboriously up the ridge, stepping high, slipping back, the snow in places thigh-deep, and at the top knelt to steady their eyes for looking. There was no smoke anywhere within the horizon, no sign of other men, no Indian village in its winter refuge; only the faint shadow of the hunters' trail along the river edge. The sun was going low, deepening the shadows.

—Wouldn't it be grand? Isaac said. Just hitch up and start, and keep on going, on to the mountains and beyond, till you reach the sunset. Nothing to stop us, we've got the whole country to ourselves.

—I like it well enough right where we're at, Bos said. Long as the game lasts and the Indians don't get us.

—Denver City's out there, and the gold mines, about straight west. It's where I started for when I first came to Kansas, Isaac said, as if talking of something a lifetime ago.

—It's three hundred miles, and you'd starve, in winter, Bos said.

The river gives out, and the game—you'd have to go north and around by the South Platte, and lucky to get there, folks say.

—You young fellows could do it, Isaac said with a forced smile, and stood up. No wife and responsibilities! Did you know I might be a father now? My wife's having a baby. . . .

—*Ave Maria, gratia plena, Dominus tecum. Benedicta tu—*. Oh, my God, my God!

—What's she saying? It was Miss Shirley's voice from somewhere by the head of the bed, fluttering past like a bird in flight. What's she saying *now?* Is it *time—?*

—Praying, my dear, Mrs Schuyler answered with authority from her chair by the window, and a good thing too, for a woman brought to child-bed. In her own language, of course—she's French, you know, Canadian French. Vinnie! the old voice came sharp again. Keep bathing her brow with that cloth. Don't let her drop off.

—There, honey, there, the black woman crooned, and the damp cloth lightly touched and smoothed her forehead, cooling, caressing, the plump callused hand squeezed her own. It's all right, you're doin *fine*, Vinnie said again, it's goin to be all right—again, again. . . .

Sighing deeply, Marie loosed the tense muscles in her neck and felt her head settle on the pillow, her whole body coming unstrung, sinking into the mattress.

She felt her eyelids flicker and forced them open: Mrs Schuyler would not let her doze, but when the spasm passed the only feeling left was drowsiness. Vinnie had run to tell the old woman that it was starting and was sent home to time the contractions with Uncle Titus' watch, and presently Mrs Schuyler sailed into the bedroom with a dress pulled over her nightgown, still in her night cap, and Miss Shirley tripping along behind like the tail of a kite. Mrs Schuyler puffed with excitement and talked of her palpitations but knew what to do from her own children and took command. Vinnie was a comfort but knew only what she was told; Miss Shirley was hopeless.

Nothing Marie had ever heard from other women had prepared her for it, much less the terrible tales repeated in whispers over tea, of babies that came wrong, of mothers torn apart—. No, not pain, but a kind of wrenching and writhing in the bowels, and you strained to evacuate, to make it get over and stop, and leave you, and it would not, and all the while floating above you the anxiety looking down, repeating—*that my babe be born strong and whole, that I may do right for him,* not knowing how to do and no one to tell you; and far off a voice wailing, cannot catch the words, and it is your own voice, crying—. And then the spasm gone and no feeling left but exhaustion, like a wet cloth wrung dry—if only it would wait another minute, let me rest for it, get my breath—oh my God, yes, pain, it is, not death-pain but life-pain, oh, oh, oh—

—Isaac! Marie cried out, where is Isaac? Why will they not let him come? They are killing my husband—

—There, honey, Vinnie said, he's *comin*. Mist Isaac's all right, he's comin. . . .

—Vinnie! Mrs Schuyler commanded, you get on down to your kitchen and warm us a basin of water, bout time now—not too hot, mind. And a little clean oil and cotton wool, and a length of strong twine. And a good sharp *knife*, when you come—step along, now!

Marie forced her eyes wide, clenched her teeth—would not let herself scream again. Miss Shirley reached across the bed and pressed her hands together. Mrs Schuyler stood looking down on her from the foot of the bed, her face severe.

—You just let *him* do the work now, dear, Mrs Schuyler said firmly. All *you* got to do is help.

—Isaac! Isaac! . . .

—There now, said Mr Durfee, sliding the grudging stack of coins across his desk. A hundred in gold, best I can let you have this time, and the rest in greenbacks, Mister Salmon P. Chase's legal tenders, which they are, of course, that's the law—eight hundred fifty. Or you can leave some on account and I'll pay you interest like I done before, and another time when you've business to do it might be the rates'll have improved and be a little more favorable—can't *promise*. I don't make the exchange. He ducked his head apologetically.

—Let's see, Isaac said. A dollar in gold's one-fifty in greenbacks now, you said. That means if I find someone that'll take paper for gold, he'll give—sixty-five cents on the dollar, more or less—

—Yes*ss*, Mr Durfee doubtfully agreed.

—Then I believe I'll leave seven hundred and take my chances.

—Very well. Pursing his lips, Mr Durfee slowly counted out the fifteen paper bills, handed the sheaf to Isaac to verify. Standing, he drew his ledger toward him, dipped his pen, and made the entries. Confidentially and in strict privacy, he said, lowering his voice and glancing over his shoulder, you'll do well to turn it into gold every chance you get, that's what *I* do—wouldn't surprise me to see gold go *double* what it is now, way this war's going. And then when it's right up there—*buy greenbacks*. For sooner or later, win or lose, it's got to come down again, and the paper convertible to gold—

—What's this new money you said?

—National bank notes—haven't any come my way yet, the law only went through last month. But there's talk of starting up a national bank right here at Leavenworth, and if they do I believe I'll take some stock. It would be a great convenience, and a benefit to trade, to have our own bank of issue—first in Kansas—

—Just sounds to me like the old state banks, with their wildcat money.

—Well—I don't know that I'd—they've started up a new bureau at Washington, supposed to superintend and make em toe the mark by the rules Congress sets, same for all—that's the national part, and this bureau gives out the charters according to law and prints the notes and don't give em out till they're backed—oh, thirty percent, I think —by U.S. Treasury stock. But the state banks now—well, they can go on banking, I guess, but they're out of the money business. . . .

—Then it ought to be good money, these national notes.

Mr Durfee tilted his chair back, reflecting.—Might be, he conceded. Only they can redeem in coin or greenbacks, either way, I'm told, I don't know what good *that* is. But I aint seen any yet, as I say. . . . But say now, Mister Pride, he continued, here we sit chatting, and very pleasant it is too, when—he took his watch out—early yet, I know, still—whyn't you come along and take dinner with me?—and we can go on with our talk and not lose any time from business—I've hired an old widow lady to cook and keep the house, and there's lots of things been happening that you aint heard of, out in the wilds. And before Isaac could demur the merchant had jumped up and was briskly reaching his hat and coat down from the rack and singing out for someone to hitch up the buggy and bring it around front.

The snow lay along the upper Solomon when the hunters started east in early March—several light snows but no big one since the blizzard in January—but the new grass was already knee-high when they reached Salina, a passage from winter into spring in a distance of a hundred and fifty miles. Marie's one letter was already a month old when Isaac claimed it, his reckoning of dates a week out. Little Isaac had been born January 27, was strong, well, a hearty feeder, slept the night through, and followed his mother with his eyes; a good babe that his father would be proud of. Isaac carried the letter in his pocketbook and conned the sparse phrases over in private. At Leavenworth Abraham Bos took his thousand-dollar share of the proceeds from the hunt, half of it from wolf pelts, and started immediately back to Salina, elated and meaning to hire a helper of his own and go on hunting from the ranch. Isaac could not think beyond getting to Burlingame, seeing his child for the first time, and his wife. When it would be sense for them to travel anywhere he could not say—Marie not for weeks yet, the little one, by wagon, on the rough, sun-hardened roads, and the hot summer coming, not for months, probably. He doubted taking them to the ranch, but if not, then where?

Mr Durfee's housekeeper was a Mrs Gaylord, a fifty-year-old Methodist lady from Erie County, New York, of inflexible ways and decided opinions, freely offered, as of coming home for dinner fifteen minutes early with an unannounced guest. She nevertheless contrived to produce a platter of fried chicken hot from the oven with a quart of gravy, a plate of biscuits and more baking, a pot of prairie honey in the comb, a pitcher of fresh buttermilk, and the best butter Isaac had tasted since Iowa.

Mr Durfee's news was mainly of Kansas land (he mentioned the new conscription law, put through early in the month, only in passing—like the new governor and most other Kansans, he expected the state to keep up its quota with volunteers). By coincidence the Atchison & Topeka land grant was signed the same day as the draft, Sam Pomeroy taking the credit, although he was not known to have any special interest in the railroad—but would have now, no doubt. It provided nearly three million acres of land, but with a serious condition: the railroad, which had yet to lay a mile of track, must reach the Colorado line in ten years or the land would not be patented. Ten days after, the Senate approved Pomeroy's Kickapoo treaty, another sizable railroad benefit, this time to his own Pikes Peak Road; all the earlier talk of the Kickapoo Fraud had somehow died away. Now he was out for the biggest thing yet, a treaty for the Osage land, fifty miles wide right across southern Kansas, and every speculator with a railroad charter in his pocket would be around to claim his share and take his profit.

—What's that to me? Isaac said, refilling his cup. I don't have any interest in a railroad, or money to put in—and if I did—

—No, no! Mr Durfee impatiently interrupted, I'm not talking of railroads, I'm talking of land. *Kansas* land. *Well,* you say—maybe this Atchison and Topeka land is three million acres, but Kansas is *fifty* million, and what's that to me? But a man's got to consider the inwardness of it. Now, that three million's only every other section along the right-of-way, so the Land Office keeps the other half to sell at a good price—and worth more, too, of course, being near the railroad—so that's *double* the land taken out. And that aint all. The law gives them *in lieu* land, another ten miles each side of the line—which means, if they pick a section in their first grant and someone's claimed it before the law went through, they get to pick another farther out—which is *double again.* Every section of it land that can't no man claim, or even buy, until the railroad makes up its mind and takes out patent, which might be ten years off—and when the time comes, it won't come cheap, if it's worth having, let me tell you, no sir! Do you take my meaning, Mister Pride? Do you begin to see?

Isaac nodded, his brows creased in a frown of concentrated calculation.—It's a lot of land that's closed to the ordinary settler, if he aint rich and can't buy from the railroads and speculators. Unless he gets in first—

—Getting first aint *in* it, Mister Pride! Mr Durfee said, thumping his small fist for emphasis. The railroads are already there. For Cy Holliday's Atchison and Topeka—that's only one, could be five or ten others before it's done, aiming to build right across the state, and what's fair for one is fair for all—they'll *all* want their share. And when they're finished, won't be hardly enough left of the public domain for a man to build a respectable pigpen on—unless he can buy from them and pay their price. *Now* do you see? Why, there's our own LP and W, right here at Leavenworth—that's the Leavenworth, Pawnee and Western—let alone this Indian treaty land in eastern Kansas that Sam Pomeroy and the whole United States Senate is helping them to—

Isaac sat back, smiling.—You sure make me glad to hear you, Mister Durfee, he said. I've got my ranch in a bend of the river twenty miles out from Salina, and improvements, and a clear claim, and a paper from the town proprietor, Colonel Phillips, acknowledging it.

—Do you now? Mr Durfee said with something approaching a grin. A good claim, is it? Well, let me tell you about our LP and W. We mean to run from here over to the Kaw and then right up to the forks, and out the Saline or the Smoky Hill, or maybe both—and land grants all the way, same as the Atchison and Topeka. *Well*, you say— but I've got a claim along that right-of-way, right and proper according to law and custom and Colonel William A. Phillips. But what's any of *that* worth, compared with—

—A good twenty an acre, Isaac put in, if the railroad really does go through. And a thousand for my improvements—*if* I'd a mind to sell. . . .

Mr Durfee made a silent pantomime of laughing till the tears came, took a large bandanna from his pocket, shook it out, and dabbed his eyes.—No, you listen here, Mister Pride, he abruptly resumed. Compared with legal title from the Land Office, signed by the President, and all the different acts of Congress assisting public improvements— and millions in Eastern and Kansas capital and a whole army of lawyers—well, maybe they'd give a hundred dollars to quiet your claim and save a little nuisance, but if it's the land you want, you'll buy from them—their price, their terms. You want to fight it—well, you can take your papers and your witnesses, get up a claim club, hire lawyers of your own, go down to Washington and beg the Congressman to put in a private bill—. Yes, sir! That's the way—and you'll die a poor man and won't own title to land enough to dig a grave in—

—But that's not *right*, Isaac said, and shoving the chair back stood up and began to pace angrily back and forth.

—Course it isn't, Mr Durfee agreed. But it's *so*. And that, he continued after a pause, is why I wanted to get you thinking about Osage land and this treaty that's coming.

—Ah! Isaac sighed and resumed his seat, slumping forward with his elbows on the table. I figured you were working around to something. You want to use me to get some of this Indian land before Sam Pomeroy and his bunch—

—Don't mistake me, Mr Durfee sharply corrected him. I'm a merchant, got to keep my trade up, build it—got to look ahead—not that I wouldn't put money in cheap land and a chance for quick profit, but it aint what I'm after. No—but look ahead three or four years, depending on this war, and there's going to be railroads running west right across the state—and bringing emigrants out, making farms and building towns. And where's your buffalo hunting going to be then, or your wild tribes, bringing in robes to trade? Cleaned out! The whole Central Plains—and that'll be too bad, because we've done good business together these last three years, you and some others out there, and I'd like you to keep it up. But you won't, staying where you are—won't matter if you get to keep your little ranch or not, it won't be *worth* anything to you, not in the way of trade. And that's where this Osage business comes in. . . .

The merchant's plan for surviving the end of the Indian and fur trade on the Central Plains was double and took some telling. On the one hand, he was going north, onto the upper Missouri, where railroads and settlers, he figured, were twenty years off and the trade likely to continue all the rest of a man's life: it meant getting boats of his own to carry trading stock, going up against long-established fur companies—set up his own posts and drive them down by underselling till they were ready to get out. The South Plains—Indian Territory, western Texas, and beyond—were the same situation so far as the duration of the trade but with a difference: no big traders since the Chouteau brothers died out; a few Indians or half-breeds did a little trading, with goods that till the war were brought in from New Orleans and up the Red River or the Arkansas. And the Osage tract was the key to the trade in this country, as he saw it: a base; and for a hunter, buffalo in plenty the year around. But if a man wanted land—well, there weren't any settlers yet, hardly, and if he got his claim staked before Pomeroy finished writing his treaty, no doubt it would hold, as claims did on most other Indian lands; money to be made all around.

—Look here, Mr Durfee said. All I say is, go on down and have your visit with your family—and then go a little farther and have a look, kind of scout it out, and come and tell me. If the hunting's what they say, the trip'll pay for itself in buffalo hides. But if you like the look of it and decide to move your trade down there—why, listen, I'll fit you out with stock and go even shares on the profits! There!—And he reached his hand out, seized Isaac's, and shook it, and it was done. But suppose it does go, down there, he continued, thinking ahead—

and suppose I make my jump up the Missouri—well, you can see, it takes a man out in the field to make the business go, can't do it alone, sitting here at Leavenworth—

—The Whitewater country, Isaac said, remembering. That's what a man called it that I hired last year. Good hunting, he said. I don't know how much he knew about it—

—And that's exactly right! Mr Durfee said, as to a ready scholar. That's one of the rivers runs through it, of course the Arkansas is the big one. They were trying to organize a county before the war, Butler County—but scared out, most of them, Confederate Indians coming up and gangs of prairie pirates and horse thieves—had a county seat laid out right in the middle—a—a—

—Al Dorado, Isaac supplied. My man told me, something about gold.

—Of course! Mr Durfee said with enthusiasm. But say—he brought his watch out. Here's an hour gone by and business to be done. Come along now, and we'll load you up for your hunt.

Calling out to Mrs Gaylord, he took Isaac by the elbow and guided him toward the door; stopped.—Look here, he said. You want to know about the Whitewater country, there's a man in town can tell you, Bill Bemis—lies on the floor and shoots buffalo out his cabin door, to hear him tell—and then about once a year comes in with his hides on packhorses, don't *own* a wagon, like the old peddlers used to come through the village, in western New York, when I was a boy. Only Bill Bemis comes in dressed all in buckskins like an Indian or a cavalry scout—and aint taken a bath or trimmed his beard since he come to manhood, by the look of him. And lays around at the steamboat landing—come on, now, we'll go look for him there, and you can talk. Drunk, I expect. . . .

—Sun's up, Isaac said with a glance at the big window to the right of the chimney. Time we were starting. He shoved his chair back but Marie held him another moment, her cool, soft hand pressing his against the table.

—Do not wear yourself down, she said, in this heat. Find yourself a nice grove of trees by the river and lie up in the shade, when the day gets hot. And your mules will be better for the rest—

—I'd like to make Sycamore Springs by nightfall, camp with Dave Ballon, he said, and stood up. That Cherokee—he's usually got a few robes to trade.

—Three wives! Marie said, smiling. What any man would want with three wives I cannot imagine. . . .

—Keeps em busy cropping babies, for one thing, he said. Or tanning robes, and the young ones help the old ones, just like sisters, which maybe they are. And say, Marie, wouldn't that be the thing for you? A fat little Indian girl to help you out, and mind the little bunny on baking day, or when you've wash to do—

—Isaac Pride! Marie cried, but grinned back at him, and the baby cooed and gurgled and reached out his fat little hands to her. She caught him under the arms, swooped him high, and laid him gently on her shoulder. The oversize head relaxed, a thumb found his mouth, and the eyes half-closed, seeking sleep.

Isaac marveled, watching. Twenty pounds he must be by now, nearly seven months, yet she lifted him and carried him around like a kitten. So slender and slight, now her figure had come back, he had nearly forgotten, and her sweet breasts swollen taut with milk— strong as a man, but different, her strength all inside and hidden, like spring-steel covered in velvet.

It was Isaac who started the pet name they used between them, Bunny—not only the smallness and softness of him, but the way he lay in his cradle after feeding, kicking his legs up—as if he was wanting to get up and run, Isaac said, and sat by the hour, watching him at his exercises, and when the baby slept and woke again set him out on a rug to roll and try to crawl, and crawled across the floor himself to show him, pretending to be a bear. It was only natural, Marie said, that a Jackrabbit should be father to a Bunny; gently teasing him with his discarded nickname.

—I'll see if Titus has got the teams hitched up, Isaac said. He pulled the door open. Marie followed him out, balancing the baby on her hip.

The two wagons were drawn up in line on the other side of the house, the mules restive with waiting, jingling their harness as they shifted foot to foot, and Titus standing like a soldier beside the outside leader; down from the loft in the dark to take breakfast in the front room while Marie cooked, Isaac still waking himself. There was the sign painted in black on a wide planed board nailed to the squared logs at the left of the door, careful black draftsman's letters, a little spindly:

Store. Isaac Pride, Prop.

and on the door another, smaller, put up last night, that said "Closed"; but though he did not want her troubled while he was away, Marie knew the prices of the stock on hand and he had said she might sell to neighbors if they paid in cash or furs, especially wolf; and there was Abe Kelly to help with heavy work, if any came. The hides and tallow were too heavy for one wagon, too light for two, but it had been on Isaac's mind since returning from the second hunt to carry what he had to Leavenworth and load up with goods to last the fall, or maybe into spring; except for the settlers scattered twenty miles both ways along the Whitewater and the Walnut who were beginning to come to Towanda for their flour and sugar, their yards of cotton cloth, he did not yet know what to expect in the way of trade down here. Marie stopped at the corner of the house and faced him in the brace-legged stance of a woman supporting her child, pillowing Bunny's head on her breast.

—Don't be lonely, he said. It won't be two weeks, with the mules, and light-loaded—won't know we've been away.

—I have the best company there is, she said, and rubbed the baby's back.

—Go visit with the Chandlers, it isn't far. Or stay the night. They've a spare bed. Missus Chandler'd like to have you.

—It is another hot day coming, she said, lifting her eyes to the clear sky. You must not wear yourself out with travel, Isaac.

He lingered, awkward with the boy standing there in silence, waiting to start; leaned and pressed his lips to the crown of the sleeping baby's head, and touched his fingertips to her cheek, in blessing.

Isaac had stayed a month at Burlingame but was soon impatient with nothing to occupy him and wrote to Titus Sexton at Topeka, offering a hundred dollars for the summer's work and enclosing the stage fare. Two days after the boy arrived, they started south with one wagon and the mule team, supplies for hunting if they chanced on buffalo or other game in the course of exploring, and Singing Bird following on a long rope. There was a traveled road as far as Emporia, a town already six years old; from there, a network of trails, some of them Indian, long-established, and worn deep, spread at random since there were no functioning settlements beyond for them to lead to. Isaac drove west to the South Fork of the Cottonwood, followed it south to its source at Sycamore Springs. Crossing a divide, they entered the Walnut valley and continued south as far as El Dorado, laid out where the Osage Trail crossed the river—the route by which the tribe reached the buffalo range to the west on its summer and winter hunts; abandoned, as Isaac had been told, except for one or two families and a pair of traders with no more in the way of stock than they could carry around in the back of a light wagon, supplying the few settlers in the neighborhood.

Taking the trail west, they passed Bill Bemis' cabin, stayed the night, and came to the big spring the Osage called Towanda, a mile east of the Whitewater River, a settlement in embryo: Charlie Chandler had brought his family and was attempting to make a farm, had put up a log schoolhouse with as yet neither teacher nor pupils, and took in the mail, carried once a week on horseback from Cottonwood Falls; another family had claimed at the Whitewater crossing, two or three others down the river—an Irish widow with two strong sons, a black refugee from the Cherokee Nation, more Indian than Negro in his looks and ways, with a wife and half a dozen small children; men and their families bearing such names as Cupp, Vann, Huller, Meser, and Harrah, an Adams, a Davis, Old Man Gillion, and Simeon Buckner, another black Cherokee, all old-line American in their assortment, as Isaac heard them, from all the states; and down where the Whitewater joined the Arkansas a half-wild Indian tribe driven north from the Territory, of whom no one seemed to know much. It was, according to Isaac's map, about the limit of organized Kansas. Below was all the immense tract reserved to the Osage Nation, except for a narrow strip, a mile or two wide, running along the south line of the state and assigned to the Cherokee, in appearance a surveyor's error thus carelessly corrected. The Osage tract accounted for such settlement as there was, and its character: the settlers were conveniently located for taking Osage land, if ever a new treaty opened it to public sale.

Isaac camped three days at Towanda, as people called the place. Mrs Chandler asked him in for dinner. Chandler for ten dollars offered him the squared walnut logs for a cabin and promised to help him build if he meant to settle. Buffalo, stragglers, he said, came occasionally as far east as the spring; Bemis' story of hunting them from his cabin door had some truth to it.

The buffalo, Bill Bemis said, were farther west now, along the Arkansas, no more than an easy day's drive; and offered to guide them in order to hunt a little himself and bring back meat enough to last till fall. The trail was plain the whole way even if Isaac had felt the need of someone to show him, but he accepted the invitation to be sociable; and then waited half the morning by the spring, packed up, till Bemis came ambling in on the bony little pinto he called his buffalo pony, leading an ill-favored pack mule, his floppy-brimmed slouch hat pulled low over bloodshot eyes. It was near sunset when they started down the final descent, succulent tall bluestem grass all the way, untouched by grazing—it was the first week in May: and now before them the narrow silver ribbon of the Little Arkansas sheathed in cottonwoods, then a prairie of buffalo grass close-cropped as a sheep meadow enclosed two miles off by the broad, shallow flow of the Arkansas itself, and beyond, a limitless plain level as sea floor from this slight elevation; and everywhere they could see, west and north and south, the bands of grazing buffalo, with here and there the stiff-limbed antelope moving among them and, coming down the riverbank to drink, a few dark, horse-like animals that must be elk. They had seen no signs of settlers since crossing the Whitewater.

They drove on down the slope, crossed the Little Arkansas at a gravelly riffle, and made their supper of salt pork and flapjacks in the dark, by firelight. Their only camp-making was to collect a stack of fallen cottonwood and spread their robes around the dying fire. The night was dry and a little cool, loud with the unremitting wind blowing strong from the west.

In the morning, a band of bulls had grazed to within two hundred yards, and it came out that Bill Bemis hunted like an Indian, on horseback, and scorned any other style. He woke, saddled up, and rode out to show how it was done: started the band moving and rode in close, yipping and singing out, picked his animal, drove his pony in among them, planted the muzzle of his big revolver behind the bull's ear, and fired. The buffalo stumbled, rolled, Bemis dodged out from among them, pulled up, and ran to the downed animal with his knife to cut the liver out and eat it hot, with a sprinkling of juice from the gall for sauce. While Isaac and Titus watched, the band ran off and escaped across the Arkansas with thunderous splashing.

Isaac rode five miles up the Little Arkansas before he found an undisturbed band, cows and their calves this time. Leaving Bird among the trees by the river, he crawled forward across the short grass and started shooting at a distance of a hundred yards; kept on, working closer, till he had seventeen down and was not thirty yards off. The buffalo cows, as if never so hunted before, milled but stayed close and did not panic, and he stood up to scare the last of them off with their young. Skinning two of the animals, he cut out as much meat as he could pack on his horse and led her back to camp, where Bemis was still occupied with his pipe and the rib bones from his breakfast. Isaac presented the meat to him, let him know there was more up the river if he thought his mule could carry it, and concluded that if he had as much as he had come for he was at liberty to return to the Walnut. Titus he sent up the river with the wagon to start skinning and followed on horseback after seeing Bemis on his way. No wolves had yet showed themselves, but they would scent fresh meat and come; and the coyotes, ravens, eagles, hawks, all the scavengers of the Plains.

Isaac and Titus stayed three weeks, hunted up both rivers, and took three hundred and fifty buffalo, a few antelope and elk, for sport; might have stayed longer but ran short of lead, and the last two days Isaac had to cut his bullets out and shape them with his knife to reload. The weight in any case was as much as he cared to haul with his wagon and his four-mule team, even the easy twenty miles back to Towanda: thirty-six packs of hides and something under three thousand pounds of tallow. They had seen no other hunters, white or Indian.

It was more of a load than he could carry through to Leavenworth without killing his mules but would keep well enough under cover, and Isaac now took up Chandler's offer of hewed logs and help in raising a cabin; and thinking a few steps farther sent off a letter to Marie by way of Cottonwood Falls and the horseback mail-man, saying that he would be along within the month to carry her and Bunny to their new home. So casually does a young man make his choices, believing, if he considers at all, that though one choice may fail he remains at liberty to go back and try another among the multiform possibilities presented as if for delight; having no thought that every fork taken or not taken on the branching road that leads across the years of a man's life is final and absolute, excluding all others; that every choice is irremediable. Neighbors within walking distance would suit Marie now she had the baby, he reasoned, never at ease in the lonely times at the Saline ranch even with Malvina for company; and he would be within a day's drive of unhunted buffalo range and white settlers, perhaps Indians too, with money or furs to pay for goods carried the long haul from the Missouri, and profit besides.

The house was built. He placed it a few steps from the great spring, on an east-west axis aligned with the sun's path at that high season; built the central block twelve by twenty feet with a floored loft above high enough for him to stand under the rooftree and the roof pitched low and extended, porch-like, on either side, supported at the corners by thick posts of walnut. These he walled in with logs to make a room on the north side eight feet wide and twenty long that would be his store; and on the south the same, divided to make a spare bedroom with a door cut through to the central cabin and a storage place for hides and trade goods. He drove to El Dorado and like other settlers helped himself to flooring, glazed windows, doors, scraps of planed lumber to finish the gables, from the abandoned houses of the aborted town; and from the thin-soil hilltops east of Towanda—the region of Kansas topography, extending north to the Kansas River, known as the Flint Hills—dug the sharp-edged gray rock for a wide-hearthed fireplace and chimney across the west wall of the cabin. They had the place weatherproof in a week and unloaded the bales of tallow and most of the hides into the storeroom. Finishing touches, such as a coat of whitewash inside, and a barn, smokehouse, other outbuildings, could wait. Before starting north, Isaac paced off an estimated quarter-section and drove stakes at the corners, with his name and the date incised. The land, as near as he could judge, adjoined the very edge of the Osage tract but lay outside it.

It was the end of May when they started for the Saline ranch, Isaac riding, most of the way, and leaving the boy to drive: up the White-water to its head, then northwest along the Smoky Hills, avoiding Salina itself—the route Harry Farris had led him from the hunt that first brought him into the country—and arrived after three long days to find Bos still occupying the stockade cabin, engaged in packing hides to carry to Leavenworth. Bos had found a partner now, an experienced older hunter named Joe Lemon, and hired two young Delaware half-blood skinners, brothers; and was for that reason, perhaps, receptive to Isaac's offer to sell him the ranch for four hundred dollars, payable over two years. Isaac next morning went into town, talked for an hour with Colonel Phillips, and returned with an imposing bill of sale conditioned on final payment by the date specified in the spring of 1865; but conditional also in the sense that Isaac sold his improvements and his right to claim title, not the land itself. Of the furnishings he claimed only the camp stove carried out from Iowa, of which the hunters made no use; and next morning drove to Salina, loaded the furniture and trading stock from the house, and took the road east in late afternoon, unwilling to stay another night there. The colonel was not in a position to buy in Isaac's part share in the town but agreed to look out for his interest, taking a ten percent commission on any sale.

They stayed two full days at Leavenworth, camping in the yard in front of Durfee's warehouse. Isaac sold the few packs of hides he had brought and from a farmer north of town bargained a nearly new wagon and a team of big, half-trained mules. After conferring at length on what Isaac had seen of the Whitewater country, the possibilities for trade and hunting on the great plain west of the Arkansas and in the unexplored territory to the south, Mr Durfee loaded the two wagons with an assortment of trade goods which he selected himself, providing an elaborate list of equivalent values in the various furs, based on his experience with the Missouri trade; it was his stock now, his credit. Isaac and Titus were back at Burlingame by mid-June. They had been on the move a few days short of two months.

They waited, partly for social reasons—a round of farewell visits, invitations to tea, a musical *soirée* arranged by Bill Shirley and his sister, concluding with a supper of prairie chicken and venison, with wines and a stone jug of whisky supplied from Colonel Titus's cellar; and at the end of a week Abe Kelly appeared on foot with his brother Jim, each with a buckskin pack on his back like a peddler, summoned by Isaac's letter from Leavenworth offering five dollars to drive the ox-team with its wagon back to Towanda—Isaac made no objection to feeding the younger boy but declined to pay extra for his company. They traveled at the restful pace of the oxen and were five days getting to Towanda, Marie spending much of each day occupied with Bunny in the bed set up behind the driver's seat in Isaac's wagon, where he had also again made a place for her straight chair and now the baby's cradle.

In three weeks at Towanda, with Titus and Abe Kelly helping and another load of boards pried loose at El Dorado, Isaac had completed all the finishings he could think of for the new ranch: shelving in the store and the spare room he now called the warehouse, liking the sound of it; a long table at one end of the store, as desk and counter, with the little camp stove near for winter heat; a large corral for the stock; a log barn with a hayloft filled with prairie hay cut by Charlie Chandler; a smokehouse; a press for hides; and had lightened all the inside walls of the house with a bag of lime Mr Durfee had been at some pains to procure for him, mixed with the pure water from the spring. Finally, although it was late for planting, dry and getting hot, with Chandler's borrowed breaking-plow he turned four acres of his tall-grass prairie and dropped corn in the furrow crossings—Simeon Buckner, a black Cherokee, kept a few hogs and had offered to trade a half-barrel of flour for a litter of spring pigs to turn into the corn, if it grew, supplying rails for a worm fence—and set out a few rows of beans and squash near the house. That done, he once more took the Osage Trail west to the Arkansas, with Abe Kelly along to help with the skinning and camp-keeping. The buffalo were as tame and numerous as before; in less than three weeks he had the wagon loaded with hides and tallow and was starting back.

So it came out that in mid-August Isaac and Titus started for Leavenworth with two heavy-loaded wagons, though with nothing yet to show from Indian trading and little enough from the settlers. They drove through Burlingame without stopping to visit and ten miles east, after crossing Hundred and Ten Mile Creek, came to a fork in the road: to the left, the main road led northeast toward the Kansas River and entered Lawrence from the west; the other went straight east to Westport and Kansas City but crossed the old supply road to the Sac and Fox Agency, little used now the tribe was clearing off its reservation, which came into Lawrence from the south, over Mount Oread—more streams to cross by the left fork but the distance about the same, and after a little thought that was the route Isaac chose, and they spent the night near the head of Camp Creek, a little, north-flowing tributary of the Wakarusa.

The wind that night was too light to relieve the heat and they both slept badly, woke before light, folding their robes up and making breakfast, and started just as the sun rose. It was the morning of August 21, Isaac noted, a Friday—no point in hurrying the remainder of the trip, and, taking their time about it, they would make Leavenworth right for the start of business on Monday. They crossed the Wakarusa at the tiny settlement of Bloomington, and by mid-morning, hungry again, stopped for an early nooning beside a spring four or five miles west of Lawrence. Isaac had it in mind to let the mules graze at leisure and go on in early afternoon, staying the night with Sam Wood, not visited since the wedding trip, more than a year and a half now. A gray haze lay low on the eastern horizon, concealing the town, the river, and although the sky everywhere above it was clear and blue, radiant with heat, did not burn away. While they watched by their small fire, waiting for the coffee to boil, the cloud darkened, thickened, spread higher, the sign of a very local tornado forming, though late in the season for it, or—

—Prairie fire, Titus calmly pronounced it, and reached the pot from the fire to pour.

It was the terror of the grasslands, but of which neither had yet any direct experience, and they watched, more curious than fearful, to see how it would proceed: the burden of every cautionary tale was the unpredictable speed with which the fire moved across the prairies, the skin-seared death that awaited animal or man caught in its path, but this was too distant to threaten and the light west wind unlikely to drive it toward them.

Isaac set his mug down, stood, peered, shading his eyes, threw his head back like an old bull, sniffing—even this far off something outlandish and distinct infused the air, wood, it was woodsmoke, the faint but penetrating aromatic sweetness of burning pine, unknown in these parts, too valuable for fuel, its useful life begun in the pineries of Wisconsin, fashioned into boards in Illinois and Iowa sawmills and planing mills.

—That's not grass burning, Isaac said with assurance. That's a house—houses—. My God! Look!

Where he pointed now rose a great glob of black smoke through the smoky haze, as if a powder magazine had exploded, but—the distance, the northeastward slant of the ceaseless, gentle wind—in absolute, magical silence.

—It's the *whole town* going up, he said. Come on!

Both ran to catch and bring in the mules, hitch up, and start, with no thought for what may have caused the wonder they were witness to; that no less than tornado or prairie fire it must mean danger.

All summer at Lawrence there had been rumors of a planned attack, intended to clean out the seat of Abolition once and for all, as the Slave-Staters' Sack of Lawrence seven years earlier had failed to do; the same bushwhacking Border Ruffians were said to be behind the new threat, now allied with the Rebels and hiding out as before in the broken, wooded, sparsely settled country of western Missouri south of Kansas City, where, despite Jim Lane's continuing agitation, Union troops rarely ventured. Spies were thought to have the town under watch, and for a time the townspeople were vigilant. A night watch was appointed to walk the streets; armed men patrolled the outskirts on horseback, Senator Lane demanded and got a small detachment of infantry. When after months no violence came, the citizens relaxed, went back to ordinary business and the comfort of their beds at night; the troops left their billets and set up camp on the north bank of the river, awaiting orders elsewhere. It was anyway only, some said, another move in Jim Lane's ceaseless maneuverings, stirring up fears to fuel a new movement for him to lead, just as in the old days of Bleeding Kansas; the people were tiring of him.

Yet the rumors persisted. The reason the attackers had so far stayed their hand, it was explained, was not that they were giving up on Lawrence but that their real target was Jim Lane—that their leader and the Senator's self-sworn enemy, Bill Quantrill, meant the town's destruction first of all as a backdrop to burning him at the stake, preferably with his wife, friends, and children looking on—that the spies' business at Lawrence was chiefly to see if Lane would stay put long enough to be caught, and for nearly a year now he had been too moving a target to hit. So the delay.

Lane's home was still at Lawrence. Unlike his colleague and sometime ally Sam Pomeroy, he would never grow rich by politics—it was power, the exercise of power, not wealth, that drove him—but he had become comfortable. When the state legislature elected him to the Senate, he left the old claim he had killed to protect and built for his reunited wife and their children an imposing two-story brick house, with an elegant brass name-plate on the front door—a mansion, people called it—on the western edge of town, overlooking the river. He was not often there. After disposing of Governor Robinson's challenge by installing Tom Carney in the governor's office, Lane controlled federal patronage within the state. Military patronage now offered the principal field for the exercise of this form of power: placing suitable Kansans in positions of command, where—since Robinson had been right on the question of law, that Lane could not serve simultaneously as a Senator and a general—they would act on his views of strategy in the West, generally supported by a weary President. In consequence, when not engaged at Washington, the Senator was on the move from St Louis to Kansas City, to Leavenworth, Atchison, Topeka, attending to military business; Lawrence, peaceably situated near the center of state population, thirty-five miles due west of the Missouri line, did not claim much of his time.

Railroads, however, were hardly less important to Kansas in the long run than the conduct of the war. In every town of any size and ambition the citizens held meetings to petition Congress and the state government for help in securing a railroad route and its profit. It was such a gathering, at the Eldridge House on the evening of August 20, that drew Senator Lane briefly back to Lawrence, along with Bob Stevens from Lecompton and others with a more than local interest in railroads. The Senator addressed the meeting. In his eloquence, his hearers imagined themselves already whirling across the Plains on iron rails at forty miles an hour, freighted with the gold of the mountains. Afterward, the Senator returned to his new house to stay the night. Bob Stevens climbed the two flights of stairs to his room at the hotel.

It was earlier that day that Quantrill started west from his camp in Missouri with four hundred well-mounted men, himself seated in a buggy with a matched pair driven by an aide and armed with four revolvers in the capacious pockets of his hunting shirt. The band's destination was Lawrence. Most likely Quantrill was moved to start his long-postponed raid not by knowledge of his quarry's presence but rather by the natural leader's instinct that no force of fighting men can be held together indefinitely without action. The coincidence of Lane's visit was a piece of his young man's luck, still on the rise. The band traveled cross-country, avoiding roads, passed undetected the border town of Aubry, where a small Union garrison was stationed. Stragglers rode in to water their horses or exchange mounts and when questioned answered that they were Union recruits bound for Leavenworth and were sent on their way. An officer, suspicious, sent to Kansas City for instructions and started in pursuit, but was ordered back by his superior, one of Lane's appointments. Runners dispatched to Lawrence with warnings met with accident or wore out their horses; none got through. Quantrill's luck held. The band kept moving through the hot night at an easy pace, sparing the horses, and as darkness waned waited near the river east of Lawrence for the coming of light.

Bob Stevens was awakened that morning by the pounding hooves of a column of horsemen coming along Massachusetts Street. A command halted them at the corner below his window. Shots rattled. Stevens leaped from his bed and ran to look out. Four hostlers, young Germans, had slept the night on the board sidewalk in front of Frye's livery stable across the street. They lay dead now, wounds visible in their faces, breasts, blood seeping across the worn gray wood.—Every man! Kill every man—let none escape! The commands echoed from the blank storefronts. The raiders' leader stood in his carriage, arms waving, directing: the column divided into squads, scattering through the town, some turning off toward the new suburb on the western limits, others dismounting, running toward the hotel. Stevens pulled on trousers, tucked his nightshirt in, slipped his boots on, and snatched money and watch from the bureau: just five-fifteen. He hastened along the hallway, hammering at doors, calling out to the other guests.

Rifle butts smashed at the ground-floor entrance to the hotel, a dozen men came clattering up the stairs, collected the guests in a room on the first floor, and went among the men helping themselves to money, watches, rings, anything else they fancied as valuable; their orders, it seemed, were to treat the men as soldiers fighting on the enemy side, and for loot, the whole town was at their disposal, but no woman was to be molested. Stevens had the presence of mind to slip his watch and a roll of greenbacks to one of the ladies herded in with the other guests (and later got them back). Presently, considering the situation, he chose a sober, older man among his captors, took him aside, and talked persuasively and at length: maybe they did have orders to slaughter the men of Lawrence, but that could not mean strangers who merely happened to be passing through and had no quarrel with Missouri or the South; he himself was from Lecompton, the Slave-Staters' capital in the old days, everyone knew Bob Stevens treated all men square and never meddled in politics—. A little later, when smoke rose outside the open windows and filtered through the floorboards—the scattered squads of raiders were not well coordinated—Stevens demanded that his chosen man bring Captain Quantrill over for consultation. The leader heard his arguments and ordered the hotel people marched to the Whitney House, which was not to be burned, or not yet, and there kept safe. As they left—besides the hotel office there was a saloon at the street level, a well-stocked drugstore—an explosion of alcohol and chemicals hurled a ball of fire and black smoke at the sky.

Senator Lane, a mile distant, was awakened by the same sound of gunfire, the trampling of running horses, that had roused Bob Stevens and needed, perhaps, a few seconds less to comprehend the threat they proclaimed. Since the trouble with Gaius Jenkins over the boundaries of their claims and the conversion that followed his rival's death, he had kept no weapons in the house, in deference to his wife. There was, however, a penknife on his dresser, and seizing it he ran down the stairs in his nightshirt to pry the brass name-plate off his front door—as if any stranger coming into town could fail to discover where Jim Lane lived. Horsemen coming along the street now: closing the door softly he got out the back and threw himself down between rows of the thick-grown corn patch at the back of the house, the blade of his small knife pointed at one eye, meaning to drive it through into the brain and, if might be, kill himself rather than be taken.

The men, rattling the front door and demanding Jim Lane, were met by Lane's wife, who, like others before in the days of territorial strife, coolly informed them that Mr Lane was not at home, she really did not know just where he might be found or when he would return, and would they care to leave a message?—exactly truthful words. Mindful of their orders, the bushwhackers were polite but insisted on a search. They went through the house, up the stairs, found Lane's bedroom, the bedclothes thrown back, the bed still warm; and ran out the back door, past the corn patch, making for the riverbank, where they calculated to find the fugitive concealed among the brush.

For something over four hours the raiders had the town to themselves; cleaned out the bank, saloons, whisky merchants, livery stables, gunsmiths, clothing stores, hatters, cigar-makers; and when they took the road south toward ten o'clock left two hundred dead, not all the bodies ever found—shot, stabbed, sabered, trampled, burned in their houses and stores. A squad of bushwhackers had themselves outfitted with new clothes, then shot the proprietor and his clerks and fired the store. The printer's son burned in the shop, his bones fused with the lead from the type cases. A small boy dressed in a sailor suit of Union blue ran frightened into a street and was ridden down by a horseman screaming—We are fiends from hell! Not every townsman or boy died that morning. A woman rolled her husband in a carpet and dragged him thus from the burning house while the raiders watched. Stout, red-faced Sam Wood hastily shaved his beard, pulled on a frock and a widow's cap to cover his bald head, and huddled in a parlorful of women—and was looked at strangely when the raiders came but was overlooked. Bob Stevens, shepherding his company of guests from the Eldridge House, stayed close to Quantrill at the Whitney, talking steadily—briskly, reasonably, pleadingly, amusingly, sensibly—and was still alive when the commander gave the order to ride out. A little after, when stragglers came back hunting "that rascal Stevens," he got away to the riverbank and hid.

Assisted by the August heat—already around a hundred when the army left—the flames made short work of the mostly wooden buildings in the center of town, and selectively elsewhere, as the fires were set. Lane's mansion was burned out inside, but the brick walls stood.

Lane himself, after the bushwhackers passed his refuge on their errand to the river, made a dash, still armed with his penknife, took the direction of the road west from town but stayed off it, and got into the first farmhouse he came to. The farmer, short and fat, furnished a shirt and trousers, which hung like a clown suit from his long, gaunt frame, and an elderly saddle horse on which he rode to neighboring farms, rallying a dozen settlers, thirty animals that might be classed as mounts—plow horses, undergrown ponies, dray mules, donkeys—and a few flintlock squirrel rifles, hay forks, horse pistols, and other weapons. Around ten o'clock, coming into town at the head of this motley column, he caught up with two covered wagons rattling along behind teams of well-fed, smartly trotting mules. The drivers pulled over and slowed to let the riders pass. Off to the southeast a dust cloud rose from a slowly moving train of horsemen and wagons loaded with plunder. Ahead, the gray smoke of the burning town floated like a cloud on the hot air. Lane rode toward the lead wagon and looked down the octagonal barrel of a large-bore Hawken rifle, its hammer cocked.

—Put up your weapon, sir! Lane commanded. Unless you are of the Rebel party, your wagons heavy with spoils—

—I'm a hunter and trader from Butler County, Mister Lane, Isaac said, flushing. My man and I are taking a load of hides and tallow in to market.

Lane peered at him.—Are we acquainted, sir?

—Jack Pride. I met you at the voting on the constitution here four years ago, with Sam Wood. And before that, when you came through Davenport—

—Of course, of course! Lane said, putting on a smile and taking a step forward, but Isaac stopped him with a shake of his head and a small, tense, negative movement of the rifle. See here, Mister Pride, he said, lifting one arm toward the town, Quantrill and his cutthroats have laid waste our city—

—I told you we mean to help, Isaac broke in impatiently. We'd best get along.

—Excellent! Lane said, smiling again. For now in this hour of peril, the Union has no greater need than for your mules, sir. *Kansas* has need—

Isaac stiffened.—No, sir! he said. These mules are my livelihood— can't be spared. But anything else—. The men of Lane's posse had all come up now and crowded behind him, holding his collection of animals in a tight bunch. Listen, men, Isaac said, lifting his eyes to them and raising his voice. I'll help you out any way I can that's right, but not with my mules. And anyone tries to take em from me— well, let me tell you, the senator here'll be the first to know I mean what I say. And he waggled the rifle again for emphasis. Besides—

Lane stared at him a long moment.—I shall remember you, sir, he said, his voice threatening, on another occasion.

—Good God! Isaac said, you've got no call to talk that way. I *said* I'd help, but can't you see these mules're no good for what you want? They're *freight* mules, trained em up myself—you try and put a saddle on, or ride em, why, before you'd gone a rod they'd half-kill you, and maybe succeed. And we stand here arguing bout a thing like that, when—

—Very well, then, Lane said, raising his hand, perhaps I misjudged. But we still have need of what help you can give. Let us fall to it and save such honor as we can from this infamous day.

Lifting his hand in salute, he jogged his horse, turned away, and shouted to his farmers to ride on. Isaac watched till they had passed and followed them into town.

The Senator halted in front of the ruin of the Eldridge House and sent runners through the streets crying up volunteers to pursue the attackers, but not many came. The men not killed or badly wounded seemed dazed with fear, stayed hidden, wandered aimlessly, or sat, heads bowed, before the smoking ashes of their homes. The women, not directly threatened, remained effectual—set up canopies of table- cloths or sheets to shade the wounded, ripped their petticoats for bandages, struggled through the streets with buckets of water from the wells. Thirty or forty men finally were gathered, some with rifles or revolvers, leading horses the Missourians had judged not worth stealing, and two of Lane's farmers carried a fire-blistered table rescued from a store and stood it in the middle of Massachusetts Street. Jim Lane mounted it.

Still dressed in his farmer's ill-fitting castoffs, no longer the polished, tailor-dressed Presidential confidant he had become but once more the penniless, rude-spoken settler who covered his poverty winter and summer with the old bearskin overcoat, whose voice and unbending will commanded the people through the Wakarusa War and all the other fights by which Kansas came to birth, he threw his head back and strained his bare arms against the burning sky.—Great God in heaven! he began in a low, carrying voice, and those who wore hats removed them at this invocation and bowed their heads. Almighty maker of the universe! It has on this day pleased the Lord to call some of us to Himself. Amen, Amen! But others He has left—and likewise for His purposes. We stand before Him here together now. What has He saved us for? What would He have us do? This much is clear—it is our task, conferred by God, to set before the world of men the infamy of this day—to proclaim and shout it forth down to time's latest date. But is that all, my brothers? Can the mighty Lord of heaven have no deeper purpose for us—us that He has saved and brought forth from the burning fiery furnace?

—No, men of Lawrence! No, I say! Our God is just! He lets no evil that men do go unavenged! And now He sends us forth to do His will. For there—one stiff arm sawed in a southerly direction, a rough-booted foot slammed the ruined tabletop for emphasis—there the murderers swagger forth—Quantrill's Missourians—staggering under the heavy plunder of our city's wealth—their hands still hot with our brothers' blood—our fathers', sons'! Wolves! Snakes! Devils!— They are not men but counterfeits, clothed in the form of men!—And there they go, with not an hour's start. And shall we let them, brothers? Carry off our goods and trample in our friends' and loved ones' blood? No, brothers, never—while we are men! Mount, and ride! And know that God rides with us—He arms us with His strength and sends us forth to smite these devils back to hell! And may God everlastingly damn their souls—

A leg of the table, which had wobbled as he stamped and waved his arms, rising toward a screaming peroration, now gave way, and the top slid toward the dust. Lane jumped clear, landed, and ran toward his horse, mounting with a leap. The men, well roused by now, raised fists in the air and let out a scattering of cheers: *Jim Lane! Jim Lane!*

—Up, men, and ride! he shouted, swinging around in the saddle.

The God of wrath rides with us—to do His vengeance on Missouri's fiends!

With a thumping kick in the ribs he surprised the old horse into an ambling trot and turned onto the road leading south. Others got on such mounts as they could find and started after him in a straggling column, perhaps forty altogether riding in pursuit of Quantrill's four hundred. Isaac watched till all were gone and, leaving Titus to guard the wagons and their teams, went off to see what help he could give—the wounded now, find them and load them in the wagons maybe, carry them where they could be cared for, and the dead, in need of burying—.

Bob Stevens, ever practical, stood on the porch of the Whitney House, now doing service as a hospital, directing the dozen energetic women he had recruited. He paused and waved as Isaac came toward him.

—Say there, Mister Pride, he called out, grinning through the sweat-lined soot that stained his face. Aint you riding out behind General Lane?

—I'd have been tempted if I'd brought a decent horse along, Isaac answered. Looked like there was enough to do, though, right here in town.

—My view exactly! Stevens said, looking serious again. The wounded, in this heat, and some terrible burns besides, people trying to rescue things. And—he lowered his voice—the dead—we don't get em in the ground—the bad air—it'll bring a plague to finish off what Quantrill started.

—Anyhow, Lane's sore at me now, Isaac said. Wanted to take my mules and I wouldn't let him—weren't any good to *him*, and I can't get my hides to Leavenworth without em—

—Leavenworth?

Isaac nodded.—It's where we're headed. I figured to stay the night, get there for business Monday morning.

—How long could you do it in? Stevens said, taking his elbow and leading him off to one end of the porch.

—I've two wagons, good load in each, Isaac said, thinking it through. Four-mule teams. We start now and go through the night, we'd be there in the morning—have to rest the mules some on the way, but I wouldn't take time cooking. I've got a sack of dried buffalo meat for that.

—Well, now! said Stevens. There's the answer, then. Next thing worrying me was, how do we get a message to the troops when there aint a horse in town that's fit to ride? And—what do we do for food? Because, you know, what those vipers didn't burn they carried off or spilled out on the ground and spoiled—aint hardly left enough to feed a family of kittens. . . .

He had Isaac by the arm again, propelling him back along the porch and down the steps.—Where'd you say you left your wagons? he said, all energy. Because, you see—well, ought to be started *right now*—get up there in the morning, get your hides off, load you up—and I'll have to run around town, hire maybe half a dozen more to load—because my credit's heavy enough at Leavenworth for *that*, I reckon—

And steadily elaborating his plans, smiling and gesturing, he marched Isaac along toward Massachusetts Street, almost running.

XV

Towanda

In the fall of 1863 the Wichita came up the Whitewater to the crossing of the Osage Trail and camped below the spring called Towanda and down the east bank of the river. A few days later, the Osage arrived from their main village seventy miles east on the Verdegris, following the trail west for their seasonal buffalo hunt, and led the newcomers as far as the Little Arkansas.

This arrangement had been negotiated in the spring with elaborate mutual diplomacy: the Osage were bound by custom and pride to take in the helpless and unfortunate, whether an individual or a whole tribe, but could tolerate no Indian intruders except by deliberate consent (the whites were another matter, steadily encroaching, but as individuals, not a tribe, and therefore a perplexity); and judged it politic to locate the Wichita on the Little Arkansas, by now the eastern limit of the short-grass country and the buffalo in that part of the South Plains—but also about as far east as the wild tribes were ever known to venture. Beyond for another hundred and fifty miles the country was still nominally Osage, according to treaty and tribal claim, but not so acknowledged by any Kiowa, Comanche, Cheyenne, or Arapaho, enemies all.

Marie was the first to see the Wichita when they reached Towanda in the course of their new migration: two fat old lank-haired men slumped on scrubby horses, riding slowly toward her from the riverbank, one wearing a grimy, collarless shirt with vertical blue stripes, the other with a frayed red blanket over one shoulder; and beside them, trotting, a slender, bare-chested, dark-skinned youth, shapely and tireless as, young, they might have been, with the fringed ends of a buckskin breechcloth flapping front and back from the belt of his denim trousers. Marie had been hanging out wash on the line Isaac had strung for her between two cottonwoods on the south side of the house, the baby pillowed in a spare laundry basket at her feet, big and active enough at nine months to roll out and crawl but content for now to lie on his back and watch, following her movements and the billowing of the white linens in the autumnal morning light with his eyes. Marie had shaken out a sheet and turned to stretch and hang it up when she saw the three Indians silently approaching, not fifty yards off; and dropping it with a shriek, caught up the baby and ran for the open door of the house. Hearing her, Isaac in his shirt-sleeves sprinted from the barn, where he had been pitching a wagonload of prairie hay up into the loft.

The horsemen halted when Isaac addressed them in signs, but the boy kept on coming and, smiling, seized Isaac in the double-handed forearm handshake of a warrior. He spoke some English, learned in the household of the Wichita agent and filled out with signs when the words did not come, and Isaac let him talk: Towakoni Jim, the agent's wife had named him; the old men—Isaac waved them forward—were Owa-ha, principal chief of the Wichita, and Ochelot, a headman of the Towakoni. The people were camped along the east bank of the Whitewater and wanted to trade—flour, sugar, coffee, perhaps a barrel of salt pork—but were poor. Isaac ran and led Singing Bird, bridled, from the corral and getting the boy up behind him followed the chiefs down through the Wichita camp. Like other tribes, by poverty the Wichita meant not enough horses: Isaac estimated hardly two hundred in the herd, some of them wild-eyed, unbroken mustangs roped neck to neck, among as many fighting men and several times as many people altogether; Jim told how in the summer the chief Esseda-a-wa had led the men south to recapture this remnant and bring it back. Other poverties derived from this one. With their wives to work the skins, the half-dozen chiefs and headmen, a few notable hunters, had new buffalo-hide tepees for traveling and took in those they had room for; others had made low brush arbors to sleep under or would do without, lying by their fires—the days were still bright, the nights chill, but there was not yet ice in the mornings on the water pails. The cattle brought back from the Territory had been slaughtered, the meat sun-dried and mostly consumed now or packed away for emergency; there would be buffalo along the Arkansas for another month, Jim thought, before the herds left the open plains and retreated into the broken country to the south, and Isaac agreed. The new hides had gone into tepees, bedding, winter clothing. The robes the people had for trade were verminous, worn thin with use.

Isaac rode back in silence, calculating the arithmetic of need; trying to count the people in their scattered camp was like reckoning the fleas on a dog's hind parts while he scratched. The store and warehouse were stocked with goods, but no Indians had come in to trade and few settlers. Since coming back from Leavenworth in September he had occupied himself in building up the ranch—chiefly, a nearly completed double cabin intended half for storage and half for an assistant or manager if ever the trade reached such activity—with one or other of the Kelly boys helping; and had hunted days at a time to the west for winter meat, with Jim Kelly along as skinner. The trade goods, he concluded, were worth nothing to him stored behind walls, and therefore he led the two chiefs and the boy to the smokehouse and reached them down two half-cured buffalo hams to take; then to the warehouse and carried out two sacks of flour and offered what sugar and coffee they could load their horses with besides. These, he said, he would sell, and in a month would haul a wagonload to them on the Little Arkansas, and what they could not pay for then in robes or wolf skins could wait till spring. He was at pains to specify the terms in signs, not trusting them to Jim's translation. Owa-ha nodded and repeated his agreement. It was understood.

Marie watching from the house was uneasy as the old men led their loaded horses off, the boy with a sack of flour on his shoulder, but said nothing until after supper. Isaac sat at the table, writing in his account book by the lamplight. Bunny lay face down on a robe before the hearth, nursed and ready to be put to bed.

—You were most generous with those Indians this morning, Isaac, Marie ventured.

—That's how my father would take it, he said with a snort but did not look up. Charity—load em up and send em on their way rejoicing. Not that I've anything against helping some, when a man's down, and don't have anything to eat—

—Even so, I wonder, Isaac, is it wise? Marie said, coming to her point. Mister Durfee must still be paid for all those goods.

—Oh, we're still ahead with Durfee, he said, laying his pen down and leaning to blow the ink dry. And all the credit we can use, six or nine months, if we need it. Course we have to pay for that, and they will too, I talked it all through with the old chief, Owa-ha, he knows he's got to pay us out of the winter hunting—get the men out working, and the women, tanning the robes—and how much it's going to cost him, too, got it all written up.

—Then it may profit us, if they are spared.

—*Course* it will, Isaac said, and looked her in the eyes, smiling. And anyhow the stock can't bring us anything lying on the shelves, or in the warehouse, that's just *costing*, way I see it. Got to cast your bread on the waters, to get some back. But they'll pay, I reckon. . . .

He closed the book, pushed it aside, and stood up, taking her by the hand.

The Osage came through on October 20, an immense train that took the whole day going past the spring: four or five thousand people

and a thousand fighting men among them, chiefs in their finery leading, on well-fed ponies, eagle feathers erect in roached hair at the
backs of their heads.

The Wichita packed up their camp and straggled in behind like
driftwood from a riverbank carried down on a spring freshet. A
month after, as he had promised, Isaac got Jim Kelly over, loaded a
wagon with flour, sugar, coffee, tobacco, and some sides of bacon
taken in trade from Simeon Buckner, and set off down the trail to find
the place on the Little Arkansas where the Wichita had erected their
new village.

In May of the following spring, with his new assistant Jack Lawton, Isaac carried two loads of furs to Leavenworth and on the way
back put up as usual with Sam Wood. Lawrence was largely rebuilt
by now, even Lane's mansion within its smoke-smudged brick walls.
Isaac in the course of the dry and snowless winter had made two
extended hunts, mainly for wolf, around the salt plains south and
west of the Arkansas, another remnant of the sea that once covered
the land. He had stayed around the fringes of the plain, killing only
about enough buffalo for food and wolf bait, but from the January
hunt brought back seven hundred dollars' worth of wolf pelts, at Mr
Durfee's inflated greenback prices (the legal tenders were now down
to fifty cents in gold, and the speculators were betting they would go
lower still); and on both these hunts by luck and watchfulness had
missed the bands of Comanche marauders that amused themselves by
cleaning out and generally scaring other Butler County hunting parties in the area, though so far without any known deaths, since none
had dared resist. Since then, his Indian trade, at the ranch or among
the grass lodges of the Wichita near the mouth of the Little Arkansas,
had been running two or three hundred dollars a month, and besides
Lawton he had taken on Jim Kelly full-time at twenty-five a month
and was looking for others; and as the business grew had returned to
his former arrangement with Mr Durfee, buying his trade goods on
his own account and mostly for cash, setting his prices for himself—
and keeping all the profit. The Wichita had turned out men of their
word and diligent.

Sensible men at Lawrence and Leavenworth that spring, like their
practical counterparts elsewhere in the North, many of their newspapers, were saying the war would last another four years, could not be
won; that Uncle Sam had taken on too big a job. For nearly a year
now, since Vicksburg and Port Hudson, the Mississippi had again
gone "unvexed to the sea"—Lincoln's majestic phrase, announcing a
rare but undoubted victory—but carried little enough traffic, and the
Red River campaign in April, aimed at capping that success by sub-

duing Arkansas, Texas, and, of moment to Kansans, the Indian Territory, had already guttered down to failure. Elsewhere in the West the armies in Tennessee lurched back and forth in battles of a bloodiness unprecedented in the history of battle, proclaimed as Union victories, though to sensible men they had gained nothing worth gaining. In the East the capital remained as open to threat as in the war's first days, Richmond and the heart of the Confederacy no nearer, despite ambitious failures by a succession of commanders. The President in March issued a draft call for half a million men, and this time, the talk was, the Kansas quota would not be met by volunteers; and two days after appointed Grant general of all the Union armies, a subject for caricature in polite journals, like Lincoln himself, but a fighter, a winner of victories; and another plain Westerner, from Illinois, Ohio-born.

Although Congress was not yet in recess, Jim Lane had quietly returned to Lawrence—a state election coming also in November and an insubordinate governor to be replaced, besides his own succession in the staggered four-year term as Senator from a newly admitted state. Isaac was astonished to hear from Sam Wood that Lane had inquired particularly for him, had said he wanted to see him when he came through from Leavenworth; and curious, rode over to Lane's rebuilt house after supper to call—something no doubt to do with the coming election.

Mrs Lane let him in, took his name, came back, and led him down the hall to a parlor. The Senator sat motionless in a red plush chair too short and low for his bony legs, face gaunt with shadows from the single lamp. As if expecting him, he waved Isaac to a chair but did not speak. His wife went out and softly closed the door.

—How old are you, Mister Pride? the harsh voice came from the silence.

Isaac hesitated, flushed—what business was it of his?—and answered—Twenty-seven, in October.

—I liked how you stood up for yourself, that day we had our little business with Quantrill—gotten clear through to Ohio now, they say, still raiding—? And practical too, taking your wagons to Leavenworth and bringing back food and medicines and clothes, what people needed. Me, I couldn't do that—man gets kind of boxed in by what people expect. They needed to show some fight, someone out front, leading, so they could get their pride back.

—I didn't mean disrespect, Mister Lane. It's just—

—No, I understand, the Senator stopped him with a wave of his hand. Grit—I like that. Man needs to know his mind, know what he wants, and what he *don't* want, before others'll follow along behind and help him get it. That's what we need out here—active men that can do things, and know what *needs* doing—that men can trust, and

follow. You ever thought about that, Mister Pride? Giving yourself to
the people's service—politics? . . .

—No one ever asked me, Isaac began, and stopped. But if they did
—well, there's my wife to think of—and the little baby now, and my
business coming along—

—I remember, the Senator said, smiling for the first time. Lovely
young lady—your wedding trip. Mary—. But that needn't stand in
your way. Man's got to make a start—sooner the better, if he's got it
in him.

—What was it you were thinking of, Mister Lane?

—I'll tell you plainly, the Senator said, sitting forward in his chair.
There you are down in Butler County—aint hardly organized, no
proper boundaries according to law, on account of it's still Indian
title, some of it, and settlers coming in every day—well, there's work
to be done, someone's got to take it up. I want a sound man in there
for the legislature, do things right. It's the sixty-seventh district.

—You want me for state representative?

—That's the size of it—and I don't see anyone else down there
that'd do for the job. Needn't stand in the way of your business, he
pressed on before Isaac could protest. It's only a two- or three-month
session at Topeka, and a man can do himself some good while he's
seeing to the public business. Well, there you are, trading with the
Indians, and this refugee tribe come up from the Territory—

—The Wichita?

—Yes, Wichita—haven't had a proper agent for two or three years
now. I don't know why you couldn't fit that in—they give you a clerk
and assistants to look after things—

—You want me for Wichita Indian agent?

—Think about it, Mister Pride—two thousand a year, and the Indian office puts up a proper house—and contracts to be let, and rations passed out. A man can do right by the Indians and still do
himself some good. And it leads on to things, of course. All I ask is,
you stand with me—and stand *against* the renegade Republicans, the
copperheads and Democrats—when my election comes before the
legislature.

It was a large dose, more than Isaac could take in one gulp, but the
Senator got it down him all the same, swallow by swallow, with a
painless dexterity the young man would remember and admire him
for afterward. No, it was too serious a matter for an answer all at
once, but he would think it through and write his decision to the
Senator at his lodgings at Washington City. . . .

His business done, the Senator had no conversation and was impatient to be alone again. By way of dismissal—You understand I don't
promise about that Indian agency, he said, there's others got some say
with the Indian department. But I'll do what I can for you—because

it's my judgment you're the man for the office—and besides, you're down there, save the government some travel money, and you know these people, trading along with them like you do, know their needs and how they think.

He stood up, gave Isaac's hand a hard shake, and steered him toward the door. Isaac held back, curious now whom the Senator had in mind to run for Governor in November, and allowed himself the question.

Again Lane stopped, looked hard, considered, and drawing himself up said—Why, Sam Crawford, of course, I reckon that's no special secret—and will win too, against anyone the other bunch has got. Sound man, he added, lawyer at Garnett, came to Kansas seven or eight years back. You ever met him?

Isaac shook his head, wanted to ask what Crawford had been promised, but kept the impertinent question to himself; and then Lane unconcernedly told him anyway.

—Sam wanted to do his duty by the Union, he said, and I put him up for colonel of one of my colored regiments. Man wants to go in politics these days, it don't hurt to get a little reputation for soldiering, if he thinks he's up to it. Course, he concluded with a wink, keeping a ranch and Indian trading, away out on the frontier somewhere—well, I reckon that'll do about as well.

A few weeks later—Marie had listened, commented on practical details, but refrained from advising on the central question—Isaac put his decision in a letter, as he had promised: he would attend the county convention, would accept the nomination if it came, and if elected would give Jim Lane his vote for another term in the Senate. The Senator did not reply, but an answer of a kind nevertheless came, toward the end of July.

A little earlier, with four teams and wagons, Isaac had followed the Osage beyond the Arkansas on their summer hunt, and when he came back loaded with robes and raw-tanned hides found the river flooded half a mile wide by the spring rains and runoff from the mountains and had to wait ten days on the river's west bank, until Towakoni Jim and a gang of enterprising young Wichita swam across to his camp and helped float the wagons over, only for the sport and challenge of it; and by then moths had gotten into the packs and half-spoiled the furs, no telling what they would bring when finally he took them to Leavenworth to sell. The summer since then was turning out dry and hot; it began to look as if this year's corn would burn up before it came to harvest.

It was out of this shimmering, south-Kansas heat that a gentleman of military mien came driving one afternoon to the door of Isaac's store beside the Towanda spring, in a trim but dust-white buggy, with a light wagon loaded with baggage following a mile back, and introduced himself as Major Milo Gookins, retired, of Indiana, newly appointed agent to the Wichita and affiliated tribes; a spare, gray, straight-backed man of perhaps sixty who seemed to have made himself as familiar with the numerous regulations of the Office of Indian Affairs as he must once have been with those of the Army. Sitting at the table in the main room of the house while Marie poured tea, his broad-brimmed blue campaign hat politely perched on one thin knee, he informed them that Mr Pride and his ranch had been especially recommended to him. Since his Indians were camped, he understood, somewhere to the west, beyond the frontier, he proposed to establish his agency at Towanda, if Mr Pride had suitable buildings to offer. He would require quarters for himself, a clerk, interpreter, two teamsters, storage for rations and other goods; for which accommodations he was authorized to reimburse eighteen dollars a quarter. If Mr Pride proposed to trade with the Wichita, he would of course require a license. The major was prepared to forward his application to the superintendent, just now headquartered at Fort Leavenworth, accompanied by the appropriate penal bond.

Two months after Major Gookins took up his arcane duties, Isaac loaded a wagon with goods and with Jack Lawton started west to visit the Wichita, leaving Jim Kelly and Marie to see to the store. Although for a year now he had done what trade he could with any whites or Indians who came through, including the Wichita, since the agent's arrival he had felt constrained to await the granting of his license, and that had taken time: weeks of inconclusive correspondence between the agent's and the superintendent's clerks, still carried on horseback the circuitous route through Cottonwood Falls (since June Jim Lane had put Isaac through as postmaster, but that did nothing to speed the mail); until the Wichita sent Towakoni Jim to complain and Isaac, exasperated, dispatched a letter to the Senator. Ten days later, hastened, as Isaac heard later, by a telegram to Fort Leavenworth from the Commissioner of Indian Affairs, the necessary document arrived, bearing the superintendent's conditional approval and valid for a year, and Isaac took his departure.

A mile east of the Little Arkansas the Osage Trail crossed a nameless creek and descended the gentle slope to the gravelly riffle known as the Osage Crossing, fordable even in the rare high water, the trail's goal and the reason for its direction; a very modest eminence, but such things are relative in generally flat country. From that point an observant wagon driver could look out on the meeting place of four natural zones. Behind him lay the tall-grass prairie belonging to the Flint Hills, ungrazed a short distance either side of the trail. Beyond the two rivers, enclosed by the immense northwest curve of the Arkansas, the Plains proper began, little bluestem mixed with grammas and buffalo grasses, dusty-green sages, in low clumps, thinning and interspersed with earth-hugging prickly pear as the flat land rises to the High Plains and dries out. North of the crossing, the riverbank growth declined to scrub—slender cottonwoods widely spaced, patches of willow, a few stunted, dry-land elms. To the south, both rivers were sheathed in the luxuriant flood-plain forest that to settlers from the woodlands of the East still meant rich soil, once cleared, and logs for the first cabin. Six miles down from the crossing the two rivers funnel together in a broad, shallow valley: the big one, called the Arkansas since before the first American traders followed its course to Santa Fe. Isaac eased his team down the gradual slope, made the axle-deep crossing, and followed its west bank down to the Wichita village.

A short distance above its mouth, the Little Arkansas doubled back on itself before joining the main river, the oxbow enclosing a grove of large cottonwood and other mature trees. This sheltered site on the lesser river's west bank, cooled by the placid flow of the two streams, shaded and airy even in the hot days of July and August, the Wichita had chosen for their village, the women's garden patches scattered across the open prairie west to the Arkansas. Isaac drove through to Owa-ha's lodge, recognized and greeted by the people as he passed. Stooping, he entered by the east doorway and found the old chief alone, reclining on the sleeping platform near the opposite entrance, propped on layers of buffalo robes. Owa-ha rose, smiling, wrapped him in a short-armed hug, and stood back to shake his hand. Bringing his pipe from a shelf, he crouched by the fire pit at the center of the lodge, and Isaac produced a sack of tobacco. The ceremony completed, Isaac had Lawton bring in the gifts—sacks of flour and sugar, tobacco, ten yards of calico for the wives—and the chief came out to examine his stock and agree on prices; although greenbacks were now down to forty cents, the relative values of furs in flour, sugar, yards of cloth, were little affected. Owa-ha made the signs of his agreement and as usual directed the traders to the lodge of Ochelot, the Towakoni headman, over on the riverbank.

Ochelot had taken the boy known as Towakoni Jim into his own household, which already included three wives and their adolescent sons and daughters; but the lodge was spacious for all, the Towakoni chief was a considerable hunter, and his sons were learning. Years back, while the tribe still lived south of the Red River in Texas, Kiowa had carried the boy off in the same raid in which they killed his parents. He had learned their language, some Comanche, but remained himself and, half-grown, escaped, wandered months alone, but survived and found his way to his own tribe's new location, his dead parents forgotten. The agent's wife had taken him in, an orphan, taught him English—he was quick as well as self-reliant—and called him Jim; whence the name by which he was now known, Towakoni Jim, no longer answering to any other even in his own language. Although still no more than a slender youth when Isaac first knew him, perhaps seventeen, he was already recognized by the chiefs and headmen as useful, for his languages, his knowledge of the ways of other peoples; showing promise in the skills of war and hunting that in time would confer the authority of leadership.

A similarly mysterious youth figures in numerous legends of the Wichita, as of other tribes of the Plains: the scorned, impoverished undergrown orphan boy of no known parentage who in solitude discovers the supernatural aid to overcome monsters, demons, save the village, sometimes claim its loveliest maiden. Why these tales of unlikely transformation were told and preserved—the pattern is not Plains or Indian but universal, traceable among the roots of European myth—cannot be truly known, but their usefulness is clear: an emblem of hope for any boy undergoing the coming of manhood, attempting to master the forms of competence while his strongest feelings were of dependence; a practical lesson for adults in cultures where dead parents and their surviving offspring were commonplace; a moral counterweight, perhaps, to the natural tendency of any warrior culture to make hereditary its chiefs' authority, its shamans' ceremonial mysteries, its warriors' right to lead and command. Jim already knew some of these stories, and as trust grew and became friendship would retell them, making them his own, to the young white trader some older tribesmen called by the Kiowa name Pai-tal-ye.

That afternoon, Jim's tale was of a new arrival in the country, the Cherokee trader Jesse Chisholm, come north with his people from the Territory a week or two back, building a ranch in a hackberry grove on a little creek on the other side of the Little Arkansas, two miles east of the village—a man known to all the tribes of the Plains, though not yet to Isaac. The boy talked on, almost voluble, mixing Wichita and English with the hand signs, while Isaac and Lawton carried in the goods, Jim helping, and arrayed them along the north side of the lodge. At length, it was what the boy seemed to want, Isaac proposed that they ride over for a visit, and Jim ran grinning to bring in a pony.

Before leaving, Isaac set aside flour, sugar, and coffee for the use of the household, according to custom—the women would cook and provide the meat while he stayed; and turned out his mules for the boys to herd with the tribe's horses.

The man known across the South Plains as the Cherokee trader Jesse Chisholm was born around 1805 in what was still acknowledged Cherokee country in southeast Tennessee, but only half his blood was of that nation, his father a Scot married into the tribe. Probably in the 1820s, he went west to Arkansas, in company with a Cherokee faction that resisted assimilation and sought to preserve the old ways in the wilderness, possibly already as a trader, bound to the people who provided his livelihood. In 1832, Chisholm contracted to cut a military road from Fort Smith, on the western border of Arkansas, through the forested uplands of the eastern Indian Territory to Fort Towson on the Red River, work that came to him, probably, through trading and the concomitant business of freighting supplies in his wagons. A little after, through marriage with a half-blood Creek, he secured a site for a trading post in the southeast corner of the Creek Nation near the place where the Little River enters the Canadian. In 1836 he knew the South Plains well enough—and was well enough known—to be hired as guide to adventurers seeking a gold mine, or possibly a buried Spanish treasure, shown on an old French map near the mouth of the Little Arkansas; they came back safely, but no richer. Sometime later, eighty miles northwest of the home ranch but still in Creek jurisdiction, he established a second post called Council Grove, on the North Fork of the Canadian and convenient to the wild tribes that supplied him with buffalo robes.

Chisholm was said to know fifteen Indian languages besides English and Spanish. Having no children of his own, he ransomed and raised the boys—Mexicans mostly, probably some white Texans—carried off by the Kiowa and Comanche and, when he moved camp, traveled like a chief with an entourage of these youths, dependent Indians adrift from their villages, a few men hired for wages. But when the Wichita fled to the Osage country and the war disrupted his supplies—up the Mississippi and the Arkansas from New Orleans, over the wagon trails along the lesser streams—Jesse Chisholm gathered his people and followed, in the early fall of 1864; and chose a pleasing site for a new trading post, on a small tributary of the Arkansas by a hackberry grove a little east of the new village.

These particulars of personal history Isaac learned or guessed in the course of years, much as he also learned Jim's life and his tribe's. As he swam Singing Bird, bareback, across the middle of the Little Arkansas, then scrabbling up the clay-hard, sun-cracked bank, and dared Jim to a race, he knew only that a formidable presence had come into the country, admired by the people; another trader and perhaps a rival.

They jumped the little creek nearly together and turned toward the tall grove where the trader was camped. Isaac, laughing, let his horse go now, and as they neared the camp there were three lengths between them. There came a high-pitched screech of anguish: a large half-built cabin at the edge of the grove and three shirtless, dark-skinned boys attempting to lever a squared cottonwood log up a ramp of saplings, and the weight was too much for them, too high to reach, they strained and stretched, cried out, the log was slipping, starting to roll back—

—Hold on there!

Isaac galloped up to them, pulled his horse up, leaped down, and ran to get his shoulder under the log, shoving, the boys shouted encouragement. Jim was beside him, pushing, arms straining, the log inched forward, up, half-rolled, and settled with a thump. Seizing a crowbar, Isaac pried the notches into place and stepped back to judge.

The taller of the three dark boys took Isaac's hand in his and pumped it, panting, drops of sweat running down his cheeks, his arms.—Ah, señor! he began. You have save—

Back among the trees there were three buffalo-skin tepees of unusual size, thin smoke rising from the smoke hole of one, and off to the east a large corral holding a herd of mules and horses, with half a dozen battered, canvas-topped wagons drawn up to one side. The flap of the nearest tepee jerked open and a man stooped through the oval doorway and came purposefully toward them.

—Didn't I tell you, boys, California? Leave that job till the men get finished their siesta. Could have got yourselves killed. He frowned, but with concern, not anger, and drew the boys to him, enveloping them in his arms. You all right, boys? You all right?

—I'm Jack Pride, Isaac said, stepping forward and offering his hand.

—Chisholm's the name, he said, Jesse Chisholm. Nodding to Jim, he sent the three boys running—Get along with you now, boys, you can water the horses till the men get up—and turned back to Isaac. Say now, he continued, I've heard about you. Pai-tal-ye—. Isaac scowled. What's the matter? Chisholm said. That's a good name, don't you like that name?

—It's just—that was a fool thing I did one time, I guess it'd serve me if I'd got myself killed.

—Heard about that too—Mathewson, old Sin-pah-zil-ba, aint seen him since this war started up. . . . The words came slowly, thoughtfully, in the singsong of an Indian speaking English, but with a rolling burr marking some that was perhaps his father's Scottish. Now, looking Isaac in the face, he spoke to him in another tongue. Jim understood and nodded, smiling.

—What's that? Isaac said. I can use the sign language pretty well, but I aint learned any of the languages much—a few words—

—Just Kiowa—don't talk it much myself. He pursed his lips, thinking: shrewd, thin-lipped mouth turned down at the corners, outlined by a drooping white mustache, wide-set, reflective eyes that seemed to look through, focused on distance, white hair trimmed roughly short, cheeks pricked with a week's growth of white whiskers. He wore a rumpled, work-stained suit of dark gray homespun, a collarless blue flannel shirt buttoned neatly to the neck, a red bandanna loosely knotted; a big man, heavy-shouldered, still handsome in his age; slow-spoken, slow in thought, in act.

—Now, Chisholm said, smiling as the thought formed itself, didn't I hear you got a place over on the Whitewater? Trading with the Wichita, and give them credit—

—By the spring, Towanda. I was out on the Saline till the Indians scared my wife, and the Rebels came through, raiding—came down last year—

—Now that's how my wife took it too, same thing down on the Canadian, and a woman don't like upsetness. And then I couldn't get no goods—. Say—the smile enlarged—I kept going to ride over for a visit when I got this place fixed, and now you've come—been wonderin where I'd get my stock, but if you got goods to sell—well, say, there's business we can do. . . .

Taking Isaac and Jim by the arms, he led them toward his lodge to talk. His wife, he said, had coffee on the fire.

Isaac was not averse to some arrangement with Chisholm, but he was having thoughts of setting up another trading station farther west for Jack Lawton to manage. So he returned from Topeka after his first winter as a legislator, which in truth he'd found confining, and suggested a hunt. He would look for a suitable site for a new trading post. Marie was pregnant again, but he would be gone only a month, and back well before April, the probable time the baby was due.

Isaac stayed three days at the ranch and started west on the Osage Trail with two wagons, Jack Lawton and Jim Kelly. Towakoni Jim joined the party as guide and companion and led them southwest from the ford below the mouth of the Little Arkansas, across the Ninnescah, the Chikaskia. They hit the Salt Fork of the Arkansas just across the line into the Indian Territory, at a meandering, peculiarly formed creek: the channel had doubled back, cut through, forming an island enclosed by flowing water. It had no name that the Indian knew. Isaac called it Round Pond: Round Pond Creek.

Here, at the edge of the Great Salt Plains, as on Isaac's winter hunts the year before, they found a few small bands of buffalo and their attendant wolves in numbers. All bulls: the cows, Jim said, would be farther south. Isaac ranged far, hunting, leaving the skinning to Jack Lawton, the care of the pelts and camp to the Kelly boy; the Indian provided meat, mostly deer, and Isaac let him keep the skins. After three weeks camped at Round Pond they had taken three hundred wolf pelts and two packs of hides, half-filling one wagon. Isaac determined to go farther south after the herds of cows Jim had talked of, perhaps meet them coming north with their calves—worth less than bulls, of course, but there would be wolves again; for good pelts Mr Durfee had been paying up to three dollars each. The Indian was skeptical: might be four days' drive and anywhere, now winter was past, they could meet a war party from one of the enemy tribes, Kiowa, Comanche. Isaac insisted. He would not go home with his wagons empty.

Rain began the first night and kept up all the next day, not hard, a gentle, soaking rain. The iron tires of the light-loaded wagons cut the trackless carpet of grass, the rust-red skin of earth oozed mud, clinging at the wheels, and they drove abreast, avoiding each other's tracks, and kept to the high ground between streams flowing south to the Cimarron. They went slowly, the mules tiring as they pulled through, becoming balky, and Jack and the boy grew angry and beat at them with their whips till Isaac made them stop, and they camped early, to wait it out. In the morning the rain had ceased but the gray clouds hovered low, damp, cold, clinging as ground mist, and the wet wood of their breakfast fire spat and sputtered and gave little heat. In mid-morning they entered a westward extension of the zone known as the Cross Timbers—several species of stunted oak, thick-grown, impenetrable except where pierced by what had once been deer or buffalo trails, kept open by Indians passing through, occasional traders, and having no sun they held their course south by the lie of the land, making for the Cimarron.

The river stopped them, known in this country to whites who knew it as the Red Fork of the Arkansas, which it joins a hundred miles east: the river was in flood, not, probably, from the light spring rains but from snow-melt high in the mountains to the west where it has its source. Isaac and Jim took their horses, left Jack and the boy to get the wagons turned and back up the trail to find a place where they could camp, and led them among the slender, tight-grown, bristle-branching trees, seeking a view of the river and its course. Half a mile east the forest gave way, they climbed, and came out at one end of a low, open, rocky bluff. Upstream in normal water the river ran broad and shallow between sandy mud banks perhaps a hundred yards across and here narrowed, deepened, speeded up, as for a mile it entered a kind of half-formed, rock-walled canyon. Up and down now as far as they could see, the river was over its banks, spreading three hundred yards wide among the stunted timber, its current strong and swirling.

Jim shook his head and looked solemn.—Still coming up, he said with finality, can camp here a week and we don't get across with horses, wagons. . . .

A little below them on the other side the river had overflowed behind the low bluff opposite and made a narrow island five or six

hundred yards long. There were four horses on it, tied by their forelegs to small trees.

Squinting, Jim stretched out one arm and pointed: above the island
on the far side of the river stood four Indians watching the trapped
horses, three men and a woman distinguishable at this distance by her
shapeless, ankle-length dress of pale, fringe-trimmed buckskin.—Kiowa! he said. Better have em over there, not this side. They see us, we
got to start back now today, get a week's start of em so they don't
never catch us.

Isaac nodded a grudging agreement but did not move, his eyes on
the little group of Indians, Bird's bridle loose in one hand. They were
arguing about something, the horses: voices lost in distance and the
hissing rush of the river, but you could read their gestures—the
woman pointed at the horses, the men shook their heads, looked
away, she made fists and shook them, stamped her feet in rage and
frustration.

Abruptly the woman undid the belt from her waist, bent over and
with crossed arms drew the dress over her head and flung it aside.
Straightening, she loosed the ties that held the square undergarment
between her legs, knelt and removed her knee-high leggins and moccasins. For a moment she stood erect and naked, looking out across
the churning water. The men watched her but made no move. Resolved, she walked forward into the water, knee-deep, thigh-deep,
pushed off with hardly a splash and swam out with strong, smooth
strokes, head up, her long hair floating out behind.

—Brave God-damn fool! Isaac said.

Jim shrugged.—She do it, maybe. Maybe she do it.

They mounted, walked their horses along the bank, curious, keeping pace, but it was already apparent the woman had misjudged: had
gone in too far above the head of the island, and the current had taken
her out into the main stream, was carrying her along twenty yards
out, thirty. She swam harder, throwing up a muddy-white spray as
she struggled to get across the current, but it carried her along, at an
angle, like a piece of driftwood. Now a tree came toward her, riding
low—Watch out! God damn it, watch out! Isaac had time to shout—
and seemed to roll across her, back, shoulders, head, she ducked, for a
moment was gone, the floating tree passed over; head popped up,
arms lifted, thrashing, shouting, went down again, one hand grabbed
at the passing roots—.

Isaac trotted the horse a few steps forward, jumped down and
stripped off his coat and shirt, sat to pull at his boots, trousers, drawers—sprinted down the shelving, grassy bank like a schoolboy let out
from school, and entered the water in a flat, hard dive. Jim took Bird's
bridle and settled back in his saddle, watching. Isaac's arms and legs
beat the water in a strong, inelegant crawl that carried him in a slow

arc down the river and across the current, toward the floating tree and the Indian woman, still clinging to a root with one hand, head down—reached it, grasped with both hands, kicking, trying to drive it like an overturned canoe toward the shore of the island—. She let go, slipped off, sinking, he saw, dove, brought her up, hands under her arms, lifting—struggle, the water spraying upward, open hand smacking her face, hard, one hand now clutching at the trailing wrack of hair, scissor-kicking, scooping at the water with his free arm, towing her toward the shore—. Near the foot of the island the main stream met the lesser current of the inner channel and began to eddy out and he got her into it, hands under her shoulders, dragging, felt for the bottom and stood, waist-deep, dragging her up the bank. . . .

Isaac pulled her up the sodden grass, leaned and rolled her over, head down, and crouched astride her waist, leaned forward, hands on her ribs, pressing with the weight of his body, and a coughing gust of water came forth from her mouth; sat back, leaned and pressed again, but no more came. Scratches, scrapes, little cuts on her back and shoulders: blood oozed, pink and transparent, diluted in the wetness of her skin. He slipped off, kneeling, turned her on her back and stood. Not a woman but a girl, smooth-skinned and slender-waisted, tall as he was, broad-shouldered, hard, flat-muscled belly under the girl-fat, strong arms and thighs, taut breasts. And not Indian but white: face tanned golden under the traces of vermilion paint on cheeks and forehead, but her body pink and fair, pale aureoles circling the untried girl's nipples starting from her breasts, and a delicate spume of reddish hair flowering from the triangular mount between her thighs; and her hair, darkened with grease and dirt, was blond at the scalp. A small, narrow-bladed knife lay in a beaded buckskin sheath between her breasts, hung from a cord of rawhide around her neck.

The eyelids flickered open, closed, and opened wide, seeing him.

—You're no Indian, he said. You're white.

She answered something he did not understand, Kiowa, choked, gasped.

Isaac took a step back, frowning, hands resting on his hipbones.— Come on, get up, he said, his voice harsh. White girl! You aint drowned yet, and there's still your God-damn horses. Get up!

The girl lay on her back unmoving, only the tight-muscled breasts faintly lifting and falling as the breath came, watching him as if she slept with her eyes open.

—Get up and walk, God damn it! he said. You know you're no Indian—understand English as well as I do. Now get up!—

Obediently she heaved herself forward, sitting, turned on her knees and pushed up, arms trembling, and fell flat. He stooped, lifted, got her limply to her feet, and drew one arm across his shoulders, pulled her close with a hand on her waist. He walked her slowly up the island, matching his steps to hers, thigh pressing thigh, toward where the horses whinnied and strained at their ropes. The island was smaller now, narrower, the water still rising.

When they reached the horses he let her go. She stood for a moment, then slowly her knees doubled under her and she sat, torso upright, hands in her lap, head tilted back a little, watching him. When he bent over to take the knife her arms came up defensively, covering her breasts, and he slapped them aside. He cut the tether of the nearest horse and gathering a handful of mane led it toward the channel, into the water, hock-deep. The horse stopped, held back, withers trembling. The muddy current eddied and pulled at its legs. He startled it with a smart slap on the rump and it stepped forward a few nervous steps, belly-deep now, feeling the lift of the current, whinnied, reared, eyes rolling, and came down afloat, shoulders working as if at gallop and head high, swimming. The current rushed the horse twenty yards downstream before it found bottom again and scrabbled up to dry ground, and one of the Kiowa boys, watching, ran and caught it. Isaac turned back, released the second horse, and drove it across. The girl still sat. A tremor went through her upper body, shaking her shoulders.

—Get up, move around, Isaac commanded. You're cold—it'll warm you. Then as she did not move: What's your name?

—Pat-so-gate—

—That's not your name, he said, furious, that's an Indian name. What's your real name?

—Pat-so-gate.

Isaac shook his head in exasperation.—Listen, Patsy, he said, we got to get you across now—get you up and moving or you're going to drown. Come on now—

When she did not move he stepped behind her, lifted, and set her on her feet. She stood there. He started her with a smack across the buttocks, led her by one arm, and went back to bring the third horse, a small, spotted mare with black ears.

—Current aint that strong, he said, maybe you could ride her across, but—what you got to do is, when I start her, grab her tail and hang on, and she'll get you over—

The girl shook her head and her mouth rounded in a wordless cry. He slapped her, hard, one cheek, then the other, and the moaning stopped. He led the horse into the water and tentatively the girl gathered the long tail in one hand and as the horse pulled, stumbled forward, made a grab with the other hand, and fell with a splash as the horse pushed off, swimming. Isaac watched them across. As the horse came out, the girl let go, went limp, and lay at the edge of the

water, face down. Two of the Indian boys ran and caught her,
dragged her up. Isaac went back for the other horse.

When he came up from the water behind the last horse the girl lay
on her back, eyes closed, and the three boys stood over her with
lugubrious expressions. Her flesh was pale as stone, prickled all over
with goosebumps, and the tremors had come back, drawing her legs
up at the knees. His own skin tingled, pink with warmth.

—Can't you see she's freezing cold? he said. Don't any of you know
enough to make a fire?—and when they looked blank repeated in the
passionless language of signs—make fire—girl sick—cold—

One of the young men ran among the timber and came back with
an armful of wet sticks and another produced a knife, feathered one
into a fur stick, knelt, struck a match, and lighted it, and snapping
twigs and laying them across slowly blew the hissing flames to fire.
Isaac jerked a buffalo robe from one of the Indians' shoulders, made
the girl kneel up, facing the fire, and wrapped the robe around her.
Another gave Isaac his own robe and went to bring the girl's dress
and moccasins.

Pat-so-gate was still huddled at the small fire, naked except for the
robe draped down her shoulders and back, but finally warming, the
chilled blood returning color to her flesh when an Indian came riding
from a trail leading south and, seeing her, leaped down with a cry and
ran toward her. She stood, pulling the robe close, and went to him,
and he seized her, drew her in, and held her; a big, broad-faced man,
straight black hair worn loose, a hair-fringed buckskin shirt hanging
to his thighs and a blue blanket draped from his shoulders like a toga.
The girl freed herself, stepped back and spoke at length, telling her
story. Brusquely the man turned away and came toward Isaac with
arms outstretched, took both his hands and held them, looking into
his eyes. Isaac spoke his name and in signs explained himself: a
hunter, trader from the Whitewater country, after buffalo and wolves
with his men—he pointed across the river where Jack, Jim, and the
Wichita watched from the bank with the two horses. The Indian was
Set-im-kayah, a name which in signs came out "bear runs over man,"
and after a moment Isaac remembered: one of several notable Kiowa
leaders of his generation who had taken a bear name and a famous
warrior, but in defense, known as chary of promises or of putting his
name to treaties, but his word once given, honorable, comparatively,
in keeping them; commonly Stumbling Bear in English. He knew, of
course, of the fight at Mathewson's post and the attack on the supply
train, Isaac's part and the name the Kiowa had given him there, Pai-
tal-ye; folly that had killed or maimed too many of the tribe's young
men, in which he had refused to join—he had no quarrel with Sin-
pah-zil-ba. The girl, he said, was his daughter—half-daughter, step-
daughter. His people were camped a short distance up a creek to the

south; Isaac must come to his lodge and stay, two or three days, till
the river went down enough to cross, or if not then, he would make a
buffalo-hide boat to carry him back. Isaac went to the river's edge and
saw that it was so: the island where the horses were tied had dwindled to a narrow hump breaking the current like a fish's back, its few
small trees all awash. In slow, exaggerated signs he told Jim what he
would do and that they should camp and wait, and the boy signaled
that he understood.

Seeing that Isaac went barefoot, Set-im-kayah knelt, removed his
own moccasins, and placed them on Isaac's feet. He took Isaac by the
arm and led him toward his horse. Evening was coming now: sun low
to the treetops in the southwest, an opaque brightness diffused in the
mist-gray of cloud flooding the horizon.

After two days of rain at Towanda the clouds cleared, followed by a
drying wind, and the sun burst forth, bright and warm, not hot—
delightful weather! Marie was sitting in the sun sewing, where she
could watch the little one playing along the edge of the spring: he
walked everywhere now, or rather ran, with forward-leaning, tum-
bling steps and arms out for balance, and only lifted his arms and
pouted, asking to be picked up, when very tired and hungry. He
played at words too, *ma-ma*, very plain, and *pa-pa*, sometimes said it,
pointing, at Abe Kelly and then shook his head *no*, a man but not his
father, he knew. A lovely, golden-headed, active little boy, as Isaac
must have been.

Marie looked up from her work. Where was Bunny? Searched with
her eyes and found him, and the moment of indrawn breath sighed
from her lips, calling—Bunny, come back here, darling, you've gone
too far. Bunny!—down the little stream that flowed out from the
spring, dappled with shadow of spring sunlight through the trees. He
crouched at the edge of the stream, examining a handful of pebbles,
oblivious as a puppy that hears a command and will not mind. She
started toward the little boy, still calling—Bunny! *Bunny!*—
Stopped. What was it, beyond? Someone's big yellow dog, who had
such a dog? or—a deer, lying down, sick or wounded, yes, and the
hunters after it, somewhere down the stream—. Stretched crouching,
tawny in the mingled black and gold of the dappling light, a long soft
form not twenty feet beyond where the boy sat playing, paying no
mind: great wedge of cat's face lifted, sleepy-eyed, thick velvet rope of
tail twitched at the end, taking notice—panther, Isaac had told her,
seen once on Paradise Creek, and again, on the winter wolf hunt on
the Salt Plains—

She cried out, running—Bunny! Come back here, Bunny—and this
time the little boy looked up, saw her, puzzled, stood but did not
move, making a fist of his pebbles. She fell on her knees beside him,

pulling him to her, soft body pressed against her swollen belly: looking, eyes wide and staring. Lazy and deliberate, the mountain lion rose, stretched, thick-padded paws pushing at the worn grass, pale eyes staring back, indifferent.

Abruptly, with fearful grace and quickness, it had leaped the stream, another rolling bound, she tried to follow with her eyes but could not in the deceiving light, under trees, such utter silence; gone, as if dreamed, and she had wakened from her dream. She still held the boy tight to her, panting, he squirmed to get free.

—Miz Pride? What is it, Miz Pride?—Abe Kelly's hand touched her shoulder, polite and concerned, and she held her breath, let go the boy, and got herself up.

—Panther—not twenty steps off from little Bunny—lying down by the stream—

—They're shy, they say, won't ever go for a man. *I* never seen one.

—She just looked like a big old housecat lying in the sun, Marie said.

Marie led the boy back to the house, nursed him, set him on the rug by the cold hearth to play till he was tired, and tried to go on with her work but made mistakes. She made up the fire in the stove and mixed batter for biscuits. When supper was done and the child in his cradle she lighted the lamp by the bed, and lay down, still dressed and propped on a pillow, to read. The roiling wind that had followed the rain gusted around the house, tearing at the big trees beside the spring—she could not follow the familiar story, laid the book aside, leaned at the cradle. She drew the knitted robe an inch up, smoothed it across his narrow shoulders. She closed her eyes and saw again the panther crouched by the spring to leap, must have dozed, till something startled her awake. *What was it, was-it, was-it, was-it?* reverberating through her mind like birdsong: she lay rigid, not breathing, listening—where? Through the log wall, the store on the other side, the sound as of a door pulled to, drawers sliding, slamming shut—how could that be, through walnut logs squared eight or ten inches thick, all two strong men could strain to lift and set in place? must have dreamed, imagined—. Steps moving, one, two, three, across plank floor, soft, whispering—the cat, the great cat, had it got in?—a muffled crack of wood on wood, a chair leg, momentary, scraping the floor—

—Abe! Abe Kelly! Is that you out there?

The door flung inward, crashed against the wall, and a man took a sliding step across the sill, leaning against the doorframe. With two running steps Marie reached the end of the bed and placed herself between the cradle and the intruder, and—

—You! Get out of here! she cried. You can't come sneaking in my house—making shooing motions with her hands and arms, and the man slumped back against the door: squat and broad, scraggy hair falling from a black, broad-brimmed hat around the creosote duskiness of his face, greasy buckskin hunting shirt hanging down over denims, unsheathed bowie knife carelessly stuck in his belt, mudcaked moccasins. But the eyes: like two spoiled eggs in a bowl, wide and staring, blinking in the lamplight.

—Go on now, Marie said in the calm, firm voice she used in talking with the Indians. If you want to trade, you come to the store in the morning, when the men are about. Not sneaking in my house, in the middle of the night.

She took a step toward him, another step. He backed away, stumbled, lurched backward into the main room and caught himself against the table edge.

—Get away from there! Marie said sharply. The lamp—

He leaned back, hands flat on the table, sick eyes staring, did he not understand? Or sick, wounded, starving—

—If something is wrong, she said, if you want food—well, I have meat put away, I will cut you some to take, and cold biscuit, there is still some coffee on the stove—

She stepped briskly past him, touched her fingers to the coffeepot, still warm, and knelt at the fire door to stir the coals, add sticks from the woodbox beside the oven.

—Money! the Indian said in a thick voice. White man—money—

—We are traders, Marie said over her shoulder, poking at the fire. We give money to Indians that have things to trade, you can come in the morning. Or—you have business maybe with the agent, Major Gookins, he lives in the double cabin. Come. I will show you where.

She straightened up, turned—persuade him out the door, shut it, quick, jam it with a chair, a chest dragged over—. The Indian had come around the table and faced her again, still leaning back, and then it reached her, the air he breathed was reasty with the putrid smell of half-digested whisky, vomit; drunk, he was only drunk.

Both his hands slipped under the waistband of his trousers and brought out his long, limp, hooded member, held it, waggling it at her. A jet of urine spurted at her in a long arc, pattering a dark spreading pool on the unfinished boards, like a horse making water. Grinning, he took a step toward her, arms outstretched, another, the flabby end of his pizzle hanging down from under the tail of his shirt.

—Baby—make baby—

Marie backed away, stooped with a rush to the woodbox, watching him, and brought up the handax—a little, short-hafted tomahawk with an ugly spiked poll Isaac had taken in trade and kept sharp for splitting kindling. She raised it over her head, backing, turning, watching his eyes, his reaching hands—

—Get away now! Get out of my house!

She felt the table, a chair back, jerked it out with her left hand and swung it around, getting it between them. He ducked his head, paused, then sudden as a leaping cat lunged forward, knocking the chair aside, arms reaching for her legs, and her arm fell sure as chopping stovewood, the blade struck his spine below the neck with a soft *chnk* as of sharp steel buried in rotten wood. She went over backward, the haft tight in her hand, pulled free, got on her feet, still holding the ax. He lay face down, arms reaching, legs for a moment twitched like a fish brought to land and were still. She looked down at him, motionless, limp, arms hanging. The baby wailed from the bedroom, wakened.

—My baby!

The ax dropped from her hand. She ran to get him, left the house still running, door standing open, pale light from the two lamps— outside in the dark a great ghost shape, horse, the Indian's horse, reared, screamed, she dodged, ran on, holding the baby, crying out for *Abe! Abe Kelly!* his cabin fifty yards off in the starlit darkness—. And stumbled, twisting as she fell, and struck the soft earth on one side, hip and shoulder, the baby clutched to her breast and safe, and then for moments knew, felt, nothing more. . . .

—I could get you across in the bull boat, Patsy, Isaac said, take you back to my ranch—you could stay with my wife till this war's over and then—well, I've got the Indian agent on the place, he'll find your parents for you and we'll send you home. . . .

Isaac had been two days in the Indian camp now, had taken a horse and ridden to the river to look, and the girl Pat-so-gate came along: no longer rising, perhaps starting to recede, the island showing again above the whirling water, and Set-im-kayah, as he promised, had made a round frame of saplings lashed with rawhide and covered it with green buffalo hide; Isaac had occupied one afternoon whittling a short paddle to steer with, telling the Indian how they made their dugout canoes on the Mississippi, when he was a boy. In the morning Isaac would cross the river and start for home.

—At first, the girl said, I wanted to run away and was afraid. Terrible things—they do terrible things to girls that run away. Now Set-im-kayah is kind, and loving—the young men come to our lodge and sing, in the night, and want me for wife, and one who is rich, a warrior and a hunter, staked twenty horses outside and left a stack of buffalo robes, but none has pleased me and Set-im-kayah will not make me choose. The horses and the robes he gave back. Now I do not know. Maybe inside I am Kiowa now. If there should come some beautiful young man that pleased me—that wanted me—

She reached and touched Isaac's damp hair, stroking it, until he pushed her hand off with an impatient shake of his head. They sat apart on the sloping, grassy bank, watching the river rushing past below. Earlier, they swam. She had been afraid, he wanted to show her, make her understand, and lose her fear: a strong swimmer, she had mistaken the current, then tried to fight it and it wore her out, and then the driftwood hitting—you have to use the current, let it carry you, he said, and he showed her, floating on his back and paddling to steer, caught hold of one of the little island trees as he drifted past and held on to rest, and she followed, they swam hard across the channel, ran back up the bank, hand in hand, laughing, and tried again, and came out, got dressed, and he made a fire to dry by. It puzzled him: he had never looked on a woman in her nakedness to study the curious convolutions of her body, nor been looked on. In the lodge at night he lay on the men's side, naked under the buffalo robes, and heard the women's breathing, the chief's two wives and the girl, and slept badly, dreaming of her naked, muscular body lying limp on the wet grass; and in the morning woke and dressed, and they left their clothes in two piles on the bank to swim, and none of it seemed strange but like a life remembered and returned to.

The girl for the afternoon and night when Isaac came to Set-im-kayah's lodge would speak no English but seemed to understand when he spoke to her; and then in the morning was voluble, as if her language had returned in sleep. She was twelve, still ignorant of the woman's mystery, when a party of raiders led by Set-im-kayah took her from the farm in the hill country north of San Antonio. It was spring; none hurt or killed, the Indians assured her later, though there had been a chase. Patricia Thomson her name had been—Pa-tit-siah Ton-sone she said, making it Kiowa. That was six winters back. The chief from the first treated her as a daughter, not a wife, a future wife, to his wives' relief, and called her Pat-so-gate, a kind of play on her American name, meaning "Looking Alike"—for a beautiful daughter of about her age, dead of smallpox a year before.

She was intensely curious to know everything concerning Isaac's wife, what kinds of work she did and whether she could ride a horse or tan a robe, and particularly what clothes she wore down to slippers, stockings, corsets, underwear; matters of which he discovered he could give no very clear account. She insisted also on knowing how they—here, having no English for it, she made the universal sign for copulation, applied indifferently to humans and the various animals: did she lie on her back and spread her legs, or the other way, and she straddled him like a horse, or—? Isaac told her stiffly that white people did not talk of such things. Again she tightened her lips in a puzzled frown, disbelieving, but too properly brought up to say so; she told him that in the village they often talked of it, since it was interesting.

—I will come to your ranch if I can be your wife, Patsy said with a shrewd look.

—You know I've got a wife—a white man can't have two. Your father never had two wives—your real father, Texas father.

He took her hand, turned it up, and traced the callused mounts of her palm with the tip of his index finger, hard, thick, and rough as a man's with her Indian work.—Don't you know, Patsy, he said softly, you've got a mother, father, down there grieving for you yet, all these years? Set-im-kayah wouldn't stop you, going home now, it's where you ought to be. And something else—you go there, I bet right now there's some young man, strong and brave and handsome, that'd jump to marry you, give everything he has just so you'd let him set to work and make you happy. . . .

For answer, the girl leaned and pressed his hand with her lips, then on her knees laid fresh wood carefully on the fire, turned back and lay down, stretching like a cat, eyes closed, head cushioned on his lap, serenely smiling. Propping his shoulders on his arms, he was comfortable and at peace, and he let her stay.

The first morning Set-im-kayah with no explanation produced a pair of nearly new trousers of cavalry cut, light blue with a darker stripe down the sides and a brass-buckled belt, for Isaac to wear; and an oversize buckskin hunting shirt that fell to his knees. They sat facing each other over a small fire in the center of the tepee, conversing seriously and sharing a pipe—a merely companionable smoke, not ceremonial; Isaac, not a smoker, politely touched the stem to his lips, held the hot bowl in his hands, and passed it back. The chief knew of Pai-tal-ye's trading places, on the Saline and now on the Whitewater, but had visited neither, too far to go: if the trader would bring goods to trade, he would inform the other bands of Kiowa gathered at the Sun-Dance camp in the summer that he was not to be molested. While they talked and passed the pipe, men of the chief's band scratched at the door flap, came in, made greetings, and sat in silence, watching—and women, boys lifting the tepee's outer edge to push their heads in—curious to see the golden-haired cold white man the people called Sun-Boy. Isaac described the place he called Round Pond, and Set-im-kayah knew it: if the Kiowa brought robes and other furs, the next winter, he would build a cabin there and have goods to trade—had meant to visit Chisholm's ranch on the North Canadian, but the flood stopped him, and later would trade there too, if it would serve the tribe—if Chisholm would allow him. First rule: no promise that cannot be exactly kept; or if qualified, the saving reservation must be expressed. The chief appeared content.

—Pai-tal-ye, the girl said, opening her eyes.

—You know my name's Isaac.

—You have two names, like me—I can call you which I like. But—

keep your Kiowa name, you come and live with us and be Kiowa, and
Set-im-kayah take you for his son, and then . . .

Her voice trailed off. He did not answer; more of her girl talk.

—Ees-sak, she said, making his name Kiowa and giggling. We have
different stories—*Kiowa* have different stories. Man live in one world,
woman in another, and they try to come to each other and they cannot, or cannot stay: worlds on top of worlds. Listen—. She sat up,
turned and faced him, kneeling. You go to that world and be Isaac,
but also stay in this world and be Pai-tal-ye, Kiowa. Be two men, and
I will marry one.

—You know that's just fairy tales. In the morning I'm going across
that river and starting home. I'd still take you if you'd go, whatever
Set-im-kayah says, and get you home to your family somehow. . . .

She was silent a long while, eyes half-closed, imagining.—When
you have gone, Pai-tal-ye—the women will go out, bringing in wood,
like they do every day. I will go by myself where they cannot hear
and sing sad songs, and cry. You will be in your white man's world
with your wife and babies, and I will be here, Pai-tal-ye, and I'll cry.

He should have stopped her then with harshness, threats: Don't
need any white Kiowa squaw that aint used soap in six years—got
one wife and that's enough—you get on home where you belong,
because it's *right*—and if you won't, by God, I'll beat it into you. He
answered nothing. A man wears down, gets tired. He did what a man
does, faced with a girl's tears, the threat of tears: reached and caught
her in his arms and pulled her close, and with his lips caressed her
ears, cheeks, eyes, her mouth.

Kneeling on the robe in front of the cold fireplace, the big Indian
tossed Bunny high in the air and as he came down caught him at the
last instant under the shoulders, for a moment held him off the floor,
legs kicking, and then gently lowered him and set him on his feet.
The little boy screamed with excited laughter, wide eyes sparkling in
the light from the lamp set high on the chimney piece.

—More, more! he shouted. Again!—

Beaming, the Indian started a different game. Marie in the straight
chair cradled the sleeping baby in her arms and smiled and felt no
anxiety for her son. Satanta! the great war chief of the Kiowa, the
name more than any other the frontier women used to frighten
naughty children to bed, and yet so gentle, so loving a father he must
be, playing and laughing with Bunny on the floor. It was because he
was a boy, of course; the Indian had shown only the most superficial
interest in the new little girl, Mamie.

Satanta now was playing a horse game, jouncing the boy on his
knee, his fingers become reins; too exciting, he would never sleep, and
it was late, full dark out the window. Leaning forward, Marie caught

the Indian's eye, pointed, and tilted her head to a sleeping gesture of
her hands. He nodded, gave the boy a final hug, and sent him marching toward his mother like a toy soldier come to life. Balancing the
baby on her hip, Marie took his hand and led him to the bedroom—
his own bed now that fitted under theirs, and the cradle had come
down to Mamie. Satanta rose, stretched, broke wind, yawned, and
noisily scraped Marie's chair across the floor to join the others at the
table, scowling now, arms folded on his chest.

Isaac had been excessively busy ever since the spring hunt, much of
his business in cattle. First a party of Wichita had gone south to their
own country or beyond for a cow hunt and come back with a hundred and fifty head they said were theirs or anyway repayment for
cattle and horses stolen by Indians and Rebels—most carried Texas
brands or had their ears peculiarly cut in jinglebobs for the same
purpose. Isaac bought them for under five dollars each in money and
goods and then after some discussion with Major Gookins kept them
around Mr Chisholm's new trading post between the two rivers, with
one of the Mexicans to herd. Then Mr Chisholm went down to his
home ranch on the Canadian and came back with another four hundred head, and Isaac bought them too and hired two more boys to
keep them; six dollars this time in money, but Mr Chisholm threw in
his trading post for the cowherds to stay in, a corral, and a small cabin
beside a grove of walnut trees two or three miles above the mouth of
the Little Arkansas. Isaac carried over a load of goods to store there,
for trading with the Wichita. Besides that and the store at Towanda,
he had set up Dave Ballon, the Cherokee trader, at the Caddo village
on Cowskin Creek, ten miles south, and sent Jack Lawton and the
Kelly boys still farther down, to the place he called Round Pond, to
build the post he had promised the Kiowa and the other wild tribes.
After bringing in his own herd, Mr Chisholm loaded all the rest of
Isaac's Towanda stock and went south again, buying cattle for a man
with a military beef contract for the forts in New Mexico, paying for
them with Isaac's goods, on credit; and returned with three thousand
head.

In June Isaac put his brand on his cattle, a jagged sunburst on the
left hip with a line coming down through it, ending in feet, which he
said was a cipher of his initials, I P, but also a sign for his Indian
name, Sun-Boy, in the circle of the sun; and drove the herd through
to Leavenworth with all his wagons. Mr Durfee was alarmed when
Isaac came in and told him he was holding more than five hundred
head on the prairie west of Leavenworth—he was not, he said severely, a cattle dealer but a merchant in Indian goods; but nevertheless for a five percent commission contrived to find a buyer in the
quartermaster department at Fort Leavenworth who gave fifteen dollars apiece. Isaac came home in extravagant spirits, talking of selling

out his business and going into cattle. He was hardly back with the goods to supply what were now four trading posts when Major Gookins gave him the news of the treaty-making in the fall: it meant presents, of course, and by custom food to sustain the Indians during the week or two of counciling, it might be ten thousand people if they all came in; and the chance of contracts for rations and annuities if the tribes agreed to go on reservations in the Territory, as they were intended to. Isaac and Mr Chisholm went partners: started immediately for Leavenworth with all their wagons, and this time came back with thirty thousand dollars' worth of goods—more than they could unload and store at the Walnut Grove post until Isaac built a new warehouse as big as the entire house at Towanda.

And then Colonel Leavenworth arrived.

So since April Isaac had been home hardly two days running, and when he was, so tired out from work and travel, so burdened with letters to write, accounts to bring up, she pitied him. Pity: it was why she had not taxed him with her anger.

The anger was very real—*if Isaac was here, if Isaac was not off on his hunt.* She left the house running, fell, but did not hurt, and Bunny was unharmed; got up and went to Abe Kelly's cabin, woke him, and he brought a lantern and led her by the arm to Mrs Addie Chandler's place to stay the night, and went back to the house and sat up till dawn, the lamps burning and two revolvers, loaded, in his lap, but there was only the one Indian, lying dead all night on the floor, and his horse; in the morning dragged the body out and dug a grave under the trees across the creek and put the horse in the corral, and scoured the little blood from the floor with a pail of water from the spring and a flat stone. In the night the pangs came and in the morning the baby, little and wrinkled and red, too soon, but it could nurse, and lived.

Two days after, Isaac came in with Jack Lawton, the Kelly boy, and Jim, so penitent she forgave him, but the anger remained. If he had been there she need not have killed—the Indian was drunk and foolish, sick, and would not have gone for her if Isaac was there, she wanted to feed him, put him to bed. Settlers down the river knew him as Horse, Man Afraid of His Horse, his Osage name unknown— a thief, a beggar, sick with whisky, a half-blood outcast from the tribe; an old man with no relatives to fulfill the tribal duty by killing a member of the killer's tribe, a white, any white; unmourned except by Marie.

They called the baby Mary Elizabeth, for Isaac's mother and his sister. The pet name was Bunny's trying to say it: May-mee. Isaac promised latches and locks for the outside doors, next trip to Leavenworth—or might as well have ordered them from Mr Durfee by letter, but Marie refrained from nagging him about it; while he was in the house, she felt less urgent for such security.

Marie in the bedroom watched the children till they slept; came out, remade the fire, and stood at the stove while fresh coffee boiled. Satanta was loud and rude, thumping the table with his fist. From what Colonel Leavenworth said, he was talking of rations: he would bring his people to talk if the white man gave rations—plenty to eat—a feast every night of the council. The one called Stumbling Bear scowled and said nothing.

XVI

Down Chisholm's Trail

Major Gookins lay propped on pillows, dressed in his usual dark broadcloth and outmoded ruffle-front shirt, sheaves of prepossessing documents spread around him on the coverlet and a battered portable writing desk inset with panels of worn morocco across his lap: a long, thin, gray, proprietous man who had a way of winding around a subject with skeins of courteous circumlocution as if to come too suddenly to the naked point would cause him actual pain. For some days now he had kept to his quarters. Isaac had wasted a good part of the afternoon sitting by his bed without discovering the nature of his indisposition, which for all he could tell might be gout, a touch of the frontier fever and ague supposed to be brought on by new-turned virgin soil, even cholera; or only an unsettling dose of offhand rudeness from his illustrious colleague Colonel Leavenworth. What he was endeavoring to communicate had something to do with the Wichita and the other refugees under his care: not invited, of course, not officially—to the council, but certainly they were interested parties, were they not? and would attend, no doubt, invited or not—if only to share in the rations the Department expected to furnish all comers, as what Indian wouldn't? But supposing now some matter of interest to them came up in the proceedings—and their agent not in attendance, since certainly he was in no condition to attend—and Colonel Leavenworth having expressly declined to commission an interpreter for the Wichita. But then who was to make them understand when the proceedings touched, as it might be, their vital interests? And who was to communicate their views of the same?

Isaac, looking into the mild, depthless gray of the old man's eyes, received a glimmer of meaning and nodded his assent: he was to be deputed. With a drawn-out sigh, the major dipped his pen and in his

flowing official hand wrote out the appointment on the agency letterhead, blotted it dry, smoothed it, held it up to reread, and nodded.
Isaac took the paper, folded it away in his pocketbook, and with
wishes for the agent's recovery excused himself.

Isaac had been attending to his trading post between the two rivers
at Walnut Grove when the Indians began to gather early in October,
too occupied this year to get home to Towanda and take note of his
birthday: a few families at first, traveling together, then whole bands,
hundreds of warriors trailing a thousand or more women, children,
old men, coming up the Little Arkansas in a broad, straggling, not
quite military column, chiefs and headmen leading, according to their
eminence, and the priestly pipeman out front, on foot; and not only
the five tribes the government meant to settle with but, as he learned
when they came in to trade for sugar or gingham, some of all those
names that had been drawn into the vortex of Kansas, Wichita and
Caddo, Delaware and Shawnee, Sac, Konza, Potawatomi, a few Osage
fresh from what they considered hard bargaining on a treaty of their
own, a little earlier in the fall. The prospect looked good.

The council was to be held in a grove of big cottonwoods a mile
above the Osage crossing of the Little Arkansas, and Isaac drove there
on his way back from Towanda, to present his letter from Major
Gookins. Colonel Leavenworth had been installed in the growing
official camp for a week—representatives from all levels of the Indian
office, their clerks, stenographers, confidential secretaries, interpret-
ers, a company of cavalry, teamsters, and two generals with their
escorts: John Sanborn, sent to uphold the interests of Sherman's command in the West, which he had retained since the war's end; William
S. Harney, lately retired, for his imposing presence—he stood six feet
four, a massive, white-haired ramrod of a man—and the respect in
which the Indians were supposed to hold him. Isaac found the colonel's tent, let himself in, and stood in silence before the folding camp
table, proffering his letter. After a moment the agent looked up severely, as at a stranger, took the paper, spread it out, stared, and,
handing it back without a word, resumed his writing. The council,
Isaac tried again, when was it starting? but Colonel Leavenworth
only muttered—something about two of the commissioners, coming
down from the upper Arkansas and not yet arrived, and some of the
tribes—without glancing up from his work and left his visitor to
work out the answer for himself. As Isaac left, the aging voice, har-
ried into sharpness, was calling for his clerk.

Two days later Towakoni Jim rode past Isaac's post with a party of
Wichita, Owa-ha and three other chiefs, with two women to gather
wood and cook. Word had come down through the Indian camps that
the last of the white chiefs had arrived, Colonel Bent from his adobe-
walled palace in Colorado, General Carson from Taos, in an ambu-

lance accompanied by six troopers. No more Indians were expected. The great council was to begin in the morning.

The Indians were camped along the east bank of the Little Arkansas for three or four miles above and below the Osage crossing. There were ten thousand people assembled, perhaps twenty thousand, no one could say—a city on the move, an army at temporary rest, with uncountable herds of horses roaming the ripe plains for miles on both sides of the wooded riverbanks, and the women stooping under their bundles of firewood, leading loaded packhorses through the avenues of tepees, the packs of dogs racing and yipping, the boys with their toy bows and arrows playing at war and hunting, and the chiefs resorting to one another's lodges, sumptuously dressed and painted, to engage in grave and politic converse over the pipes, pausing as they entered for a critical sniff at the steaming cauldrons of meat, wo-haw, white men's meat, butchered daily from the bawling cattle herded in from the east and south, and here and there a splash of blue among the painted tents, an off-duty cavalryman discreetly hunting a squaw who would offer a neat-sewed hunting shirt or smoke-tanned buffalo robe, perhaps other, more personal commerce for a government-issue knife or haversack; and the little camp of the officials' regulation canvas tents around which whirred this ceaseless human movement set going by the white men's purposes and promises—implied promises, not yet set forth in words or written on the sheets of paper.

Yet for those same officials, charged with guiding the council to its predetermined goals, the actual numbers of Indians who had consented to come were of less moment than the absences. Most of the Kiowa seemed to be present. The Arapaho likewise: perhaps because their comparatively small numbers heightened the value they placed on peace, the price they would pay for the promise of it. On the other hand, the still smaller tribe of Kiowa Apache—speaking a language related to that of the Apache farther west but otherwise unconnected —after generations of living as one with the Kiowa had fallen out and were camped with the Cheyenne. The Cheyenne in turn were represented by that part of the tribe, perhaps half, that followed the peace policy of the head chief Moke-ta-ve-to, Black Kettle, the unprovoked slaughter of whose band at Sand Creek had both demonstrated the folly of attempting peace with the white men and encouraged the pacific elements in Congress and the Republic to insist on this hopeful gathering on the Plains. As for the Comanche, the two most intransigent bands had not appeared at all, and of the three others, only one, often allied with the whites against their fellow tribesmen, was largely represented. Men like Jesse Leavenworth had therefore reason to be querulous: unless all consented, whatever treaties resulted would be repudiated and of no effect, like so many other Indian treaties labored for in the past; not, probably, that their failure would make any more practical difference to the result than their success.

Two new tents had been set up in the official camp since Isaac's visit, two groups of tents: the great bright gaudy-striped pavilion that would be Colonel William Bent's, Turkey-carpeted inside, where, it was said, he dined with silver tableware and painted china arrayed on stiff linen and drank his wine from crystal goblets, and grouped around it, only a little less grand, the tents of his two half-Cheyenne sons and his daughter, convent-reared at St Louis, and of the servants; and over by the river the two plain canvas tents of General Carson and his escort. In front of one of these a man in a blue military tunic, unbuttoned on the white shirt, sat slouched on a camp stool when Isaac and the Wichita rode past, hunting a grassy spot to spread their buffalo robes for the night. He stood up, waved: a small, compact man, short arms and legs, who looked to be an inch or two shorter than Isaac himself; perhaps fifty years old and getting thick around the middle, silky hair receding from the forehead and worn to the shoulders, light brown with a glint of red as he stepped forward into the afternoon light.

—Fine-lookin horse, the man said in his quiet voice, looking up with eyes of palest blue between sun-wrinkled, narrowed lids. Them your Indians?

—Wichita—I trade with em at their village down by the mouth of the river. Their agent stays at my ranch, only he's sick, wanted me to come along with em to the council.

—Same with me—don't know what they wanted me for, like the Indians'd listen better if I talk than Harney or their own agents—he laughed—but they did, and I done my duty and come. . . .

—Could you be General Carson, then? Isaac doubtfully asked.

—Kit's good enough—Old Kit, he said and reached his hand to shake. The pictures aint much like, I'm sorry to say—them writers and sketch artists, they think they know more of a man's looks, and his business too, than he does himself. But say—if you're lookin for a place to sleep, I've got a camp cot you can put your robe on—and a wagonload of rations for the women to cook. And them chiefs—.

Isaac turned and explained Carson's offer to the politely waiting Wichita, and it was accepted. Isaac stayed the ten days of the treaty-making, riding back to Towanda on Saturday night for the Sunday when the council held no sessions. With a small keg of military whisky—no more a drinker than his young guest, but it represented his notion of the hospitable duty expected of him at such a gathering —Carson turned out companionable, answering Isaac's respectful questions freely enough, though often with a self-deprecating story told against himself, deflating the exaggerations of the books and magazines: like the time in his green youth, bound for Santa Fe with a train of wagons and camped at Pawnee Rock, set to guard duty and dozing off, and when the stock turned restive in the night, he roused, raised his rifle, and fired at a shape—and in the morning found he had shot his own mule through the head. He had perhaps no more of proficiency and selfless courage than a thousand others of his time. What he did have in uncommon degree was luck in surviving where others did not, and an effectual dutifulness coupled with intense modesty that endeared him as much to ambitious commanders as to writers remaking the current history of the West as popular fiction. Carson fitted the heroic role required of him. If he did not seek it, if he modestly corrected when he could the romancers' carelessness with the facts of his life, neither did he refuse to wear it, nor did he demean it, once he had put it on, by unworthy acts.

Carson was born on Christmas Eve of 1809—the same year as Isaac's father and the late President—the eleventh in a family of fifteen children that presently followed the westward drift from hill-country Kentucky to frontier Missouri, pulling up at Franklin, the earliest jumping-off point for the route to Santa Fe. At seventeen he escaped apprenticeship to a harness maker by joining a train bound for the Southwest; tried trapping up and down the mountains and years at a time in Spanish California, married an Arapaho woman and acquired some of the languages, and when the beaver trade declined made his living as a hunter supplying meat to Bent's Fort on the upper Arkansas. In 1842, taking a boat down the Missouri for a visit home, he fell in with a well-connected young lieutenant of the Topographical Corps, John C. Frémont, and agreed to guide an expedition commissioned by the U.S. Senate to map the Oregon Trail. Frémont's father-in-law was Senator Thomas Hart Benton of Missouri. The partnership continued, young liege and faithful squire: two further explorations, an expedition aimed at separating California from Mexico.

Frémont's career continued the upward trajectory—a fortune in California gold, then governor of the state, Senator—that would carry him within reach of the Presidency; and Carson's too, modestly and at a distance. He was appointed to the new agency for the Ute Indians of northeast New Mexico and settled at Taos. When the war came he raised a regiment of Union volunteers and received the rank of lieutenant colonel; saw action in the winter of 1864, leading a small force into the Texas panhandle to chastise the Kiowa, and was nearly crushed when he met the entire tribe camped near an abandoned trading post of Colonel Bent's, known on the South Plains, from its ruined condition, as Adobe Walls; where he was saved from massacre by determination, luck, and two twelve-pound howitzers. After the war he was promoted to brigadier general and called to assist in establishing a peace with the wild tribes.

The diffident modesty that made Carson a natural foil to an elegant, confident, self-destined man like Frémont had its roots in the un-schooled poverty of his frontier childhood: Interviewers generally reported his voice as "soft and effeminate," meaning not the quality of voice but the style of speech, slow, deliberate, and considered, avoiding the harsh, loud, blustering rant that passed for manliness in that age.

Sleeping in Carson's tent at the council grove, Isaac was struck by the ways in which the actual man differed from the romancers' tin-type. He noticed too but did not understand the bloodshot eye, red threads radiating like the spokes of a wheel from their blue-gray pupils, and the preternatural alertness, the older man sitting up on his cot in the night when a horse stirred outside the tent, a footstep passed; signs of the coming of age and sickness, of the time when a man no longer sleeps much but holds himself quiet in bed, listening and remembering.

The grove had been cleared of undergrowth and thinned some-what, the new-cut logs dragged into place and laid in rows as benches to accommodate the chiefs and headmen of the five tribes; common tribesmen, their women and children, led to the scene by curiosity, and others unofficially present, such as the Wichita, were left to squat or stand at the back and sides of this improvised theater, a vast throng humming with gossip and much coming and going, occasionally throbbing with grunts of approval at a chief's apt phrase or unan-swerable accusation. In a clearing at the front, facing this audience from behind a long bare table set up on trestles, like actors pantomim-ing the Last Supper or ministers in a sanctuary, sat the seven commis-sioners, with secretaries, clerks, and translators ranked at camp tables on either side.

Isaac spent most days crouched behind the last row of chiefs. He found the proceedings tedious. There were three treaties to be gotten through: with the Kiowa and Comanche; with the Kiowa Apache, affirming their new affiliation with the Cheyenne and Arapaho; and with the Kiowa Apache, Cheyenne, and Arapaho together. Each was preceded by days of speech-making. Usually General Harney spoke for the commissioners, sometimes after whispered consultations. The chiefs answered him tribe by tribe, any others who cared to be heard —rising in place, one hand on the breast holding robe or blanket in place, the other arm oratorically extended, sometimes only to express pleasure in being present, willingness to agree to whatever was to be agreed; or to make public obscure quarrels within the tribe. The force of the oratory was impeded by the necessity of translation: sentence by sentence into five other languages. Start and stop: the speaker spoke his measured words, then waited. Colonel Leavenworth occu-pied himself with documents from the copious supply in his overcoat pockets, Kit Carson sat sober-faced and glassy-eyed, as if asleep. Only General Harney remained alert and seemingly attentive to the end, huge and upright in his chair at the center as if observing a military exercise from a reviewing stand.

The council was dull for another reason: its outcome was foreordained. There might be adjustments of detail, but the treaties were already drafted before the first orator raised his voice, were indeed prescribed in form and substance by the hundreds of earlier treaties made between Indian tribes and the American government during the preceding seventy-five years. All that remained was for the attendant chiefs of the five tribes to signify their acceptance of what was offered.

What was offered was first of all "perpetual peace": the tribes were to refrain from "depredations" against whites or other tribes friendly to the United States, and any of their members accused of attacks were to be delivered to the authorities for punishment; where the tribes suffered, as they insisted they did, from whites or their Indian allies, they were to make their complaint through their agents to the President, who would arrange to resolve the dispute through binding and impartial arbitration. In return, the tribes were to settle as soon as practical within the boundaries of reservations established by the treaties. The Cheyenne and Arapaho, for now united with the Kiowa Apache, were to occupy a homeland vaguely defined between the Cimarron and Arkansas rivers. The Kiowa and Comanche reservation would lie to the south, between the Cimarron and the Red, extending west to New Mexico—pretty much all the territory they claimed but excluding the plains of western Kansas where their claim was disputed by enemy tribes. The five tribes would be secure from white settlement within these boundaries and conversely were not to leave them, for hunting or any other purpose, without written permission from their agents. The treaties did, however, qualify their rights to this land in several ways: the President was free to redefine the boundaries; roads might be run through the reservations without interference—the Santa Fe Road in particular, where many of the recent depredations had occurred, but also the railroads whose routes had been debated for a generation; and much of this land already belonged, by treaty and purchase, to other tribes, notably the Five Civilized Tribes of the Indian Territory. As an inducement to settle, the tribes were to receive annuities—trade goods of a specified dollar value. All five tribes promised to induce the bands that had not come in to accept the terms they had agreed to.

After supper on the evening of October 17, Carson and Isaac sat in silence by their cook fire while the older plainsman enjoyed a last cigar. The camp around them was quiet. The business of the council was about finished. In the morning the chiefs of the Kiowa and Co-

manche would "touch the feather"—make their X-marks, duly witnessed, the name spelled out beside each cross, on the last page of the
fair copy of their treaty—and the gathering would disperse. Suddenly
Carson was on his feet, backing away from the firelight, the half-
smoked cigar clamped in his teeth.

—What is it? said Isaac sharply.

The other pointed, and from the darkness a bulky figure astride a
lean black horse emerged, slumping in the saddle, a buffalo robe
pulled loosely around his shoulders, slipped to the ground, and with a
long stride seized Isaac in his heavy embrace.

—Set-im-kayah! Isaac said, pulling free. General Carson, this
here's—

The Indian stepped around the fire as Carson came back into the
light and gave his offered hand a fierce two-handed shake. For a minute or two they talked back and forth, nodding, with tight smiles.
Turning away, Stumbling Bear threw himself down beside the fire.

—Never did learn any Kiowa to speak of, Carson explained, but we
can both talk Comanche. He was sayin, I had me some luck, getting
out of that fix that time at Adobe Walls last year—hadn't been for
them cannon, throwin grape mongst the Indians, he'd a had my scalp
hung up in front of his lodge right now, and mighty pleased with
himself he'd be, too—. He's right of course, he added. That was a
darn-fool thing to get myself into. . . .

Carson leaned forward, held his cigar to the flame, puffed, and
remembered his manners; felt in his shirt pocket, produced a fresh
cigar, and reached it across to the Indian. Set-im-kayah bit the ends,
spat, pulled a stick from the fire, and pressed the coal to his cigar tip.
For a time he sat hunched in his robe, looking into the fire and smoking, his face troubled. Clearly he had not ridden in from his camp to
exchange pleasantries with Kit Carson, but what he wanted he did
not say. The two white men waited in silence.

At length, laying the cigar on the bare earth, the Indian turned and
addressed Isaac, his hands moving slowly and mournfully. His heart,
he said, was heavy with the paper the chiefs must put their names to
in the morning. Did this paper say good things? He did not know.
The Kiowa and Comanche would have a country where the soldiers
promised to keep white settlers from coming. It was not a large country. In ten days a man traveling slowly, wives and children and baggage, horses and dogs, could ride from one end to the other. But the
Kiowa had always gone everywhere on the Plains, it was necessary, to
follow the buffalo. How could they live when the buffalo in spring
and summer went north out of this narrow belt of country where the
white men wanted them to stay? How then could he put his mark on
the paper that said these things?

Isaac hesitated, turned to Carson—he at least had had some say in what went into the treaty—but the older man shook his head: it was Isaac the Indian wanted to answer.

He had listened to the same speeches as Set-im-kayah in the ten days of the council, and the mealtime talk among the commissioners, officials, soldiers. He tried to think through what he could answer. The buffalo, people claimed, were getting fewer every year, not only the Indians hunting as they always had but white hunters, more and more, for trade or sport: in time they would be gone, no way to build up the country anyhow while they lasted, and the Indians who lived by them would be gone too if they did not learn in time to live like white men, farming. That had been the idea for decades, generations: settle them on land, send them agents, schools, teach them to grow crops, raise cattle, maybe sheep; or get them out of the way of the settlers that would come in. But that part about the buffalo—it maybe sounded right enough in Congress when they were debating policy or ratifying treaties—he didn't believe it any more than any Indian hunter would. And turning them into farmers: he had grown up farming, could make his living at it well enough if he wanted, but let someone set him on a piece of ground and try to make him—. He thought of the Sac and Fox: farmed their own way back in Iowa and Illinois, between hunting seasons, and the settlers moved in, took the land, and when they wouldn't clear out called up the militia and had a war about it; and Seoskuk and his son in Kansas, making a farm like a white man, and it seemed they wouldn't put up with that either, and where were they gone? But Set-im-kayah now—what choice did he have? Take what's offered and try to make something of it. Or stay and fight till they kill you off.

—Set-im-kayah! Isaac said aloud and, looking him steadily in the eyes, began to try to explain. Among the Kiowa, all the tribes, he said, there were some men always wanted war, but others always peace. The Indian nodded. White people were the same. Some wanted only war, go on fighting till there were no more Indians left to fight—like that crazy soldier at Sand Creek, cutting up women and little babies—. Here Set-im-kayah glowered, struck his fists together, and Carson, watching the meaning of Isaac's hands, broke in with angry words in Comanche. So, Isaac continued, that was bad, and all the Americans were ashamed, and now the peace people had their chance —make a treaty of no more fighting, and a country for the Kiowa where the white men will not come, and a country for the whites where the Kiowa will not come, so they will not meet, misunderstand, and kill each other. But if the Kiowa will not stay in the country apart from the whites—if they let their war people keep on fighting—then the Americans will be ashamed of their peace people and will let their war people do what they want—

Isaac broke off. He wanted to say how, now the war was over, there were millions of trained soldiers free to kill Indians, if they went on fighting, millions more settlers to fill up the buffalo land, and fight for the land they got their living by, till there were no Indians left. The numbers were beyond the reach of the sign language, even if the Indian would believe: clear enough for counting on fingers, ten buffalo robes to trade, tens of robes, maybe even a thousand horses in a herd; not for the scale of the Civil War battles. He therefore resorted to similes: the white war people would send soldiers numberless as the stars in the heavens, the leaves of new grass in the spring. Now it may be every Kiowa will kill one soldier as a man kills the grasshoppers that swarm in the hot summer after a wet spring. But the soldiers will keep coming, and when they have passed over, the country will be empty of Kiowa as the prairies are stripped of grass where the hoppers have been.

He did not say what he would do if himself Kiowa but left it as a choice: sign the treaty and do what it says, and your children, their children, can learn the good things from the white men and be Kiowa still; or don't sign, go on fighting, and your tribe will vanish off the earth, like the snow on the hilltops where the spring sun pours down.

Set-im-kayah sat cross-legged, looking into the fire. Sun-Boy, he said finally, I know you do not lie, you say what you think is true, but you say as the white chiefs say. And what you say is death.

After a time, he found the dead cigar, held it close, examined it, sniffed, and laid it on the dying coals.

The Wichita were supposed to be starting south any day now, finally, and for days Isaac had been meaning to ride over for a last visit —wasn't just sentiment, though he was sorry to see them go, Jim especially, and they had had hard times enough already, but he meant to go on trading with them once they were settled again in their old country on the Washita—and could not make the time. It wasn't the cholera, anyhow: ran up against that with Sam Carter—fell off his chair at supper and Isaac and Abe Kelly sat by his bed all night, as he gagged and choked on his vomit, his belly tightening in painful knots, and fouling the bedclothes with something that didn't look like the diarrhea or smell it either, but like a thin rice soup; dosed him with calomel and morphine and whisky, made him keep drinking the pure water from the spring, but nothing helped and in the morning he was dead. They washed the body, got his good suit on him and buried him deep, back from the stream, with a slab of walnut planed smooth for a headstone, name and date, and purified the cabin floor with lime, white-washed the walls and burned the bedding, as the army surgeon said you should—and never caught the disease himself, never a twinge. It was as people said: the cholera poison might be all around you in the atmosphere, but it wouldn't take if you didn't give it a chance, what the doctors called the predisposing condition—weaken your constitution with too much bad whisky and spoiled meat, loose living—

It was the soldiers brought it.

There had been no real cholera scare anywhere in the country since the war started, nothing you could call an epidemic since 1849, but all the summer of 1865 the disease raged through Europe and sooner or later would cross the Atlantic, people said, as it had before. In the spring a ship sailed into New York Harbor and the master reported seven dead and buried at sea; cholera.

Some thousands died but still it was not an epidemic as in the times before; but the disease spread west, along the Ohio and the lakes, the railroad lines, from the West Indies across the Gulf and up the Mississippi.

In the fall of 1866 when Isaac was at St Louis on a buying trip they were having a thorough scare and deaths every day; wintered over somehow, it seemed, and in the spring when the emigrants started west and the troops to garrison the new forts along the emigrant roads, the cholera reached the Plains, and in the fall, at last, the Wichita village at the mouth of the Little Arkansas.

The cholera started among the soldiers. By early fall half the men in the detachment showed symptoms, Major Barr said, twenty or thirty had the actual disease, and they set up a big tent for a hospital and a dozen died. When it crossed the river and spread among the Wichita, there were at least a hundred deaths, the graves scattered up and down the Little Arkansas on both sides, some of the chiefs among them, Sam Houston of the Towakoni and Owa-ha, the fat old head chief of the Wichita; and still the Indians would not leave but stayed on to make their crops—and too leached by the sickness, probably, most of them, to travel if they wanted.

Cholera was not the only thing the soldiers brought. To free himself for buying and freighting, Isaac had sent Jack Lawton to Walnut Grove with Jim Kelly and got hold of Titus Sexton, fresh from a six-month enlistment in the Kansas volunteers at the end of the war, and sent him down to Round Pond with a boy called Caboon, one of Chisholm's ransomed Mexicans—like moving counters around a checkerboard. And then Lawton had a dispute with a mule skinner that came along with Barr's command, something about a horse, and the man was drunk and brought a little peashooter derringer out from his boot top and shot him through the heart; and got clean away, never caught. When Dave Ballon abandoned the Cowskin Creek station, Isaac drove there to retrieve the few remaining supplies but could not think of replacing him, and had not anyhow earned much profit there: still had three active trading posts to see to and another planned, and two of his men gone—and Sam Carter, just started at

Towanda, best clerk he'd had yet—and all that summer and fall found hardly time to sleep; and Marie, who could keep the books at Towanda as well as clerk and look after the trading with Abe Kelly to help, had spent the summer at Burlingame with the children, and needed it, of course, the change of atmosphere.

The trade had grown up since the treaties. Isaac got the Commission business, rations and presents, not all of it but a good share, out of his normal stock of Indian goods, and it kept up, Indians coming in with robes and furs and the Indian traders, Delaware and Shawnee, Caddo, that he outfitted to trade with the wild tribes in their winter camps in the Territory. He was putting most of his time in buying and freighting, nearly every month to Leavenworth, sometimes ten thousand dollars in a lot, hardly ever less than five, and when Durfee hadn't the stock or his prices didn't sound right he had only to take the cars now to St Louis and buy direct.

Isaac no longer had the country to himself. Right after the treaties Bill Greiffenstein came down the Walnut with Jennie and two little light wagons, a span of mules to each, and stayed a week at Towanda; had given up their station on the Great Bend, too many Indian troubles and not enough trade to risk their scalps for, and Isaac fitted them out for a winter of trading in the Territory. They came back in the spring, paid off and restocked, said they had camped at the old Wichita Agency on the Washita and were setting up a trading post there year-around; a year later Bill was trading regularly between the Little Arkansas and the Washita and for convenience moved into Isaac's Cowskin post when Dave Ballon left it, and Isaac let him, having no use for it himself. Others came in off the Plains and built their cabins along the Little Arkansas or between the rivers, and then toward the end of the summer of 1867 Bill Mathewson came through driving a train of goods intended for the Wichita when they moved and had a promise to supply Leavenworth's agency and the wild tribes wherever they settled, once they agreed to their new treaties. Lizzie Inman had gone ahead and married him all right, first Isaac had seen of either of them since that time at Salina five years back; got along very well, it seemed, with the Indians coming in to trade—when she introduced herself formally as Miss Lizzie, the Cheyenne transformed the outlandish name to one that matched Bill's Kiowa, Mar-wissa, "Golden Hair," which was about right for color but also another kind of Indian joke, being the name of Black Kettle's sister.

The traders going south followed the trail Jesse Chisholm had made hauling Isaac's goods: easier than striking out fresh, the wagon tracks had marked the prairie grass indelibly as an engraver's burin on a steel plate, and it ran straight into the heart of the Territory, good water all the way and easy stream crossings; *Chisholm's* Trail they called it, in distinction from others to the east. Now there were cattle coming up besides trade goods going down. Chisholm and the Wichita started that too, with their few small herds brought up toward the end of the war, and then in 1867 the legislature closed eastern Kansas to Texas cattle for fear of Texas tick fever infecting the settlers' domestic stock. Since there were still no long-distance rail lines into Texas, however, the new railroad across Kansas remained the necessary means by which to connect Texas cattle with the markets of the East, where beef had been in short supply since the Civil War; and Chisholm's Trail, known and proved, was the natural route to follow in making this connection while avoiding the quarantine zone—north across the Red River to the Washita, then by Chisholm's route up the west bank of the Arkansas to the crossing just below the mouth of the Little Arkansas, and from there the old West Shawnee Trail along the edge of the quarantine line to Abilene.

The cattle, changing Chisholm's Trail from a traders' route to a cattlemen's, were a good part of what Durfee was after in locating on the Little Arkansas. They were also the reason Isaac had to see Towakoni Jim before the tribe went south. He had an idea for a new trading post where the trail crossed the Ninnescah, a pretty, wooded stream that joined the Arkansas down toward the Kansas border, whose Osage name, "good spring water," the whites made into Clearwater when they did not use the Indian word. The Clearwater crossing was a natural camping place; with a station there and a stock of goods, a man could sell what the cattlemen needed before they reached the Little Arkansas.

So on a morning at the end of October finally Isaac left Marie to manage, saddled Singing Bird, took the Osage Trail west and down the east bank of the Little Arkansas to the village, arriving about midday. He had to stop at the first lodge he came to for directions and got a boy to lead him; in the summer Jim had married and according to custom moved to his wife's mother's lodge. The whole village was silent, in mourning, the young widows keeping inside, hair cut short and dressed in worn-out garments, the children forbidden to laugh and shout at their play—hardly a lodge but had lost a relative to the cholera.

Jim greeted him in the doorway of the lodge with a long hug, stepped back to shake his hand and led Isaac in. In the half-light it seemed they were alone, but a girl crouched by the fire pit looked up as Isaac passed, tiny sharp-chinned face framed in silky-dark hair, quick with intelligence but solemn now before the white trader who was perhaps a kind of chief; Jim's new wife, maybe fifteen years old and not yet fat, and her cheekbones marked by round spots of vermilion touched there by her husband's fingertips, signifying honor and affection. A boneless chunk of buffalo ham was roasting on a spit over the fire. There was cornmeal batter ready in a pot, a flat slab of stone heating at the edge of the fire.

Jim's wicker sleeping platform was to the left of the entrance, mattressed with buffalo robes. He lay back, at his ease, waiting. Isaac sat at the other end.

—So, Isaac said. You starting for the Washita? Tomorrow? Next week?

Jim shrugged.—When Mister Chisholm say—when Major Shanklin say—we start. Too many people still too sick to ride, have to haul em behind horses, maybe put em on Chisholm wagons.

—Listen, Isaac said earnestly, why don't you stay when the tribe goes south, you and your wife? You know where the trail goes across the Ninnescah? I'm going to build a station there, stock it with goods, and you could run it for me—say twenty dollars a month and a share in the profit, and you've got the English for it, and the Indians that come in to trade—. The Indian looked back politely, eyes half-focused: futile, he could see it now, foolish to bring it up—well, he could put Titus in charge of the Clearwater station then, find someone to take over at Round Pond, or give it up, more moves on the checkerboard—but, having started, Isaac persisted, outlining his idea.

—I cannot live in cabin, Jim said. My wife—her mother, father.

—You could make a grass lodge, same as here, or use your buffalo-hide travel lodge. I've only got to have a cabin to store the goods in— and a good door with a lock.

—One Indian trading with white cattlemen—

—Chisholm does it.

—Ah, Chisholm! Jim said. Your man Jack Lawton—white man kill him, for a horse, and one Indian. . . .

Isaac had nothing more to argue. Jim sat forward on his couch, took his hand, held it.

—Wichita go home to Washita, he said. Wife got to have man to get meat, make garden—mother and father, old. Whole tribe maybe, someday. You want me be white trader, I can do that, maybe, but I go Indian road—going to be Wichita, all my life—.

He smiled, nodded. The girl knelt with a wooden tray of sliced meat, corn cakes flat as pancakes, face solemn at the serious talk in the strange language, her eyes holding back their laughter; and in the eyes also worship—the man her parents gave her, who guided the white traders and never came back from the hunt without meat, reclining on his couch like a chief, counseling with the white chief Sun-Boy, and would be a chief one day himself. Isaac, remembering his manners, drew his knife and speared a piece of meat from the trencher.

It was mid-November when the Wichita started south. Chisholm left his cabins beside the little creek that flowed through the hackberry grove, now known by his name, Chisholm's Creek, as the trail was also Chisholm's, and led the tribe south with all his people, his wagons loaded with rations for the journey. Major Barr, anxious to return to his wife in the rented cottage at Leavenworth, procured orders to break up his camp on the Little Arkansas and march north but detailed a squad of men with horses and a staff lieutenant to go along by way of escort for the agent, Major Shanklin. The tribe's misfortunes continued. They traveled slowly, making hardly ten miles a day, stopping over at the camps to rest. The weather was turning cold, though as yet there was no snow. At the Clearwater crossing they camped for two days around Isaac's new station, doing a little trading. On the second night a prairie fire roared down on the camp driven by a fierce north wind, rumbling over the dry grass like a freight train. The people got across the river, most of them, but the fire destroyed tepees, bedding, food stored in parfleches, tools, and surrounded the screaming herd of horses at the crossing, killing eighty animals; what started the fire was unknown, perhaps one of the boys set to guard the herd, trying to get warm in the furious cold wind. The trading post, manned by Titus Sexton and a young emigrant, Andrew Hansen, a Dane who had wandered to Towanda one day on foot and alone, dazed by his ignorance of English, was only scorched; Isaac when he built the cabin had taken the trouble to bring a breaking-plow and turn four wide furrows in the surrounding sod. Hansen did not know much, but enough to drive a plow.

The exodus continued, with painful slowness, however the advancing season urged haste. At a camp on a stream just over the line into the Territory, disease broke forth again, violent, killing, swift, and cholera named it as well as any, whatever it may have been in fact. Another hundred died, possibly more, the people now too weak in numbers and in blood to bury their dead, leaving them where they fell: the whole tribe dying as it seemed, but at least by a warrior's death, in the Wichita view of things; wounded in battle and like to die, a man saved honor by leaving the camp and seeking the open prairie, offering his flesh to the wolves. December now: few tents, few robes, though resourceful hunters like Towakoni Jim had green hides from deer taken along the line of march; at night they threw up brush arbors to keep the weather off and slept close by their fires. They were still some days' travel from Chisholm's abandoned ranch on the North Canadian and the wooded trails through the Cross Timbers country beyond, both offering shelter of a sort, when the blizzard struck: that abrupt, north-driven storm that besets the grassland winter, transforming the sun-warmed day in an hour to aching cold and blinding swirls of drifting snow. Jim's new wife was half a mile from the camp, collecting wood to carry back tied up in a square of home-spun on her back; hurried with the load, dropped it, lost her way, fell. Jim found her in the morning, not a hundred yards off, one stiff arm reaching above the snow, the frozen hands still clutching her shawl.

Of the fifteen hundred or more members of the tribe driven north five years earlier, a thousand survivors reached the site of their former village and agency on the Washita, in late December. Jesse Leavenworth had chosen the place for his camp and, careless as ever of regulations, offered such supplies as he could spare from his own stock, although the tribe was not his responsibility. In any case, since the wild tribes had promised at Medicine Lodge to come in and settle, he had more supplies ordered, was negotiating for herds of Texas beef to feed them.

Some particulars of this journey Isaac heard from Chisholm in the spring, others later from Jim in the rebuilt village on the Washita. At the beginning of February the Cherokee sent a boy called Yonitob on mule-back to Towanda with a laconic message, laboriously drafted: wife and most of the boys gone to the home ranch on the Little River, but he was wintering at his old place on the North Canadian, below the salt spring where he used to make his salt for trade, maybe two thousand Indians camped all around, five or six tribes. It was the camp people called Council Grove, from earlier gatherings years past when he first set up to trade there, and if Isaac could bring some goods, the boy would guide him. Isaac loaded a wagon and started down the trail with Abe Kelly and the boy. The weather was like spring now. They made it through in a week of easy travel.

There was a grand council of chiefs around the fire in Chisholm's lodge the night Isaac arrived. Those tribes or parts of tribes that were inclined to peace—or were at least prepared to keep the winter truce till they knew what the new agent would offer—had gathered around the trader's camp: most of the Kiowa, Ten Bear's band of Comanche and one or two others. Ten Bear, an elderly, white-haired, humorous chief who wore steel-rimmed spectacles and dressed in citizen's clothes, with a portrait medal of Lincoln on a ribbon around his neck, given him by the President when he joined a delegation to Washington during the war, was known all his life for keeping a strategic peace with whites of all stripes. The Caddo had sent a delegation to confer with Colonel Leavenworth at his camp on the Washita: it was their report—of rations, clothing, *wo-haw*—that the chiefs had assembled to hear that night. Most of the Cheyenne were missing. Black Kettle and his band had cautiously made their winter village far up the North Canadian. Other bands were somewhere between Chisholm's camp and the Arkansas but considered themselves still at war. Two traders' outfits were camped along the river nearby, Mathewson's and Greiffenstein's.

Isaac and Abe spent the next day arranging their wagonload in a tepee that Chisholm, chief-like, had set aside for trading. When they finished the trader stooped at the door of his lodge and beckoned Isaac to come in for a talk. He had a lengthy list of goods he wanted from Towanda. Isaac wrote cross-legged by the fire in his pocket account book; pretty much all his stock, all his wagons to carry it. Starting next day, he figured to be back in two weeks if they had no troubles with river crossings.

—Not for me, understand, the old man said. This Leavenworth—good man, but: all this winter I send out messages to the bands—*come in to Washita camp like you promise in the treaty.* Now they come, some of them come—but this agent, he aint give presents, they say he liar, go away, start war again. I sell him goods, and what he don't buy, I give to Indians that trust me. You understand? All my life I been a peacemaker—Tennessee with the Cherokee and whites, Arkansas, the Nations—now the wild tribes from the Plains. What's the sense, people killing each other?

He sighed. Closing his pocketbook, Isaac studied him: white hair bleached of all color, slack cheeks veined with red, benign eyes staring into abstract distance: age, to grow old, weak, tired—what was it? —and the pity.—You aint sick, are you, Jesse? he said. Some of that cholera poison from the Wichita?

Chisholm shook his head.—Just old—just getting old. . . .

—You look worn out—bringing the Wichita home, and now this business with the treaties. Aint you afraid you'll make yourself sick? Your age—you're older than my father—

—Listen, boy, he said, I don't listen to preachers much, but all my life I done what my heart said was good—man never went from my camp hungry or barefoot—couldn't walk, I give him a horse. Now, if the Great Spirit says it's time, I aint afraid to meet him in the other world. That's how I've lived. . . .

The old man sat in silence for a time; smiled, roused himself, stood up.—Come on, he said, we got to eat—maybe I got sixty more years of things to do. We ride over to Satanta's lodge, see what his women's cooking. . . .

Isaac was three weeks returning to Chisholm's camp, not two. He closed the stations at Round Pond and Clearwater and took the four men back to Towanda, would need them all to drive. Going south again they ran into two of the Cheyenne war parties Chisholm had mentioned. When they crossed the Arkansas there were dust clouds, horsemen approaching, far out on the plain to the west, tracked them as far as the Ninnescah, five or ten miles off, but came no closer; at night, camping, Isaac kept the mules and his horse close, set a watch all night with revolvers loaded, but the Indians, Cheyenne most likely, made no attempt on them. Then for two days as they neared Round Pond they met scattered bands of buffalo moving urgently north—too early yet for the spring migration, something down there, Indians, hunters, had disturbed them, run them off.

They were making for a nooning at Round Pond when Isaac, riding out in front of the train, saw horsemen galloping hard up the trail toward them, long war bonnets trailing and whipping in the wind, lances poised; Cheyenne. Ordering his men to get down and each stand at the head of his team, holding the lead mules in, he dismounted and faced the charging Indians, one hand on Bird's bridle. One rode straight at him, lance aimed at his breast. Isaac stood straight and did not move, and in the final moment the Indian reversed his lance so that the butt thumped his breastbone without hurting much and the loose-held shaft slid harmlessly through the Indian's fingers. He veered off and the warriors circled the wagon train, perhaps fifty of them, whooping, threatening with their lances, but making no move to attack: the fat old war leader riding heavily on an overtaxed pony, bringing up the rear, had given no command. Dropping the bridle, Isaac took a step forward and raised his hands in signs expressing peace, friendship. The chief pulled up hard in front of him.

The Indians escorted the train to their camp on the north bank of the Salt Fork of the Arkansas, opposite Isaac's Round Pond station. The camp was guarded by a picket line of Indians organized in squads, dressed mostly in cast-off uniforms acquired at the Medicine Lodge council in the fall, armed with the usual assortment of weapons, from antique trade muskets to a few modern cap-and-ball revolvers and one or two repeater cartridge carbines. Sitting cross-legged on a mat of buffalo robes under a spreading cottonwood, Isaac spent the rest of the day in delicate negotiation with the band chief, who gave his name in signs as Tall Bull. Isaac's men waited nervously by their teams, raising a cry when one of the Indian soliders made to get into a wagon and help himself. Tall Bull did not threaten to rob the train. Rather, he told at length how long his men had been away from their village, ranging from the Platte south into Texas: hungry now for different food, flour, coffee—. Isaac explained that he was going to Jesse Chisholm at Ten Bear's camp on the North Canadian and had promised them the goods; but could spare some for a friend. Then the chief wanted to trade some ponies from his herd for Isaac's draft mules—needed also powder, lead; again Isaac excused himself without refusing—Ten Bear and his warriors would be displeased if he did not keep his word. Eventually Tall Bull let him go for three sacks of flour, one each of coffee, sugar, and half his lead and powder, poured out on a robe and carefully divided. The soldiers at the chief's command saw the train across the river and offered no further threats, but Isaac cautiously drove off the trail a few miles south and went on to Chisholm's camp by a slow and circuitous route.

The council grove was deserted when they reached it the first week in March. Isaac spent an hour going over the ground on hands and knees but could make no sense of it: only that the tracks were a day or two old—there had been no rain—and went off in all directions, some apparently crossing the river and going south. Perhaps it had been a quarrel, a chief killed, by accident or in anger, and the bands, intent on peace, had scattered to avoid a pointless fight. The traders' wagon tracks, however, led down the river. Isaac recalled that Chisholm had another place a day's drive farther where he liked to camp sometimes, a broad, low hill the Indians called Little Mountain, half a mile back from the North Canadian, with a fine spring issuing from its base. It might be the traders had gone there. He determined to follow and try to catch them, get an answer.

They drove till nearly midnight, the trail clear even in the darkness, and started before light, arriving at Little Mountain by midmorning. There were buffalo lodges in among the trees along the river and scattered across the rising prairie to the east, without order, a smaller camp than the previous one. Isaac recognized Satanta, Satank, and Set-im-kayah, that made three bands of the Kiowa. Chisholm's big lodge was set up on the hilltop, the doorway facing west and closed with a buffalo hide, and Ten Bear sat before it on a pile of robes, calm as a bank president in his spectacles, smoking a long-stemmed pipe. That was a band of the Comanche; he saw no others of the tribal leaders. But where was Chisholm?

A little below the brow of the hill, toward the spring, there was a mound of fresh-dug earth beside a pit. Dutch Bill Greiffenstein stood beside it, stooping a little, judging the work with a critical eye. Isaac rode over. A tall, bearded white man rose in the grave, chest-deep, Bill Mathewson, easing a tired back, and reached the shovel up to Dutch Bill.

—Reckon that's deep enough to keep the wolves out, Mathewson said, and raised a long arm for the German to help him out. Wiping his hand on a pants leg, he gave a short, hard handshake as Isaac dismounted.

—Who died?

Dutch Bill gazed mildly back, holding one hand to shade his watery, pale, myopic eyes against the searching afternoon light.— Chisholm, aint you heard? he answered finally. Two days ago, and he say, he want to be buried here at Little Mountain, and we do it—only, don't nobody know what is Cherokee custom—and them Mexican, *they* don't know, so Mathewson dig American grave, and Ten Bear say, lay im wit his head east so when time come to go to sunset land, he get up easy. . . .

Bill told what had happened. A week ago Chisholm felt weak and stayed in his lodge, called for the remedy for too much lean meat, a cup of melted fat, but there was none—end of winter, fresh meat of any kind was scarce. An old woman remembered a brass kettle with old bear grease in the bottom, put aside at the back of her lodge and forgotten. She brought it, melted it on the fire, and gave it to the trader to drink. He turned sick with signs as of cholera and after two days was dead. They loaded him on a wagon and brought him to Little Mountain as he asked.

Ten Bear came over, stoop-backed, with short, arthritic steps, inspected the grave, nodded, and went slowly back to Chisholm's lodge. As eldest among the chiefs, he had washed and dressed the body, taken the ceremonies upon himself; when Satanta wanted to kill a horse at the burial so the trader might ride to the land of the dream-people, Ten Bear refused—an old custom, abandoned, never the way of the Cherokee. Now he threw back the covering of the lodge entrance, summoned four of Chisholm's Mexicans, and the boys went in, carried the body out awkwardly between them wrapped in a buffalo robe; knelt at the grave head and let the body slowly down by the corners of the hide. The white men removed their hats. Ten Bear stood at the foot, in silence. Raising his eyes to heaven, he lifted up his voice, praying, his hands signing the words of his prayer as he spoke:

Earth! Our mother! You contain all things, produce all things. All the roads of a man's life he travels across your body. As all life springs from your life, so you have taught us to revere all life, and at its end, when man has traveled to the end of his road, with reverence to bring him back to you, that everything coming forth from your body may be reunited with your body. So now this man: we give him to your body, cover him with your flesh. Earth, our mother—take him.

Set-im-kayah came forward with moccasins and a pair of buckskin leggins that looked new, perhaps made for the occasion by Pat-so-gate. Kneeling, he laid the garments on the body. Ten Bear nodded, but when Satanta brought a rifle, a bow, a quiver of arrows to put in the grave, he raised his hands and shook his head, denying, spoke at length. The Kiowa scowled and finally turned his back and walked heavily away. Facing the crowd, Ten Bear politely explained in signs: this Chisholm was always a peace-man—he does not go to the Great Father carrying weapons for a fight. Here—. Removing the Lincoln medal from his neck, he held it up for all to see, then let it fall on the body's breast. Rising, he spoke to Mathewson, and the white man put on his hat, came over with his shovel, and began pushing the loose earth in. Removing his spectacles, Ten Bear wiped at his eyes and limped back to Chisholm's tent to sit. Satank brought a bundle of peeled cedar poles and set about fencing the grave: forked sticks at the corners, cross-pieces, picketed with uprights all around. Greiffenstein had made a gravestone of a slab of oak, carved with what he said were Gothic letters soot-blackened against the dark wood and nearly illegible, with a Christian cross cut above:

JESSE CHISHOLM
1805 – March 4, 1868
No man went from his lodge
hungry or barefoot

He pounded the slab in at the head of the grave inside Satank's fence, facing west. It was finished. They had done what they knew.

Mid-afternoon by now, long shadows, hunger quickened by the smell of cooking meat. Buffalo had been scarce here for weeks, months—turkeys in thousands, thick as sparrows in the trees along the river, but the Kiowa ate no birds. Someone, however, had brought in two bucks and some of the women were cooking now below the hill to the east: haunches smoking on spits, great kettles stewing on the coals. There was a general movement of men toward the cook fires.

While they stood around, cutting outer slivers of meat as it cooked, dipping from the pots, Dutch Bill went back to a wagon, wrestled a flour barrel out, opened it and felt inside, and returned with a ten-gallon keg on his shoulder and a tin cup at his belt: whisky, forbidden by numerous statutes, in the Territory or for trading with Indians, but carried by every trader, ingeniously hidden—taken immoderately it could bring on the cholera, no doubt, as people said, but in small and frequent doses was considered preventive, curative, and therefore necessary.

—Come on, boys! Bill shouted. Drink up, for Jesse—best Kentucky, and I've got more! and with his revolver butt pounded in the top, took a drink by way of invitation, and handed the cup to Ten Bear.

The keg was soon empty. Dutch Bill went back to his wagon, found another and brought it. Satanta recovered his good spirits and embraced Ten Bear, laughing. His lieutenant now was a young man nearly his opposite in appearance that Isaac found himself disliking: slight and slender, fair-skinned with some admixture of white blood, smooth regular features and the lounging insolent feline grace of one who has heard his looks too often praised; Ado-e-et-te, Big Tree, who already on raids with Satanta had gained a reputation for faithlessness and needless cruelty, but not yet as a fighter the warriors' society would follow.

In a loud voice Big Tree was challenging to a race: any man in the camp who *was* a man and thought he had a fast horse. He pointed to a lone tree a quarter-mile east on the prairie—race to the mark, around it, and back. A dozen Indians ran for their horses. Big Tree's was a pinto with black ears, a desirable trait, and big for an Indian pony.

Isaac stood off to one side as if he had not understood. Satanta with a stick had drawn a starting line in the grass and the riders were lined up behind it, waiting for him to start them, but he did not. The women had grouped themselves at one end of the line to watch, Pat-so-gate tall and lithe among their squat middle-aged Indian forms, her face and unbound hair darkened with paint. Big Tree wheeled his horse to face Isaac and said something derisive in a loud voice.

Mathewson came over to Isaac and laid a heavy arm across his shoulders.—Go on, he said in a low voice. You're the one he's after—says whites are afraid to race with him and Pai-tal-ye's the biggest coward of the lot.

—I can see well enough what he's saying, Isaac said. I don't need to race against any burnt-cork nigger to prove I can ride a horse. And they're drunk, some of em—someone'll get hurt.

—You got to do it. You don't, you'll just have trouble with him—all of em. Besides, he needs taking down—it'd do us all some good.

Isaac straightened up, working his shoulders, arms; only one swallow of Dutch Bill's liquor, he was all right. The Indian still slouched in his saddle, watching him with sneering lips. Isaac looked him in the eyes, nodded, turned. He had left Singing Bird on the hilltop near the grave, placidly nibbling grass, still saddled. He gave the nickering calling cry and the horse pricked her ears, answered, came toward him at a loose-limbed walk, and stood beside him. The crowd of watchers at the starting line was silent as with held breath; then a long collective sigh, a babble of voices raised in wonder. Isaac mounted, positioned himself at the outside of the line of racers, to Big Tree's left. The Indian pulled back on the reins, reared and pranced his horse. Satanta let out a deep-toned bellow, and they started.

The riders stayed in close as far as the mark, and Isaac went along with them, holding her in, and eased through the pack and over, moving in close for a tight turn. As he came around, Ado-e-et-te was up beside him, crowding, slapping at his horse's flank with the loose end of his reins, and to get clear Isaac let her out a little and pulled in front, a length, two lengths. The white men, watching, let out a cheer which some of the Indians joined.

Halfway back to the line there came a crash, a scream behind him, and across his shoulder Isaac saw a horse go cartwheeling over and a boy flung forward, landing stiff and flat, and two lengths back Big Tree on his black-eared horse, then the other racers in a bunch. Isaac pulled up short, jumped down, ran, and threw himself on the fallen boy, covering his own head with his hands. He could hear, feel, the Indian's horse lifting over him but dared not look, then the others, veering to either side. He got up. The downed horse did not move, the boy lay as he had fallen. Isaac knelt beside him, turned him over, felt along the bones—bruises, cuts, he could not tell what more. Calling Bird to come, he lifted the boy up in front of the pommel, mounted, and rode back at a slow walk, holding the boy, head lolling, with both arms. As he crossed the line there was a long cheer. Satank ran and reached the boy down, carried him in his arms and laid him on a robe, kneeling beside him.

Mathewson came over, offered Isaac a hand, and helped him down.

—There now, Isaac said. I told you somebody'd get hurt—and a pretty good horse killed besides. Horse racing and foolishness—it's just trouble. . . .

Satanta had carried a buffalo horn of whisky to Ado-e-et-te, who took it, drank—he had won, after all—but still sat his horse, face set in a scowl.

—Look at him! Bill said with a sharp nod. Aint done with you yet, Sun-Boy—and get a little more of Griff's spider juice in him and he *won't* be, till he's made you fight.

—He can't if I won't.

—You watch him now. He aint got feelings, that one, about going for a man unarmed.

Isaac wiped abstractedly at the horse's steaming back and sides; whispered to her, and started up the hill, the horse following. He was conscious of something else behind him, at his left side, and then an Indian voice, haranguing. Turning abruptly, he faced Big Tree, and the Indian, startled, backed his horse a step.—Don't talk your language at me, Isaac told him, shaping the words slowly, I don't know it. You wanted a race and got it and you won. Good. All right.

No, the Indian was saying with vehement hands, that was no race: Sun-Boy blocked the finish, or Black Ears would have beaten the ghost horse. If the white man was a man of honor, he would run again, one to one.

Isaac stared him in the eyes a long moment, face flaming: nothing but a little puffed-up, overdressed runty Indian, ought to joke him out of it, he knew that, but it just made him mad—Couldn't be Satanta putting him up to it, they were friends, but then—. The Indians and traders standing around watched in apprehensive silence. Finally Big Tree dropped his eyes and with a scornful toss of his head turned and started walking away.

—All right, God damn you, Isaac shouted after him. You want a race, by God you'll get it! and mounting, he turned the horse and followed.

At the starting line Set-im-kayah got in front of them, arms raised: would bet ten robes on Sun-Boy to five that anyone would put on Big Tree. He repeated the offer aloud in Kiowa, then Comanche, and Satanta took it. The two men went off to their lodges at a trot and a few minutes later came back stooping under the weight of robes and threw them down in two heaps in back of the line. The riders waited, six feet apart, not looking at each other. Then suddenly as Satanta was taking his position to call the start, Big Tree lashed at his horse, it leaped across the line, and they were running toward the mark at a muscular, uneven gallop. Bird followed, running smoothly, and made up the two lost lengths.

Again Isaac held her in, just off the other's left flank, let him make the turn, then eased off and let her come up. With a glance over his shoulder Big Tree pulled hard toward him, to the left. Pressing lightly with his knees, Isaac swung right without a break, and the Indian with a hard jerk at the reins veered toward him again. Isaac made a feint to the left, and as Big Tree started to follow circled past him in a wide arc to the right and, lying forward on the horse's neck, talking steadily, loosed the reins and felt the surge of energy between his legs, the sense of flight, as of a bird set free and flying, scorning the slave earth forever, that he rarely granted her now.

Twenty yards from the finish, Isaac pulled her in again and crossed at an easy canter. The Indian horse came up lathered, at a stumbling trot, blowing through flared nostrils, beaten. There came the trilling of a woman's sweet soprano, as for a warrior come home with many scalps, a clapping of hands. Isaac jerked his head around: Pat-so-gate, eyes shining, feet making shuffling dancing steps in the moccasins; that was it, the trouble. He held her eyes, frowned, shook his head. She stopped. The women around her covered their mouths with their hands in embarrassment. Isaac sang out for Abe Kelly to come take his horse, rub her down and cover her with a robe; and yes, a pail of shelled corn—she had earned it. Mathewson came over to him.

—I reckon you took him down some that time, he said.

—Maybe, Isaac said. But God damn it, Bill, she's eight years old, about. Every time I let her run, it's one less she's got in her. He wiped his knife on his boot sole, pointed: a dozen Indians were loudly gathered around the second keg, tipping it to pour, nearly empty. I've got one of my own, he said—never want it, but sometimes a chief thinks it's polite. But if I get it out, there'll be killing here before we're done.

There was a commotion behind him: Stumbling Bear giving out the pack of robes he had bet, the half pack he had won. And something else, silencing the rejoicing: Big Tree had his bow strung, three arrows arrayed in his left hand for quick firing. He twanged the string menacingly at Isaac. Satanta with a look of concern went over to him. Big Tree spoke earnestly and at length, his voice rising; the Indians near him uttered grunts of disapproval. Satanta shrugged, came toward Isaac with a puzzled look, his young retainer following: Big Tree, he said, allows that Sun-Boy owns a pretty good horse— Isaac let out a scornful snort—but says he cannot shoot; will shoot against him, arrow against bullet, and if—

Isaac shook his head vehemently. Tell him, he said, I'm not playing any more little-boy games. Besides, he said, I came to trade with friends and help out Jesse Chisholm—didn't bring my rifle, only a light carbine about good enough to shoot birds with.

Satanta turned to Big Tree to convey this message. Isaac looked around for Mathewson but could not see him. The negotiations continued through Satanta, neither contestant speaking directly to the other. Mathewson came back with a rifle, powder, shot; a Hawken, a little longer, heavier, than Isaac's own. He hefted it, raised it to his shoulder; nothing special about it, Bill said, it just hit where you aimed it. Eventually it was agreed: one shot each, Isaac to pick the mark, Ten Bear to judge. Big Tree wanted to bet Black Ears and a herd of ten ponies against Singing Bird, but Isaac was angry again, refused to consider it, and Mathewson backed him.

A hundred yards off on the rising ground to the northeast something dark protruded among the pale tufts of winter grass, something white beside it that looked at the distance about the size of a half-dollar: a sun-bleached buffalo skull half-buried in the sod. Isaac pointed. Big Tree went through the arrows in his quiver, selected one and laid the rest aside; sighted along it, flexed it slightly, straightening. He braced his feet, nocked the arrow, drew his bow, aimed, waited, let the string slip from his fingers—. Long arc of flight as if driven by in-held breath, released, a distant thump. Ten Bear peered and started with painful slowness across the grass to the target, walked all around it and slowly returned: Big Tree had hit, his arrow through the skull bone.

Isaac measured powder, patched the ball and rammed it down. Best shoot standing, a little better angle on the mark; no wind, he waited, could not hear it, feel it—but something interfering. He let the gun down: Pat-so-gate, a few steps off, watching him, face solemn, eyes half-closed.

—Get away from me, Patsy, he said. You'll spoil my shot.

He set the hammer, brought the gun up, held, breath held, knew how he had to do it, little prick of arrow wood in the sight, cool silky smoothness of the much-worn trigger on his finger—should have tried it first, but nothing special about this gun, Bill said, like—

Gray-black jet of smoke, spreading, rising, slap of the gunshot echoing back from the rising ground. Isaac reached the gun away and someone took it.

Ten Bear again limped forward, dutifully, reached the target, looked, stooped, knelt, crawled all around it. He stood up, making the signs broadly, to be understood: no arrow left. Sun-Boy had shot the arrow. With a shout the Indians ran toward him, the traders' men. Isaac stood alone, disarmed, Mathewson behind him, Satanta and Big Tree with his bow, facing him. The girl was between them and a little to the south, rebuked yet glowing, trilling softly to herself.

Now, if he wants to try it—my skinning knife anyhow, dodge the first shot and give a jump—you aint a man-killer, Mathewson told him once—well, by God, let him try me—

Bill Greiffenstein lurched down the hill behind them, singing, a rifle trailed, powder horn and shot-pouch dangling from one hand: meant to have his turn too, shooting at the mark. Mathewson let out a whoop, shouted in Comanche: Dutch Bill was going to shoot. The Indians came swarming off the prairie, got behind him and up the slope, and Ten Bear last, with slow but urgent dignity. Greiffenstein pounded the ball down with his ramrod: his eyes weren't weak, he said, he never owned a pair of glasses in his life and could tell a man from a horse at a hundred yards as well as any man, and anyone who said he couldn't was a damn liar!

Isaac slept that night in Dutch Bill's tent. They lay late in the night on their robes, talking by the dim light of a candle lantern hung from the ridgepole. The German took occasional sips from a stone jug saved for his own use, which Isaac refused: not drunk certainly but replete, serenely satisfied with the send-off they had given Chisholm and his own part—and the shooting! no doubt at all he had hit the mark as well as Isaac, two or three times—hit something, anyhow—and Isaac did not dispute him.

—Bill, Isaac said, I'm sorry he's gone—didn't know him that long or well, but I had the same feeling as the Indians: like a father, the kind of man you'd have for a father, if you could choose. But still—

—The best! Best man on the Plains. . . .

—But still, and all in all—well, it sure leaves me in a fix. Three thousand dollars he owed me from this winter—and a whole train of goods I brought down this time, pretty much cleaned out my store and warehouse, and cost me another five thousand. What am I going to do for my money?

—Take the goods back, Bill suggested. They sell all the same, in time.

—Have to get by that gang of thieving Cheyenne Tall Bull, I told you about him, cost me three sacks of flour to get away.

—You don't got goods to pay, he kill you, Bill said quietly. That's all. No more worry after that.

—How about Leavenworth and his agency?

—Sure, he take some, I bet. And what he don't, you leave wit Jennie at my station—she pay what furs she got, you give credit and I pay the rest when I come up in the fall. All right? Isaac nodded. But listen, Bill said, sitting up and putting his jug aside. Know what *I* do, I got a train of goods like that? Give em out to Indians, that's what Jesse going to do. They pay you something, maybe.

—Oh, come on, Bill, said Isaac, smiling, but the other was serious.

—I mean it. Old-time Indian trader—Jesse's last, the end. All these Indians—going to clear the buffalo, fence em up in Indian Territory. Aint going to be no more Indian trading, cep maybe little agency contracts, every man undersell every other man—what's the good in that? And settlers coming like flies at spoiled meat, fill up Kansas, all the Territory. *No more trading—*

—You talk like you're getting out.

—You damn right I'm getting out—sell off my goods, let that Washita station go to hell: any money I get, I put into land, maybe start a town, sell shares. That Wichita village by the Little Arkansas —ever thought of that? Hell of a place for town site—man get his claim on that, cut it up in lots, start up a town, he going to be rich, don't never got to risk his scalp or work *no more*. You think about that sometime?

—Oh sure, I've *thought* about it, Isaac said cautiously. And I reckon it's an idea too, if a man likes that kind of life, though what I've seen in Kansas—well, starting a town, it looks like the straight road to the poorhouse if it don't take with the settlers. . . .

—Nahh, Bill said with emphasis. It aint no risk. Besides, the land— you always got the land. He reached out, pulled the cork, and took another swallow from the jug.

A town where the two rivers came together: it was a matter about which Isaac had his reasons for not talking, and Bill, half drunk, having let the idea out, did not pursue it.

Much later, the candle out, Isaac lay wakeful in his buffalo robe, listening to Bill's snorts and snores on the other side of the tent. And now something else: a surreptitious rustling in the grass along the tent wall, what was it—snake? some small nocturnal animal? He lay taut, listening, reached out one hand—. A hand gripped his, warm, strong, held it, he rolled toward it—faint scratching of the canvas lifting, warm breath touching his lips. Where did he lay his knife?

—Isaac! in a voiceless whisper, the breath-shape caressing his cheek.

—God damn it, Patsy! Set-im-kayah catches you—or Ado-e-et-te either—he'll kill you. Kill us both!

A tiny snort of laughter, barely suppressed.—They *didn't* catch me, she said. Ado-e-et-te!—another in-drawn snort.

He reached with his other hand and pried gently at the clutching fingers.

—Isaac! Let me in! It's cold. . . .

There was an incautious scraping of canvas, clashing of dry grass as she began to move again. What else is a man to do, giving thought to the alternatives? He sat up silently, reached with both hands to lift the loose tent wall and let her in, carefully lowered it again, and felt the burst of warmth as at the door of a furnace opened, naked legs to his legs, breasts to his breast. He pulled her close, drew the robe across them both, and stopped her mouth with his hand.

Her lips lay against his neck, her loose hair wreathed his chest in utter repose. He held his breath, listening: Bill still snored, would sleep long and heavy. And the night: some hours yet, it might be three or four hours till the first light came.

XVII

The Wichita Town

Isaac for once had been cautiously reticent when whisky and circumstance revealed Dutch Bill's ambition to start a town near the site of the Wichita village. The reason was that for nearly two years already, with several prominent Kansans, he had been party himself to just such a plan. Nothing had yet come of it. The partnership remained informal, awaiting ratification of the Osage treaty to clear the legal obstacle to settlement and town-building, and the actual removal of the tribe that would follow.

The idea had been Sam Crawford's in the first place: an idea in several men's minds about the time, perhaps, but it was the Governor who first groped it into words—that the place where the two rivers came together, big Arkansas and Little, where the Wichita had built their refuge village and planted their corn, would make a good spot for a town.

Early in July of 1866, with his term in the legislature behind him and his mind set against running again, Isaac rode through to Topeka, left his mare to board at a livery stable, and took the cars to Leavenworth. It was an experiment. The Union Pacific, Eastern Division—the Kansas Pacific, as it was commonly known and would presently be officially named, having begun life as the Leavenworth, Pawnee & Western—had been running to Topeka since January and in May finished a spur from Lawrence to Leavenworth. Isaac had started Sam Carter with a train of furs by the usual wagon route and come on to meet him. If the arithmetic suited—if the railroad would rebate for carloads to Topeka and a regular contract—he could save time and possibly money by freighting halfway by rail.

All the talk at Leavenworth when he got there—in the newspapers, along the hotel bars, among the merchants Isaac called on—was of

Jim Lane shooting himself. There had been a strong anti-Lane faction
when he came up for re-election at the legislature's January session in
1865—only his luck in getting the credit for turning back Price's
invasion had carried him through, with Sam Crawford and the rest of
his allies—but organized around politicians' self-interest, not principle. Since then, however, he had given his enemies the opening they
wanted by standing with Johnson in his soft notions of reconstruc-
tion in the South, earning the enmity of the radical Republicans in
Kansas, and Sam Pomeroy had come forward to outradical the radi-
cals. Since that was the kind of open fight Jim always in the past
seemed to enjoy, they went at him roundabout. Nothing had come of
the charges of trading votes in the legislature for offices in the gift of
the Indian department. This time the accusations in the anti-Lane
papers were of outright money payments from "Indian traders" repaid by profitable contracts to supply dependent tribes, with particulars that sounded like E. H. Durfee at Leavenworth or, occasionally,
the freshman legislator from Butler County. Even in sibylline hints
that stopped short of libel, the charge had soured Isaac's term at Topeka, dull work at best, gave him the feeling that someone out of
reach at Washington City was watching him closer than he liked, and
cautious inquiry confirmed it—Dave Kilbourn was in fact still clerk-
ing for Senator Pomeroy and keeping his secrets.

The slander, not true if it did have some scruples of truth behind it,
like a gob of spit on the cheek that does no harm but shame, had not
really bothered Isaac—it was only another reason why politics would
never be his life; but Jim Lane it cut deep. He came home to Kansas
to gather evidence that would exonerate him—as if a man can prove
he has *not* done a thing; wrote to Isaac at Towanda, and Isaac answered with a careful statement of the plain truth and said he could
publish it; and secured a similar testimonial from Mr Durfee. Such
gestures did not help much. What mattered was that the people, who
in the old times of struggle and the war had hung on his words,
followed him like a Caesar where he led, were turning from him. In
June he started back to Washington with his evidence in hand but
much dejected.

At St Louis Lane complained of dizziness, numbness in his limbs,
and took a room at the Southern; called for a doctor, then a minister
—there was none in town of the Methodist calling—and when the
doctor came tried to jump out the window and was caught and held.
After twelve years of living with death he had become fearful of
dying; he told the story of an admired older brother no one had heard
of before, an army officer in the Seminole wars, thirty years dead in a
swamp beside Tampa Bay—crazy with fever, he had run a sword
through one eye and into his brain. At night the harsh, compelling
orator's voice came through the door of his room in prayer.

Lane persuaded the doctor to accompany him back to Kansas City, then up the Missouri to Leavenworth where he would visit relatives on a nearby farm. The doctor left him there, enjoining the household not to leave firearms around; when he demanded a loaded shotgun or confinement to a madhouse, they cheerfully ignored him. On July 1, a Sunday, he seemed better, rested, they said, and the family took him for an afternoon drive. When they stopped to open a gate, Lane got down, spoke a brief farewell, and pulling out a pocket derringer somehow found in the farmhouse put the barrel to his mouth and pulled the trigger with his thumb. After all the years of threatened suicide, the meditation on the modes of death, it seemed that Jim Lane had not seriously attended to the subject: the ball splintered the roof of his mouth, passed through his brain and out the top of his skull, but failed to kill him. When Isaac reached Leavenworth two days later, the wondering talk was of how Lane had finally blown his head off but lingered, was conscious and could talk; and in whispers of how his real complaint had been syphilis, implanted by youthful indiscretion and now at last exacting its due in the form of paresis, a medical term new to Isaac, meaning that the disease had penetrated his brain and softened it—there was by now, the wisdom gossiped, not much brain to kill, and it made a small target for a little peashooter pistol.

Governor Crawford was alone in a private room off the Planter's House dining room when Isaac came in to take supper, spooning up a bowl of soup with half-a-dozen newspapers for company. The governor nodded, pushed his papers sociably to one side, and Isaac sat down opposite: a narrow-faced, balding, chin-bearded, sharp-cheeked man with the glaring, intractable, tragic eyes of every man of his generation who had gone through the war and tasted the bitter wine of command; not burdened by great intelligence, but dogged in the petty maneuverings of politics, and Isaac judged him honest. He had one quirk that his stay in the governor's office had aggravated: a hatred for Indians constantly reiterated. His feelings for Negroes were opposite: when the subject came up, it generally reminded him of some favorable incident from his service with his colored regiment.

—You heard about General Lane, I reckon, the governor said when Isaac had sent the waiter off for another plate of the bean soup.

—Aint heard hardly anything else since I come to town.

—Sad! the governor said with a whispering sigh. A great mind done to death by his enemies. . . .

The waiter took their order for beefsteaks and, after some discussion, a bottle of claret.

—You know, the governor resumed, I've hired a carriage for tomorrow morning, mean to drive out to the farm and kind of pay my respects. You want to come along, Mister Pride? You organized things for Jim last time he was up, I remember.

—Well, I don't *know*, Isaac hesitated, and then—I mean—they say half his head's gone, hardly nothing but the bandages holding his brains in—

—Sam Crawford never went back on any friend that treated him white, said the governor sententiously, mistaking Isaac's meaning. Don't care how folks talk or what they think, when it comes to *that*, no, *sir!*—. And besides, he concluded with a heavy wink, that Jim Lane, he's a tough old turkey. Wouldn't surprise me none if he fooled us all and got over it. And then—well, you can see for yourself. . . . .

Their duty call the next day was less distasteful than Isaac had feared from all the morbid talk of the Senator's condition. The wounded man lay on a narrow cot in a small room on the first floor at the back of the farmhouse, darkened by green shades drawn at the windows, the covers pulled up to his chin despite the July heat. His wife sat at the foot of the bed, her voice that rose in prayer stilled when they came in. She stood up, took a step, leaned—Jim! It's the governor and Mister Pride, in a muffled voice—and left them, dabbing at her eyes with a handkerchief: a woman—you saw it in the downcast eyes, slumping shoulders, thick waist, knowing little enough of her history—that had known no great joy in marriage.

—General! Sam Crawford began, leaning close. I didn't come out here to say good-bye—nor ask any favors neither, I reckon you've had as much as man can bear of that, but—Jim, it's just, you've done more'n any man living for Kansas, but—well, God damn it, Jim, there's more, the job aint *half* done, Indians to clear off the land so we can settle, and railroads to get built, and—maybe you've got enemies, can't any man stand up in the crowd and not make enemies, but there's a whole lot more that's *friends*, all across the state, just waiting for you to say which way to go, and—damn it, Jim, you can't just die on us—

The governor broke off, overcome by his rhetoric; plucked a handkerchief from his tail pocket and honked his nose. Lane lay motionless as before, his narrow hands flexed on the turned-back sheet. The days since the shooting had drawn the flesh from his face—probably he could not eat—leaving the bare bones covered with pale, stiff skin in an effigy of life; coarse bandage folded his forehead like a nightcap.

Isaac reached out, took one cold hand in his and held it.—It's Jack Pride, Senator, he said. The buffalo hunter. We had some business at Lawrence once, in sixty-three. . . .

The whole head moved or seemed to move minutely on the pillow, in recognition, assent, and for a moment the eyelids raised and Isaac looked into the passionless depths of eternity and death. For another quarter-hour of indeterminate time the two men sat on stiff chairs at the bedside while the dying Senator dreamed away their presence but gave no further sign.

—I don't believe I'll run again, Isaac said, breaking the silence as they drove back to town. Too much time out of a man's business and his family, and no one appreciates it anyhow. Oh, you needn't worry, Mister Crawford, he assured him as the governor turned, frowning. I'll find you a sound Republican when we hold our county convention in the fall.

—Well, sure, Crawford agreed. Stay out of sight and let the other fellow do the work, that's the ticket. Still, he nodded, you could go another term, and then the state senate—and then, well, Congress, if you want it, or secretary of state—now there's the thing, all the state corporation records under your hand, and a man can't make money out of *that* is blind, deaf, and dumb.

—That's about how Jim Lane started, Isaac said. And we've seen where it got him. Or Pomeroy!—

It was not a line the governor cared to pursue. Changing direction, he demanded that Isaac tell him about the Whitewater country and the lower Arkansas—not a passing sentence or two but everything, from the beginning, that Isaac had known, felt, observed, experienced in the three years since settling at Towanda.

—You ever thought about getting up a town down there? the governor asked. On the Arkansas, about where you've got this new station of yours.

Isaac admitted that he had, but cautiously. The town company fever was no longer what it had been in the fifties, before the war, but it remained one of the standing jokes: hardly a man pre-empted his quarter- or half-section but dreamed his land would attract a settlement and turn his acres into twenty-five-foot town lots at a hundred or two hundred dollars apiece, and it seemed half of them had incorporated and printed up maps and made an effort, at least, at selling off shares. Sure, he had *thought* about it. Who hadn't?

—There's only two rivers in the state amounts to anything in the way of settlement and commerce, the governor said, not counting the Missouri, and the Kaw's about towned up, as far out as is practical to build. And the other's the Arkansas, right about where you've got your station—virgin country, ripe for settling and town-making, and a hundred thousand emigrants crowding in *right now*, if there was any place to plant em. Oh, there's forts on it farther up, guarding the Santa Fe Road from the cursed savages—but the Arkansas don't count for much, that far out on the Plains—not much more to it than the Platte—and you know what they say, "a mile wide and an inch deep!" But down where you are—good water at every season, and timber on the bottoms, for cabins and fencing—

—One year it flooded so below the mouth of the Little Arkansas,

Isaac said, I couldn't get my wagons across for a month. And another year—so dry I camped on the riverbed and had to dig for water—. I told you about those times.

The governor shook his head at this objection.—It's all in the geography, Mister Pride. A town about there—it'll be like a funnel, drawing all the commerce from the whole South Plains and carrying it right on through—the Territory, Texas—to the Gulf. It's what this state needs—don't have a town yet that'll carry its weight.

—Sounds like you mean to settle there yourself.

—I mean to start a town and make some money and do something for *Kansas*, Mister Pride! But can't even make a *start* on it with—what's that tribe squatting by the river mouth?

—The Wichita—and some others.

—Yes, Wichita. Well, we've been hospitable, let em stay—too occupied to do anything about em anyway, though all the years we've spent trying to *settle* this country, and then to have some stranger tribe moving *in* on us from the back of beyond—. But the war's over now, time to clear em out—the whole lot of em—back where they come from. And that's only the first step on the way. You know what it says in that Osage treaty they're putting through? They mean to auction the land to the highest bidder, for the benefit and civilizing of the Osage tribe!

—Only you mean to straighten em out so you can start a town, Isaac said, but the governor did not return his smile.

—It's just too much land to lock up like that. All we want is, open it to settlement same as any other public land, according to the general land laws. It means a new treaty—get the Indians back for a pow-wow.

The governor talked on, enlarging on his idea. He was not out for any backwoods farming town or county seat but a real city—full square mile of town, and sections adjoining to be annexed as the place built up. That way, he reasoned, they would draw the railroads when they came, since they had to build in the general direction anyway, and if they had a town in place to build to—why, it meant freight business and passengers, emigrants, straight off, and land prices rising—because, of course, when they fixed the Osage land for settlement, they'd have to set some aside for the railroads too, for an inducement—but there was plenty enough for all comers—

—Sounds like you've got it pretty well figured, Isaac said as the governor eased the buggy down the long slope into town. What is it you want from me?

—Why, Mister Pride, you're on the ground—all you got to do is, keep your eyes open, claim up proper when the time comes—in a year maybe we'll get the surveyors through and you can organize a county—and then come into the company with your land. I've talked it out with Elias Durfee already, he's coming in, there's others. No sense you shouldn't join up too. . . .

Isaac gave his assent—no sense not to, as Sam Crawford said—and remembered to thank him for inviting him into the enterprise. A grand idea certainly, and the ability to conceive it and think it through this far raised the state's chief magistrate a notch or two in Isaac's estimation, but too many obstacles in the way for it to come to anything, most likely. Probably anyhow Crawford was only going on about it by way of pastime, to turn mind and memory from the indecent spectacle of Jim Lane's drawn-out dying; or as a first step toward persuading Isaac to run for the legislature again in the fall, a Jim Lane sort of promise that cost him nothing and would be no loss to anyone if not kept. It was his own land partly the governor was building his castle in the air on and grandly proposed to let him make money from.

Lane lasted another week, dying on July 11. The Leavenworth, Lawrence & Fort Gibson provided a boxcar to carry the coffin home for burial, on a hill behind the town. So ended the tumult of his life, in a modest funeral on a peaceful hilltop. He left his much grieved wife the rebuilt mansion at Lawrence and an infant son to live on for and raise.

For nearly two years Isaac heard little directly about Crawford's town scheme. There were nevertheless signs that amid the cares of state the governor was not neglecting his private interests. In March 1867 a new law went through Congress, redefining the legal means by which settlers could establish towns on public land. That summer the surveying contractors went to work on the Osage lands, staking the townships and sections and submitting their Land Office maps, which in due course the map dealers printed up and published, essential tools for land-lookers; it was from one of the new sectional maps, ordered by mail from Leavenworth, that Isaac learned that his Towanda ranch was indeed laid out over the line onto Osage land, subject to the same restrictions as any town they might try to start in the vicinity of the Little Arkansas. That fall, with the help of a detachment posted from Fort Leavenworth, the governor realized his goal of clearing the Wichita from their village at the mouth of the Little Arkansas; then in the winter E. H. Durfee sent his train down from Council Grove and built his considerable establishment across the Little Arkansas from the Wichita village site. Something was beginning to happen, but still the Land Office showed no sign of offering any Osage land for sale, and the Osage treaty remained as an obstruction, precluding pre-emption at the traditional minimum price, $1.25 an acre, and making no provision for town-building.

Something else happened late that same summer of 1867 in which

Sam Crawford played only an incidental part. All that year the Kansas Pacific was laying track west at nearly a mile a working day, right out on the true Plains by now: in April, it reached Salina; by fall it was a hundred miles farther and the railhead had created another mushroom town, known as Hays. In the spring an Illinois cattle dealer named Joe McCoy came prospecting a Kansas market on the railroad and settled on Abilene, a town left slumbering by the westward advance of the Kansas Pacific.

Abilene is about eighty miles north of where the Little Arkansas joins the Arkansas. Chisholm's Trail became a magnet for the herds coming up from Texas, connecting at the Arkansas crossing with the West Shawnee Trail for the final leg to Abilene. Isaac now had two stations along this route, at Round Pond and Clearwater, and, just off it, at Walnut Grove; for the next season, he would have to improve his stock with suitable harness and saddlery, ready-made clothing, up-to-date repeater pistols and ammunition. The drovers were also the most immediate reason why Mr Durfee that winter decided to move his southern outpost from Council Grove to the Arkansas.

The legislature that spring had quarantined eastern Kansas against Texas cattle, drawing the deadline so as to exclude Abilene by thirty miles. Crawford, when asked about this difficulty, made known the view of the state's chief magistrate: no one seeking to sell cattle at Abilene need fear prosecution for ignoring this particular law.

At the end of March 1868, when Isaac came home from Chisholm's death, there was a long letter waiting from Sam Crawford. The time had come to move on the town company, and on March 18 he had registered the corporate charter with the secretary of state, putting down a list of eight incorporators: himself and Durfee, Isaac as promised, Bill Lawrence, the secretary of state, four others. The plan remained as ambitious as the governor had first conceived it: they would lay out a section and a half between Durfee's new place on the Little Arkansas and Chisholm's Creek a mile and a half east, Section 17, according to the land map, and half of 16; capital stock of twenty-five thousand dollars in 250 shares but no hurry about paying in, beyond some immediate expenses for advertising—the company was to meet in a month at Emporia to organize and plan, and they could divide the stock up then. That evening after Marie went to bed, Isaac, much excited, sat by lamplight at the table, sketching and calculating on a sheet of brown wrapping paper—streets and avenues and blocks and twenty-five-foot town lots—yes, and parks and churches and a courthouse square, a school for the children; with lots selling at say a hundred each, really nothing for town property, every hundred-dollar share in the company would pay back a thousand easy, maybe twice that. He would put in for twenty shares—or why not thirty, since he would be on the spot, putting in the work?

There was one difficulty: Isaac was longer on credit just now than he was on cash. His time since Chisholm's death had been taken up with settling the old trader's debt and disposing of the last big train of goods. Isaac rode east to Chisholm's ranch on the Little River and arranged with his widow to pay off in stages, as she could, then west to Greiffenstein's station on the Washita, between the revived Wichita Agency and Fort Cobb. Jennie, there alone while her husband toured the Indian winter camps, was prepared to take two thousand dollars' worth of Isaac's stock but even for that had not much in money or furs on hand to pay with. Isaac conferred at length with Jesse Leavenworth, who had established his own camp nearby: officially the agent to the Kiowa and Comanche but, as one of the peace commissioners for the Medicine Lodge treaties, considering himself responsible for all the wild tribes who had signed there as well as others in process of removal from Kansas, particularly the Konza, expected in the summer; and, as Chisholm had said, short of supplies with which to induce the tribes to settle on their assigned reservations or to meet the commitments of the treaties. The consequence was that Isaac came away with an order signed by Colonel Leavenworth for the remainder of his goods, at a price that would make up the profit he would lose on trading them for furs; and a contract for another four thousand dollars in rations to supply the Konza and others as they arrived. So the difficulty was solved, though it would be a while before he was paid in full. Chisholm's widow and Greiffenstein would pay off in the course of the summer, most likely in robes and hides and wolf skins, not cash, but it came out the same, around five thousand dollars. The sales to Leavenworth's agency would not be payable until the contract was complete, but he could expect another eight thousand dollars sometime in the fall.

Isaac started for Emporia on April 22, seventy-five miles, a long day's ride—the meeting was next day—but it saved a day putting up at a hotel or settler's cabin; the country was getting a little settled up for him to feel comfortable camping just anywhere. It was the week following Marie's birthday. She had been silent and disappointed when he failed to surprise her with a present—not that he had forgotten, but it had been all winter since he had been near a town where he might have bought anything suitable; he promised to bring her back something—a shawl, a bonnet—as long as it would fit in a saddlebag.

Governor Crawford opened the meeting by explaining why he had rushed ahead with the town company: Ed Ross, appointed to fill out Lane's term in the Senate, who himself had done sharp bargaining with Kansas Indians in years past, had sent word that the President intended to reopen the Osage business, and it had seemed well to organize the company and put in a claim for land before someone else got the idea. Hence the company's first meeting. Once more Isaac was impressed. The governor was not a man to underestimate.

Crawford handed out printed copies of the corporate charter registered with the secretary of state, with a set of standard bylaws adapted to Kansas law. The document, run off by the state printer at Topeka, occupied one page; until the new Osage treaty was settled, there had seemed no point in spending money having stock certificates engraved. All that remained to bring the company into being was to elect a presiding officer and secretary and assent to the charter and bylaws; except for Durfee, all the incorporators seemed to have had experience of proper legislative style.

—Mister President! Isaac called out, rising, when they had voted Lawrence into the chair and he had taken his place at the head of the table. What's this on this charter about *Town of Sheridan?* Does that mean we've got to call the place Sheridan?

—That was my idea, Crawford said. It's got tone—I like the sound of it. Besides, the general don't object—might even put some money in.

(Little Phil, hero of the Shenandoah Valley and other campaigns in the late war, was now commander of the Army's Department of the Missouri, responsible, as they all knew, for carrying out the new military policy of pacifying the wild tribes and ending their depredations; a suitable name for a new town on the Kansas frontier in 1868 that meant to benefit by that policy—and no doubt the governor had other reasons for picking it.)

—Those are good reasons, Mister Crawford, Isaac said, but it's already got a name—the Wichitas' Town. That's what everyone on the Plains calls it. Wichita, for years now. . . .

—The two sections I specified aint right where they had their village, Crawford said, if I read my maps right, they're *east* of the Little Arkansas. After that cholera scare last fall I figured folks'd be shy of coming if we platted too close. Besides—Wichita, that's Indian. What do we want with an Indian name when we can have a good Anglo-Saxon name like Sheridan?

—Half the names in Kansas are Indian, if it comes to that, Isaac said. Topeka's an Indian name. *Kansas* is Indian.

The governor looked dark, the others non-committal, indifferent what the place was called, so it made money.

—There is substance in Mister Pride's view, Durfee put in, and something to be said for it, as I know from experience. When I sent my men down last winter to build my new trading post, Wichita, I told them—build as near to Wichita as you conveniently can, on good land, of course. That is what I said, *Wichita.* It might seem odd if we—

The governor did not care to contest the name, and it was settled: Wichita. Mr Bancroft, chosen temporary secretary and treasurer, went around the table correcting the printed copies of the charter. The bylaws were voted without change. There was not much further business to do till they knew what the commissioners would put in the new Osage treaty. Isaac, knowing something of surveying and mapping, was appointed to draw a town plan for the chosen section and a half, putting in streets and avenues and numbered lots; Mr Bancroft would have it lithographed with suitable flourishes, parks and churches, perhaps a small steamboat on the river, and a surrounding hinterland of thriving farms, with an adjoining half-section for suburban development in lots of four or five acres, depending on how Isaac's block plan came out—the city of the imagination which in every town company anticipates the actual. He was authorized to distribute three hundred copies to newspapers and land agents. The incorporators assessed themselves fifty dollars each to cover these and other expenses. Since Isaac had his own business to attend to, no less than the others, Governor Crawford would arrange for a reliable man to occupy the town land and constitute a claim club—to keep order in any pre-emption claims made nearby, of course, and more particularly to discourage strangers from pre-empting on town land; and to sell lots if any wanted them. These services would require no outlay of cash, the governor suggested, since the manager could be paid with a share or two of stock in the town company, when issued, and doubtless would consider himself sufficiently rewarded for his pains. The meeting was adjourned.

Isaac spent a week camped near Chisholm's Creek, sketching the plan for Bancroft's map, and while he was at it staked an adjoining quarter-section of prairie with his name and the date and hauled the four cottonwood logs to arrange in the form of the foundation for a cabin, making good his claim according to the established customs of pre-emption—assuming, of course, that the new treaty with the Osage would finally open the land. Before he had finished, Crawford's man arrived from Topeka in a wagon drawn by two span of mules: Darius S. Munger, known as Dave, an easy, bearded man of perhaps forty who affected an innkeeper's lazy affability—his last employment had been managing an hotel—but seemed not to know much about starting from scratch on the frontier Plains. Borrowing a man from Durfee's ranch, Isaac worked with him at putting up a cabin on the west side of the townsite, which on his plan he had named Waco Street, for an affiliated subtribe of the Wichita.

It was not till he came home to Towanda to send off his town plan to Mr Bancroft that Isaac got news of the new Indian outbreak, in some ways the most ominous yet in Kansas: ten days earlier, on June 4, a party of raiders, Cheyenne, it seemed, had attacked the Konza reservation at Council Grove, about midway between Towanda and Fort Riley, the principal base for defense of the Plains. To get there, the sizable war-party had had to slip past the half-dozen forts guard-ing the main routes of travel through Kansas and had succeeded in coming farther east than any hostile Indians had been known for decades. To the governor and others of his mind, the raid served as a fresh and urgent argument for a general campaign to quiet the wild tribes and drive them once and for all from Kansas; and incidentally for hastening the removal of the tame Konza (not to mention the Osage) to the supposed safety of the Indian Territory.

The same Kansas newspapers also reported the Osage treaty nego-tiations, supplemented and amplified by a furious series of private letters from Crawford and Durfee. The terms had come out when the document signed by the Osage chiefs went before the Senate. As in the earlier treaty, the only exceptions were to be "actual settlers"—those already squatting a living from a patch of Osage land—in the usual distinction from the "greedy speculators" bent on acquiring public or Indian land for resale at a profit. The treaty made no provi-sion for town-building.

—Is it the end of Wichita? Marie asked when Isaac had finished his reading and thrust the papers from him.

—Not only Wichita. Towanda's on Osage land, it turns out—all our stations except Round Pond, which is over the line in the Terri-tory.

—I suppose there would be no profit, buying from the railroad company, Marie suggested. She had the baby on her ankle, little Ma-mie, playing horse, her fingers as reins. The little girl laughed, and Marie laughed back. Bissy was out by the spring with his ducks. Serious and quick and five and a half years old, he had learned read-ing from his mother, and Isaac had rewarded him with a flock of ducklings to manage; and writing too, to the extent of his name, in full, in a graceful, rounded script, and that had led—through admira-tion for his own name, then a parental attempt at distinguishing the two Isaacs, and finally Mamie's struggle to pronounce the difficult syllables—to his new nickname. Bissy: Bunny was childish, and he no longer answered to it.

—Well, I don't know about profit. If they'd let us have our townsite at a reasonable price for unimproved land—ten dollars an acre, say—it wouldn't hurt much. He did some figures on the back of an enve-lope. Actually, he continued, it looks like there's so much money in selling lots, it don't hardly matter what we have to pay, even *ten times* ten dollars an acre—we'd come out about as well, if the town takes—if people settle and buy. Only, you get up around that high figure and it gets to be a lot of money for the eight of us to raise, or even borrow, all in one jump—or we'd have to pay on time, and a pretty fair inter-est. . . .

—Could you not issue more shares, raise more capital?

—Oh, I reckon we could do that, Isaac agreed and went to figuring again. But the way it looks—the more stock you put out, the less profit you get on a share. You pretty soon reach the point where you can do about as well or better, putting your money in something else, with less risk—the Indian trade, or buffalo hunting, and we're back where we started. Which aint so bad, is it, Marie? He grinned. But the big thing is, the others are going to fight it, no matter what, cause they're set on getting the land at the minimum rate for pre-emption. And the other, I don't doubt but Senator Ross and his railroad gang have ideas for a town of their own and never would let us take the land to go against them at any price. Or they do, and they finally get tired of the land game and lay some track, and they don't come *near* our town, why, it's dead, just goes back to prairie, like El Dorado when the war came, or a whole lot of other Kansas towns that won't ever come to anything—just aint room for two paying towns in this country, and we'd be left with a section-and-a-half of pretty good corn and wheat land, grazing land—only it cost us ten times what it's worth—or a *hundred* times!

He laughed, stood up, and took the baby, swung her high and pulled her in close, cradled in his arms.—Nothing I can do about it by worrying, anyhow. . . . But, Marie! he said abruptly, as if a new thought had just come to him. Why don't you take the little ones and go up to Iowa for the summer? Never met you—you'll like them, and they keep asking for you to come for a visit. Go on. We can afford it.

—Oh, Isaac, she said, frowning. You know I have nothing to wear.

He knew by now that the trunk full of garments beside their bed did not count as anything to wear; but she had not dismissed the idea, was prepared, perhaps, to bargain.—There's shops at Davenport where you can buy things. Or my mother—you could make things together, she loves to sew, nothing better in the world.

He set the baby down to crawl and reached to hold her but she pushed free, refusing to be hurried.—Would you come, Isaac? she soberly asked. It is you they have been begging to come—you owe it.

—Too much to do down here, he said. Got to get my goods assembled and freighted down to Colonel Leavenworth, so we can fill that contract and get our money out—and that aint the half of what's before me this summer. . . . But listen! he said as she frowned again —there's things I ought to be doing right now at Leavenworth too, I can drive you to Topeka and put you on the cars—might even ride through to Saint Louis and see you on the boat—it's a lovely trip up the river, and how they do feed you, on the steamboats!

She studied his face—not, certainly, a face in which ever thought or feeling could be hid. Now it showed wanting, wanting her to agree and go, since the idea was his, and pleasure, anticipated, her pleasure —he was thinking of her and meant her to enjoy it; and something more, not after all quite clear, that if he would not go home himself, submit, she could go for him. So at length, gravely as fitted the occasion—I shall write in the morning, she said. I suppose we could be ready in a week, if they will let us come. But Isaac! What will you do about Bissy's ducks? And with a fluting laugh she now let him hold her.

Marie was a month at Rockingham before she began to feel at ease. It was not that anyone was unkind, only so different in their ways from any she had known, and yet she had become connected with them, a part of them, through Isaac, through her children. The house itself was bigger than any she had lived in, bigger than Uncle Titus' at Burlingame or the Schuylers', set into the top of the slope above the Mississippi, with the fine view up and down the river that Isaac had talked of, and from an ivy-mantled window in Lizzie's apartment (as she called it) you could look right up the mouth of the Rock across the way where once the Indians had their great village, Saukenuk: built on in every direction from the original cabin of thirty years ago.

It had been a restful time, with only the two children to think of and Mamie still put down to nap after lunch and when up running after Bissy. The boy, serious and purposeful, used all the daylight exploring the farm and had to be hunted and led in to meals; Mr Pride had given him a motherless foal to care for, and Bissy fed it and brushed it, had made it a bridle of rope and with limitless patience taught it to come and follow like a dog, it came after when he went in to meals and had to be tied to the back porch railing while he ate— and said before the summer was out he meant to ride it, though Mr Pride soberly told him it would still be too young to carry anyone, even a little five-year-old boy.

Mr Pride's affairs seemed to be prospering: some of the old settlers had lately sold out and gone to western Iowa or Nebraska in search of cheaper land, and within the last year he had bought two such tracts adjoining his homestead, south-facing but steep, and one of them wooded and had to be cleared and the stumps removed by blasting, work that had taken till planting time that spring. He had four men on the place just now, old Henry, hired from year to year to look after the milking and the pigs, and another for the season, also boarding, besides two men who came in by the day, at present for haying and would stay till harvest, and Mrs Pride, with a summer kitchen set up in back, complained of the work.

Imagination had failed to prepare Marie for meeting Isaac's father —Isaac himself, perhaps, had given her too few particulars. A Protestant minister and missionary on the Iowa frontier, even if cast off by his church: despite her childhood warnings against Protestant subtlety to lure the faithful from the way of salvation, Marie had expected a man of severe and brooding virtue, living at a remove from mankind and his family, speaking, when he spoke at all, with fierce, black eloquence—not, certainly, a man to stoop to common talk with an ignorant young woman. But he talked easily with her from the start, mixing his talk with gentle little self-mocking jokes—of her journey from Kansas, of the children, the Wichita town company and the rascality over the new Indian treaty—only at times he broke off in mid-sentence, as if his mind ran through subterranean channels and now had withdrawn again, eyes looking vaguely into distance, unfocused; and came to himself with a faint smile and asked what they had been saying.

He stood perhaps a head taller than his son, long-faced and heavy-boned, slow and deliberate where Isaac was quick and graceful in all his movements; and even now, near sixty, with the strength to take down a two-foot oak in minutes with his ax or heave a mired wagon wheel from the rut.

Twice since Marie had come he had brought a tramp home from his marketing at Davenport, sent him to the kitchen for the girl to feed, and given him a night's bed in the attic; and in the morning sent him on his way with bread and meat and a cast-off coat or patched pair of trousers. Mrs Pride contemplated these charities in silence. She had grown used to them.

What Isaac had told of his sister inspired an awe which Lizzie in person did little to abate. Graduated from a female seminary in the East, wrote lengthy poems which were often published, painted—landscapes and houses, flowers, disliking human subjects—besides performing at the harmonium, organ, or piano, and singing: Marie had labored anxiously at her dutiful letters to Rockingham, but her hand looked childish to her, half her spellings wrong—Isaac was hopeless about such things even if she had cared to ask him, wrote his letters out in haste and impatience and sent them off without correction, and how he wrote was exactly how he felt at the moment and good enough; Marie's letters in consequence were brief, formal, and few, it seemed to her when she was obliged to write that she had nothing of interest to tell. Lizzie, in her minutely written engraver's script and now in conversation, had news of a concert by the Norwegian violinist Ole Bull, a Petroleum Nasby lecture, a week of sermons at the various churches by Reverend Dwight Moody, an appearance by General Tom Thumb and his wife; it seemed that Davenport was a very cultured place. Yet Marie only partly envied her sister-in-law's gifts. She had turned thirty-two in May, five years older than Marie, and for all her graces, her elegant ripe figure and abundant dark hair, she remained unmarried, her prospects uncertain.

Lizzie was in the family but not of it, so Marie put it to herself. There was still a building on the road along one side of the farm that the family called "the school," perhaps once a grainery, which for a few months after coming home from the seminary she had refurbished and set up as a school for a few small neighborhood children; the work did not agree with her and she had given it up. Apart from practicing her various arts, Marie could not see that she now did any work. Occasionally she would make an unusual pie, strawberry, sweet potato, or tomato, all abundant in the garden according to the season, which she then carried off to her apartment to consume in solitude. In the spring she had acquired a lamb from a neighbor and from somewhere a shepherd's crook, and, contriving a shepherdess costume, she led the animal with her on painting expeditions until it turned out a ram, ugly and stupid, and she lost interest and gave it back. Now she had reverted to the vaguely Spanish style which, she said, best suited her coloring, with a new basquine Mrs Pride had spent some days sewing for her.

It was sewing that made Marie easy with her mother-in-law, as Isaac had predicted. Her afternoons were taken up with the children or excursions with Lizzie, then many days with elaborate teas to which Mrs Pride invited chosen friends among the neighbor ladies and, twice, Mrs Patience Newcomb, with the Prides among the county's first settlers, whose husband had made a fortune in wheat, then land and money-lending, and retired to a great house on the bluff above Davenport surrounded by three acres of blue-grass lawn. The mornings Marie had to herself, having no special duties in the household, and occupied them in the family parlor cutting and sewing cotton goods she had brought in her trunk from the stock at Towanda: new roundabouts for Bissy and Mamie, shirts and underwear to take home to Isaac. Mrs Pride looked in and approved and suggested Marie would like something for herself, and Marie, remembering Isaac's offer, agreed. They drove to Davenport, made the rounds of the dry-goods merchants, and selected some yards of an extravagant silk, tiny pink flowers on a dark blue ground, and took tea with Mrs Newcomb on the way home. Mrs Pride had a pattern from a New York ladies' magazine that she had been wanting to make, but it did not suit Lizzie just now. The pattern called for an elaborately gathered bodice that Marie did not know how to do, and some mornings after, having finished the skirt, she watched while Mrs Pride worked at it.

—Is it wise, do you think, the older woman said, to allow your son such freedom with that colt?

Marie, sitting forward in the straight chair, eyes on the supple fingers pricking the glinting needle at the dark fabric, drawing the thread through, felt a prickling at the nape of her neck: an edge to the question. Never an unkind word, and yet never a word of unqualified praise. No one ever entirely pleased her; except, perhaps, her own wayward, unmarried daughter.

—I see no harm in it, Marie said. He is very careful, have you watched him? And he does everything he is told.

—Oh, I have watched him. Isaac was little older when he got his first pony, a little Indian pony, a reprobate old Indian gave it him— we hunted him all the afternoon and thought him lost. And then— Mister Pride would never after control him. It was the beginning.

—If he had not started young he might have had no place on the Plains. Do you know, they say he is the finest horseman in Kansas? None can outride him. I have ridden with him. It is like following after a thunderstorm.

—He was ever a willful child. It was because we thought him sickly —*I* thought him so: we allowed him greater freedom than perhaps was right. God, I suppose, willed him to be small and neat, not a large man like his father—but oh, to bring one's child into the world in a little one-room cabin in the wilderness, no relatives or friends by to assist one's strength—. You were fortunate, my dear, to have your uncle to go to, and a wise old woman to see you through—certainly your first-born.

—I should have rather my own house, however humble, Marie said. It was only—we had given up the Saline ranch, because of the Indian scare, you know, and then the Rebel raiders from the mountains, we were like birds on the wing, no place of our own.

Mrs Pride nodded gravely but insisted:—I should have been less fearful at home. For he *was* sickly too, more than his share of colds and frontier fevers when he was small, and even growing into boyhood. It is *not* a healthful climate, not like my home, in Vermont. And then the stipend the Board of Missions allowed—hardly enough to feed a man with no family, and they took it amiss when a missioner, like the Apostle, sought his bread by his own labors. Cabbage—and Irish potatoes, of course, because they keep in the root cellar—the potato bugs were not pesky as they have since become, and we had never heard of the blight. And what Mister Pride could get with his gun—prairie chickens, and pigeon in season, and squirrels for stews and pan-fried and every other way, and once in a great while venison—

—Isaac does as well as an Indian, getting our living by his gun, Marie said, smiling. A mother cannot but feel anxious, watching her child grow, yet now—you must feel proud at all your son has accomplished, making his way in a new country like his father before him. I should like, one day, to have such pride in—

—I am *glad* of his success, Mrs Pride corrected her. If it be not too dearly bought. She held the nearly finished bodice to the light, turned it, peered close. My eyes, she said. Growing to an old woman's eyes, I

have found no spectacles that help for work like this. To think of it!
She sighed. That a time might come when I could not sew. . . .

—He will go to the state convention this fall, he wrote in his last
letter—I shall start back and meet him there, we can travel home
together. And, he said, some want him for state senator from our
district—he says he does not know if he will do it, he will see who
they pick for governor.

—I had an uncle once was Senator—for Vermont, Mrs Pride mildly
observed. In the national Senate, at Washington.

Marie gave a short, impatient shake of her head.—We shall have a
heavy interest in the new town, she said. If the new Indian bill goes
through: Wichita. Isaac named it, I expect he was too modest to tell
you. The others talked, this name and that, and he said, *Gentlemen, it
already has a name.* Wichita. We shall build a city there, and live. . . .

—Ah, child! . . . She put the dress carefully aside and lay back,
closing her tired eyes. Rockingham was to be a city once, would you
think it? Mister Pride came out and looked and took a claim above the
townsite, came home and said we should found a church and have a
part in building the capital city of a new state, and I came, what could
a wife do but follow where he had chosen? . . . When we lost the
vote for county seat, the people began to move away—one winter, the
houses where the town was, the Davenport merchants used them for
storing grain, then pulled them down, for the lumber, you would not
know unless you looked on the recorder's map and saw how the land
divided. And the church: Mister Pride preached through New England, raising money for it, on a corner of our land, and when the
people left we kept it for a carriage house. And then Lizzie, when she
wanted her school—.

For a long moment in silence they contemplated the vanished town
her words called forth, vanity of vanities, a text for a sermon. There
had been lively talk at the supper table about Wichita and the Osage
scandal, as it was now called in the newspapers; Marie had supposed
it a local matter, a Kansas matter, but now Senators from other sections had taken it up, and it seemed certain the new treaty would not
be voted. Isaac wrote that Governor Crawford was working through
the state's representatives for an act of Congress specifying the selling
of the Osage land to settlers at pre-emption rates, within the frame of
the old treaty—Ross was lost, but Pomeroy, whatever his hidden motives, would publicly back the Kansas interest—and if he succeeded
Wichita would yet be built. Marie had been puzzled by Mr Pride's
seeming knowledge of town building, and now she understood. He
had been Isaac's age, not old, not gray, imagining a city to build on
the empty land and his part in it. The one way they were alike, father
and son: the energy—but different there too. Mr Pride went off like a
load of bird shot dispersed among a flock roosting in a treetop; his

son, a rifle with the same charge, but aiming its ball at one target. Marie at twenty-seven felt certainty he would hit whatever he aimed at, and pity for the mother left behind by the town that had not come to pass.

—Missus Pride, I think that Isaac—

Isaac's mother roused herself, sat up.—There now, she said, we're almost done, and then I must see to dinner. We'll try the fit this afternoon.

Marie gravely regarded her: the mouth drawn down in stiff seams of habitual disappointment barely contained, not forgiven, the weary eyes.

—Would you mind, Marie said, if I call you Mother? I feel awkward, otherwise, and having none of my own—

Mrs Pride looked her in the eyes, softening, and sat forward, taking Marie's hand in both hers.—My dear child! . . .

Isaac felt dull without Marie, no one to talk to. He was stretched on a bench, digesting his dinner in the shade in front of the Walnut Grove cabin, when Bill Greiffenstein came riding in at the head of a train of three mule wagons. He had seen him a mile off, coming across the softly contoured buffalo-grass prairie, and as he came near recognized him and walked out to meet him.

—You look like a man that's bringing me money, Isaac said as he reached his hand up to shake. *There's* the way to make sure of your welcome! Catching the horse by the bridle, he led it toward the house, calling out for the boy to take it around to the corral and give it some corn.

—It is true, the German said gravely as he dismounted. What Jennie did not have to pay in winter, I pay you now. He drew a memorandum book from an inner pocket of his formal black coat, opened it, found the page, and held it close, peering.

—Let's see what you've got, Isaac said and ran to climb in the back of the first wagon as it came up.

It was wolf skins, still good as money, and robes, made up in packs, that looked to be all from this summer, thin, worth perhaps twelve dollars at Leavenworth; about half a load and the other wagons the same.

—You mean to throw in the wagons and the mules too? said Isaac, grinning, as he climbed down. I mean, he said, when Greiffenstein's eyes widened in vague incomprehension, I aint counted up exactly, but it don't *look* like enough to cover two full loads of Indian goods I took you last winter. Course I could carry you through till fall again, if—

Bill shook his head.—I pay in money, also, he said.

Together they worked out a value for Greiffenstein's furs—slow-spoken work, at each step he paused to consider and pencil a note in his pocketbook; and the balance, nearly half, in national bank notes of a new Topeka bank. While the men were unloading, Isaac led the German into the cabin and wrote out his receipt. Greiffenstein then wanted to look over Isaac's stock and in the warehouse out back selected a half-dozen sacks of flour, sugar, coffee, a box of assorted glass beads, a case of light hatchets—standard items in the Indian trade but no large quantity of any; and offered to pay cash, for a consideration, and they at length settled on five percent off. Returning to the store, he looked through Isaac's guns but shook his head.

—They're what the drovers call for, Isaac said. Light single-shot carbine you can hang on your saddle horn and scare a wolf off with, or kill a snake. And cheap.

—The Indians—they want modern rifles, repeaters. Now, you had a case of Henrys—next time, maybe?

—I might consider, Isaac said slowly, thinking it through. But, Bill, that Henry, with its fancy cartridges and spring-loaded magazine— that aint a practical gun for out on the Plains. I tried one, last time I was at Leavenworth—too light for buffalo, don't have the range for antelope or even deer—don't seem to me it's good for anything but killing men with. What you want, trading that kind of gun to wild Indians that'll turn around and use it against white men?

—I don't sell guns to bad Indians. Moke-ta-ve-to, Black Kettle, the Cheyenne peace chief—he want good rifles, I get him good rifles. Or my wife's brother—or Set-im-kayah, the Kiowa peace man. Besides, they don't buy from me, they buy from somebody else, just like whisky—or steal from soldiers, or when they go raiding, Texas, Mexico. . . .

—Damn it, Bill! Isaac said. You know what it means—the Indian agents get wind of it, you lose your license—or me supplying, the same—and never get it back, and what kind of business have you got then? I'll tell you frankly, it aint worth the grief for the kind of trade I get from you—not that I don't appreciate it, mind. But just now—it don't amount to half a wagonload, and you going out to the buffalo camps to trade, thousands of Indians—.

Greiffenstein shrugged.—Most things, I get better prices at Durfee's ranch, credit as long. I buy from you what I can.

Isaac in his mind ran through possible offers but held back: it was like a game of chess; it might be the German had given the same story to Luke Ledrick, Durfee's manager, in the morning.—I'll think about that, Bill, he said finally, and the guns too. But my prices are fair, and my terms too, and I'm in no hurry. What you don't take, the drovers will, or the Indians, when they come back in the fall. . . .

Greiffenstein's long face was expressionless, volunteering nothing. Their business at an end, Isaac offered a drink of whisky from the keg under the counter, coffee from the large pot on the back of the stove, but Greiffenstein declined. Sitting straight-backed in the one armchair, he produced a long-stemmed pipe, then a tobacco pouch, worked a strip of cut plug between his palms, and with concentration loaded and tamped the bowl. The pipe lighted, he gazed amiably at Isaac through the haze of gray smoke, prepared for general conversation. Isaac leaned back against the counter, facing him. Kelly's voice came through the open door of the cabin, wordless, directing the teamsters at their unloading.

—That little stock of guns, the German observed. How much powder you keep for them guns? About fifty pound, I bet.

The powder was an anxiety: a good price, Isaac had gone a little heavy in buying. He said:—It sells right along. I've got about a *ton* here, in kegs, and a thousand pounds of bar lead. And as much again at the three other posts—just laid in, for the summer and fall—

The German's face showed concern. He puffed at his pipe.—Too bad, he said. Them cartridge rifles—everybody got to have cartridges, ordinary powder going to be cheap. I could take some, help you out, sell to Indians in the Territory, in winter. . . .

Isaac became persuasive. Eventually Greiffenstein agreed to take fifteen hundred pounds of powder and lead in proportion, at a moderate profit, and paid in cash. Isaac, grateful, went out to give further orders about loading the wagons.

It was the following morning before Isaac rode down to Durfee's ranch. The notion that Durfee was underselling him rankled, but he calculated he knew Ledrick well enough to secure a straight answer; and he and Durfee were after all partners in a manner, at least in the town, and had done business since the first day Isaac came into Kansas, more than nine years now—not but that he had on occasion taken his trade to Kansas City or St Louis when to his advantage, but in all their dealings through the years there had never been anything underhanded or behind-the-back that Isaac knew.

—You seen anything of Dutch Bill lately? Isaac asked when they were comfortably settled in the room that served as office, built into one corner of Durfee's extensive, open-ended stockade.

Luke nodded: a gaunt, dark man, Tennesseean once, who had served a boyhood apprenticeship in the old fur trade in the western mountains, then in the war joined a Kansas regiment of mounted infantry as sharpshooter; not quite the silent, immovable presence of Bill Mathewson, say, but a man of similar stamp.—Night before last, Luke ventured after a pause. With four wagons. I gave him a bed. And let his mule skinners camp in the plaza, he added, crimping the corners of his mouth in an intended smile.

—*Four* wagons, Luke? Isaac said. He only had three when he came by my place.

Ledrick reflected.—It was four, he said. Left one to rest, maybe, save his mules driving out of the way, cause it was loaded up already, much as it would carry.

When finally Isaac got him around to the matter of prices, it came out that Mr Durfee himself set them at Leavenworth, a written list that changed every month and, allowing for distance and the cost of transportation, was different for each of his posts; but here at Wichita about the same as Isaac charged for most items, higher for some.

They sat in silence for a time while Isaac pondered.—You sell him any guns? he asked.

—Couple old cap-and-ball Colt's carbines I had around—about like the Navy revolver, only—

—I know the gun, Isaac said. That all?

—Seemed like Bill was kind of nosin around after repeaters— Henrys, or this new one, the—. Mister Durfee don't carry any such, but I said I'd write him a letter and see what he says. Only—well, I don't care what he says, I don't believe I'd sell one of them so a bunch of murdering Indians can come raidin with em right into central Kansas—like them Cheyenne last month—

—That's what I think—went through the whole same business with him. And powder—you sell him any powder?

—Well now, there's the funny thing, Luke said, almost voluble. Here we about done with our business, I figure, and he says like it kind of slip his mind, You got any powder you can let me have? And lead? Cause his stock was down at the home place on the Washita, he says, and he heard the price might rise, and—. Well *of course* I got powder, and—to make it short, I about filled one whole wagon for him—would've cleaned me right out if I let him, only it'd be a month to get more, from Leavenworth—*and* paid up in paper money—. How about you? You sell him any?

—*Some,* Isaac admitted, lowering his eyes for a moment. Not any wagonload, anyhow, I don't carry that much at a time—. Luke! What's he want with it all?

—Aye, there's the nub on it. Aint givin it out for charity, I don't guess, not Dutch Bill.

—Where then?

—Old Bill's a mite close about that too, but one of his mule-busters let it out. Luke leaned forward, lowering his voice. Seems all the tribes is gathered along Medicine Lodge Creek, bout where they had the Sun-Dance last year and the treaties—might be ten thousand Indians. Been there a month, kind of hangin around—all had their Sun-Dance, and then the buffalo's plenty and they're huntin, aint been so plenty on the Great Bend this time of year for years back, seems the railroad goin through has kind of milled em back, ahead of season. And then the government has promised annuities, a whole trainload, delivered at Fort Larned—only the Army and the Indian office is havin a debate. Some say, since the Council Grove raid, no presents to any wild Indians, or not till they come on the reservation like they promise—and others say, give em cloth and rations accordin to treaty but no guns—and a few, everything they's promised, no matter, *includin* guns—. And the Indians kind of waitin around to see how it falls, but gettin out of patience, as you might say. . . .

Two days later Isaac started west with three wagons and three men, Milo Kellogg, Jim Kelly and Andrew Hansen; closed the Walnut Grove station and padlocked his stores, made an early start, and when Luke Ledrick hailed him at the Arkansas crossing said he was going south with supplies for Round Pond and thinking of opening another place farther down Chisholm's Trail. The same morning he came on fresh wagon tracks plain as mileposts in the dry summer bunch-grass and followed the trail all the way up the Ninnescah to its source; an untraveled route with the buffalo thick all around, as Luke had said, but except to get meat they pushed along and did not hunt. On the third day out, Greiffenstein's trail diverged northwest and Isaac left it, crossing the divide and turning south to Medicine Lodge Creek, and late the following day came into Set-im-kayah's camp.

The Kiowa had broken the great camp circle since holding their Sun-Dance at the end of June and were camped by bands along the stream. Ten Bear and his Comanche band were across the river, Black Kettle and the Cheyenne within a day's ride to the north; and Arapaho, Kiowa Apache—all the tribes of the South Plains spread across the dry grasslands enclosed by the Great Bend of the Arkansas. Isaac consulted with the headmen and settled Kellogg and young Kelly in the two nearest Kiowa camps with a load of goods to trade; Stumbling Bear assigned him and Hansen a lodge near his own. Satanta himself was absent from his village, somewhere vaguely west, and Isaac did not insist on knowing what was not readily told. Except in Stumbling Bear's village, it seemed that many of the warriors were missing from the Kiowa camps, only enough remaining to guard the women, children, and horses; possibly hunting, more likely on war parties.

Isaac stayed a week, but the trading was dull. Except for those too old for it, most of the men actually present in the camps were occupied in hunting, and the women followed to cut up the meat and care for the skins. Pat-so-gate passed around the platters of roast meat one night when her Indian father invited Isaac to his tepee for a feast. He saw her again, two mornings later, as he went to the creek to bathe and swim according to the Indian custom but had no chance to talk. Like the other women, she was occupied with meat and the tanning of hides for the winter.

At the end of the week messengers arrived from the north: a great train of treaty goods had reached Fort Larned, all that the white chiefs had promised the year before, including guns; issue-day would be held in ten days' time. Criers ran through the camp the same afternoon, announcing departure in the morning—the village, traveling slowly, would need the full ten days to get to the fort on the Arkansas, nearly a hundred miles. Isaac told his men that they would be starting back the same morning. Their trade had been no brisker than his own. If they could not fill the wagons by trading, he had concluded to camp somewhere on the Ninnescah and spend a week or two hunting for hides.

Isaac led his train southeast and the second morning left the Great Bend flatlands and entered a new country gullied by many small streams flowing into the South Fork of the Ninnescah: good grass etched with a checkerboard of buffalo trails and shelter in the creek heads for bands of buffalo, it might be he had come on a part of their wintering ground, and why not cattle too? though no one he knew of had yet tried keeping even the wild Texas cattle through the winter this far into the shelterless Central Plains. It suited him anyhow, and he chose for his camp a bend of the river, water on two sides and an open scrub of low-spreading elms and cottonwoods across the south. It made him think of the place he had picked for his first ranch: not the lush green sweetness of the Saline country as it stayed in memory from that first hunt, but not far off it, either—and the buffalo plentiful and so placidly feeding they seemed tame as sheep, and never a sign of other hunters, Indian or white. What the devil did a man want with a string of trading stations to keep up, and men to pay and feed, debts to meet and orders to give, when not a hundred miles off there was naked land for the taking.

The hunting here was as brisk as the trading had been dull. Isaac left young Hansen to mind the camp and peg out the hides and took Milo and Jim as skinners, but they could not keep up. By dinnertime on the second day he had made a stand of fifty buffalo and left his rifle in the wagon to help with the skinning out. Bird, grazing fifty yards off, gave a warning nicker and Isaac straightened up, looked around. Milo Kellogg, working near him, pointed with his bloody skinning knife, and Isaac saw her, a half mile distant, outlined against the western light, coming down the shallow slope at a walk on a pale horse patched with black, and knew it was her.

—Indian, Milo said.

Isaac nodded.—Only a woman, looks like she's alone. I'll see what she wants—don't reckon it's *good* news, anyhow. He sang out for Bird to come. You, Milo, he said, mounting. Keep on with your skinning—but keep your eyes out too. You see any others, you and Jim get over by the wagon and get your guns ready, but *don't shoot*. And let me talk to them. . . . .

He trotted the horse toward her and fifty yards off turned toward the river and waved for her to follow him in among the trees. She came on at the same unhurrying pace. He waited, facing her up the river bank, and she slipped off the horse, walked slowly toward him, arms reaching out to him, and he took her, held her.

—God damn it, Patsy! he said and held her at arm's length. She was wearing a robe and skirt of fine buckskin washed and scraped and pounded nearly white, pale as old spring snow, a garment such as a woman would array herself in for marrying, and she had washed the paint from her hair and face. Except for her dress, worn like a costume put on for a ball, the deep summer tan of the Plains, she was a white woman again.

—God damn it, Patsy, don't you know they can trail you as easy as you followed me? And I *know* the things they do to a girl runs away—cripple your feet so you'll never go again is only the start. Even Set-im-kayah that loves you like his natural child—especially him, to show the others the proper decorum and old-fashioned manners—

—I do not care. But on the march Set-im-kayah will have other concerns, and he will think I travel with a different family, another band. He will not hunt me till they camp at Larned, and then—

He brought her to him again and led her, one arm at her waist, to the riverbank; did not want to hear it all again—impossible! there was nothing he could do, and he sat, leaning back on his elbows, staring helplessly into the slowly moving water.

—I did not come to talk foolishness again, she said. What you call foolishness. . . .

That was something anyhow, if she meant it, and he let go a small sigh of relief. There was only the one thing he could truthfully offer her: find her parents somehow, maybe the Indian office could help, or the Army, and send her home to Texas.

—There is a great war coming, she said. All the whites on the Plains will be killed—settlers and station masters on the stage lines—buffalo hunters. Isaac! They will kill you also. . . .

She stood straight as a scout giving a report, only the facts of things seen and known, looking out across the river to the north. He lay back, head cushioned on his hands, eyes closed.

—War! he said. I've been hearing that since I first came on the Plains and it aint ever happened. It don't seem the Indians have sense enough to get together for a real war—just some of the young ones running hither and yon on their little raids, bout as much bother as a bunch of blue flies buzzing.

—This will be different. Tall Bull, the Cheyenne war chief—he will lead and the Cheyenne have sworn, or nearly all—Sauts, that the whites call Roman Nose, has sworn, and there are many will follow him: after issue-day, when they get the new guns. And Isaac—

There was a faint rustling of her skirt and he reached out, found her thigh, and left his hand there: she was kneeling beside him, leaning close, he could feel the sweet breath of her voice on his cheek.— I've run against both of em, Isaac said. Roman Nose at my old place on the Saline, years ago—and Tall Bull just this past winter—

—Not only Cheyenne, Isaac. Kiowa and Comanche also. And Isaac! —terrible things have come to the Kiowa. After Sun-Dance, Set-daya-ite, the great medicine chief you call Heap of Bears, led a war party against the Ute—Comanche also. He is the keeper of the Tai-me, the grandmother gods which are the life and power of the tribe, and he carried them with him. And the Comanche warriors did evil against the Tai-me—killed a bear and ate it, wore little mirrors on their shirts, for signaling—and the Ute caught them, killed many—killed Set-daya-ite and stole the Tai-me, the life of all the Kiowa. . . .

Isaac sat up. She was telling real news now.—That's bad, he agreed. But it don't sound any reason the Kiowa should go killing white people—maybe the Comanche that let em down, is what *I'd* do—or the Ute—

—For honor—they must make war to wipe out the shame. Without honor, the tribe cannot live. . . .

—But listen—most of the people in Kansas, they're just waiting for the Indians to step off the peace road, any of em, and they'll take after the lot like hornets swarming from a broken nest—and the governor's the head dog of all, I hear from him nearly every week and he's half crazy over Indians—or not Indians so much maybe if they aint in Kansas, but he just can't stand them, getting in the way of building up the state. So some young fool Kiowa goes raiding a stage station, you know what happens? They've been building up troops and supplies since last fall, every fort on the Plains, but can't turn em loose as long as the Indians stand by their treaties. But *that* happens and sets it off—let me tell you, Patsy, you won't know what a war is till you see a couple of regiments of heavy cavalry come riding down your village —and when they do, they won't make any difference between big war chiefs and women and children—or pretty little Texas girls that only *look* Kiowa. And they won't stop this time till they've cleared the Indians right off the Plains, penned em up like cattle going to the slaughterhouse. . . .

—Then what can they do but fight, since they will die in any case?

—Damn it, Patsy, you aint listening. You talk as dumb as—oh, as *Satanta*, for pity's sake! If the Kiowa go by their treaty and try to learn the new ways, there's lots'll stand by em and help, because it's right. But they go killing white people for no reason, that never did them harm, why—I tell you, I believe I'd go out there myself with my rifle and join in the fun. . . .

He lay back again, trying to think what he should do. He could not do nothing—set the girl on her horse again and start her back, which was the same as nothing: it did truly seem that the general Indian war might this time come, and if it did, the girl—if not the white troops, destroying the village, then the Kiowa themselves, some of them—.

Something delicately touched his ear, fly or spider, and he brushed at it with his hand. Then on his cheek—he looked up and Patsy giggled, holding out a blade of grass to tickle him.

—I will tell you what I think, Isaac, she said. I think we should go far away in the western mountains—no Indians, and no white people either, making wars. You will build a cabin, and you can hunt—buffalo, they say there are different buffalo in the mountains, bigger—and deer, bear, moose, every kind of animal. And if you will not let me be your wife, I will be your woman and work for you—make the buffalo skins into beautiful robes for you to sell. And when you come home at night from hunting, I will have the cabin swept out clean as an Indian lodge, and meat cooking for you to eat, and warm water to wash your feet. You will lie back on your robes to rest, and I will kneel and wash your feet. . . .

He listened, eyes closed, and for a moment it seemed possible: go off and never heard of again. He tried to force his mind back to what had to be done. The thing was to get the message through to the Kiowa headmen, and soon—Stumbling Bear was sensible, a man to reason with, Satanta too, if you could put it to him right. They wouldn't any of them listen to the girl though, too young, and white besides. He would have to tell them himself, and anyhow knew more than most what was in Sam Crawford's mind—and it might be they would listen. Go back with her then—only, leave his men and the wagons to get home by themselves, wild Indians roaming about and a war coming? No—

Her sly fingers were at his shirt front, loosing the buttons, her cool hands cupped on the tense nipples of his breasts, sliding along the lines of rib and muscle toward his—

—Damn it, Patsy! he said, slapping her hands away. It aint any time for *that*, now.

He jerked to his feet, pulling his shirt together, smoothing the shirttail back under his belt. She knelt before him, head bowed.

—What we've got to do is have a talk with Stumbling Bear and the others, persuade them to stay out of it, if we can. And can't have you riding back alone, if there's trouble coming—but I've got to get my men back too, so—. We'll start east in the morning, you'll have to come along, and then I'll ride back to Larned with you and speak my piece. All right?

He crouched, touched his fingers to her cheeks: wet with tears, he wiped at them, lifted her chin to look her in the eyes.

—Is it all right? he said.

For answer she reached out and pulled him close, face radiant through the tan, and kissed him on the lips.

XVIII

The Tribes Depart

Issue-day that year at Fort Larned was actually several days at the end of July and beginning of August, as the bands came in to receive the first installment of the annuities promised the year before in the Medicine Lodge treaties. The debate over giving out guns was finally settled in the Indians' favor by the arguments of Edwin Wynkoop, agent for the Cheyenne and Arapaho: that the government's good faith could be maintained only by exact adherence to the treaty terms; that a limited supply of guns suited to hunting was essential to the Indians' subsistence until they could be persuaded to settle on their reservations and take up farming; that the Cheyenne for their part would refuse all annuities if guns were not included; and if so, they would consider the treaties nullified by the failure of the whites to keep their part in the bargain and with their allies would once more take the warpath. The agents and other officials at length agreed to hand out something over three hundred of what were called Lancaster rifles, with quantities of lead and powder. This was not the long-barreled, medium-bore muzzle-loader such as Isaac's father had taken with him to Iowa in the 1830s—associated with the Kentucky woodlands but originally designed and for a century manufactured at the Pennsylvania city; rather, a lighter, shorter descendant convenient for hanging from a saddlehorn—a cavalry carbine to the Army, a Plains rifle to most others, but still with the accuracy and nearly the range achieved by the older design. In defending the good intentions of his charges, Colonel Wynkoop evidently did not consider that, like the other Plains tribes, they got their livelihood by hunting the buffalo on horseback, with bow and arrow or lance; and valued a gun of any kind chiefly for man-killing, at a distance.

After all this, issue-day was nearly broken off before it had begun.

A Kiowa youth was shot dead when he attempted to run off horses from a Great Bend trader cutting prairie hay on contract for Fort Zarah. Whites who knew Bill Mathewson judged that any Kiowa fool enough to try robbing him deserved killing. The Kiowa apparently agreed: the obligation of vengeance against a member of the white tribe picked at random was in this case neglected. After an anxious day or two, the agents proceeded with the distribution of their bounty, under the watchful eyes of the 7th Cavalry, detailed for the purpose. The tribes were impatient to load their annuities and be gone.

The events that followed appeared to confirm the gloomiest predictions of critics such as Governor Crawford who had insisted all along that the Indian department's peace policy was folly. On August 10, a few days after the tribes had left Fort Larned, Indians raided a small settlement on the Saline. It was the first in a long series of such raids, spreading across western Kansas—the Solomon, the Republican, the Pawnee Fork of the Arkansas—and into eastern Colorado Territory, many of them so closely spaced as to be probably the work of the same small, fast-moving band. Although the raids generated wealth in the form of horses and cattle, just as in the old days—about fifteen hundred run off in the three months—there were differences in style: the raiders generally took the trouble to kill all the white defenders before departing; and the women were less likely to be carried off for ransom or possible adoption than to be raped, chopped up, scalped. With one exception (a wagon train of emigrants caught and burned out at the Cimarron crossing of the Santa Fe Road), all the attacks were on attempting settlers—ranchers, farmers, town-builders. If it was not in fact the "general Indian war" that had been a recurring nightmare on every frontier since Massachusetts and Virginia, it did appear to be a comparatively deliberate and systematic effort to drive the whites off the Central Plains by terror.

This outbreak took its timing and its general urgency from the railroad and its effect on the buffalo. By now the Union Pacific, Eastern Division, as it was still officially named, had followed the Smoky Hill west to within forty miles of the Colorado border. The tribes in their treaties—at any rate those chiefs and band leaders who actually signed their assent—had agreed not to interfere with roads through their country, including railroads, but it is doubtful that the white commissioners had anticipated in any concrete sense how the railroads would affect the country.

The tolerance of the buffalo for the rail lines was much exaggerated by promoters eager to build traffic by depicting the wonders of their routes: tales and pictures of herds in the seasons of migration thronging across the rails, blocking traffic for days at a time. Actually, although the buffalo in the mass were blindly unstoppable once stampeded, they seem also to have been highly sensitive to any regular human passage across their range. The earliest traders along the Santa Fe Road recorded, a few years later in the 1840s, the apparent dwindling of the herds: what they in fact observed was not significant decline in numbers but rather a drawing back beyond reach of hunters on both sides of the route, at least within the season of heavy travel to and from Santa Fe. The coming of the railroads made this withdrawal permanent: the "great herd," however that may be understood, became a northern herd and a southern herd, divided by the railroad line running up the Smoky Hill River, and every emigrant trail or railroad that followed from it produced further withdrawals, further divisions. It appears that the "great herd" was indeed an entity in one sense: it would not survive in fragments cut off from communication with one another.

The railroad had a more immediate effect on the survival of the buffalo: it greatly accelerated the rate of kill. The crews that built it were fed chiefly and abundantly on buffalo meat supplied by hunters such as Buffalo Bill Mathewson's former apprentice Bill Cody; so were the troops who came to defend it—and on the march could hardly be restrained, when they chanced on a herd, from breaking ranks for the sake of killing a few. To promote traffic, the railroad organized excursions for trainloads of sportsmen; conductors on through trains carried guns and handed them out to passengers when buffalo came in sight. More seriously, every rail town that followed the line west from the old buffalo frontier at Salina became a base for hide-hunters and a shipping point for hides which now, with the discovery of a new tanning process, had become a cheap raw material for the making of leather. Although buffalo hunting was still, as when Isaac fell into it, the means by which a young man of few resources could get a living and generate capital, intensified hunting drove down the prices paid for hides. The more the market fell, in turn, the more implacably the buffalo were hunted. The process of extinction, once set in motion, was irreversible.

It was late afternoon that day before Marie came to think seriously of supper—had to pause for a moment and with an effort think where the day had gone: breakfast and dinner and washing up, beds to make and laundry, the ironing put over till next day, and then the house to sweep out, and two Indians came in, leading a pack-mule with wolf skins to sell, and she had to consult on the price; and now it was time to call the children in for their baths and supper not thought of. Sister Lizzie was company certainly and a change, and every day cheerfully but vaguely offered to help, but when the time came was elsewhere or otherwise occupied, and Marie found it easier to do for herself. And now supper: nothing yet in the garden though the early peas were already flowering finely, but still potatoes in the root cellar—. And the meat? Buffalo steaks would be easy and there was still plenty in the smokehouse, but Lizzie only picked at buffalo, however Marie thought to cook it. . . . So it came down to chicken, fried perhaps: it made her tired to think of, running after chickens and getting the heads off, plucking them clean. Perhaps tonight Lizzie would like to make the biscuits. The men at least were not fastidious about their meat, so long as there was plenty.

Marie stooped for the basket, straightened with an effort—back worrying her some, really she felt tired all over though she did not calculate the baby to come before the end of April, but it seemed she was heavier than with Bissy or Mamie and it must be big, a boy for certain this time and a little brother for Bissy—and went out to bring in the potatoes. And she would ask one of the men to catch the chickens for her.

It was Isaac that insisted on asking Lizzie. Marie had seen no need, she could manage well enough by herself if she had to, and there were always the neighbor women to help when the time came, but he said they must think of Lizzie too—the change from Iowa, seeing new country, would do her good—and that decided it. After an exchange of letters that began before Isaac left for the session of the new legislature, Lizzie agreed to come and started from Davenport at the first of March, stopping several days at Topeka to visit her brother at his boardinghouse, and coming on by stage to Towanda with a trunkful of new clothes. It was not that Lizzie was difficult to get along with—she called Marie Sister, often kissed and complimented her, and was loving with the children, inventing new games to play, telling them old rhymes and bedtime stories, but she did not take thought.

Lizzie was, as she said, quite capable of occupying herself usefully. Taking note of Marie's ripe figure, she spent two days alone in the spare room, writing a long poem in couplets on "Motherhood" and gave Marie the fair copy, finely written in purple ink, to put away with her things. Since then she had painted views of the ranch house from three different locations and was occupied now with a fourth; watercolors, she explained, convenient for sketching, but more difficult in their way than oils, which she had left at home. Marie had looked over her shoulder at one of these, pale browns and grays and greens on creamy thick paper, but even from the unaccustomed angle hardly knew it as the square, broad-roofed cabin that had become home, something awry in every dimension with the—what was the word Lizzie used once?—*perspective:* in her watercolor all the lines Isaac had built square and plumb as a draftsman's plan wandered and leaned together, and the house squatted on the grass like a great limp toad, too lazy to hop, the gray splintery roughness of the squared logs that you could feel, even standing at a distance, smoothed away like the painted flats of a stage set. "I don't paint only what I see," Lizzie explained with a gentle smile, "but what I *feel*." Marie had not inquired into these feelings.

The session ran longer this year than before, the legislature meeting for the first time in one half-finished wing of the new capitol, built on land Mr Holliday had given, with a curtain down the middle to divide the Senate from the House. Isaac wrote often but briefly and each time signed his letters "In haste," till Marie longed to tell him just once to make time to write her at leisure but did not. He wrote on Senate writing paper, sometimes at his desk in intervals of state business. They had voted him chairman of Senate Ways and Means, also something about a state insane asylum, no end of work but at least no speeches. There was also his own business with the Kaw contract: twice he had taken the cars to Atchison to consult with the superintendent of the Indian office but had not yet been paid for the trade goods he'd take to Fort Larned; a question of jurisdiction that would have to be resolved at Washington, they said.

Isaac was getting on finely with the new governor, Jim Harvey, had known him some the time before in the legislature and now it turned out he too had started life as a surveyor, so they had things to talk of besides state business: he was favorable, Isaac said, to organizing a new county west of Butler and making Wichita its seat. Ten days after Lizzie's arrival, Marie wrote him a letter of unusual firmness: this time, she wanted her husband home when the baby came, and in good time too, Kaw contract and Ways and Means or no; first week of April, say, at the latest.

Marie was peeling the potatoes, sitting to ease her back, elbows on the table, when the door slammed open and Lizzie came in, puffed with running.

—Indians! Lizzie cried. Coming up the creek. A whole war party of them. All in paint. And—oh, Sister!—scalps!—

Lizzie at home had followed attentively the accounts of the Indian war and now in the Emporia paper; and remained anxious, though no fighting had been reported for months—at night before retiring she patrolled the house in her nightgown, cap, and wrapper, candle in hand, examining each door and window, testing the locks. Marie finished a potato, dropped it in the kettle of salted water, and laid the knife aside. Wiping her hands on her apron, she went to the door to look out.

—It's only Little Beaver and his scouts, Marie said, coming home from the war and all dressed their finest and mean to trade—the Osage Trail goes past our ranch. Go and tell Mister Kelly, Sister, will you? And tell him, mind, no whisky—

And while Lizzie went around to the store to convey this message,

Marie walked slowly toward the advancing horsemen, a dozen of them, in gaudy shirts and headbands, some decked out in wide-brimmed campaign hats or other articles of military issue, and provided with sturdy cavalry mounts and saddles. Little Beaver was in high spirits: the Army had outfitted them for the campaign, they had defeated and humbled their enemies the Cheyenne and now had been paid and sent home in time for the summer hunt. The hoop of long black hair swaying from his lance-tip was that of Moke-ta-ve-to, Black Kettle, the great chief of the Cheyenne; one of his young men had taken the scalp of Black Kettle's wife. Little Beaver spoke some English, Marie by now had learned the rudiments of the sign language, and between the two she managed to congratulate the Indian and explain that her husband was attending the great council at Topeka and would be pleased to know that his friend Little Beaver had driven the enemy tribes from Kansas.

As Abe Kelly came around the corner of the house trailed by Lizzie, the chief dismounted, opened a saddlebag, and brought out a fat jackrabbit, then another, and held them out dangling by their long ears: a present for his friends; coming along the trail from the Little Arkansas, they had been lucky in their hunting. Marie thanked him—the question of meat for supper was answered and no bothering Abe now about catching chickens. Lizzie followed her into the house.

Marie built the fire up in the stove while Lizzie sat at the table and discoursed on the Indian problem telling nearly all she knew, which was considerable. As she laid the skin back on the rabbits, Marie considered how best to do them and decided on a nice fricassee in the big iron kettle, really not as meaty as they looked, with the fur off, and they would go farther that way, and a thick, dark gravy for the potatoes—getting late and oh! she was tired, plain boiled potatoes and she would not bother making them into salad—. She leaned and sniffed at the meat: a little high, Little Beaver did not get those rabbits this morning, coming from the Little Arkansas, but yesterday, the day before, and should have known to clean them fresh but they liked their meat strong—what was it in an Indian that made him lie so? Marie felt for the joints and removed the paws, then with one deft cut opened the belly, tore the guts loose in a handful and shoved them aside. Really very warm with the fire up in the stove and her hair coming loose around her ears, her hands slippery with rabbit fat and stained with the thick, half-dried blood, what a sight she must look to her elegant sister-in-law, talking on and on, and the smell! really too strong, but once it was cooked—. Something walked across her cheek like a fly, and she brushed at it with the back of her hand, the drops of sweat trickling down her cheeks, her nose, into the corners of her mouth. Wiping vigorously at her face with both hands, Marie finished disjointing the rabbit, cut the back up, and laid the pieces on a platter.

And now the other: drew it to her and began to clean it, wiping at her face and working in haste. But oh! the prick of the knife point at her fingertip and a ruby gout spread and mingled with dark animal heartsblood and frantic with carefulness and hurry—if only Lizzie would be quiet for a little or *do* something!—dabbed it with the inner hem of her apron but it flowed again and hurt and no matter—finish and get the meat on the fire or she would simply have to stop, sit down and rest, and they could *sing* for their supper, all of them—and plunged her hurt fingers into the clammy cavity and ripped the bowels clean.

He went out from the light of the house and down the creek into utter darkness, stumbling on the rough ground, wet grass licking at his legs, and blundered against a tree trunk and stopped, looking up: not absolute dark but the void of heaven pricked with spring stars and as his eyes drew in the light a lighter haze of cloud floating between sky and the velvet depth of blackness where the stars grew.

The feeling he had now was like the one that came with the dream he had often as a boy, about the wolves: riding home from the prairie and lost his way, and the pack got the scent and came after, yipping and snarling, no powder left, and he beat at the pony, calling out, but she could do no more, he felt her slowing and sinking under him, and the eyes all around him, glaring, the ivory click of teeth snapping, ravenous, closing in—at that moment he woke, crying out, the mattress clammy with sweat and fear, and sometimes his mother sat there beside him, saying nothing, and would not hold him.

It was because he could not bear to wake her from the half-sleep the sickness sank her in: because he could not bear the mournful, whispered faces, Widow Kelly and the women, waiting for the dying to come: because he could not let them hear his voice lifted in futile prayer.

Great God! I know I've given cause—haven't been to church or kept the Sabbath but about twice since I came to Kansas—or attended to my prayers or, to tell the truth, given You much thought. And then that girl, Stumbling Bear's white daughter—well, of course I know that's wrong any way you look at it, but let's be fair too: it wasn't just myself I thought of, but her, trying to do what was right for her as it looked at the time. Well, I admit it—I've gotten in the wrong and got it coming to me, but listen: is that any reason for taking it out on my wife, that hasn't anything but goodness in her? and lies in bed this moment grieving, and the tears running from her eyes, not for herself and her own life but for her dear children, left motherless—yes, and her husband too, that will have no wife—. Because I don't see how a man's to take it but she's punished for wrongs she never did. But me now, well! You know I haven't much, and everything I've got is Yours to take, anytime You want it—the home ranch and the stations, trading stock, wagons, cattle, horses, mules, and harness, and one little buggy I wanted to please

*her with and the little ones—what good's any of it to the Great One of the
Universe? Or my life, the strength and health of my body: take it all! but not my
wife—not those innocent babies that aint hardly started on the first leg in the
great race. . . .*

When Isaac went back to the house Lizzie met him at the door and
in her hushed sickroom voice told him the fever was a little better
now, she thought, and if he meant to sit with her some more he
should keep on sponging with a damp cloth to bring it down and
then, perhaps, the fever would break at last—the thing Dr Kohn had
said they must wait and hope for.

Softly closing the bedroom door, he resumed his seat beside the
bed. Marie lay in the middle, propped on two pillows, the covers
drawn up to her chin and tucked in tight so only her face showed,
wreathed in a dark aureole of unbound hair. Very quiet now, breathing slow and shallow so you could barely see, but even that worried
him: in natural sleep the sleeper stirred, changing expression as
dreams came and went; but better than the times the breath came
quick as if she'd been running a race, and from so deep within it
seemed her ribs would crack, and it hurt her. It was the marriage bed
he had hauled in his wagon from Junction City to furnish the little
house at Salina, in which she had borne Mamie and now little Willie:
William Aplon Pride, the name they agreed on months ago for a boy,
as Marie insisted it would be; mostly because Isaac had liked the
sound of it but for Bill Mathewson too.

Isaac got home from Topeka a week earlier than he promised and
found the ranch in an uproar: the baby come only the day before, it
might be a month before its time if Marie had figured right, and
Marie herself sick as death. That was what brought her to labor, it
seemed: the sickness came on with terrible suddenness—a hoarse,
loud, painful, uncontrollable coughing and then bleeding from the
nose, not any ordinary nosebleed but as if the cough had burst veins
deep in her chest, and the dark blood poured out, gagging and choking. Those first violent symptoms had passed off by the time Isaac
arrived, he learned of them only in the frightened gravity of Lizzie's
description. They were followed by burning fevers that came and
went from day to day, with chattering chills, night sweats that soaked
the mattress and bedclothes, left Marie too feeble to sit up—and Isaac
knelt by the bed, holding her head up, to spoon small portions of Mrs
Kelly's chicken broth to her lips, and it was all the nourishment she
got. When tormenting headaches joined the fever, Isaac drove the ten
miles to El Dorado to get help. They had a doctor there now, Dr
Jacob Kohn, some kind of German, not a stolid Rhenishman like Fred
Weyerhaeuser but a neat, dark, little point-bearded man educated at
Dresden who spoke a precise and literary but strongly accented En-

glish larded with allusions to Heine and Shakespeare; he charged by the mile. Dr Kohn took an hour examining Marie in private and at the end pronounced it a case of typhus, only unusual in exhibiting no rash, and prescribed calomel, camphor, and, for the fever, laudanum, of which he had brought doses in his bag; more often than not, he said, the patient recovered. The medicines had no effect Isaac could see, except that the opiate heightened the fever-dreams—he sat by the bed and wept while she became a girl again at St Louis, dressing for a ball, and sang—and he took the bottle and poured the liquid out on the ground by the house door.

He rode to the Army post at Wichita, now called Camp Beecher, and at word that the 7th Cavalry surgeon would be passing through from the Indian campaign waited for him two days at Walnut Grove: Major Sternberg, trained at Columbia, with a reputation for producing cures where others despaired. He prescribed champagne in small doses and ice to suck on—Isaac rode to Emporia and brought back two bottles, and a cake of ice from a butcher, wrapped in straw and burlap—and the sponge baths to contain the fever.

And there was the baby to think of: long-boned and thin but seemed well-formed if it was a month early, and in the first days healthy, only: Marie was scant of milk, and attempting to sit up to nurse left her so entirely prostrate that for the first time Isaac was badly scared. Mrs Kelly advised cow's milk thinned with spring-water, sweetened, and sucked through a bit of sponge, but when Lizzie tried it the baby took little and coughed back most of it. They kept the child by Marie's bed—she was fearful if she woke and did not see it—and Isaac took turns with Lizzie trying to make him eat and some days succeeded. He never cried; as if, Lizzie suggested, the babe sensed its mother's perilous condition and would not disturb her.

The Bible says a man will not be tested beyond what he can bear; not that his strength is not hedged by limits on every side, but that a residue will be left him, as the burned-over prairie starts up green in the spring again, as the storm-shattered oak sends forth sprouts from its roots. In the pride and strength of young manhood you make promises—what had the words been, if it mattered? *Between you and every evil that the world holds, dearest, I will put my life like a shield.* But the evil comes and carries you regardless as a grain of sand tossed on the wind, and the strength of flesh and mind is no more to stand against it than the dust of the earth. So in the end, having done all you know and weighed as nothing in the balance, nothing is left you but to sit by her bed and watch her die.

Isaac leaned forward and touched his lips to her sleeping brow, burning hot, and drew back: the damp cloth in the basin at his feet, he was forgetting. He wrung it, folded it to a pad, and wiped it across her forehead, made the circuit of her cheeks, chin, lips. All over, the doctor said, draw off the animal heat, chest and limbs too. Setting the cloth to soak again, he lifted the sheet by its hem and laid the covers back. So many buttons, from her neck down, chaste and tiny as pearls in their loops of silk braiding: frowning, he concentrated on his clumsy thick fingers, not to wake her.

—Dearest Isaac! Her voice weak but clear, her eyes drowsily watching him.

—Hush. Save your strength.

—I did not sleep. I knew when you came back—so glad. . . .

He shook his head. He could not speak.

—Isaac, is my birthday passed? the faint voice asked. Did you forget?

—Today's your birthday. I remembered. . . .

—I should not tax you if you had—tired, too tired to celebrate or think of anything, I only want to lie here, resting. . . . But tomorrow, Isaac—do you know, I feel the fever going?—I shall be better, dearest—for your sake and the children's, and dance with you, to keep my birthday—.

—I'll dance with you, my darling. . . .

—Oh, dearest, are you weeping? . . . Must not let our little Willie see his great father so—tears running down his cheeks. A man must never weep. . . .

Her eyes closed again. He knelt and sank his wet face in the pillow by her cheek.

—Dearest Isaac, hold me, she said, her voice sinking as if drifting into sleep. Your hands—so gentle, ever. I want no other medicine in this world. . . .

It was a bright Saturday toward the end of April when Abraham came home from marketing a load of eggs and butter in Davenport, very cheerful—soon now the strawberries would come in, a fine year for them, by the look of it—and bearing in his pocketbook a thick letter from Towanda. Before he would allow the girl to bring dinner in, he had his wife join him at the table while he read it out. With ceremony he fitted and adjusted his spectacles, brought the pen-knife forth from his pocket, opened the blade and slit the envelope; and paused to savor the moment. News of their new grandchild, it came to him, but such a fat letter, for Isaac, perhaps news also of the town they were starting—daughter Marie, praise God, had passed through childbed twice without incident, and surely this time, hmmm—. And of course a month, was it, since his last, so much to write of, senate matters and his business to keep up, and perhaps something concerning General Custer's Indian campaign, so near. The house was empty, he had frequently observed, with Lizzie gone, only themselves —and the kitchen girl and hired man, of course. Not long since, he

had ventured that his wife might wish to invite them for the summer
again—oh, when Marie and baby were in condition to travel, of
course, a month or two perhaps, but travel was wonderfully easy
now, not like the old days, and Lizzie coming home of course, she
could share the journey with them. And Isaac—perhaps this time,
Isaac—yes, and fill the old house up with people—.

So with many small flourishes of anticipation and turnings aside, as
his thought started one possible happiness and then another, Abraham produced the folded pages, opened them to Isaac's familiar hurried scrawl, and read—

My Dear Parents

*I sit by my dear wife's side, fulfilling the Sacred promise made at the Bridal, to
stand by her in death as I have endeavered to in life. Our heavenly Father has in
his wisdom laid his hand upon us and called her to that place where is no pain, but
everlasting peace. Seeing how the anguish which for twenty days has tormented
her, is banished her sweet face, I would not if I could, recall her gentle spirit back
from the abode of the blessed, from whence it came—*

*It was—it is—her birthday today, now doubly so, into this earthly world, and
now the world beyond, April 17th, which I shall keep for a day of thankfulness &
sorrow, so long as I live—*

*The malady which the skill of two physicians was powerless to arrest, was of the
Typhus form. It fell on her*

He laid the papers on the table, removed his spectacles, and brought
out a handkerchief, covering his eyes.

—God in His mercy! he said. Our dear son—

Mary watched him, her face set.—Let me see it, Husband, she said,
with a sharpness in her voice, and when he did not answer reached
and took the letter, and read it slowly through.

—The babe, she said. He does not say how it is with their new little
son.

They buried Marie on Sunday afternoon the day after she died.
Isaac sat with her to the end except when the women came in to wash
and dress her body. Abe Kelly dug the grave and made the coffin of
sweet Wisconsin pine and when the time came nailed it tight; Lizzie
had gathered flowers along the creek and plaited them in her hair,
and that was the last he saw of her, dark hair laced with the pinks and
blues and yellows of April.

The baby remained feeble and passive, eating little, putting on no
flesh. Dr Kohn came again but could name no specific complaint;
prescribed calomel in minute dosage and for strength a diet of meat
broth, weak tea with milk, potato mashed through a strainer. When
after a week the weather warmed, Willie was feverish, vomited again

and for a day squittered death and corruption in yellow streams from his bowels and could not be stanched or cleansed. Lizzie was in panic, could not bear to watch while the life placed in her hands ebbed away, but—home, Mother, all her life resourceful at caring for ailing neighbor women, and familiar doctors, the Davenport hospital— must do something. She caught the stage to Topeka in the morning, with a few necessaries in a carpetbag and the baby, closely wrapped, on her shoulder, and Isaac let her go. Next day, waiting for the train to Kansas City and Willie perhaps a little livelier, hopeful of the journey, she carried him on the omnibus to the office of the Topeka *Times*, introduced herself to the editor, and left a poem.

The editor printed the poem, unsigned, and, being acquainted with Isaac, sent him a clipping with a sympathetic note. It came within a day of the letter from his mother saying that Lizzie had arrived safely, but the little one failing in that struggle from which a merciful death had now released him. Isaac's father had administered conditional baptism—Lizzie did not seem to know—and had seen to the little coffin and the burial.

Isaac flattened the clipping on the table to read.

> *The Dying Wife.*
> *Prop my pillow, dearest husband,*
> *Help me catch my failing breath.*
> *Never dread those shadows stealing,*
> *They are only shades of death.*
> *Will you sit once more beside me,*
> *Let me clasp your darling hand?—*
> *Hand that me has ever strengthened,*
> *'Mid the frontier of this Land!*

There were five more stanzas. Poor Lizzie! He refolded the clipping and placed it in his billfold to read sometime and keep. Little enough to keep out of twenty-eight years of a life: the picture taken with the children at Davenport a year ago, some of her letters, the few garments she had owned and worn; the trunk of linens and blankets, a box of clothes she spent the winter making, for Bissy, Mamie, the baby she carried, while he was away at Topeka. But the children—of course the children—.

The Wichita town still hung on what the Congress decided about the Osage land. Sam Crawford, no longer preoccupied with Indian matters, once more turned his persuasions on the two Kansas Senators and the Congressman but had little influence now he was out of office. The incorporators raised another small assessment among themselves and freely promised stock in the town company that on paper would be worth something if the town itself ever came into being, but it did not seem that so distant a possibility carried much weight with Sam Pomeroy and his colleagues—certainly not in the face of the railroad lobby, on the one hand, and the Indian faction on the other, which, now the hostile tribes were pacified, had turned all its fervor to protecting the Osage—had the tribe not aided Sheridan and Custer in ending the depredations? In January 1869, the Congress by a joint resolution had reaffirmed the Osage treaty of 1865—the new treaty, aimed at handing the land to the railroad combine, was now officially laid to rest, as it had been long since in public opinion. On April 10, the Congress spoke again, somewhat softening its rejection of the treaty: the Osage land was to be disposed of in accordance with the body of law governing the public domain; the process would begin in August at the nearest Kansas land office, Humboldt, a hundred and ten miles east of Wichita. Settlers now could claim the land in quarter-sections at the minimum price, $1.25 an acre, in accordance with regulations and long-established custom (but not the newer Homestead Act); there was still no provision for anyone attempting to organize a town.

Although the town company had come to nothing, its brief life and its lithographed map—perhaps the idea alone, the name—had attracted a few settlers and the town had begun to have its own life, a dozen sod-roofed structures of logs, pickets, adobe scattered across the prairie beside a bend of the Little Arkansas, on either side of a track that ran along the western limit of Dave Munger's claim, a few others just beyond it—four saloons, five trading posts, including Durfee's imposing establishment, a picket cabin put up as a schoolhouse and serviced Sundays by an Episcopal missionary, five homes of settlers; and the cattlemen still crossed their herds below the mouth of the Little Arkansas and skirted the village driving north to market on what was now officially the Kansas Pacific, the KP to every Kansan. These circumstances combined to solve Isaac's problem of caring for his children and finally to rouse him from his grief.

Late that spring Bill Mathewson established his post at Fort Sill, far south in the Indian Territory, licensed to the Wichita and Kiowa, and Isaac supplied him from Towanda. The partnership had become a reality. Isaac persuaded Mathewson's wife Lizzie to stay at Towanda—an impressively competent woman but so far childless— to care for the children and incidentally oversee the store, a task that had fallen to Marie since Sam Carter's death. In recompense, Isaac staked in Lizzie Mathewson's name the unclaimed quarter-section east of his own at Wichita—no harm done if she did not finally take it up, and even the right to claim was recognized by custom and worth something. In August when the Osage land opened to sale, Isaac stirred Dave Munger—still from his grandly named Munger House keeping track of claims within the township and occasionally selling a lot measured off with lengths of rope and marked on a much-worn copy of Isaac's original plat—and together they rode to Humboldt to file the claimants' first papers: each a standard form giving the land description according to survey, with a sworn statement of intention to settle and pre-empt.

Isaac had now come to another choice, another fork in the road. There was the tract enclosing the Towanda ranch, well watered and handsomely wooded, promising land if a man meant to farm when the Indian trade ended; and the grassy quarter-section adjoining Wichita, so far with no more improvement than the conventional four logs hauled into place as foundation for a cabin. In addition, while at Topeka for the last session, he had put down four dollars an acre for a quarter across the river from the capital, unbroken land but not far from the KP right-of-way and worth the price; this land he had put in Marie's name—a gift, a dower, a kind of insurance policy —and now it was his again. Although the Land Office would sell an individual as much of the public domain as he could pay for, it could not under law allow him to pre-empt more than one quarter-section: additional land he would be obliged to bid on in competition with others and therefore, probably, would not get at the minimum price of $1.25 an acre; or, perhaps more seriously, any quarter-section after the first that was not yet patented might be validly pre-empted by another claimant swearing himself an "actual settler." Isaac at any rate would have to choose between Towanda and Wichita, both claims on Osage land, but not till spring, when the six months' residence was up; the choice was not urgent. And there was still Marie's land at Topeka.

In November the detachment of troops at Wichita was withdrawn and Camp Beecher, which in its year and a half of existence had filled no other function anyone could see than as a place of exile for officers out of favor with their regiments, was abandoned. About the same time the settlers took steps to form a government: a census, which counted three hundred citizens at Wichita and twice as many in the surrounding county-to-be; an organizing petition; and an election of county officials, to meet pro tem at Wichita. Someone had suggested John Sedgwick, a Union general vaguely connected with Kansas, to honor in naming the new county. Isaac, who had rashly talked of his acquaintance with Jim Harvey, was picked to carry the papers to the governor. Leaving Mrs Mathewson at Towanda with the children, he drove to Topeka, meaning while he was there to put a cabin on the land across the Kaw and rent it to a settler in return for sod-breaking.

Jim Harvey was cordial as the chairman of Ways and Means could have wished, *delighted* to hear of another county getting organized—promised to study the papers personally before submitting them to the attorney general as the law required—but Isaac went away reflecting that the governor had expressed no opinion one way or other as to the legalities, of which, he realized, he knew little enough himself. A formality, no doubt. The people had acted, after all, defining boundaries, choosing their county commissioners, a surveyor, sheriff, justice of the peace, representative to the legislature. For two weeks Isaac was occupied with his land and through an agent found a young man who since the war had lost his farm for debt and come to Kansas to start fresh, with a team and wagon, tools, possibly enough money to see him through the winter and pay the fees for a quarter-section under the Homestead Act: Ebenezer Day, from Muscatine, down the river from Davenport, with a wife and baby left behind at his parents' home. Isaac gave him the land till harvesttime next year, with a promise to ship seed corn from Towanda in the spring, in return for eighty acres of plowing, and then they would see about a new lease; and spent a week with him, building a cabin with a lean-to shed behind for the horses.

Isaac was another week at his old boardinghouse at Topeka and twice called on the governor, but it seemed that making a county took time; Harvey still had no answer for him. Several times at a distance, he saw what looked like Bill Greiffenstein, sedately driving a prosperous new buggy, with an elegantly dressed lady at his side, dark enough for a Mexican, but had no chance to talk and did not know where he was staying. But courting, surely: a widower too now, Cheyenne Jennie dead in the Territory about the time he lost his trading post.

Then a letter came from Dave Munger, written in his florid lodging-keeper's hand:

Mr Pride—

  Beg to advise you get yourself over to Wichita at earliest convenence as your Claim is in trouble—one W'm Whiteman is the party by name, was mule-skinner to 5th Infantery 'til they left & Dispensed with his sarvices—Well he has taken & squatted on your quarter, cut him some squares of prairie sod with a matock and cut up your logs that you had laying there and made him a litle shanty about suitable for a dog house—says he means to set there as Actual Setler & not beholdin to any absent Speculator tho' what he w'd use for money to buy with at Land Office I don't know I am sure—I rid over to reason with him as to squattin anothers Claim—told him of Claim Club—and list of land in Wichita T'ship—NW Quarter Section 21 & so and your Name Jas A Pryde writ next it right and proper, all staked out and first papers filed. Well—CLAIM CLUB AINT LAW! says he bold as dirt & is a hard case, no mistake, but a little money to hand paid would move him off quick enough, is my Opinon—Would help him to land if he wanted as there is still some clear and vacant only it don't apear Land is his requirements—

Trustin this finds You in Health, busyness in hand and Sidgewick C'ty goin ahead like a six-wheel Engine—

> I remain
> D S Munger,
> Prop.

Isaac left in the morning for Wichita.

As it happened, Bill Mathewson had come up for a visit and was starting back with a load of goods from the Walnut Grove warehouse, which Isaac was closing out. Isaac saw him going past the Munger House, talked for a few minutes, and they rode together to Isaac's claim. It was as Munger had written: a low, windowless soddy set back from the cattle trail that ran along the south line, about as big as a chicken coop. From a little distance it looked more like a natural hummock in the prairie than a habitation for a man, but there was a scrawny Indian pony staked to one side and as they rode up a thick-set man emerged from the cavelike darkness of the doorway, one trouser leg stuffed in his boot top and the other hanging loose, a week or two of black bristles on his face and a season's grime, grease, and cook-smoke on his garments; a man of the same kind and calling as Jack Lawton's uncaught, anonymous killer, if not the man himself.

—Mister White-man? Isaac politely inquired.

—*Whit*man, the man said, eyes half-closing in rims of fat. *Bill* Whitman from Paducah. What's your business?

—Mister Munger, who's secretary to the Settlers' Association, informs us you have a little misunderstanding about your claim, and—

—Aint no misunderstandin! I come on it fair—man he says staked it aint made no improvements and has abandoned, and I claimed. That's law.

—Now that's *good*, said Isaac sweetly, cause we're the Law Committee of Sedgwick County, and it's our job and appointment to see that folks settle their disputations according to law and don't get carried away by their violent and sinful natures.

This was a little more than Whitman could take in at one jump, but he caught the drift.—Violence! he said. Any violence bout this claim and Bill Whitman'll be on the *givin* end.

He slapped a hand meaningly on the revolver hanging from his belt and let it rest there. Mathewson reached one hand and took the wrist, gripped till Whitman's hand turned white, levering him so he could not move, and with his other hand slipped the gun from its holster. He held the gun up, examining it—spun the cylinder, flipped it out, removed it and dropped it in his pocket. He handed the revolver back politely, butt first.

—Neat little pistol, he said, making conversation. But you ought to be careful, carrying it around loaded. We aint got much use for guns in this county.

—Fact! Isaac said, taking the cue. A gun is the *last* thing, cause we've got *law*, and a Law Committee. Like that poor stranger that squatted on Tim Meagher's claim over east of town on Chisholm's Creek—all from just one little misunderstanding—.

He turned away, with a sweep of one arm made a gesture of covering his eyes.—But it's too horrible for one Christian white man to relate to another—why Mister Whitman, the stranger's own mother—. But I reckon, if you've been around long enough to claim land, you've heard it all anyhow. . . . When Whitman's fat eyes widened in interrogation, Isaac proceeded: Well now, Tim came in the spring, chose out land, staked his corners and sent in first papers and laid the foundation for his cabin, and then he went over to El Dorado to carry seed or flour or lumber—some such. And this stranger came, poor man, and saw the quarter abandoned, as he supposed, and he raised up a little sod house and squatted. And Tim Meagher came back, he said, That's my land you're on, but the stranger said No, it was abandoned and I took it by Law. Well, sir, the citizens, they were a little perturbed, but they had the Law Committee looking on, and they went by Law, said—You want land, stranger, you've *got* land, and will *stay* on it too and be buried. And they kind of gathered around and invited him to stay, right where he was. And after a week, the man was starving, says, All right! I'll go, and let the other fellow *have* the land, cause a man's got to eat. And the citizens said, We'll *help* you go then, and good as their word. What they did, they hitched him by the legs behind a horse and run him across the prairie as far as the river. And then they turned him over and turned him around, hitched him by the arms and run him back. Kind of wore him down like the eraser on the end of a pencil—and when he got back to Tim's claim, which he'd only squatted out of innocent misunderstanding— there wasn't enough left of him to shoot. That's why we don't have much use for guns in Sedgwick County. But we do go by Law. . . .

Whitman was very quiet as Isaac finished this invention, his eyes opened their widest.—I believe, he said, a little louder than a whisper, I'll throw the saddle on old Kate, ride out and take the air for a spell.

Mathewson looked grave.—Go away? he said. Couldn't let you go without you paid your assessment. That's Law. Assessment's *fifty* dollars—every man, woman child, brother-in-law and maiden aunt that wants to claim, makes no difference. Law don't come cheap in Sedgwick County.

—Can't get blood out'n no turnip—Whitman started with a feeble smile and caught himself, and his whiskey face went pale.

—Course there's the Law Committee Loan Fund, Isaac put in, and Mathewson nodded. Since it's only an innocent misunderstanding anyhow. He drew out a coin, spun it in the air, and returned it jingling to his pocket. Whitman's bewildered eyes followed the flash of the gold-piece in its flight and sank again when Isaac put it away.

—Pays a man so's he can meet his assessment, Mister Whitman, Mathewson explained.

—And if he's business elsewhere, Isaac said, he can pay it off when he comes back, whenever he does come.

—Fifty dollars! Mathewson said. It'd pay a man's fare on the Butterfield Line to San Antonio.

—Fifty dollars? Whitman said, wondering, and for answer Isaac produced five coins and lined them glinting across his palm.

The consequence was that Isaac and Mathewson assisted Mr Whitman in saddling his pony and tying up his worldly goods in a bandanna and then rode with him as far as the beaten track that led north from the river into town—so that any citizens who chanced on him would not be roused to righteous excitement by the notion he was going his way without having paid the due assessment of Law.

—You been real white, Mr Whitman said to express his gratitude as they parted. What'd you say your names was?

—Why, this here's General George Armstrong Custer, the famous Indian fighter, Isaac answered him. And I'm General Phil Sheridan, I reckon you don't need to be told who that is—folks wanted to name this town for me, but I'm a modest man. . . .

Mr Whitman looked doubtful, trying to connect these familiar names with the two men before him, but he concluded with a little bow of his head, as of a man too politely reared to question the word of a newfound friend.

Mathewson as they rode away made known his displeasure at being likened to the boy general, but Isaac assured him it was in a good cause, and for the sake of verisimilitude and upholding the Law. There wasn't a fool on the Plains, he said, didn't know that Custer was the tall one and Sheridan was short.

Mathewson the truth-teller joined in improving Isaac's claim: identical twelve-by-twelve high-peaked cabins but weatherproof and serviceable such as each had often built elsewhere, squared cottonwood logs neatly fitted, slab rooves and puncheon floors, each with a fireplace of river-stone, clay, and logs across the west end. Isaac at least was decided: settle on the Wichita claim in fact, or lose it.

Governor Harvey's letter was waiting when Isaac returned to Towanda: the Sedgwick application was rejected. There were reasons enough—the papers careless and irregular, not enough people yet to organize a county or a county seat, and some of the petitioners, such as Isaac himself, known to make their homes elsewhere; a scandal the governor would not risk. Possibly Jim Harvey was only dutiful and cautious, taking his lead from the attorney general, but as Isaac reflected on it he found other motives: the Atchison and Topeka was now laying track along the north of Sedgwick County and it might be the governor had an interest in a county seat on the railroad; or maybe it was only some business to be bargained from the Senate Ways and Means Committee in the coming session of the legislature.

On the dark day of the year, still a few days till Christmas, Greiffenstein arrived at Wichita with two handsome carriages pulled by matched teams of horses. Since the trouble with Bill Whitman, Isaac had observed the Land Office rules with care, dividing his time between the new cabin and the Towanda ranch so that in June there would be no difficulty proving the six months' residence that allowed him to pay for his claim and receive preliminary title. Isaac was at Wichita building a barn to store the remainder of his stock from Walnut Grove when he heard of Greiffenstein's arrival in town. Dutch Bill, so Dave Munger reported, had lost his trader's license following his contraband trade in powder with the Indians. He'd a new wife and had moved into Durfee's ranch. Isaac rode over to make a visit.

Her name was Catherine, the same dark young woman Isaac had seen driving around Topeka, but when she brought the coffee she said something to her husband in what Isaac recognized as German. Had he taught her the language already? Isaac wondered. Pretty quick!—
—Didn't have to teach, Bill said slowly. Got German mother, Indian father—Abram Burnett, Potawatomi chief, lives at Topeka on rent from his land—whole section on the Kaw, across from town, where the railroad goes through. So, he concluded, Catherine, she know to work like Indian woman, but smart and obedient like German.

He puffed at his pipe with grave satisfaction. Not as old as he seemed: Isaac had asked him once, only a year or two past forty; it was his slow manner and air of grave deliberation—and the weak eyes that bothered him in bright sun, the thatch of gray in his hair and long beard.

—You going partners with Mister Durfee! Isaac asked.
—No partners. Bought him out—don't want to be on South Plains no more, got his fur company up the Missouri, two or three boats to run.
—You going to keep up his trade? Looked to me he did so well with it there wasn't any point keeping my place at Walnut Grove—I can do as much with just the stations on the cattle trail, and less bother.
—Sure we trade—give good prices too, you want to buy from us. But you ever get this town going, we claim on land and join on. You know, he said—getting a little old to go taking wagon train after wild

Indians, and Catherine—she live all her life in town, she want a town *here* or go back to Topeka, she says.

—Sounds like she's got some pretty definite views of things, Isaac politely suggested.

—*Sure* she does, Bill said with a prolonged smile and then closed one watery blue eye in an astonishing wink. Was her money bought out Durfee—she got things to say bout how we do here. And other thing—she use *her* money for ranch—so I keep *my* money and buy in town when you start her up. Now what you say to *that*, Isaac Pride? The smile became a kind of chuckle, and blowing a slow stream of pipe smoke he lifted his cup and drained his coffee.

Isaac went away puzzling over the German's notion of a joke: a new young Indian wife who could talk to him in his own language, was rather stronger-minded than she let on, and could put down the money to buy out the heaviest trading establishment this side of Bent's fort. He had not seen much of Dutch Bill for a while but had supposed he made enough selling illicit powder and guns to the hostiles to repay his loss of trader's license several times over. Or had the soldiers possibly cleaned him out after all—and his prosperous air now was all bought with his wife's money?

Isaac went home two days before Christmas and on the Eve, as a special treat for a serious boy who had mastered his letters and would soon be seven years old, bundled Bissy in front of him on the saddle and rode slowly down the Whitewater, scouting for their Christmas dinner, holding the reins with one hand and his son with the other. It was venison he had in mind and had promised Mrs Mathewson but— lifting the boy down, getting on hands and knees to instruct his attentive eyes—found only a few tracks and droppings, a week old. Coming back up the river through the evening light, he discovered dark shapes of turkeys roosting in the cottonwood branches, got off a shot from the saddle, reloaded in haste and got a second bird before the flock scattered: a brace of hens fattened on walnuts and acorns, each as heavy almost as the boy could drag through the frost-stiff grass, and they rode triumphantly back to the ranch, the birds hanging loose-winged from his saddlehorn.

They were ten crowded at the dinner table next afternoon. Partly to console Lizzie Mathewson for her husband's absence at the Kiowa trading post, Isaac had brought in all the men from his own stations —and Widow Kelly, Bissy sitting up on a chair stacked with books, very proper in the new little suit Mrs Mathewson had sat sewing by lamplight after the children were in bed, a good dark serge with long trousers and a jacket that buttoned neatly to the neck; and Mamie on her lap. The fireplace blazed with logs of walnut till the warmth was like midsummer Kansas; Mrs Mathewson and Bissy had scissored bells of red paper which hung from ribbons tacked to the rafters. She had boiled one of the turkeys with an oyster stuffing, roasted the other with plain bread and sage; and roast potatoes, mashed potatoes, corn pudding, trays of biscuits, ginger peaches. She had declined to make pies or cakes but provided instead two good English plum puddings of large size, with a sauce made of Kentucky whisky and butter —Isaac weeks earlier had ordered the ingredients from Leavenworth, several kinds of nuts and dried fruits but strangely no plums. Lizzie Mathewson before she would let Isaac carve insisted he produce a grace, and the words came, his father's, unused since he left Iowa—

Bless, O Father, these gifts of Thy Providence, and make us mindful of our fellows, and truly thankful for Thy mercy. For Thy Name's sake.   Amen.

And afterward, finally, before the two women dealt with the washing up, Bissy was allowed to help his father pry open the box from Iowa: apples and nuts, cookies and fudge, mittens and warm socks knitted by Grandmother, an elaborately dressed doll Aunt Lizzie had made for Mamie, a crock of butter, scarce and expensive in Kansas, and four bottles of port from the grapes that grew on the arbor behind the house at Rockingham; all wrapped in brown paper and padded with shavings. The men sampled the port, smoked, and talked while the women washed.

That winter while Isaac did his duty at Topeka, Munger and some of the others conducted a new census of Sedgwick County and counted nearly a thousand citizens, half of them adult men eligible to vote. They wrote out a new organizing petition and sent it to Isaac with a hundred signatures to present to the governor, this time in a more cautious form: Harvey was invited to appoint commissioners to supervise an election for public officers and a county seat. At the beginning of March he responded with a proclamation naming three commissioners, and Sedgwick County now formally came into being with Wichita as its temporary seat. The election would be held in a month. Meanwhile, punctually on February 2, six months to the day from the opening of the Osage land for pre-emption and sale on the first Monday in the previous August, Dave Munger traveled to Humboldt, paid in his two hundred dollars and fees, and became the first in Wichita Township to secure preliminary title to his quarter-section. Uncle Eli Waterman put in for his, the quarter adjoining Munger's on the south, twelve days later.

When the session ended and Isaac went home, he discovered that the innkeeper had done nothing more toward securing the town's legal existence: preoccupied with his hotel and lot sales, the county census, the start of the new cattle season, and did not know what to do or did not care, since he now owned the land and could at last give valid title to those who had already bought lots and built. It was a matter first of showing proof of ownership and depositing a town plat with the Butler County recorder of deeds, Sedgwick having no such official until the election and no office to house his records. From his original map Isaac made a clean copy covering Munger's quarter-section, showing blocks, streets, lot numbers, and those lots already sold and built on, not omitting the blank spaces set aside for a town park and the courthouse square; and headed it "City of Wichita—The City of the Plains." Late in March he drove his buggy over from Towanda and with the promise of a night at a hotel and supper persuaded Munger to come with him to El Dorado to settle with the Butler County recorder. The election was barely a week off, and there were two other incipient towns contending for county seat and recognized in the governor's temporary appointments, one ten miles up the Arkansas, the other in the north end of the county but with the advantage of lying on the Atchison & Topeka right-of-way. Although Isaac did not know their status, it seemed reasonable that Wichita if it had no legal existence would lose out, fading as his father's dream of Rockingham had faded thirty years before, and once more grass would flourish where the seeds of a city had fallen on stony ground.

It is a good half-day's drive from Wichita to El Dorado, even with a smart new buggy and a lively horse, and Isaac did not succeed in rousing Dave Munger to an early start. It was mid-afternoon on March 25, last Friday of the month, when with a certain air of justified importance the two men entered the little store-front building rented for the recorder's office and stepped up to the counter. The official was a small, bald-headed man whom Isaac knew slightly, face masked in a flowing beard grizzled with tobacco stains.

—Mister Boggs, Isaac announced in his senate-chamber voice, you join us this afternoon in an historic occasion: the formal founding, according to the laws of Kansas, of the great City of Wichita, future seat of your sister county of Sedgwick.

Munger produced his duplicate and the redrawn plat and laid them on the counter. Mr Boggs chewed reflectively a few more moments, arced an accurate glob of red juice at the spittoon, and shifted the quid to his other cheek.

—Have to pick a different name for your town, Senator, he said. Wichita's taken.

—Wichita *Township*, Isaac said, still smiling. We're talking about the *City* of Wichita, not the whole township—not yet, anyhow!

—City—town—village, the recorder said with an indifferent little shrug. We've already got a Wichita in Sedgwick and can't have two—twould be confuseratin.

—Stole our town from under us! Munger gasped, finding his voice. Dirty, low-down, thievin—

—Mister Boggs, said Isaac reasonably, Wichita by now is known all through Kansas—and *beyond* Kansas, Sir!—town company organized two years ago and maps and advertisements extensively circulated— why, sir, we've got four hundred citizens, two dozen substantial dwellings and business establishments—cattlemen coming in for supplies and stage line coming through, and you can buy your ticket at Topeka straight to *Wichita.* It would be gross misrepresentation to assign that name—

—Now I don't know about *that,* Mr Boggs said. It's all done and recorded, right and proper, accordin to law: *Wichita.* That's what it's called, and only this morning—gentleman was very particular I put the time in my books as well as the date—nine-fifteen, right after we opened. Aint that coincidence?

—Where is this place that wants to call itself Wichita? Isaac demanded.

Mr Boggs sidestepped along the counter, opened his record book and read the description: east half of northwest twenty, township twenty-seven south, range one east of the sixth principal meridian. The two partners stood in silence for a time.

—Why—that's *Waterman's* claim, Munger said when he had gotten his voice back—or half of it, south of town on the cattle crossing—

—It aint Waterman, Mr Boggs put in. Name's Grife—Grief—

—Greiffenstein! both shouted at once.

—Dutch Bill! Isaac broke out, grasping at a straw. He can't make a town if he don't own the land! and he don't own a stick of land, told me himself—made his wife pay for Durfee's ranch, and maybe the claim, if there was one. After the cavalry confiscated his goods—

—He's got a deed for this, Mr Boggs informed him. Endorsed by Waterman, witnessed, notarized by Jim Steele—one dollar and other good and valuable consideration—.

Isaac with another thought demanded to see the plat and the recorder produced it: matched up well enough with the original town plan, but with some differences. For one, he had changed all the names of the north-south streets, Lawrence, Market, Main, and Water, where Isaac had called them Texas, Chisholm, and, for the two public squares, Court and Church; and his east-west streets were not named but numbered, First, Second, Third. In a practical way, Greiffenstein's plat came out with more lots to sell—he had made his blocks longer, and there were none set aside for parks, town buildings, or other public lands; and had picked the cattle trail for the principal commercial street, which he named Douglass, with all his shallow little lots facing on it. All considered, it was not a bad plan to make money from. Isaac nevertheless was furious at being scooped by an elderly German and was for making a fight of it: they would keep on with their own town, where there were already settlers and lots sold, only change the name. Mr Boggs leaned patiently on the counter

while they argued what to call it—Munger was for going back to
Sheridan, while Isaac favored Chisholm City—and finally, as the afternoon declined to suppertime and closing—

—Why don't you, he suggested, just call your place an *addition?*
Thoughtfully with thumb and index finger he removed the pale plug
of tobacco from his mouth and dropped it into the cuspidor. You're
bang by Greiffenstein's eighty anyway, he continued, and if the town
goes like you say, you'll all come out square—and if it don't, why, you
can still plant your town with corn and get back to earning a living.
Don't matter much anyway *what* you call it, just a convenience to
keep the land records straight, cause you got to call it *something*—and
the legal part has to go through the courts, trustees and incorporatin,
and then a special bill through the legislature sayin what kind of
town it is, and what offices you can have, what you can raise in taxes
and bonds—. But I reckon you know all them kind of things, Senator,
being you're in the town-building trade—

It was getting late, Isaac was hungry for supper, tired of the argument. Without another word he seized the recorder's pen, scrawled
"Munger's Addition to" above the careful lettering at the head of his
plat, he and Munger signed their names a few more times and
watched while Mr Boggs wrote the record in his book and filed the
plat, and it was done.

What Greiffenstein had given for the one-eighth section that forever would appear on the county land records as the Original Town
of Wichita was never known. Guesses ranged from a broken-down
span of mules to two thousand dollars—twenty-five an acre, Isaac
perceived, a handsome profit on land sold at the Land Office for $1.25
—but the German cannily neither affirmed nor denied. A little later
that spring when Waterman entered his remaining eighty acres as
Waterman's Addition, it was reasoned that he had demanded more for
the whole quarter-section than Greiffenstein could pay and that,
therefore, the two-thousand-dollar guess was likely for the Original
Town. On the other hand, he had money later that year to pre-empt
in his own name the quarter-section on the bank of the Arkansas
south of the Original Town. Wherever the money came from, it appeared that Greiffenstein was betting on Wichita but, like a careful
gambler, hedging his bets: the town might grow in any direction, but
so long as it did, he (and his wife) would have land to sell at profit.

The lesson that afternoon in the recorder's office continued useful.
The town did grow, and as it did Greiffenstein's nucleus was surrounded by layers of additions bearing the names of various early
claimants, among them Isaac Pride's.

In April the citizens of Sedgwick County chose their first lawful
slate of officials and Wichita as the county seat. The backers of the

rival towns naturally grumbled—that the election was carried by Texans paid with a glass or two at Cadero's Buckhorn Tavern—but their allegations went unproved: the paper ballots and other records were never produced. By some it was said that they had floated down the Arkansas, by others that they had been put away for posterity on a quarter-section beside Dry Creek in the southeast corner of Wichita Township.

XIX

The City of the Plains

Independence Day that year got started in the early evening of July 3 with a dance at The Buckhorn, where a man named Henry Vigus had installed a piano since taking over from Charlie Cadero. It was a double celebration, as several pointed out: not only the national independence but that of Wichita as well, which by petition to the county's newly elected probate judge, Reuben Riggs, was completing the formalities for incorporation as a town under state law. And "You call that independence?" Dutch Bill Greiffenstein rejoined, only half joking. "Town council to make laws and put out bonds and pay interest—and a treasurer to collect taxes, and a marshal to arrest us when we don't pay—and a jail to lock us up in after that! Wichita had independence when everybody squatted their own land and did like they please. . . ." As the summer dusk settled on the prairie, blotting the last glow of sunset across the wide bend of the Little Arkansas, Dutch Bill climbed an unsteady ladder to the sod roof of the tavern, balancing a crate of fireworks ordered from Kansas City, Doctor Lewellen, one of the new town's dozen storekeepers, followed with a lantern, and the crowd gathered out front to watch: five or even six hundred people, more than half the citizens residing within the newly certified corporate limits of Greiffenstein's eighty-acre Original Town and Munger's quarter-section Addition. Gangs of children scampered and twittered through the crowd like prairie dogs. Isaac had lifted Mamie high on his shoulders. Bissy stayed close, holding his father's hand with dignified restraint.

Groping his punk by the lantern light, Dutch Bill started with a string of small crackers, then another, popping in accelerating series, another, like the sounds of an Indian fight heard at a distance, but harmless, no war cries or screams of frightened horses, only the children's high-pitched admiring squeals and hurrahs. He went on to Roman candles to please the ladies, bright blobs of yellow, blue, and green fire like shooting stars, hissing against the dark sky, and ended with a dozen rockets: basso cannon-thump, then the whistling trajectory as the missile rose above the river, and the final star-burst explosion of falling light. It was not, Isaac reflected, as grand or extensive a display as they had mounted at Davenport when the railroad came through, but a good deal closer, more intimate, and now it was his own town they were celebrating.

Three horsemen rode out of the darkness, complaining in accents of Texas that they had a herd bedded down by the cattle crossing and all the shooting had roused them till they could hardly be held, and if they stampeded, they would repay the compliment by turning their cattle through the town. Bill shouted back that even a Texan taking a herd to market oughtn't to be working on the national holiday but stay and join the fun, and led them into The Buckhorn for a glass of refreshment at the bar.

Only half the crowd stayed for the dance, the young parents bedding their little ones in the wagons ranged along the dusty track Isaac had called Waco Street on his plat, a name the cattlemen heard with approval. Even so there was hardly room for all to get inside at once, let alone move around or dance. Two Irishmen with interchangeable names—Malony and Mahoney, with claims at the north end of the township on a fork of Chisholm Creek—alternated on fiddles or occasionally joined together; Lucy Inman, a much younger sister of Lizzie Mathewson's visiting from St Louis and helping with the children, pounded an accompaniment on Vigus's battered upright.

Bissy and Mamie still stayed with Miss Lizzie, as most people respectfully called her, in the cabin on the claim Isaac had staked in her name; Isaac calculated to plat the west half of his own claim and farm the rest and to that end had taken in a moneyless land-looker named Converse Waters to make a first crop of sod corn on shares and his wife to cook, but with four little ones of their own there was no room in the cabin for Isaac's children (to accommodate his tenants, he had cut a shed kitchen through at one end of the cabin and curtained off a corner for his bed but was not home half the time to occupy it). In the spring there were enough families with children to get up twenty-five dollars a month and board for a session of school in the picket cabin of the Episcopal mission church, taught by Billy Finn, who had arrived on foot with a pack to claim his quarter in the township and, having the mathematics, eked his income with jobs of surveying new streets and twenty-five-foot lots according to plat, and Miss Lizzie delivered Bissy to the school punctually each morning in her buggy. The arrangement could not last indefinitely, of course. Miss Lizzie was staying out of friendship but chiefly to establish residence and secure preliminary title to her land, and meantime had put wire fence around part of it and taken in forty head of stock cattle to fatten, bought at ten dollars apiece from passing drovers, which she declared would be worth thirty at Abilene when she was done with them; but would be more use to her husband at his trading post at Fort Sill. Just now Bill Mathewson was up from the Territory with a train of robes and hides and had stayed on for the holiday and a visit with his wife.

Twice from politeness Isaac danced with Miss Lizzie when waltzes came up, but she had definite ideas about dancing as about other things and he was clumsy as a boy with her; perhaps the steps were different since he learned them. The Texans—the herd owner, his trail-boss, a son—stayed and gracefully in their oversize silver-plate spurs and high boots led what they said was a Texas reel when Malony or Mahoney sang, in a clear, penetrating tenor, and the other Irishman played the new comic song:

> *If I'd a cow that gave such milk,*
> *I'd clothe her in the finest silk,*
> *I'd feed her on the choicest hay,*
> *And milk her forty times a day!*

And all with much foot-stamping joined in the chorus:

> *Ha! ha! ha! He! he! he!*
> *Little brown jug, don't I love thee!*
> *Ha! ha! ha! You and me,*
> *Little brown jug, don't I love thee!*

As the crowd thinned and there was room in the tavern for more spirited dancing, each to his fancy, Isaac's melancholy increased. He stood for a time by the bar, watching, not drinking, then went out where someone had dragged a settle by the hitching rail to take what cool the evening afforded. Mathewson, an early riser, had already left with the children; his wife stayed for her sister, and Isaac had promised to see both home but was heavy with sleep. In truth he had not been fully himself since Marie was taken from him—oh, he went where he had to go, did what he had to do, but it seemed with only half a mind for it, his attention always elsewhere: a part of him missing as truly as if hand or foot or eye were cut away. So a man and his woman unite one energy greater than the sum of the two apart and, sundered, become less. What good from that life freely given and expended? What can any man claim of life who walks the earth, in whatever season death takes him hence? *Naked I came, and naked I return:* life itself I cannot possess, it is a loan.

Leaning forward on his knees and his back stiffening, finding no ease on the cushionless bench, Isaac stood up, stretched, and drew his watch out: after midnight and the big day still to come; the ladies maybe by now would be ready to go home.

There were hardly a dozen couples left, most sitting quietly around Vigus's rough tables, no longer dancing. The Irishmen had departed with their fiddles. Lizzie's sister was still at the piano at the far end of the room, back to the door, softly singing in a high sweet voice, inspiriting the outworn instrument with soothing clusters of guitarlike notes.

> *The grass is growing on the turf*
> *Where Willie sleeps,*
> *Among the flow'rs we've planted there,*
> *The soft wind creeps.*
>
> *We laid him there in wintertime*

Isaac strode the room's length, boot-heels thumping the packed clay floor, and laid a hand heavily on the girl's shoulders. Her voice ceased, hands resting in a dying chord, and her smooth young face turned to his, questioning.

—Please don't, not that one, he said in a muffled voice. I can't bear it. He took his hand away and stepped back, awkward.

—Is it very late, Mister Pride? she asked, still looking him in the eyes.

—Past midnight.

—Ah, *very* late, she said, and we are keeping you. And then with a small but assured smile: Well now, Mister Pride, we shall have one more song, and I hope you will like it better, it is new at St Louis now. And *then* we shall let you drive us home. And turning away she paused, straightened, and her hands found the first notes:

> *There's a land that is fairer than day,*
> *And by Faith we can see it afar,*
> *For the Father waits over the way,*
> *To prepare us a dwelling-place there.*
>
> *In the sweet by and by,*
> *We shall meet on that beautiful shore,*
> *In the sweet by and by,*
> *We shall meet on that beautiful shore.*

And under her voice the last chord swelled like a peal of trumpets.

The picnic next day was at Waterman's Grove on the bend of the big river below the mouth of the Little Arkansas—the unsold half of the old man's claim between Greiffenstein's Original Town and the cattle ford: the whole town invited, if they brought their own food and drink; Uncle Eli had freely offered the shade of his woodlot and all the dry wood they could gather. The Mathewsons were taking little Mamie. Isaac wanted the boy to go with him but had not said why; it was to be a surprise all around. It was time Bissy, eight years old he would be in January, learned some riding so he could take himself to school and not have to be driven like a baby; Isaac had taken time with him already, sitting him up on Bird with the stirrups pulled short, leading him in a circle at the end of a long rope, but that was not riding. In the spring at Fort Sill he had traded with Towakoni Jim for an undergrown pinto with black ears he had named Washita, thick-legged and heavy-bodied but a mare and gentle; and since then, when in town, had been training her and had ordered a boy-size saddle of Indian style, with a high cantle, trimmed with red leather and a profusion of brass studs. Accordingly at mid-morning, leading the little horse by a rope looped to the pommel of his saddle, Isaac presented himself at the door of Mathewson's cabin. Lizzie's sister answered his knock.

—Miss Inman, Isaac gravely addressed her, removing his hat, I owe you an apology. Breaking in on your song last night like that. I had no right. And of course it's a lovely song.

—It's I as should apologize, Mister Pride, she said, her eyes wide, her seamless girl-face reshaped by lines of sympathy. Sister told me your sorrow, I wouldn't in the world've given pain by my singing. Your own little darling boy!—. She clasped her hands tight, looking down.

Isaac stood on the smooth slab of river-stone Mathewson had set for a doorstep, looking up at her, but found nothing more to say on that head: fair like her sister but short, no taller than Marie yet with the full hips, pinched-in waist and expansive bosom of an older and bigger woman—as if a master sculptor had started with the one basic female form and amused himself by altering it in every detail. Sixteen, she gave her age out, but that was vanity, Miss Lizzie had confided; she had only turned fifteen in June. She wore her skirts short in the current mode, showing some inches of white-lisle calf above the high-laced boots; today, for the occasion, a dress of sheeny striped gingham, white on pale blue, ruffled at hem, wrists, neck, with a dark blue half-apron.

—Well, now, Miss Lucy! Isaac said, stepping through the door as she stood aside. You got that boy of mine dressed for riding? For ride he shall, on his first own little Indian pony!

Bissy came forward without a word in the suit that had been new at Christmas, already looking short in the sleeves and trousers, and stared soberly out, eyes wide with wonder: his father's great beautiful blond Singing Bird and placidly beside it in the dooryard the sturdy little long-tailed mare with its gaily trimmed saddle.

—Pa! the boy said, still looking. Is she for me? My very own pony?

—You get up on her and we'll *see* if she's yours, Isaac said. It's riding makes a man's horse his own.

The boy did not at once do as his father bade him but with deliberation, while Lizzie and Bill stood in the doorway and watched, and Lucy with the little girl in her arms, walked all around, examining, then faced her, reaching out one tentative hand to pat the velvet pelage of her cheek; and only then lifted foot to stirrup, grasped the reins, and swung his leg up, settling in the saddle. He turned to look at them.

—Oh, *Pa*—, he said and smiled, eyes gleaming between laughter and the verge of tears.

It was half a mile back to Isaac's cabin, then about the same on to Waterman's Grove, and hot, the loose earth rising from the trail and kiting on tides of south wind across the ripe summer grass. Isaac did his son the honor of loosing and coiling the lead rope but kept both horses to a cautious walk till the last two hundred yards, when he let Bird into a light trot, and the pony followed, Bissy jouncing in the saddle and holding the reins tight, his face set. They pulled in and stood for a minute in the shade of the trees, the boy's face etched with dust and sweat. Isaac reached out and patted him on the shoulders, man-fashion; not a little boy any longer to be chucked under the chin or let anyone tousle his neatly brushed hair.

—Did all right, boy, Isaac said, your first time out and riding on your own. Now come along over to the river and we'll let em drink— just a touch of your heels is all she needs to start her. Only mind, don't let her fill her belly—aint many horses got sense enough like Bird, not to drink themselves foolish if you let em.

—*Washita's* got sense, the boy gravely answered, and started after his father.

There were plank tables set up on sawhorses all through the grove where men had cleared undergrowth, some of them dancers from the night before who had not troubled to go to bed; and out in the sun around the edge fire pits dug and the day's meats cooking according to each party's style. There was one fire bigger than all the others, ten feet across and burned down to coals now, beside it an immense skinned, headless carcass and standing around it, well back from the heat, half a dozen men in postures of indecision: small forked trees set on either side of the fire and through the animal, vent to neck, a stout peeled shaft—evidently they meant to roast it whole, as on a spit, but could not think how to get it up, half a ton or more even with the guts out and the head off. Curious, Isaac left his son to mind the horses in the shade and went over.

—Looks like an elephant got loose from a circus! Isaac's voice rang out. Give you much fight, did she?

The silence stretched out.—It's a buffalo, one of them said. A bull buffalo.

—Now by jingo! said Isaac in a tone of amazement, shoving his hat back and shading his eyes to look. I'd have taken it for a dromedary, now I see the hump. And you're starting early to have it ready for Christmas—or *next* Fourth—cause if you mean it for today you'd cut it up and cook it piece by piece. Any of you men got a butcher knife?

He looked from face to face—others had come over to look and listen—then crouched and poked with a stick: the stick sank as in a pudding, moist flesh falling away, swollen, gray with a greasy coating that was iridescent in the noon light.

—It don't look like it'd be fit to eat if you *did* cook it for a year—been that long by its look since it was on the hoof. Where'd you get it?

—Off a nigger cook from a cattle outfit, a voice cried. Cut it out from a herd, coming up through the Territory.

Isaac swung around: big dark man with raging heavy-lidded eyes, shadow of blue-black beard outlining mouth and jaws and a slouching way of hunching his shoulders forward as if offering to fight; a face seen somewhere that he could not put a name to.

—That's a month's drive from Red River, Isaac said. Nigger traded it off some Indian before that—or found it dead of old age along the trail.

—That'll cook out. It's only well aged, and we mean to season it and cook it right.

—And salt it with strychnine, might as well, Isaac said. You feed that spoiled meat to our townsfolk, there won't be enough of em live to make up the school tax.

—I've et worse in my time, the man said with dignity.

—I haven't! Isaac snapped. Prairie dog and coyote, hedgehog and skunk, and every kind of meat that grows on these plains, but none of it spoiled. Why man, if you didn't have a nose to smell with, all you got to do is look—

A buggy was coming along the trail from town, Mathewson and his family, and Isaac waved. He turned toward them, reined in, got down with deliberation and walked over.

—Bill, what do you say to that? Isaac said, pointing at the carcass. These fellows want to cook it and feed it to the citizens.

—*That's* what it was, Bill said. Now I *thought* I smelled something, clear from town.

—You want any? Isaac insisted.

—If I was a Indian coming home from a year of raiding, Bill said, I'd think it a little high for my taste. Or if I was a pig or a goat—

There was a murmur of cautious approval from the onlookers, by now a considerable crowd: Jack Pride might run on till a man couldn't tell if he was joking or what, but not Buffalo Bill the truth-

teller; what he deemed not fit to eat no other would touch. Doctor
Lewellen had been observing from a distance. He now walked off and
came back a few minutes later driving a span of big horses unhitched
from the wagon that had carried him to the grove, with a doubletree
dragging behind and a set of chains clinking softly in the dust. The
crowd parted to let him through.

—Come on now, boys! Doctor cried. Reckon now we're a town we
don't have to eat just buffalo anyway—ham and pig and mutton and
beef and fried chicken and every kind of civilized meat there is,
plenty enough for all. And them as aint hungry yet, there's a full
barrel of Dave Munger's whisky with its head stove, back in the
grove. Come on now!

Someone started a cheer, which was followed by many-voiced mas-
culine laughter, and the crowd began to scatter. Without waiting for
answer from the dark man Doc chained up to the tainted carcass and
with a great show of cracking his whip set his team off at a trot
toward the river bank, meaning, as he said, to send that critter back
where it came from.

In the afternoon Isaac joined the Mathewsons at a table in the
shade and was showing Bissy how to manage a long strip of roast
tenderloin with one hand and a sharp knife when Greiffenstein am-
bled past, picking at a breast of chicken fastidiously wrapped in a
clean white handkerchief. Isaac went over to him: what did Dutch
Bill know of that fool with the buffalo meat?—thought he'd met him
somewhere but couldn't think—.

Bill nodded and went on chewing, mouth full; after a time swallowed, tossed the bones aside, wiped his fingers. Sure, that fellow, he
knew him, he said: had taken a quarter-section over east in the county
by land warrant but also put a hundred dollars on a town lot and
meant to build; had been a cavalry scout sometime, then in the war a
teamster and later joined a company of sharpshooters—

But the name, Bill, the *name*—

—Why sure, that one, I thought you knew—says he knows *you:*
that's Mister Dave Payne, Greiffenstein concluded, and resumed his
progress among the picnic tables.

Besides the varieties of cooked meats, there were great heaps of
green roasting ears, tubs of potato salad, limitless trays of biscuits, a
whole wagonload of watermelon, and a dozen kinds of sweet pies and
cakes, again in astonishing quantity and sampled along from table to
table among neighbors. In late afternoon, replete, the people gathered
along the cool of the riverbank to sing, and the Irishmen reappeared
with their fiddles: all the old emigrant songs, "A Life in the West,"
"Uncle Sam's Farm," "Ho! for Kansas," and "We Cross the Prairies as
of Old," still to Isaac the most stirring of the lot, and he was moved to
get up in front of the crowd and lead them through all the verses; and

"Little Brown Jug" that had seemed so comical to dance to and now brought whoops of bass laughter from around the whisky barrel. By comparison, a new song celebrating the completion of the Pacific railroad the year before seemed pale and tame, but it was perhaps only that by now most were sung out and too full of good food. The women now were getting to their feet, smoothing skirts, brushing away wisps of grass and gathering children, pots, and leftovers for the drive home.

Isaac and Mathewson, in no hurry to go, found an empty table and were taking their ease in silence with cigars when Dutch Bill came toward them with an air of purpose.

—Those Texans, he said, leaning heavily on a table plank. They're gettin up a horse race—that's the owner, Major George Stone of Stag Ranch, Bexar County, it's his son, Young George—. We figure, Isaac, if you'd run, for the honor of Wichita—

Isaac cut him off with a sharp shake of his head, then a laugh and a joke to soften the refusal.—No, Bill, he said, not an old widow-man like me—I'd break my neck coming round the pole. And anyhow, it seems every time I get talked into one of those things, it's only trouble. But I tell you—get someone else to run and I'll judge your start and finish, and you can have a Texan judge the turn. That fair enough?

The Texas horse was a nondescript gray, not big, slender-shanked but heavy in the shoulders, with sharp ears twitched back; a mean-looking animal, possibly smart, that could turn out a sprinter for the man that could stay on him. The Stone boy had mounted up and sat like a jockey with the stirrups set short, holding the horse in tight and scowling defiance across the crowd of Kansans. Someone had scratched a starting line between two wagons and there was a post set up for the turn perhaps two hundred yards south toward the cattle crossing, but since Isaac still refused, it did not seem there would be a race, and Major Stone scowled and muttered derogations. Then—

—I'll take your challenge, boy, a voice boomed, and all turned: Dave Payne in shirt-sleeves, coming forward on a big black that stood a hand or two taller than the gray, a pretty fair cavalry mount in its day, Isaac judged, but no racer.

Considerable betting ensued: the Texan's stock cattle at their home price, twelve dollars a head, against anything of equivalent value the Kansans cared to lay—greenbacks and some gold, a buggy and a couple of wagons, a pile of revolvers and rifles, a settler's breaking plow, Doc Lewellen's draft team; altogether around a thousand dollars on each side. Payne and his horse were newcomers, equally unknown to most of the Wichita people. After some discussion, Stone's trail boss, a tall, dark-bearded man with a livid scar across his forehead, was appointed to judge the turn.

Isaac counted the start and the two horses were off, but with a groan from the crowd: the gray went off like a jack rabbit and stayed in front. Payne's black, once he was moving, went along like an express engine, closing up, but slowed at the stake and lost a full length; came on again, closing toward the finish, and might have passed if the race had gone another hundred yards or two. The Kansas groan became a drawn-out sigh. As the riders circled back, Isaac went over to the Stone boy and announced him the winner in a strong, clear voice, then swung around to his father.

—That's a pretty fair race your boy run, Isaac said, raising his voice for all to hear, though what a man would want, encumbered with plows and plow-horses and such truck, driving a herd to Abilene, *I* don't know, but—. How many head you say you brought over the Arkansas, Major? Isaac demanded.

—Twelve hundred, more or less, the man answered in a low voice. Aint counted for a week—

—And of course your bills of sale and registers of brands, made out and witnessed, certified by the inspectors—not that any of us here would make a gentleman *prove* his word—

The major was inaudible.

—But since you're a *sporting* gentleman, Isaac continued, and to save you trouble, driving to Abilene, here's what: I'll run against your boy for your whole herd—and all the stuff, of course, the citizens just lost—against the Original Town of Wichita, eighty acres of prime real estate. How's that? Your boy wins, you can change her name to Austin and move your capital—or anything you like. And if *I* win, why then I reckon—

There were sputterings on either side of him, the Texan's face red, Dutch Bill's white.—Or if that's too heavy for you, Isaac went smoothly on, I'll settle for your winnings. Only—you got to stretch the course out some. My old mare—she takes two hundred yards to get her bones moving. Say, move the post out another two hundred yards.

Major Stone could not refuse. Men ran to reset the pole.

—And one more thing! Isaac said, raising his voice again. Mister Mathewson here's to judge the start *and* finish. And either party goes off previous before he calls, that's a false start, and we start again.

Isaac gave the nickering call and Singing Bird came trotting from the grove and halted beside him, expectant, and Bissy after, running, with his new pony on a lead. Miss Lizzie and Lucy were standing back of the starting line with the little girl. Isaac went to them and gave Lizzie his coat to hold.

—You reckon you can beat, Mister Pride? Lucy anxiously asked, her eyes bright.

—At that distance my Singing Bird'll go with any horse in Kansas or the Territory. It's only just a kind of formality, so the Texans can allow the citizens their farm-making tools back without insult or disputatiousness. . . .

Isaac mounted up and stood at the starting line waiting, the horse perfectly still except for a little excited flickering of the ears, forward and back. Mathewson was halfway down the count when young Stone let his gray break, and Bill roared him back for a new start.

The second start was clean. Isaac was conscious of two things: the swiftly accelerating pole sighted along the horse's neck, then the smooth turn so close he might have reached and picked off a splinter of bark from the post; and the crowd coming back to size as he ran the return, girls and children jigging up and down in excitement, the men raising cheer after cheer. He had meant to hold her in a little, make it look like a race, not too humiliating, but Bird had never been one to hold back, it was months since he'd given her a good run, and he let her go, greathearted, giving all her speed. What the watchers saw and remembered was as much beauty as some of them would ever know: the great smooth-flowing stride of the creamy-blond mare centaur-backed by her golden-headed rider moving to the same beautiful motion, two nodes of energy united; and behind—a length, two lengths, three—the little gray, legs churning, stretching his lithe body across the trampled sod like a prairie coyote with its heart set on outrunning a bullet. Singing Bird made the turn so close it seemed she had merged with the post, then she was clear again and coming back, still gaining speed.

Thirty yards out, it appeared that Isaac had pulled his horse in sharp and made her stumble and slow. No one had observed him to look back, but the gray had come hardly half-way down the second leg, slowing in a gasping, raddled, wind-broken gallop audible clear to the finish line. As Isaac crossed, the horse with a great shudder sank under him and rolled to her side, and he jumped clear. Mathewson was already shouting the outcome, over and over, *Isaac Pride, the winner, on Singing Bird,* excited for once as any boy in the crowd, but the horse opened her mouth in a gurgling snort and spilled a glob of dark blood on the grass. Isaac threw himself down, one ear to her ribs, and for a long minute lay there, limp. As he got up, Dave Payne had shouldered through the now silent crowd of onlookers and seized his hands to help him to his feet.

—I reckon we're even now, Jackrabbit, Payne said in a low voice. I don't know how I'd've ever showed my face at Wichita again, letting them Texans fool me that way.

—*Even!* Isaac said, staring back hard-eyed. There aint any way on this earth you and me can ever be *even*, Payne. I'd've soon've taken both hands off with a meat-ax as run that horse to death in a fool race, if the whole state of Kansas was laid on the winning—

The other flushed dark but managed to hold his voice down, having some few words more:—All the same, Jack, he said, you done me a turn I'll remember, same as if you saved my life. But I know what a man's horse is to him, and I tell you before God in His heaven, I never meant to make you any horse-killer doing it. . . .

Isaac turned away, shouting for Doc Lewellen.

A boy standing near heard part of what was said. A murmurous chant of boys' voices rippled through the crowd: *Horse-killer Pride! Horse-killer Pride!*

Lucy Inman huddled against her sister, cheeks wet, shoulders quivering. Choking, she found his eyes.—Oh, Mister Pride! Your lovely horse—your beautiful golden horse—

—You mustn't grieve, Lucy, Isaac said gently. Hadn't so many years left anyhow, and she went doing the thing she loved best in this world, and all in a rush—no years out to pasture, growing old and feeble, swayback, blind—

A hand touched his arm: Doctor Lewellen.

—Listen, Doc, Isaac said, now you got your team back, I'd appreciate you do me the kindness of sending old Bird after Payne's buffalo —don't see what else we can do—

—Of *course*, Isaac, Doc said respectfully. I'll get the saddle off and bring it by your cabin, next time I—

—No! That saddle, it was hers, had it made special—let it go with her, let it all go. . . .

Bissy had come up beside him with his pony. Isaac swooped him up in his arms and hugged him close as if still the toddler he had been.— Looks like your pa's fixed himself for a long walk home, Isaac said. But you'll ride, anyhow, boy. You'll ride.

—Oh, Pa! the boy cried, and wrapping his father's neck in his small arms pressed a kiss to the rough cheek. We've got *Washita*. You needn't ever walk as long as I've got my horse.

A town, like a man, turns to whatever at hand will provide a livelihood. Wichita for a start had the cattle trail distinguished by Chisholm's name. The modest wagon tracks connecting the village of the Wichita with his ranch on the North Canadian had now been driven south across the Red River into Texas, to San Antonio and by many branchings clear to the Gulf coast, and Wichita had become a profitable station on the road to Abilene. The improvident ambition that launched Abilene as a cattle market in 1867 had not so far, however, brought any measurable profit to its originator, Joe McCoy.

Texas had been cattle country since the Spanish early in the 18th century drove herds of long-horned Castilian stock to that remote province of their Mexican domain. The cattle drive became the means of taking surplus beef to market. The Civil War put a stop to this commerce: Texas cattle were enemy contraband in most of their former markets; the ranchers and their hands were otherwise engaged. When the war ended, there were millions of cattle running loose on the Texas plains, unclaimed, unbranded, presently known as "mavericks" for the man who had the notion of gathering them and burning his own mark on them. The huge supply meant low prices, perhaps three dollars a head in Texas, and it was said that a rancher's poverty was in direct ratio to the size of his herd. On the other hand, beef of any kind was short in the cities of the North and East, worth fifty dollars or more delivered in New York. The difficulty lay in connecting the Texas supply with the Northern demand.

The country through which the Texas cattlemen had to pass to bring their herds to markets and railroads in eastern Kansas, Missouri, Illinois was now settled by farmers with shorthorn stock of their own—"native" or "American" cattle as distinct from the Spanish-descended Texas variety. The native cattle were subject to a generally killing disease that seemed somehow to be transmitted by longhorns but to which the longhorns themselves were immune: Texas fever, sometimes tick fever, in Texas known as Mexican or Spanish fever; properly, splenic fever because the spleen was particularly affected. During the Civil War and in the years following, most states in the central Midwest passed quarantine laws against Texas cattle: on the same principle as with cholera and other human epidemics. County sheriffs were empowered to enforce the quarantine by arrest, fines, jail, often, in turbulent Missouri, with practical assistance from armed mobs of citizens and local cattle rustlers.

It was the Illinois cattle dealer Joe McCoy—Joseph Geiting McCoy, of an age with Isaac Pride, born to a well-off family of cattle dealers in Sangamon County—who conceived a solution to this dilemma: a cattle market at the nearest railroad point to Texas unaffected by quarantine law. Since Texas and its cattle country were not yet within hundreds of miles of a railroad connection with the rest of the nation and the cattlemen had already learned the drawbacks of attempting to trail their herds through Missouri, that goal could be met only by a place somewhere in western Kansas. McCoy spent the spring and early summer of 1867 scouting the new railroad building west up the valley of the Kansas River; considered Salina and Junction City but was rebuffed at both by citizen-farmers unprepared to welcome fever-bearing Texas cattle; and settled on Abilene, a village halfway between the two, too small to reject any scheme that offered a livelihood and having no other prospects. All three towns were well within the deadline established earlier that year which Governor Crawford was not disposed to enforce.

Having made his choice, McCoy consulted with the railroad. Its president made no objection to his providing a stockyard and other amenities, at his own expense; in return, he offered a railroad siding and a commission of one eighth of the freight on cattle shipped over his rails to Leavenworth (whence they would go on to Quincy and Chicago by other lines)—five dollars on a carload of twenty head of cattle. On the strength of this promise, Joe McCoy went to work at Abilene and by September had built a 250-acre stockyard west of town, big enough to hold a medium-size herd of a thousand animals; a three-story hotel that cost him the considerable sum of fifteen thousand dollars, which he modestly named The Drover's Cottage; a sizable livery stable, a bank. He hired surveyors to mark the route to Abilene, wrote letters to Texas newspapers and to connections in the cattle-buying trade at Kansas City, St Louis, Chicago, sent agents down the trail to carry the message in person, armed with circulars. Although not ready for business till near the end of the season, he drew perhaps 45,000 head to Abilene by his ceaseless tub-thumping; of which nearly half, a thousand carloads, were sold and shipped east by rail—enough to push prices down—while the rest were trailed on north and west as stock cattle to fill new ranges in Nebraska, Wyoming, the Dakotas. The next year, 1868, McCoy sent a kind of Wild West show east to the market cities by way of publicity—trick riding, roping of wild longhorns and a few captured buffalo—and put out (he said later) five thousand dollars in free hotel rooms, meals, and livery service for cattlemen and buyers.

These efforts brought 75,000 head to Abilene, of which 2,500 carloads were shipped east, embarrassing the railroad for rolling stock; and it responded by cutting his commission in half. The 1869 drive to Abilene was no greater in numbers than the year before, but delay due to high water at the Wichita crossing of the Arkansas pushed prices up—as much as twenty-five dollars a head at McCoy's stockyard for beef of average quality. The 1870 season, aided by more favorable weather and a market that continued strong, doubled the previous year's drive to Kansas; in 1871 it doubled again. About the time it seemed that Joe McCoy was on the way to getting his investment back and turning a modest profit—through freight commissions but also through trading on his own account and that of the family cattle business back in Illinois—other Kansas railroad towns were competing fiercely for the growing trade; and more seriously, the Kansas Pacific declined to pay even its reduced commission on cattle freight. Creditors learned of this embarrassment and demanded payment. Both to meet their demands and to finance his suit against the railroad, he was obliged to sell the stockyards and The Drover's Cottage. Eventually he won his case and collected what was owed him, but by the end of 1870 his business at Abilene had ended as abruptly as it began.

Wichita's benefits from Joe McCoy's enterprise were modest but

real. The 1870 season, when 150,000 head of cattle were trailed to
Abilene, meant around 150 outfits making the Arkansas crossing and
passing through Wichita, perhaps two thousand hands, each provided
with four or five ponies in the remudas. Wichita was the first town
north of Fort Worth where after eight or ten weeks on the trail the
drovers could resupply with groceries, feed for their horses, clothing,
harness, blacksmithing and wagon repairs; perhaps relieve camp life
with a visit to a barber, a restaurant, a saloon or billiard parlor for an
evening's entertainment. By the fall of 1870 there were fifty or sixty
business establishments set up at Wichita, coming in almost faster
than they could be counted, though most would be as quick to close
up and move on if the prospect showed signs of cooling; an election
brought out 449 voters from a population that had reached two thousand.

With a share in the cattle trade, the Wichita founders were ready to
consider the obvious next step: securing a railroad of their own. It
was a goal they had dared to imagine before the not yet incorporated
town first began to show signs of attracting settlers and becoming a
going enterprise, but it remained elusive. There were probably as
many motives bound together in this aim as there were citizens, but
the cattle trade was immediate and overriding: with its location on
the Chisholm Trail in combination with being the nearest shipping
point to Texas, there would be no reason why Wichita should not
succeed Abilene as the leading cattle market. Cattle at Abilene in 1871
represented around four million dollars changing hands, quite possibly a great deal more. Much of that swift-moving money went back to
Texas with the cattlemen or was sponged up in Kansas Pacific freight
charges, but a decent portion remained—with the banks and outfitters, the saloons on Texas Street, the dance houses, brothels, and gam-
ing establishments set apart from respectable Abilene in the district
known as Hell's Half Acre. To the Wichita founders a commerce on
that scale would necessarily mean a wonderful rise in the value of
their land—a hundred thousand dollars, perhaps several times that,
realized on a quarter-section that had sold in the first place for $1.25
an acre; the sort of calculation that had fevered Isaac's imagination
when the town was first thought of.

The railroad possibilities continued to tantalize. In the summer of
1870 a crew of Santa Fe surveyors came through Wichita conducting
a route survey, led by Thomas J. Peter, a stolid Cincinnati German
who came to Kansas originally with the construction firm that secured the Santa Fe contract and stayed on as the railroad's construction superintendent and general manager. T. J. Peter agreed that the
well-drained trail with its easy stream-crossings first marked by Jesse
Chisholm's wagon wheels was as suited to the iron tracks of a railroad

as to the hooves of the cattle that now in their hundreds of thousands had packed it hard as city pavement; but the general manager went back to track-laying, and no word came of Santa Fe plans for a branch to the south.

What Peter and the Santa Fe directors were waiting for, the founders now reasoned, was a subsidy in the form of a county bond issue; no Western railroad, it seemed, ever laid a foot of track without a guarantee of its construction cost from the towns and counties that would benefit, and since part of the twenty-five-mile right-of-way between Newton and Wichita would lie within the Osage Trust, the railroad would not have the usual incentive of free public land. Someone—it may have been Bill Greiffenstein—argued that if the railroad could exact conditions for doing what, after all, was in its own interest, building traffic to a promising new town, then Sedgwick County was entitled to conditions of its own: they would not lay the bond issue out in advance, like a simple farmer buying a hoe from a hardware merchant, but would award it to the first line to carry its tracks to Wichita, the county seat—let them compete for the favor! Besides the Santa Fe, there appeared to be three candidates: the Santa Fe's great rival, the Kansas Pacific; Bob Stevens's Missouri, Kansas and Texas—"the Katy" and the St Louis and San Francisco or possibly the Missouri Pacific.

The presidents of the five lines, duly informed, did not reply; they declined the competition.

In May of 1871, when the silence had lasted five months, Isaac traveled to Topeka to consult with Cy Holliday: half a day on the stagecoach to Newton, then the cars to the capital. Holliday was sympathetic.

—*Of course* it would pay, Mister Pride—right on the cattle trail, and the nearest point in Kansas that's on the railroad, only—I don't know what we'd want with *two* cattle towns not twenty-five miles apart, now we've got Newton started up, and Mister Joe McCoy advising how to go about it and bring the buyers and the cattlemen together—

—Aint only cattle, Mister Holliday, Isaac put in. Way our county's settling up, in a year or two you'd be hauling as much in wheat and corn, and settlers and their goods coming in, and every kind of supplies they'll need. And we've got about the whole of the Indian trade from the Territory and out into the Southwest, robes and hides coming in and trade goods going out, Indian contracts with the agencies —and now there's people say there's money too in gathering buffalo bones off the prairies, grind em down for fertilizer and the lime in them, if they had a railroad they could get them to. He paused to take breath.

—Now if that aint what Mister Peter was telling me when he came back from his surveying last year—and I agree with him, too. Drawing a cigar out from a vest pocket he leaned back in his chair, gazing reflectively past Isaac's head; except for a fresh coat of paint, it was still the same neat, modest frame building he had used for his offices when Isaac first met him eight years earlier. Out his front windows, when he chose, he could contemplate the hilltop twenty acres he had given as an inducement to locate the seat of government at Topeka, on which now rose the nearly finished structure that was to be the east wing of the capitol, creamy Shawnee County sandstone in the general form of a Roman temple, pedimented porch supported by a row of columns reached up a broad flight of steps; surrounded by a barren waste of builder's rubble and a crude fence of fragments of leftover stone, put up to keep the pigs out.

—Yes, sir! Holliday continued when he had his cigar properly lighted, if it was only Cy Holliday's say-so, or Mister T. J. Peter's, why, sir, I can tell you, we'd be laying track to Wichita tomorrow, or anyhow next week. But of course it aint—we've got directors to answer to and stockholders to answer to, big money-men at Boston and other points east, and I can tell you frankly, Mister Pride, they'll not hear of it, for we've put it to them: "Finish your main line to Colorado and *then* we'll talk about building little branches hither and yon," is what *they* say—for you know, sir, the way Sam Pomeroy wrote his dod-burn law, if we don't have track open to Colorado by the last day of December, eighteen seventy-two, which is near three hundred miles still to go, we lose every mile of our land grant. No, sir, we just aint got the resources—

—Resources! Isaac burst out. We already drilled and marshaled our voters and got em agreed on the bond issue, two hundred thousand dollars—why, sir, that's eight thousand a mile, and if you can't lay a little one-track branch line for *that*, why—why, I believe I'll take up railroad building and do the job myself!

—You might do that, Mister Pride, Holliday said with a hard little chuckle. Oh, I read your bond authorization, he continued, frowning and puffing fiercely at his cigar. *Payable upon completion*—just the kind of thing some farmer'd think up that don't know no more of business than maybe which end of the ox to hitch his plow to. As if you'd get a team of railroads running a race for a paltry little sum in county bonds—

Isaac felt his face warming but answered nothing.

—No, you're damn right they won't, Holliday growled. But suppose one of us *did* start in to build your little branch line for you on those terms, know what it'd mean? Why, I'd have to go to the New York or Boston banks and borrow the construction money—*at* twelve or fifteen percent—and be surprised if they'd lend. Because why? Because they'd think me and my directors was gone soft in the head, is why. And I'd have to agree—.

—All right! Isaac said, we'll get up a new election—a month or six weeks, say—

—You see the trouble you'd've saved yourselves? Holliday said, smiling again. If you'd talked with us first about the practical side of things—

—And we get your bonds authorized: well, what I want to know is, when would the Santa Fe start construction, when would we—

—I already *told* you, Holliday snapped. The Santa Fe aint in it—directors won't hear of it, not for two or three years anyhow, at the soonest.

—Then how in the nation—

Holliday silenced him with a raised hand and deliberate as stern schoolmaster to laggard scholar explained: the directors' caution did not mean that he and Peter were against taking a hand personally—as he had already indicated. All they had to do was get up a Wichita railroad company, get their bonds approved by the voters, and then they could *hire* the Santa Fe to build for them—and operate when the line was finished—and the board of directors would have nothing to say about it. Sound business!

Isaac sat in silence for a minute or two.—I can see how your people would like that arrangement, Mister Holliday, he said slowly. If Wichita pays like we think it will, the Santa Fe makes money. And if it don't—why, it aint cost them a cent to find out!—not to mention a little profit in the first place, from running the crews and buying the iron for the track-laying—.

Holliday smiled—the scholar was not entirely hopeless after all—but said nothing. After a further silence, however, he opened his watch impatiently, shoved his chair back, and stood up.

—Mister Pride, he said, a railroad man's got to run by the clock. Now, if this Wichita branch is too heavy for you to take in all at once, you go back to your hotel and think about it.

—I reckon I've done my thinking, Isaac said. I believe we can get up our railroad company, like you say we have to—and I believe we can get our bonds through again—but I can't go back to my people and even start till you put down in writing what you'll do to keep your end of the bargain. So if—

—Of course, of course! said Holliday with enthusiasm. Sound business all around—you write to Mister Peter at Osage City and tell him what *you're* prepared to do—and he'll answer and tell you what *he'll* do. Exchange of letters—good as a formal contract in any chancery court in the nation.

And before Isaac could think of more to say, the big man had his hand under his elbow and was propelling him amiably toward the door.

Bill Greiffenstein in particular seemed taken with the railroad scheme: Wichita was special—railroad coming to her, not the other way around, one more Kansas town springing up like mushrooms where the iron horse had left its droppings; and would have her own railroad company besides. Isaac tried several drafts of his letter to Mr Peter, each longer and less satisfactory than the last, and finally reduced his message to two lines with no superfluous words to look foolish or ignorant to the railroad men. He wrote a fair copy on the new letterhead Marsh Murdock had run off for him on his hand press at Burlingame—*From the Office of Isaac A. Pride, Dealer in Real Estate*—and sent it off on June 2:

Mr T. J. Peter
Superintendant & General
Manager
Dear Sir—
   Upon what terms will you build a branch of your Road to Wichita?
                                             Most respectfully yours,
                                                   I. A. Pride

The reply came three days later, equally terse:

Hon. I. A. Pride
Wichita, Kan.
Dear Sir:—
   In answer to y'rs of 2nd inst. will say, If your people will organise local Company & vote 200,000$ of County Bonds—I will build you a Rail Road to Wichita within six Months—
                                                   T. J. Peter
                                               Supt. & Gen'l Mgr

Isaac collected a list of citizens who were prepared to have their names put down as directors and went back to Topeka: Bill Greiffenstein; Charles Gilbert, who was starting a plow factory; and Jim Steele and seven others who had been drawn to the town by the prospect of county courthouse law and a steady business in land titles and transfers; the three other founders pleaded the press of their own affairs. Cy Holliday guided him through the drawing up of the corporate charter to be recorded with the secretary of state. He was indifferent to the resounding name the Wichita men had picked for their railroad, as they thought it—Wichita and South Western Rail Road Company—but had decided views on other matters. The branch was to be capitalized at five hundred thousand dollars, of which two hundred thousand dollars would go to match the county bonds and the rest to Holliday and Peter—couldn't get into it, of course, if they didn't keep control. Isaac went into the record book at the head of the list of directors, as president. Of course, Holliday explained with a chuckle, the office carried no compensation since this little railroad company really would have no income of its own but was only a legal and fiscal convenience, a kind of fairy-tale gotten up for the benefit of Wichita and all concerned. And Isaac agreed, of course, without quite following his reasoning.

Isaac was still pondering next morning as the Santa Fe train clattered along to Newton at twenty miles an hour: whether the railroad man hadn't played him for a fool with his self-assured certainties. Looking at the matter all around, he really could not see why in justice he should not get something—director's fees, a little something a month for warming the president's chair—for the trouble he was going to in organizing the branch line and bringing the voters around; Holliday had a way of taking the starch out of a man—made him feel that Wichita needed the road a great deal more than Holliday or the Santa Fe needed Wichita. Still, it ought to bring about equal benefit to both parties, which is the essence of any bargain: for the Santa Fe, two shots at the cattle trade; for Wichita, another jump in land prices. That, for Isaac and the others with land in the town, would be worth far more than any fifty or hundred dollars a month he might have demanded for lending his name.

Armed with his charter duly endorsed and dated June 22—and a very plain corporate seal, a box of printed stationery and envelopes, a thin sheaf of stock certificates engraved with a diamond-stack locomotive steaming across a prairie pulling a baggage car and three passenger cars, and a small, leather-bound ledger in which to keep the stock records, though there would be only two or possibly three stockholders—Isaac went home to collect signatures on a petition for a vote on the new bond issue. The election was set for August 11, most of the signers from Wichita itself.

From the first announcements, the railroad plan and the renewed bond question stirred an opposition centered on Newton, which, founded on the prospects of the cattle trade and exclusive rail traffic for the whole county, had not yet enjoyed a full season's profit from either. At the end of June a delegation took the stage to Wichita for a meeting at Greiffenstein's house on his reserve south of Douglass Avenue: S. J. Bentley, who in the spring had built the town's first hotel, the Newton House (there were already three or four others); Cy Bowman, Newton's first and leading lawyer; and Mike McCluskie, a bad-tempered Irishman employed as yard boss by the Santa Fe.

The meeting came about partly because each side had an interest in learning how far the other would go to gain its objective. The Wichita group had all the arguments, and Isaac, the only one with experience in the legislature, presented them: that Newton would actually gain by becoming a junction and transfer point rather than just another stop on the main line; that anyhow, if they cooperated, there was enough in the cattle trade for both towns, and both would benefit by Wichita's growth; and on the other hand that Wichita already had the votes to win. Mr Bowman could answer only that Newton could hardly be expected to take a hand in its own hanging; and that he thought they would find the votes one way or other—not only every resident of his town but half the farmers in the county, who, like their kind everywhere, hated on principle bond issues and the taxes that went with them. The meeting was courteous enough, but it did not seem there was any way it could resolve the conflict of interests. When nothing remained to say on either side, Greiffenstein offered whisky or fresh-made coffee all around and led Mr Bentley away to another room to talk, he said, about the hotel business. What else Greiffenstein had to say on that occasion he did not hint until much later, but the Newton people quieted. Farmers throughout the county continued to oppose any bond issue and found a voice in Dave Payne.

It was the first week in July of that year that the unclaimed remainder of the Osage land was opened to general sale. The Land Office responsible had by now moved west as far as Augusta in Butler County, a half-day's easy ride from Wichita, and no doubt would locate at the Sedgwick County seat itself if the railroad scheme finally came to anything. Wichita was the natural point from which to prospect much of the offered land, and the lure of cheap land and profit in a settling country drew the usual mixture of people: the gentry with money to put out on land for resale or on mortgages at perhaps twelve percent for two or three years, the rates being just now low compared with the territorial days; the salesmen of various implements and the gamesters, some accompanied by overdressed ladies known as "soiled doves" in the polite language of the newspapers; and, predominant, the travel-grimed farmers who had left wives and children on failed and mortgaged acres in any of the Eastern states and come to Kansas intending to change their luck, though not, if they could help it, at the price of railroad land, however easy the terms and the interest rates.

In such a crowd, so assertive, self-conscious, one of the new arrivals passed nearly unnoticed: a small, gray, mild-eyed, clean-shaven, unobtrusive man of perhaps forty, wearing a dark suit of vaguely clerical cut and a broad-brimmed black hat pulled low on his brow. The coach from El Dorado jingled to a halt in front of the Empire House, the passengers descended, went in to take rooms, departed in their manifold directions. Brownie Brown, the conductor, stood ready to slam the door shut; and then from the dark interior leaned the small man pressing a worn leather valise to his breast, stepped a tentative foot to the board sidewalk, and stood blinking in the harsh afternoon light, breath coming short and shallow like a dog panting in the heat. Shifting his burden to one hand, he blotted his upper lip delicately

with a handkerchief and eased his head back to look. Brownie had
forgotten him; went around to the boot, extracted the last heavy carpetbag, and handed it to his final passenger.

Mr Ezekiel Blood, the hotel manager Greiffenstein had persuaded
from St Louis, slicked-back hair and a handsome pair of mustaches
waxed to points, lounged at the high desk while the guest balanced
his way across the lobby—where had that boy got to?—the small,
worn valise in one hand, the bulging carpetbag in the other: might at
first glance be taken for some kind of traveling preacher, the way he
kept his eyes cast down, looking every way but front, as if meditating
a text.

—The Empire House at your service, Reverend! Mr Blood announced in his innkeeper's voice as the small man set his bags down
and straightened up.

—A room, the man said with a momentary raising of his eyes. Only
two or three nights, that's all I'll be.

—Second floor front, Mr Blood suggested, caressing his mustaches.
Light, airy, new-furnished—fine view out on this growing City of the
Plains, and only three dollars—or by the week—

—Something more modest? the man said, pursing his lips. I can
view the town on the feet God gave me, at no extra charge.

—The wing at the back, the manager offered, lowering his voice.
Two dollars, but it overlooks the barn, of course—

The man hunched his shoulders in assent. Mr Blood opened the
register and slid it toward him, the pen, the ink-pot, and read upside-
down while he wrote in a clear and flowing hand, schoolmaster's or
forger's—*J. C. Fraker, El Dorado, Butler County, Banker.*

—That's in advance, of course, Mr Blood carelessly added.

Mr Fraker with a small sigh brought out a purse and, holding it
close, withdrew the two heavy silver coins, which he laid silently one
atop the other on the counter. For a moment he looked the clerk
firmly in the eye.

—You are *not* Mister Greiffenstein, the guest said with assurance.
He wore a beard, last time I saw him.

—Ezekiel Blood, at your service, sir! Mr Blood said, flushing. General manager to Mister Greiffenstein.

—I shall be calling upon him while at Wichita. We may have business.

—Of course, of course! I'll be sure to tell him, Mr Blood said, and
hammered the brass service bell, Room twenty-one for Mister
Fracker—he shouted

—*Fraker*, the man softly corrected him, J. C. Fraker, and took up his
bags and started across the room toward the hallway and the stairs.

The servant met him as he entered the back hall and politely
reached to take the bags.

—Please allow me to assist you with your luggage, Mister Fraker, the porter insisted as the little man made for the stairs.

—Let go my property! Fraker hissed, pulling the bags close, and gave a shove with his elbows. I can find my own way to my room without your charge.

The man jerked back and froze as if a wedge of rattlesnake head had showed itself among rocks.

Through most of July and right down to election day, Isaac traveled the county speaking in country schoolhouses, from a wagon bed stationed at a crossroads—wherever he could gather a modest crowd of listeners—to expound the advantages of the railroad and therefore the necessity of voting for the bond issue. At the same time, there was the delicate question of the railroad right-of-way. The general route was settled, following the cattle trail, but exactly where the line entered the city of Wichita and built its depot, stockyards, and sidings involved something more than surveying and engineering. Isaac took the initiative by offering his own land. The Wichita corporate line for now ran down the middle of his claim, the west half already within the town, the east eighty acres held back according to the founders' informal agreement for a later addition, which for now he made a little money from by keeping Converse Waters to grow corn. Mr Peter wanted a two-hundred-foot right-of-way: just under thirteen acres it amounted to, Isaac calculated, sliced out of his undeveloped east eighty, but it would enhance the value of all the remaining land on both sides of the corporation line. Isaac persuaded Nathaniel English to give land for the stockyards, while John Hilton donated right-of-way north of Isaac's claim; there was little land clear to Newton that actually had to be paid for in money—the occasional obstinate farmer was brought around by a pass promising unlimited travel between the two towns.

It was early August, just before the vote on the bond issue, when Lizzie Mathewson announced that she was going south to join her husband in the Territory: they missed each other; she would manage the trading post, perhaps stay the winter, and he would have more time for traveling around, trading directly with the Indians. It was nearly a month since Isaac had been home long enough to take time for a visit with the children, and he was disappointed to find that Lucy had taken them to town in the buggy to buy household supplies. He could not object to anything that helped Mathewson in the trade, but his own part in the Indian business, on top of the railroad and his dealing in land, had become a burden. Although Mathewson was exact in settling his accounts and invariably produced an ample profit, it was the nature of the trade to tie up Isaac's money, five and ten thousand dollars, for six months at a time, and until Mathewson came in with a train of furs to sell he was frequently embarrassed for cash. Now there was the matter of farming the east half of his claim: Converse Waters could not very well cross the railroad line every day to work the land, once the railroad was through—he did not seriously consider that the bond issue might be rejected after all his efforts; did not much care to lose the little income the corn brought in, but on the other hand did not want to build another cabin over there for Waters and his family—no time to do it himself, it would mean hiring the labor, and a competent carpenter came high at Wichita now, two or more often three dollars a day.

Lizzie had a pot of fresh coffee boiling on the stove when Isaac arrived. She poured two mugs, set them on the table, politely slid the sugar bowl toward him; and informed him of her plan.

—Ought to be good for the business, of course, Isaac observed, and I can't blame husband *or* wife, wanting each other's company more than two or three times in a year. Still, Lizzie—I can't help wondering what I'll do for a woman to trust my children with—take em up to Iowa to my parents, I suppose. They say there's a good school near for them to go, and Mamie's of an age now—

—I thought Lucy would manage well enough on her own, Lizzie said. Sixteen now, though she *says* seventeen—old enough to take a woman's part when she needs to, yet not so old but she can join in their games too and enjoy them.

—I don't know that I'd like her *or* them off here by themselves, no neighbor closer'n half a mile—. But say now, he said abruptly, I've been thinking how Mister Waters can keep working my land, once the railroad's come, wanted to talk with you about it—and there's the answer.

And while Lizzie heard him out in silence, Isaac explained: Waters and his family would come over to the Mathewson cabin and work the two parcels of land together—turn Lizzie's pasture and put in sod corn, or fatten cattle for her again if she liked. And Lucy and the children would move into his own place.

Lizzie gazed steadily back, her face expressionless. At length she drained the mug and set it down with a little thump of having made her mind up to something.—Well now, Isaac, she said, There's certainly points in favor all around, only—I don't know how the four of you'd fit in your one little cabin, even if I *did* see my way to trusting my little sister's good name under the same roof with Wichita's most eligible widower.

Isaac stared in his turn, but there was nothing in her face to show she was making a rough joke in the Kansas style, and he blushed.—*Lucy?* he protested. Why, good heavens, Lizzie—if I'd married a little sooner, I could have had a daughter of my *own* her age. But listen—I'll build on another room just for her and the children, with a door and its own stove for winter—and a lock too, if that's what you want. And I can bring a sofa over from Towanda to sleep on in the main room when I'm home, which aint *that* often just now —and some of my other furnishings, fix it up nice as our first little house at Salina—. And stopped himself short, like a boy that has let himself run on too long.

—You'd better put it to Lucy when she comes, Lizzie said finally. I won't have her take a place against her inclinations—for all I know, she's tired of frontier living and wanting to go home to Mother and begin thinking of marrying. But one thing, Isaac—if you want the girl for a housekeeper, I wouldn't consent without you paid her something.

—Why, of course! Isaac meekly agreed. Whatever you think would be right.

For election day Isaac bought a wagonload of watermelons, abundant and cheap that year, for two hundred dollars, stationed himself at the Wichita polling place, and gave them out to any electors who would accept the ballot favoring the bond issue. It carried by three hundred votes.

Lizzie Mathewson packed her battered, brass-bound leather trunk and took the stage for Fort Sill a week later, driven by Isaac to the Empire House—would have started sooner but it was that long before Isaac could finish the new room to his cabin he had promised and furnish it from the Towanda place, including his own marriage bed for the girl and the two children. The Towanda ranch itself he disposed of cheaply: three hundred dollars for the buildings and claim and the loan of another two hundred to pay for the land and fees.

Lucy turned out to have been well trained by her mother and latterly by her formidable older sister: could produce acceptable biscuits, pies, and cakes, keep up with the household laundry, and knew enough sewing to provide the children's everyday garments, though nothing so difficult as the suit Lizzie had made Bissy, now outgrown and discarded. Whatever parting advice Lizzie had left her with, she seemed awed by her new responsibility: rarely addressed Isaac unless spoken to and then with downcast eyes and "Mister Pride" in every sentence; but he was too occupied with other matters to give much thought to ways of putting her at her ease.

It was the beginning of September when Isaac first heard of the toll bridge Greiffenstein was getting up to build across the cattle ford at the west end of Douglass Avenue. Jim Steele told him about it: had not gone in himself, but his partner Gerry Smith was on the list of directors; Greiffenstein had hired a Topeka lawyer to secure the cor-

porate charter. Isaac rode immediately to Greiffenstein's house. The
prospect rankled—and doubly so, that he had not had the idea himself. In the nine years now that he had been in the country, the
Arkansas every year or two had flooded over its banks in spring and
through much of the summer so that for months at a time no wagons
could cross. He thought of Colonel Titus and his little bridge at Burlingame, sitting on the porch with a toddy and watching his money
come in. Greiffenstein's bridge would be a thousand feet across anyhow and ought to be worth that much more.

—Bill! Isaac demanded when they were alone in Greiffenstein's
parlor. What in the devil are you up to with this toll bridge?

The German gazed mildly back, sucking at his pipe.—You heard
about that, did you? he said.

—About the last in town that did, it seems. Bill, you son of a bitch
—you *know* that aint how we agreed: anything touches the whole
town, we go together. Didn't I let you in on the railroad, straight off
and aboveboard, no secrets? And then worked like a mule skinner all
summer to get the bond issue past the voters?

—That railroad! Greiffenstein said with a frown and laid his pipe
aside, leaning forward. That railroad—put my name down on the
board and don't give nothing in return—and *you* got the right-of-way
through your own land, which got to be worth something, maybe.
No, it don't look to me I owe anything to man that make *that* kind of
bargain—*and* call me son of bitch. . . .

—I didn't mean that, Bill, Isaac said, ducking his head. It's just—
you know I wasn't doing that for personal benefit but the good of the
town, all of us. And now this bridge—don't seem to me that's any
different, I'm *glad* to lend a hand when another fellow's got an idea
for the general good, and if there's money in it, why—

The German nodded and considered for a time in silence.—We got
our twelve directors all made up for the charter, he said slowly.
Course the stock aint all subscribed, if you wanted in that way.

—You figure it'll pay?

—We going in it mostly for the town and the land prices—and give
the drovers more reason against taking herds to Ellsworth. But sure—
I don't know why it don't pay for itself, in a year or two, and pay
back profit.

—What can you charge?

—What they'll *pay*, Greiffenstein said with a misty smile, taking up
his pipe again. I don't know—five cents, ten cents a head, for cattle—

—That could be twenty-five hundred a season on fifty thousand
head—or double that, or double again, if the river don't run dry.

Greiffenstein nodded.—Wagons, he continued. We figure they got
to run all the year, wet or dry, and we let em cross for fifty cents

loaded—which aint anything to a man with hundred bushels wheat to sell that he don't want spoiled—and half that, coming back empty.

—Which is the same as the cattle all over again, Isaac said quickly. So we're taking in ten thousand a year, maybe twenty thousand, and nothing to spend it on but a couple of men to take tolls, and once in a while replace some worn-out planks in the roadway. What can you build it for?

—Capital is four hundred shares—forty thousand dollars. Don't figure to spend it all, but something over for upkeep. Or make money lending out on land. . . .

Isaac was silent, reflecting, his anger quieted, though he remained puzzled at the German's devious ways.—I believe I could go for fifty shares if I had my money from my Indian goods, Isaac said slowly. But that aint for months—this winter sometime.

—Sure! Greiffenstein said affably. I put you down for fifty and you take what you can—and what you don't pay, you don't get! Aint nobody paying in anyway till we get our bids—they come in too high, maybe we don't build. I figure we don't have to start till spring, like your railroad—just so we're done when the cars come through.

—Who else did you get? Isaac asked.

Greiffenstein puffed thoughtfully for a time as if checking off the names on a mental list.—For directors, he said, there's Uncle Eli Waterman—that's his land this side we got to build from, paying him five shares for the privilege and perpetual easement. And English and the two Smith brothers. And Dave Payne—

—*Buffalo Payne*, God damn it, Bill! Isaac exploded. What you want with him? I've known him since the first day I came to Kansas, and never anything but trouble, every time he turns up.

—Sure, Greiffenstein agreed, I know what you think—just kind of booms along like a big bass drum that somebody else's beating on, only—some of them farmers out in the county, they listen, and what I think is—we get him *with* us, not against. Only down for ten shares anyway, and I be surprise if he pays in so much when time comes.

—All right. Who else?

—Well now, our heaviest is a new man, says he'll take a hundred— got implement business at Emporia, and El Dorado, and farms, and the way he tells, he's the one behind this El Dorado bank starting up. So in July—you're out campaigning—he comes over, takes a room at the Empire—only stopping few days, look around, he says, and here it's two months already. And now he says: Wichita's ripe for bank of its own, and I believe him—

—What's his name?

Fraker, Greiffenstein said, James C. Fraker. Got a house rented and bringing his family and means to settle and start a bank, and I told him about you, says he wants to meet. Now, I don't know much about banks, but somebody does know, I put money in—and do the town good, too. Wouldn't you, Isaac?

XX

The Wichita Bank

Isaac on a Monday morning in mid-October went on foot to the bank meeting at the Empire House, making the circuit, four blocks from his house down Lawrence to Douglass, then two blocks over and back up Main to the hotel on the corner of Third Street. Ten o'clock they had agreed on, a leisurely banker's hour, and presumably the men from El Dorado who were to put up most of the money had come in the night before on the stage. He walked the town these days more often than he rode or drove, leaving the new horse in the barn—Towakoni Jim he had named him, a three-year-old chestnut gelding and on the big side, the first not a mare he had ever kept for personal use, brought back that summer from Topeka and cost him a hundred and fifty dollars; a horse men turned to look at in admiration when you rode past but never with the breathtaking wonder Singing Bird had stirred, the horse was only a means of getting around, a little better than most, not a creature to feel attachment for.

When a man came looking at lots, of course, he took the buggy and made the rounds with Old Tom in the traces, knew the stops by now about as well a milk-wagon horse, and how long to wait while Isaac talked.

The important thing, Isaac had discovered in this new business, was simply to keep on talking till you came on the particular truth the other fellow was looking for. The visitor in time would let out what he really wanted and meant to pay, if he was serious, and Isaac more often than not could show him just the piece of ground that would satisfy and come to agreement.

The City of Wichita Isaac extolled on these tours was still largely the city of his imagination. The churches were not yet started—the Methodists had fallen into factions and some now talked of giving their lots back and building elsewhere; the school Bissy attended, two blocks from home, amounted to no more than the first little sod-roof picket cabin they had put up two years ago over by the Little Arkansas, already pulled down for the windows, doors, and firewood. Yet everywhere on that fall morning came the sounds of the actual city rising, the random metallic thump of hammers driving nails, the rasping whisper of handsaws, the creak and whinny of the wagonloads of lumber and millwork and kegs of nails moving along the dusty streets.

That was why more often than not he made his rounds on foot: the sights and sounds of the city growing from day to day and the little useful things that came into a man's head, moving at that slow pace, such as trees—the absence of trees along the streets and how the summer days burned and sweltered without them, and maybe if he could find a good source for seedling elms, say, he could offer three or four to any who bought a lot. Before God truly in his life he had never known feeling to equal it for strength, day by day waking in the mornings to go out and walk the town in the delight of it: the rising city belonged to him, or the best part of it, to shape and put his mark on, like a farmer shaping his land to his tilth—the exhilarating pleasure, he recognized, that had drawn his own father to Iowa in the hope of himself becoming a city-builder after the generations of life in a city already entirely built by others past and nothing much more to be done, like a fine painting with only a touch of color here and there still to be put in; and the disappointment ever after, that was the look he remembered in his father's eyes at Rockingham, the county-seat-to-be come to nothing, he had seen the old plats in the county recorder's office at Davenport, the lots laid out for warehouses and mills along the river, all now abandoned. Davenport was twenty years old when it got its railroad, he remembered the fireworks and the church bells ringing, the celebration; Wichita would be hardly two.

He wished his father here to see: what he had started, his son was finishing. When this bank meeting was over he would go home and write, invite him—grand if he could come down on the first train to Wichita, though it might not be till April or May, the way Mr Peter was talking; but had to be finished in time for the opening of the cattle season.

Isaac turned up Main Street, Greiffenstein's land: the Southern Hotel, a cigarmaker and a restaurant, a liquor wholesaler, a tinsmith and stove merchant; better built up than Isaac's commercial blocks on Lawrence, but the merchants had taken only every other lot—looked like a man with a sick mouth, half his teeth missing—and left the intervening lots to throw their garbage and feed their pigs, and only the Southern was all saw lumber and painted, on the front, two stories high, the rest built from the dwindling stock of cottonwood logs along the Little Arkansas. There was not yet a sidewalk anywhere in town, except in front of the Empire, and when the wind blew the dust chased along the half-built streets: bright days now in October, Indian summer, cool at night, but the wind still blew and the dust clouds raced. Isaac in his forthright efforts at selling property had made, repeated, and elaborated jokes about the wind and the dust: Wichita real estate is moving nicely just now and, if wanted, will be found along the coast of the Gulf of Mexico or in the Yucatan; but wait a day or two and it will be back, at the corner of Douglass and Main.

The half of Isaac's land that so far was in the town divided into sixteen long blocks, six hundred by three hundred feet, with a narrow alley down the middle of each—that had been Bill Greiffenstein's idea, said it was how they laid out a town in Prussia where he came from. He had calculated it to go commercial on the outside avenues and divided the frontage into thirty-foot lots, except twenty-fives on Douglass; and the interior streets in fifties, for houses, with room for a vegetable patch and a stable on the alley at the back, though most who meant to build wanted at least two lots. It came to nearly three hundred residential lots and half as many commercial but about the same in money, say thirty-five thousand each if all sold, since naturally he could ask more for commercial property. He and Dutch Bill were the only ones so far doing much trade—Mr English a little on his side of Douglass, but Hilton and Munger were just not in it. Isaac had given title on nearly half his Douglass Avenue lots, at good prices, though none yet over where the depot was to be; and about a third of the rest. Sixteen thousand dollars it footed up to and another twenty-five hundred on time, two and three years at ten percent— often at the end of the week as the money flowed in he had ridden the hundred miles to Emporia with his saddlebags stuffed with gold and paper, to get the money banked and earning. He would no longer have to carry his money to Emporia for deposit, anyhow, now Mr Fraker and the El Dorado people had gone ahead with their little Wichita bank, though in the month since it opened he had done little business there and had yet to transfer his funds.

All this was rational, it was how he consciously thought of his land dealings, with calculation, yet looked at another way it was only a kind of play, not the reality of trading—you sat in the chief's tent and gravely smoked, making compliments, and the women carried trays of choice buffalo meat, and you came to agreement—so many cups of sugar and coffee and flour and yards of cloth for a robe, you came with a load of goods to trade and you went away with a load about equal in weight and volume, and it was all real, a real exchange; though of course in another part of your mind you carried at the same time the abstractions of money, what the goods cost you, what the robes and furs were bringing just now. But the land business was at a remove, abstracted from that clear reality—it was all paper, words and numbers on paper, not land itself but a plat ruled in the rectangles of streets and blocks and numbered lots, and a man wanted one of those little rectangles for his own and gave bank notes and greenbacks and sometimes gold, one dollar and other valuable consideration, and you gave him for his money a piece of paper written out in proper legal form by Henry Sluss or one of the others doing Isaac's legal work: *To all people to whom these presents shall come, Greeting . . . All that certain piece, parcel or tract of land . . . To have and to hold the above granted and bargained premises . . . unto the said grantee, and unto his heirs and assigns, forever, to them and their own proper use and behoof;* and carried the deed to Mr McIvory, the registrar, to make abstract of and record in his book.

Forever: sometimes in the night lying on the sofa in the main room of his house Isaac had a kind of vision: the plat of his addition, Pride's Addition to the City of Wichita, spread out on a table and covered with a pyramid of money, then the west wind blew, and the money lifted and scattered, swirling across the Plains like dust. Nothing human is forever, not man's written symbols of permanence, whatever they claim, not perhaps the land itself—certainly not what a man makes of it.

That was part of the reason he had been free in giving his land, the church lots and the school, the railroad right-of-way and depot, and uneasy too, as if even in giving he was putting something over, offering an only pretended value that had cost him $1.25 an acre and a little work and time and now through the mystery of other men's wanting would very likely bring a thousand; and the other part of course, the calculation, reasoned and conscious, that what he gave free would make up by enhancing the value of what remained.

All the past summer the money had come in fast enough, and would again next summer when the railroad came and no doubt another year or two after that; and went out again nearly as quick, and when it was gone there would come no more, as if carried away by the Kansas wind of his bad dream. The necessity now, therefore, was to find things to put his money in as it came so it would stay together and go on making money. He had raised his subscription in the bridge company to a hundred shares, the same as Mr Fraker, and paid in enough in cash for the St Louis engineering firm to send men to do surveys and plan the design. Greiffenstein and the others were more cautious—Bill planning another big hotel, this time on Douglass at Water Street, two blocks from the bridge, to be closer to the cattle trade—but Isaac figured the bridge to earn back its cost in two years and thereafter to pay thirty or forty percent, good even by Kansas standards; if his guess at the construction cost was anywhere near right.

Another five thousand had gone out in goods to supply Mathewson at his trading post—paid well enough, but slow and not without risk, and that trade too would come to an end, the buffalo fewer every year. The Indians would not outlast the buffalo, and then the white hunters would finish off the strays, bringing in not the beautiful Indian robes worth twenty or thirty dollars apiece but only their own green hides to sell by the pound for cheap shoe leather, and the more they brought in, the lower the prices went. The Kiowa anyhow looked to be about finished, fiercest of the lot that no one on the Plains thought would ever give in. It was Satanta that did for them, wanting to be the great chief over all, and finally the people trusted him and followed, or a lot of them, the young men, wanting to know war, and now he was done for and they were left with no one to follow. Satanta had been on the reservation two years since Custer brought him in, stood it peaceable enough, going in to the agency every week or so for his rations of beef and flour, taking a new wife and getting a child on her. And then this very spring of 1871 he got up a party of young men that had never been in a real fight and took the road to Texas, just like the old days, and old Satank went along and that young chief Ado-e-et-te, Big Tree, that thought himself such a catch and hated Pat-so-gate because she wouldn't have him. In Texas they came on a mule train hauling supplies for the Army and the young men got their fight: tore the train up pretty thoroughly, killed seven drivers and stripped them, cut them up and took the scalps, and got clean away. But Satanta couldn't leave it at that: got back to Fort Sill and boasted to the agent how he'd showed his men some fighting all right. Only the agent he made his boast to was a new one, Laurie Tatum, a very plain Iowa Quaker that had never set hand to any weapon more threatening than a coffee spoon. So all Mr Tatum did was to have the soldiers arrest them, Satanta, Satank, and Big Tree, and take them off to Texas in chains to be tried for murder, each locked in a separate ambulance. Satank got loose and got himself killed the first day out from Fort Sill, buried beside the road, but the others were tried and sentenced to hang. And then such a cry! and petitions for justice to the Indians, and talk how the Kiowa would be worse than ever without their leader Satanta to keep them in line— just the kind of thing he was claiming himself, ever since Dohasan died and left the tribe with no head chief. In the end the governor commuted to life: Satanta and Big Tree packed off to a very ordinary Texas prison.

That was the past: Satanta and the old unchanging ways of the Kiowa, finished—and buffalo hunting and Indian trading would follow, and anything else that could not change and make way for the new time coming. But if all that was past, the question remained whether this bank was the future, for Isaac and his land that was turning into money: even now, walking to the meeting at which they were to settle on terms and swear their names to the papers that would create a national bank of Wichita according to law, he considered that he had not made up his mind to it one way or other. He was persuaded in a general way that the city, to grow and make something of itself, needed a bank no less than it needed the railroad and the bridge and merchants to supply the cattlemen—and lumber yards, a register of deeds, a court and lawyers and the U.S. Land Office, promised for the spring, and all the rest—but did not understand very specifically, as he understood the town's other enterprises, the kind of work a banker actually did.

The common wisdom concerning banks was that they only had money to lend at reasonable rates in easy times, when no one needed it; but let the times be tight, there was none to be had at any price—nor extensions on notes and mortgages to carry a man through till he was earning his way again. That matched with what Isaac knew from his own experience: Ebenezer Cook at Davenport ruining the mill in order to hold his father to a discounted note carelessly given and made worthless by fraud, because that was law and would make a little profit. Two sides of the same business, in neither of which he could imagine himself playing any part: not laying himself open to the vengeance of a mob; certainly not stifling another man's enterprise for the sake of profit. On the other hand, if they had to have this bank, to build up the town and uphold its property values, well then, as a kind of public duty he might have to lend a hand—.

The other thing was, he did not just at the moment have much money to put in, and whatever else there might be to banking, money was its stock in trade: maybe a thousand dollars he could spare and still keep two or three thousand aside for Mathewson's needs, fresh opportunities, and ordinary living, not cheap on the frontier. By spring it would be different: property moving again and Mathewson coming in with a trainload of robes, and entirely possible the Indian office finally would settle his old claim for supplying the Konza on their move to the new reservation in the Territory, nine or ten thousand it was worth by now, with interest and expenses. Greiffenstein, however, said it was not money the bank wanted of him, Mr Fraker's El Dorado backers could supply all they needed. But if not money, what? That, really, was the unanswered question.

Mr James C. Fraker in that October of 1871 had only just turned forty, six years ahead of Isaac. Born in Indiana, he was commissioned a missionary of the Methodist Episcopal Church in 1858 and chose the year-old town of Emporia in Breckenridge County as the field of his labors. A year later, married, he forsook the cloth, a decision that in later years he attributed to delicate health, though the dilemma he faced was no different from that of many another missioner, such as Isaac's own father, the impossibility of supporting a family on his stipend. Mr Fraker remained, however, a very proper, earnest, moral man.

He acquired land near Emporia, tried cattle-feeding, then wheat, and prospered; turned his profits to dealing in farm implements—the Civil War did not greatly inhibit Kansas immigration, and Northern factories not adapted to producing weapons responded to the shortage of farmhands with a continuous flow of improved mowers, reapers, harvesters, and threshers exactly suited to the broad, level fields of the prairie counties. When the war ended, he left a brother in charge of the business and a substantial warehouse at Emporia, and followed the frontier south to El Dorado, just outside the limits of Osage land, and repeated the process: bought a dozen town lots as a speculation, claimed land nearby to farm, and brought in machines to sell. About the time Wichita was beginning to look like a town, he joined with others at El Dorado in organizing the first state-chartered bank in southwest Kansas, which they named the Walnut Valley Bank. It was a sequence that might well give a man exaggerated notions of his own perspicacity, but Mr Fraker remained, to all appearances, a very modest, moral man. And is there after all any fundamental difference between dealing in land or machines and dealing in the money with which both finally must be paid?

So in July 1871 Mr Fraker came on to Wichita to look things over; stayed a few days at the Empire; departed and returned in September to commence business in a narrow store front on Main Street north of First, with the name The Wichita Bank painted in chaste white letters across the show window, a modest stock of money for loans, and himself as president, cashier, and principal clerk. The bank presumably had been chartered under state law; its capital, it was said, was supplied by the partners at El Dorado. It was never known if the idea was his or theirs, but the opportunity was obvious to anyone who had observed the connection between moneylending and the cattle trade, at Abilene and lately at Ellsworth and Newton. Mr Fraker, at any rate, gave every sign of intending to stay: had rented for now a small house on Water Street a block from his office and brought his wife and children but also had put money on a two-acre tract across Central Avenue from Isaac's reserve and of the exact size, where he meant to build a suitable home. It did not seem that Mr Fraker in personal matters possessed great imagination: had looked on Isaac and the other founders and only meant to furnish himself a situation and a dwelling as ample as theirs.

There was really no limit to the information a man could pick up, making the rounds of his city, if he talked to his neighbors, and listened. The banker himself Isaac had met only two or three times, informally, never for serious discussion; it was Greiffenstein that persuaded him to attend the meeting, telling something of the bank's plan to reorganize and enlarge its business. Isaac had agreed to come and listen but had promised nothing.

The door opened to Isaac's second knock and—Come in, come in, Mister Pride! We was just starting, all our official papers spread out to examine and approve of, and very punctual you are indeed, I must say, as behooves a railroad man!—and closed softly behind him: Mr Fraker moved with hasty, nervous energy and spoke in a kind of whisper of downcast, desperate earnestness. Behind him, one of the Empire's better rooms, looking down on Main Street, with the bed shoved back against the window and a table carried up from the dining room, three men were seated in plush-upholstered straight chairs: Greiffenstein, long-faced and inscrutable, and two that must be the investors from the El Dorado bank, a young man of perhaps twenty-five and an older one, full-bearded, dark, and severe on whom Isaac lingered for a moment—something threatening and absolute about him, immovable, yet just because of that to be trusted as one not likely to give his word without meaning to keep it.

Mr Fraker was breaking in with introductions. The young man was Mr Albert H. Gossard, not intending to become an investor himself, not yet, but here to represent the interests of his father and uncle, Mr William P. and Mr John G. Gossard, stayed at El Dorado to see to their bank matters and besides, elderly gentlemen both, did not much care to travel about by public conveyance. The older man was James S. Danford, cashier at the Walnut Valley and meant to go in heavy at Wichita, but equally important, proposed to spend half his time at the new bank for the first few months or year, overseeing the daily operations—at a reasonable salary to be agreed, of course—till he was satisfied things were going smooth and young Gossard ready to take up his appointment as cashier and his father's seat on the board of directors; but would start as assistant cashier—that much was agreed and indeed a condition on which the elder Gossards would put money in. And Mr Greiffenstein, of course, Mr William Greiffenstein, Mr Pride already knew by long acquaintance. Isaac pulled out the empty chair and sat.

The papers Mr Fraker had referred to were standard forms furnished by the Comptroller of the Currency, elegantly printed in script, with blanks to fill in. Isaac drew them to him and scanned the pages while the banker talked steadily, explaining and commenting in his breathy voice. There were four of them, each on heavy paper that had the crisp feel of money: an Organization Certificate in which a fluent hand, evidently Mr Fraker's, had already written the bank's name, First National of Wichita, and its capitalization, fifty thousand dollars in five hundred shares; Articles of Association, bylaws; a Certificate of Officers and Directors, naming them and giving their official signatures; and finally an Oath of Directors, in which each swore that he would uphold the banking law and was the bona fide owner of the number of shares credited to him in the bank's record book.

Isaac turned back to the Organization Certificate. Article Four was a long page ruled in three columns for the names of the directors, their places of residence, and the number of shares held by each. Mr Fraker had written in the names—his own, the two elder Gossards, Danford, Greiffenstein, and I. A. Pride at the end of the list—but had left blanks for the numbers of shares.

—Fifty thousand dollars, Isaac said pleasantly. That's a good sum of money—more'n I've ever had my hands on at one time.

—Fifty thousand's the minimum to start a national bank on, Mr Danford answered in his threatening basso. If Wichita was more of a town, law says the capital'd have to be bigger.

—And how much did you figure me for? Isaac continued, keeping his eyes on Mr Fraker. Supposing I conclude to go in—. Matter of fact, I wasn't aware I'd given anyone authority to put my name down.

—That's up to you, Mister Pride, Mr Fraker said quickly, entirely up to you—but there aint that much stock left unsubscribed, though we're provided in our charter to enlarge capital at some future date, the Lord willing and we're all spared, but—. Well now: the Gossards, Mister William and Mister John, they're set on a hundred shares each, and Mister Danford here the same. And I would very much like a hundred for myself—

—That leaves a hundred over, Isaac said. How many're you good for, Bill?

—I take half, Greiffenstein answered after a pause. Fifty shares.

—So five thousand dollars, Isaac said. There's a lot of things I could do with five thousand dollars. What kind of return you figure to pay?

Mr Fraker drew breath and puffed his cheeks out like a toad preparing to snap a fly.—A very good question, Mister Pride, and let me say —and pardon if it takes a little talking through to answer—. We pay in our capital of fifty thousand and put it on deposit with the Comptroller, and he allows us our ninety percent in bank notes—

—That's forty-five thousand.

—Forty-five thousand, circulating money, and then depositors come in, say another *two hundred* thousand—nothing to say it mightn't go two fifty or three hundred, but taking it cautious and conservative, and allowing for—. Say two hundred forty-five thousand dollars assets to trade with—

—Deposits aint assets, Mister Fraker, Danford growled, they're *liabilities*—got to be paid back.

—Of *course*, Fraker agreed, and have to pay interest too, so we can't let em lie idle, got to put em to work. So they're *resources*, to make money on, for the benefit of them as puts their trust. Now, Kansas interest is ten percent, and some of our *resources* we let out at that rate, on good security. But take cattle—man comes in and got to pay off his crew and send them home to Texas, so he borrows. And ships his cattle to Philadelphia or New York for the best price and got to pay the freight, he borrows again. And say it takes him six months to sell and pay off, that's nine percent at the going rate, eighteen a year. Or he only uses the money three months, he pays *seven* percent, that's— that's—

—Twenty-eight percent annual.

—Twenty-eight percent, Mr Fraker agreed, not looking at Isaac. But of course we can't get that on everything we lend. And there's expenses—salaries and stationery and postage and suitable premises, though we can rent part and make that come out even. And interest to pay on deposits at six percent. And prudent reserves on our circulation, and allowances for profit and loss—. But take it all in all, I don't know why we can't come out with ten thousand clear, or twelve thousand, in a average year. So on fifty shares—

—That's twenty or twenty-four percent, Isaac said. Nearly as good as I figure our bridge stock for, so I wish you could put me down for fifty shares, only—

—Law don't allow us to put you down for a director without you take *some* stock, Mr Danford said.

—Well then, Isaac said, that being the case—and point's well taken, I'm sure—I'd best let you go along without me—not that you've got any great need of the little money I can spare just now in any case. Then in the spring we'll see how you're going, and if you've stock to spare or you decide to enlarge, like your Articles say you can, why, maybe I would go in for five or ten thousand—for the good of the town and the bank, and make a little money back on it for myself. But I don't anyhow see why you want me sitting on your board. You gentlemen know something of this trade. Me, I don't know any more of banking than—I don't know, than piloting a steamboat across the seas to China!

He straightened up and shoved his chair back as if preparing to excuse himself.

—Now just a *moment*, Mister Pride! Mr Fraker said, restraining him with a plump and urgent hand. The sentiment does you proud, and handsomely expressed it is, I may say, but altogether too modest— yes, entirely so. For it's our view, Mister Pride, you have an important and, let me say, decisive part to play on our board. If I may put it so—

—Fact is, Mr Danford broke in with an irritable shake of his head, getting this charter past the Comptroller aint any Sunday evening church social. We sign our names and send it in, we aint any more to him than five country folks away out beyond the frontier of civilization, and he won't pay any more mind than—

—But if it carries endorsements, Mr Fraker continued, from responsible gentlemen mighty in the councils of the Republican Party—

—The Kansas Senators and our Congressman—

—Listen here, Isaac, Greiffenstein said, speaking up for the first time. Aint nobody in this room's had your advantages for this job—maybe in all Wichita: two terms in the legislature—and friends with every governor since Robinson—and controlling the county convention, and *state* convention, two years running—

Isaac silenced him with a faint smile.—All right, Bill, he said, I got you. All you want is for me to go to old Pommy Pomeroy and Alex Caldwell and Congressman Lowe and persuade em to put a little of the fear of God and the Republican Party into this Comptroller. And then go lobby your charter through Washington. . . .

There was a stealthy shifting of posteriors around the table, signifying assent.

—But it may be, gentlemen, Isaac resumed, you're asking more than you know. Sure, I'm acquainted with the Kansas delegation—Pomeroy longer'n the others, and maybe he'd remember he owed me a little thing or two. But there's just the thing, Gentlemen: aint any little favor I can ask those men but they'll come back and want something in return, and maybe more'n a man intended to give. It's why I didn't go on with politics. And you don't pay back when the time comes, you'll never have credit with em again, and a whole lot worse, as opportunity affords. . . .

—I'm sure, Mr Fraker said, breaking the silence, the Board would authorize any reasonable recompense, expressing gratitude for assistance rendered, as you might say. Within the law, of course, and sound business practice. And your expenses to Washington—

—Law! Isaac said. Those men are law*makers*. They don't stand on any little fine points of right and wrong. But no—you'll just have to let me go and trust my judgment, what I can promise, or I can't. But there, you see, gentlemen! You're asking me to put my hand in the fire. I've got to have a little more in return than just the opportunity to give my money for your stock.

—We can't give it free, Mr Danford said. We give our oath—every share on the books is paid for and truly owned.

—Aint asking you to give—just in the spring, when I've money coming in, sell me anything up to a hundred shares, out of what you all take now. At the initial price, of course, a hundred each. Will you do it?

—That's a complicated business to reduce to writing, Mr Danford said doubtfully.

—Don't have to *write* it, Isaac said. When I give my word, I reckon to have the same of you. Do I?

There was a murmur of acquiescence.

—How about you, Mister Gossard? Isaac said, turning to the younger man. You speaking for your father and uncle?

—I am authorized, he said, swallowing. Yes—we will get up the hundred shares among us, when you are prepared to take them, in the spring—

—How many you good for *now*, Mister Pride? Mr Danford demanded.

Isaac waited, not thinking, turning the numbers over in his mind, but to let the others appreciate: he would come in on his own terms or not at all.—Ten, he said quietly. A thousand dollars.

—That leaves us forty short of our minimum, Mr Danford said—couldn't start business. We could try Sol Kohn, take him in. Or go back to the Gossards—. He turned heavy-browed questioning eyes on young Albert Gossard.

—I'll take up the forty, Mr Fraker said softly. Understood I'm the first to sell, when Mister Pride comes in heavy in the spring. At a hundred, of course, at the initial price.

Mr Danford gave a wary lift to his shoulders.—Anything else, Mister Pride? he said, finding Isaac's eyes with his own.

—Well now, since you're *asking*, Isaac said. Yes, if I'm to take my chances with the politicians, I believe I'd fancy something a little more official in the company than just a seat on your board—

—President aint to offer, Mr Danford said quickly. It's already taken.

—No, Isaac agreed, and I doubt I'd give satisfaction. But in the Articles there's *vice*-president mentioned.

—Of course, of *course*, Mr Fraker said with enthusiasm. Shall we consider Mister Pride elected and write his name in? he concluded with a smiling, downcast glance around the table.

The men's voices mingled in agreement. Isaac stood up, reached, and soberly shook hands all around.

—Course you understand, Mister Pride, Mr Danford said, it can't pay anything much beyond ordinary directors' fees, not at the start—

Isaac turned this objection aside with a smiling wave of his hand.—Since we are starting, he said, what's our first step?

—Why, I believe we can finish our morning's work by putting our names to our papers, Mr Fraker said. If someone could go and invite Mister Steele to come and notarize—and bring his official seal—.

Greiffenstein silently left the room on this errand. The others rose and stood back from the table. The president collected the documents, resorted them, and laid them out in order in four neat piles. He brought out a pen and ink pot, dipped ink and prepared to sign, then remembered—waiting for the notary—and nervously fell to turning the pages over, pausing to write Isaac's name as vice-president in the appropriate blanks.

After preparing the way with letters, Isaac began his journey of persuasion on November 1 with several days at Topeka and polite calls on Cy Holliday, Bob Stevens, Sam Crawford, and the current governor, Jim Harvey. He went on to Leavenworth and secured a carefully written letter of endorsement from Senator Caldwell, then down to Fort Scott where Congressman Lowe granted him a brief note urging the Comptroller to approve the bank's application. He continued to Washington—Sam Pomeroy made his main home there and rarely visited Kansas and the sizable estate he had assembled from railroad and Indian land, except at election time.

Isaac the afternoon he got in went to the Senator's house near the Capitol and after a quarter-hour's wait was shown into the warmly draped, lamplit parlor. It was some years since they had met, but Pomeroy not only remembered his name and something of his affairs in Butler County and at Wichita but addressed him politely as "Senator": Pomeroy stone-bald by now, the long fringe of hair, the heavy brows and bulging side-whiskers turned a uniform gray; only the practiced benignity of his expression, shaping the smooth-fleshed contours of his face, was entirely unchanged, the look of the deacon and Sunday-school superintendent he may once have been, grown old in service but not poor. The Senator wasted only a minute or two on Kansas gossip—had his own sources of information—though he showed a certain interest in Wichita's promising fortunes. Isaac stated his business and spread the bank documents on the Senator's desk.

—Seem to be all in order, Pomeroy said after glancing through the papers, yes, very much. And of course your town needs a solid bank —*Kansas* has need of banks everywhere. No reason at all that I can see why the Comptroller should make any objection or delay—.

In that case, Isaac suggested, for the sake of his fellow citizens of Kansas, perhaps the Senator could find a few moments of his time, in the midst of his many duties to present the bank's application to Mr Hiland R. Hulburd, the Comptroller—

—Why, of course I could do that, Pomeroy said, for Kansas. But I hardly think—here!—

Pulling out a small notehead of the United States Senate Chamber, he wrote, in a large, untidy scrawl—

Mr Hurlbut
Compt of Currency
Sir
I herewith
present Papers in case
of Nat. Bank at Wichita
Kansas— and recom-
-mend they be ac-
-epted— as They are
evry way right

and unlike his two Kansas colleagues, who signed themselves "very respectfully," "yours very truly," put only his name at the bottom, S. C. Pomeroy, in the same emphatic, self-assured hand.

—There now! the Senator said, blotting the note and handing it to Isaac. And if that don't fetch him, Mister Pride, why you come back here and tell me, and *then* we'll see—. For a moment his face was hard. Then it gentled again, he talked politely for a minute or two longer about Wichita's prospects and Isaac's partners in the bank, whose names and peculiarities, perhaps, would earn entries in the very confidential notebook he was said to keep. Rising, he suggested Isaac meet him that evening at the levee at the President's House, and he would introduce him to General Grant; and dismissed his visitor with a soft handshake and a saintly smile.

Isaac went away dazed at the ease of the thing, so much so that he hardly noticed, passing out through the entry hall, a tall, bearded man descending the stair from an upper floor of the house who greeted him with a curt and silent nod. It was not till he was driving in a cab to call at the Treasury building that he realized it could only have been Dave Kilbourn; and that Dave must have seen the letter he had written Pomeroy three weeks back and refrained from interfering—or perhaps more likely the Senator for reasons of his own had deemed it politic to support the bank and had overruled his secretary. It took him a little longer, thinking over the few words Pomeroy had let fall in the course of the interview, to work out what those reasons must be: that the Comptroller had incurred his displeasure, that he had a candidate of his own before the Secretary of the Treasury and the appropriate committees on which he sat, and that Isaac could be useful to that end; he went now, with the letter, as Senator Pomeroy's emissary—a test, a dare, the bait for a complicated little trap. Politics, but lucky too, he still had his luck.

That night, flushed with the President's handshake and the crowd trampling the worn carpet around the punch bowl in the great public parlor at the White House, Isaac wrote to his father on the elegant stationery of the Willard Hotel—he saw no good reason why an officer of the First National Bank of Wichita should not be dignified by a night at the capital's best hotel before taking the cars home to Kansas:

My Dear Father—

I have come through to Washington to see to passage of our Bank Charter, appears there will be no objecton and will comence buisness First of year— Of course we have some now but no Currency. Starting back in morning and would go by way Davenport and visit, if time permited—

I wish you to think if you have money idle you can put in Stock of our Bank, or Mother and Lizzie too—now I can obtain Shares at par where when we commence they will surely rise—Say 5.000$, which is 50 shares secured by deposit of Treasury bonds, I see no reason why they should not return you 1.000$ per Annum on that sum, the way the town is growing and cattle shipping coming our way with our Rail Road— Can you do so well from Farming? My thought is only, to secure you some ease in your advancing years—

Of course a bank's prosperity is the prosperity of its Town, I wish you come and see for yourself how we prosper—make us a visit for Christmas and see your Grandchildren who are grown a handsome young gentleman and lady. Of course I still live in my little cabin I built to hold my claim—wings added for comfort and convenence but we can make you comfortable, you have been a Pioneer in your time your self, Have you not? Also a chance to hunt Buffalo if near, Mr Peet and my men will organize a hunt if you like—

But think about best use for your money— Where in Iowa now can you earn Twenty Percent on money, secure?

Will obtain pass for Rail Road to carry you to Newton and send, if I can—it is only a morning by the coach 'til our branch is built.

Excuse this rambling letter, I have not leisure to order my Thoughts—

Your loving Son, in haste
Isaac A. Pride.

There was another thought about the bank stock that Isaac neglected to mention. Of course the main thing was to help his parents to security through a good return on a safe investment. On the other hand, now that there seemed to be no further obstacle to the bank's charter—Pomeroy's curt little note had worked like a magic passkey, unlocking the multiple doors into the bureaucracy, and Mr Hulburd had been most courteous and encouraging—Isaac felt great urgency about getting his stock immediately, not waiting till his money came, in the spring, so as to have a perhaps decisive say in the bank's affairs from the start: how better than by buying on behalf of his parents and sister? He would have to take it in his own name of course, that was how he understood the agreement, and would have the voting of it, but there was nothing against transferring it in due course to members of his family. He had a kind of vision of the five hundred shares in their combinations: the others had promised to make up another hundred from their own, in addition to his initial ten, and probably Fraker would unload his extra forty first, which he had seemed reluctant to take on, and the rest from the two elder Gossards; so his extra ten would be deciding—a hundred and ten shares that he controlled if not owned, and Greiffenstein's fifty, and Danford's hundred, that made a majority on any matter where it came down to a fight. He inclined to trust the El Dorado cashier in anything serious, just because he made no effort to be likable, agreeable; the Gossards—he still had not met them, they had not come to Wichita to sign the Organization Certificate and Articles of Association till after he had left for Topeka, and the completed documents had to be sent on to him at Leavenworth—impressed him as old men interested only in a peaceable return on their capital, while young Albert Gossard was too young and inexperienced to carry solid weight as an ally. Fraker, a little excitable perhaps, certainly showed energy and sense in matters of business but kept his inner thoughts to himself in a way that made him difficult to judge and weigh. Presumably he knew his way around the workings of a bank, or Danford and the Gossards would not have put their money behind him.

There had been a by-election while Isaac was away, Dave Payne running as a Democrat to fill out the term of Sedgwick County representative to the lower house of the legislature, against Henry Sluss, whom Isaac had induced to lend his name as corporate secretary of the branch railroad and now gave all his title business and other legal work. Payne, it seemed, had won, a surprise considering how rarely the Democrats carried anything outside a few of the old Missouri-border counties in east Kansas.

Sluss drove to Isaac's house the morning after he got back, in high indignation over ballot-stuffing, fictitious voter lists, lost records, and other irregularities, of which he claimed to have proof, as if he had discovered practices unheard of in Kansas politics.

Isaac listened sympathetically, though with several other matters pressing for his attention that morning. What did Henry propose to do about it?

The lawyer, thoroughly rattled, seemed to be trying to go off in several directions at once: he would petition the governor, place his evidence before the legislature and demand that they refuse to seat Mr Payne; file suit to have the election nullified by court order and rerun—

—Now in the first place, Henry, Isaac broke in, elections aint Jim Harvey's job, that's the secretary of state—and not much he can do when a county election board certifies a result, except ask em to go back and make sure they counted right and send it in again. And the legislature—well, you send your evidence to the speaker, and he'll hand it along to the Committee on Credentials—and the only kind of election fraud really upsets them is too much money being passed out to the electors, cause they wish they had it themselves, which I take it you aint prepared to prove. And in a year or two they come in with their report—Well, they say, it does appear there were questions raised, and things here and there not quite proper about that election —but on the other hand, we haven't any wish to go against the will of the people. And by then there's been a new election, and a new man in, and all your complaints and proofs don't mean a thing. And same if you go to law, I reckon, though that gets beyond what I know much about, thank God.

Henry C. Sluss was a small man of exceptional neatness, starched collar, mustaches waxed to points, hair lightly pomaded, every strand in place. Listening, he seemed to wilt all over.—Then is there nothing to be done about this outrage?

—Why sure there is, Henry! Isaac said, slapping him on the shoulder. Get yourself nominated again next year—and this time speak up so the electors can hear you, and run the rascal out of office. Buffalo Payne! You know he aint fit to run on the same track with a man like you. . . .

Sluss brooded on this for a time, gazing steadily back, calming himself.—I expect you're right—still, it does go against the grain—just don't seem fitting, to let it pass without doing *something*—

—No reason you should. Get it on record with the secretary of state—not that he'll do anything, but next year you can use it against Payne as fair as if you'd proved it in a court of law—"serious charges of fraud surrounding his earlier election"—

—All right—only I wish you'd help. A letter from you, since you know him some. . . .

Isaac considered for a time. Probably there was nothing he could do to make Dave Payne any less an enemy than he already was—or any more a one, either; and no reason anyhow why a private communication to an elected official should ever come to Payne's attention.

—Sure, I'll write, Isaac said—and stand by what I say next November, if you run—. Here, tell you: I'll come by your office this afternoon, after dinner, and look at what you've got on him. So I'll know better what to put in my letter. . . .

Abraham came the week before Christmas. It was twelve years since Isaac had seen his father face to face. He had thought and written of him as growing old, reaching a time of life deserving of ease from labor, but the reality of aging had not touched his imagination. To a man who has attained the maturity of his years, his own father seems as changeless, invulnerable, as in his heart he believes himself to be. *All others are mortal. Only I am not.*

Abraham's journey became elaborate. It was now possible to travel from Davenport to Newton by railroad, though with interruptions about every hundred miles for changes of train and line, often requiring an overnight stay. He determined to improve these stops with visits to old friends, former Iowa neighbors, acquaintances of his son's—subjects for further exchanges of letters producing an elaborate itinerary. From Cy Holliday Isaac procured and sent a pass good from Leavenworth; arranged for the best room at the American House at Newton and passage the next morning on the stage line to Wichita, in which he had put a little money.

Abraham took the cars down the west bank of the Mississippi to Hannibal, then across Missouri to St Joseph and down to Weston, paralleling the route Isaac had followed in his wagon when he first came to Kansas. At Weston he put his leather trunk on a freight sled and, invigorated by the prospect of entering new country, walked across on the Missouri River ice to put up at the Planter's House and wait for his train in the morning. The river was low, hardly half the width of the frozen Mississippi at Davenport, but it was cold, as cold as Iowa, and halfway over snow started to fall, coldest winter yet known in Kansas, everyone was saying; by morning a heavy rheum had settled on him, but he was provided with remedies—Jamaica ginger, Hostetter's bitters, a pint flask of brandy Lizzie had insisted he pack in his trunk, for emergencies. He stayed three days at the Eldridge House at Lawrence, making visits to a Yale classmate now a lumber merchant, and to a family connection from Connecticut; twelve thousand people now, nearly as populous as Davenport, and more churches; and at length took the cars south, Burlingame, Emporia, Florence, and finally Newton, and in the morning was much impressed, crowding into the coach with a dozen other travelers bound for Wichita and points south, when Mr Brown the conductor refused to take money from "Jack Pride's old dad." Isaac was waiting for him in front of the Empire House to drive him home for dinner.

Isaac was excessively occupied all through his father's visit. One day it was an icehouse to be built over near the depot site and stocked with a ton of ice hauled from the Arkansas. Another day a gentleman from Ohio arrived on the stage, bought a pair of lots, and for another eight hundred dollars contracted for a small house, to be ready in a month when he returned with his family; and departed the next day. Abruptly one morning Isaac was off on railroad business, gone four days, to Topeka, Kansas City; grading and clearing of the right-of-way was complete, the cast-iron rails stored in the railroad yard at Newton—track laying to start in February if the winter broke up, and there was hopeful talk of bringing the first cars through to Wichita by the end of April. He was home a few days, then off again, this time St Louis—something concerning the bridge over the cattle crossing, and purchasing government bonds for deposit with the Treasury; to secure the bank stock, as Abraham understood it, which certainly made the investment seem safe as his son had assured him it would be. Isaac, however, had not directly raised the question of putting money in since his father's arrival. The bank did some business already under its old name, The Wichita Bank, but was due to reopen the first Monday of January as the First National, and *then* they would see activity, Isaac said—though there was some question if the Treasury would have the bank's currency ready in time.

Abraham contrived to occupy himself. When the sun shone, he walked the town, curious, such activity, more going on than he could keep in his mind together, a sign no doubt of getting old. The cold had settled in his chest with a cough that was often painful. Every day or two fresh snow covered the ground but did not last. For heat there were three stoves going constantly in the house, the logs chinked with brick, but the drafts came through, the cold. He kept by the stove in the main room and read, a packet of books brought in his trunk, the little Wichita weekly paper, others from Davenport Mrs Pride sent in her frequent letters. He discovered a Presbyterian preacher and on Sunday mornings went to hear him, but that was all the service offered.

Abraham was divided in his mind, another sign, perhaps, of aging. On the one hand, the town growing day by day, quite literally, and his son's leading part, the people when he walked around, to the post office to send off a letter home, treated him with deference for his son's sake, best head for figures in all Kansas, they said; it should have filled him with joy, if he felt entirely himself. Yet so rough too, unfinished, everyone in haste, and Isaac resembled the place. The frontier: he heard the word often, in explanation of Kansas ways. In Iowa in the settling time they had not as he remembered it thought of themselves as planted beyond the pale of civilization but rather as bringing civilization with them, establishing the ordered New England way in fresh but compatible country—oh, hard times and inconveniences, but all to be set right in course of time as the country grew up; and not all New Englanders, of course, but a leaven in the lump. Here the people were all mixed up, from every part and several nations, no telling what to expect of a man by his looks and dress.

Isaac ran through his days without ease, without grace—said, when he had the railroad built and the bank, the bridge, the money coming in and the town built up, maybe he would settle back some, it was how they all talked. Abraham had formed, he saw, an exaggerated view of his son's life here; not that he did not seem to be dealing in large sums of money, of course. But the whole house—a cabin really, hardly bigger, and less well built, than their original Iowa one—would fit in the kitchen at Rockingham: the one main room where at night they made the sofa up in a double bed to share, and at one side a sort of shed, partitioned, a little room for the housekeeper and the children to sleep, another to eat in, and a sort of alcove with a stove for cooking.

The housekeeper Lucy was a disturbing presence, surrounding him with wordless commotion when he drew a chair to the stove to ponder a passage in *De Senectute*—Cicero, he understood, had been about his own age when he wrote it, a book he had not appreciated when young. Eighteen she gave her age once but might have been fifteen or twenty-eight, Abraham found he no longer could judge such matters. She possessed an immense bosom, indeed she bulged behind and before like a ripe plum bursting its skin; marriageable—time she was settled with a vigorous and provident young man, though none of Isaac's affair to take any hand in, so she performed the services he had hired her for. The children: he had hinted, the young woman was not raising them up, they merely grew; of course school was out, he did not see much of them, Bissy off every morning after breakfast, on his pony, or to the river with his skates and Mamie running after. Lucy, he had asked her once, do you not read? "I can read the *Vidette,*" she answered, rather pertly, referring to the little four-page Wichita weekly Isaac said he meant to replace with something more nearly worthy of a rising town. But do you never read to the children? he persisted—so improving to young minds and such a pleasure, to hear and be exposed to suitable literature, it was how Mrs Pride raised ours up—Mother Goose of course for a start, perhaps some of Hawthorne's children's tales, or try Bissy with Mr Longfellow's *Hiawatha*, Indians, you know, and see how it takes—; concerned for his grandchildren's well-being but meaning also to be kind, but she turned away without a word, toss of her ignorant young head and sway of her fleshy hips, and returned to the kitchen. It was where she was comfortable and belonged. He considered how she would fare under Mrs Pride's tutelage but concluded she would not be one of the kitchen girls who stayed long.

There was a masquerade ball a week after Abraham came: on Christmas evening, at the new school erected on Isaac's land. Isaac produced a worn-out, mismatched suit, a broken straw hat suited to a cab horse, and a corncob pipe to clamp in his teeth, and declared he was going as a Vermont Yankee, a solution Abraham considered not in the best of taste. Lucy's costume was Spanish, a black velvet gown specially made in the town, cut rather low, with a black lace shawl and her hair held up in heavy wooden combs, the dark garments contrasting pleasingly with her complexion, nearly as fair as Isaac's own. Abraham was doubly impressed. She wore the gown with ease and conviction, not at all the bulging young partlet she appeared in her workaday dress but quite the *condesa* she announced herself as. At the same time, she must be more serious and frugal than he had judged her, to have saved the price of having the gown made—ten or twenty dollars, he supposed, no judge of such matters—from the wage Isaac allowed her for keeping his house.

Isaac insisted his father go, though he would have preferred staying home to keep the fire up and read himself to sleep over Cicero. They drove the short distance crowded on the seat of the buggy under a tight-wrapped buffalo robe of special fineness, elaborately painted on the flesh side, which Isaac was then at pains to conceal when they went in, for fear it would be stolen. The music was performed by two Irishmen with more vigor than art. There were printed cards for the ladies, supplied by the *Vidette*, and Lucy soon had hers filled, much sought by the young men, and for an hour Abraham stayed with his son by the punch bowl, enjoying the patterns of movement, the colors interchanging: one of her partners was a buyer of wheat, another dealt in wholesale liquors, a third was set up in hardware, Isaac said, and the girl moved lightly among them like a dark moth on the wing, bosom and shoulders pink with her exertions and her piled hair glowing like polished brass. Any one of them, it appeared, would suit, and then of course Isaac would face the difficulty of finding another housekeeper in so small a place—far better for a man in his situation, still in his prime, to marry, not carry his grief on.

When the fiddlers started a waltz, Isaac excused himself and went to lead Lucy in the dance. Abraham found his way back to the cabin on foot. It was two o'clock when Isaac came in, arm in arm with his housekeeper and both much elated, whistling and humming together. Abraham had banked the fires for the night, made up the sofa, and enjoyed his first sleep, the cough less troublesome. Isaac turned up the lamp, bade Lucy goodnight and sweet dreams at the door to the little bedroom, and, still humming to himself, poured out a large glass of whisky to take before retiring.

Mr Peet returned in late January with a partial shipment of robes, having left half the teams and wagons with Mr Mathewson to bring up in the spring. He reported herds of buffalo fifty miles south at Round Pond, where formerly Isaac had conducted a trading station, and no Indians around, all staying quiet in winter camps on their reservations. Isaac proposed to outfit a hunting party, Mr Peet and any of the men who cared to go: raw-cure the hides and barrel up the meat, and he would take half to sell and the hunters could do what they liked with the rest. Abraham by now felt entirely well—perhaps there really was something in his son's repeated boast of the life-giving properties of the Kansas air—and laid out an extravagant sum for a sixteen-shooter Henry rifle with a box of metal cartridges. They had two wagons loaded with provisions, meaning to start the next morning, when the bank's currency and stock certificates arrived by express, both the same afternoon. The cashier lived at El Dorado, only thirty miles but mail took a week, and he had gone to Topeka: Isaac, impatient, concluded to carry the money and stock to him for signing; Abraham and the hunters departed without him.

When he returned ten days later—the Henry had not done the execution among the herds that he anticipated and hoped for—Wichita was seized in a new excitement: dividing the county, a petition gotten up by people at Newton and a vote to be held in the spring. There was a public meeting in the evening at the schoolhouse. Isaac put on his best suit and went, and Abraham accompanied him, curious, having taken his part in Scott County affairs, at home, when called to.

Three hundred men came, half the town's electors. Isaac addressed them—hardly an oration, but sober, ordered, and persuasive, given without notes, in the approved Western style, setting forth the folly and extravagance of creating two little counties out of one medium-sized one when Newton was already a railroad junction and needed no county of its own to be seat of to ensure its prosperity—and at the end they polled unanimously against division. As they were leaving, Mr Greiffenstein came up, two or three times Abraham had met him but was not at ease, too devious in his thoughts, too hidden.

—That was good speech, Isaac, the German said. Like you meant it. Folly of political rivalry—two little counties where one might hold its head up in the community of Kansas. That's good.

—*Course* I meant it, Isaac said rather sharply. I don't say what I don't mean. You don't think there's any sense cutting off the northern twenty miles of Sedgwick just to make law business and county offices for Newton. Do you, Bill?

—No, I don't, Mr Greiffenstein gravely agreed. But that aint the question. It's all settled, I thought you knew. Wichita got her bond vote and her railroad. Now Newton got to get her county seat. Didn't you never know that, Isaac? And his eyes widened in sympathetic astonishment.

Driving home from the meeting, Isaac was angry and tight-lipped, for reasons his father did not fully comprehend: worked all summer like a rooster to get the railroad bonds voted, he said, and here Dutch Bill had put another one over on him—counted his effort as nothing, and laughing in his beard all the while. He had as well have spared his pains.

Abraham had been away six weeks, truly time he was starting for home, and he would be taking the stage early in the morning to Newton, to connect with the train for Lawrence. Several times he had thought to leave but felt no urgency, and Isaac persuaded him to stay on. But there were the grape vines on the arbor to prune, each year about this time in late winter, hardly work to trust to the hired men. He had for once no building in mind, but the fences, barn, and outbuildings wanted careful looking over after the deep cold and heavy snows; if might be the house should be painted again. He did not contemplate new things so readily as he had when younger, getting old, another sign. So the evening before he was to start, trunk packed and strapped up tight, he sat with his son by the stove, Lucy and the children in bed, Isaac taking whisky in small, infrequent sips, and Abraham to be companionable his last night joined him with a very mild toddy. It did not seem they had had so much time together, an hour or two unspoken for, since he came to Wichita, and their thoughts wreathed and circled like smoke and at intervals thickened into words.

—And what's your impression, Father, Isaac said, now you're packed and ready to start for home? What do you make of us and our prospects? And when Abraham looked vague: The town, Wichita, he said. And our bank, of course.

—It does seem a place for a young man to make a solid start, Abraham said. Promising country for agriculture, what I've seen of it, when it's settled and built up—makes me think of our Iowa prairies and our own prairie farm, only a longer season, so far south. The town will surely profit by it.

—Say, listen, Father, Isaac said abruptly, why don't you and Mother come down here to live—Lizzie too, if she'd like? Sell the farm and you'd come out ahead. You're not too old for a change. . . .

He gazed at his father in the shadowy light: looked the same imposing, quiet-eyed reverend gentleman he had always known, hardly any gray yet in his hair, yet moments came back to memory from this visit—laboring out of bed in the mornings, shifting the stiff joints into place, or getting up from a chair where he had sat too long meditating on a book, coming in from woodchopping with his face set and aching hands tucked under his arms. Pain: he had known that kind himself in his winter camps, snaking through the snow after meat and hides, but you paid it no mind and it passed, but stayed longer the older you got, the human destiny.

—*Please*, Isaac, he said, shading his brow with his hand. You know not what you ask.

—Why *not?* Half your Iowa neighbors have sold out and moved to town, or handed on to their sons—wouldn't be any bigger thing, packing up for Wichita, than going into Davenport, and you'd gain by it. I'd *give* the land, any you choose that aint spoken for, and build at cost, good as you've got now, and our lumber won't be much more'n Iowa, once we can bring it the whole way by rail—

—Isaac, I have made my choices—not done all I meant and hoped, when I was your age—when I was young—but it is done. I can no more change my home than I can change my wife—. He looked his son in the eyes, embarrassed. I mean, he said, we are one, so far as two humans can be—no more than I could cut off my hands or pluck my eyes out from their sockets. It was the best I could give, and she loves the old place as well as any that is not her first home—and sometimes in the spring mornings, looking out from our hill-top, and the river in its aeons flowing, and the mist rising like the Holy Spirit of immortal God, walking upon the waters, in the first day—. He felt for a hand-kerchief, still looking, and wiped at his eyes. I shall be happy, seeing our home again, he continued quietly. It seems months since I left.

Isaac let out a snort, and Abraham, refolding the handkerchief, found his son frowning on him with the hard, appraising eyes almost of a stranger, a rival. What was it? that if *he* had been the one joining his life to hers, Mary would have had the worldly success and posi-tion he had not given her—something more like her Vermont home, perhaps even that home in fact? would not have drained the joy from her life with failed promises and hopes and made of her the cool, sharp-tongued, practical, never-pleased woman she had become? Yet if all sons judge their fathers so, in their secret hearts, then all in their strength share the like illusion, which growing old lays bare as inexo-rably as winter strips the trees of their leaves.

Isaac lowered his eyes, his face cleared, and with a little shrug he felt for his glass.—I only meant to suggest something reasonable, he said, sipping his whisky. Get your money clear from your land and your home for nothing, or nearly so, and I mean to help you all you'll let me, now I can—mustn't judge us by our dirt streets and our false-front stores, cause we're going to be the grandest city on the Plains. Money from your land—you could buy in this county at two or three dollars an acre. Or put it—put some of it—in our bank and get double the return. You thought of that?

—I *have* given thought, Isaac, but cannot see my way to it. I have the mortgage on the prairie farm due this spring—it will be paid off, some other debts. We shall be clear, owing no man, the first time since the mill went under. Some thanks to you, my son, he added with an austere inclination of his head. The beautiful robes you have sent us over the years, to sell.

—That's all well in principle, get out of debt and stay out, and I'm for it. But it depends what else there is you can do with your money. Now what're you paying for it in Iowa, ten percent? Well, you could *go on* paying ten percent, and put the cash in our bank stock that'll pay twenty-two or twenty-four—and take it now at the start at par and likely go up—and in four or five years you'll have your debts all paid *and* your capital still in hand and earning, every six months, enough to live on if you want. Or sell out and you'll find takers, I don't doubt, to pay twenty or twenty-five a share premium—I'd take it off you myself at that rate, make you an undertaking in writing, if you like. . . .

Abraham absently lifted his glass, then set it down without drinking, looking into the distance; the alternative Isaac offered was beguiling, would never have occurred to him—keep the money and earn twice from it what he was paying at the bank, and Mrs Pride had her inheritance, something over five hundred dollars put aside—. He drew back from the vision with a little shake of his head and looked his son in the eyes.

—Nothing, I suppose, can be *entirely* certain, where money is concerned, he said. I have not found it so.

—Well, of course, Isaac said impatiently. But our prospects: thirty thousand of capital paid in and the rest coming month by month in installments—and *twice* that in deposits and only just got our currency.

—But if another panic should come, such as we had in fifty-seven—no money to be had and trade dries up, and the merchants fail and their banks with them, *Western* banks—

—They don't all—depends on judgment and good managing, what they take for security, and maybe too the good will of the people they trade with. We've got reserves to carry us through anything, growing every day.

—Judgment and good managing, Abraham repeated. That is a great deal, Isaac. Are you so confident of your associates?

—Wouldn't've gone in if I wasn't, let me tell you, Isaac answered him with a self-conscious smile. They know their business, near as I can judge.

—Mister Fraker—is he ever so—voluble, so overflowing with projects? I do not doubt but he is a sound Christian gentleman, as he appears, and chosen by his church to carry the Gospel into new lands, yet I find it impossible to hold any connected conversation with him. He makes me—

—That's only his way, Father, Isaac said with a grin, and his job, too. Takes some getting used to, I grant, but it suits.

—A man full of words, Abraham said. You recall how Scripture warns us: *A fool is known by the multitude of his words.* And again: *In the multitude of words does sin come forth, but the wise man restrains his lips.*

—Now Father! Isaac said, frowning, that's too hard altogether. Danford and Fraker—I wouldn't've gone with either of em alone, but together—well, they just suit each other. Danford, he's just a bulldog where it comes to keeping our books up so we know every day where we are, and steering the bank along according to banking law and good, careful practice. And Fraker, he kind of stands above the everyday to look the whole scene over, consider what's needed and how we can serve the need, so as to make money. *Course* he's got a thousand ideas going through his head—hardly two years since this was naked prairie, and here we are, a city, but still got nearly everything to build from nothing.

—And what of yourself, Isaac?

—Why, that's the best of all, cause there I stand right between the two, hand on the rudder, you might say. Danford, if he gets a little too slow and cautious, bulldogging our assets, why I'll give a little shove to Fraker, to let out sail and turn those assets into income. And Fraker, if he gets to running along too fast and heedless, I'll lever him back in Danford's direction and hold her on the straight course. You needn't have any fears for your money when you've got me here to watch out for it. . . .

He paused and took another sip of whisky, satisfied with the direction the conversation was going: could not indeed recall when he and his father had talked so seriously and at length, on such equal terms. The arguments were practiced: on men thinking of buying at Wichita and settling, the town's prospects and the bank's; not that there was any stock to spare just yet, but the certainty that there would be in time, as the bank prospered and enlarged its capital, provided one more inducement for the sale of his land.

—It is you I am concerned for, Isaac, the heavy weight of responsibility you have taken on yourself. Do you feel yourself sufficiently prepared? Are you apt for this work?

—Oh now, look here, Father—! Isaac said, his ears flushing red. Well, I know you don't mean that derogatory, of course, but look at it from where I sit. We don't any of us know the whole business of operating this bank, but we've each got things we're good at that the others aren't—that's what I was explaining—and I reckon to carry my weight. Like getting our charter through the Comptroller—the others couldn't've done that. I'm not going in to keep the books, we've got Danford for that, we can *hire* bookkeeping—. His father opened his mouth to interject some further caution, but Isaac held him with a raised hand and pressed on. And look at it another way around, he said. Here I'm trading twelve years in Kansas now, started from nothing and worth seventy-five thousand, maybe a hundred, if I was fool enough to want to turn it all into cash. Indian trading: that aint just swapping cups of sugar and flour for robes and wolf skins. It's trust, first of all, on both sides—. But you know what's behind that? It's money, same as banking—money put out six months or a year at a time, and calculating to come back and give a return, that's the thing every trader's got to learn, if he's going to make a go—. He paused to draw breath. *Course* I don't know all there is about banking, he concluded. But it looks to me I've got a start—and I reckon to get what I don't know pretty quick, and—well, if a man was to wait till he was *really* ready when a thing comes along, I don't reckon anybody'd ever start anything.

Abraham was silent for some minutes, then cautiously—Isaac, you must not think I spoke in a spirit of detraction, he said. I *see* you have done well—perhaps I did not fully appreciate—letters hardly convey—

Isaac drained his glass in a swallow, noisily rose from his chair and turning his back went to a side table to pour himself another dram, carefully measured by eye.—That's right enough, he said. Father, you never did appreciate—nor Mother neither: nothing I ever did all my life was good enough to suit. He sat again and set the glass down with a thump on the rough floor beside him.

—Isaac, it is I who failed to please—failed to find the right way for you, when it was in my power. When I saw that you would have no call for ministering the Word, I labored to improve and add to my land, for you to have in your time, for to till the land and bring forth its fruits is also to serve God: *Replenish the earth, and subdue it, and have dominion over it.* And when I saw that the land was not to be your way—

—I knew what you were after and appreciated, if I didn't show it, all along.

—Not what I wanted, Isaac, but what God meant you for: to help and guide you in the way you were meant to go. If ever I was harsh— if I seemed so, if you thought me so—it was to turn you from the harsher judgment of the Almighty. In life we are granted opportunity to correct our faults, if so be He arm our conscience with correction. Afterward, we cannot.

—Don't Scripture teach us never to judge, not even our own self?

—*Judge not that ye be not judged.* Yet I cannot reconcile that law with the duty of a parent, who will answer for the child's fault at the Last Day—and his every failure doubled by his debt to his child. Think what I must look back on in my life, Isaac! Called with a glorious calling to plant churches in the wilderness, turn souls to God, and what good gifts have I now to lay before the throne of grace? Cast out by my own church—prevented from carrying the Word—

—Father! That's too hard altogether—why, there must be a dozen Iowa churches that you started and still going—hundreds of people you brought in, spite of all—and four hundred acres of woodland and wild prairie cleared, brought under plow and made productive. Don't you think that all weighs for something in the balance of a man's life?

—Land ill-chosen, never out of debt—to have spent my strength on that, and now, grown old—. No, if I do not—must not—judge myself, as you remind me, it may be only that strength fails me, begins to fail —that I know, whatever I have attempted, whatever failed in, I can only cry God's mercy on all my acts, when finally I stand before the judgment seat. Men in their vanity distinguish this man's intentions from another's, good consequence from evil—the difference is as nothing in His sight—all, all have failed and fallen short. All are unprofitable servants. . . .

—And make no difference between the man that takes the hungry in, sets him by his fire and feeds him, and the one that robs and murders him? Father! That don't sound like any Gospel I know. And don't you blame yourself about me, or anything I make of my life, either, cause it's mine, and I aint shy of speaking for myself when time comes. And as for how you raised me—well, I don't reckon it'd mattered how you tried to steer me, I had to get out and see and do for myself, and never'd've been worth a damn if I hadn't. But the things you taught—well, there aint much that hasn't turned out useful, one way or other, and I doubt I'll do much different with my own boy, allowing for difference of time and place and circumstance.

Isaac took a slow pull at his glass, wiped his lips with fingertips and brushed his mustaches smooth, savoring the whisky smell.

—Your mother blamed me: letting the boy run wild, she said, riding out on the prairie, hunting, alone. It has made you a man of the frontier, as they call it, rough and hard. Your ways are no longer our ways, nor your speech our speech. And yet—

—I talk the way the people talk here, so's to be understood, get em to do things when they got to be done. I know we aint elegant as Davenport or Greenwich. He lay back wearily in the chair, eyes half-closed, looking up through the rafters where the nails came through the slab roof like stars pricked in a milky sky.

—And yet beneath that harsh exterior, Isaac, I believe you are still the same trusting, innocent, gentle nature I knew in the child I reared. Some men seem born with an instinct for shrewdness, a quick perception of the smallest advantage and the means of seizing it and turning it to themselves. I have never seen or known that quality in any of our Pride men—possibly my younger brother Theodore. I do not see him enough, now he has come to manhood, to—

—Shrewd enough anyhow to do you of your inheritance and get the old home place at Greenwich for his own, Isaac said, still lying back in the chair. It was yours by right. You'd be preaching now, at the Greenwich church, like you always—

—*Please*, Isaac. It is done—it seemed right at the time, for Theodore and for us, and I had every hope our mill would prosper. Besides, we came to a settlement—

Isaac with an impatient shake of his head sat up, drank, and held the glass in both hands, looking into it.

—But I was thinking of Fred Weyerhaeuser, Abraham continued. Now *there* is a man of instinct—

—He does seem to be coming right along, Isaac gratefully agreed.

Hear of him even out here—some of our lumber that we bring in comes clear from his mill.

—I think of you these days, Isaac, and that raft of lumber you took to Saint Louis. You remember—

—That was *fourteen years* ago nearly, I don't know why you'd bring that up—I wasn't but a green boy, no experience of the world, but I took the raft down and sold every stick and brought the money—

—At prices that hardly repaid the value of the logs: because you were trusting by nature, Isaac, and shrewd men took the advantage, in every transaction. That is what I meant. It was our last hope to get through.

—Fred was along that time, you recall. We worked every sale together and he did no better'n I did—not so well. I did all I could—

—I have never blamed you, Isaac. Probably we should have failed whatever you did. The times were against us and our capital insufficient, all along—and then Mister Cook going to law with his spurious note, where if he'd had the decency to extend, even a few months. . . .

His voice trailed off. Isaac finished his drink and stood up.

—Well now, Isaac said briskly. I don't know how we've led so far from where we started but I do know—what's past is past, aint any way of changing it or setting it right. And if you're catching that stage for Newton in the morning, we'd both best be in bed. But I want to say, Father, if I wasn't plain: I've got a hundred more shares of bank stock promised me, I made that a condition of going in—I can take em in now, or any time this year at the original price. And I thought—maybe it'd suit you to get some and do yourself some good, and purchase some ease in your life. But if it don't, why, I'll still buy em in before summer's out, when I get my returns from the Territory, and it won't make any material difference to me one way or other—and I'll find other ways of helping out, as I can, when opportunity comes—.

—There now, that's my promise, he concluded, silencing his father before he could say more. And I reckon we've both talked enough for one night, and time we were in bed.

Isaac lay sleepless for hours afterward, holding his body rigid, simulating sleep lest his stirring wake his father: still angered at his refusal yet reminding himself also it was not his place nor any decent respect of son for father to force him to decision, the thought circling. It was now he resolved to build the house: so grand and spacious visitors to Wichita would go to view it—Jack Pride's place, built on buffalo hides and a good horse and a Hawken rifle, don't *that* show what a young man can make of himself in this country?—second to nothing in Kansas or Davenport, Iowa, and proper servants to keep it up. Of course it would be fall before he could think of starting on it—the bridge, the railroad, and the bank would take up every minute of time till then, not to mention money, but by fall, September or October and the cattle drive settling down—; and all the more time for careful planning, it might be on a trip to St Louis about the engineering of the bridge he could look up an architect, hire him on and set him drawing plans, though he knew already well enough what he wanted. Certainly he would tell none of them at home his plan—but keep it for a surprise, and then: why don't you all come down and make us a visit, Lizzie too? Room? of course we've room, *twenty* rooms, and our front parlor about the size of your whole house—like to invite our solid people in of an evening, believe you'd enjoy meeting them, and of course the children and their friends—.

For a moment he had a glimpse of Marie, young and slim and dark, presiding at her end of the table, serving, and the servant girl in her uniform carrying the loaded plates around to the guests. The vision faded: such a household, it made no sense without a wife at its head.

There was a sour taste in his mouth, had neglected to brush his teeth and the whisky was giving him a headache. Would the light never come? And he slept.

XXI

Pride's Reserve

The First National Bank appeared to be prospering through this accelerating spring. Mr Fraker told the directors severally that the bank's assets footed up to nearly two hundred thousand dollars and he saw no reason why they should not vote a ten percent dividend on the first six months, at the end of June, but was understandably vague as to precise figures: Mr Danford had not been able to get away from El Dorado as long or frequently as he had intended, and young Mr Gossard, the acting cashier and a principal stockholder since his father's death, had been occupied in settling the estate; since January Mr Fraker had hired and dismissed three different bookkeepers but found none satisfactory and naturally had difficulty keeping up with the day-to-day bookkeeping, on top of his other duties. He had, however, found a Mr Maxwell to start work the first Monday in June, of whom he held the highest expectations. As it happened, that was also the day scheduled for ground-breaking for the new bank building, on three of Greiffenstein's lots on the corner of First and Main a block north of Douglass, next to the modest frame structure, a former saloon, in which the bank had done business since January. The directors had approved the president's plan for a substantial brick building of two stories over a half-basement (the brick furnished from Greiffenstein's kiln at cost), to be completed for six thousand dollars. The estimate, Mr Fraker explained, was net—much of the actual cost they would get back by a long-term lease to the Masons, who wanted the second story for their hall; the basement, half below ground and enclosed by several courses of brick supporting the upper floors, would do very well as premises for the city police court and jail—the block designated on Munger's plat as Courthouse Square, three blocks north, still stood empty, along with most of the rest of his addition.

The directors were all out on the sidewalk with the new young bookkeeper, observing the ground-breaking that morning, June 3, when a gentleman approached from the direction of the Empire House, identified Mr Fraker, and presented his card: A. M. Britton, cashier of a national bank at Kansas City; and a letter from John Jay Knox, the new Comptroller of the Currency, appointing him to examine the bank. It was nine o'clock. The examiner stayed till closing at three, a careful, gray methodical man of perhaps fifty who freely questioned matters he found on the books and did not understand but avoided direct statement.

Isaac was in and out of the office all day, meeting land-lookers come down on the train, pausing to look on at the digging of the foundation for the new building, not much interested in the bank's books beyond assurance that they were properly kept, but overheard: sometime after dinner and the examiner occupying the president's room at the back and the ledgers spread around him on a table, and Mr Britton patiently explaining—had gone over all the accounts and could not get a balance, out by two hundred and twenty dollars, to be precise, and it did not appear the books had been balanced in three or four months, was that possible? And Mr Fraker drew himself up, said two hundred and twenty dollars did not appear a large amount in two hundred thousand of assets, it was little more than—well, not a large amount, they might have that much in postage stamps or damaged currency, but—putting on a look of determination—he would find the discrepancy himself if it took all night; and began a very circumstantial account of the three bookkeepers and the difficulty of obtaining qualified help in frontier Kansas, everyone new and untried, to which the examiner listened with patient attention. Isaac went out.

He looked in again just at closing. Fraker had gone home. The examiner appeared to have found an apt and agreeable pupil in the new bookkeeper, was showing him with sketches how the various ledgers should be set up, explaining with little smiles of encouragement how it would be necessary to go over all the records from the beginning in order to get his balance, say to the end of June, and then best start fresh, with new books, from July—and *keep* them up, every day, even if it meant staying through supper some nights. He nodded courteously and held out a sheet of printed paper with Isaac's signature on the back: Greiffenstein's note for $5,000, which Isaac had endorsed. Was the vice-president aware that the amount of the note equaled the amount that law, Section 29 of the National Bank Act, 1864, deemed it prudent for a bank to lend any one borrower, ten percent of its capital? And was Mr Pride aware that Mr Greiffenstein appeared as borrower or endorser, the same position under law, on several other notes, totaling—he consulted a slip of paper written over with figures—$22,066.63? Isaac was not aware but pulled up a chair and entered explanation: how Mr Greiffenstein needed cash for his new hotel, and his brick works and other projects, and had title to the Original Town and two further additions, heaviest property holder in the township according to the list of taxpayers published in the *Eagle*, and his holdings turned into cash would go *ten times* what he owed the bank, which surely was good security by any standard—. Mr Britton lifted both hands in schoolmasterly encouragement, but Isaac could think of no more to say and was uneasy. He was getting the habit of running on like Mr Fraker.

The foundations of the new building were up by the end of June. Isaac stopped by every day, sometimes staying an hour or two, and on occasion, if Mr Fraker was away, approved a small loan when he knew the party taking it. It was about this time that the president asked him to write the El Dorado directors, calling a meeting for the purpose of approving the bank's first six-month dividend, or if they preferred they could simply give their proxy; he himself so occupied he was hard put to keep up his ordinary correspondence. No reason not to make it ten percent, though, as he had been saying all along, and really they were very nearly obliged to start out with a substantial return—support their stock and assure it a ready market when the time came to enlarge their capital, as they surely must in another six months—. Isaac, curious, since the dividend had to come out of profit, wanted to know how much they had actually made. Mr Fraker leaned back in his chair, looking up at the ceiling: pay out around four thousand, he thought—the stock had been paid in at various times and would be apportioned by time, not quite all of it in even now—and set aside another thousand for the surplus fund, as the examiner, what was the gentleman's name, had advised they should— and of course cash going out for construction, and would continue all the second half of the year, but properly that was an asset account, and would grow in value too, very probably—.

But surely, Isaac insisted, if Mr Fraker was talking of paying out profit, he could say what the profit amounted to? Well, no, not precisely, not to the penny, or the dollar either—as if there were something inconsiderate, rude, in demanding such precision—but in round numbers, of course, perfectly plain; but of course the books had not been closed for June. It was a manner of talking that made Isaac impatient: numbers in their columns and combinations flowed through his mind as naturally as the breath from his lips, comforting, orderly, definite, yielding answers that were irrefutably correct, once reached—he thought sometimes of taking a hand himself at the books that had proved such a continuing annoyance, if ever he had the time and patience to master the principles—but whenever he put a question that seemed to require just such a clear, numerical answer, Mr Fraker went off into mystifications of debit and credit, profit-and-loss accounts, surplus accounts, the exchange account with the correspondent bank at St Louis, until it was difficult to put a handle on his meaning. But if number was not the very substance of the banking trade, then what was?

The little man now rose, went on tiptoe to the door of his room, looked out, softly closed it, and resumed his seat. Lowering his voice and in strictest confidence, he said, he explained that he had been looking over the books himself with some care and was astonished and dismayed to discover that Mr Maxwell still had not brought them up—really had demonstrated no greater diligence or competence than his three predecessors. He would have to be let go at the end of the month.

—Then what we going to do? Can't run a bank if we can't keep our books accurate.

—I know, I *know*, Fraker agreed, earnestly clasping his hands. Mister Albert Gossard will simply have to take a hold, can't carry him along and not take his active part—and perhaps if Mister Danford could see his way to giving a day or two again, every week or so—. But we shall still have to find a bookkeeper to assist.

—Someone from Topeka or Kansas City the other banks recommend? Isaac suggested. Or maybe we aint paying enough—offer a bonus for moving down, fifty or a hundred dollars. And Wichita's got things to offer an active young man besides money.

—But there's just the difficulty, Mister Pride—oh, very difficult—not *at all* the sort of place to attract a serious young professional gentleman that we can train up for our service, if you believe what they print in the newspapers—and now *Harper's* with those scandalous illustrations, baboons in big hats and spurs and revolvers at their belts, dancing with their lewd women, like Wichita was, I don't know, some depraved mining camp high up in the Rockies, some hellhole in the jungles of the Amazon—

—Now, Mister Fraker, Isaac said with a smile. You know the *Eagle's* printing good things right along and exchanging with papers all over the country, and the others the same—Wichita cattle prices quoted in Chicago and New York—only they like to put in a little color to stir up interest. The *Eagle* was Marsh Murdock's new venture, recently settled in from Burlingame.

—And the worst thing, Fraker continued, casting his eyes to heaven for witness, much of it true, from what folks say—saloons and dance houses that never close their doors, day or night and the Sabbath included—other things too offensive to decency to—

—Well, I don't know about *that*, Isaac broke in. Just sounds to me like the boys coming off the trail and looking for a little change, a little fun, and the people over there arranging to provide it, but orderly too—don't want their premises shot up, or broken up, no more than any other man of business. You ever gone over to West Wichita since it's been going strong?

Mr Fraker gave his head a vehement shake: wife and children and a regular churchgoer, leading his family to their place in the front row, and his position to keep up—

—Neither have I, Isaac said, and don't reckon it'd do to come down hard in my opinion till I've seen for myself. You know what the Bible says about judging others. . . .

It was the way their conversations often went: start with some practical question concerning the operation of the bank and end up a mile or two distant.

Isaac that night on the bank letterhead wrote his parents with some satisfaction of the dividend about to be declared. A week later his father's answer came, with a draft for two thousand dollars on the Davenport bank: had reflected on his son's advice last winter and about concluded to take it—extend the mortgage and, well, they had assembled the money from various sources—and the splendid news of the bank's progress had confirmed his decision; and perhaps too the investment would be of some assistance to Isaac in his venture. He wanted ten shares for himself, five each for Mother and Lizzie, and perhaps in time they would be able to undertake more. Isaac called the stock from Mr Fraker and listed it in his own name in the bank's records—to any but himself it commanded a premium of fifteen dollars a share, now the news of the dividend was going around, and none apparently to be had; time enough to make the transfer in January say, when the next dividend came due—which he would make over to them, of course, and pay the Kansas tax on stock too, while he was at it, so they could enjoy the entire amount, with no deduction.

Mr Fraker spent the morning in his office at the bank, occupied with a delicate matter of correspondence. The bank examiner's report had in due course produced a stern admonition from John Jay Knox, the Comptroller, concerning Mr Greiffenstein's notes. The bank president had not actually seen Mr Britton's report, but had stayed by him throughout the day of the examination, conversing, answering questions, offering every assistance, and had shared an amiable dinner with him at the Empire. He had felt confident the report would contain nothing awkward, and the tone of the Comptroller's letter was therefore unsettling. He cited Section 29 of the currency act, concerning liabilities owed to national banking associations, as the act called them:

That the total liabilities to any association, of any person, or of any company, corporation or firm for money borrowed, including in the liabilities of a company

*or firm the liabilities of the several members thereof, shall at no time exceed one
tenth part of the amount of the capital stock of such association actually paid
in. . . .*

Mr Fraker labored at the draft of his reply, went over it with care,
inserted emendations, and at length wrote out the fair copy. Mr
Fraker read his letter through again and was satisfied: *dont desire either
to violate any law or your instructions,* that was the tone to take, perfectly respectful to the high office of Comptroller but all the same
remind him that strict adherence to law was the rule all around. He
addressed an envelope and inserted the fair copy. Pinning his draft to
Mr Knox's letter, he put it away at the back of a desk drawer to await
an answer.

The other matter now seemed easier to deal with. The expenses of
setting up at Wichita had run to more than he anticipated. There had
been the land where he meant to build on Central Avenue, then getting started in a new implement business with his brother to manage
—a set of lots over along the railroad line, a warehouse and a little
building for an office, and of course the stock of equipment, on credit
but that cost money too; and he had taken up several likely opportunities in cattle and wheat on which he was only beginning to realize.
The consequence was that when the time came in the spring to pay in
his stock so that the bank could take up its bonds and secure the
remainder of its currency, he had only two thousand dollars that he
could spare; twelve thousand dollars short. That difficulty he had
solved rather neatly by drawing up three notes of four thousand dollars each for six months—deposits had come in so well the first few
months that they were amply covered. The notes had been properly
entered on the books, and Mr Britton, having so many lesser matters
to occupy his thoughts, had asked no questions, if he noticed them—
they were individually within the limits permitted by the National
Bank Act, were not past due, and the accrued interest had in fact been
paid, out of the July dividend on the stock; and finally it appeared that
the examiner had made no mention of the notes in his report to the
Comptroller. Had he demanded to see the original paper, kept locked
in a strongbox of which Mr Fraker had the only key, he would not
probably have found anything irregular. Each note was approved by
the bank's president, in accordance with the authority granted him
by the Articles of Association. They were made out to JFC Co., his
own initials, rearranged; First St Louis, which sounded like the
bank's principal correspondent; and Central Ave. Assoc., suggested
by the land where he meant to build his house, opposite Pride's Reserve.

Unfortunately, the notes were all due in August, and, waiting on
his cattle and wheat money, he was still pinched. He could extend, of

course, but as a last resort; Mr Gossard was still not giving full time as acting cashier but might well demand explanations and particulars —why these three notes, representing a substantial amount, should receive special accommodation. Young Mr Maxwell, the bookkeeper, attempting to get the books up, had showed curiosity that way and persistence, had hunted the original notes everywhere, and Mr Fraker had talked at mournful length about the carelessness of previous bookkeepers in filing important papers but assured him they were somewhere and would turn up. Now Mr Gossard was demanding a replacement to carry on the day-to-day work.

Fortunately there was a solution ready to hand: consolidate the three notes in one with another bank. Then they would be cleared from the bank's records, his stock would be paid in in fact, and the asset would be free to earn; and none the wiser. It was not a thing to attempt as if begging a favor, but bold, businesslike, and brief. He took a sheet of the half-size letterhead with his name at the top and in his fluent hand addressed the cashier at the St Louis National, a Mr T. N. Eldon whom he had not personally met but looked on as an acquaintance and friend through frequent correspondence over bank matters:

Sir

I have oportunity to do some good for our Bank and yours if you have funds for short term at moderate premium not otherwise engaged—say six months at 10 per cent. Would not go outside except demands of Cattle buyers uses all our resources at this season and wish to do something in wheat besides. Since many of our Setlers are still breaking prairie, the plantings not large yet as they will be but talk is of 30 bu. an acre on that planted—

Would require $12,000 to take advantage, suggest in form of Certif. of Deposit, to draw on demand. Send papers properly drawn at yr convenence and I will execute and return.

Our N.Y. correspondents have been demanding to share our Prosperity but I concluded, we owed St Louis National first offer—

Awaiting your early response,

> *Yours respectfuly*
> *JCFraker*
> *Pres.*

Mr Fraker made a brief note of the contents in his private daybook and locked it away back in its drawer.

The Honorable John Jay Knox sat rigid at his desk, reviewing the day's correspondence with his chief clerk; hardly a patient man but orderly, even methodical. The rooms assigned his bureau in the Treasury building were not sumptuous but afforded an imposing view down Pennsylvania Avenue to the Capitol, to which he kept his back turned while at work, as he was now. He shoved a letter across the desk.

—Here! What d'you make of that?

—Ah! said the clerk, his face lighting as he recognized the letterhead of the First National Bank of Wichita. It's the one upset Mister Britton so when he examined. Country preacher turned banker I believe he described him as.

—I remember. Can you make out his meaning?

—Well, sir—. The clerk scanned the writing. He appears to demand your assurance that—that the limitation on loans to individuals or corporations does not apply to commercial paper or to—the clerk was here unable to restrain a smile—to demand deposits in the hands of a correspondent to facilitate exchange.

—God damn his eyes! Hasn't he read the law he does business under? Didn't we quote the essential part when we wrote him before?

The clerk nodded.—I am afraid he has things quite muddled, sir.

—Well, tear the scales from his eyes, man! Tell him, if he ever again lets out more than ten percent of his capital on loan to *anyone*, we'll hang him. I shall myself make the journey to—what's it called, Wichita?—to preside at the springing of the trap. I wonder if it would be any use sending him the whole law, in pamphlet form.

—I had made a note to enclose a marked copy.

—*If* he's capable of reading it. Dear me, I sometimes fear that no one in the Republic has read and understood that law—not the bankers nor the two houses of the Congress and certainly not the President. Except me—and you, of course, my dear Jeffreys. National banks indeed! It is like attempting to keep order at a party given for ignorant and ill-natured children.

The clerk ventured no opinion.

—Well, now! And put him on the list for examination again in a year, if we can fit him in—if he's not dead or bankrupt. Country preacher my foot! That letter is the work either of a great fool, or a great scoundrel.

Drawing the next item of correspondence from the pile with a snap, the Comptroller smoothed it flat before him on the desk to consider.

Three weeks after the bank examiner's visit Isaac left with two wagonloads of goods for Mathewson's post near the Kiowa Agency. They arrived mid-morning on the second day, and Isaac sat with Lizzie Mathewson long enough over coffee to relay the news of Lucy, the children, Wichita, then borrowed a horse and, leaving Mathewson to superintend the unloading and storing away of the freight, rode down Cache Creek to visit Stumbling Bear. Satanta and Big Tree were still in prison in Texas. Even so muffled, Satanta made his eloquence heard, proclaiming to any who would listen and report that with Satank dead he was now the sole paramount chief of the Kiowa, true successor to Dohasan, that he alone had the authority to keep the tribe at peace and on the reservation in accordance with their treaty; a number of influential whites were persuaded—officials of the Indian office, Congressmen, members of the commission of church leaders that had taken responsibility for recruiting honest Indian agents, mostly Quakers—and argued that the Indian should be pardoned and released. As if to substantiate Satanta's claims, some of his admirers among the tribe's younger leaders had attempted to compel his release by drawing their old allies, the Comanche, into a general outbreak against the whites, and when they were refused, had carried out, earlier that summer, several highly successful raids; up to Fort Supply in the northwest corner of the Territory, then down through the arid, broken plains of the Texas Panhandle. The raiders ran off hundreds of horses and mules; a few whites and two Kiowa were incidentally killed, some of the leaders captured and transported to a military base in Florida for confinement. Isaac and his men had been cautious coming south—traveled and slept with loaded guns handy, kept the mules staked close to camp at night while half the party stood watch in two-hour shifts and kept a fire up—but made the journey unmolested.

Isaac found Stumbling Bear's lodge, announced himself—had brought a ten-pound sack of coffee beans as a present—and was invited in. The Indian sat alone at the back on a heap of robes supported by a backrest, the lower edge of the lodge's buffalo-skin cover tied up to let the breezes come through; was cordial—brought out his pipe to smoke, called for the women to bring meat, inquired of Isaac's affairs, his son—but preoccupied, aging, perhaps unwell, letting his hands fall silent for minutes at a time. Isaac asked about Pat-so-gate. Stumbling Bear after another silence told him a little: had not gone away but lived apart, a small lodge back in among the trees a mile or two down Cache Creek. Trapped some, claimed rations from Mr Tatum, the agent; when he had buffalo meat, Stumbling Bear took her some. Isaac politely stayed another hour and departed.

He rode a slow three miles without finding the spot Stumbling Bear had described, then started back, leading the horse, searching with his eyes among the trees along the creek, and discovered a narrow path worn in the grass as if by muskrat or other small waterside animal. A pale, coyotelike Indian cur came out to meet him, yapping. Isaac crouched, offering his hands to smell, the dog circled, going for his heels, and he sent it back howling with a kick. He tied his horse and picked his way cautiously through the trees along the path the dog had taken, coming out before a low tent half hidden by the slope of the bank, its flap closed with splints of wood despite the heat. Pat-so-gate knelt in front, flensing a skin that looked to be about the size and color of beaver. Her hair was bound smooth and tight against her head by a single long braid down her back, streaks of gold showing through the layer of charcoal and grease she had darkened it with.

—Patsy.

She answered two or three words without looking up.

—Here now! he said. Is that any way to greet me? I came a long way to find you, Patsy, and you know I can't understand a dozen words of Kiowa.

—Pai-tal-ye—

—Damn it, Patsy! You can stop that!

He dropped to his knees facing her, reached and caught her wrists and squeezed till she dropped the scraper. She tried to jerk free, then sat back, tense but acquiescent.

—That is all played out now, she said, looking him at last in the eyes. You must go back, Pai-tal-ye.

—Not till I've said the things I came for. He let her go and she folded her hands in her lap, waiting. He swallowed, cleared his throat, breath coming short and shallow till he could hardly speak. My wife died, since I saw you last, he said. Three years ago this spring, don't suppose you'd've heard of that down here—. Oh, Patsy, I've thought long and hard on this, but where you belong is your own people, and if—

—Kiowa are my people, she said with a lift of her arms and let them fall again.

—No they *aint*, Patsy! You aint any more Indian than the first day I saw you, however you get yourself up and pretend. Kiowa don't want you, I can see that, or you wouldn't be hidden away off by yourself like this.

—I did a bad thing, could not help myself, but it was wrong. Now the people are shamed, or afraid. I keep apart, to spare them.

—*Course* they don't want you, it's what I said at the start. I don't know what it is you're ashamed of, but—well, you don't look any different to me, and it won't *make* any difference, whatever it is. And if it's the only way, why, I'll take you, if you'll come, I can do that now—take you and make you my wife—. There now! It's said, and it'll happen at last, the way you wanted. . . . Patsy!

He leaned toward her, softly took her hands again and held them.

—Isaac—for a little time I believed we might travel the same trail together, which is life. We came to a branching—you went by one fork, I by another. Now if we travel a thousand years—cross all the plains and forests, the great mountains of this earth—take our way through the heavens and reach the farthest stars—our roads cannot cross again.

—I don't know how you can say that to me when I'm here before you. And what you're talking about is destiny—a man's life all settled and laid out for him before he starts and no way to change it. I don't believe that, and it aint Christian, either. What I believe—it's all up to you. Things hit you, knock you flat, but you can always get up, go on the way you've chose to head.

From inside the tepee came a faint catlike cry, then a scrabbling at the flap and a small blond head emerged from a corner of the opening, sleep-dazed, wakened from sleep by their voices. A little boy pushed through, crawling, raised himself on fat arms and stood balancing, legs wide, arms out, naked: might be three years old and off the cradle-board by now. Isaac held out both arms, as to a puppy, and the boy tottered the remaining steps, reached a soft hand to touch the shaggy tip of Isaac's mustache, slid it across his cheek, seized a lock of hair behind his ear and gave a sharp tug.

—Hey there, boy! Isaac caught him in his arms and cradled him close, and for the moment he lay there, sleep-warm and supple as a kitten.

—He is why I will not go with you, Isaac.

Isaac swung the boy out and set him on his feet, clamping his shoulders with his hands to look him in the face.

—I don't know how you can look at him and say that, if I take your meaning right—looks as much mine as my own boy home at Wichita. *He* thinks so too.

Pat-so-gate spoke a word or two to her son and—made no answer, surely could say things by now but shy, hearing unknown language— he wriggled free, took a step back, eyes still on Isaac's, and with a little crowing gurgle of surprise went over backward on his bottom. Turning over, he crawled off slowly through the dusty grass to play beside the creek.

—His hair and color are of the man I think his father, Pat-so-gate said, and when Isaac turned sharply back to her, face hardening in a frown: George Custer. General Custer—

—That braggart! Isaac burst out. That newspaper general, that crow-beaked woman-killer! Why, Patsy, I wouldn't trust him to drive one of my mule-teams on the Plains, let alone command a regiment of the U.S. Cavalry!

—I was at Black Kettle's village when he attacked, she said softly. One of his prisoners. . . .

He was silent. Finally, his voice tight—I already told you, Patsy. Whatever it was happened, I wouldn't let it make any difference. I'll stand with that—whatever I say, I'll do, you ought to know that. . . . Then, with another thought, almost cheerful: Besides, he said, that don't settle it, his growing up towhead. I've been told time and time that Custer and me are like as two brothers that way, except some inches of height. But it's you he looks like, Patsy, in his features *and* his hair. I don't see any other resemblance. What'd you name him?

—Tunk-aht-oh-ye, that is *man-makes-thunder*, only his first baby name. In his first months he was strong but suffered sickness that made him cry out in rage, like thunder. She smiled faintly, remembering.

—Do you love him?

She nodded.

—Then if you love him, what do you keep him off here for, like you were quarantined for cholera? He ought to be running and playing with other boys—yes, and grow up talking the language of his own people.

—When he is grown he can choose.

—Sure he can—like the weakling chicken in the flock that the others peck to death because it's different from them. To the Indians he's a white man that happens to know their language. To the whites he's only another Indian, though he does have pale skin and yellow hair. But what he needs is a father, to show him the way to be a man. You can't do that, Patsy—you'll make a woman of him. . . .

—Ado-e-et-te, she said, pronouncing the syllables with care. That you call Big Tree—

—That fool and cheat! Isaac shouted with a barking laugh—that wasn't any more a man than to run Satanta's errands for him. Not fit for hanging—

—I hid from him with Black Kettle's people, but when the baby came, he said he would have me still, and my son, even if we should live as outcasts from the tribe. I will go with him if he will have me—

He sprang up, caught her under the arms and pulled her up and her face close to his.—God damn you, Patsy! You can't compare me with that snake-eyed scalp hunter—

—There! she said. I know you are strong—can drag me from my lodge, tie me to your horse and take me, like an Indian—like the raiders did when I was a girl in Texas. . . .

Her face flushed through the deep tan. He felt her ribs heaving between his hands and let her slip loose and slump to the ground. He took a step back.

—There isn't anything I'd make you do. But if you'll come with me of your own to be my wife, I'll build you the grandest house in the grandest city of the Plains to queen it over, and cherish little Thunder dear as your life, and dearer than my own. . . .

—You will build these things for yourself, she said in a faint voice, head drooping. And my son: maybe for a time you will love him, as you promise. Then a time will come and you will see different: seed of him I hate who defiled the body of her I love. You will hate the child too, and wish him dead. . . .

—That just isn't true, he said. He's a lovely boy—a man couldn't help loving him, or blessing God for giving him such a son, however he came by him. Any more than I could help loving you when I first saw you—when I wasn't free, and it was wrong, to have such feeling. . . .

The sun was getting low, compressing the darkness among the trees where she had made her camp. He was tired; hungry too, it did not look as if she had meat, or none she would spare from feeding the child.

—I'm staying with the trader, Bill Mathewson that they call Sinpah-zil-bah, four miles up the creek—a day or two longer till the stage comes through going north. You decide you'll come with me, you can leave your tent and bring the boy and come—or send someone from Stumbling Bear's people to tell me and I'll come and get you. There, now! he said, smiling a little and raising one hand as she seemed about to answer something. You've heard all the promises I've got, but don't answer me yet. Only come when your mind's made up.

He waited a minute or two, looking down at her submissive head, but she said nothing. He turned and pushed his way back out through the brush, into the sunset.

Isaac let the borrowed horse carry him home unguided, unknowing, when finally it arrived, where it had indolently wandered, cropping the ripe grass, until finally, itself hungering for hay and shelled corn, it stepped into a careless, jolting trot. It was dark when he reached the trading post, ten o'clock, bedtime. He decided against going in to stay with Mathewson and Lizzie, did not want to disturb them, so late in the night; the hayloft over the barn, where Mr Peet and the men were to sleep, would do as well, and no reason the trader should think he had not stayed the night with Stumbling Bear. The train captain came to see who had arrived, took the horse, scraped the last of the stewed deer meat from one of the cook pots, and brought it to him on a tin plate by the dying fire. Isaac recalled feeling hunger when he started back, ate some, then set the plate aside. He remembered to say good night all around and climbed to the loft to sleep.

Sleep did not come. He groped a spot in a corner, spread and settled the prairie hay, removed his boots and lay back—hot, a hot night still, the hay seemed to hold and steam with heat, and the dust got into his clothes and swarmed along his skin like columns of ants on the march.

He had not known—had not intended—that he should ask to let him take her for his wife: saw her and the words came, as of themselves, and said, could not be taken back. It was a whole chain of things unknown, hidden link by link within his will: that he had gone to Stumbling Bear only to find her; contrived to come with his wagon train to Mathewson's post at the Kiowa reservation on the chance of seeing her once more; that for three years at Wichita he waited for such an excuse, wanting her, and put off finding it. Pity had impelled his words: beautiful and strong as that day he watched the flood carry her and swam to get her out, the beauty not diminished but magnified in the beauty of her child, and to see her alone and wronged, cast off by all, and himself as denying as the rest, dear God forgive me—it made him want to shield her with his arms, to keep off harm, forever, and change her sorrow into joy, if he could, if she would let him, would have him. Love: he found he did not know much of love, but those were of it, pity and protectiveness, sorrowing in her sorrow; and joy. It did not seem there was much or often joy in any life, but, merciful God, it came, in moments, a mystery, unwilled, unconscious. He wanted only to be with her, for as long as life lasts; forever. . . .

She had answered him, but in words opposite her meaning. The desire he had felt in her heart, in the sweet recesses of her flesh, was for the one thing he had refused: that he seize her, drag her, compel her to come, tie her to the horse if need be. That moment was now: rouse yourself, take a pair of horses and go, get there by first light—. His skin prickled in the dark with sweat, he trembled all over as with the ague; and tired, so tired, when he tried to lift an arm to wipe his face it was as if his whole body had been weighted with lead clamping it to the dull earth. . . . Then in the morning: when the light came he would gather his strength and rise and go with the horses to get her, and the child. . . .

He had not, it came to him, thought where. Now objections to Wichita marched in file before his eyes, and the house he had promised her—what did she know of such a place or care? But his parents would no more comprehend or forgive such a choice—ruined girl and her bastard, however beautiful and true, however disguised in dressmakers' garments from Kansas City to take a place at his mother's tea table, but Kiowa in her heart forever—than if he came home to them with one of Towakoni Jim's half-sisters. And Lucy: come in the door of his house leading this strange woman and turn her out—so the act came to his mind in words, setting one cruelty right by doing another, and her sister Lizzie would take it as poor repayment for having come into his household to lift the shadow of Marie's death from his children and himself. It was not a thing she or Bill would forgive, no more than his parents, and the partnership he had often chafed under would come to an end not of his choosing. Nor till this moment, it struck him with shame and remorse, had he given serious thought to his own son—little Isaac, bearer of his name, his claim strongest of all: what man worth his manhood would set that child of doubtful birth against his only son's life?

So all that could truly follow from his promise was flight, a new life for the two of them alone, a cabin in the far mountains where he could get what food they needed with his gun, maybe at last revive his old dream of prospecting for gold; but a life cut off equally from past and future and from all the world. It was no more serious or possible than Patsy's own girl's fancy once, of going away together, turning their backs to the two opposing separatenesses of their lives so as to fashion one new together, for themselves alone.

He was like an animal in a trap, unable to go forward or withdraw, struggle and struggle, but the jaws hold only tighter till you drown. What he had vaunted Patsy that afternoon of the strength of a man's will to raise him from defeat and drive him on in his chosen direction —that had been a lie. She it was spoke truth, had known. He had reached his limit. No choice remained to make. Tears mingled with the sweat that filmed his face. In the morning, he told himself, it would be over, he would find his strength again and the way through. And the horses—take two horses, saddled, leading one, and go and find her, take her home. No, not force, only demand, but in words she could not this time deny. Till morning, then. . . .

Mathewson found him, shook him awake in the first light. *What are you hiding out here for, Isaac? Heat too much for you, is it?*

Between them they could have the robes sorted, counted, loaded on the wagons by day's end, if the men kept at it, start the train north in the morning—and sooner they reached Wichita, the sooner they would both get their money. There was a stage coming north from Texas, due at Fort Sill probably in late afternoon; not another going that direction for a week. Another reason for finishing the loading: the coach would save him a week's travel against staying the night and going with the wagon train.

It was an hour after a hasty dinner when they finished with the wagons and Isaac had time to recollect the intention that in the night had seemed indelible. Pat-so-gate had not come, nor any message. About time enough remained before the stage was due to wash, change, select a few necessities for the journey from his trunk.

Mathewson himself led the next train of robes and furs to Wichita, arriving at the beginning of October. Isaac shipped them out consigned to Morehead & Young, St Louis, calculating to come out with five thousand dollars clear when the sale was completed and the summer's stock of goods finally paid off, depending somewhat on just how they hit the market. He and Mathewson went on to Leavenworth to replenish their stock, then St Louis and through to Philadelphia before they found all they needed at satisfactory prices. Returning to Wichita, he saw the trader off on the south-bound stage and on Sunday, a duty rarely performed, drove with Lucy and the children to hear the new preacher at the little Presbyterian church recently completed on another of Isaac's donated lots, an unsold fifty-foot residential on Fourth Avenue over toward the railroad.

Afterward, as Lucy led them out, a child firmly grasped in either hand, and Isaac lingered to greet friends and shake the preacher's hand, Bissy, impressively silent and attentive all through the service, broke away and ran ahead to climb up on the buggy seat.

—Mama Lucy! Mama Lucy! he cried in his clear boy-man's voice as they came toward him. Let me hold the reins, do, on the way home. Can I, Mama Lucy? Can I?

Lucy turned to Isaac for permission, faintly coloring under the pale blue bonnet tied and decorated with pink ribbon that he realized must be new, put on for the occasion. Turned eighteen, was it, in June, but a grown woman now, whatever her age, guiding the children with dignity and firmness through the departing crowd.

—Well, now! Better take me along home like you're used to, then. Boy's nearly ten, handles that pony like a man and time he was learning to drive too, and I reckon that's the way of it, with his pretty little Mama Lucy to teach him. And smiling he took her arm, led her to the buggy and helped her up, and went around to the other side to get in, with little Mamie snug on his lap.

The bank's directors had of course approved the new issue of stock, a hundred shares, ten thousand dollars, thereby enlarging its supply of currency by nine thousand dollars. Isaac's father sent another draft for two thousand dollars, the stock to be divided as before; borrowed money, no doubt, at least his father's part of it, but he thought it not proper to ask. Albert Gossard took in twenty of the new shares—still dividing his time between Wichita and El Dorado, but Mr Fraker had made no further complaints about the bookkeeping since hiring a young man named J. P. Campbell for the job. Isaac took it on himself to dispose of the remaining stock: to Billy Thomas, a genial, strongly accented German who had arrived about the time the railroad was completed, set up in groceries, and by now was reputed the heaviest wholesaler at Wichita; and to Jim Steele and others around the town but also to a merchant acquaintance of his father's at Quincy—all glad to accommodate and incidentally to buy at par stock whose original issue was now worth $120 a share and scarce, and Mr Fraker already maintaining there was no reason their second six months' dividend, due in January, should not again go ten percent.

Isaac himself took no further shares. In the course of the summer and fall he had claimed the balance of the hundred promised him by the other incorporators, in addition to his original ten: from returns from the partnership with Mathewson, from a steady sale of lots. In mid-October he considered himself sufficiently ahead to contract with a builder to start work on the completed plan of his house, the same partnership that had lately finished Greiffenstein's Douglass Avenue House where Ezekiel Blood now presided, having left the Empire House as he promised. The brick was delivered and stacked—Isaac held Greiffenstein to his word and bought at cost; the contractors' laborers turned up to commence digging the cellar. The house was to stand in the center of the reserve, a hundred feet back from Central Avenue, surrounded by his already planted hedges and fruit trees, cuttings sent him by his father. Isaac faced his house west and planned it with few rooms but spacious: a formal parlor across the front surrounded by a covered porch, over it the main bedroom, of the same size, behind it in the central block a dining room and family parlor with bay windows at either end; three more bedrooms on the second floor and above them an attic enclosed by a slate-covered mansard roof to drain sun-warmed rainwater into a cistern to feed a shower bath in the bathroom on the second floor, an unheard-of innovation in a Wichita private house (there was also to be a furnace in the cellar supplying steam heat, supplemented by fireplaces in the main rooms); at the back, a twenty-four-foot wing housing kitchen and pantries, with four small rooms in an attic above for servants.

Isaac felt a certain uneasiness at starting without all the money in hand, six thousand dollars the builders had estimated, not counting the brick. The builders, however, working their crews around other jobs, made no promise of finishing before late winter or early spring, and by then the prospects were excellent. Mathewson now calculated to go one more winter in the Indian trade and sell out, meaning perhaps ten thousand dollars as Isaac's share. At the worst, he could borrow on his stock or even sell some, at a profit, but the house would be built. It was not a great risk.

The new bank building was completed in December. Its temporary quarters reverted to a saloon, but buffered by an unsold lot between. The total cost, as near as Mr Fraker could calculate at the January directors' meeting (at which he recommended a ten percent dividend, to maintain the value of their stock), was sixteen thousand dollars—with another six thousand dollars for suitable furnishings, to which all had agreed in principle, and an unbreakable vault. The city had, however, agreed to occupy the half-basement with its police court, constables' office, and jail, on a long lease, while the Masons had taken the second floor. Eventually the building's cost would be earned back in rent.

At the same meeting the president announced that Mr Danford had asked to be relieved of his responsibilities as director, since his work at El Dorado was now taking up all his time; and his proposal to replace him with young Mr Campbell, whom Mr Gossard was finding so satisfactory as assistant cashier, was duly voted, so as to fill the board out to the number required by law—eventually they would have to find a few shares for him, no doubt, but there was no hurry about it. Since Mr Danford had said nothing of disposing of his considerable holding, he would no doubt continue to take a practical interest in the Wichita bank's affairs.

On the evening of February 2, 1873, a Sunday, the Presbyterian minister married Isaac to Lucy Ann Inman, at the home of Dr A. H. Fabrique, Wichita's second physician, who at Isaac's urging had built on the southeast corner of Munger's Addition, diagonally across Central Avenue from Pride's Reserve. Marsh Murdock recorded the event in two paragraphs in his new weekly wishing heaven's blessings on the union. Mrs Murdock and Mrs Fabrique furnished a supper. Isaac had arranged with the doctor's wife to take Bissy and Mamie for the night.

He had intended taking the morning train to Newton and on to St Louis for a week, by way of a wedding trip, but had after all concluded he could not well spare the time; and Lucy, although furnished with clothes for the journey, had shown little interest, talking rather of how the children would fare in their absence. He was determined, however, to spend the night in the new house, as planned. It was closed in and weatherproof but probably two months from finishing. At ten o'clock he said goodnight to the doctor and his wife, Marsh Murdock and the other guests, and, taking Lucy's hand in his, led her across the rutted street, past the old cabin, and in the front door of the house. Remote light greeted them, coming around corners, through empty doors, abated, and the wet-lime smell of half-cured plaster. Two days earlier Andrew Hansen had helped him carry the new double bed into the back parlor and set it up and now had left a smoky fire of Kansas coal in the fireplace and a lamp on the mantelpiece. It gave him pleasure to lead her through the shadow-dancing dark. She gave a shiver, seeing the high-posted bed like a throne facing the dim fire. He led her to it, stirred the coals with a stick and laid on splits of cured cottonwood for light and warmth.

—I wanted it finished for you, Lucy, he said, but just couldn't hurry the builders along fast enough. So think of it like a tent out on the Plains, only we've a weatherproof roof over our heads. Crouching at the hearth, he opened his arms to her, drawing her to the warmth.

Hidden in shadow at the foot of the bed was a small, square trunk in which she had assembled her best clothes to travel in, mostly new. She found it, slid it over in front of the fire and sat, shoulders huddled, resting her chin on her hands. He crouched uncomfortably beside her, thought he had swept up carefully all around the fireplace but the unfinished flooring grated his hands with dust and grit, too dirty to sit on; should have carried over a rug too while he was at it but had not thought. His whole insistence on spending their first night in the unfinished house now seemed an empty gesture, devoid of feeling and dignity; better sense to have started modestly in the familiar cabin and enjoy the house when it was really ready—he had wanted her in this way, by this propitiatory act, to have her part in its building, make it as much hers as his own, but all she felt was unease. She shivered again.

—Cold, Lucy? he said. Better get a shawl over your shoulders, if you've got one in your box. Can't have you coming down with something now, can we?

—Yes, Mister Pride.

She got up, opened the lid, and felt down through the layers of garments.

—Now then, he said. I don't know that we need to be quite so formal now we're man and wife. Course in the old days, that was how they did, my own parents for instance, but it's a new age we live in—. She darted an uncomprehending glance over her shoulder. I should like you to call me by my Christian name now, Lucy, he said, raising his voice a little. Isaac—

—Yes—Isaac. . . .

She closed the trunk, stood, the black lace shawl she prized trailing indifferently from one hand, eyes glistening in the lamplight. He reached fingertips, felt tears spilling from her unwilling eyes. He took the shawl, drew it across her shoulders, and pulled her to him, closing her in his arms.

—There now, my dear, he said—mustn't be sad—here's all the best of life before us.

He drew her down to sit again, crouching close beside her, one arm gently circling her slender waist.

—I've not minded, coming over to see, when the workmen were everywhere, she said, looking around. But now—I hadn't thought— only the one lamp and the firelight, it's like a great empty cave filled up with darkness, cold. Oh, I know it shouldn't fear me, no different really now from daylight, and I'd find my way, I expect, but. . . .

—Don't have to sit here feeling cold, he said, if I can get that fire burning. He rose, gave the fire two or three encouraging pokes, and returned to her side. It's not strange you should feel so, Lucy, he continued. A house hasn't any life of its own, any good or bad of itself, it's only an empty shell, a mold you can use to make things— oh, a kind of abstract of its builder's intention to build strong and true as he knows, with what means he has and for the purposes he aims at—. He glanced at her sideways but she stared blankly into the reviving fire, face empty as a mask.

What this house needs, he said, is filling up with life—babies of our own. Why, young and strong as you are, Lucy, I don't know why you shouldn't have a dozen, if you want, and suit me very well too, I can tell you—fill the place up with babies, in every room and running up and down the stairs, pestering the cook at their games—. Except, he added with mock gravity, we could run out of names we'd both agree on before we're finished, if we don't start in right now, collecting. What names would you like best, Lucy, for a start? One for a little boy baby, and one for a girl.

When she did not answer, he reached his fingers with a tickling motion under her chin, wanting her to smile for him if not laugh, and turning her face to his, touched her soft cheek with his lips. She stared gravely back, as if he had assigned her some task, and next she would be calling him Mr Pride again, and if he was not careful he would be annoyed.

They sat in silence until he began to wonder how, if she did not, he could raise the delicate question of going to bed. He could recall no such awkwardness with Marie. Once she made her mind up to the idea he was to be her husband, they had advanced through the moments of their life like two soldiers marching in step, each sensing the other's wants with least resort to words and their clumsy and imperfect mediation—nothing marked off as peculiarly belonging to him, or her, but only to them both, in the commonalty of the married state, by shared and mutual discovery; or so, in this moment, he remembered. That first night together at the Schuyler House, for instance: probably it made it easier, old friends and wise women all around, the music, the dancing, the bowls of punch, old Vinnie to lead her up and help her dress when the time came, and then going off early the next morning on their little trip through Kansas, all they could afford. It had been selfish and a mistake, not getting up something like that, for Lucy's sake; but done now, never to be undone.

—I've got some whisky here someplace, he announced, getting up. Believe I'll try some—quiets the nerves, they say, and helps a body off to sleep.

Two days earlier he had bought a bottle of what the dealer assured him was best Kentucky bourbon, the sort Colonel Titus had favored, and left it on the mantel for such a moment, if he felt the need. He lifted the lamp, found it, and realized he had neglected to provide glasses.

—Forgot the glasses, he said, holding the bottle out to her with a diffident smile. Distracted as a young groom—a wonder I didn't forget my pants too! Still, when we're camping out like this, I reckon we needn't stand on ceremony—

She watched wide-eyed while he pulled the cork, tilted the bottle up and drank, a long slow swallow, then another. He held the bottle out to her again but she shook her head. He shoved the cork down and replaced the bottle on the mantel.

—Now then, Lucy, my girl! he said, his voice louder than he had meant, resounding from the high ceiling, echoing in the empty room. Getting late—he brought his watch out—and time for bed, I reckon. I'll just step around the corner with my cigar while you get your night things on. Everything you'll want in your trunk, I expect, have you?

She nodded faintly, still sitting. He drew the cigar from his vest pocket, cut the ends, found a match, lighted, and left her, moving cautiously toward the front of the house and the room that was to be the formal parlor, finding his way to a window by the dim glow of his cigar. He stood looking out, hands clasped at his back. Gradually, as his eyes adapted and the glimmer from his cigar tip brightened at each puff, he made out his own face looking back from the glass in transparent outline, an image fit for a ghost. He felt the heat scorching his fingers: half-smoked. What was taking her so long? Oh, getting her hair out, no doubt, that always took time, and no mirror to see to brush it out in. Perhaps he could offer to help, put her at her ease somehow—he was not entirely ignorant of such matters, after all—

—Isaac! Isaac!—her voice, not a scream, but loud, pitched high, echoing up the empty house.

He turned at a run, slammed against a doorpost, and came back into the yellow, shadow-filled light. She was in bed, only her face showing, under a lacy cap that covered her hair, and the fingers of her two hands clamping the coverlet pulled up to her chin. She lay on her back, eyes closed.

—What is it, dear?

—Something!—there was something—.

With his eyes he made the circuit of the light that did not reach the room's far walls. Throwing the cigar stub in the fire he took the lamp and followed the walls all around, holding it high, then along the hall to the kitchen, back to the front of the house.

—There's nothing, Lucy, he said when he returned. All the windows tight and the doors bolted. Only the two of us in an empty half-built house that, please God, we'll fill with life, and the joy of life, beginning this night. She had not moved. Her eyes were still closed. He spoke to soothe but could not see that she had heard. A woman she looked, but only a child afraid of the dark and the shapes dancing, just past the limits of sight. A man must be doubly strong, wasn't that how he saw it? Here now, he said. I'll make the fire up and come to bed, and that's really camping out—go to sleep by the firelight, and no sweeter sleep I've tasted on this earth.

He lowered the lamp to blow out and replaced it, threw on logs and a careless shovel of coal, and carried her little trunk around behind the head of the bed. He was down to his underdrawers and bare feet, folding his suit and shirt on the trunk lid as best he could in the weak light, to stay off the gritty floor, when it came to him that his nightshirt too he had forgotten, where was his mind these last days? but all the same done and no helping it: let her take him to her naked as an Indian.

He lifted the edge of the sheet, dusted the grime from the soles of his feet, and slipped in on his side of the bed. He lay flat, keeping his distance. He found the pillow that supported her head and got his arm under; both horses and women, have to gentle them along—a harsh word or any forgetful, impatient roughness and you'd be weeks or months getting their trust back, if ever. That was the thing favoring a mature man marrying young, whatever the jokes about an old fool and a girl—not that at thirty-five a man could be counted old by any standard, whatever his wife's age, but experienced, certainly. His right arm moved in silence under the dome of bedclothes, hand lightly rested on her belly—felt muscles tighten through the flannel of her gown, rigid legs clamp shut, she was not asleep—and pursued its stealth till it found the small of her back and with the strength of his arm turned her toward him, taut but unresisting. He placed a cool kiss on each eyelid and let his head fall back. He felt a tremor run down her, enclosed in his arms, felt it in his breast, arms, legs.

—You're cold, he whispered. Let me warm you, Lucy. . . .

He resolved to hold her so, giving her his sleep, all the night, till she woke and trusted. With his eyes he followed the flicker of firelight up till it was lost in the gray, unpainted plaster of the ceiling. . . .

He had not meant to sleep but woke with the fire out, chill damp air touching his face and cold light refracted through the bay window at the room's west end. Lucy still lay rigid but perhaps had slept, was sleeping. Both arms ached, the left numb with the weight of her head. What made her so fearful? Last child of an aging mother, unless one or two came after and had not lived, he had not much sense of the whole family, but the lastborn so usually cheerful and loving, living life easy. Lizzie, of course, fifteen years older more or less, had partly raised her. Was it Lizzie, so competent and kind, who planted her with follies of men's brutish lusts and the woman's sorrow in childbearing that follows the joy of child getting? Eight years married and she had yet given Bill no child.

He got his arm free, raised himself on his elbow and felt the covers slip from his naked shoulders: his breath pressed the shape of her name to her lips, naming her—*Lucy, Lucy.* His other hand entered the yielding cleft where her legs joined, pulling, forcing them apart, drawing her gown up—*damn it, woman, we're married, it's my right.* . . .

He swung his right leg over, the other, lowered himself on his knees, thighs pressing outward at thighs, not so very different from mounting a horse: the place, *there*, he could feel it, groped, found, pressed—. Her eyes opened wide, looking up, looking past him.

—It hurts! she cried, her voice not loud but reverberating in the emptiness, and letting himself down on her he tried to stop it with his lips. Oh, it *hurts!* she cried again.

XXII

Cattle Paper &
Winter Wheat

The winter of 1872 was dry—so dry that the cattle and farm wagons had no need to use the toll bridge. The toll collectors idly watched the cattlemen take their herds across the river at any point. The bridge earned nothing, and Isaac's ten thousand dollars in bridge stock was worth half its original cost. The town people, too, were complaining about the toll; they thought the bridge should be free, and not by floating a bond issue, either.

During the summer that followed, the number of cattle coming through Wichita hit a new record. The bank, though it could loan no more than ten percent of its capital, had no limitation on commercial paper. Cattle paper was the heart of the bank's business that year. The bank itself occasionally invested in cattle for the three months or so of fattening and transport and sale in eastern markets.

About this time Isaac learned that Bill Greiffenstein had sold his stock and resigned as director of the bank. His place as director had been filled by one of Fraker's partners in a new mill he'd invested in; an enterprise which promised well, certainly, with the growing amount of land being put to wheat. Fraker had also invested in the new Occidental Hotel, said to be the grandest in the state, and certainly competition for Bill. These were events that caused Isaac unease.

The grasshoppers came in August and devastated the land. Even the wooden handles of farm implements were eaten where man's sweat was ingrained. This was followed in September by the run on banks set off by the failure of Jay Cooke of Philadelphia, who had tried single-handed to finance the Northern Pacific Railroad. The panic spread, and in Wichita it necessarily centered on the cattle trade. The First National Bank stood in delicate balance between the cattle dealers and the cattlemen. With requests for restraint in demands for cash, the bank managed to get through the fall and until the bulk of the cattle had been sold and the loans, many much extended, paid off.

Mathewson finally closed out his Indian business early in 1874. Isaac's interest in it came to eight thousand dollars, with another thirty-six hundred dollars still owed on a mortgage taken on Mathewson's claim east of Wichita. Except for a little to operate on, most of this cash he put into certificates of deposit of the St Louis National at three and six months; in the face of his continuing anxieties over the progress of the Wichita bank and his parents' investment in it, he was in no haste to put his money to fresh risk. What wise and continuing use to make of money that came at intervals with the appearance of income—money from the sale of lots, now Mathewson's money—but was in reality capital, unregainable when spent.

He thought vaguely of going in with E. H. Durfee somehow, he had been unwell of late, would welcome a vigorous and active partner, and the brother-in-law he had brought into the firm hardly carried his weight. Then in September the question, half formed, was answered: the report came of Mr Durfee's death, at home at Leavenworth, of nephritis, three months short of forty-six years old.

Events kept turning his thoughts to cattle. It had seemed to him in the old days that if ever the buffalo diminished, their place would be taken in natural succession by cattle herds fattening on the same rich grasses: no reason they should not winter through on the Plains— except for the occasional blizzard, the Kansas winters were mild enough, the ripe grass cured on the ground and made nourishing pasture for horses, oxen, wintering buffalo, and why not the half-wild Texas longhorns? In his mind he had already settled on the country he would take his cattle to. Sedgwick County was now too settled to provide the large blocks of range land needed for a herd of reasonable size, but a little farther west the country was cleared of Indians and as yet uninhabited by whites, only a few drovers passing through, coming north along a recently opened branching of the Chisholm Trail. He thought of the upper Ninnescah and Medicine Lodge Creek—a river, really, by its size and constant flow, and properly so called— only eighty miles southwest of Wichita, where the last great council of the wild tribes was held, where he himself had gone for trading and hunting, even then it was country that brought cattle to mind.

Isaac in August allowed himself ten days from Wichita for a leisurely ride out toward the river's headwaters alone, to see if the country was as he remembered. He came home encouraged and enlivened: good grass hardly touched now the buffalo were gone, timber along the river and its tributary creeks that would do for the two or three cabins needed for a winter camp, and shelter in the creek bottoms to get the cattle into if the weather turned stormy; and near enough to Wichita that he could ride over every week or two to protect his interest without having to stay out all the winter.

The arithmetic of the scheme gave him more pleasure than he had felt for months. In the fall, at the end of a slow season, he could take his pick of prime Texas beef at, say, ten dollars a head, trail them north to fatten through the winter, and in May, like a farmer with early fruit, bring them in to Wichita to sell ahead of the market, twenty-five dollars easily and no dickering, maybe higher with any luck. Expenses he calculated at twenty-two hundred dollars complete, but say twenty-five hundred to allow for accidents, crew fares home at the end, maybe losing something on reselling the string of thirty or forty horses he would have to get up: no reason he could see not to clear twenty thousand dollars on a herd of medium size, say fifteen hundred.

The difficulty again was shortage of capital: would need to put in close to eighteen thousand dollars to cover an operation of that size— it was part of his plan to get the best stock and price in Texas by paying cash, not buying on credit or otherwise going into debt. He had about enough in his St Louis certificates to cover five hundred head and expenses—could hardly do with a smaller crew, and the small herd would cost nearly as much as a big one to keep, cutting the profit to where the thing was hardly worth going into.

Isaac's spirits flattened again after two days at home: when has a man ever the money for the opportunities he reaches out to take? He spent dull days at his office on Douglass, gloomily meditating other investments, but his thoughts hovered on cattle, and he sketched out on paper and discarded, one after the other, schemes for raising the money; none worked out. In September came a laconic letter from H. H. Hackney, a Pittsburgh merchant and speculator in Western land Isaac had come to know through a younger brother practicing law at Newton, had visited at his home on a trip east and persuaded to take fifty shares from the last issue of bank stock: did not understand all the talk of hard times, he was finding it as good a time as any for making money and in fact had some lying idle this very moment —could Mr Pride perhaps put him onto something in his section of country, not too long-term?

With the feeling his luck was not dead after all, Isaac answered with two careful pages outlining his cattle scheme, the figures set out in detail, and proposed that Mr Hackney put in twelve thousand dollars to his own six, splitting the profit in return for Isaac's managing the undertaking—on fifteen hundred head, he figured they would clear ten thousand each. Mr Hackney answered with a formal contract offering ten thousand and a division of profits in proportion to investment by each. Isaac signed and returned the agreement without change, figuring that if he ran short on expenses for the trail crew he could cover himself with overdrafts, up to a thousand dollars or so. Mr Hackney responded with a draft of ten thousand dollars to Isaac's favor at the Wichita bank. At the end of the month he started for San Antonio, going the roundabout route by Bob Stevens's former railroad—the Katy, bankrupt since the panic and now in process of acquisition by Jay Gould—through the eastern Indian Territory as far as Red River and on through Texas by stagecoach.

San Antonio at first sight was the recognizable original from which Wichita and the other cattle towns derived: half the population seemed to be cowboys and cattlemen, the rest Mexicans—eight or ten hotels, dozens of gambling saloons, some of great elegance. Isaac put up at the Central, a little more modest in accommodation and price than the Menger, but had no time for diversions. He had written ahead to a half-dozen ranchers outlying the city and the morning after his arrival hired a horse and rode out to make the rounds.

Isaac did most of his cattle business with André Long. Isaac found he did not know much about judging cattle on the hoof: whether a jut-boned three-year-old steer would survive the drive and the winter, put on respectable weight to be worth selling in the spring—the little he learned as a boy from his father's cows did not apply; buffalo he had taken chiefly for their hides, not meat. For four days he rode among Long's herds, dodging the vicious pointed horns, with the rancher, his foreman, three or four hands, and steers he chose the men cut out and turned into a fenced holding ground, Long made an entry in his pocket notebook, and the sale was accomplished: fifteen hundred head exactly. Long helped him assemble a crew—an assistant foreman who would do for boss, a cook, the ten hands he said it would take to get the herd to Barber County, most from his own ranch. They were a week trail-branding—Isaac had the ranch blacksmith forge two irons in his Sun-Boy emblem, drawn with a stick in the dust outside the shop, the same he had years ago devised for the cattle Jesse Chisholm brought up from his home ranch in the Territory.

Isaac had decided to make the whole trip back by stage, four days. Beyond Fort Worth the stage diverged from the general route of the cattle trail and toward evening of the second day out was rolling along beside Cache Creek approaching Fort Sill and the Kiowa Agency store for a supper stop and a change of horses. Isaac, dozing alone in the rear seat, no other passengers since Red River Station, roused himself and pulled back the curtain to look out: a little square sod-roofed windowless cabin that would about do for a buffalo hunter or an Indian, surrounded by an acre of dry yellow cornstalks clashing in the October wind and a fat old gray-haired, parchment-skinned woman coming through it, bent under a load of sticks for the evening cooking, tumped in a blanket on her back, a gang of dogs and children roiling the dust by the doorstep; a woman such as Pat-so-gate would in time become if she persisted in her Indian ways, her hair no longer golden, indistinguishable from all others. The coach pulled up at the store—the trading post Mathewson had built and operated and Isaac had financed, where now it was sold there was probably no one left that he knew. He got down and started toward the building anticipating the usual fried salt pork and watery coffee, a long night ahead, you had to eat something.

The new owners made Isaac welcome. In the morning he borrowed a horse and rode to find Set-im-kayah's camp. He recognized the chief's lodge, set off by itself on the bank of a little stream flowing into Cache Creek a mile above the fort. For a quarter-hour he hung back, sitting the horse at a distance, looking all around, but could see no one: a trickle of smoke spilling from the smoke hole of the tepee— getting to be an old man now and the morning chill, he was in there by a small fire, warming himself—and in front of the doorway a cook fire smoldering with a chunk of meat over it on a spit; beyond, three Indian pintos tethered. There was a lightness and quickness pressing upward from his belly, filling his chest, tightening his throat till his breath came short and his skin prickled with warmth under the close-fitting city clothes he had worn since leaving San Antonio. He walked the horse toward the lodge, a pony nickered at his approach as if it knew him; dismounted, stooped, scratched politely at the door-flap and softly called Set-im-kayah's name and his own, Pai-tal-ye. After a moment the Indian answered and he let himself in, crouching in the luminous interior dark.

Set-im-kayah, drowsing on a backrest with a worn buffalo robe pulled across his legs, gestured Isaac to a seat beside the fire. When he had prepared and exchanged his pipe, he called out, then, getting no answer, heaved himself up, went to the door to look out, and came back frowning.

—Pat-so-gate? Isaac said aloud, taking a guess.

Yes, the Indian asserted, No other would have her. Now she shamed him by having no meat to offer when his friend came—

Isaac said he was not hungry, had come out of respect for Stumbling Bear and to talk, not eat. He asked about the baby—

Man-makes-thunder, Stumbling Bear said—Tunk-aht-oh-ye, the name she gave him, too big a name for a little boy, unlucky. Did Pai-tal-ye not know the boy was dead?

Isaac shook his head.

The Indian told: when Big Tree joined the Comanche war party, Pat-so-gate went with him. Women do so sometimes, permitted if the warriors make no objection. She insisted on taking the baby, to make him a warrior, she said, to match his name, which was disapproved by all but her husband, the women especially; many would have kept and nursed him. It was at Bent's old post which the whites call Adobe Walls, a stray bullet that carried half a mile, while she held him in her arms—so small, yet a warrior's death. She came back alone carrying the dead child, buried him beside the creek where Stumbling Bear now made his camp. The Comanche Coyote Droppings blamed both for the failure of the war against the whites: the baby had spoiled his medicine.

—That might have been my own son, Isaac said, eyes throbbing with tears that spilled and stung his cheeks. Could not have been more like—

Set-im-kay-ah reached awkwardly across the smoky little fire and gripped his shoulders, expressionless, eyes staring: She did not think that, he said, shaking his head, maybe did not want the boy to live, because of that, maybe Big Tree too.

They lay back for a time, exchanging no more signs. Then the Indian stiffened, straightened up, threw the robe off, rolled, and got cumbrously to his feet. Isaac felt a chill as of spirit swirling past him in the permeable confines of the tent, departing, and shivered. He stood up.

You must go now, Set-im-kayah told him, cannot stay longer. We will not meet again, we that have been friends, that have wanted much good, each for the other, and have done little good. He caught Isaac's hand in both his and held it.

Isaac got his billfold out, drew forth the sheaf of bills, a hundred dollars and some, all that remained from his cattle buying and the trip, and divided them, reaching half across to Stumbling Bear.— Here, he said aloud, in English, you know what that's for, money, buy things with at the store—if I had more, I'd give more, but I can't and get home.

Set-im-kayah nodded, accepted the bills, folded them once, and slipped them in the pouch strung at his waist.

Buy her something, Isaac went on in signs, a good horse, blankets, or for both of them, and don't tell it's from me—but something—

He darted out the entrance. The borrowed horse, he had been careless, hadn't had his mind on his business, had wandered off with the others, cropping the late grass.

Three horses, the thought exploded in him, three Indian ponies! She had seen him coming, in front of the lodge, cooking the old man's dinner, and ran and hid, down along the creek, among the trees and

brush, or crouched beside the tepee listening, lifting the edge of the
buffalo hide to look—

—Patsy! he called, his voice rising. For the love of God, Patsy!

Isaac ran at the tethered horses, stumbling in the tufts and hummocks of drying grass, crying out, no words left him. The horses
reared and screamed, fighting the rawhide ropes that held them to
their stakes, as at the smell of mountain lion hunting them, the black
smell of prairie fire burning through the grass.

He was home for Christmas with Lucy and the children, bringing
in a brace of turkeys shot on the way. Isaac stayed on for the New
Year and went out again, five trips back to the range before he was
done: camped with the men a week at a time, hunted meat for them,
even one solitary tough old buffalo bull; rode the rounds, learning the
skill of cattle-holding, and felt better than he had for a year or two,
maybe years back.

The arrangement for the new herd in the fall was a little different
from the year before. Mr Hackney wanted his Kansas brother's son
involved as trail-boss: Bill Hackney, twenty-five, earnest, well-edu-
cated, shrewd enough to insist on a share in the eventual sale rather
than a boss's wage, thirty or thirty-five dollars a month. Isaac met and
liked him and agreed, figuring that being able to speak for the owners
would make up for his inexperience in leading the trail crew; and Bill
seemed a ready student of matters about which Isaac felt a growing
and systematic curiosity, the fossils of the Plains, Indian artifacts, the
rapidly changing wildlife. They traveled together to San Antonio,
going around by rail this time as far as Dallas, beginning to compete
with Wichita despite the disadvantage in freight costs. Riding the
range land with André Long, they bought two thousand head at
prices that this year averaged twelve dollars, and fifty ponies for the
enlarged trail gang they would need.

Isaac's knowledge of the bank's affairs was vague and intermittent.

In the early spring, while Isaac was making a visit home and doing
a desultory trade in lots, nearly all on time, his luck took a fresh turn.
A Topeka investor made a low but serious offer on the quarter-section
farm across the Kaw from the capital, first bought for Marie and now
defensively put in the children's names with himself as trustee and
unsatisfactorily rented, which for years he had been wanting to sell.
He took the cars, met the gentleman, and came to agreement: something over $21 an acre for the 160 acres. Talk and anecdote at Wichita
were no longer of cattle but of winter wheat. It was the easy and
unexpected sale of the troublesome Topeka farm that put wheat in
Isaac's mind as a matter of personal interest, not merely a topic of
polite conversation about which to keep informed over dinner at the

Occidental. In the thousand square miles of Sedgwick County there was probably by now no unclaimed land, but there was much held on speculation, never broken to plow or improved, that under the promise of wheat was beginning to sell. Isaac in March had the luck to find a half-section of unplowed prairie a scant five miles south of town, rich bottomland in sight of the Arkansas, so level you could stand in the center and see the four corner stakes a half-mile distant; offered the claimant $1,200, under $4.00 an acre, an average price for such land, and got it; and missed the adjoining quarter by a day or two. No reason he should not get thirty bushels an acre in time but say twenty the first season, estimating cautiously. Breaking the sod would come to $800, around $1,100 for plowing, seeds, implements, and planting, another $600 for harvesting, $250 each for threshing and haulage to town. He figured a profit of $1,800 the first year, $5,200 the second year. Isaac copied his estimates into a letter to his father and challenged him to keep them and compare when the wheat was cut and sold.

When he closed out his herds at the end of May, Isaac was left with twenty-five thousand dollars clear, beyond what it would cost him to develop the new farm and harvest the first crop; money on call and earning at a moderate rate while he thought what to do next.

Isaac, busy with the buildings on the wheat farm to be gotten ready in time for his tenant to move in and start planting, had frequent demands on his cash. Wages for his workmen, were running nearly two hundred dollars a week; the suppliers of brick and lumber insisted on payment on delivery, nearly all of them in cash, not by check. Anticipating, he went to the bank to draw a thousand dollars from his account. Edwin Wright, the bookkeeper, was at the teller's window, an earnest, agreeable young man Isaac had always found careful and accurate with his figures as well as anxious to please. Wright glanced at the check and with a shake of his head pushed it back across the counter.

—Something wrong with it? Isaac asked. I keep over four thousand in that account, long since collected on. Look it up and verify, if you've any doubt, I can wait. . . . He had another thought: If it's inconvenient somehow, I could get by with five hundred today and the balance on Monday. How's that?

Wright with a nervous little smile again shook his head: was aware how Mr Pride's account stood, no need to look it up. If Mr Pride could take his withdrawal by cashier's check—several checks, if more convenient—

—No, it *aint* convenient, not at all. I can't do with checks—got to have cash to—

It was a rule, Wright said in a low and hurried voice, with an anxious glance past Isaac at the two other customers behind him, waiting. A new rule only just gone in and no doubt temporary. If Mr Pride would care to take it up with the cashier, Mr Eldridge—

—You're damn right I'll take it up! Never heard of such a rule—

And seizing his check, Isaac stepped past the customers, let himself through the gate, and marched over to Eldridge's desk.

—What's this about a rule against drawing cash on my account? Isaac demanded, dropping the check on the cashier's blotting pad.

Eldridge for some moments studied the check: a soft-looking, dark, laconic man with an air of amused superior knowledge that stopped short of insolence. He looked up, faintly smiling.

—We're asking directors and stockholders—any that's got a special interest in the bank—to hold withdrawals down to a hundred a week, he said quietly. Reckon we'll be freer again in a week or so. And no limit on cashier's checks, of course, if that'd suit.

—You know damn well it don't suit! Isaac shot back, trying not to shout. I've got men to pay—and the brickyard, the lumberyard, stonecutters and every kind of trade—and they've got to have cash. Why— I offer them checks, they'd stop work on me, I'd be a fool and laughingstock to the whole town, and my credit gone—. And let me tell you, Mister Eldridge, I'm damned if I know—when I've put my good money in this bank and given it my business and put in my time— you tell me why I've got to be handicapped more than any ordinary customer that walks in off the street.

—I'm a director same as you, Eldridge said, and up against the same limit. And my father and me, between us we've put about as much money in as you have.

—Maybe you have, Isaac said, but haven't the same need just at present. No, sir! That's money I can't do without—

Eldridge with a shrug handed the check back.—You can take it up with the president, he said. In his office, I believe—it's his rule, and I reckon he can make exception, if he likes. . . .

Isaac, jaw set, face dark, strode to Fraker's door, gave it a sharp rap, flung it open, and closed it sharply behind him. The president looked up from his papers with a smile of humble inquiry. Isaac slapped the check down on his desk.

—That's my check for a thousand dollars that your two clerks out there just refused, he said, against over four thousand in the account. Mister Fraker!—no man can carry on his business in that fashion—

—Oh, I *know*, said the president, still with his soothing smile. *Terrible* awkward for all of us—and Mister Thomas and Mister Kincaid and me, all in the same position as yourself, and the mill only just starting to earn, and demands on our resources coming right along— but of course, having the good and safety of the bank at heart—

—Now you know that's my sentiment same as yours, Isaac broke in. But not if it's going to ruin me. I've got a gang of men's got to be paid on Saturday, got other bills. I can't have my money—

—There's shipments of currency coming in next week that'll put us right. And cattlemen that have sold, bringing in deposits right along, and some of the farmers—

—What're we down to in currency? Isaac demanded.

—Three thousand something when we counted this morning before opening. And three twenty-five in specie that there's never call for. And fractional money, and stamps, a hundred or so—. We'll get through the week, I reckon, if we all pull together and exercise restraint. And then next week, I don't see why—. Say now, Mr Fraker said, reaching out his short arms in entreaty and embrace: I don't know why you shouldn't take three hundred to make your payroll, and your suppliers—well, given em something on account if they got to have it.

Isaac nodded agreement, but his mind raced down the branches and turnings of the road that now opened before him. Rewrite the check for three hundred, and yes, the rest could be put off a week or two, though he hated it. Then close his accounts at Wichita, but no—that wouldn't do either, look bad, and he had to have the cash for day-to-day call, if he could get it. Most of his money was in certificates of the St Louis National, he had meant to cash them at intervals through the summer to pay his building costs, but best to get some of that in at once, keep it at the office in the cash box.

Mr Fraker was going on about his latest fight in the city council. He was still leading Wichita reform: the year before, on the issue of using city money to promote the cattle trade, had run George Harris, a saloonkeeper, for mayor against Jim Hope, a likable wholesale-liquor dealer first elected in 1872, and had won, and put through ordinances that were claimed to have driven gambling from the saloon and prostitution from the houses of ill-repute. Now Hope was back as mayor. . . . What the devil connection was there between his political games and the bank? Or Isaac's own money on deposit that he would not pay?

—What happened to the reserve fund?

Isaac stood up, leaning his fists on the desk, breath coming short and quick.

—Demands on our cash all summer has been—

—In March you said we had fourteen thousand put aside, money that came from reducing our circulation, and our profit-and-loss—so much we'd get through anything. How much've we got left?

—I *told* you, the count this morning. Mr Fraker popped from his chair and started for the door. I'll have Mister Wright take a fresh count, so we'll—

Isaac gripped his soft shoulders, pushed him back, and held him against the wall.

—You're going to show me how much is in your tin box, he said.

The president's eyes darted.—I hardly think it proper, Mister Pride—

Isaac let him go, stood back.—I'm vice-president of this bank, I've got the right, he said, aint any matter of our business that's *not* my affair. And if that don't open that box, I'll be back here this afternoon with a court order for it. And if that don't do it, why, by God, I'll—

—Of course, of *course*, Mister Pride, Mr Fraker said, drawing himself up with a shake of his shoulders like a wet dog.

Isaac made him take the key off his watch chain and hand it over. They went together to the vault. Isaac carried the strongbox back to the office, set it on the desk, fitted the key, and pulled back the lid. Instead of neat stacks of crisp new banknotes and legal tenders tied up with red tape, little slips with the count for each, there was only a thin sheaf of printed forms on white paper, each apparently bearing Fraker's smooth-flowing, confident signature. Isaac turned the box out and shook it, scattering the contents across the desk; at the bottom, three or four hundred dollars in dirty, mutilated bills unfit for circulation and not yet sent in to the Comptroller for replacement. He closed the lid and set the box down on the carpet.

The papers were promissory notes to the bank, all given by the president, a thousand dollars, two thousand, some going back a year —even in March when he was swearing the amount of the reserve and showing the cashbox that held it, there had probably not been much left. Isaac riffled through the notes, looked to foot up to around eleven thousand, and—my God! it came to him—when they put their report in the *Eagle* at the end of June, as law required, they had claimed thirteen thousand for profit-and-loss and surplus, as usual not reporting their actual reserve: but maybe two thousand cash and eleven thousand of Fraker's notes was about what it must have meant in fact.

Mr Fraker stood at the window with his back turned, plump hands clasped, contemplating the empty lot behind the building.

—I only done what seemed right at the time, for the good of the bank, Mister Pride, he said in a faint voice, you can understand that, I know—I hadn't gone in that mill, they'd've failed, we'd be out the whole eight thousand of our loan, and then—then, I don't know what—.

Isaac leaned wearily on the desk, sorting, smoothing the notes, putting them in order; there were nine.—I've read that the streets of hell are paved with good intentions, Mister Fraker, he said softly. I don't see we could be any worse off if the mill did fail. Our reserve cleaned out and our cash turned into worthless paper.

—*Worthless*, Mister Pride? Mr Fraker indignantly demanded, swinging around on him.

—*And* it's some thousands over what the law says we can loan to an individual or enterprise—and I don't doubt your partners borrowed what *they* put in, which makes it three or four times over.

—But don't you see, we've come through with the mill? Mr Fraker said, taking a step toward him. Only barely started up and we're doing a thousand a month—it'll go fifteen hundred in the fall when harvest comes, two thousand—

—And you'd be two or three years paying back out of your share, *if* it was all profit. We'd be broken up by then, long since. And interest aint even specified.

—Why, Mister Pride, you know I'm good for it—everybody knows —I'm worth *many times* that modest sum, I can tell you, can give all the security in the world, if it was deemed right and necessary, though I hardly think—

—Such as?

—Well now, I can't think, here and now—

Isaac took a step toward him. Mr Fraker backed away.

—Well, there's my interest in the mill, and the Occidental—

Isaac let out a snort.

Mr Fraker hurried on.—And farms in Butler County and Lyon County, and town lots at El Dorado, and the warehouse at Emporia, and the implement business, of which half is my brother's—my very home, if I was called on, for the sake of this bank and my good name—

—Which you know state law don't allow us to touch, Isaac said. But the rest of it—would you make it over in proper form to secure these notes, as much as it takes?

Mr Fraker hesitated, then—Anything I give my word to, I'll do, Mister Pride, he said with dignity. And put it in writing too, this very hour, if you insist. As the head and founder of this enterprise, you must know, I live my life as a book open to the eye of the public, always have—can't do with any little, hidden—

Isaac took him by the arm, propelled him to his chair, and sat him at his desk.—Write out the list, he commanded, legal description and encumbrances. I'll have Henry Sluss draw it all up in proper form— trustee deeds is what I think of, and don't revert till the whole debt's paid, but he'll know how best to set it out. . . .

He took the list when the president had finished and read it through, already wearily thinking ahead to the time and effort it would take; he folded the sheet of paper around Mr Fraker's notes and slipped them into his coat pocket.

—Say now! Mr Fraker protested. Those are resources of this bank. I can't allow—

—Sluss has got to see them too—maybe he'll want to incorporate them in the agreement he draws—or rewrite so they're worth something. But here—he reached across the desk, took Mr Fraker's pen and a fresh sheet—I'll write you a receipt, and a copy for myself, and you can keep it in your strongbox with the spoiled currency till I give them back. And while I'm at it—a check for three hundred dollars, and I'll tear up the old one. And you go tell Wright and Eldridge they can pay. . . .

Isaac was stepping briskly down Douglass toward Henry Sluss's office, aiming to catch him before he went out to dinner, when it struck him Fraker had not put his bank stock on the list of property, still a hundred shares, so far as he knew, but among his other worries could not drive his mind to search out a reason. Just an oversight, no doubt, Fraker had worries of his own after so lively a morning. And the real estate ought to be plenty to cover what he owed.

XXIII

Liquidation

Isaac was at breakfast a little after eight one Monday morning in late August, when there came a knocking at the front door, the little kitchen maid ran to answer, and a moment later informed him that Mr Fraker wanted him. The president was waiting on the porch, would not come in, and cut him off in the midst of an invitation to join them at table for coffee.

—The most terrible thing, Mister Pride! Fraker said. We don't get some cash in within the hour, we can't open our doors.

—What's happened? Some bank robber violate the Sabbath peace by working his trade on our premises?

—Mister Pride! Worse—far worse: the express of currency we're expecting—neither has come. Called at the depot to inquire on Friday, twice on Saturday, and again this morning—

—Now what in mercy's name, Mister Fraker? Isaac demanded. What's become of the cash we still had Thursday night? Five or six thousand, Eldridge told us, I recall—

—Some optimistic perhaps, Fraker said. But pretty near—but what with withdrawals Friday and again Saturday morning—nothing big, you understand, but all proper claims we couldn't refuse—and nothing much coming in—. We don't have much over five hundred left, counting in stamps.

—Any idea what's holding this currency? Two different shipments?

Fraker shook his head in dejection, then brightened a little.— Surely by the afternoon train—tomorrow morning at the latest—. I shall telegraph—

—How much'd't take, to get us through?

—Five thousand to make us comfortable—or, supposing deposits come in—though Mondays aint generally lively that way—or persuade some of our friends to pay early on notes, for a little premium —well, we might do with half that sum—

—So you come to me, figuring I've got more cash than sense, Isaac said, stamping his boot heels. Cause you've no money of your own left to put in, and those others you've got on the board now, the same, all laid out on the mill, or God knows what—.

He stopped himself, pacing angrily up and down the echoing porch while the banker leaned by the door, head hanging. Probably he did have the minimum Fraker was begging him for, two thousand or twenty-five hundred, in the little safe at his office—had kept cash on hand all summer, since the last scare, and let his account at the bank go down to a few hundred; but could not risk it all without calling off the building crews, by now within three weeks of finishing. On the other hand, he could borrow—still, thank God, no shortage of friends or credit. It was the old dilemma, souring all his dealings with the bank: let it go, and fail, as now seemed likely, to judge from Fraker's frantic manner, and lose all he had put in, ruin and disgrace his parents; or go still deeper, but make time for hope, some chance of recovering or at least getting clear and beyond harm. . . .

Isaac stopped his pacing, seized the banker by the lapels of his coat and pulled him close.—Listen, he said in a low voice, I'll get the money for you—enough, anyhow, if all's as you say, maybe more later in the day, if I can. But I've got to have security for it, good as gold. And something more—proof this currency is really on the way. And if you don't—well, by God, you and the bank can go straight to hell, but I'll have your hide before I'm done, if we all go up—

—Of course, of *course*, Mister Pride, Fraker cried, eyes glaring as if the threatening words had evoked the beatific vision. And only businesslike and proper—

Isaac let go, shoved the door ajar, and called out to Lucy that he was going downtown with Mr Fraker.

By the private side door on First Street Mr Fraker let them straight into his office and from a locked drawer of his desk produced the proofs Isaac had demanded: statements a week and ten days old from the St Louis and New York correspondent banks, other national and state banks, showing among them a net of around eighteen thousand dollars due First Wichita; letterpress copies of his letters, dated a week past, instructing the correspondents to draw two thousand dollars and three thousand dollars respectively on the accounts and ship in currency by express. To secure Isaac's cash, the banker proposed a draft on the St Louis account up to three thousand dollars, the balance, and if he brought in more, the remainder on any other bank he chose from which exchange was due. It was as much as Isaac could think of to ask, and he started for the door to let himself out and do what he had promised. Halfway he stopped, came back.

—Those notes of yours in the strongbox, he said softly, almost whispering. Little private matter between you and the bank, never entered on the books. That wasn't all, was it? Every time, all these years, you ran short of cash, you just helped yourself till you didn't know which was which, bank money and your own—

—I kept accurate record, Fraker said defiantly. Every penny, proper and in order, to be paid when the time comes. And you know I never acted from any motive of personal gain, but only for the good—

—Why didn't you tell me there was more?

—You never asked.

Isaac tried to think back: was it true? had he been such a fool and baby?—How much? he said. Fraker got around on the other side of his desk. *How much?* Isaac shouted, the roar of his voice rattling back from the window glass.

—Around twenty-one thousand, something over—I'd have to add it up on paper to be exact.

—I want a list—amounts owed, dates made and due, rate of interest —everything, no quibbling, nothing left out. And the paper that backs it up—and if the property you've already made over aint enough to cover, why, I'll take my money back where I got it, and you and the bank can go to the Devil!

He was back in an hour with $2,000 in worn tradesmen's bills tied with twine in a brown paper sack: $400 from his office safe and the rest borrowed on seven-day notes, though it made him sick, rehearsing the story of the delayed shipments of currency. Ed Wright was throwing open the main doors, raising the blinds, ready for the day's business. Fraker in silence showed him the list and the supporting notes: with the previous lot, still open, it came to $21,167.17. Isaac folded the papers away in an inner coat pocket and handed over his cash.

He loitered the whole day at the bank, keeping watch. He was as unobtrusive as he could manage—chatting with customers he knew, twice urging particular friends to restraint in withdrawing. Business was slow, as Fraker had predicted—no sign of a run, no panic, just ordinary business of a Monday at the end of August—but hour by hour a little more money went out than came in: by the four-thirty closing time, they had still not suspended, but Isaac's two thousand was gone; they were left with the four or five hundred with which they started the day.

Isaac took Fraker's buggy and himself drove to the express office, but the agent knew nothing of any package addressed to the First

National Bank of Wichita. On the way back he stopped at Henry
Sluss's office.

—Those statements he showed you, the lawyer said when Isaac had
told him of the money borrowed to keep the bank open. All a week or
two old? Isaac glumly nodded. How do you know the balances
weren't already taken up by bills in transit? Or drawn against to
settle accounts with other correspondents? Those statements—they
don't prove a thing, there's a hundred ways they could be wrong.

Isaac, leaning on the lawyer's desk, head down, said nothing for a
time.—What can I do?

—Start taking my advice! Henry Sluss briskly answered—or get
yourself a new lawyer. We'll go to the bank. I don't know a whole lot
about bookkeeping, but I can make sense of a balance sheet. We'll get
you through!

The lawyer was two hours with the president and cashier going
over the closing balance for the day, then reviewing the bank's assets
—loans and discounts, amounts due from various other banks—and
the supporting notes and statements. At the end, Mr Fraker seemed
entirely at his ease again: taking the most cautious view of what notes
could actually be collected, Henry Sluss judged the bank's assets sufficient to pay all deposits—sixty thousand dollars in good loans and
another twenty-five thousand dollars in exchange from banks, making
no allowance for the bank building itself, original cost over twenty
thousand dollars with furnishings, now carried on the books at its
valuation for tax purposes, twelve thousand five hundred dollars,
though where a buyer could be found at anything near that price was
another question. Isaac, looking on, noted but said nothing of the odd
fact that the bank's position in every account had worsened in the
short weeks since the last examination: deposits up by five thousand
dollars, dues from correspondents down about the same; loans, despite Fraker's assurances they would be called in and reduced, had
risen by eleven thousand dollars and those likely to turn out uncol-
lectible in proportion by the simple process of notes falling due and
remaining unpaid—where Fraker had vehemently disputed the examiner's total of nearly twenty-five thousand dollars in doubtful paper,
he now cheerfully agreed that for present purposes at least thirty
thousand dollars could not be relied on and was likely to be written
off.

The difficulty, then, seemed not to be the balance between asset and
liabilities but simply a shortage of cash to cover demand deposits; no
more was said of the tardy shipments of currency—for whatever reason, they were not coming.

—You can't open tomorrow, that's plain, Sluss concluded, surveying the sheets of ledger paper covered with figures that were arrayed
across the president's desk. You do, your cash won't last the morning,

and when you suspend, you'll have depositors crying round you like a pack of wolves, putting in court judgments, protesting to the Comptroller, and other banks will stop payment on what they're owing, and the Comptroller will have a receiver in to take charge within a week—and then the fun starts. He'll discount your paper to the first comer that'll put up cash, sell your property for half what it'd bring with a little prudent waiting—and write off loans that might cost something in court fees to collect—all so's to turn your assets into cash to distribute to depositors with the least delay, and you'll pay him a hundred or a hundred fifty a month for the privilege, *and* expenses and a clerk's wage. And when he's done you'll find your assets shrunk by a third or half what you count today, and land it on the shareholders to make good, twenty or thirty thousand dollars maybe, any of em aren't lodged already on the county poor farm.

Only Isaac, the onlooker, appeared much troubled by this recital: Fraker smooth and unruffled, checking and rechecking the columns of figures with a freshly sharpened pencil, making notes on a tablet, tunelessly humming or whistling to himself in small, breathy, birdlike notes; Eldridge dark and immobile, apparently immune to surprise; and Henry Sluss himself, exhilarated by his own unselfconscious competence as he led them along the paths of argument to necessary conclusions.

—Then what's to be done? Isaac said, giving him his cue in a throbbing voice. Have we got to sit here while they bleed us dry? Not that I can't meet any assessment to the full value of my stock—my parents' too—. But it'd clean me out.

—That's how it'll go, more or less, if you leave the Comptroller to take charge, the lawyer said. But you don't have to—you can start voluntary liquidation, run the show yourselves, and come through with your skins intact, pretty much. Of course the Comptroller will put someone in for an independent audit, but if he reads the books same as we do, the law's in your favor and he can't stop you winding up. But you got to start it immediately, this very night. . . .

The first step was a telegram to the Comptroller announcing their intention, to be followed by a letter stating the bank's present condition. For the moment, Sluss was less concerned about the legal steps than the practical matter of how depositors and citizens would take the news—Wichita was of a size to offer many recruits to any mob a few hotheads might choose to lead. To head off any such development, he proposed they put the bank management in the hands of a committee of depositors and leading citizens, none shareholders or present officers or directors; trusted, public-spirited men like Greiffenstein, Charley Gilbert, perhaps Bill Mathewson, a minister or two, a lawyer of course, though Henry Sluss thought it not proper to serve himself—the officers would stay on, but the committee would assure all claimants that assets would be fairly distributed and accounted for. And finally, by way of precaution, Sluss drew up a further deed by which the president made over his property to Isaac Pride as trustee for the bank, to be canceled only when the liquidation was complete.

The final step, drafting a formal statement to go in Thursday's *Eagle* and be distributed to customers, took them as long as all that had gone before. Fraker wrote it out, several florid pages of argument and justification; Henry Sluss revised, shortened, generalized. They debated for some minutes how to refer to the president's deeding his property to make good any deficiency, an act to which he seemed to attach great importance, and at length agreed to let the paragraph stand in the form of a challenge to cautious creditors:

> *If there are any Depositors who are uneasy, and think they will not be paid, I am willing to back up my judgment to the extent of all my private property, not even excepting my homestead. I therefore make the following proposition: I will sell, at fair and reasonable valuation, my property, to any depositor of the First National Bank, and I will take your claims against said Bank, in payment. No man appreciates his Home more than does myself, but I will cheerfuly part with same, if it will satisfy claims of Depositors of this Bank.*

Isaac knew as well as any of them that in the present slack state of Wichita real estate, no one would give anything of value for so doubtful a title, even if there were a depositor with a claim for the nine or ten thousand dollars his house was reasonably worth—and if, strictly speaking, it was still his to sell, as he insisted on putting it, but wearied of objecting—the words would go over Fraker's signature, let him say what he liked.

It was ten o'clock when Isaac got clear of the bank building and walked north on Main Street through the summer night, crickets thrumming, pigs and stray dogs snuffling in the empty lots, toward Marsh Murdock's house with the fair copy of Fraker's statement in his pocket, something material at last to accomplish. The publisher, called puffy-eyed and disgruntled from his bed, declined to run the statement as editorial, with any comment or endorsement of his own; would take it only as a card, cash in advance, and made no objection to running it off as a broadside for distribution. Isaac produced the money from his billfold and drove with Murdock to the printing office on Douglass; sat while he roused his compositor to set the copy, pull proof, and run off five hundred copies on cheap paper, the type to be held for a week in case more were needed.

Haven't You paid me back enough already? Took her that was dearer than everything to me, but You take and take, for one little fault—his own voice echoing through the darkness of his mind, but too drained of energy to sustain the argument. It was after midnight when Isaac got home.

Isaac was back at the bank before eight the next morning, and the other officers, Henry Sluss, the two other directors, soon after. The citizens persuaded to join the oversight committee had assembled by nine, headed by Bill Greiffenstein, to hear once more and at length the rehearsal of the bank's condition and begin to grasp the duties they had accepted; Mathewson had declined to take a hand, and Isaac had no heart to argue him into it even if that were possible. From Murdock's proof press, Isaac had procured a set of cardboard signs printed in end-of-the-world type and had them posted in the glass panels of the main doors and in every window: BANK CLOSED. Ed Wright was stationed at the door with a supply of the printed statement which he handed out to recognized customers, repeating its message: the bank, embarrassed for cash due to circumstances beyond its control, was liquidating but had assets to cover all it owed, and all depositors would be paid, in time. Mike Meagher—reappointed marshal—stood behind him with a pair of revolvers holstered on his belt, a shotgun cradled in his arms, no one let in unless approved by Isaac or another officer. The marshal had posted his half-dozen constables on the sidewalks around the building.

Depositors came singly to the door, accepted the statement, heard the teller out, and went down the steps again, but lingered, watchful, curious, baffled, two and three together quietly consulting across Main Street and around the corner on First. By noon, like wolves with their escort of coyotes and other, lesser scavengers drawn by the smell of fresh-killed meat to the ground where a hide-hunter had made his stand, there were a thousand onlookers filling the intersection, blocking traffic, but Meagher judged it best to keep his men close and not attempt to clear the streets. Despite its numbers, the crowd remained quiet and unfocused. Among them, Isaac, peering from windows, recognized members of the vigilance committee, who had closed their stores and offices and taken positions in the interest of order, though most were not armed, customers too, many of them; and around the fringe, cowboys drawn from the Douglass Avenue saloons, the camps beyond the Arkansas, in hope of entertainment— and gamblers and their fancy women from West Wichita, farmers in broad-brimmed straw hats and earth-stained overalls, come to town with wheat to sell, supplies to purchase, and finding not much business to be done that day.

—Where's Wright got to? Isaac demanded, passing the front doors and seeing Meagher standing alone.

The marshal cocked his chin outward. Near the middle of the intersection a dozen or twenty men were packed close, and at the center, the teller, hatless, waving a packet of his broadsheets in the air—fists raised around him, angry shouts rising, jeers.

—Said there were customers out there hadn't come in, Meagher said, and his duty to go talk to them. I figured I hadn't no call to stop him.

—Damn fool! I'll have to bring him in.

White faces under broad hats turned, like flowers turning and swaying in the fall winds combing the grasslands, as the door clicked open and banged to behind him. Isaac descended the steps, boots ringing on the metal. Cries, pulsing through the crowd in waves like fire starting in a wheat field, spreading, leaping, dancing—*There's one of em*—*Taken our money, the son of a bitch*—*Built his fine mansion with our money*—

And silence again, like the smoke rising in wisps from the black earth where the fire has passed: he walked unhurried, straight, looking neither right nor left, toward the thick center, where he had seen Ed Wright, and men made way, crowded back as from a man condemned and marching to the scaffold, as if to touch him would confer a share in his doom and the long train of luck from which it came. Two large men held the teller close, looking small, young, and badly scared between them: arms pinned back, a sleeve of his coat ripped loose at the shoulder seam, and his sheaf of broadsheets trampled at his feet; a third stood behind, hands heavy on his shoulder. Isaac looked the three in the eyes, slowly, one to the other, lingering.

—I don't recognize a one of you gentlemen as customer of our bank, he said quietly, and I don't know what cause you've got to come interfering with one of our officers. But if you did have money with us—you wouldn't get it a minute sooner if you tore his arms out from their sockets—! Isaac spat in the dust. Three big men and one little fellow aint hardly more'n a boy! And a thousand more standing behind you, backing you up to make you brave!—all cause he tried to do you some good and do his duty, according to his lights—.

The men, shamed, let go, took a step back. Isaac reached out, took the teller by the wrist, and with a shove sent him swaying back along the open corridor of bodies toward the bank.

—Now get along there, Wright, he called after. And this time stay at your post like we told you—

The voices again, all around him, in crescendo: *Little bastard*—*Wouldn't tell us when we get our money*—*Holding back on us*—*Come on there, Pride*—*Where's our money got to?*—*Give us our money back!*—*Our money*—*Money*—*Money!*—

—Gentlemen! Gentlemen! Isaac cried, his voice rising through the choric voices that enclosed and taunted him. You can't make the young fellow tell what he don't know—and there's none but the Lord God, that carries the everlasting roll of future time in His hands, can tell you *when*. But I'll tell you this—you'll *get* your money, every last cent, and every one what's justly his—just as fast as we can settle our affairs and get our money in and verify accounts—

What's he saying? Can't he talk any plainer than the other bastard?

—Boys! If I'm going to answer you, I can't do it one by one or we'll never get through—got to get where I can answer all together, let everyone hear and see—

He turned abruptly. Several, pressing close, staggered back as if threatened. Again he marched through the opening crowd, mounted the sidewalk, climbed the steps, and faced them, back to the glass doors. The crowd closed up behind him, pressing in. Below him and a little to the right, in front of the steps down to the marshal's office, one of the officers straightened up nervously, a hand resting on the handle of his revolver, one of the new ones, Earp was his name, Wyatt Earp. Isaac breathed deep.

—Men of Wichita! he cried, feeling his way toward the pitch, the volume, to carry and be heard. Fellow citizens! Fellow Kansans! He paused, turning his head, letting his eyes rove the mass of faces up-turned to the noonday light. Why, if I'd known we'd have such company here this morning, he said, dropping his voice a little, almost conversational, I'd've ordered in a load of watermelons and a barrel of whisky. But since I'm all the entertainment that's provided, I'll just have to get on with it and do what I can to oblige—

A sigh of collective breath let out rippled through the crowd, as of an engine heard at a distance, coming into the depot, blowing off steam. A few laughed. There was a general shifting of feet, a settling back of an audience preparing itself to listen, maybe to be entertained as well.

—Boys, I know a lot of you are customers of this bank—come here cause you've got money with us and you want to know, as is your right and interest: where's my money got to? and, am I going to get it back, and get it all back? and, just as much to the point, *when am I going to see it again?* And some of you just curious, I reckon, though it aint any of your own money that's in question—but that's all right. Since we started up, we've done our best to assist the business of every citizen of this city and this county, and there aint many we haven't done business with, sometime. And anyhow, we're all friends here, or mean to be, and friends don't have any secrets to keep from each other—why, I doubt there's many of you I don't know, or don't know me—for I've watched you come in, and settle, go to work build-ing up this town—Yes, boys! since this town was thought of—since there wasn't nothing where we stand today but the buffalo grass—

Shouts stopped him: *Where's the money? Get to the point! What's hap-pened to our money?* taken up, repeated. He waited them out, arms crossed on his breast, eyes hunting eyes he knew: the thing you learn your first session in the legislature or hold your tongue and don't come back—talk to them one at a time, a word or two for each, if you will be heard; no man can speak with men in the mass, the mob, and open his heart. He began to find individuals: Buffalo Bill Mathewson looming immobile as a pillar of stone and golden-haired Lizzie at his side, Marsh Murdock taking his words in shorthand, Andrew Hansen, who ought to be occupied at Pride's Reserve, pruning the ruined fruit trees, spading in what the hoppers had left of the garden, and George Stone and André Long, must have come up from Bexar County with a herd to sell, and William A. Phillips, in the Congress now but still made his home at Salina like an honest man, down for a visit; others less friendly: Dave Payne standing up with his haunted eyes under the threadbare campaign hat, Kilbourn wearing the bushy black brevet-colonel's beard he never earned.

—Boys! I'm *coming* to the point, but it takes some telling. The bank's got around eighty-five thousand dollars in deposits, which is money our customers have put in, and they want, and we mean to pay. And what we've got to pay with is, money owed us by others— twenty-five thousand from other banks and the U.S. Treasury, and sixty thousand from individuals and corporations that we've loaned money to and expect to get. Now, you can do the arithmetic as well as I can: we *owe* eighty-five thousand, and we're also *owed* eighty-five thousand, so it comes out even, and it is my firm belief that every man that we owe will be paid. Only, though our accounts look good, same as most others in Kansas since the panic, we don't have the cash to pay with all at once, and *won't* have till those that owe us pay, which may be three or six or nine months, according to terms of agreement. So—as fast as the money comes in, we mean to pay it out to all that's owed, and have placed our affairs in the hands of a committee of citizens and depositors to make sure it's done and all receive their due —and Dutch Bill Greiffenstein has taken the committee in hand to see all's done right and proper and according to law—

He paused to breathe, flushing his lungs with the dusty air. They were still with him, listening, but would they understand? He looked beyond the ragged fringe of the crowd, west along First where the street ended in the mud-flat bank of the Arkansas, and still a few big cottonwoods growing there that no one yet had bothered to cut for firewood or lumber, leaves yellowing in the summer drought. Off there, standing apart, it seemed he saw, plain as if he were leaning across his desk in the Santa Fe office at Topeka, chewing a cigar and stating the terms on which he'd support a branch line to Wichita, Cyrus K. Holliday, and Thomas J. Peter on one side and Bob Stevens, his rival, on the other—now, there were three who knew the ways of money and the delicate touch to entice it into new enterprise and make it go, but hardheaded, too, as a Sedgwick County farmer, no argument or excuse would answer till they were paid what was theirs. Off to one side by himself stood E. H. Durfee, one hand resting inside his oversize coat like Napoleon reviewing his troops, who knew of money that he could turn it into hairpipe beads, powder, lead, and knives to buy furs of the Indians and make himself master of the trade on the upper Missouri, to earn the respectful title of Commodore, for his steamboats, carrying Indian goods up in the spring and bringing out furs—*Mister Pride, take charge of my post in the Yellowstone Department, it's a fine life for a young man starting his family and his wife for company, and you make it go, in three or four years you'll have a share in the Firm, quarter interest, third interest—*. There was Captain Andrew Jackson Smith coming up through the cottonwoods in his dress uniform mounted on a cavalry plug tall and stiff as a circus elephant, and Israel Titus in his white linen suit, rolling back in his rocking chair with his feet up on a keg and a glass of toddy big as a milk pail beside him, saying he'd never accept a toll from a brother officer crossing his bridge. Out on the river, booming down the Upper Rapids from his great new house on the bluff at St Paul, came Fred Weyerhaeuser, manning the steering sweep of a raft that covered five acres of water, built all of dollar bills in stacks, framed together so tight and thick with limber withes of gold you could jig a hornpipe on it and never dampen your feet, and along the Rock Island shore ran old Colonel Davenport, blood streaming down his face and begging to be taken off before the river pirates finished him. Bill Wood was coming along the street with a sack of shelled corn for brother Sam's mill, and Andy McHarg looking on with tears in his eyes, homesick for Iowa, promising they'd meet again, be friends, remember how they drove their wagons through Missouri, taunting the slavers with their Free-State songs. General James H. Lane stood tall on an empty whisky barrel, wrapped in his bearskin and the light of death glinting in his eyes, saying he'd let Jack Pride have his say, but what the citizens had got to understand was, money was nothing to a man upholding the honor of his cause, for when his money was gone there were always ways he could think of to get some, but honor, once lost, will never return—and Sam Pomeroy standing below him, writing names in his private account book, let those who make speeches lead the fight, he would take what was owed, for favors and services rendered, in Kansas land and railroad stocks. Abraham Bos, Bill Whitman, and Harry Farris came riding through a swirl of dust, bandannas shielding their faces, at the head of a column of horses and pulled up short before Don Carlos Cadero, a long-barreled pistol in either hand, demanding where they'd gotten those horses and if it was settlers or Indians they stole them from, but answered nothing till Tommy Thorn came at them—chapfallen bloody head and empty eyeholes, and arrows sprouting from his naked belly like a porcupine's tail—then turned and rode back into their dust-cloud. His father, Abraham, stood back among the shadows, shading his eyes against the cruelly slanting sun—*Isaac, I never truly believed I'd get wealth by putting money in your bank, I ask your forgiveness for my little faith, it was because it seemed you needed it, but the Lord gives and also takes, if only He will spare us the home place to live out our age on,* and Mary, his mother, stiff and dark, slim as a girl, standing close but not touching, protesting by her silence the waste of her father's inheritance, all that was left of her life in Vermont; and sister Lizzie dancing past with a basket of wildflowers gathered by the river to plait in her hair.

Isaac let the silence hang a full half minute, holding the thousand faces motionless and concentrated, rank after rank of eyes like polished jewels sparkling in the light as from the universal source and center of energy and heat—almost too long, seconds more and he would lose them—

—As I told you, friends—and taking the most conservative—I will say, the most *pessimistic* view of our circumstances—it is the best judgment of the officers of this bank, as also the judgment of those sober and responsible citizens who have volunteered to assist in winding up the bank's affairs—our resources are more than sufficient to meet every call. But some of you may point out—those having experience of money loaned in time of need or opportunity, and of the ways of men in repaying when the need is past—and who of us has not, to his sorrow, had such experience and eaten of the fruit of knowledge which it bears?—some of you will say, and rightly: those resources he talks of so confidently, they're mostly loans—promises to pay a certain amount by a certain date, written out in lawyers' language and entered on the account books of the bank. But then you say—and it's your right to say it and bespeaks the wisdom a man carries off from his experience—you say: supposing some of them fellas you loaned money to *can't* pay when time comes, cause they haven't got it any more, or they *won't* pay. *Then where's our money coming from?*

A groan sighed through the crowd, rolled back, turning angry. Isaac waited it out, felt the sweat dampening his brow, trickling on his cheeks like flies walking.

—Don't think we haven't considered that, friends, and taken steps to meet it—for, you know, we've had experience of our own with men and their loans, and a sight more, let me tell you, than some of us bargained for!

—But to give you your answer—. Now the first thing is, all of us that put our money into stock of this bank, to start it up and make it go—and I don't mind telling you, since we're all friends here, I've got about eleven thousand dollars of my own in—all of us that took stock are liable for the *full value* of our stock if the bank comes up short on what it owes. That means, we could each of us be called to pay off as much as we paid in already, if we don't succeed in getting our loans in and turning them to cash so as to pay off our debts. You may think that's pretty hard, squeezing a few more drops out of them that's already bled white—but it's the *law*, boys, and we mean to go according to law.

—But maybe some of you are still feeling cautious—and I don't care for that, these are cautious times, and times for thinking clear. So just suppose: we collect all we can on our loans, and assess our stockholders, and it *still* aint enough to meet what's owed. What then? And I'll tell you what—and our president Mister James Fraker has already said it in a general way, in the printed statement some of you have read, and put his name to it: will make over all his property by deed of trust to meet the obligations of this bank—if we go short on our other resources, we sell his property off lot by lot till all's paid, right up to and including that fine new house where he lives with his dear wife and children—which can't be taken under law, as you know, being his homestead, but he'll *give* it and no haggling over law, if that's what it takes to save the bank's customers and our Wichita fellow citizens. And having some experience of Kansas real estate myself, I don't hesitate to tell you, I'd figure the president's property to bring thirty or forty thousand, even in these slow times, if we come finally to the point of selling. But I don't consider that likely, seeing all the other resources we have to call on first. . . .

—Now, you can say what you like, boys, every man entitled to his opinion, but mine is, that's handsome, and beyond the call. And you know? it sets me thinking—and all of you that know me, know I've never been shy where work's to be done—and if he *has* been president of this bank and I'm only vice-president, I'll match him, and throw all my *own* property on the table to make good, so far as needed—lots and buildings and wheatland—and some of you make your home and business on land made over from my Wichita claim, fair price and easy terms and no hurry about paying off, you recall, and there's schools and churches stand on land I *gave* and never took a cent for—but plenty more where that come from, as you all know: but be my witness today, *I'll give it all to see you through.* . . .

He lowered his head, eyes on the iron plate of the step worn to a shine by shoe leather, bringing the words forth, forcing his mind forward to what remained to say, and looked up again to sweep the crowd and hold them close, and saw—no crowd of half-acquainted strangers, no little frame houses, brick business blocks, hotels and saloons along Douglass—. The cottonwoods were thick along the bottomland as when he first came down the Osage Trail and the rich grass standing belly-high to his horse, and down from Chisholm's camp in the hackberry grove was the faint track, little used, leading to the ford below the mouth of the Little Arkansas, and Jesse himself coming across it from the west, lifting the hat from his gray head to shout and wave, and his gang of Kiowa Mexicans driving his herd of goat-thin contraband cattle from the Territory to pay his debt. Away out on the Plains beyond the river, John Sarcoxie was coming in to trade, leading a string of mules swaybacked with their packs of beaver from up in the Paradise country, and Seoskuk riding along beside him for company and guard, the golden horse he called Singing Bird naked of bridle and saddle, carrying the man for love, pleasure, and forbearance. From the Wichita village—the old head chief, Owa-ha, thick and heavy as iron from the forge, and Towakoni Jim, lithe and young, naked chest above his white man's jeans and his feet beginning to step to the rhythm—the sound of drums came, summoning to the dance, the celebration of harvest and survival, and strangers coming from the four directions of the world: Redtail from the north at the head of his remnant of Otoe with the Cheyenne Roman Nose and old Black Kettle on either side; from the south, a rumble of wagon wheels and a horn blaring, Satanta standing up in his ambulance with his blue general's uniform coat over his shoulders like a buffalo robe and Big Tree guiding the ponies in the traces, and coming to meet them, Carson with his volunteers from Santa Fe and Custer at the head of a column of peace commissioners sent from Washington. Set-im-kayah sat motionless in the door of his lodge and would not join the dance, sucking at his cold pipe and grieving his two lost daughters, one dark of skin as he was, the other pale, twinned by their shared name: *Pat-so-gate.* The river rose, waves roiling their sinews where the rocky ford had been, and a golden girl lay limp beside it, soft hand lapped by the rising water—light flickered, the girl was lissome and dark, and her straight black hair done up in a prudent bun at the nape of her neck and naked still, spreading her legs and lifting her knees to let the life forth as a woman must to accomplish her part in the mystery of generation, however flesh cry out at such sundering—*Marie, my darling, my wife, forgive*—

—Put it in writing! a voice called.

The voices were all around him, calling him back, wolf-like, tearing at his cheeks like ravens at a carcass.

—Say listen, boys! Isaac shouted above the babble and wind-eddy of the voices. It's seventeen years since I come on the Plains, an ignorant, inexperienced boy, and that first season, heaviest merchant at Leavenworth, he trusted me for a wagonload of goods for the Indian trade, on nothing but my word—cause he knew I'd make good on it, to the penny and the day, if I died for it—and aint nobody in Kansas since ever doubted my word or credit—

—Bout time they did, *Mister Pride!* a voice cried in the silence he took for breath, the last word drawn out, rebounding from the store on the opposite corner of Main Street: -ster *Pride;* pride.

—Jack Pride never put nothin in writin!—a different voice, hateful. He searched the crowd for it.

—Say! I know that voice! he cried, his own voice rising, piercing the thousand voices flocking and twittering around him. That's Dave Payne out there leading the chorus—Mister Poison-Buffalo Payne! Come on up where folks can see you, Dave, and speak your piece—for if there's any good you mean the citizens, now's the time—and every man in Sedgwick knows you aint any interested party in this bank's affairs. Why, if ever you had enough money at one time to stuff a worn-out sock—let alone make a bank deposit, or invest, or the trust any sensible banker'd give a loan on—there's no man knows it. So come on, Dave—

Put it in writing, Jack! Put it in writing!—The voices, drowning his own, became a chant, the crowd of citizens a thousand-voiced faceless mass in which neither Dave Payne nor any individual could be distinguished—

Isaac, arms raised to call down silence, voice strained to cracking:— All right, boys! But all at the proper time—sure I'll write it, however law and the Comptroller at Washington requires—. But what counts is, you've already got my word on it, written or not. . . .

It may be some heard him, crowded in close. From out there in the now seething, screaming mass a brickbat came flying in a slow, high arc, exploded with metallic clatter on the step below where Isaac stood. He looked down, saw the constable with his gun out and raised, maybe to fire a warning over heads, maybe to try a shot at the next arm lofting a stone.—God damn you, Wyatt, put that gun up! Isaac shouted. We can't do with any killing here—

There was an instant of silence, then cries of protest, outrage, shame, but met and canceled by fists shaken in the air, hats tossed, screams of scared horses, and answering cries: *Get the little yellow-hair bastard!—Taken our money!—Tar-and-feather!—Get our money out!— String him up!*—

—Listen to me, boys, I aint finished, I've more to tell, but I gave you my word! Isaac screamed, waving his arms at them, face purple with rage and strain and despair. Wrecking this bank won't get your money back! Killing me won't get it!—

The door clicked open behind him. Mike Meagher stood beside him.—You come on in now, Isaac, he said, they aint going to listen to you anymore. But long as nobody gives em the idea and they've nobody special to be mad at, I reckon they're in too much perplexity to try anything—and they do, why, there's a whole lot goin home with lead in their bellies before I stand aside and let em walk in. . . .

His heavy hand on Isaac's elbow turned and drew him through the door. The marshal slammed it and slid the bolt across.

EPILOGUE

Energy Darkened and Dispersed

All the lights went out at once. It was like waking in a close-drawn room in the darkest hour of night, no match or lamp to be found, and you grope, hands out, shoulders hunched, bruising toes and barking shins on nameless, hard, inimical objects, set down directionless in unknown space—or like the children's game of blindman's buff, the scarf tight-covering your eyes, and soft hands touch and shove and turn, you reach out, grasp empty air, and the voices surround you, mocking, laughing, like the spirits of all the dead: the slow months, more than a year, succeeding the bank's failure. There came a time, late winter or early spring, you had an appointment at nine with the receiver and Henry Sluss, to make the final settlement, had risen with the light, endured a shower bath of chill water from the attic cistern, had toweled yourself, and wrapped in the deerskin robe and feet in the beaded Konza moccasins, stropped the razor, and paused to examine your face by the hard morning light in the shaving mirror—did not seem there was a time since boyhood you had troubled to look close, only taken looks for granted like the size and shape and strength of your body, a vanity not to be indulged, but now: transparent pricks of white in the red-gold stubble on your chin and cheeks, never did come in thick enough to make a proper manly beard, though the silky-soft mustache was well enough, daily trained and pointed with wax. Something wrong with your eyes this morning, could not seem to focus sharp: dull haze of dust talcumed over hair, and squinting you perceived distinct strands of white scattered through the changeless endowment of darkening gold, like weeds in a neglected garden—*the very hairs of your head are all numbered*—and at the corners of eyes and mouth the engravure of lines that would go shadow-dark when you smiled or talked.

He was thirty-nine, six months short of his fortieth birthday. Two uncles had died untimely, not yet fifty, but his father at sixty-five and in spite of the Iowa winters had the vigor of a man half his age; seen together they could be taken for brothers except for the difference in size and bearing. Possibly he had got through half the life he had yet to live. Stirring the lather in his mug, Isaac applied the brush to his cheek.

The Bureau of the Currency was at a transition when the bank came to its crisis, its affairs in the hands of G. S. Langworthy as acting Comptroller, John Jay Knox, the actual holder of the office, being indisposed. He nevertheless responded zealously to the directors' plea for voluntary liquidation, sending off a telegram to the bank's last examiner, Tom Eldon, designating him temporary receiver. Eldon reached Wichita four days later, armed with his appointment, took possession, receiving the keys, the combination to the vault, and the books from Mr Fraker and dissolving the citizens' committee. While attempting to calm the clamorous depositors and setting about the long task of reconciling the books with the mass of supporting paper—notes, loans, the statements of correspondent banks—he ran formal notices in the *Eagle* and in papers at Topeka and Kansas City, calling on creditors to submit proof of what they were owed.

A week later, Eldon called in the officers and directors one by one for questioning under oath. Mr Fraker had urged them all to volunteer nothing; Henry Sluss, who came with Isaac to the interview, advised him to confine himself to fact and exercise his right to refuse to answer any question whose purpose was to incriminate. Isaac largely ignored this advice; it was not in his nature to refrain from telling what he knew in response to a direct question. He told at length, the lawyer corroborating, of his discovery of the empty cash-reserve box, of the accounting of Mr Fraker's borrowings he had demanded, and the trustee deeds taken to cover them. Tom Eldon was cool, distant, but not unfriendly—there would be no making over of the deeds, let alone any step toward Isaac's keeping his promise to make good any further deficit, until the receiver submitted his own sworn statement of the bank's assets and liabilities. Of that, Eldon spoke freely enough from what he had learned so far. On the one hand, he took a cautious view of what could be realized from the bank's outstanding loans, judging more than half of them worthless, nearly fifty thousand dollars, of which Fraker was maker or endorser of more than thirty thousand dollars, while only twenty thousand dollars was certainly good and collectible. At the same time, Eldon was optimistic about Fraker's property—had consulted various citizens on the value of Wichita real estate, Greiffenstein in particular, though not Isaac, and judged that with his interest in the Occidental Hotel and even calculating the house at only five thousand dollars, half what it cost three years earlier, it would bring thirty thousand dollars altogether. Henry Sluss, as they left the bank building, ventured his opinion that Isaac would end up liable for no more than five thousand dollars. More to the point, if Eldon had found evidence in plenty of careless and unfortunate banking, it did not seem that he inclined toward recommending criminal charges—Fraker's borrowings and endorsements, if excessive, were at least all supported, apparently, by notes in proper form on real security, thanks to the lawyer's own foresight and skill.

A few days after, with the Comptroller's approval and for the sake of his knowledge of Kansas banking in similar circumstances, Eldon called in as his assistant the receiver of the First National Bank of Topeka, which had failed more than a year earlier in the aftershock of the panic. Isaac discovered that the new assistant was H. B. Cullum: had not seen him since Marie's death. Isaac remembered him clearest from that first hunt, fat and jolly by the campfire, an easygoing peacemaker among the other young men, nothing he could recall from those past years' acquaintance to mark him as an enemy, and it might even be he could be looked on now as a sympathizer, a friend, in an hour when a man needed all of both he could find. It was a candle lighted in the darkness: perhaps his luck was not dead after all. He wrote Pomeroy's successor, Senator John J. Ingalls, urging endorsement of Harry Cullum for receiver of First Wichita. Cullum was the son of early settlers, had seven years' experience of Kansas banking, and had carried out the Topeka liquidation to general satisfaction—not to mention Tom Eldon's firmly expressed confidence in his assistant. In October Cullum formally took up his duties as receiver; and Tom Eldon departed for St Louis.

In the few days of grace that fell between the bank's closing and Eldon's arrival to take possession, Fraker, Eldridge and Wright had been occupied with the citizens' committee from early morning till lamplight, reviewing the books. Isaac took the opportunity to put his parents' stock in his own name, forty-four shares among them as near as he could determine, backdating the transfer to April, and then, since the others were doing the same, protected himself by recording a further transfer of these shares, a day later, to Bissy with himself as trustee, therefore not assessable. It seemed to him a small matter. He had given his word before the assembled citizens to make good any deficiency; his word did not include leaving his parents liable for the bank's losses. To complete this transaction and diminish the assets that could be called on, he put the last of his cash into a draft of two thousand dollars for the stock, and sent the payment to Rockingham. Henry Sluss about this time was alarmed to discover that his client had carelessly left the title to the new farm in his own name and hastily drafted a trust deed to Isaac's children and had it recorded—and entirely proper, he said, since it was bought with the proceeds from land held in trust for them in the first place.

These arrangements remained private, but rumors originating most likely with Dave Kilbourn in the county register's office went through the town: that Isaac was making his property over to nonassessable relatives and offspring; that the herds of cattle he had managed on shares through the winter, the last not sold till August and September, had been his own, that like all the bank's other officers he had hoards of cash put aside, if only it could be called on to satisfy the bank's creditors. Harry Cullum, less friendly than Isaac had hoped, heard and demanded settlement: Fraker's property, held in trust, and Isaac's own, according to promise. On the last Monday in October, Isaac went to the bank building with Henry Sluss to hear him out.

The receiver's case was briefly made. The accounting was not final, still many complications and uncertainties, but he made it to date $90,000 in proved claims, another $15,000 in deposits and liabilities to correspondents shown on the books but not yet proved, and $8,000 in miscellaneous charges, taxes, costs of redeeming currency. All in all, he concluded, a deficiency of $58,000—say $60,000, to round it out and make allowance for unforeseen costs.

—Sixty thousand! Isaac exclaimed. Why, only two months ago when we concluded to shut down, we calculated around eighty-five thousand in claims and ample to cover in dues from correspondents, bonds, and good notes coming in—and that, I recall, was writing off twenty-five thousand or so in notes we weren't sure of. Where's it all gone?

Cullum shrugged.—Maybe there were claims you didn't know of, didn't show on the books, but they've come in, and I've proof they're good. It's why I can't do with any more delay on those deeds of Fraker's. I'll have your signature on the transfers this morning, or—

—Now hold up there a minute, Isaac said. He studied the banker's impassive face: round and gray, clean-shaven, eyes narrowed by creases of fat and masked by small gold-framed spectacles under a balding skull traced with wisps of hair, you would take him for past fifty though he could not be a year older than Isaac himself; a patient toad's face, awaiting the imprudent fly. A thought formed: I don't suppose you've got anything in there for Fraker's property, since you aint got it yet, in a manner of speaking—though I won't hang back, of course, once I'm satisfied—

—It's in there and allowed for. Fifteen thousand.

—Fifteen thousand! Isaac exploded. Why, I know that list of property as well as I know my own, and that aint *half* what it's worth by any careful estimate—. Of course, he reflected, quieting a little, if you noise it around you'll take the first live offer that comes with cash behind it, you naturally won't get much, but that's no way to deal in real estate—

—I aint *dealing* in real estate, Cullum said. My orders is, turn assets into cash and pay proceeds to creditors as expeditious as possible. I get forty thousand for the property, I'll take it, and reduce assessment accordingly. Or fifteen, or twelve, I'll take it all the same. What I *can't* do is wait around, two or three or five years, and the property idle, not bringing anything in, till someone comes along with—

—You *had* any offers that you base this estimate on?

Cullum nodded.—Nothing definite—nor can it be, of course, till I've got the deeds, which is why—assuming they're all proper and in order and will give good title—

—Now see here, Cullum! Henry Sluss broke in. I wrote those papers, and I can tell you, they're not in question. What *is* in question is your accounting for the assets and liabilities of this bank you're trusted with—and till you give us that, my client'd be a fool, and betraying his own trust, to turn over one inch of ground. Or maybe he'll give some and hold back the rest, till he sees how you prove up. . . .

At the lawyer's insistence, Cullum went through the list. A Mr Houck had offered five thousand dollars for the house, which had cost twice that, but it turned out to be encumbered with a mortgage for one thousand dollars which would have to be paid from the sale. The Butler County farm, 320 acres of improved wheatland, he carried at ten dollars an acre, less commission and expense of sale. His estimate on the Emporia farm-implement storehouse was three thousand dollars, about the original cost some years ago, although Fraker had often spoken of refusing twice that for it. The three partners had put ten thousand dollars each into a water mill, but Cullum had yet to find anyone who would pay half what it cost. He saved the conclusive item for last: the Occidental Hotel. It had cost twenty thousand dollars or more. Cullum, like Isaac, had expected Fraker's share to bring seven thousand dollars or eight thousand dollars. Now it turned out to carry a fifteen-thousand-dollar mortgage which had slid into default, and within the past three days the parties at Topeka who held it had started proceedings to foreclose. Besides Fraker's share in the company, the bank was out a note for forty-five hundred dollars he had taken with his hotel stock as security.

—That's one we never heard of before, Isaac said with a nervous glance at Henry Sluss.

—I believe there's a good many of Fraker's notes, and his other

affairs too, that you aint heard of, Isaac, Cullum said. I've been working through this tangle six days a week for six weeks now, and *still*
haven't sorted it to my clear satisfaction and understanding. But what
is clear—whatever Fraker's turned over, it's just swallowed up in an
ocean of liabilities. And whatever I can get out of stockholders—and
whatever you put in, Isaac—well, maybe all in all it'll just about
settle. But that's why I got to have those deeds now, every one and no
quibbling, so I can get on—and clear commitment from you, written
down and collectible, as to what you'll do, and then maybe I'll know
how I stand with the rest of the stockholders. And you keep putting
me off as you have, let me tell you, I'll do my duty by you, go to law
and take you into court, and we'll see if that don't hurry you along
some—

—With permission, Mister Cullum, Henry Sluss quietly interrupted, I'll offer professional opinion and no fee billed: you might be
some cautious, threatening my client with law and the courts in presence of his attorney. You talk of assessing the stockholders—why, you
can assess Fraker all you like but it won't bring you anything, he's
nothing to give that I or anyone knows of but the real estate, and I
don't doubt all the others in like condition, except Mister Pride. And
him—that's only a hundred and some shares, ten or eleven thousand,
and anything beyond that strictly voluntary, in accordance with his
honor and his promise to the citizens. But you try to compel him by
law to do what he's already promised, before the proper time and
your own obligations in the matter fulfilled—why, sir, I tell you, I
won't stand for it. I'll tie you so tight in law, you'll be ten years
getting unwound, *and* never see a cent. Coming down on just one of a
dozen or two of stockholders, that's given his word to do what's right,
and never known to go back on a promise! Why, I should like to put
you before a jury of Kansas farmers—Mr Sluss kneaded his hands
together in anticipation—I should be pleased to hear you explain to
them, sir, how you took Fraker's half-section of improved Butler
County bottomland, farmhouse and barn and storage bins for grain—
that will produce ten or fifteen thousand a year with ordinary good
management, and worth twenty or thirty an acre even in these times
—and conspired to let it go for not much over the price of unbroken
prairie! You'd find you had more than civil matters on your hands
before you'd done: wasting of assets by trustee. . . .

Harry Cullum appeared to reflect on this tirade.—It's odd, he said,
you should hint at criminal matters, Mister Sluss. That statement
Mister Pride alluded to just now—posted in the door of the bank,
handed out to every customer that would take it, printed in the paper.
Fraker says he wrote it with your professional advice and approval,
after careful examination of the bank's records.

Mr Sluss gave a silent assent.

—It's odd because, go at it from the books every way I can think of, it don't make sense except to conclude you left out of consideration the biggest item of liabilities: the circulating currency.

The lawyer's intent face went a shade of gray.—I don't believe we'd have much difficulty showing, he said finally, we were addressing the depositors, talking of the amount on deposit that was owed—and amounts owed other banks.

—A one-dollar bank note is a liability of the bank just the same as any other kind of promissory note. Forty-five thousand dollars, more or less, Mister Sluss: that's how much you understated the bank's liabilities by—or put it another way, overstated assets. The biggest part of the deficiency—scattered and vanished on the wind like dew in the morning sun, never to be recalled—. So—you talk of criminal matters, and *honor*—and your client here as much a party as all the others. . . .

—I believe we're getting a little off the main subject, Henry Sluss said, breaking the lengthening silence with a smile and a little deprecating bow of his head. If we're talking of criminal matters, and deficiencies that can't reasonably be accounted for, why—Fraker's had the control of this bank and all the benefit, and my client can't be compelled to make up what another's taken. You got to show us what Fraker's liable for.

—That's evidence for the U.S. Attorney—can't take the chance I'd prejudice his case. Besides, my examination aint completed—there's matters coming in every day—

—In confidence and between these walls, not to be repeated, Henry Sluss softly suggested. That's not prejudicial, among men of their word. And if you don't—well, make your choice, Mister Cullum: show us some cooperation and Mister Pride'll cooperate to the extent of his resources—or fight us through the courts and, as I promise, you'll get nothing, and less than nothing when you've paid your legal fees, for the Comptroller or the creditors of this bank. . . .

Cullum considered for a time, then slowly, in a dry, irrefutable voice, began to recite the shortages he had discovered so far. When he had finished, the whole shortage, as near as Cullum could reckon to this point, came to $61,700—about the deficiency of assets to liabilities, and something over.

There was a long silence at the end of this recital.

—Why, I congratulate you, Mister Cullum, Henry Sluss said at last. I believe you've got a case even a jury of Kansas farmers will comprehend—that he got away with all the bank's circulating currency—and—and something more—why, don't it appear, the difference is about the value of the stock he was down for?

Cullum agreed, that was how it looked, whether it could be proved or not. He could not find, at any rate, that any of Fraker's stock had actually been paid for as bank law required—besides the ones Isaac discovered, he seemed to have covered his stock by loans taken at various times from other banks, but all had been made obligations of the Wichita bank, not personal. In addition, on the morning of the last examination, as the cashier and teller both admitted, the books had been reopened from the previous day and extensive alterations and erasures made in order that they should appear correct, although in fact it was nearly two years since they had actually been balanced.

—There now, Cullum gently concluded. Have I made my point, gentlemen? Do you see why I can't wait on those deeds? And why I've got to know what Isaac Pride's good for?

—I can tell you straight off, Isaac began, I haven't any forty-five thousand to give—

Again the lawyer silenced him. He talked on, soothingly, persuasively, but Isaac could no longer force his attention. Sluss was agreed on making over the Fraker property, produced the papers from his portfolio for Isaac to endorse. As to Isaac's own commitment, he firmly refused to go beyond what was already said: that Isaac would meet any proved, final deficiency to the extent of his resources—but no amount specified, no date set, no inventory of property drawn up. They would do nothing more till the receiver's accounting was complete, accepted by the Comptroller, and verified, if need be, by independent audit.

—I suppose you see what I was after with him, Henry Sluss remarked as the two men slowly descended the steps of the bank building, dinnertime come, the whole morning consumed.

Isaac numbly shook his head.

—Keep him guessing of course, Henry Sluss cheerfully explained. Like a game of poker, though I don't personally indulge, not often, anyway: hold back your good cards, if you've got any. Now if you'd given him the list he wanted and put it in form to collect at pleasure, twenty thousand, thirty thousand, whatever it is you can raise, why, it's that much less he figures he's got to squeeze out, and maybe he'll let up some—whereas, this way, well, we kind of give him reason to keep at it, hard as he can go, or maybe he don't get anything out of you, do you see? And it's only tit for tat anyway in this game, for I believe there's things Mister Henry B. Cullum aint favored us with yet, that he knows or has in mind to do, however frank and open he talked—. Say now! he said, seizing Isaac by the elbow. How well do you figure you know him, anyway?

Isaac shrugged.—Knew his partner better—Aaron Schuyler, folks friendly with my first wife's uncle.

—I believe you'd be mistaken to count on him for any special favor, the lawyer softly advised—even if he didn't seem to take a most pertinacious, and I may say unbending, view of his duties. Which is another reason against playing all your best cards just at present—till we see all he means to bring out in the way of court action and, I don't doubt, criminal indictment. He'd be a fool to touch you, so long as he can do better without going to law. . . .

A week before Christmas, Cullum sent off his completed report to John Jay Knox, once more in charge as Comptroller: thirteen closely written pages setting forth his findings of misapplied funds to the amount of $58,691.14; with the recommendation that if the Comptroller agreed action was called for, the report be submitted to the U.S. Commissioner at Emporia or Topeka, since Henry Sluss, the lawyer who held that office at Wichita, was already employed by a party to the case, Isaac A. Pride.

Whether he somehow learned the drift of the receiver's report or had merely tired of the Wichita climate, James C. Fraker did not stay the holiday with his family. A day or two later, it was noted that he was no longer among the city's residents, and the U.S. Marshal's office set about the tedious process of ascertaining his whereabouts, putting Charley Jones, the Wichita deputy, in charge. The *Eagle*'s first issue of the new year, which reported Fraker's absence without comment, also carried a small advertisement over his wife's name, offering private board and pleasant rooms. That the solicitation was indeed hers and not a typesetter's joke or an anonymous instance of Kansas humor was confirmed by the announcement a week or two later that she would entertain applicants for a private school to be conducted in her home. Contrary to the rumors of hidden Fraker wealth, the two facts gave assurance that all there was had been made over to the bank and its creditors. Mrs Fraker, at any rate, evidently had none of it.

The sixteen hundred dollars in borrowed cash Isaac had supplied the bank at Fraker's beseeching immediately before it closed became an inordinate difficulty in the way of settlement. Isaac had paid his notes with drafts on the bank's account with First National of St Louis—which, however, were not honored when the bank closed and its accounts were everywhere frozen. The merchants Isaac had called on for help took his notes to court in self-defense, secured judgments, and attached a sizable part of the real estate by which he intended to make good the bank's deficiencies. There the matter lay till February, when Henry Sluss proposed that if the receiver would persuade the Comptroller to order payment of the drafts, lifting the attachments, Isaac would settle without waiting for the findings of the Grand Jury.

Late that month, therefore, Isaac once more presented himself at the bank in company with his lawyer. Between them they reckoned Isaac's list of property at more than $50,000, enough to make up the entire shortage even if the receiver persisted in his unreasonable valuing of Fraker's assets. Cullum took a different view. The old Kaw claim, now up to around $11,000, with interest, which Senator Ingalls had again revived with a private bill, he flatly refused as having no sale. He put the bridge stock down at $2,000, twenty cents on the dollar—the citizens in January had voted $6,400 to acquire the bridge, with some chance of more forthcoming. There was no argument about Isaac's $2,000 in cash, but considerable about the rest of his property. Listing everything at his miserable valuations his total came to $18,700. It became apparent in the course of the discussion that Fraker's property, still unsold, had dwindled further in his estimation, as Henry Sluss had long since predicted it would.

Henry Sluss took his client aside: these arguments were abstract; even at Cullum's niggardly valuations, he had met his assessment and more, and his home, Pride's Reserve, was exempt by law, while the farm was in his children's names and unchallenged; if the property in the end yielded more than was due, the law would give recourse.

Isaac signed the necessary papers, prepared in advance, and took his receipt. Marsh Murdock saw fit to report the conveyance in the *Eagle:* Isaac Pride had paid his due in full.

In April at Topeka, George R. Peck, the U.S. Attorney for the District of Kansas, submitted the receiver's evidence to a grand jury, with Tom Eldon and H. B. Cullum as principal witnesses. The jury returned three indictments. The first, in five counts, charged that on dates from May 1, 1875, to the day following the bank's closing, James C. Fraker "unlawfully and feloniously did then and there embezzle abstract and wilfully misapply . . . moneys funds and credits" amounting to $55,276.32. The second indictment charged the cashier, John W. Eldridge, aided and abetted by Fraker, with eight counts of making false entries in the books of the bank, with intent to deceive the examiner, T. N. Eldon. The third, of five counts of false entry in similar form, was against the teller, Edwin Wright, Fraker again aiding and abetting.

Eldridge and Wright were released under bond of three thousand dollars each for appearance at Leavenworth for trial on October 8. Isaac, considering the teller ill-used, was among those who went surety for him, offering, after some argument with Mr Peck as to what he would accept, the east half of Pride's Reserve still in his name, valued at ten thousand dollars, and horses, harness, and assorted personal property worth five hundred dollars. Except for honor, of which the judicial process could take no account, it was all he had left.

Fraker himself remained a person of whereabouts unknown. The

U.S. District Judge issued *capias* for him to the Kansas marshal under nine thousand dollars bail.

Assisted by a printed description with a careful sketch from a photograph, run off in hundreds on one of the *Eagle*'s presses and circulated through the West, Charley Jones in the course of the winter succeeded in tracking his quarry across eastern Colorado—Las Animas, Pueblo, Fort Garland—and thence to Taos and Santa Fe, where he seemed to disappear, and Charley came home empty-handed. Then, at the beginning of April, from the sheriff at Ysleta, in the far southwest corner of Texas, came word of a man calling himself James Franks who fitted the deputy marshal's description. Charley Jones answered with a telegram instructing the sheriff to hold the suspect till he arrived and sent along a photograph to confirm the identification. He was two weeks securing the necessary papers and started a few days before the indictments were handed in. It was a slow journey: the railroad by now through Dennison and as far as Austin, but something approaching seven hundred miles from there by stagecoach; sixteen tedious and impatient days. For the same reason—Austin was the nearest location of a U.S. Commissioner—the Ysleta sheriff judged it useless to make the arrest until Jones arrived with his papers: the accused would be released by *habeas corpus*, wade or swim the shallow Rio Grande, and be gone forever into Mexico. Since "James Franks" had explained his presence by an interest in buying a cattle ranch, the sheriff endeavored to occupy the time and keep him in sight by driving him around the county day after day, inspecting likely land.

A day or two before Marshal Jones finally made his appearance, the man calling himself James Franks decided to look elsewhere for his ranch and slipped away with a train of wagons bound for Fort Davis, two hundred miles east. The sheriff, by now assured by another delayed telegram of the marshal's imminent arrival with the requisite papers, judged it proper to track the suspect and rode off with two Mexican deputies. At dawn the next day, sixty miles down the trail, they caught up with the train. The suspect, already up, took a guess at their purpose, mounted his horse, and made a run. The sheriff and his deputies were the best part of the day tracking him, thirty-five miles through the chaparral, and might yet have lost him but that his horse stumbled and went lame. He leaped down and ran, plump legs pumping, throwing up dust like a stagecoach passing through. As the Mexicans on their jaded horses closed in, he turned, drew his revolver, and emptied its chambers in their general direction. The deputies answered in kind, but none of the three was much use with a gun, and there was no harm done. The suspect, still protesting his name was James Franks, allowed himself to be led back to Ysleta, complaining all the way of improper arrest and the violation of his rights. Charley Jones was waiting at the sheriff's office when the trail-weary party came in.

—Mister James C. Fraker? Charley Jones inquired, *pro forma*.

—Charley Jones! James Fraker exclaimed, seizing the marshal's out-reached hand in both his. You can't think what a sight of good it does, setting eyes on a friendly face from home, after all these weary months. How's things at Wichita?

—Pretty fair, Charley admitted. Last fall's hoppers hatched out pretty thick but seem to have departed. Rain come along, not too much nor too light, and opinion is, those that replanted will make a fair crop of wheat.

—Wonderful! said the suspect. And Missus Fraker and the children, any word of them? Only a family man knows the heaviness of heart a man feels, with the miles and days between him and his home and loved ones, and prevented by circumstances from passing the joyful season of Christmas—. A tear brimmed at the corner of one eye.

—Well now, Charley said. Your wife has got two or it might be three boarders living on the place, as I recall, young gentlemen that pays their rent. He closed a handcuff around the delicate, out-stretched wrist. And as I was leaving, she was starting up a school for little children—in the house, you know—

—Wonderful, resourceful woman! said Fraker. Just the sort of thing would suit her!

The other ring of the handcuff snapped shut.

The former bank president continued voluble through the sixteen days of the return to Wichita. At the end of May, Marshal Jones delivered his prisoner to Leavenworth to hear the charges. Fraker in lieu of bail was consigned to the county jail to await trial.

Mr Winkler, Isaac's tenant, completed the wheat harvest by the first of August, two thousand bushels—an average of little over eleven bushels an acre on the 180 acres. Charley Jones then appeared with a court order in favor of a Chicago bank, taking possession of the wheat. As Henry Sluss explained it, the Chicago bank had discounted a note given to secure one made by the Wichita bank to repay the cash Isaac had put in to see it through its final day; now, acting on infor-mation from Dave Kilbourn, Mr Cullum seemed to have arranged for the Chicago bank to get full payment on the note from the wheat, while Isaac would eventually recover from the assets of the Wichita bank, perhaps half what the wheat was worth—. Isaac left it to the lawyer to untangle the legalities, if he could. He wrote to Senator Ingalls urging him to demand an independent audit of the Wichita receiver; and perhaps, after a year in office, it was time to replace him with someone better informed by experience of conditions at Wichita.

The three trials and their attendant formalities lasted two weeks. Isaac put up at the Planter's House in Leavenworth and duly appeared for every session but was only once briefly called to testify. As in the grand jury proceedings, Eldon and Cullum were the chief witnesses in all three cases. It was found before it came to trial that the indictment concerning Edmund Wright was defective by reason of errors in copying the multitude of figures that constituted its substance, it was hastily corrected and rewritten, resubmitted, again approved by the grand jury, and after four days he was found guilty and sentenced to five years at Jefferson City. Fraker sat through a week of damaging testimony, then through his lawyer submitted a plea of guilty to all charges, and his parts in the three indictments were ordered consolidated. Eldridge's trial was more complicated, and the jury failed to reach a verdict; the trial was put over to the April session. Meanwhile word went around that Cullum was now determined on indictments of others connected with the bank, notably its vice-president, but on what grounds Isaac was unable to discover.

Fraker's sentencing was set for the morning of October 18. He availed himself of the customary right to make a statement to the court before sentence was passed. Isaac for the occasion took a seat on a bench in the last row of the cold, dusty courtroom and sat with head hunched low, as pained to witness this performance as to be witnessed in its presence.

Fraker, plump and fit in a well-cut suit despite the months of vagabondage and his prolonged confinement since, by reason of his inability to make the bail imposed under his three indictments—it was the first Isaac had seen of him since December—took his stand to the left of the judge's bench so as to face the jury box and at the same time keep judge and spectators under his eye.—*May it please the Court!* he began in his city-council voice, the formulary no doubt prescribed by his lawyer.

I have no words to express the great humiliation—the self-abasement that I feel— in being brought to the bar of this Court, to answer the charges brought against me, of violating the laws of my country. [Here he lowered his head and seemed to meditate for a time, then drew himself up with resolution, swept the jury and spectators with his eyes, and lifted his head to gaze directly at the judge.] *I would endure in silence the judgment of this Court, were it not that, should I so meekly accept the fate which has so heavily befallen, my motives and my purposes, in doing whatever was done, to improve the failing fortunes, and, if possible, to prevent the failure, of the bank with which I was connected, would be grossly misread by my enemies, and would likewise be misunderstood by the Court, my friends, and the world. In the course of my adult life, I have endeavored to take my part in the councils of men according as called to—yet now I find nothing in past experience to prepare me to address a proceeding of the present kind.* [Here, a modest inclination to judge, jury, audience.] *I have never in my life been a juryman, or a witness in a criminal court—certainly was never before now charged with the violation of any law, in any court of justice. For nearly twenty years I have been a citizen of Kansas, during most of which I have actively engaged in mercantile and other business pursuits. A part of that time also, I have held important, responsible, public trusts. As to how faithfully these have been discharged—as to whether, up to the time I am charged with this present offense—my conduct has not been that of a quiet, orderly, law-abiding citizen—and my influence ever laid to the side of law, and order, and upright public morality—it would be for tongue otherwise than mine, to speak.*

Now, first, as to that matter of five thousand, one hundred twenty-five dollars and fifty cents. . . .

Isaac rose softly from his place, went stooping inconspicuously out the door, hat trailing from his hand, and eased it shut. Fraker gave every appearance of settling to an extended discourse which, if he had a mind—Marsh Murdock was in the front row, taking it all in shorthand—he could no doubt read *verbatim* in next week's *Eagle;* but to no more meaning or consequence than the late-summer singing of the host of cicadas in the cottonwoods along the Arkansas.

John Eldridge appeared at Topeka in April 1878 to change his plea to the original indictment to guilty, but his lawyers persuaded the judge to postpone sentencing until trial could be held on the second body of charges in the fall. He was released on nominal bond but failed to appear when the witnesses were reassembled at Leavenworth in October, his doctor sending in a sworn statement of his inability on medical grounds to stand trial. James Fraker by then had begun the process that would lead to his parole the following spring.

Isaac's wheat harvest that summer of 1878, untroubled by grasshoppers, came to something over four thousand bushels on a full planting of three hundred acres, double the previous year. Apart from riding out to visit Winkler and his family, sometimes with Bissy for company—he had given the boy his own horse, Jim, and bought himself a big Morgan gelding—he no longer had much to occupy him: no real estate to deal in as times improved, nor the little storefront office where he had done his business; no building in hand, no bank, no branch railroad. He worked with Andrew Hansen improving the gardens and fruit trees of Pride's Reserve; the house, he found, although built all of brick except the porches and the trim around eaves, windows, doors, required upkeep. He filled the time with long walks around the town, with slow, mournful, and largely silent visits to Mathewson and Greiffenstein, the few others left from the old days.

As the summer drew in and cooled, became fall, the dry leaves, wind-wakened, rattled and whispered together along the branches of the trees and in their season fell and mingled with the dust devils careering down the unpaved streets; trees sprung from the wagonloads of seedlings he had given out hardly five years past to advertise his lots, still sapling-limber, unacclimatized, but growing tall. Once or twice a day now Isaac made what had become his customary tour, expected, waited for, sometimes distantly greeted by those who lived along the way: east along Central to the railroad track, down Fifth Avenue to the depot, back along Douglass and up Lawrence and home, the boundaries of Pride's Addition; as if patrolling the limits of his former domain. The city was built now, fairly started, and would begin to grow again now real estate was picking up and money easing. In hardly ten years from first conception the few of them had joined to plant and people a city on the naked prairie, a task measured in slow generations of his father's Iowa, or centuries in the Greenwich of his Connecticut ancestors. For a time he had lived and let his dreams run as if he owned it all—and of course had, in part, but only in the way recognized by law, by right of property. Now he neither owned nor belonged: had no more connection with the place and its on-rolling life than the desolate dead leaves of the cultivated foreign trees with which he had lined his streets, keeping him company on his morning and evening strolls—except that he was anchored here by the extravagant house, by the wife and two children it housed, by a few other dependents; and by Marie perhaps, lying beside the beautiful spring in Towanda twenty miles east. They would go on, of course, he and his city, but on parallel tracks now, like childhood friends growing their separate ways, yet so intertwined by shared consciousness that each retains a share in the other's life apart—in imagination, in love and longing—so that, meeting again in afterlife, each will still recognize the other and know the essence of what the intervening years have been. So the city, built, was saved, for now, the debt paid, or if not entirely paid to the limits of law and bookkeeping, yet to the limit of honor and his power to give. Finished, done: and then, *O God that tonight I might lie with her there, at Towanda;* except that while one of us lives, the other also lives, immortal in memory, and that is love's final gift and meaning, not to be taken back, because whatever a man has known and given of love before, each in its time, is pale and imperfect by comparison with that gift; and therefore, for love, while love lasts, a man's death must not be of his choosing, must not be sought.

Lucy celebrated Isaac's forty-first birthday by roasting a brace of geese he and Bissy had shot a week earlier, hunting miles up the Little Arkansas beyond the former Osage crossing; his father sent two bottles of his heavy, sweet wine from the Rockingham grapes. Lucy, supposing her husband would not welcome company, had re-

frained from inviting even her sister and Mr Mathewson; only the
two of them facing each other from opposite ends of the mahogany
table, Bissy and Mamie between, and Andrew and the girl taking
their share in the kitchen.

Late in the afternoon, when the cheerless celebration was finished,
drowsy with the dark, oily meat and the wine, Isaac went out for a
walk while Lucy and the girls cleared up, and Bissy came with him.
There was hardly a lot they passed but reminded Isaac of someone, of
some event in the town's brief history that now seemed remote and
ghost-guarded as the pyramids. Bissy of course knew most of the
stories as well as Isaac did himself, he need not repeat them unless
particularly asked. A hint, a word, did as well, evoking and confirm-
ing shared memory.

At the corner of Lawrence, Bissy stayed him with a light hand on
his arm: didn't want to go home yet, couldn't they walk on, past the
courthouse and along the riverbank? There were still a dozen kinds of
ducks and geese coming over, making for the Gulf, and the great
sandhill cranes, and only the other day he had spied a box turtle,
digging itself into the mud for the winter—

Strong persuasions, but Isaac shook his head:—I don't like going
that way anymore, boy. Built too many hopes there—and gone now,
all gone—

—Pa! the boy said. *We can get it back.*

Isaac turned to look at him: getting his growth now, sixteen in
January, a fine strong boy, gentle and grave, and already tall as Isaac
himself, and when he filled out might end big as his father; it did not
seem he saw enough of him of late, attended to him enough, grieving
in himself over things that were done, never to be undone.

—Why, of course we can, boy, Isaac said, gripping the strong
young shoulders. You don't think, cause a man's turned forty, he's
finished, do you? I've got plans, boy! Get the money out of this wheat
of ours and I'll take a share in another herd of Texas cattle with my
friends in the East that have stood by me. And then next year, when
we're ahead from the cattle—and Wichita's about finished as a cattle
market, unless a man wants to drive to Dodge and sell among strangers—we'll do the thing I started for when I first come to Kansas. We'll
go to the gold regions out in the Colorado mountains, buy us a mine
or two—silver, too, out there, though gold's so plenty they don't
hardly bother with it. Together, boy! We'll go in together!

—Oh, Pa! the boy cried. We can do it—we'll get it back! We'll get it
all back. . . .

His eyes glistened with tears nearly past holding, his smooth young
resolute face shadowed with resemblances from all the blood of the
past that formed him: Marie, his mother, father, grandparents, others
past knowing in the backward-ascending endless chain of family. An-

other minute and he would be crying, they would both be crying, and what kind of display was that to make on the public street, a graying man and his half-grown boy, father and son? And to stop him, Isaac pulled him close and hugged him, pressing his face to his shoulder.